I0788194

A SPY AMONG THE FALLEN

BOOKS 9-11

DEMONS OF FIRE & NIGHT

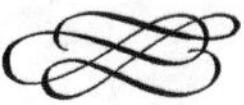

C.N. CRAWFORD

COVERT FAE - BOOK ONE

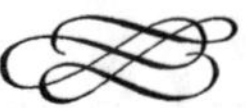

CHAPTER 1

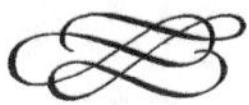

The day before the world ended, I dressed up in sequins and white feathers.

Of all my burlesque routines, the "stripping angel" was the biggest crowd-pleaser. I wasn't sure if it was the shimmering silver dress that I peeled off slowly, the creative use of wings or just the innocent-girl-gone-bad vibe. Or maybe the feigned shyness. In any case, at *Madame Francine's,* the "stripping angel" killed even more than the "naughty Puritan."

Backstage, I looked at myself in the mirror as I threaded white crystals into my blood-red hair. I'd piled my locks high, securing them with a silver hairpin. My false eyelashes swooped over my eyelids, and frosty makeup shimmered over my cheekbones. A hint of purple eyeliner brought out the pistachio-green in my eyes.

My alter-ego was nothing like the legends of the angels I'd been told growing up—those mythical spirits who dwelled in the heavens— but New York's cocktail drinkers didn't need to know that.

I liked my job. Granted, I didn't make a ton of money performing, and most of the money I did make went right back into costumes. But it covered the rent for a tiny apartment in Brooklyn—just enough room for my younger sister and me.

In the backstage mirror, I applied ruby-red lipstick—what my fellow dancer Tommy Sugar jokingly called my "whore mouth"—then arched an eyebrow at my reflection. *Nearly perfect.*

Reaching above my head, I adjusted the hairpin that held my hair in place, secure in the knowledge that its tip could cut through flesh and bone. Call me paranoid, but whenever demons were around I liked to have at least one or two weapons at my fingertips. I'd had this hairpin specially-made, and I could ram the tip of it right into a demon's heart—carve the fucker straight out if I needed to.

These days, demons were always around. Even if humans didn't recognize them.

I scrutinized myself in the mirror, wondering if I could still live up to my stage name: *Angela Death.* It had been a long time since I'd actually needed to fight anyone, and I might have gone a little soft. A perverse part of me almost hoped that something would kick off soon to give me the chance to test my skills again—to draw blood—but maybe that was a dangerous thing to hope for.

"Are you going to stand there all evening, Lady Death?" Fanny Fluffer stood behind me, her arms folded, her dark eyes narrowed. Her dress of shimmering black sequins and feathers glinted in the pulsing white lights that streamed in from the stage. A feather fell from her corset, and my eyes tracked the movement, strangely mesmerized.

Feathers falling from the heavens...

"Hey Ruby?" she prompted, snapping her fingers in my face. "You're nearly on."

I popped my lipstick back in my bag and tucked my makeup bag into the corner of the counter.

"Right. Sorry. I'm done." I lifted a set of large white wings from the table—important props for a classic fan routine. As I crossed through the dark passage to the side of the stage, my body hummed with anticipation. From here, I could see Tommy performing. With his cheeky grin and russet-brown skin, he had to be the cutest boylesque dancer in New York, and his soldier performance always brought a smile to my lips.

As the music pulsed through the club, I peeked at the crowd. My heart thrummed at the sight of Marcus. Even for a vampire, he was stunning—despite the fact that he'd been alive for four centuries. His tousled, chestnut hair fell into his eyes, and warmth sparked in my heart, which still raced at the sight of him even after all our time together. Part of me wanted to skip the routine altogether and curl up in his lap.

He was sipping a Manhattan, watching Tommy Sugar's routine—not quite as interested as he usually looked when I took to the stage, but clearly enjoying himself. When he caught a glimpse of me peering at him from behind the curtain, he smiled, his cheek dimpling.

I ducked back behind the curtain, returning to watching Tommy as he peeled off the last of his colonial soldier's costume to reveal tiny, sparkling shorts. He was nearly at the end of his act.

Before I crossed the stage, it was time to summon my *piece de resistance*. As a fae, I could glamour myself as any other kind of supernatural creature. Any demons or fae in the crowd would recognize the faint hallmarks of the succubi, and the sight of a dancing succubus would thrill them beyond measure. There weren't many *actual* succubi left in the world, so rumors of the legendary seductresses could draw a real crowd.

Standing behind the curtain, I summoned the glamour, feeling the thrilling tingle of magic ripple over my skin and curl around my ribs. When I finished, my skin had taken on a faint golden sheen. Even without looking, I knew my irises had darkened, black as the night. I couldn't see magic very well, but powerful demons would sense tendrils of charcoal magic curling off my body. It wasn't real succubus magic, but looked close enough to fool people.

I took a deep breath, smiling in anticipation. Fae were hedonistic creatures, each with our own vices and pleasures. Some fae liked food, some the texture of silk, some perfumes. For me, it was dancing—feeling that precision of getting each movement right, the visceral thrill of my own body's movements. That was my high.

I stepped onto the stage, catching Marcus's eye. Smiling, he lifted his cocktail and took a sip, toasting to me.

As the stage lights gleamed off my silver dress, the music began: Rihanna's *Love on the Brain*. The gentle beats vibrated through my core, and my hips began to sway to the drum beats. Fluttering the fans behind my back like wings, I let a tendril of my hair fall in front of my eyes. Each movement was perfectly choreographed, each movement of my hips designed to hypnotize and entrance. The music beat through my blood—a deep, rhythmic thrill.

I shifted one of the fans in front of me, gently moving it so the feathers pulsed like a heartbeat. As I did, someone else in the crowd caught my eye, and my *actual* heart skipped a beat.

I could tell the guy was a demon—the sheer, muscled size of his body made that clear. More than that, his close-cropped golden hair seemed to glow as it framed his head, gleaming like a crown of fire. His skin was sun-kissed; his deep, burnt-amber eyes penetrated me to my very core.

Everything about him exuded power. The hard glint in his eye—and the sensual curve of his lips—promised conquest and pleasure all in one terrifying package.

A sun-demon. I couldn't think of any other way to describe him. Kinda made the glamour of my *Angela Death* persona pale in comparison. No one would outshine this guy. Was he aligned with Emerazel, the goddess of fire? Maybe one of her twelve high lords? He must be a demigod from her Sun Court.

That was when I noticed the two bodyguards sitting behind the sun-demon, and by the sickly yellow glow of their eyes I immediately pegged them as dragon shifters. A hot rush of fury ignited in my blood, and I had to restrain myself from crawling off the stage, glassing them, then stabbing them with the broken shards. Maybe take out the sun-demon while I was at it.

Maybe that sounded like a bit much—but the last time dragons had visited New York, they'd razed the city to the ground, burning buildings, massacring humans and demons alike. Even among demons, dragons were a class all their own, terrifying agents of chaos and slaughter.

My parents had died fighting them—something I tried every day not to think about. But it was kind of hard to forget it when dragon shifters showed up here, in my place of work.

I spun, twirling one of the fans over my head. Stopping with my back to the crowd, I wiggled my hips, trying to forget who was watching me.

I faced the audience again, holding the two fans in front of me to completely cover my body, waving them gently like the opening and closing of a clam shell.

No matter what resentments New Yorkers harbored, we weren't allowed to attack dragons. The city had formed a sort of truce with them over the past few years, and the dragons had been on their best behavior ever since. I wasn't about to start a new war right here in Madame Francine's—even if I desperately wanted to.

I caught Marcus's gaze, subtly nodding toward the sun-demon and his dragon buddies. Already, Marcus's muscles were tensed, his dark eyes locked on them. He'd spent several centuries fighting in vampire armies. If anything was about to kick off, I was in good hands.

I twirled in my high heels. The sun-demon's golden gaze pierced through my comfort zone. Obviously, he liked the succubus glamour, but he was looking at me with the predatory gaze of a snake sizing up a mouse. The power rolling off him made me want to flee in the other direction.

What *was* his deal? I tightened my jaw. *Stay focused, Ruby.* I had a show to put on, so I tried to bury those distractions in the back of my mind. Tuning in to the music, I felt its vibrations pulsate over my skin and sank deeper into the thrill of the dance.

With the fans shielding me, I let the strap of my dress fall off one of my shoulders. The bass drum pounded between my ribs. I undulated my hips behind the fans, making the feathers twitch.

For just a moment my gaze flicked back to the demon, who twirled his wine glass between his fingers. A faint smile curled his lips. As the lights shifted to a deep red hue, I thought I glimpsed phantom wings cascading from his back, and a gleaming bow slung over his shoulder. A voice in the back of my mind whispered, *Not a demon...*

I blinked, clearing my mind, and twirled to the corner of the stage, reveling in the feel of my feet moving across the stage.

Block him out, Ruby. Bury those thoughts.

Of course he was a demon. Just an ordinary, run-of-the-mill demon of some sort.

Swallowing hard, acutely aware of his eyes on me, I let my dress fall to the floor in the corner of the stage. Under it, I'd worn shimmering white stockings and a white sequined corset with feathers over the bust. Two sheer strips of tulle reached from my hips to the floor in front and back, and the shimmering material covering a silver thong.

I kept the fans raised, moving them until they pulsed like violent storm clouds, swishing my hips behind the feathers. Then, with a twirl of my wrist, I spun one of the fans over my head, giving the audience a glimpse of the corset.

I glanced at Marcus, flashing him a smile. A beautiful rosy blush colored his cheeks, and warmth pooled in my ribs. More focused now, I turned in my high heels, looking at the crowd from a profile view. Smiling coyly, I extended one of my legs beyond the fans, slowly pointing my toe into the air.

As they cheered, I dropped my foot to the ground, and extended the other leg, arching it high into the air. For just a moment, I forgot about the demon, thrilled at the feel of my own body's movements and the warmth of the lights on my skin.

A small smile curled my lips, and I turned back to the crowd. The rhythmic beats thrummed over my body, and I swirled a feathered fan above my head. Smiling at Marcus, I spun in my heels. As I moved across the stage, the tips of the feathers tickled my skin.

So far, I'd kept to the routine, each movement precise and planned —but for some reason I was having a hard time working up the resolve to pull the fans away. I think it was the sun-demon's eyes burning a hole into me.

Focus, Ruby. He's just a regular demon. Nothing to get worked up about.

I spun, my back to the crowd, one fan covering my backside. I puffed it in the air, bending over just a bit—a faint glimpse of thong beneath the sheer fabric. The crowd whooped.

I spun again on my heels. Usually at this point I'd worked up a serious buzz from the dancing, but tonight I felt strangely empty. Maybe this classic burlesque style of dance was growing old. It was too coy, too gentle. I needed something with a little more teeth.

Or maybe the gods-damned dragon shifters were making me feel aggressive.

Whatever the case, I wanted to draw blood with my dance. Tonight, I didn't just want to entice. I wanted to terrify.

I tried to focus on the routine—every footstep in the right place—and held both fans in front of me, my gaze darting back to the sun-demon. As I met his eyes, an unwelcome ache pooled inside me, and an electric rush rippled over my skin. Despite myself, when I looked into his amber eyes, I was starting to feel it again: the thrill of the dance.

My body grew warmer under the hot white lights. A sheen of sweat covered my skin. I shot a glance to Marcus again, taking in his stark beauty; that hot thrill intensified further.

I swished the fans through the air until I held them both in front of my body with one hand. With the other, I reached behind my back to unzip the corset, fluffing the wings as I did so.

Anticipation rolled off the crowd.

Shielding my body with the gently waving feathers, I wiggled out of the corset. Now, behind the delicate wall of feathers, I wore only a white sequined thong, feather pasties, and the swaths of sheer fabric.

I turned on my heels, shifting the fans again—one in front, one behind. The wings swayed.

I spun again, this time crossing my arms in front of my chest, hiding my breasts. I gently beat the fans behind my back like wings—a slow, undulating pulse. Then, as the music changed, I turned to the side, one fan in front of me, soft against my skin. I arched my back, lifting a fan with one arm and extending it over my head. The crowd cheered, and I pivoted again.

Each footstep in the right place, a calculated dance. Precise and expected. I waved the fans before me, nearly giving glimpses of my body, but not quite.

I turned my back to the audience again. This time, I raised the fans completely above my head, my thong nearly visible under the fabric that draped from my hips. I arched my back and undulated my hips the way I'd learned in my belly dancing class.

Turning again in my high heels, I faced the crowd, the fans covering the front of my body. With a few beats of the feathers, I pulled them away, holding them over my head. I curved my back, and the lights of Madame Francine's washed my body in pure white, shimmering over the white pasties, the sheer fabric.

I looked out at the crowd. To my relief, the golden-haired demon had left the club, and his table sat empty.

Still, that phrase once again rang in my mind: *Not a demon...*

While the crowd cheered, I crossed off the stage and into the hall that led back to the dressing rooms. I sucked in a deep breath. I felt strangely shaken by tonight's performance—dazed, almost—and after five minutes of putting every footstep in the right place, each twitch of my hips perfectly calculated, I tripped over my own damn feet— right into the arms of the sun-demon.

He deftly caught my arm, fingertips clenching on my wrist possessively, like he was claiming me. His thin, coppery sweater had felt like a combination of silk and cashmere wrapped over pure, muscled steel. His clothes probably cost the same as one month's rent for my shitty apartment.

The sun-demon arched a dark eyebrow, and my stomach clenched. I felt an overwhelming urge to submit to him, to drop to my knees in front of him. Still, I managed to wrench my arm away from him and stepped away from him. His two enormous dragon-shifter bodyguards stood behind him, their yellow eyes locked on me.

"A succubus dressed as an angel." His accent was English, and extremely posh. "How deliciously perverse."

As he spoke, light seemed to shine from his body, warming the air around him. I wasn't sure what his game was, only that I needed to get the hell away from him—even as he seemed to lure me in. But he and his dragon-thugs were blocking my path back to the changing room.

As I glared at him, his eyes swept over my body, heating my blood. Something about him exuded pure dominance.

Of course it didn't help that I was practically naked. I quickly shifted my fans in front of my body.

Irritation sparked. "Is there someone else you could bother right now? Maybe you need to put your lizard friends back in their cages, feed them some mice? I've got somewhere to be."

He cocked his head, the movement nearly imperceptible. "Trying to get away from me already? That's a shame. I was hoping to get to know you a bit better."

I glared at him. "I feel I should warn you that I haven't had a snack in a few hours, and I'm feeling a little aggressive. You know what I've never tried? Roast reptile. Then again, I hear the meat is vile."

He took a step closer, forcing me back a step. "Aggression—something I appreciate well. But I'm curious. What are you going to do? Tickle us to death with your wings?"

"Maybe a stiletto through your eye. I haven't decided."

"Not very friendly, are you?"

A feather fell from one of my wings, drifting to the ground.

Seemingly entranced, his eyes tracked the movement, until his hand shot out. He caught it between the tips of his fingers. "Don't you know that angels are supposed to be loving? Moral?"

Warning bells rang in the darkest recesses of my mind. This didn't happen often with demons, but it almost seemed as if his raw power was strong enough to vibrate through my body, curl around my bones. It beckoned me to my knees, and I fought the urge to kneel.

An intrusive, terrifying sort of magic. He shoved the feather into his pocket, then continued to peer down at me. Up close, I could see that his amber eyes darkened to burnt copper at the edges.

I sucked in a deep breath, considering my options. I could hold the fans before me and try to shove past his enormous frame. Or, I could threaten him with my hairpin—though I wasn't sure he'd display the appropriate amount of fear at my threat.

Fighting the urge to drop to the ground, I glared at him. "Angels should be loving. Got it. Thanks for the performance notes."

The strobe lights of Madame Francine's pulsed over the perfect planes of his face, and he kept peering down at me, rooting me in place with his penetrating gaze. Whatever his game was, it struck me that he used his sheer, stunning beauty as a predatory tool, a way to control and distract his prey.

I had no idea what he wanted from me, but my fingers twitched, ready to rip the hairpin from my tresses. I could ram it right through his heart before he knew what was hitting him. No matter what kind of demon he was, a blade to the heart would put him out of commission at least temporarily.

"Do you need something?"

He quirked an eyebrow, inching even closer now. "Not much, honestly. Just total conquest, the worship of the masses, and the end of the world."

The worship of the masses, the end of the world. His astonishing arrogance aside, his words sent an icy shiver of fear licking up my spine—so cold I actually shivered, goosebumps rising on my skin. It was the same sort of crazy shit my parents had talked about—except when *he* said it, I was left with the impression that he meant it. Never before had it been so clear to me that I needed to stay far, far away from someone.

"But until then," he continued. "Maybe I could interest you in a drink with me."

"No."

The stranger's eyes took in the dimpled skin on my shoulders. "Oh, dear. Did I say something to disturb you?"

"No," I lied. "I'm just wondering how long you're going to block my path and if I'll need to stab you to get back to my clothes."

He raised his eyebrows. "Are you threatening to lay your hands on me?"

I was about to respond, but as I stared into his eyes, for just a moment, I saw a flash of stars whirling among the darkness. A pit opened in my stomach. *When the stars dim and the earth rips apart...*

Shivering, I took a step closer, staring into his eyes. He wanted to scare me, and I wasn't going to give him the satisfaction of dropping my gaze. "What are you?" I asked, steadying my voice.

With a feather-light stroke, he ran the back of his finger down my cheek—a lover's touch that tingled over my skin. Golden light whorled in the air around him. He leaned down, his breath warming the shell of my ear.

"I'm your worst nightmare." His whisper caressed my skin.

My worst nightmare.

I believed him, certain to my very marrow that he was telling the truth. I pulled the fans closer to my own body, taking a small step back.

Then Marcus stepped from the shadows—or rather, leapt from the shadows. In a blur of movement, he was standing before the demon, fingers poised just in front of the demon's heart.

Sun-demon here had no idea just what Marcus could do with his fingers.

"Is he bothering you, Ruby?" Marcus asked, without taking his eyes off the stranger.

I ripped the hairpin out of my hair, and it caught in the flashing lights. "Marcus, my love. You know I can take care of myself."

"And you know I like to be a gentleman," he said.

The stranger seemed completely unperturbed. "Ruby. It's been lovely to meet you." He turned to walk away.

It was cute when Marcus got protective of me, but I had to remind him of what I could do. And more importantly, I needed the sun-demon to know. As he turned to walk away, I narrowed my eyes and aimed. The hairpin struck him exactly where I'd wanted it to, pinning his $1500 sweater to the wall, just above his shoulder.

He turned to look at me, and surprise flickered over his beautiful features, filling me with a sharp thrill of satisfaction. But in the next moment, his eyes flashed with white-hot rage, and my stomach dropped.

He plucked the hairpin from the wall, twirled it in his fingers. He shoved it into his pocket, masking his face with a pleasant expression again. Flanked by the two reptiles, he disappeared into milling crowds of Madame Francine's.

CHAPTER 2

The sun was setting on Brooklyn. Marcus had surprised my younger sister and me with a picnic in a botanical garden. Ivy and wildflowers climbed the rough bark of a towering oak, threading through its branches and reaching for the skies. We sat under the rosy canopy of a cherry blossom tree, its boughs rustling gently in the breeze. Nearby, lily pads gently floated in a pool of dark water.

Now, at dusk, the sun tinged the sky with shades of violet and strawberry. Marcus was rare among vampires—a born daywalker, whose milky-white skin remained untouched in the light of day.

As we sat on a small, red blanket, Marcus opened a wicker basket and pulled out a baguette, camembert, and strawberries.

Hazel rested by his side, frowning at a book about a sorceress queen. Given how much she'd been talking about the book, I should have had the whole thing memorized by now. But I'd been making an effort to tune her out when she rattled off all the spoilers, because she had a tendency to give the whole plot away before I got to read it.

I frowned at her, wiping a smudge of butter off her cheek. She didn't look much like me—at fourteen, she was already six inches taller, with long, black hair that curled down her back. Only our pale skin and shared literary obsessions marked us as sisters.

Hazel's dark tank top was fitting her a little too snugly now, her skin showing when she bent over, and I yanked it down. I was pretty sure she'd never notice that sort of thing, and she'd wear the same thing every day if I let her.

With her wide-set eyes and porcelain skin, she was beautiful, even if she didn't know it yet. When it came to her appearance, the only thing she seemed to care about was adding little signs of self-expression: the safety pins artfully arranged in the shape of a star on the front of her shirt, the "tattoos" she drew all over her hands with black markers, the white nail polish that was actually Wite-Out.

At last, she looked up from her book and peered into the basket, grinning. "Oooh. Chocolate graham crackers."

"Of course," Marcus said. "I know you're obsessed with them."

And that was my favorite thing about him. He *always* remembered what people liked. I could make one off-hand comment about a delicious lemonade I'd sampled at a shop, and within days he'd pick it up for me. He knew I loved surprises—that I loved sunset and strawberries and spending time with Hazel—and he'd arranged it all for us. So for just an hour or two, I didn't have to worry about making rent money, or the bullies who'd been targeting Hazel in school and writing horrible things about her online.

I touched Marcus's arm. "This is perfect."

The dying sunlight sparked in his dark eyes. "So are you."

My cheeks warmed.

Hazel looked up from her book just long enough to roll her eyes. "Do I need to go somewhere else? Maybe you can just give me the champagne and I can sit by myself and drink it in one of those garden nooks while you both tell each other how perfect you are and then touch each others' boobs or whatever."

Marcus smiled, his cheeks dimpling. "That sounds lovely and romantic. I'm so touched you noticed my boobs. Perhaps when you're older you can give me some of your seduction tips." It had been a few centuries since Marcus had lived in Scotland, but I could still hear his accent. "Have you picked them up in your books?"

She rested her chin on her fist. "All I know is that if you want to get laid, you need to wear a kilt and kill people."

Marcus nodded thoughtfully. "I can manage both those things beautifully."

I poked Hazel on her upper arm. "Go back to your sorceress queen and her gnome army."

"Troll army," she mumbled, swiveling to face away from us. She hunched over her book, no longer listening to anything we said.

A floral breeze whispered over my skin, toying with strands of my hair. I plucked a strawberry from the basket, and bit into it, the sweet and tart flavors dancing over my tongue.

"I have a job tonight," Marcus said, his mahogany eyes catching the light. The golden flecks around his irises never failed to take my breath away. "I'll be out late."

I took in his muscled arms, his sharp cheekbones, the powerful set of his jaw. He was a soldier through and through—but one without an army. Since he'd moved to New York a hundred years ago, he'd been working for a sort of supernatural police force, helping to keep demons in line when they started to feed on too many humans, or to keep the peace between warring factions of light and shadow demons.

"Anything dangerous?" I asked.

He shook his head. "Since when has anything posed a serious threat to me?"

I pulled another strawberry from the basket. "Cocky. I like it. Do you ever miss your days in the vampire army?"

It had been nearly a century since he'd left Lilinor, the vampire city.

"Yes and no. I was the only daywalker in the Lilinor, and people started to resent me after a while. To them, I wasn't a real vampire. Our king, Ambrose, resented me. The only one who didn't have a problem with me was Caine, the general—probably because he wasn't a vampire."

"What was he?"

"Incubus. Demigod. We were close, once, but I haven't spoken to him in years." Marcus's brow furrowed, and I could see him thinking about something. "Lilinor has changed, though. Maybe we could go back there, you and I. And Hazel, too."

"Changed how?"

"The entire city has changed, transformed from vampires into demons that can walk in the light. Fae, incubi, valkyries… They had to transform themselves in order to fight the Brotherhood."

I nodded. "Ah. The Battle of Boston."

"Exactly." He shrugged, almost imperceptibly. "Maybe there's a place there for me now, among the other daywalkers. I do miss it. I miss being part of something larger."

"I'm not sure I want to leave New York."

He snatched a champagne flute from the basket and set it before me. "You'd love Lilinor." Gently twisting the bottle, he popped the cork. "Once, you'd have hated it—they lived in perpetual night. But now the sun rises over a sparkling ocean and sets over the old stone fortress. Food is cooked by fae chefs. It's really quite extraordinary."

I sipped the champagne, the bubbles tickling my tongue. "Right. It sounds lovely. We can visit, but Hazel and I are happy in the human realm. She wants to be an archeologist or something." I gestured at the park. "Plus, you can't possibly tell me Lilinor is more beautiful than this."

"I want to go to the vampire world!" Hazel said, without looking up from her book. "Human boys are so lame." Now, she fixed me with an intense stare. "Like, you would not believe how lame they are. They stink, for one thing, and for another, they're basically monosyllabic. I want to meet some demon guys."

I shook my head. "No. You don't need to meet demon guys until you're eighteen, at least."

She nodded. "Four years, then. We go to Lilinor in four years, instead of college."

"See?" Marcus flashed a brilliant smile. "It's settled. You can dance there, and I can kill fire demons and witch-hunters openly, like I'm meant to. Caine would have me back in the army in a second."

I brushed his hair back from his forehead. "Sounds dangerous. I'd rather you become an accountant or something."

"Yeah that's not going to happen. I'd rather chew my own legs off."

"That's a bit dramatic."

"I didn't spend my childhood in Fife dreaming of sitting behind a desk thinking about numbers. I had a wooden sword, and enemies made of sackcloth and hay."

He hardly ever talked about his childhood, and I loved getting a glimpse into his past. "Did you spend a lot of time on your own when you were a boy?"

He nodded. "It was either the hay soldiers, or my uncle was beating me for some offense I didn't understand."

I took a deep breath. "You never told me what happened to your parents."

"Both dead of the plague. I was the only one who survived. My uncle took me in, but he resented the money he had to spend on me until I was old enough to work."

My fingers tightened into fists. I'd seen the scars on Marcus's back, the ones that had survived even his transformation to vampiric form. It was a shame my fae powers didn't involve the ability to go back in time and beat the shit out of drunk Scottish uncles.

"Well," I said, "I don't want to stand in your way completely. You could still fight sackcloth enemies."

"I don't think they'd satisfy my bloodlust."

I frowned. "You do realize that normal people try to disguise impulses like *bloodlust,* right?"

He opened his mouth, baring his fangs. "What made you think I was normal, my darling? And anyway, you'd hate normal. You just don't realize it. You need a man who can draw blood."

Absentmindedly, I plucked another blade of grass. "You must be scared of *something,* right?"

He arched an eyebrow. "I'm not sure I know you well enough yet to betray my weaknesses."

"Oh, I already know your greatest weakness. And if you knew how to flatter a woman, it would be on the tip of your tongue."

"I'd rather you were on the tip of my tongue."

I cocked my head, studying him. "What do vampires fear?"

He sipped his champagne. "Boredom. Unfulfilled dreams."

I rolled my eyes. "Whatever it is, I'll keep you safe."

He ran the tip of his tongue over one of his fangs. Maybe he was right about the fact that I needed a man who could draw blood. The sight of his fangs always sent a spark of heat through me.

"There's nothing I could do to persuade you to do something safer?" I asked. "What if I promised to wear the succubus glamour every night?" Closing my eyes, I summoned my glamour, letting it wash over my skin in a wave of tingling magic.

When I opened my eyes, I knew my irises had gone dark. A faint hint of charcoal magic whispered around my body, and my skin had taken on a faint, golden sheen.

Marcus licked his lips slyly. "Maybe I could be persuaded."

I ran my fingertips up his arm. "What is it about men and succubi? I look the same as I did before. Just with slightly different colors."

He took a sip of his champagne. "I don't know. Succubi are just dirty—or so I've heard. I've never been with one, obviously."

"Right. You were celibate for several centuries before you met me, isn't that right?"

"Of course. I was saving myself. I wore hair shirts and whipped myself every night to cleanse myself of impure thoughts."

I plucked a handful of grass and threw it at him. "You are such a liar." I bit my lip, shooting a glimpse at Hazel to make sure she wasn't listening. "Though the self-flagellation thing *is* kind of interesting. I don't suppose the succubus could see how that works?" I reached for him, stroking my thumb across his cheek, faint hints of my glamoured magic curling off my body in pale, dark tendrils.

A ghost of a smile crossed his lips; his eyes darkened even further. But in the next moment, his body had gone tense. His gaze flicked to the skies, and his brow furrowed. He frowned, setting down his champagne flute.

I turned, trying to get a glimpse of what he was seeing, but the sky looked normal to me.

"What's wrong?"

He sucked in a sharp breath. "We should get inside."

"What's happening?"

Hazel looked up from her book, her muscles tensing. "What do you see?"

"Fire," he said quietly. "I see fire in the skies. Dragons, I think."

The hair rose on the back of my neck. They had come back.

It had only been a few years since dragons had last razed the city to the ground, and we'd hardly had a chance to clear the rubble. Apparently, the truce we'd formed didn't last long.

Already, Marcus was pulling me up to my feet, spilling my champagne. But Hazel had frozen, her eyes wide with horror.

I knew why, of course. This was how our parents had died. Hazel had been old enough to remember the screams that ripped through the city, the scent of burning flesh. She remembered the terror of running through the subway tunnels while the dragons hunted the city streets above.

And now it was all coming back.

"Hazel!" Marcus barked, his military training emerging in full force. "We need to move, now!"

Clutching her book, her face pale, she leapt up. Her eyes were panicked as she started to reach for the basket.

Marcus's hand shot out. "There's no time for that. We need to leave now. We need to get to shelter. You two run ahead of me. The Brooklyn Museum is nearby. We can hide in there. Go!"

I had no idea what was going on, but I trusted Marcus. I snatched Hazel's hand, breaking into a run over the park's grass. We were nowhere near the exit. I pumped my arms, turning my head to face Marcus. "Should we tell the people around us?"

"You can try," he said, hardly breaking a sweat.

As we ran, I cupped my hands around my mouth, shouting "Dragons!"

Marcus joined in, shouting along with me. A few people strolling through the parks stopped to stare at us, then to look at the skies. Screams pierced the air.

It only took a few moments for the chaos to begin. The sky began to darken; cauldron-black clouds rolled in. The temperature dropped, and cold winds whispered over my skin. Hot streaks of fire streaked the sky. The winged forms circled overhead.

Dragons were drawn to beauty, and had a tendency to capture women. I didn't think they had many scruples about underage girls, and they'd come after Hazel in a heartbeat.

So much for the gods-damned truce.

Thunder rumbled over the horizon, and heavy drops of rain began falling from the sky, hammering against my skin. I could see the museum in my sights now—the enormous, classical stone structure, the size of several city blocks. It would be the perfect place to hide. I turned to Hazel, who was starting to fall behind, tears streaking her pale cheeks.

"Hurry!" I shrieked, slowing my pace.

Hazel had frozen again, staring up at the sky, her entire body trembling. She was pointing. "They're coming!" she whispered.

I stole a glance at the sky, and my heart threatened to gallop out of my chest. Darkening the skies above us was a horde of dragons, more than I'd ever seen in one place.

This wasn't a repeat of New York's prior attack. This was much, much worse.

Given how low they were flying, and the speed at which they were racing through the roiling clouds, I wasn't sure we'd make it to the museum.

A single, coppery feather floated from the sky. Light from a flash of lightning sparked off the quill, and a hollow opened in the pit of my stomach. I didn't know what I was looking at, but the ancient part of my brain told me to run—now.

Marcus's hand was on my back, soothing me. "We won't make it to the museum." He pointed to the right, at a small, glass-walled building. "Head for the cafe. It's not perfect, but we just need to get inside."

Hazel was still gaping at the oncoming dragons, her entire body trembling.

I grabbed her arm, pulling her along. "Hazel! Snap out of it!"

Marcus—my savior—swooped in to pick her up, carrying her in his arms. We turned, ready to run for the cafe, and a thundering crash trembled the earth behind us. The sound sent a shock of fear into my heart.

Pulse racing, skin cold with fear, I turned to see a dragon standing directly behind us, his yellow eyes locked on me.

CHAPTER 3

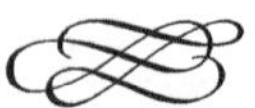

$\mathcal{I}$ knew better than to look directly into its eyes. To look a dragon in the eye invited a total mental breakdown.

But no matter where I looked, there was no way to run. Turning your back on a dragon meant instant death. Unfortunately, to stand before a dragon merely meant a slightly slower death, but perhaps it would buy us some time. Maybe someone more beautiful would distract it.

Lightning cracked the sky, gleaming off the creature's dark, oily hide. The thing was the size of a city bus, its spiked tail swishing lazily behind it. Inwardly, I cursed myself for failing to kill those two dragon shifters in the night club.

In human form, they could be killed as easily as any other demon. In their dragon forms, not so much.

In the driving rain, Marcus stood before us, shielding us with his arms outstretched. He didn't want the dragons to see our faces—to see our youth, our beauty.

Marcus had bragged that nothing was a threat to him, that he'd survived for centuries without so much as a scratch. But dragons were different. Dragons hides were practically invulnerable, susceptible only to destruction with one sword—a sword we didn't have.

What did I have? A damned hairpin.

Still, the hairpin could have its uses. The only other option was the eyes—those large, golden orbs.

Slowly, his eyes on the dragon, Marcus shielded us with his arms and began inching backward. Moving slowly, trying not to alarm the creature, I pulled the hairpin from my hair.

"Stay behind me," Marcus whispered.

Hazel's fear was palpable, her breathing coming in short, sharp gasps. Her fingers were tightened into fists, knuckles white.

"Glamour," I whispered. If she could turn herself into an aged hag, the dragons would leave her alone.

She turned to me, staring, her eyes wide, and that was when I really began to panic. By the look on her face, her mouth agape, I could tell she was losing it, completely shutting down inside. Even if I screamed at her to glamour herself, she wouldn't listen.

"We have to run, Ruby!" she shouted, too loudly.

I pressed my finger to my lips, trying to silence her. But she was already turning to run. She took one step, two—

My heart slammed against my ribs, my body surging with terror.

The dragon threw back his head, his scream ripping through the air, piercing me to the bone. The earth shuddered and lurched.

I summoned more of the succubus glamour, intensifying the illusion—the midnight eyes, the deep golden skin. Marcus tried to shield me from the dragon's view, but I slipped in front of him, hitting the dragon with the full force of my succubus allure.

"Right here, dragon!" I shouted, silently praying Hazel would get away.

The rain pelted my body, making my dress stick to my skin. I stared into the dragon's ancient, reptilian face, barely managing to avoid its eyes. He paused, no longer looking at my sister. His golden eyes were locked on me now, my sister forgotten.

"Ruby!" Marcus shouted.

My gaze flicked to him. He'd drawn a knife—a thin, silver blade. If the dragon got too close to me, Marcus would try to stab him.

But no one could aim like I could. I narrowed my eyes, staring at the dragon through the rain. With a lightning-fast movement, I threw the hairpin, and it found its mark—right in the dragon's eye.

The creature's scream rent the skies; its body bucked and flailed. Marcus leapt into the air, catching hold of the spikes that lined its spine.

My breath caught in my throat as I watched him shimmy into position on the dragon's back, his dark hair soaked with rain. The monster reared up, trying to throw him off. Marcus was yelling at me to run, but I ignored him. No way was I leaving him here alone.

Moving in a blur of darkness, Marcus shifted his position, climbing higher on the dragon's neck. Gripping the creature's spiked head, he reared back his arm and slammed the knife into the dragon's remaining eye, completely blinding him. As the dragon flailed, trying to throw him off, Marcus drove the blade in further, trying to reach the beast's brain.

Gods below, he was breathtaking.

At last, with Marcus's arm rammed into its eye—nearly up to the elbow—the dragon staggered. It heaved and fell to the ground, slamming against the earth. Marcus ripped his arm from the dragon's skull, his skin coated in oily, crimson blood. Dragon's blood stained the earth, mingling with the rain.

Tears stung my eyes as I looked at Marcus. "Let's go find Hazel!" I shouted.

He nodded, gripping his blood-stained knife.

Around us, dragons swooped down to the earth, their vast wingspans blackening the skies above us.

We hurried to a nearby cherry tree, shielding ourselves a little from the view of the dragons that circled above us. From here, we could try to plan our route. With Marcus's sensitive vision, he might be able to catch a glimpse of Hazel.

I scanned the horizon, trying to tune out the destruction around me. A large, crimson-scaled dragon swooped lower, opening his mouth to sear the sky with a white-hot stream of fire.

I knew that dragon. He wasn't like the others. He was the Drake, and he'd burned half of New York to the ground once before. A silver sheen covered the front of his blood-red scales—that was the sword Excalibur, formed into part of his body. The Drake alone was the only creature who could hurt the other dragons—too bad he was on their side.

"Marcus!" I pointed at the Drake, who was heading for the museum. Cold dread welled in my chest. "Is that where Hazel went?"

The Drake swooped lower, breathing a stream of flames onto the stone building—a sharp line of platinum flames streaking across the iron gray sky, hot enough to melt rock.

"I don't see her," Marcus said quietly. "I can't smell her, either."

Icy fear rippled over my skin. She'd gone to the museum, hadn't she? My heart thrummed in my chest. "Let's run for the museum. We have to get her out of there before the Drake burns the whole thing down. You remember what happened before."

He turned to me, cupping my cheek, stroking my skin gently. "You stay here under the tree. Try to hide from them. Glamour yourself. Can you glamour yourself as a tree? I've never known what your limitations are."

"You've got to be kidding me. I'm not sending you out there alone. I helped you take down that last dragon."

"You're fresh out of hairpins, my love."

I held out my hand. "Give me your other knife. I know you always carry two."

His jaw clenched, and he reached behind his back, pulling out his second stiletto.

I grabbed it from him. "Not the kind of stilettos I'm used to, but I still know how to use it."

He leaned in, kissing me hard on the lips—quickly and deeply, as if it would be our last. His warm, cedar scent enveloped me. He pulled away, staring into my eyes. "Just glamour yourself. Before we run for the museum, glamour yourself as something ugly."

"Right." I closed my eyes, summoning a glamour: an old man with a beer gut, dressed in a mustard-stained wife-beater and sweatpants. White whiskers sprang from my chin and cheeks.

Marcus stared at me, his lip curling slightly. "Mr. Owens from the bus stop? I'm glad I kissed you before."

"Mr. Owens at your service. Let's kill some dragons, shall we?"

We broke into a sprint across the park's rain-slicked grass, moving faster this time, our footsteps pounding the earth. Side-by-side, just the way we belonged. Hazel hadn't been able to run as fast as us, but as a fully grown fae I could move as swiftly as a vampire.

The wind whipped over my skin. I might look like Mr. Owens, but it was just an illusion. My body was still mine.

The Drake was circling the museum, breathing fire onto its roof. From here, I could see lights flashing in the library, hear the alarm bells ringing loudly among the screams. Humans were running from the building now, and I tried to sharpen my vision, searching for Hazel's pale skin and dark hair.

Then again, if she'd glamoured herself like she should have, who the fuck knew what she looked like?

Through labored breaths, I asked Marcus, "How will we recognize her?"

He sniffed the air. "I'll smell her when we get close enough. She smells like blackberries."

"Right."

We were closing in on the Brooklyn Museum now, as everyone else fled in the other direction—moving toward the stately steps that curved around the front of the building.

Marcus sniffed the air. "She's here. I smell her. Hazel!" He shouted into the fleeing crowd.

An older man was running toward us, his eyes wide open with terror. Then Hazel dropped the glamour, raising her arms in the air. "Marcus! I'm here!"

I ground to a halt. "Hazel! Keep your glamour up!"

Claws of dread sank into my chest. I couldn't let the dragons destroy my world again.

CHAPTER 4

efore the front steps of the Brooklyn Museum, a green-scaled dragon swooped lower, claws outstretched. He landed with a boom on the earth behind Hazel, then a long, pointed tongue shot out as he licked his teeth.

I shot a nervous glance at Marcus. We'd have to use our knives again, maybe take him down through his eyes. "Glamour!" I shouted at Hazel.

Within moments, she'd raised her glamour again, taking on the guise of an old man—grizzled beard spilling over a ripped flannel shirt. But it was too late. The dragon had already seen what she was, was already closing in on her. In her panic, her glamour was fading already, her black hair shining through.

I had to act fast. I summoned my own glamour, letting it ripple over my body in waves of magic. The succubus with the cherry-red hair—a dragon's favorite—was back.

I waved at him seductively. "Oh, dragon, over here!"

Marcus shot me a look of death. He did not appreciate my diversion tactics. But he already had another dragon to contend with—an orange-eyed creature that crawled up behind him.

I blocked that one out, focusing on the first one. This time I would try to climb the dragon's back. I could throw the knife, but I didn't want to lose my only weapon. I just needed to get it a little lower.

I stepped back, swishing my hips as I moved, trying to hypnotize the creature and avoiding looking into its eyes. Growling, it lowered its head to my level, prowling closer. I had to get everything right, every step in the right place.

When its neck was only a few feet off the ground, I leapt—a dancer's leap, graceful and precise. I grasped its spikes, then hooked my leg over the back of its neck, careful to avoid impaling myself on its dorsal spikes.

Bucking, the creature tried to throw me off, and I had about two seconds before it succeeded. I gripped Marcus's knife, slamming it into the first eye. *One.* The dragon screeched, lifting up on its hind legs, and I clung onto it for dear life. My fingers slipped over its scales.

Nearly there.

I reared back my other arm, slamming it into the dragon's second eye, my fingers tight around the hilt of the knife. The dragon bucked frantically, and I lost my grip, flying through the air until my body slammed against the ground.

Pain splintered my ribs, but I glanced over at my hand. I was still holding the knife. I hadn't been able to jam the blade into its brain the way Marcus had done, but I'd blinded it. That would do for now.

I pushed up onto my elbows, staring as the dragon thundered wildly over the grass, its enormous body writhing in pain and confusion.

In the next moment, Marcus was by my side, his own body covered in blood. He slipped an arm around my back, helping to lift me up. "Are you okay?"

I nodded, glancing at Hazel. Her glamour had completely fallen away, and she stood in a pool of dragon's blood, hugging herself, shivering. Her worst nightmares had come to life today.

I let Marcus help me up, and I eyed the horde of dragons that swarmed above us. Not far from us, the Brooklyn Museum blazed, an inferno in the rainy, gray horizon. A road cut along to our right, and from here I could see cars speeding along the pavement, desperate to flee the dragon's attack.

I touched Marcus's chest, feeling the warmth through his soaked T-shirt. "Let's get Hazel out of here."

He pointed to the road. "Let's see if we can get to a car. I can punch through the window and maybe start the engine. If nothing else, we can at least shelter inside one, out of view."

I turned, beckoning to Hazel. "Let's go! We have to get out of the park."

She nodded mutely, and I let her run ahead of us so we didn't lose track of her. She ran faster this time, speeding across the sodden grass, her black hair plastered to her face in the storm.

As I sprinted, my breath grew ragged in my throat. Around us, the sounds of dragon's screeching rent the air, sending icy dread right through my bones.

We drew closer to the park's edge, our feet slamming over the pavement as we ran into a parking lot. My heart slammed against my ribs; adrenaline snapped through my nerve endings. On the road just before us, cars sped and screeched, frantic, too fast for the slick road. Two sedans slammed into each other, glass smashing all over the asphalt.

Still, we were nearly there, nearly free.

A row of parked cars lined the road just ahead of us, only twenty yards away. We just needed to get to one, and Marcus could get us inside.

"There!" Marcus shouted, pointing to a black sedan. "I can rip the door open."

Nearly there. Once we got to the car, we could huddle down, and—

The sound of beating wings interrupted my thoughts, and I whirled, my heart stopping.

Three dragons surrounded us, one of them larger than the rest— his body a deep crimson, eyes burning like fire. Lightning flashed, sparking off his blood-red scales, his silver armor.

The Drake.

The blood drained from my head, and I gripped the knife tighter.

CHAPTER 5

he Drake spread his wings—fifty feet at least. When lightning struck again, it shone through the leathery skin. Flanking him were two dragon bodyguards, one with a scarred face.

Marcus stood before me, his arms outstretched protectively again. Lightning flashed in the sky, sparking off the Drake's silvery scales, the sword that had transformed into armor over his body.

If we tried to run now, the Drake would unleash a stream of fire, incinerating us where we stood.

Fuck fuck fuck.

The blood-red dragon stared us down, ready to burn us to ash, and all we had was a set of knives. If we'd known this was coming, we could have avoided the mistake of bringing a knife to a dragon fight.

My legs trembled, and I stared up at the monsters, my brain starting to shut down. The dragon with the scarred face was inching closer, hissing.

Marcus raised the knife, whispering to me, "Get back, Ruby. Back away."

I swallowed hard, not entirely sure what he had planned. But I trusted him. Turning to Hazel, I tugged on her arm, pulling her back.

We moved slowly, carefully, as Marcus blocked us. The two smaller dragons flanked the Drake, like some sort of reptilian bodyguards.

"The Drake," Marcus's voice boomed. "Is that what they call you? Tell me about something I've always wondered. Are you a reptile in every way? You're a bit lacking in manhood, aren't you?"

The green dragons seemed to rear back, horrified and transfixed at the same time. Clearly, no one spoke to the Drake this way.

And suddenly I was getting an inkling of what Marcus had planned. He was right—we needed to back away fast.

"No wonder you're a bit tetchy," Marcus went on. "You've never gotten laid, have you? Must be awful wondering what all the fuss is about, never knowing. What have you got, just a hole—"

Fire blazed in the dragon's eyes, and Marcus's sentence fell short. The dragon was about to loose a stream of fire at him.

Hazel and I had backed up all the way to the car now. The Drake opened his mouth to breathe fire, Marcus lunged in a blur of black and white, zooming between the dragon's legs. The Drake loosed a torrent of fire over the pavement, scorching the earth, searing the air.

But Marcus was already on the other side of him, waggling his knife. "I do believe you interrupted my thought. I was going to ask about your hole. What do you do with it, exactly?"

Hazel and I pressed against the car. We'd made it now, and if there was any chance in hell we could all get out of this encounter alive, we had our hiding spot.

Snarling, the Drake turned, its heavy footfalls rumbling over the pavement, shaking the leaves in the nearby trees, and the sound rumbled through my gut. In order to stay here, pressed against the car, I had to fight the overwhelming instinct to run from that sound, a primal urge to flee at the thumping footfalls that trembled the earth.

Hazel grabbed my arm. "What is Marcus doing?" she whispered.

"Saving us. Watch. He knows what he's doing."

Marcus's hands were in his pockets as if he hadn't a care in the world—but as he strode toward the dragon, I remembered what it was that all vampires feared.

Fire, their one weakness.

I felt an overwhelming surge of love for him, and fought the instinct to run over and throw my arms around him, to bury my head against his chest and listen to his heartbeat.

Casually, masking his fear, he rolled the knife's hilt between his fingers. "You know what they say. The bigger the dragon, the smaller the—"

The crimson dragon opened his mouth again, but Marcus was already moving in a blur—this time dodging past one of the other dragons.

And this is where Marcus's plan came into play, as the Drake roared a hot stream of fire all over the scarred dragon. As the dragon's body blazed, the scent of burning flesh filled the air. Black smoke curled off the body.

Marcus didn't need to taunt the Drake anymore; it was already enraged. When Marcus zoomed past the second dragon, his movements too fast to track, the Drake released another surge of flames— missing Marcus, and hitting the second bodyguard.

The green-scaled dragon burst into flames, his smoking body flailing around the parking lot. The scent of singed flesh overpowered me.

As the Drake opened his mouth again to breathe a stream of fire, Marcus threw his knife, landing the blade in the Drake's tongue. Black blood streamed from the Drake's mouth, and it howled—an ancient, otherworldly scream of agony. Frantically, it swatted at its own mouth, trying to knock the knife free, but its talons weren't dexterous enough.

Staggering, the dragon stumbled away from us, clutching its snout. A trail of black blood streamed over the pavement, and in the next few moments the Drake outstretched his wings, lifting off into the darkened skies.

I sighed in relief, and tears welled in my eyes as I looked at Marcus. He'd just faced his worst fears, and he'd done it for us. I couldn't have been prouder, and I couldn't have loved him more.

"He did it," Hazel whispered in awe. "He saved us."

Pride welled in my chest. Marcus hadn't been kidding. He really was a terrifying predator who outmatched nearly everyone—including the Drake and two of his dragon henchmen.

As he crossed to me, I held out my arms to him. Within moments, he'd scooped me up in his powerful embrace, and I breathed in his smell of cedar and leather. Warmth radiated from his body, and I felt his heart pulsing through his shirt. I could lie on top of him, feeling his heart beat for the rest of his life, and not complain.

Or maybe I'd give him the full succubus treatment later.

"I told you I'd keep you safe," he said, his accent faintly lilting.

"Actually," I said, against his chest. "I promised to keep you safe, but I won't complain."

"Guys?" Hazel said. "Let's get the hell out of here before someone lights us on fire."

I unlocked my arms from Marcus. "Brilliant idea."

Marcus nodded at the car we'd been hiding behind. "Step away from the vehicle. I'll get the door open."

I pulled Hazel back a foot, and Marcus stood before the window. He punched once through the window, smashing through the glass. "No time to jimmy the lock." Then he reached inside, unlocking the door. "I might be able to start this thing. Let me just clear the glass."

He opened the door, brushing fragments of glass onto the pavement.

I was so relieved, so close to escape that I didn't even notice the shadow looming behind him until the last moment, when the stench of ancient caves and rock dust alerted me to the presence of a dragon. I whirled, just in time to see the dragon lunge.

I screamed a warning, but it was too late.

My world tilted as the dragon clamped Marcus in its jaws, its teeth piercing Marcus's flesh. Blood streamed over the pavement. My mind nearly shut down at the streaks of red streaming from the dragon's mouth. My chest clenched with pure, raw panic.

This *monster* was hurting my Marcus.

Screaming, I leapt into the air, trying to get a grip on the dragon, but it was too tall for me, and my fingers slipped off its rain-slicked scales. I slammed back down onto the ground, knocking the back of my head on the pavement.

A clawed foot plunged toward me, and I rolled to avoid it, then sprang up to my feet.

The dragon had Marcus's body clamped in its jaws; fear ripped my mind apart. I'd told him I'd protect him, hadn't I?

Frantic, I hurled my knife at the dragon's eye. Somehow, I managed to hit it just at the edge of the iris, even as it flailed its head around.

With its maw clamped around Marcus, it screamed, rearing up on its hind legs. Still, it didn't open its mouth, and the pain only seemed to enrage it more.

The dragon tossed Marcus into the air. Blood poured from his chest, his ribs. A dark voice in the back of my mind screamed that it was too late. The dragon caught him again in his jaws, and the knife fell from Marcus's hand, clanging on the pavement.

I ran for the second knife, snatching it off the pavement. Tears were blurring my vision, and this time when I threw it, it went slightly wide, bouncing off the dragon's hide.

I had a vague sense that I was screaming, calling for Marcus as I scrambled for the knife again, but I couldn't hear my own voice.

I could feel my world being ripped from me, torn apart by dragons again. I grasped for the knife, the rain cold on my skin. Gripping the hilt hard, I ran, leaping on top of the dragon. Its neck was lower this time, and I scrambled onto its back. It had been a sloppy jump, frantic, and I pierced one of my legs on its spikes—but I still managed to grip it.

I couldn't look down, couldn't stare at what the dragon was doing to Marcus. I had to bury those thoughts, lock them up in a mental coffin—but it was hard to clear my mind, and a haze was clouding over it.

I had to protect Marcus like I'd said. As the dragon flailed, I shimmied higher on its neck, blocking out the blood, my thoughts becoming fragmented. I had to block out the terrifying limpness of Marcus's limbs, block out the sounds, the ripping—

Not many ways to kill a vampire but if you ripped through the spine, the heart—

No, Ruby. Block it out. Lock it in a coffin, bury it under the earth.

Marcus in a coffin...

My blood roared in my ears, that icy haze clouding my mind until I couldn't see Marcus, couldn't process what was happening to him. With a feral roar, I reared back my arm, plunging the knife hard into the dragon's eye, my icy rage forcing it deeper, all the way into its socket. Its head thrashed, lolling, until its whole body tilted over and slammed against the pavement. I slipped off its blood-slicked hide, my legs shaking, and rose.

The haze in my mind began to clear as Hazel's shrieks pierced it. I kept my eyes on her, unwilling to turn around. Hazel was screaming Marcus's name, hysterical now. I didn't want to turn around. I knew what I'd see if I turned around. I'd see my whole world ripped apart.

"Ruby!" Hazel screamed, tears pouring down her face. "Marcus is dead."

My breath caught in my lungs, and an icy numbness spread through my body. I forced myself to turn around, my legs shaking.

That was when something in my brain shut down, the haze clouding it again. I could no longer process what I was looking at. I had a vague sense that there was nothing left of Marcus, that the dragon had torn him to pieces, but I just stood there, staring at a pile of wet ash.

Marcus had turned to ash...

My world seemed to go black, the ground tilting beneath my feet. Tears rolled down my cheeks.

I'd gone numb inside, couldn't figure out what to do next. Rain hammered against my skin, grief ripping my mind apart. As I stared mutely at the ground before me, I tried to grasp onto a single, clear thought.

Hazel was screaming incomprehensibly, her nails piercing the skin on my arm. I turned, catching a glimpse of her panicked face. And then the haze in my mind cleared again, as if a lightning bolt had hit my brain. I couldn't fall apart completely now. I still had to get my sister out of here.

Lock up your terror, your grief. Bury it in a wooden coffin next to your parents.

I didn't know how to hotwire a car, but we could still hide inside, shield ourselves from the dragon's view. I pushed her toward the car, but already her eyes were on the skies. Drawn by the screams and blood, by the still-burning bodies of their compatriots, four dragons circled overhead. My heart leapt into my throat. They'd already spotted us.

"Get in the car," I whispered to Hazel.

She shook her head, her expression grave. "It's too late." Her calm, resigned voice suddenly sounded much older than her fourteen years. "You know it's too late." She fixed her dark gaze on me. "The best we can hope for is that they abduct us and don't kill us."

As she finished her sentence, a taloned hand curled around me, yanking me from the earth. I reached for my sister, shouting her name.

Hazel screamed, and the dragon lifted me into the air, wings beating the air around me. He'd pinned my arms to my chest, and I couldn't fight him.

"Hazel!" I screamed through the rain, the wind whipping over my body.

When he'd carried me twenty feet into the air, he hurled me back to the pavement, and fear blazed through my nerve-endings. My body slammed on the ground, pain ripping through me. If I'd been human, the fall would have killed me instantly.

I rolled over, unwilling to look at what remained of Marcus, trying to block out the pain.

I lay on my back, staring up at the sky. From my place on the ground, I stared, horrified, as a second dragon swooped down.

He wasn't coming for me—he was coming for Hazel.

I struggled to push myself up on my elbows, to stand, but I stared in horror as the dragon lifted Hazel higher into the sky, clutching her hard in its talons. His wings pounded against the wind as Hazel screamed for me.

"Hazel!" I shouted again, a useless scream into the void. The dragon was already taking her away, and there was nothing I could do about it.

I stared, heaving a sob as the dragon took her away from me, watching their forms grow smaller and smaller in the stormy sky, until Hazel and her captor looked the size of a small bird, then a black dot against the clouds.

Grief cut me to the core.

Hazel was gone.

Tears poured down my cheeks, and I forced myself to stand. Why weren't the dragons taking me, too?

From where I stood, another taloned hand curled around my body; the dragon lifted me into the air a second time, wings pulsing in the stormy skies. A faint spark of hope lit deep within my chest. Maybe it would take me with Hazel, and I could protect her.

Then, the dragon let go again, and I plummeted.

And at last I understood. The dragons wouldn't be taking me with them. They wanted to toy with me, then kill me slowly. They weren't taking me with Hazel, because this was vengeance for the dragons I'd killed.

I slammed against the earth again, the fall knocking the air out of me, and my body screamed with pain. I pushed up onto my elbows waiting for the next attack, waiting for the talons to pierce my flesh. An entire horde of dragons now surrounded me, yellow eyes gleaming as I struggled to rise. I'm not sure what compelled me to rise, but I didn't want to die on my back. Grabbing my ribs, I rose, glaring at the dragons who surrounded me.

The world seemed to have gone silent; the air was colder now.

As I stood in the center of the dragons, a single, coppery feather floated down from the heavens. I didn't know why, but I reached out to snatch it, as though it were a lifeline.

Then I looked up at the skies.

There, like a gleaming angel of death, flew the sun-demon, his golden hair gleaming like a crown of sunlight below the iron-gray clouds.

CHAPTER 6

The dragons seemed to sense him, their necks craning up to look at him. He was flying lower, heading for me. My mouth went dry, and I swallowed hard. He wore black military clothes, with a silver bow slung over his back. If I hadn't been halfway dead, the sight of him would have sent a cold shiver of fear up my spine. As it was, I was just hoping he'd end my life quickly instead of letting the dragons torture me to death.

I stared at him as he swooped down. My fingers found their way to my side. As the Sun-demon landed, I clutched my battered ribs protectively.

He peered down at me, his amber gaze cold and hard. "A succubus against a legion of dragons. Seems you've held your own for a while."

"What?" I could hardly process what he was saying.

He leaned in, stroking a finger over the golden skin on my forearm —the one patch of skin not covered in red and black blood. "A succubus," he repeated. "One who dresses like an angel. Too intoxicating to waste as dragon food."

Of course. I still wore the glamour of a succubus, and maybe right now it was saving my life.

One of the dragons snarled, moving closer, his eyes locked on me, blood dripping from his jaw. Whose blood, I had no idea, but it seemed to want mine also.

The Sun-demon pivoted. Then, he lifted a powerful arm, slashing his hand through the air. As he moved his arm in an arc around us, an invisible blade seemed to cut through the dragons, ripping through their necks, their chests. Screeching, a few of the dragons flapped their wings, trying to get away before the Sun-demon cut through them, too, but he was too fast.

He slashed his hand through the air, slicing through the dragons. Tons of severed dragon flesh slammed against the earth, shaking the pavement.

And just like that, the dragon horde around me lay dead.

I turned to stare at the Sun-demon, his body glowing with a golden light. My stomach dropped. What sort of demon could do that? Not even a demigod had such power.

"Who are you?" I whispered.

He took a step closer, his velvet voice brushing over my skin. "I am Kratos."

"Are you an angel?" I stammered. It was a stupid question. Real angels were incorporeal. They never came to earth, didn't speak to humans.

"According to you, I'm a rich prick. Isn't that all you need to know?"

I swallowed hard, clutching the copper feather between my fingertips. "I need help. The dragons took my sister." But even as I said the words, I knew I was pleading to the wrong man. The man before me wasn't my savior.

He stepped closer, and I could feel the heat burning off his body. He leaned in and whispered, "Well then, you'd better find her, hadn't you?"

"What's happening?" I stammered.

He narrowed his eyes at me. "You could come with me. You could amuse me. I won't stay in this hellhole long."

"Come with you where?" My voice sounded hollow.

"To London."

I shook my head, trying to block out the pile of sodden ash that lay a few feet from us. The grief washed over me so completely I could hardly remember how to speak. "I have to find my sister."

"Suit yourself."

"What do you want from me?" I breathed.

"I told you, my little succubus. I demand only worship, and the end of the world. I think you'll find the world a very different place now."

I grabbed his arm, my fingers leaving smudges of blood over his black clothing. He was terrifying, but desperation spurred me on. "I need your help."

Cold fury flashed in his eyes, and he pulled his arm away from me. In a burst of honeyed light, he spread his wings, his hair gleaming like a halo. Then, he lifted off into the darkened skies.

CHAPTER 7

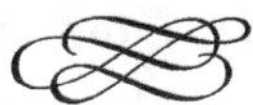

I huddled in the corner of the abandoned sanitarium on North Brother Island, warming my hands over a fire that crackled in an old steel drum. The other survivors and I called this place The Fortress—a Victorian brick hospital that we patrolled at night, protective of our meager horde of canned food and venison, our moth-eaten sleeping bags and filthy blankets.

Nearly all the Fortress inhabitants were men, but they pretty much left me alone. For one thing, I could hunt deer on the island better than any of them, by setting traps and using my knife. I didn't even need the two guns we kept in the fortress. And for another, I'd beaten the shit out of three men who'd tried to grope me during the first month. No one bothered me after that.

For six months, I'd been living here, curling up into a ball in the corner at night, sleeping among the rags and burning barrels. When the winter sun rose, streaking the freezing Hudson with milky white light, I'd leave to search for Hazel. The dragons wouldn't care that she needed water by her bedside at night, that she had to read for twenty minutes before falling asleep. The dragons would not accommodate her nut allergy, or provide her with her asthma medication. They wouldn't soothe her when she woke up from her nightmares at night, screaming for her parents, and they certainly wouldn't give a fuck about the crippling menstrual cramps that laid her out every month. They didn't care that every Saturday, we sat together on the sofa watching superhero shows and stuffing our faces with pizza and popcorn.

I had to get her back. There was no other option.

Every day, I roamed the ravaged streets of Brooklyn, Manhattan, Queens. Dragons had destroyed most of New York—most of the northeast, in fact, from Maine to Delaware. And then, as far as I could tell, they'd simply left.

The last time the dragons had come to New York, they'd made their dens in the bowels of the city, taking up residence below the Statue of Liberty and beneath bridges. Not this time. Where they'd gone, none of us knew, but they'd probably taken Hazel with them.

My decision to stay in the city had been the wrong one. Now, it was painfully clear I should have gone with the sun-demon when I had the chance, but I'd had no way of knowing that at the time. He'd have been a link to the dragons, at least. If I'd bided my time, maybe I could have learned something from him, found my sister again.

Standing before the roaring fire, I rolled the thin, golden shaft of the feather around in my fingertips, watching the firelight flicker through it, mesmerized by its beauty. The feather almost seemed to glow with an inner light, even after all these months. It was almost as if it were made of light itself.

While I stared at the feather, a bearded man slumped down next to me, staining the air with the scent of sweat. For reasons I didn't understand, everyone called him Elvis. He was completely bald on the top of his head, with a long gray beard that always seemed to be covered in food.

"I've seen you playing with that thing before," he grumbled.

"Don't you ever touch this, Elvis."

"What's so special about it, anyway?" He perked up, suddenly rising to peer at the feather. "Is it worth something?"

"To me it is. Not to anyone else. This belongs to someone I want to find. That's it."

He furrowed his enormous eyebrows. "It looks gold. Do you see that? Like it's glowing."

"I've noticed."

His eyes glistened. "Do you know what that is?" A sense of reverence tinged his tone.

"It's a feather, Elvis."

"It's an *angel* feather."

I snatched it from his line of sight, secreting it in my pocket—a pocket with a zipper to keep it safe. "Don't be ridiculous. Angels haven't been to earth since the Fall a hundred thousand years ago. They live in the heavens. They're just spirits."

He shook his head. "Nah. You want my theory? An angel caused all this. They're punishing us. We deserve it, too, after everything we've done."

I didn't want to ask what he meant. I had no interest in his theories on the inherent wickedness of humanity.

But maybe he knew something.

"What do you know about angels?"

He shrugged. "They hate us. That's about it. Where do you think your angel went?"

"I think he's in London. And I'm not going to get there on foot, and probably not by boat, so it looks like I'm shit out of luck."

He scratched his beard. "There's a man on Long Island running flights from his private airstrip to Europe. Getting people out of the hellscape if they can pay. He goes by Lord Bristol, though that's not his real name. No idea what his real name is. Not a lord, of course."

"Right. So, how much does this cost?"

"Only a million dollars. Give the cash to his secretary, and she'll set you up."

"And where the hell am I going to get a million dollars? I have zero dollars right now." Certainly no one was paying for burlesque shows —not in the ruined husks of buildings that were all that remained of Manhattan. "I've got nothing but a few knives."

"I'm sure you can find something else to trade him for." Elvis grinned. "He likes pretty girls, and there aren't many pretty girls left in New York. I like pretty girls, too, but I don't got any money. Unless you get real lonely."

"You've got to be kidding me."

Elvis shrugged. "You're an enterprising girl. I'm sure you can think of something."

* * *

I SAT in the plush airline seat, my body deliciously free from grime. I didn't know my airplane types well. All I knew was that it looked like a super-fancy private jet, with champagne-colored leather seats— enough to fit six passengers in the roomy seats, plus a leather sofa and a kitchen.

While we waited to take off, I made three trips to the kitchen, fixing myself cheese sandwiches and grabbing fruit.

For a moment, Marcus's beautiful face flashed in my mind, and his loss hit me like a fist to the chest. Every day I remembered his beautiful cedar scent, his smooth skin. I'd never meet another man like him.

Pushing my grief under the surface, I peered out a round window at the tarmac—the pale strip of pavement that stretched out over the glimmering blue water. After seven months in the Fortress, it felt amazing to be clean, with a full belly. I didn't want to stop eating anytime soon.

Getting the money for the flight hadn't been as hard as I'd feared. First, I'd needed to identify the one person who might have a million dollars. And the one person I knew for sure who had that money was Lord Bristol himself. He'd been fleecing people left and right, people who were probably trying to save their families. So I went straight for him.

As I waited on the jet, I bit into my apple, chewing contemplatively. I peered out the window, craning my neck to look back at Lord Bristol's mansion. I could just about imagine him still tied to the chair in his room, blindfolded and gagged with silk. I'd told him that "naughty boys needed to wait," and he really hadn't noticed when I'd robbed him. The secretary hadn't asked any questions.

As the pilot made an announcement, I buckled my seatbelt. While the engines revved up, vibrating the jet, I pulled the copper feather from my pocket. Here it was. My one clue to getting my sister back.

Fascinated by its inner glow, I held it up to the buttery light that streamed in from the window. The sunlight sparked over its feathers, gilding it.

At last, the jet rolled down the runway, and a smile curled my lips.

London. I was going to find the angel of death in London, and I would pick up the pieces of my life again.

CHAPTER 8

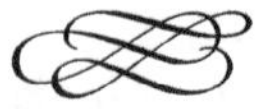

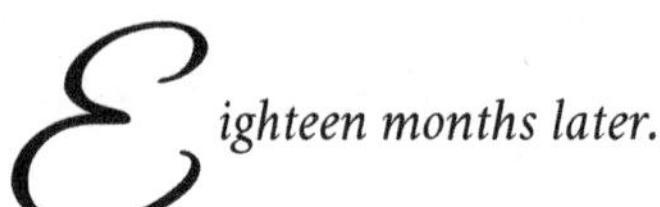 *ighteen months later.*

AT THE FAR corner of my rookery, I tiptoed over the trip wires, careful not to trigger the traps. One false step, and I'd find myself in the awkward situation of having to wrench one of my own wooden spears from my ribs. Not my favorite way to spend an evening.

Just one of the perils of living in a home with an interior design plan inspired by the quaint concepts of *maim and kill.*

When I managed to reach the door un-impaled, I peered out a hospital window at Whitechapel High Street. A few rays of coral sunlight pierced the bruise-colored clouds, glinting off the broken glass that littered the streets.

My breath fogged the window, and I cleared the cold pane with my palm. I focused on the unexpected beauty of the sunset-tinged glass, and stories began to whirl in my mind—stories of glamour and luxury from before the Great Nightmare had begun.

How long had it been since angels had first come to the Earth? Maybe a year and a half?

I let out a low whistle. A full year and a half—at least—since I'd been a burlesque dancer on the other side of the Atlantic. In New York, my Stripping Angel act killed like you would not believe. Even better than the Naughty Puritan.

Funny thing about the apocalypse was that there wasn't much call for glittery performance art. Sequined pasties, shimmering tassels, fan-dance interpretations of the Salem Witch Trials... Not exactly high on the priority list in the post-apocalyptic hellscape.

I hadn't danced a single step since before angels had razed cities to the ground. Not one twirl or arabesque after the angels' dragon-shifter buddies had kidnapped my sister right in front of me. Still, I had to hold on to beauty where I could find it, keep it alive with stories of the old days.

And more than anything else, I had to hang on to my dream of finding my sister again.

I took a deep breath, still working up the nerve to leave the rookery—the hive of homes that survivors had made in the old hospital. It was safe in here, protected by my slightly terrifying traps.

Unfortunately, I couldn't stay here all the time.

Slightly dazed from hunger, I pressed my hand against the glass a final time, staring out at the street. "Hazel," I whispered my sister's name, finding comfort in the word. "Where are you?"

Footsteps sounded behind me, ripping me away from my thoughts. I turned to see my friend Alex gingerly stepping over a trip wire in the dingy hospital lobby. "Ruby, darling. A penny for your thoughts."

Just thinking about Hazel, as usual. I smiled. "Thinking about all the delicious food we're going to eat," I lied.

"Didn't think you were going to leave without me, did you, Ruby?"

I frowned at him, studying the bruises marring his coppery-brown skin. "Alex, you know I love you, but you just got the shit kicked out of you a few hours ago. Let me do this on my own."

"You know you need my mad skills. And what kind of man lets a woman venture into post-apocalyptic hell on her own?"

I scowled. "Spare me the machismo, Rambo. I might be a woman, but I'm not human. The fae don't break as easily as humans. No offense."

His forehead crinkled. "Fine. I'll stay behind. But only because you insinuated that I was acting chauvinistic, and now I have no idea what to do. I know you Americans get funny about political correctness, and it scares me more than the gangs or angels."

Smiling, I nodded at the hallway that led back to our safe haven. "All you need to do is stay here and wait till I come back with potatoes and meat."

"Fine." He hesitated. "You have weapons?"

"Of course." Granted, all I had were scalpels from one of the hospital closets, but they were better than nothing. "I'll see you for dinner."

I pushed through the door into the afternoon light of the world outside. The January air nipped at my skin through my threadbare coat. It was still a little early to leave, but I'd started to become more and more leery of staying out at night.

When the sun set, there were worse things to fear than demons and gangs.

Danger or not, I had to get to our hidden garden one way or another if we wanted to eat. In a secret patch of grass off Brick Lane, we grew potatoes in the cold winter soil and left out traps for rabbits.

Already, I could taste the rich meat, the stewed potatoes, and my stomach rumbled.

If anyone found our garden, we'd starve in a week.

In the chilly air, I clutched the straps of my backpack, glancing at the clouds gathering on the horizon. From the front steps of the Royal London Hospital, I surveyed the main street. A light dusting of snow covered the pavement—the worst we'd seen so far in a mercifully warm winter. Plastic bags drifted languidly over the broken asphalt, and bare trees clawed at the skies. A few rays of the setting sun poured through a break in the steely winter clouds and streamed over a pile of ivory bones that lay among a pile of ash on the sidewalk. Human? Animal? Probably best not to think about it too much.

Shivering, I pulled my jacket more tightly around me and started walking. My skin prickled at the eerie silence that enshrouded the East End, and I kept close to the walls as I walked.

When I turned onto Brick Lane, a flicker of movement caught my eye. A robed figure drifted down the street, black eyes glistening like inky pools, skin the color of bone. I released a long breath. *Just one of the sentinels, out for a patrol.*

Once the whole apocalypse had started, the sentinels had arrived to roam London's streets, always watching, never speaking. Some flew through the air, and others stalked the alleys. They never touched anyone, never did anything, but we were all sure they reported to someone. To the angels, probably—the godlike creatures who never deigned to walk among us.

Shuddering, I almost regretted turning down Alex's offer of help. I needed his stories to keep me sane. I had a sudden urge to hear about his pre-apocalypse days of champagne and gold-flaked cupcakes.

"Cupcakes…" I hadn't realized that I was speaking out loud until the word was out of my mouth.

Hunger ripped through my stomach, and I wiped a bit of drool off my chin. Dignity had deserted me long ago.

Just then, a blur of movement in the distance sharpened my fae senses, and my heartbeat sped up. Two figures were moving fast over the pavement—too fast for humans.

Quickly, I summoned my fae magic. I always wore a glamour to disguise my fae appearance. But now I began to add another layer, transforming myself into a succubus with a tingling of magic over my skin. I hardly had to change a thing—my deep red hair stayed the same, and my petite frame remained unchanged. By keeping the changes minimal, I could conserve energy I badly needed.

I merely shifted my pistachio-green eyes to black, added a bit of charcoal magic swirling around my body, and *voila*—another demon roamed these streets.

Demons tended to leave other demons alone.

Maybe a succubus wasn't the scariest of disguises, but it was the quickest one to wrap around myself. One I'd used for years as a burlesque dancer.

By the time the two redcaps caught up to me, their metal boots clanking over the pavement, they were staring right at a full-blown succubus. As far as they knew.

Probably naively, I hoped they'd simply take their scrawny asses on past me, uninterested in bothering another demon. Instead, they ground to a halt right in front of me, metal boots screeching on the cold pavement.

Until this afternoon, I'd never seen two redcap demons standing side by side. And I'd certainly never seen the sinewy old creeps skulking around in London's daylight. Obviously, things had changed since the Great Nightmare had begun, since there were no police left to protect us.

Sunlight glinted off the demons' metallic boots, and their black eyes shone like oil. Apart from their strange footwear, the wiry, blood-spattered demons wore nothing but loincloths. A shudder snaked up my neck when I realized the demons' caps were glistening with burgundy streaks of gore—the felt fabric dipped in their victims' blood. If Alex were here, they'd be trying to eat him right about now.

Stay calm, Ruby. Stay calm.

"Aren't you a pretty little succubus?" one of them purred in a thick Scottish accent, stroking his tangled beard.

I arched an eyebrow. "I hope you don't expect me to return the compliment."

He chuckled, the raspy sound making me cringe.

You'd think an encounter with two ancient, repulsive demons would make for a good story. Like I said, in the world of the Great Nightmare, stories were our refuge. But I already knew I'd be keeping this one to myself. Our salvation was our happy memories, and this wasn't about to be a pleasant one.

In fact, I had a pretty bad feeling about what was going to happen next.

Mentally, I took stock of my weapons. I had three scalpels tucked into my leather belt, and… nope, it was really just the scalpels. Still, these particular demons didn't seem like geniuses, so maybe I wouldn't need a full arsenal.

One of the redcaps licked his lips, his long, pointed tongue darting out to taste a droplet of blood on his mustache. "Little on the skinny side, aren't you? Not enough meat on your bones. Not to worry, pretty thing. We've got meat for you."

Gross. I wrinkled my nose, mindful to maintain an aristocratic, succubus attitude.

I loosed a sigh. "Not a lot of Michelin-starred restaurants around since the whole apocalypse started. And unlike you two, I don't feast on human flesh. You ever think that maybe the angels wouldn't have come to Earth in the first place if demons like you hadn't been gorging on Earth's citizens for centuries?"

One of them rubbed his hands together lasciviously. "You want to see me engorged, eh?"

I shook my head. "Not even close to what I said. You're not very bright, are you?"

"Pretty thing." He stroked his scraggly beard. "You feast on humans in other ways, don't you? Maybe the angels came to Earth because of you. Maybe they want to watch you feeding, with your legs wrapped around a human male. Maybe the angels are as naughty as we are. Ever think of that?"

I gestured at the scorched husks of buildings around us. "I'd say the angels might be worse, in fact, given what they've done in their time here."

None of us really knew why the angels had come, but their arrival had coincided with the start of the Great Nightmare. I'd say there was a good chance they wanted to slaughter us all just for kicks, and they were more than capable of doing it. Redcaps and demons could be scary, yes. But angels—now they were terrifying.

One of the leathery old men crept closer to me, flashing his uneven teeth. "And that's why we need to stick together, you see. Demon on demon. Wrap those pretty legs of yours around me, and I'll give you some food to eat. Some fresh human rump. Fatten you up. You just need to be nice to me first. You know how to be nice, don't you, succubus?"

Obviously, the succubus glamour had been a bad call. Should have gone for an ogre or a troll, even if it sapped all my energy.

My stomach tightened, and I took a step back from them. I could try to run, but no one was faster than a redcap, and few demons were stronger. "A succubus chooses her men, not the other way around."

One of the redcaps grinned, sharp teeth glinting. "Times have changed in the Great Nightmare, pretty thing. Females are slaves now. Now be a good little succubus, and take off those filthy clothes. Let me see what charms you're hiding underneath."

As my blood began to boil, I took another step backward, reaching for one of the surgical scalpels tucked into my leather belt. Whipping it from its holster, I pointed it at the closest redcap.

"What do you plan to do with that?" he sneered. "An emergency appendectomy?"

Succubi weren't known for their amazing aim.

But the fae were.

I threw the scalpel, and it plunged into his chest. Wide-eyed, he clutched at the protruding metal, blood streaming between his fingers, and I reached for the next scalpel. That one hit its mark in the second redcap's neck, and blood arced through the air.

Only pure iron would kill them, but the steel would slow them down. I pivoted, breaking into a run at the full speed of a fae—far faster than a human, faster than a succubus.

Just—unfortunately—not as fast as a redcap.

I got maybe fifty yards before bony fingers scraped my scalp, yanking me backward onto the street by the roots of my hair. I slammed down on the pavement, the wind leaving my lungs. In the next second, the redcap was on top of me, his bloodied teeth bared, bony knees in my chest. The scalpel protruded from his ribs.

Frantically, I yanked the final scalpel from my belt.

But before I could slam it into his neck, he clamped a powerful hand around my wrists, the other around my throat. He began to squeeze.

I fought the urge to fade, to reveal my true, primal fae form. If this was how they'd treat a succubus, I didn't want to think of what they'd do to a feral fae.

As the burning rose in my lungs, my eyes bulged.

Running out of air... I stared beyond the redcap at the sky, hoping for a glimmer of salvation—maybe a passing valkyrie who could help a girl out.

Instead, I saw a single, shimmering midnight feather drifting to Earth, and my heart stopped. Somehow, this herald of an angel's presence terrified me more than the redcap choking me.

I have to get out of here, or I will meet an angel face to face.

CHAPTER 9

The shock of the angel feather jolted my body alive with pure adrenaline—enough to give me the boost I needed to wrench my hand free for just a moment. A moment was all I needed.

I brought the scalpel hard into the redcap's back, and the blow stunned him just enough to make him release his grip on me. I grabbed the back of his tangled hair, yanking him off me as I thrust my hips. When he fell to the ground, I leapt up, slamming my boot into his skull with the full force of my fae strength.

As I kicked him again, trying to crack his skull, a shimmering, deep-blue glow caught my attention. I froze, ice-cold fear spreading through my body.

He's here.

When I looked up from the redcap, my stomach dropped. The angel's enormous, midnight-blue wings spread out behind him, fifteen feet wide. There, in the middle of the road, stood an angel, divinely beautiful and terrifying all at once.

* * *

BOTH BLOODIED REDCAPS had crawled to their elbows. All three of us stared, seemingly frozen in time.

The angel towered above us, honeyed sunlight washing over his perfectly bronzed skin. I caught glimpses of the magic curling from his body, dark as the hair that swept over his forehead. In contrast to the shadows that seemed to pool around him, light refracted off his inky wings, dazzling me.

His clothes looked expensive, finely cut to showcase his powerful body. In the deep V of his elegant shirt, I glimpsed a hint of spiked, thorny tattoos decorating his tawny skin.

Barefoot, he prowled closer to me, his gait relaxed. In fact, his expression looked *amused,* a lazy smile curling his lips. Our terror, our filth, our savagery, our frantic will to survive—it was all probably a hilarious joke to him.

When he came within a few feet, his power thrummed and sparked over my skin like an electrical pulse. I stared into his eyes—a stormy gray that blended to deep sapphire around the edges. Flecks of silver sparked there too.

Instinctively, I knew that he was a predator, and that beauty was one of his most terrifying weapons.

He stalked closer, and his inhumanly fluid movements sent my blood racing. As he walked, shadowy magic trailing behind him, I caught the breathtaking veins of silver that shot through his feathers, gleaming in the dying sunlight.

That sensuous smile never left his perfect lips. "I'm surprised to find a goddess such as yourself squabbling in the streets with these dregs." The dangerous timbre of his voice promised death and seduction all in one. "At least you seemed to have the upper hand."

The redcap at my feet scrambled up. "She did not have the upper hand," he stammered. "No woman has the upper hand over me."

The angel arched a perfect eyebrow, his expression faintly mocking. "Perhaps you enjoy pain? Would you like some more?" The threat of extreme brutality underscored the calm tone of his voice.

The redcap pointed at him, trying to feign bravery, even though we could all see his finger shaking. "You think you're better than us, do you? You filthy carrion birds, vultures the lot of you. You should go back where you—"

The angel cut him off with a flick of his wrist, severing the redcap's head from his body in a single, brutal instant. The headless corpse thunked to the ground, blood streaming over the pavement, and my stomach lurched.

I gasped for breath, my heart slamming against my ribs. In the next few moments, the sound of clanking filled the air as the second redcap started to sprint away.

The angel turned, cutting the air sharply with his hand. This time, he severed his prey at the waist, and the two pieces of the demon's body slammed to the ground.

My jaw dropped. *Was I next?*

My blood roared in my ears, but I tried to hold his gaze steadily, tried to hide the terror that raced through my veins. My knees had gone weak, and the urge to fade into my fae form nearly overwhelmed me.

With his gaze now locked on me, the exquisite angel took another step closer, lethal grace imbuing his every move. The smell of myrrh curled off his body, along with the intoxicating scent of sycamore trees. Everything about him drew me in and told me to run at the same time, my brain a riot of conflicting emotions.

I stared up at him. He stood only a foot away from me now, his terrifying power caressing my skin. If I tried to run, I'd end up in pieces like the redcaps.

The angel reached for my face, and my breath caught in my throat.

He brushed his fingertip over a dab of blood on my cheek. At his touch, an electric jolt seared my core.

"It's been a long time since I've seen a succubus covered in blood," he said quietly. "The days of the old sacrifices are long gone. Things didn't turn out so well for your kind on Earth, did they? Pity. What fun it was to watch a naked succubus bathe in the blood of her male sacrifices. I imagine you miss the old days."

I simply opened my mouth and closed it again.

His sensuous smile deepened. "I'd ask if you wanted to recreate it with me, but for an angel such pastimes might be frowned upon. We can kill, but we can't appear to enjoy it too much."

That's right—I was supposed to be an ancient succubus. At one point, they had practically been deities. I shoved my terror under the surface, trying to summon the regal bearing of a goddess. One who'd once stood in the center of a temple, covered in sacrificial human blood. The succubi ran from no one.

Which, come to think of it, might explain why most of them were dead.

I swallowed hard. "So you remember the old days?" Unlike mine, his ancientness was probably real.

He laughed softly. "Do I look like I was born yesterday?" Arrogance laced his voice. "I've walked the Earth for thousands of years. Like you, succubus."

Of course, any man who'd spent thousands of years looking like he did would develop a bit of an ego.

He cocked his head, studying me. "I'm surprised I've never run into you before. I would have remembered."

A cool breeze rippled over us, toying with my crimson hair. "I've spent many years in hiding. There aren't many succubi left. We have to protect ourselves however we can."

The angel pulled a handkerchief from his pocket, wiping the blood off his finger. "Indulge my curiosity. Why were you fighting with those two curs?"

I met his gaze evenly. "Apparently, they wanted me to take my clothes off and wrap my legs around them."

Darkness flitted through his eyes, and I realized I'd just confirmed to him all the despicable things angels believed about demons.

As he stood before me, shadows twisted around him, swallowing the air. "So they had good taste, but poor manners."

"I had to teach them a lesson, as you might imagine. Sometimes violence is necessary. Things have changed in the past year." I crossed my arms. "Since the angels commanded dragon shifters to start slaughtering us, things haven't been great for females."

"Well, like you said." His velvety voice seemed to curl around me like a dangerous embrace. "Sometimes violence is necessary."

All right. I wasn't going to get into a philosophical debate with him about the justification for mass slaughter, or what the angels had done to the Earth. I had something important I needed to ask him, and I wouldn't get many other chances.

I cleared my throat, steeling my resolve. "Look, I have a question to ask you. I'm looking for my sister. It's the whole reason I came to London—"

Before I could even finish the sentence, he spread out his dark wings, the silver strands glinting in the sunlight. The sight dazzled me, cutting off my words.

In the next few moments, he took flight into the skies.

And with him went my only chance to ask an all-powerful being about the fate of my sister.

CHAPTER 10

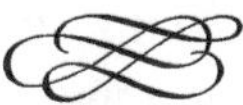

$\mathcal{I}$t took a full day before I had the nerve to leave the rookery again. And for my next foray into the world outside, Alex declared he was coming with me, whether or not it made him a chauvinist. He didn't care about being PC anymore.

Frankly, as we walked along Brick Lane, I found myself happy for the company.

The sun would be setting soon. Dusk and nightfall were when the angels usually crawled out of the shadows—when the Hunt came to East London.

But I didn't want to think about that now. I wanted the good stories—the gold-flaked cupcakes and wine—so I could forget all about what had happened yesterday.

Alex smiled at me. "You never get sick of hearing about the cupcakes, do you, Ruby darling?" The sunlight warmed his mahogany skin.

"I just want to hear the varieties again. I don't actually care about the gold; it's more the cake flavors that interest me." Anything to get my mind off the memory of the severed redcap bodies, the angel's savage efficiency. "What did the gold-flaked cupcake taste like?"

Alex squinted into the sunlight. "That one tasted like honey, but

I'm sure for enough money, you could have had any flavor you wanted."

My stomach growled audibly, and I clutched it. "My sister Hazel used to bake cupcakes every weekend. I would murder for a cupcake right now. Any kind. Vanilla, red velvet. Hell, even carrot cake with the cream cheese. I'd probably murder multiple people for that kind with the molten chocolate in the middle."

"Murder's not gonna get you cupcakes, love."

"I think she used to make molten chocolate cupcakes. That's real, right? It's not something I dreamed up, is it? Melted dark chocolate, right in the middle of a cupcake. I don't know what sort of problem the angels have, but the human race invented those, and that makes them gods-damned geniuses. Molten chocolate cupcakes were humanity's zenith before the Nightmare began, do you know that?"

He shot me a sharp look. "You okay, fairy? I feel like hunger is driving you mental."

"Fae. Not fairy. And yes, hunger is driving me mental. Ignoring hunger isn't part of the fae skill set. At least not until you reach the age of ninety or two hundred or something."

"Right. Sorry. And you're… what… eighty?"

I rolled my eyes. "A mere twenty-five. Young as hell for a fae." I rubbed my rumbling stomach. "Hence, I have no control over my hunger."

"You and me both."

I glanced at him. "You must have known about the fae for a few years, right? It's not a new concept for humans." Demons, humans, fae… we'd all started fighting each other out in the open five years ago. Years before the angels came and started killing all of us.

"Yeah, I'd heard of the fae, I guess, but I'd never met one. Mostly, once humans learned about supernaturals, everyone was focused on the demons. They just seemed a lot scarier than, you know, fairies."

"Fae. And we are plenty scary. Let's not forget the time you watched me go feral and chew through leather restraints."

"It was honestly oddly cute."

I scowled at him. "Oh, please."

Alex shook his head. "And yeah, I guess I don't know a ton about your kind. It's hard to keep up with everything we humans had to learn in the past seven years. First we learned that magic is real. Then we learned that magical creatures want to kill us, and we could protect ourselves with spells if we get them right. We were just getting used to the idea of all this, and *BAM*, the dragons come out to slaughter us all before we can do anything cool with this knowledge. Never even got my hands on those magic books to learn to make myself invisible or levitate."

"Well, I never learned that either. Really wishing I'd studied one of those old agricultural magic books at some point."

"I'm with you there. I'm just hoping we can get our bloody potatoes out of the ground unscathed today. The hunger is making me dizzy. And if the ground freezes..."

He let the sentence die in the air. If the ground froze, which it usually did in January, we'd be fucked. There was no way around it—we didn't have enough supplies to get us through the winter.

"I think I know a way to keep people away from us today." Only this time, the glamour would take a bit more effort.

I closed my eyes as we walked, summoning a powerful glamour—one that would tax my energy. As I let the spell wash over me, the ancient fae magic tingled across my skin in a satisfying rush. I disguised my pale complexion and my green eyes. I covered up my gaunt cheekbones and my skinny form.

I replaced it all with a gargantuan, scarred hulk of a man.

After the glamour fully took effect, a passerby would see an ogre striding down the street next to Alex, all corded muscle. This glamour would be a struggle to maintain, but at least it would keep the redcaps away from us. Sadly, the glamour didn't actually change my physiology—I didn't have the strength of an ogre. I was still me completely underneath it all. It was a sort of bubble of illusion around my body. Only thing I didn't disguise was the bag I carried—that would just about lay me out with fatigue.

Alex peered up at me, grinning. "You look ugly as sin, and I feel safer already."

"You know I'll protect you, my little friend."

My stomach rumbled, hunger gnawing at my ribs. We walked on in silence, and my gaze trailed over the blackened husks of pubs and apartment buildings that lined Brick Lane.

In one of the alleys we passed, the breeze lifted a few plastic bags. The sudden noise made my heart thump. I think I had PTSD from the whole angel run-in.

I could almost envision this street as it must have been: people bustling in and out of the shops and restaurants, buying trendy clothes and eating curries. Now the windows had been smashed, and a crashed truck blocked part of the road, its rotten contents spilled into the street: old cartons of eggs, blackened in the dragon fires; piles of beer bottles, half-melted.

Did the angels spend much time around this sort of depressing landscape? I didn't imagine so. They probably had a gilded palace somewhere, and every now and then they'd just fly around unleashing death on everyone for no reason.

A few blocks away, two sentinels drifted silently, their dark eyes locked on us.

At last, we took a sharp right onto Buxton Street, where an over-grown park lined a crumbling cobbled road. Part of the park was enclosed by a brick wall—and this was where our garden lay. We looked furtively around us before crossing to the rusted refrigerator door that masked the garden's opening.

When we were sure the coast was completely clear, Alex shifted the door aside.

Quietly, we slipped in through the narrow opening, my muscles already aching from the effort of keeping the glamour in effect.

In the safety of our little hidden garden, Alex began to pull up potatoes from the cold ground, while I went to check the traps. I grinned when I saw one of the wooden boxes flat on the ground.

Long ago, my parents had made sure I'd learned the old fae ways—how to live off the forest, to set snares for prey. If larger game like deer ever ran through the city, I knew how to carve a bow and arrow from a sapling and shoot the poor bastards, but I didn't see that happening any time soon.

My mouth was already watering. We'd be having rabbit for dinner tonight. I snatched up the box, then grabbed the panicking rabbit. It only took a second to snap its neck. Clutching the limp body, I wrapped it in a plastic bag.

As I did, an icy wind rippled over my skin, a shadow passing overhead. When I looked up, my stomach dropped. Under the deepening clouds, the dark-winged angel swooped low, though he didn't seem to notice us.

Tawny sunlight pierced the iron-gray clouds, gilding his powerful wings.

My heart skipped a beat. *Death, wrapped in one beautiful, angelic form.*

I smacked Alex's arm, then pointed at the sky. His eyes went wide. As the angel soared away, Alex let out a long breath.

"Bloody hell," he breathed. "That the one you saw yesterday?"

"Yeah. That's your first one, isn't it?" I asked.

He nodded. "You're the only one I know who's seen one. What the hell do you think they're doing here?"

I shook my head. "I can't tell. I'm not sure if they care whether we live or die. I tried to ask him about my sister, but he didn't even stick around long enough for me to finish my sentence. He made some weird comments about succubi being naked and covered in blood, then he just flew off."

Suddenly, Alex's eyes went wide, and he pressed a finger to his lips, arching a cautionary eyebrow. Voices echoed off the nearby bricks, and a chill snaked up my spine.

The gangs were out late today. Probably the same gang that had beaten the crap out of Alex yesterday. Didn't they know the Hunt would be coming through here soon?

I shoved the rabbit into the backpack, then peered out the craggy opening in the wall. I cast a nervous glance at the sky, clenching my jaw. Night hadn't fallen yet, but the last ruddy rays were slipping away fast.

From my vantage point, the street still seemed deserted, just a few plastic bags and old newspapers drifting in the wind. I turned back to Alex, beckoning him to follow, and we slipped out into the street. Carefully, I slid the fridge door over the opening to the garden, hiding our bounty. I tightened my grip on the backpack's straps, and we moved swiftly over the cobbles, back toward the safety of our rookery.

As we moved, the hair rose on the back of my neck. I didn't see any gangs, but I could feel their eyes on us. They knew we had food they didn't have the skills to catch. They might not be stronger than us, or cleverer than us, but they outnumbered us.

"Any idea where they are?" whispered Alex.

I scanned the streets, where nothing moved but scraps of trash blowing in the breeze.

As we turned onto Brick Lane, I heard the first footfalls behind us. I cast a quick glance behind me, my heart thundering at the sight of a large street gang a half a block away. There were about twelve of them. Judging by the looks on their faces, my ogre glamour was doing nothing to scare them off.

At the front of the gang, a pale, bearded man gripped a machete. I knew him, in fact. He was the one everyone called Dickhead, on account of the long, thin birthmark on his bald head. Exactly the man who'd beaten up Alex for his food yesterday.

I can't say humanity had gotten any more appealing after the Great Nightmare had begun.

Dickhead nodded at us. "What have you got in your little bag there?" he shouted. "Something tasty? Why don't you let us have a little peek? Feeling a bit peckish myself."

I shot a quick look to Alex. *Not giving up the rabbit,* I tried to convey with my eyes. My rumbling stomach demanded that we hang on to what we had.

Alex nodded at me, then we broke into a sprint, charging down Brick Lane. Not a brilliant plan, but a simple one.

Unfortunately for me, the glamour was using up half my energy, and already my muscles were searing, my lungs burning. Dizziness clouded my mind, and I dropped the glamour. It was running or magic—I couldn't do both.

By the time we reached Osborn Street, sweat drenched my clothes, and my breath had grown ragged in my throat.

We hung a sharp left, my throat tightening at the sound of the gang closing in on us. I reached for one of the surgical blades from my belt, grabbing the hilt.

With a quick turn, I flung it at our pursuers. The blade found its mark in Dickhead's shoulder. He screamed, grinding to a halt. Already, I was reaching for another blade as the rest of his gang pounded closer to us.

"Faster," Alex gasped.

Wildly, we veered across Whitechapel High Street. It was only a matter of seconds before we were careening through the doors into the old hospital building.

The gang, of course, ran in after us—right into the trip wire. I didn't stop to watch the wooden spears pierce their flesh, but I heard the thuds, the screams.

I sent a silent, grim *thanks* to my parents.

Without the old fae ways, I'd be dead right now.

CHAPTER 11

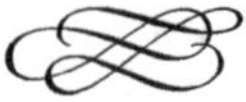

On the rooftop of our rookery, safe from the trip wires and traps, I turned the makeshift spit over our fireplace, a piece of metal speared through the rabbit. The flames warmed the winter air around us. Smoke from the roasting meat curled into the air, and my mouth watered. Tonight, no clouds darkened the sky, and a canopy of stars twinkled above us.

Years ago, you could hardly see the stars in big cities like this, but now they burned bright, gleaming sequins on a midnight fabric. In the old days, the fae had claimed they were windows into the worlds of the gods.

Across from me, Lucy twirled her blond hair around a fingertip, the firelight wavering over her skin. Before dragons had scorched the Earth, she'd been a bartender. During the long days in the rookery, she regaled us with stories of drunken brawls in the *Duke of York*—the men who fought with broken bottles, the women pulling hair. Sometimes she told us about her exes—a charming collection of men who'd cheated on her and complained about the size of her thighs.

Lucy licked her lips, staring at the rabbit. "I miss pies. How hard do you think it would be to make a rabbit pie? How do you make pie, anyway? You need flour for pies. Can you make a pie without flour?"

Katie, a thin woman with a smattering of freckles over her nose and dirt caked in her hair, sat by her side. "Are you going to keep saying the word 'pie'? We can't make them. Forget it."

I knew very little about Katie's prior life. She was a bit… off. When she told stories, they were not about her life. They were weird fantasy tales about talking arctic foxes and royal polar bears ruling Nordic kingdoms. Pure nonsense, really, but it was a nice escape from her usual ill-tempered grumbling.

Alex's stories were my favorite, of course. I didn't think I'd ever get sick of hearing about one-hundred-fifty-dollar wagyu steaks or hot tubs on hotel roofs.

And me—I could tell stories of life as a fae burlesque dancer in New York City. *Angela Death,* my alter ego. I tried to leave the tragedies out of it. In fact, I mostly kept it on the glitter and feathers, the backstage drama. Or that time I had to fill in for my friend's oddly kinky "cake smooshing" routine.

That wasn't me anymore—I didn't want the glitter or the attention, didn't want men's eyes on me. But people liked those stories. Even if I could hardly bring myself to detail such a flagrantly wasteful use of cake anymore.

Lucy tapped my shoulder. "Tell us about the angel again. Not the one from yesterday. The blond one in New York."

I swallowed hard. Like I said, no one wanted to hear about the tragedies, and that meant this story had to be edited. Heavily.

I stared into the jumping flames. "I was dancing in *Madame Francine's.* I had all kinds of routines—stripping Salem witch judges, a lonely satyr with troublesome hooves, a slightly terrifying clown routine. The seductive angel was one of my few purely sexy shows. I mean, it was back before we knew angels were terrifying, when I thought they just floated in the heavens like pretty spirits."

Alex hugged his knees to his chest. "Are you telling me the fae were just as clueless about angels as we humans were?"

I shrugged. "We knew about dragons, definitely. But not angels, even though we evolved from them. After the rebellious angels were cast from the heavens, some became demons of darkness. Some became demons of fire. And the fae—we're unaligned. We lost our wings over time, transformed. Got obsessed with the food, the clothes, the dancing—all the fun stuff you get on Earth. We've all been fighting each other for millennia, dragging in the humans sometimes. But you have to understand that the fall happened a hundred thousand years ago. None of us had seen a real angel since. It's like expecting you to know what a Neanderthal might be like, except without scientists to explain it all."

Lucy nudged my arm. "Less of the history. Get back to the sexy angel costume."

I smiled. "Fine. I had a silver dress, feathered wings, lacy stockings, the whole nine yards. Pretty and delicate. Just like an angel."

Alex snorted.

"But that wasn't the whole costume. I glamoured myself like a succubus," I continued. "If any demons came in, the succubus touches always intrigued them—the dark swirls of magic, the faintly gold skin. They couldn't get enough of the whole demonic-angel thing." I swallowed hard. "Little did I know, that night an *actual* angel came in. He didn't have his wings on display or anything like that. They can hide them, I guess. I just thought he was an ordinary demon, a powerful one, with a golden glow of magic."

Lucy gripped my arm. "Handsome, right?"

I nodded. "Very. While I danced, his eyes were locked on me. I could tell he *really* liked the whole routine. I could just see his rapt expression, like he was drinking me up with his eyes. After my performance, he came up to talk to me. I thought he was flirty, totally full of himself, used to getting what he wanted. I brushed him off. I had no idea what he really was."

A harbinger of death.

Firelight sparked in Alex's eyes. "But you saw him again. The golden angel."

A few days after my angel show, when I was picnicking in the park, I learned what the handsome, glowing stranger really was. He flew down from the heavens with his wings blazing copper, his head gleaming like a golden crown, with dragons surrounding him.

A lump rose in my throat. "Yeah. You all remember that day, I'm sure." *The day the world ended for everyone.* I straightened. "But none of us want to talk about *that*, do we?"

My chest ached, but I tried to keep my expression neutral. *Don't tell them what happened, Ruby. Leave out all the death. Put on a good show.* "The angels had come back to Earth. The blond angel told me his name was Kratos, and he invited me to join him in London. I declined his offer."

Lucy shook her head scornfully. "You could be in a palace right now."

I left out the rest—the part about dragons abducting my little sister in the midst of an orgy of destruction and flying off with her into the skies. I didn't tell them what it had felt like to watch the reptilian shifters slaughter my boyfriend, Marcus, the gorgeous vampire who'd been the love of my life. I didn't tell them that my decision to turn down Kratos had been one of the worst of my life—that without his help, I had no hope of finding my sister again. They had their own traumas. On that same day, everyone here had watched people die.

Stories were a performance, and I aimed to make people happy.

Alex rubbed his chin. "My theory is that the angels lured the dragons to kill us all, just like another weapon. They spread diseases and death throughout the world just for the hell of it, and dragons did the job pretty quick."

I glanced at Alex, eager to distract myself. "You're ruining story time with this misery. Tell us about the good stuff, will you?"

"Right. Sorry." Now it was Alex's turn to regale us. He leaned into the fire, the flames dancing over his dark skin.

He took a deep breath. "One night a few years ago—I'm not even kidding you—I woke up under a table in the Forge Bar, covered in a pile of fifty-pound notes, empty bottles of Cristal, and two pairs of rubber gloves. I'm still not sure what happened. Had to show up to work an hour late, reeking like the bottom of a pub trash bin, and close a deal with Goldman Sachs."

Katie blinked thoughtfully. "Sometimes I put on gloves and touch my own face and pretend it's someone else's hand."

Her comments tended to hang in the air awkwardly while people tried to figure out how to respond, and that one was no different. Katie was often the first to break the silence, making it worse.

"Sometimes I feel so cooped up in here," she continued. "Like I'm being buried alive in the hospital walls. Never wanted to die in hospital, now I live in a hospital, and I'll probably die here too." Wide-eyed, she stroked her cheeks. "Freckles, I say. Everything will be okay." She snapped out of her reverie, scowling again. "People call me Freckles. No idea why."

"Maybe because of…" I cleared my throat. "Never mind."

Lucy touched Alex's arm. "Did you close the deal with Goldman Sachs, Alex?"

Alex smirked. "Of course I did."

Katie scooted forward, taking her turn at the spit.

I leaned back on my hands, smiling at Alex. "In those days, Alex, you had buckets of champagne and probably some expensive prostitutes—"

"I had no such thing," Alex interrupted.

"—Cheap prostitutes, whatever. I'm not judging. But how often did you get to sit under the stars with a roaring fire pit, three beautiful women, and a roasting rabbit? *This* is the good life, Alex. Even if we're on top of a ruined hospital building in a city full of scorched trash."

He nodded. "Of course. The post-apocalyptic hell is a significant improvement on my former life of luxury, as long as I never need to see a doctor or any of my loved ones ever again."

"Well that's just being greedy, Alex. We can't have everything."

Lucy bit her lip. "What do you think the chances are any of this will get fixed? I've heard there are people working against the angels, you know. A resistance, like, in the Tower of London."

Lucy was talking about The Institute of the Watchers—the secretive group my parents had once served, dedicated to preventing the apocalypse. Hadn't really worked out the way they'd planned, apparently.

"I went to see them once," I said. I surprised myself by the admission.

"What happened?" asked Alex.

"I wanted to exchange information." Not the whole truth. I wanted to spy for them, but they wouldn't give me the time of day. "One of their wardens turned me away. Apparently, they weren't willing to even talk to me unless I could tell them something they didn't already know. And they already knew about Kratos."

"Bastards," muttered Alex.

Would my encounter yesterday be enough to get me past their gates? I didn't think so. I needed something more, and I planned to get it—if I could survive long enough.

I shimmied over to the edge of the roof, peering down at the night-cloaked streets. In the moonlight, a few sentinels drifted along the main street like phantoms. One of them turned, gaze locked on me, and my heart skipped a beat.

The sentinels saw everything.

I scooted back toward the fire, relishing its warmth. The Hunt hadn't yet begun tonight. At the first sign of the howling hounds, we'd be inside, lightning-fast. Rabbit or no rabbit.

I leaned back on the roof, gazing up at the stars.

As Katie launched into a story about a sparrow king, I reached into my pocket, pulling out a copper feather—Kratos's feather. Moonlight streamed through the downy filaments, tingeing them with silver.

This was the true reason I'd come all the way to London, stowing away on the private jet of an apocalypse profiteer. I'd wanted to find Kratos. Dragons hoarded beautiful women like treasures. Kratos had been there on the worst day of my life, perhaps controlling the dragons that had taken my sister. Maybe he knew where to find Hazel.

Crazy as it sounded, my ambitions didn't stop there. Maybe, with a little help, I could worm my way into Kratos's life until I learned the angels' secrets, their vulnerabilities. Surely even angels had weaknesses. If I was careful enough and clever enough, maybe I could exploit them.

As I stroked my fingertip up the soft side of the feather, a hound's bark bellowed through London's streets, and horror slid through my bones.

The Hunt was nearby.

CHAPTER 12

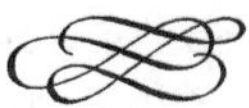

$\mathcal{A}$s the sounds of the Hunt raged outside, I curled up in my makeshift bed—a collection of blankets and rags. I didn't sleep with the others.

After we'd come inside, I'd eaten my portion of rabbit and potatoes by myself in my little room, a ramshackle Victorian outpost where I stayed on my own. This was what I was used to—living among humans, while never quite being one of them. Always a little bit separate, always holding back my true nature just a little.

My parents had left the fae realm centuries ago. The fae kingdoms were kind of backward, sexist as hell. My mom was supposed to be some sort of sex slave to a fae lordling, but she and my father had fallen in love. So they'd left and started working among the humans.

Most fae considered us traitors. Most humans would consider us dangerous if they knew the truth. I'd been lucky to find people as open-minded as Alex and my other rookery friends.

I pulled a blanket around myself tightly, surveying my familiar space. Truth be told, I was pretty sure that my corner of the rookery had once been a VD clinic. The poster on the wall when I'd first arrived, reading *No Glove, No Love,* had made that clear. But believe it or not, I'd managed to clean the place up, even decorate a little.

I had everything I needed here in the cozy little VD clinic I called home: a candle, a bottle of whisky I'd looted from the Sainsbury's, and helpful reminders about the dangers of chlamydia. I'd decorated the walls with the help of a glue gun and pieces of broken glass and aluminum that glinted like jewels in the candlelight. (You could take the girl out of the burlesque club...)

And most precious of all, tucked under a plastic waiting room chair, stood my collection of books. The dragons had destroyed half of London, but mercifully, the Whitechapel Library remained standing. Some lucky survivors had claimed the library as their rookery, but through charm and flattery, I'd wangled my own reading material from them. I now boasted a small collection of paranormal romances, a few biographies, and stacks of history books.

Apart from finding my sister again, what more could I ask for in the world of the Great Nightmare?

Maybe a bit of company at night, I supposed.

Only I couldn't sleep with the others—not with the candle burning. Katie, Lucy, and Alex slept in a part of the hospital with windows, where a flickering light would give away our presence.

I hadn't always been scared of the dark, but ever since the dragons had descended, it freaked me out. In the shadows, I saw things I didn't want to see. Lucky for me, VD clinics didn't tend to have windows, so I could keep my candles burning.

As far as the others knew, Alex's snoring had driven me to another building.

Outside, I heard the hounds barking as the Hunt tore through the nearby streets, and a chill rippled over my skin. Did the sentinels ever tell the hounds where they could find people, huddled in the rookeries?

No one really knew much about the hounds, only that they were supposed to be the size of horses, with bone-white fur. Oh, and they had the charming habit of tearing people to pieces and eating them. Worst of all, anyone caught harming a hound would be found hanging from a lamppost the next day, so you couldn't fight back without dying.

Not a single one of us knew why the Great Nightmare had begun at all, even though theories abounded. We'd sinned, and we deserved it. We were destroying the Earth and hurting each other. God was angry with us.

If you asked me, the gods were insane. Best not to worry too much about their motives.

I opened a book, trying to block out the human screams that wound through the streets. I flipped the pages, trying to read about medieval England, long before the angels had come—when people lived among living things, when they could hear the sound of rain pattering on trees or walk in the woods.

Before long, I closed my eyes, envisioning an ancient forest, sunlight streaming through verdant yew branches. Warm light dappled my skin, the earth, until sleep claimed my mind.

* * *

Barefoot, I walked through the woods. I had the sense that I was supposed to be hunting, but I hadn't brought my bow with me.

My hair whipped around my head in the forest breeze. My stomach growled, reminding me of my hunger. I needed to find a sapling, one I could carve into a bow and arrow. Then I could catch a stag.

But as I reached a clearing, my heart began to race.

I wasn't in the woods anymore. I was in New York, on the day the dragons came. On the day my soul began to wither.

We'd been in the middle of a picnic when the first dragon shadows had darkened the skies, fire streaming from their mouths. Dragons had killed my parents years ago. Now they'd come for us.

I stared at the grassy earth, unwilling to lift my eyes. Blood stained the blades of grass, splattered over my shoes. Here, in this memory, there were things I didn't want to see. Marcus lay dead nearby, ripped to shreds. By the wild panic in my chest and the shaking in my hands, I knew Hazel had already been snatched from the Earth, taken from me. I'd never felt so alone, so desperate. With a shaking hand, I plucked a single, copper feather from the grass. *Death is coming for me.*

My chest aching, I forced myself to look up at the skies, where the golden-haired angel swooped lower, filling me with a terrible sense of awe.

The dragons seemed to sense him, their necks craning up to look at him as he headed for me. My mouth went dry, and I swallowed hard. He wore black military clothes, with a silver bow slung over his back. *Not a demon, like I'd thought. An angel. A harbinger of death.*

If I hadn't been halfway dead, the sight of him would have sent a cold shiver of fear up my spine. As it was, I just hoped he'd end my life quickly.

I stared at him as he swooped down, and my fingers found their way to my side. As he landed, I clutched my battered ribs protectively.

He peered down at me, his amber gaze cold and hard. "A succubus against a legion of dragons. Seems you've held your own for a while."

"What?" I could hardly process what he was saying.

He leaned in, stroking a finger over the golden skin on my forearm —the one patch of skin not covered in red and black blood. "A succubus," he repeated. "One who dresses like an angel. Too intoxicating to waste as dragon food."

He remembered me from the other night. I was still wearing the glamour of a succubus, and it seemed to be saving my life.

One of the dragons snarled, moving closer, his eyes locked on me, blood dripping from his jaw. Whose blood, I had no idea, but he seemed to want mine also.

The angel pivoted. Then he lifted a powerful arm, slashing his hand through the air. As he moved his arm in an arc around us, an invisible blade seemed to cut through the dragons, ripping through their necks, their chests. Screeching, a few of the dragons flapped their wings, trying to get away before the angel cut through them too, but he was too fast.

He flicked his wrist, and tons of severed dragon flesh slammed against the Earth, shaking the pavement.

And just like that, half the dragon horde around me lay dead.

I turned to stare at the angel, his body glowing with a golden light. "Who are you?" I whispered.

He took a step closer, his velvet voice brushing over my skin. "I am Kratos."

"Are you an angel?" I stammered. I had the strongest urge to drop to my knees before him, to worship him. The Earth's gravity wanted to yank me down. Shaking, I resisted the pull. I wasn't going to kneel before him. He'd caused all this.

I swallowed hard, clutching the copper feather between my fingertips. "I need help. The dragons took my sister." But even as I said the words, I knew I was pleading to the wrong man. The man before me wasn't my savior.

He stepped closer, and heat burned off his body. He leaned in and whispered, "Well then, you'd better find her, hadn't you?"

"What's happening?" I stammered.

He narrowed his eyes at me. "You could come with me. You could amuse me. I won't stay in this hellhole long."

"Come with you where?" My voice sounded hollow.

"To London."

I shook my head, trying to block out the pile of sodden ash that lay a few feet from us. The grief washed over me so completely I could hardly remember how to speak. "I have to find my sister."

"Suit yourself."

"What do you want from me?" I breathed.

"Little succubus. I demand only worship, submission, and the end of the world."

Again, that urge to kneel overwhelmed me—I wanted to feel the rocky earth biting into my knees. Gritting my teeth, I forced myself to straighten.

I grabbed his arm, my fingers leaving smudges of blood over his black clothing. He was terrifying, but desperation spurred me on. "I need your help."

Cold fury flashed in his eyes, and he pulled his arm away from me. In a burst of honeyed light, he spread his wings, his hair gleaming like a halo. Then he lifted off into the darkened skies.

* * *

I WOKE, covered in sweat, my heart slamming against my ribs.

Nausea gripped my gut, and I wanted to puke. That was why I slept with the candle burning, why I did everything I could to stop myself from remembering the past.

Kratos had been there when the dragons had killed my boyfriend, when they'd ripped my sister from the Earth. He'd done nothing to stop it. To them, we were no better than animals, filthy creatures who should be on our hands and knees in the dirt before them. Once I found Hazel again, maybe I'd put an iron-tipped arrow through the lot of them.

I glanced at the candle, the wax dripping over the floor, and I pulled out a fresh one. I *really* didn't want the lights going out tonight. In fact, I wasn't sure I wanted to sleep at all anymore.

CHAPTER 13

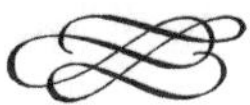

As the sun lowered over East London's charred buildings, I walked by Katie's side, my backpack full of potatoes and topped with three dead rats. No rabbits for dinner tonight.

I liked going out on these missions, feeling the sunlight on my skin. I needed the light like I needed water. London had never been known for its beautiful sunlight, but since the apocalypse had begun, the light had somehow taken on a rich, honeyed hue, so sweet I could almost taste it. Maybe the beautiful light was compensation from the angels for destroying civilization. Not quite an even trade-off, but we weren't in a position to make bargains.

I hadn't bothered with the glamour today. It sapped my physical and mental energy, and it didn't seem to deter Dickhead. Apparently, desperate, starving people didn't care much what you looked like.

As we drew closer to our rookery, Katie glowered at it. "Sometimes I feel like I've been buried alive in there," she muttered.

I was no psychologist, but I was pretty sure her mental situation was deteriorating fast.

"You're fine, Katie. Take some deep breaths. We're outside now, and we'll go into a nice, safe place with windows."

"Yeah." She scratched her cheek, pausing in her path. "But I don't want to go back in there. Feels like death in there."

"It's *not* death, though. Death is out here, if you hold us up any longer." *I'm not staying out in the dark for you, Katie.* "The sun is setting, and Dickhead wants to flay me alive. I'd rather not give him the opportunity. You know what I mean?"

She pressed her lips into a thin line and clutched her hands together, knuckles whitening. She shook her head.

Shit. I was losing her.

Before I had the chance to utter another word, she broke into a sprint, careening down Whitechapel High Street, dirty hair streaming behind her.

I cursed under my breath, sprinting off after her. The sun was beginning to set, but I really couldn't let her run off. She had most of the potatoes. Oh, and I guess I didn't want to let her die.

"Katie!" I called out. "Frecks! We can stay on the roof! Plenty of fresh air! I'll get you gloves to touch your face with!"

The sun dipped lower behind the buildings, and goosebumps rose on my skin. We were getting dangerously close to the time of the Hunt.

Katie turned to me, grunting, her expression savage. As she opened her mouth to argue, someone came barreling out of an alleyway, throwing Katie to the pavement. It took me a moment to recognize the dick-shaped birthmark on his forehead, and when I did, I ripped a scalpel from my belt.

Unfortunately, Dickhead already had a machete at Katie's neck. He'd one-upped me with the blade just a bit.

"Get him off me!" Katie shrieked.

"One false move and I'll slice your jugular." He glared at me. "My shoulder still hurts from where you threw one of those things at me, bitch. Good thing them scalpels are clean."

The word *bitch* sent a hot surge of anger through my nerve endings. When I spoke again, my voice was low and controlled, belying the fury underneath. "Put the knife away, Dickhead."

"I'm not fond of that nickname. Name's Derek. And I'm gonna need your food."

No way in hell was he walking away with our food. But I'd play along just enough to get his machete away from Katie.

I held up my hands defensively. "Okay. We'll give you the food. Put your knife away."

"And I'm going to need you to show me where you get it from."

Oh *hell* no. "Night is falling… Derek. The Hunt could start soon."

His lip curled in a snarl. "I haven't eaten in two days. I'll starve to death before any dog finds me. In fact, I'm so hungry I could eat one of them dogs raw right now."

Idiot. He'd be dead within seconds.

He pressed his machete further into Katie's throat, and she gave a little yelp.

"Stand up, crazy bitch."

My face heated, and I clutched the scalpel tighter. *That word again.*

"We're not showing you our food source!" Katie shrieked.

This situation was not good, and nightfall wouldn't help our chances of survival. We'd just have to placate the psycho until we could make a run from him. I'd hurt him some other time.

I held out my hands. "Everyone calm down. We'll all take a little walk together, okay? We'll go to the garden," I lied.

"Right," muttered Dickhead. "A little walk. Show me where you get your spuds so I can have in on the bounty."

Katie spat in his face, and the spit glistened on his cheek. "You're not getting our potatoes."

He wasn't pulling his knife away from Katie's neck. In fact, the way drool was pooling around his lips, he was looking at her like she was his next meal.

"It makes me really fucking angry, you know that?" he said. "Know your place, bitch."

"Get off me, you nutter!" Katie shouted.

"Maybe it's time someone taught you two a lesson."

Nope. I could kick him hard, knocking him off her, probably break a few of his ribs in the process. But that would risk his machete digging into her skin, severing an artery. I mastered my rage, trying to think clearly through the haze of anger. Maybe it was better to appeal to his appetite to get him away from her.

"Derek!" I shouted. "Do you want to eat or not? She's got a bag full of potatoes, and I've got a fresh rat for you, ready to be roasted. Bet you haven't had meat in a while, have you? You want some meat and potatoes for dinner?"

His groan was audible. "Meat and potatoes?"

I nodded. "Why waste your time on us when you could be feasting within twenty minutes?"

"What about your garden? I want the whole garden."

"A little plot of land right next to Christ Church," I lied. "The bodies buried there years ago have provided wonderful fertilization. You can go there tomorrow, after you fill your belly with the food we've got for you here."

Dickhead wasn't the kind of guy who had great impulse control and planning skills. He'd easily take a small meal now for a full bounty tomorrow.

He licked his lips. "All right. All right. Slide that sweet rat over to me, and I'll cut the backpack off this little maggot."

I could only hope that Katie wasn't about to do something stupid as I pulled off my backpack, dropping it on the ground. And yet even as I did, I had to wonder where this was going to end. If Dickhead intercepted our food runs every day, we'd starve. Plus, the next time he saw us, he'd know that we'd been lying about our secret garden.

He has to die. I have to kill him.

In the pre-Nightmare world, that kind of idea had never run through my head. Now... now the dark and violent thoughts flowed like the murky Thames.

I kicked the backpack over to him. He grinned at it, licking his lips. "Nice one."

Then he slid his machete under one of Katie's backpack straps. Only—her face was contorting with rage, the look in her eyes increasingly crazed.

When she screamed, "Those are *my* potatoes!" I knew it was all over.

She brought her knee up hard into his groin, then swung a wild right hook while he sputtered.

I snatched the bag off the pavement and broke into a sprint, the wind rushing over my skin. Katie's footsteps pounded the sidewalk behind me—at least, I hoped they were Katie's.

As the sun slipped behind the buildings, shadows thickened around us. A chill rippled over my skin. We'd been out here too long, and the Hunt could tear through the streets at any moment.

Sweat dampened my skin, and I cast a quick look behind me. My heart slammed against my ribs when I caught a glimpse of Dickhead closing in on Katie, his face contorted with rage. It was a look that said *when I catch you, I will bash your head into the pavement, then eat the flesh from your bones.*

How was this starving bastard so *fast?* Maybe his desperation gave him some sort of super strength.

Gasping for breath, Katie pulled ahead of me, pumping her arms wildly. "We'll lose him," she breathed. "Follow me."

My breath grew ragged in my throat. There was no way in hell we'd lose Dickhead without picking up some serious speed, but my lungs were burning.

There was one way I could move faster—if I let my true form out.

I wasn't *just* a fae. I came from a line of feral fae, bestial creatures that dwelled in the forests among the stags and wild boars. We could move fast, like the wind through the oaks. Except—as a feral fae, I didn't always think clearly or make the best decisions. Civilized logic usually went out the window when my canines and pointed ears came out.

Gasping, I glanced behind me at the maniac sprinting toward me, spit flying from his lips. In the last rays of dying sunlight, his machete glinted fiercely.

Katie swerved right down another narrow alley, footsteps hammering on the cobblestones. Crooked brick buildings loomed above us, and shadows pooled in the alley. I gasped for breath.

They'd be here soon. The hunters.

As adrenaline blazed, my rising fury told me the feral fae was taking over whether I wanted her to or not. *Fading,* I called it, when magic rippled over my skin and the human glamour faded away.

Catching in the breeze, my crimson hair lightened to its natural pale gold. A wild, ancient power blazed through my bones, setting my mind on fire, sparking my lust for blood.

But I couldn't quite think clearly anymore. An earthy haze clouded my mind, as if particles of dirt and moss whirled in my skull.

The scent of peat billowed around me, and primeval power imbued my limbs, my mind. I'd come home, no longer Ruby, no longer tame. I was blood and moss, earth and claws, a creature who'd gnaw on bones in a marshland. I didn't need to run.

As I neared the mouth of the alley, I whirled. I bared my fangs and stared at the man who chased me, fingers twitching with anticipation.

Come closer, delicate thing. I will end your pain.

Roots and bone, flesh and earth, teeth puncturing veins, the hot rush of blood, the scent of pine. Trees breathing around me, their trunks pulsing like bellows in time to the rhythm of my lungs.

I will kill to live, and I will enjoy it.

As he ran closer, my hand shot out to grab his throat. My lip curled, fingers tightening ruthlessly around my prey, and I unleashed a feral snarl. I'd caught him by surprise, and he dropped his knife.

Growling, I slammed my forehead into his nose, breaking it. Blood spattered over me, but I clung to his neck, nails piercing his skin.

A vicious grin curled my lips, and terror blazed in my prey's eyes. My gaze landed on the throbbing vein in his neck, primed for my canines.

Right then, only one thing could have cut through my haze of bloodlust—and it did. From the far end of the alley, the bellowing of hounds rumbled off the brick and cobbles. At their frantic baying, even my feral heart skipped a beat.

CHAPTER 14

The hair rose on the back of my neck. Still gripping Dickhead's throat, I froze, sniffing the air, scenting them. I smelled raw meat, and my mouth watered.

Slowly, I turned, staring at the mouth of the alley. The skinny, freckled woman had disappeared. Couldn't remember her name, what I'd been doing with her. I only knew she'd hidden somewhere, out of danger.

My pointed ears tuned in to the sounds around me—the panicked breathing of my prey, his heartbeat pattering like a frightened rabbit's. I'd been about to rip out his throat, but there were larger predators afoot now, and I instinctively stilled my movements.

The hearts of the larger creatures pounded nearby, along with a thrilling undercurrent of growls, the wet snorting of enormous snouts.

Their heartbeats called to mine, beast to beast.

I dropped my prey, listened to his footsteps skitter over the cobblestones behind me. I'd kill him later. Only a fool would try to outrun the hounds of hell. You seduce a beast's bloodlust with your back turned, with the alluring scent of fear.

In the gathering darkness, steam whirled at the alley's mouth. The hounds' heartbeats drew closer, claws tapping on the pavement as they walked.

When they turned the corner, I stared into two pairs of red eyes that gleamed like droplets of blood, faces as high as my own shoulders. Fur the color of bone, stained with splashes of crimson. Steam curled from their blunt snouts. When they growled, their teeth glistened with gore. Long, pointed ears swooped back over their heads, and they snapped their muscled jaws. A few more hounds came up behind them, snarling.

Even in my feral state, I knew I was no match for them, but I still bared my own canines, my heart thundering in my chest like a battle drum. Some rational part of me recoiled at my own savagery, terrified I'd do something insane. But Rational Ruby wasn't in control right now.

From the whirling mist, another figure appeared, looming over the hounds.

At the sight of him, some part of me understood: there was only one true Hunter.

And right now, his sights were locked on me.

From atop a bone-white horse, the angel glared down at me, his copper wings gleaming with light, golden hair shining like a corona. Leather armor, studded with copper, covered his muscled body.

Like a star, he radiated light. He wore a longbow slung over his back. Looming over the street, he looked like a god. My blood roared through my veins as I gaped at him.

Two warring desires fought for supremacy in my mind. One of them was screaming at me that he was a threat, that I needed to attack him, to dominate him. Feral Ruby, this death-seeking part of myself, wanted to fight.

The other desire compelled me to move closer, to fall to my knees in front of him and worship him like a mindless slave.

And somewhere in the hollows of my mind, his true name knelled. *Kratos.*

Dim recognition sparked. This was the man I'd been looking for.

Right now, I couldn't remember why, just that I'd been looking for him. To kill him? To worship him?

My hands and knees ached for the pavement, but I kept myself upright.

Kratos. My fingers twitched, and I struggled to think through the dark, peaty haze in my mind.

Clenching my jaw, I closed my eyes.

I was looking for someone, someone I loved. I wanted her back. My sister… she had a name. My sister was *Hazel.* I'd come here to find her. Could this man help me, for some reason? Slowly, painfully, the thought began to take root.

Along with another, clearer thought: the Hunter was probably going to kill me in a few seconds. *Right. Focus. Survive.*

I stared at the shining angel, my rational mind trying to claw through the dirt. *Stay still, Ruby. Stay very still.*

My legs began to shake, my teeth chattering, my mind unsure what I was about to do next. I needed to compose myself to ask about my sister…

Instead, Feral Ruby just snarled. I began snarling loudly, the sound rumbling through my gut.

One of the hounds prowled closer, scenting the air. His red eyes burned into me, and a crimson droplet fell from his canines to the cobblestones.

Growling, I reached up to my forehead, where human blood had spattered my skin. With disgust, I felt myself smear the blood down my face.

Ruby… no. I withered inside as Feral Ruby licked the blood off her fingers.

The hound paused in its tracks, flattening its long pointed ears against its head as if staring at a ghost. Feral Ruby had managed to creep out even the hounds of hell. Maybe she was on to something, because the hounds didn't seem to want to come any closer.

Slowly, my rational mind began to claim more territory, digging its way out of the dirt.

The angel leapt from his horse, eyes glowing amber in the gloom.

Slowly, he stalked over to me, his gaze intent. His fluid movements suggested a tightly coiled violence just under the surface. My hackles rose, ready to fight.

What do you think of a feral fae, Kratos? Primal violence roiled within me as he moved closer. I longed to sink my teeth into his perfect neck, to grow powerful on the blood of an angel.

But Kratos was the first to attack.

When he reached me, his hand shot out, and he gripped me by the collarbone, thumb grazing my throat. In one smooth motion, he had me pinned to the wall, his golden eyes penetrating right into my hazy mind. I bared my teeth, snarling at him, and yet I knew if he moved his thumb and pressed down, he'd crush my throat in an instant. Hot magic curled off his body, vibrating over my skin. He smelled like burning cedar.

What does the blood of an angel taste like?

His grip on my throat relaxed, but he moved his hand down to my shoulder, still pinning me in place with his impossible strength. With his free hand, he stroked my face, the light touch searing my skin. For a lethal angel, he was so gentle. I hadn't expected him to be.

He stared down at the blood staining his finger. "It's a fae. A corrupted angel. See the blood, the pale hair. See her fangs, so much like a beast's. I imagine these things rut in the street like vermin."

I had a vague sense that he was insulting me, but I could hardly focus on the words. Up close, his power washed over me, overwhelming me. A dark sweep of lashes framed his burnt-gold eyes, rimmed with umber. The urge to attack him had dissolved completely, leaving behind only the urge to get on my knees. For some reason, I resisted.

"I knew the fae had fallen from the heavens," he said. "I just didn't realize how far. She's a complete animal."

What was that thing I needed from him…?

Hazel. The word rang in my mind again. Why did I have to encounter him like this, half-crazed, unable to control myself, when there was something I *needed* from him?

He still pinned me against the wall, one hand on my collarbone.

Slowly, his gaze slid down my body, then up again. He sniffed the air. "A skinny thing, bony even. She has those strange fae eyes, an unnatural silver. Yet somehow beautiful. If she weren't so depraved, she'd actually be tempting. That is how the fae fell in the first place, you know. Lured by earthly temptations. Unable to control themselves."

Silver eyes. I'd faded completely. I gripped at his wrist, but it had no effect. I wanted things from him, but I couldn't put them into words.

He cocked his head, unperturbed by my struggle. "Strange that she should have such delicate porcelain skin." He lowered his face, breathing in my scent. One of his hands stroked down the back of my hair, as if he were soothing me. "But do you know? I think she's been eating rats."

For an instant, I saw myself through his eyes: a bestial fae, golden-haired, red of tooth and claw. Irises gleaming silver. Through his eyes, I almost felt disgusted by myself. Once the fae had been angels like him, but we'd fallen to Earth, trapped by its temptations—by our love of food and dance, of sex and sunlight and the feel of rain on our skin. We'd changed over time, becoming more bestial, more animalistic.

We weren't angels anymore.

He pulled his hands away from me, stepping back to study me. Then he brushed a strand of pale hair from my eyes. "I'm not wrong in thinking there is something strangely alluring about this beast, isn't there, Culloch? Is that perverse of me?"

It took me a moment to realize he was talking to his dog—that he'd been talking to his dog the whole time. That's where I ranked in this hierarchy. Somewhere below his dogs.

He frowned, cocking his head. "Adonis hates the fae with an unparalleled passion. I wonder what he'd do with this one?" Kratos's lips curled. "Perhaps I'll leave her alive for him."

With the immediate danger averted, my mind began to clear a little more, my rational self digging its way free. What had he said? *Adonis.* Through my murky thoughts, I tried to cling to the name, to store it for later use.

Kratos stepped away from me, pulling out a gold handkerchief.

"Leave her, Culloch. She's more beast than human. A perverse temptation of the flesh, but one that will pollute your body."

Thanks, asshole.

But as the fog cleared, I realized something about his tone—the note of affection when he spoke to his dogs. He *loved* his demonic hounds.

Slowly, the hounds turned from me, disappearing into the swirling mists. Kratos mounted his horse again, his movements swift and graceful. He pulled his horse's reins, and its footsteps clopped away over the pavement.

As the sound of bellowing hounds faded, the sharp tip of my canines receded from my tongue.

Apparently, all I had to do to survive in this world was to be absolutely disgusting.

But I had another mission now. I had important information I could give to The Institute. I had another angel's name. And more importantly, I knew what Kratos truly loved. In this world, love was a vulnerability. It might be enough for The Institute to recruit me.

At the other end of the alley, two sentinels glided, their glassy black eyes watching everything.

CHAPTER 15

I didn't know a ton about the world of espionage—just what
I'd learned from my parents when they'd started to train
me. Most importantly, I'd learned to be very careful whom I trusted.

As you might imagine, my paranoia hadn't eased at all since the
angels had come to Earth. Supposedly, some humans fed information
to the sentinels in exchange for food and protection. If I divulged my
plans to anyone in my rookery, I risked exposure, or left them open to
some kind of angelic torture.

Plus, Alex would try to thwart my plans in an instant. He had a
little overprotective streak when it came to me.

So I tucked myself away in the VD clinic and made my own prepa-
rations. I'd found a hospital blanket and used my magic to glamour it.
I pulled it over my head like a cloak, then stared at my reflection in
the only shiny surface I could find—the glass window at the check-in
counter.

This time, I was going to The Institute with valuable information,
and I could only pray I wouldn't be leaving empty-handed. I had the
name of another angel, and I'd identified Kratos's weakness.

And if The Institute of the Watchers couldn't tell me anything about the dragons, I had another plan in my arsenal. One that involved using my skill set.

I stared at my features—my green eyes, my red hair, my heart-shaped lips, the cheekbones that stuck out more than they should. I summoned my glamour, feeling it prickle over my skin. I gaped at myself as my eyes transformed to glassy black orbs, my skin paling to the color of bone. After a few more seconds, I looked exactly like one of the sentinels.

Now I just needed to slip out of the hospital unnoticed. Shouldn't be too hard, since I was the only one here. Katie had gone south to the river for water, and Lucy and Alex were out on a food-gathering mission.

I snatched a candle from the ground, folding it into my cloak.

Wrapped in my blanket, I crossed slowly to the clinic door, pushing it open to survey the scene before plunging into London's streets. For just a moment, a wave of dizziness washed over me—a side effect of the powerful glamour magic.

A hard rain fell over the city, washing the land in a dull gray. I shivered, pulling the cloak tighter, then closed my eyes. As soon as I was outside the door, I had to behave like a phantom. No shivering, no wincing, no frowning. Just a vacant, glassy-eyed stare.

Sucking in a breath, I pushed through the door. I walked carefully, trying to give the illusion of gliding. A bit of additional glamour helped to smooth out my stride, so I appeared to be floating like the other sentinels.

Hunger rumbled between my ribs, but I ignored it, staring straight ahead as I glided onto New Road. The cold rain slid down my pale skin, dampening my cloak.

Just like a burlesque act, this was a choreographed routine. I'd watched the sentinels long enough to know how fast they moved, how smoothly, how they swiveled their necks.

As I drifted onto Commercial Street, I glimpsed another sentinel on the far side of the road, and my stomach clenched. Would he sense that I was an imposter? Could they smell each other?

I peered at the other sentinel from the corner of my eye, and his head rotated toward mine—the movements owl-like. I imitated the swivel, turning my head to stare at him in the same way. After a few moments, his head turned straight ahead, and I followed suit.

Soundlessly, we passed each other on opposite sides of the street. Rain drenched my cloak as I skimmed by an old, derelict music hall. I was going to need some of this rain to let up if my plan was going to work.

No one else was walking nearby, but when I looked up at the sky, I glimpsed a sentinel floating above me, watchful eyes burning. I couldn't let down my guard here, not even for a second.

The quiet streets unnerved me. I depended on the constant chatter and stories in the rookery to keep my mind off everything I wanted to forget. I needed the fear of the Hunt, or my vampire books. I needed bright lights and dancing candle flames. I needed, above all, to forget the things I'd seen. My mind craved distractions.

Here, with only the sound of the rain to occupy my thoughts, it was hard not to think about Marcus.

He'd been my first real love, my first relationship where we'd communicated like grownups. With Marcus, I'd never had to guess what he was feeling. I'd known when he was annoyed, and exactly when he'd fallen in love with me, that he'd wanted to marry me. That had been true love.

Marcus was a rarity—a vampire who could walk in the light. But I didn't want to think about him, his beautiful face, or the way he'd pursed his lips when he thought. I didn't want to think about our summer vacation in Georgia, swimming with him under the moonlight, the phosphorescent waves dazzling against his pale, smooth skin.

That way madness lies.

A lump had risen in my throat, and I swallowed hard. That's what the Great Nightmare had taken from me: Marcus and Hazel, and all the memories of them that would drag me under the surface.

Block them out, Ruby. Bury the thoughts.

If I was going to survive in this world, I couldn't let my emotions overwhelm me.

And if I was going to convince The Institute to help me this time, I needed to keep my wits about me.

The stormy skies darkened as I walked, and goosebumps rose on my skin. It wouldn't be long until Kratos and his hounds tore apart the city, but I needed the cover of nightfall for my task tonight.

I crossed Tower Hill Garden, glancing at the scaffold. Here, long ago, kings and queens had once executed heretics and traitors. After the Great Nightmare began, the sentinels brought back the scaffold, for old times' sake. We never knew who hung the victims, just that bodies appeared hanging from ropes in the dead of night. Mercifully, none swung there today as I glided past the gallows.

As I approached the Tower, the rain began to let up, and I loosed a sigh of relief. If I was going to contact The Institute of the Watchers, I'd need to be able to light a candle. I wouldn't have much time to linger in front of the gatehouse trying to strike a match.

As I approached the Tower's stone gates, I swiveled my neck from side to side, checking the landscape for the presence of sentinels. One drifted over the grasses of the old moat, and another glided slowly in the cloudy skies.

I peered at the Tower again. Really, *tower* was a funny name for the constellation of buildings before me. According to one of the history books in my little STD clinic, it was actually made up of at least twenty towers, some of them connected. I'd read about the Bell Tower, the White Tower, the Salt Tower, and the disturbingly named Bloody Tower, where someone had murdered two young princes...

Now I approached the first of the towers—the Middle Tower— basically a gatehouse without the gate. I strode right through the arched entryway.

I understood why they didn't bother with the portcullis here. If the hounds wanted to get to the next gate, they'd just go around it, using the moat. Only the tower directly in front of me served a purpose in the world of the Great Nightmare—this one formed a part of the imposing medieval walls.

The hounds were terrifying, but they weren't capable of leaping ninety feet in the air. Neither was I, sadly, so I just had to hope I could get in there before the hounds arrived for the night.

A heavy wooden door and an iron gate barred the arched entrance to the Byward Tower. High above the door, narrow windows were inset into the stone walls. In the gloom, I couldn't see anything in them. I had to hope *someone* was in there, watching—a fae, perhaps a human.

Anything but an angel.

My eyes flicked to the skies. The sentinel had swooped over the Tower until I was no longer within its line of vision. I glanced to my right, where the other sentinel was approaching. When the creature reached the wall, he pivoted, turning in the other direction.

Now, without any sentinels watching me, my chance had arrived.

With shaking hands, I reached into my cloak, pulling out a candle and a lighter. I flicked the lighter, igniting the wick.

A gust of wind blew it out again.

"Shit!" I whispered. I lit the candle a second time, my pulse racing.

Distantly, I heard hounds baying, and hairs rose on the back of my neck.

I held the candle up, hoping anyone watching the gatehouse could see what I was doing. I needed to cover it three times with my hands and—

The damned thing blew out again in a damp gust of wind.

"Balls!" I hissed, maybe a little too loudly.

Flick. My heart raced, and I lit the wick again, this time managing to shield it with part of my arm. The shaking in my hands surely wasn't helping the situation, but this time, the wick stayed lit. I glanced up at the tower windows, then blocked the flame with my hand.

One... Two... Three.

One of the old signals of The Institute of the Watchers. Last time I'd come, it had gotten me as far as an audience with one of the Watchers.

I blew out the candle. As the smoke curled into the air, I shoved the candle and lighter back into my cloak. *Ordinary sentinel here. Nothing to see here, folks.*

When my gaze flicked to the right, I saw the moat sentinel turning, heading back toward me. Had he seen my ungraceful movements, the frantic lighting of the candle? Had he noticed that I'd been lingering here too long? Sentinels always kept moving, and I'd just been standing here.

Maybe I needed to drift—just until someone opened the gods-damned gate. Hadn't the Watcher been faster last time? I *needed* that gate to open. My chances of getting home alive at dusk weren't wonderful.

But instead of the creaking of the gate, silence greeted me.

I slowly pivoted like a sentinel, gliding over the cobblestones. The sound of barking hounds drew closer, and my heart began to slam against my ribs. Maybe I could fool the sentinels, who were all eyes, but the hounds would sniff me out in a second.

Slowly, I glided back over the cobbles toward the first tower. I did my best to act like a normal levitating, soulless being. I drifted slowly through the first arched door, occasionally swiveling my head like an owl. Desperately, I listened for the sound of a door creaking open behind me.

Please open the door.

As I got to the edge of the cobbled path, a tendril of pure fear coiled through me. There, across a stony expanse, Kratos rode atop his bone-white horse, surrounded by his mob of ivory hounds. They were going to tear me to pieces if I didn't get inside the Tower.

I pivoted, heading back to the gate, moving a little faster than a sentinel should, no longer able to keep control of my movements. A cold sweat drenched my body. Behind me, the sound of the hounds moved closer, their barking ripping through the silence. From the corner of my vision, I caught a glimpse of the sentinel moving closer, eyes locked on me now.

My cover was blown, and the hounds had scented me.

CHAPTER 16

I sped up, practically running for the wooden door, frantic now.

At the last moment, just as I reached the iron gate, it began to heave open with an ear-piercing creak.

Behind the gate, the wooden door swung open. My heart thrumming, I ducked, rolling under the iron gate as it rose.

From the ground, I heard the iron gate slam down again. I scrambled out of the way as the wooden door banged shut. Someone in a cloak was bolting it.

On the other side of the door, the dogs howled into the night. They wouldn't be able to get to us. Magic protected these walls. At least, I was pretty sure it did.

I shivered.

As my savior secured the door, I slowly rose, trying to calm my breathing. When she whirled to face me, I took in the woman's elegant face, hints of chestnut hair tucked under her hood. She held up a lantern that cast a warm light over her brown skin.

Her brown eyes glinted as she stared at me. "You're a fae," she said evenly. "You glamoured yourself."

"You really waited till the last minute there." I let my sentinel glamour fade, my face returning to its normal hue, bright red hair shining through the gloom. "Last time I was here, the warden was a bit faster."

"Even if you knew our signal, I couldn't be sure that you weren't a real sentinel until I saw the panic written all over your body. Sentinels don't panic." She shoved the lantern closer into my face. "What do you mean, the *last* time you were here?"

"I tried to get information from you. I was told I needed to bring some in return. So I have information for you." I glanced around the Tower's stony interior. Why didn't The Institute extend some of this security to the other Londoners while the hounds devoured them every night? "It must be nice to have all these walls here to protect you."

"How did you learn our signal, fae?"

"My parents were members of The Institute of the Watchers. They tried to recruit me and train me before they died."

The Watcher held my gaze for a long time, then nodded curtly. "Where were they stationed?"

"New York City. They were killed in one of the random dragon attacks, long before the Great Nightmare even began. Look, I'm not here to give you my life history. Like I said, I'm here for an exchange of information."

"The Institute once depended on fae like you. Now we have none left in our ranks here in London." She cocked her head. "What's your name? Your full name?"

"Ruby Hudole."

She frowned, still gripping the lantern aloft. "An unusual name."

"Not for a fae." Silence fell as a chilly wind rippled over us, and her gaze continued to bore into me. I started to lose patience. "Look, I have some information about Kratos and another angel. I'm hoping in return, you can tell me what you know about the dragons."

"Why dragons?"

"I'm looking for my sister. A dragon shifter abducted her."

She tapped a fingertip on her lower lip as she studied me, and I felt like I'd shown up for an oral exam I hadn't prepared for.

"Wait here." She pivoted, heading for one of the gatehouse doors.

As the door slammed behind her, I hugged myself, surveying the Tower. I stood between two sets of walls, medieval structures looming over me on either side. Droplets of rain fell on my skin, and I glanced up at the gatehouse tower. Her lantern light burned warmly in there.

What is she doing?

After several minutes in the icy rain, I huddled by one of the Tower walls, though it didn't offer much protection.

At last, the human woman returned, her lantern burning warmly in the gloom. She peered at me inquisitively. "Ruby Hudole."

"Yes?"

"Your parents were Orla and Rayne Hudole?"

So that's what she'd been doing in the gatehouse. Checking up on me. "That's them."

"Sister named Hazel."

My throat tightened at the sound of her name. "She's the one who is missing. And... do I get to know your name?"

"Yasmin," she said abruptly, then glanced at the gatehouse. "The new shift will be arriving soon. We can leave. I need to show you something. Chop chop." With that, she turned on her heels, marching over the rain-slicked cobblestones. Wordlessly, she led me past the Traitor's Gate as I hurried to keep up, teeth chattering. I looked up at the narrow windows, finding candlelight flickering in a few of them.

"It's practically empty here," I pointed out. "Maybe you could have let in a few more humans instead of leaving them to the killer dogs?"

She shot me a sharp look. "We moved in here after the Great Nightmare began, and some of our sorcerers helped to shield the Tower with magic. We tried allowing in more people. The experiment didn't last long."

"Why?"

"You've been out there. You've seen how untrained people behave when they're scared and desperate. You've seen the gangs, I'm sure— the violence, the desperation. We couldn't control them. The strong stole food from the weak, the men tried to overpower the women. We are trying to achieve something here, and they were frustrating our objectives."

I thought of Dickhead and his gang. I mean… she had a point. "But what about families with kids?"

"We let some families and young children remain in the White Tower, but we couldn't accommodate them all. We had to secure our borders. If we're going to figure out who's attacking us, we need to survive first. There are families out there, and innocent people. But we have to help them in other ways—long-term ways."

Okay, so maybe this was their version of the hidden garden, or the traps around my rookery. Just—a much more elaborate hidden garden, with thousand-year-old fortress walls and dungeons.

"What are your objectives, exactly?"

She didn't answer. Instead, she led me up to another tower. She yanked open an enormous door with a creak, and I followed her into a narrow spiral stairwell. Here, candlelight wavered over the rough-hewn walls. Our footfalls echoed off the stone ceiling.

"Where are you taking me?" I asked.

"If you're going to pass on this intelligence you claim to have, we're going to a secure place. As long as we remain outside, the sentinels can watch us. They can listen."

She led me through a narrow, arched hallway until at last we reached a door. Yasmin pulled a skeleton key from her pocket, clicking open the lock and opening the door to reveal a cozy, white-walled bedroom. A portrait of a knight hung above a fireplace, and papers lay strewn over an old wooden desk. Just in front of the fire-place, two wooden chairs flanked a table, set with wine and a few glasses.

Yasmin gestured to one of the chairs. "Have a seat."

I did as instructed, and she pulled up a chair directly across from me, lowering the hood of her cloak. A fire burned in the fireplace, and the flames warmed my body. Gods-damn, it felt nice in here. The angels and shifters had left the whole Tower intact, and I knew that magic protected its walls. A girl could get used to this place.

I studied the rest of the room, trying to learn what I could. A bare dresser stood against one wall, with a door to its left. To the right of the dresser hung a tapestry—a depiction of a forest scene.

An examination of the bed gave me an idea of where the second door led: a raggedy stuffed monkey lay on the covers beside a slightly tattered copy of *Mother Goose's Nursery Rhymes.* Yasmin had a child nearby—a young one.

"I'm surprised you let me into this secure enclave," I said.

"Some of the Watchers feel differently, but I value the fae above all other operatives. You were rare before the Great Nightmare began, and now we don't have a single fae among us. Not here. Not in the Tower." She reached for the bottle of wine, popping out the cork. Without asking, she poured me a full glass.

No one in the hellscape of the Great Nightmare would share their wine unless they *really* wanted something.

"But there's something I need to tell you," she began. "If the information you want is about the location of the dragons, I can't help you. Dragon shifters are notoriously secretive. We have Watchers and spies all over Europe searching for angels, but none of them know where to find the dragon shifters. Their lairs are dripping with gold. You can imagine why they'd be secretive. I can only tell you we haven't seen any dragons in the south of England since the Nightmare began. You should tell us what you know anyway. We're on the same side."

My chest welled with disappointment, but I'd been expecting this possibility. "I know the dragons must have a lair or a fortress or someplace they take their women. That's what I remember my parents saying. Dragon shifters hoard gold and beautiful women in their lairs. You don't have any way to find where these lairs are?"

Sympathy shone in her eyes. "There may be a way I can help you find your sister. But before we get into that, I need to know exactly what you've come here to tell me."

Some of the tension in my chest unclenched a little. I knew The Institute would have *something* up their sleeves.

I took a sip of the wine, letting it roll over my tongue. The wine had been open just a little too long—she'd been saving this, even when it started to taste too acidic. And yet—gods—I didn't really want to leave here.

"The last time I was here, I tried to tell another Watcher about Kratos. The Institute already knew about him."

She nodded. "This is our objective—learn about our enemy. What makes them tick, why they're here, what they want to protect. And when we've learned their weaknesses and vulnerabilities, only then can we fight them."

"That's where I can help."

She leaned forward. "Oh?"

I wasn't giving up my leverage so easily. "Before I get to that, tell me more about how you can help me."

"We might have a way to get a message to your sister through magical means, if it was important. We just won't be able to get any information back from her." She tapped her fingertip on the wineglass.

It wasn't much, but hope bloomed in my chest anyway.

"What is it that you've learned?" she asked.

I leaned forward. "I've learned one of their vulnerabilities. Kratos was talking to his hounds like they were people, like he loved them. Perhaps we could use them to set a trap for him." I took another sip of the wine. "Have you ever heard of an angel named Adonis?"

Her brow furrowed. "Adonis?"

"I don't know who he is, but I have a theory. An angel with midnight wings and gray-blue eyes. He hates the fae. I watched him kill two redcaps in front of me. He seemed..." *seductive* "... like the name would suit him."

"Ah. We've seen him, but didn't know his name."

I frowned. "How many angels do you know of?"

"Here's the strange thing. We only knew of one by name—Kratos. We've seen him around London, and one other from afar. Our Watchers have reported few angel castles in Europe."

"There were none in New York either after Kratos left. Just the demons that took over the city." I bit my lip. "So there aren't many of these apocalyptic angels as far as you know?"

"London seems to be a headquarters of sorts, from which just a few angels wreak their chaos all over the world. No one is safe. The dragon shifters did some of the work, yes, but the angels did more to create this hell. Shockingly, it seemed to only take a few of them. Only a few to spread disease, famine, to destroy crops across the Earth. We have reason to believe they cause plagues, widespread death and destruction in every corner of the globe. We need to stop them before there's nothing left." Passion glinted in her eyes. "You understand, don't you?"

My fists tightened, and the gears were already ticking in my mind. "I understand."

"You're already providing us with information we didn't have before. But what did you mean about trapping Kratos?"

"I'd considered the possibility that you wouldn't know where to find the dragon shifters. So I have another plan. I want to spy on the angels. I think I know how I can get into their world, and when I do, I want to learn everything I can: the angels' powers, what they want, what they know about the dragon shifters… I can feed information to you, and you can tell me what you know about their weaknesses to keep me alive."

Her eyes glinted. "No one has been able to get close to them. What makes you think you'd be able to do any better?"

"I've met Kratos three times now. The first time I met him, it was before the Great Nightmare began. I was dancing at a burlesque club in New York, glamoured like a succubus. It was one of my acts." Gods, it seemed a lifetime away. Another Ruby, one who didn't exist anymore. I swirled the wine in my glass, watching the light spark off its surface. "Kratos seemed fascinated by me. He liked the idea of a succubus dressed as an angel. Must be a weird angel kink."

I could practically see the gears working in her mind. "I see. And the next time?"

"It was the day the Great Nightmare began, the day the dragons took my sister. They killed…" I let the sentence die on my tongue as grief slammed into me. I managed to master my emotions again. "That's not important. The important part is, Kratos was there. He saw me again, glamoured as a succubus. In the middle of all this blood and death, the scorching bodies…" I practically choked on the words. "He invited me to come to London with him. My world had just been ripped to pieces." The raw memory still clawed at my chest. "I didn't know I'd need him. I didn't know he'd be my only link to Hazel."

I let out a long breath. "I saw him one more time, but he didn't recognize me. I was in my fae form. His hounds came after me, and Kratos just let me go."

"And when you met Adonis, did you appear as a fae or a succubus?"

"Succubus again. They've both met me as a succubus. If I play my cards right—if I gain just enough of their trust—I could buy myself an invitation into the world of the angels. Then I could learn what I need about the dragon shifters. And the angels in general, of course." Maybe I could even find a way to destroy these angels of death before they slaughtered the rest of the world, but I didn't want to sound like a lunatic by suggesting something so bold.

"And you'd be willing to give us information? Right now, knowledge is our only weapon against these angels. There are those who want to fight the Hunter with armies. In fact, the gods are raising up armies of humans and demons together. But we won't defeat them fighting blindly. We have to understand the magic that binds them, what can truly destroy them. This isn't just about you, or me, or Hazel. We're fighting for the very survival of humanity right now." She blinked. "And for the fae, as well."

"If I'm going to help you, I need everything you know about the angels. I'll need to know what weapons I can use, and what to do if one of them corners me. I've seen the angels slaughter creatures with a flick of their wrists. I don't want to be one of their victims."

She paled for a moment, then leaned back in her chair, her gaze never leaving my face. "Of course. We've never targeted angels before, but already the information you've given us is invaluable. Until you told me about Kratos's hounds, we didn't know if angels were capable of affection at all. We can use that now."

Truthfully, the thought of spending more time around those angels turned my stomach in knots. These weren't the glorious, ethereal angels I'd imagined as a child. These were gods of death, who apparently held a particular animosity toward the fae. And worse—since Eimmal was coming up, I risked exposure if the real me came out.

Still, it was like Yasmin had said. This was bigger than her, or me, or Hazel.

This was a fight for the very survival of our species.

CHAPTER 17

Yasmin rose abruptly, heading for one of the wooden doors in the wall. "Follow me. One, two, three. Let's go."

I was beginning to get the impression that Yasmin didn't spend a lot of time talking to adults and had forgotten the basics of normal human communication. Still, I stood and followed her into another shadowy hall—this one narrow and unlit. I ran my fingers along the damp walls to steady myself in the darkness, my heart hammering.

Here, the Tower's shadows crept over me.

At last, a door creaked open and a chink of moonlight streamed through. Yasmin's silhouette moved into a silvery room. Old, warped window panes lined the ceiling and walls. It seemed to be a small greenhouse of sorts—I'd never imagined something like this existing here in the Tower.

I breathed in the glorious aroma of soil and plants, the air heavy with the scent of foxglove, sage, lavender, and marjoram.

I traced my fingertips over a flowering plant with pink blossoms, the damp petals transfixing me. "This place is beautiful," I breathed. "It's been a long time since I've seen anything with flowers."

"That plant is turmeric. It treats asthma."

I glanced at another plant. In the faint light, I could just read the hand-scrawled label. *Feverfew.* "So you've got your own elaborate medicine cabinet in here."

She nodded. "The gods give us what we need."

I crossed my arms. This idea that the *gods provided* didn't really gel with my recent life experiences—experiences that included starving and watching people die of infected wounds. "I was always under the impression the gods were just batshit."

Yasmin was gently, lovingly pruning a plant. "And what do you know about the gods?"

I tried to remember what my parents had taught me. "The seven earthly gods were once archangels. When some of them passed on the Angelic language to humans, the lesser angels decided to punish them. The seven were cast to the Earth, and with them, their angels fell, turning into demons—valkyries and hellhounds and whatever else. They hate it here, hate being trapped and tormented on Earth. My people—the fae—were different. Angels who actually *wanted* to be here. I like the feel of having an earthly body, dancing, eating the food... Earth isn't hell to the fae. Or at least, it wasn't."

A sudden sense of loss gripped me. I hadn't danced at all since the last time I'd seen Hazel.

Yasmin eyed me from behind a flowering plant. "Good. You know your history. And you're right, the seven gods will not help us. But you don't know the whole history. I speak of different gods."

I blinked. "Wait... *who* are you talking about?"

Moonlight bathed her in silver. "The gods who lived on Earth before the angels' fall. The gods born from the Earth itself."

"What? I've never heard of them."

"Most people haven't. We call them the Old Gods."

This kind of sounded like some bullshit, but I'd go with it. "And how are they supposed to help us?"

She crossed to another plant—one with indigo flowers. Reverently, she stroked her fingertips over the blossoms. "This plant is known as Devil's Bane. Some call it the Queen of Poisons. Incidentally, that is what the other members of The Institute call me."

"Good to know."

She met my gaze. "Kratos, the Hunter, lives in an ancient castle just outside London. It's been glamoured for centuries, but we know where to find it. Now, in the forest outside his palace, Devil's Bane has begun to grow. We hadn't seen it in centuries, but the Old Gods give us what we need. We believe that Devil's Bane is one of the only substances capable of weakening the angels."

"Can it kill them?"

She shook her head. "No. It may put them out of commission for weeks or months. But they would recover."

"But I could use it as self-defense if I needed to."

"Yes. And I'm certain that there's more in that forest—another gift from the Old Gods. Maybe even the key to their defeat. But we haven't been able to explore the grounds there. The angels slaughter anyone who gets too close. Nearly all missions to the forest have resulted in death. We can't get past the outer boundaries."

Great. "So that sounds promising." I frowned. "I must say, I was hoping for something more concrete than potential gifts from imaginary gods that may or may not be in the forest."

"They're not imaginary. Look—" she held my gaze steadily. "We *need* you, Ruby. If you really can get into the angels' palace, you could tell us why they're here, what their plans are. Are they planning another large-scale slaughter? Disease, a massacre? We don't know, but you could help us find out. Help us prepare for it to save lives. And give the Old Gods a chance. Find out what they are trying to tell us. Angels were never meant to walk the Earth. They were meant for the heavens."

Remembering Kratos, his otherworldly strength, a shiver of dread ran up my spine. And Adonis was even worse. "What else can you tell me?"

"In order for you to convince them to trust you, you'll need to shed your former self completely. Become the succubus you pretended to be—a demon who doesn't care about humans. Prove to them that the Great Nightmare has changed you. You're as ruthless as they are. You thrive on death like they do. You value beasts more than human lives.

You can be our beacon of light, but first, you must descend into the shadows."

I nodded grimly. "I understand."

Little did she know I was terrified of the dark and had to sleep with candles lit.

With my arms folded, I tapped my fingertips on the crook of my elbow. "How would I communicate with you while I'm in their castle? And how will you get a message to my sister, like you said?"

"That, unfortunately, is a little difficult. We have only one scryer, and he wasn't fully trained before the Great Nightmare began. I can make contact with you through a reflection—you'll be able to see us, but we can't see much back. Just blotches of light and shadow."

I frowned. "That doesn't sound very useful."

"We'll make contact with you just after dawn, every day. It's a risk every time. You need to let us know if the sentinels can see us when we appear to you, so we can find another reflection. Flicker the candle once to tell us it's unsafe, or five times to let us know it's okay."

"And then how do I communicate any actual information?"

"When you have something important to tell us, signal with a candle again. For a meeting, flicker the candle *three* times. One of us will meet you at the forest's edge. On the north side of the forest, you'll find a grove of mulberry trees, with hellebore and cockle weeds growing around them. Wait until there are no sentinels overhead, then glamour yourself as a fox. We'll meet inside the cave of pines."

Plants. Of course the *Queen of Poisons* gave directions by way of plants. "When can you send my sister a message?"

Her brow creased. "What do you want me to convey?"

I thought of all the things I wanted to say to Hazel, from a reminder to eat her fruit to a simple message letting her know I was okay. "Just… can you just tell her I haven't given up on her, that I want to find her? Maybe find a way for her to signal where she is?"

Yasmin let out a long sigh. "If that's what you want me to do, I will do it. But you should think about this first: we'd be opening up a scrying portal without knowing who is watching. If dragons are surrounding her—if they know she is communicating with The Institute—it could end very badly for her. You should wait until you have something important to communicate."

Her words sent a lick of dread chasing up my spine. "I don't know any other way to find her. And if you can contact her—if you find the blotches of light and darkness when you search for her—at least I'll know she's alive, right?"

"Yes. We will work on finding her, and you work on finding an escape route for her. But don't risk her life just to reassure yourself—risk her life when you think it's the only way to get her back."

My chest tightened. She had a point. "Fine."

"Charm the angels. Seduce them. Make them want to please you, and steal information from them when they're not looking. Whatever it takes, find out what you need to know—for Hazel, and for all of us."

Wordlessly, Yasmin crossed to a shadowy alcove in the corner of the herbarium. If I strained my eyes, I could just see a wooden box resting there. Yasmin pulled it from the shelf. When she opened it, the box almost seemed to glow from within.

"If you want to save your sister, save us—you're going to have to become a new person. A seductive succubus. But I won't send you there unprotected." She pulled a silvery knife from the box, and the moonlight sparked off its lethally sharp blade. "This is Nyxobian silver, so sharp that it can cut through anything. Including angels' bodies, their wings. Hide it on yourself as protection. If an angel seems like he's about to slaughter you, plunge this through his heart. It won't kill him, but it will certainly slow him down."

I shuddered, taking the knife from her. "Let's hope it doesn't come to that, shall we?"

CHAPTER 18

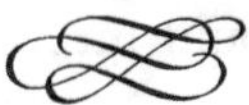

*B*ronze light slanted through the street, washing over the fading graffiti. I walked along the ruins of Whitechapel High Street, dressed in a form-fitting satin dress—garnet in color, to match my lips. The outfit was completely unsuitable for winter, but I did my best to keep my teeth from chattering.

Hidden safely behind the walls of the Tower, I'd prepared myself for my appearance on London's streets. With Yasmin's help, I'd raided the contents of an old pharmacy by Liverpool Street for makeup, then a department store.

In crimson high heels, I now strode through the city with a freshly painted face: black eyeliner, mascara, blush on my cheeks. I'd painted my nails to match my dress. Curled into soft waves, my red hair cascaded over my shoulders, and a bit of glitter glinted from my eyelids.

I had the strongest urge to find Katie, Lucy, and Alex, to tell them I was okay, that I had a plan.

Yasmin had been a hard *no* on that idea.

Trust no one, she said. *You'll only endanger them. Let them think you died.*

I'd spent three weeks in the Bloody Tower with Yasmin, gorging on their reserves of food in order to put a bit more meat on my bones. I could glamour a few curves onto myself, but new glamour took mental and physical stamina. The closer I could get to looking like a curvaceous succubus in real life, the better.

As I walked, my glamoured succubus aura snaked through the air. I could hardly see it, just hints of shadows from the corners of my eyes. An angel like Kratos would see the thick, charcoal tendrils undulating from my body. The sight would lure him closer, like a butterfly to nectar.

Once, succubi had been goddesses, queens among demons. And therein lay the fascination. Powerful creatures like Kratos wanted to take something beautiful and crush it in their fists. In fact, the sight of a seductive, powerful succubus striding through this hellscape would inflame his thirst for conquest. He wouldn't rest until he'd quenched it.

Right there is the reason the world had few succubi left. They'd been hunted out of existence by males terrified of their allure.

But I'd come armed. A bow and bull-skin quiver of arrows hung over my back—not in the fae style. That would give the game away. No, these were the weapons of a demon—a Carthaginian bow, hewn from wood and silver. Arrows carved with the symbols of the Night God. A silver-tipped baton, its hilt made of engraved elephant tusks from thousands of years ago. And of course, the knife of Nyxobian silver strapped to my thigh.

A quiver was a handy thing. Not only did it hold my weapons, but I'd stuffed my makeup and a few handkerchiefs in there.

In the guise of a succubus, I already felt more powerful, as if a thrilling, ancient magic flowed through my blood. That was the thing about disguises. Sometimes you wore them—and sometimes, the disguises wore you.

As Succubus Ruby, I had three tasks. One, gain Kratos's trust. Two, seduce him until he invites me to his castle. And three, survive the hounds.

Simple, right?

First I had to put on a little show for the sentinels who watched my every move as I strutted through Whitechapel. I had to prove my ruthlessness, that I didn't care about humans—and I had to do it all without seeming too much of a potential threat to the angels. As far as the sentinels would be concerned, the Great Nightmare had turned me into a great monster.

To prove that point, I needed Dickhead.

Only an idiot would be out at this time of day, with the sun about to set behind the buildings. Lucky for me, Dickhead was an idiot, and one with very predictable patterns. When I reached Brick Lane, I found him traipsing along the sidewalk, carrying a plastic bag stuffed with food. In fact, potatoes were protruding from its surface.

Were those—*our* potatoes? Oh *hell* no. He'd found the garden. I'd been gone for weeks, eating proper meals in the Tower, while my old rookery friends were probably starving. A tendril of guilt coiled through my ribs.

Sauntering behind Dickhead, I whistled my favorite pop tune—an old Taylor Swift song. He whirled around.

"Hello, hello, hello." A grin spread across his features. "Isn't this my lucky day. First I found the secret garden, and now I've found you."

Oh good. He's only just found the garden.

He didn't seem to recognize me at all, but then again, he'd mostly seen me either as a glamoured ogre of a man or as a scrawny waif running through the streets. He'd never seen the glamorous, well-fed succubus before him.

I glanced at the skies, looking for a sentinel. As the sun disappeared to the west, the moon's glow seemed to brighten. A shiver rippled over my skin.

I can do this. I can handle the night.

But I didn't see any sentinels. Where were the bastards when you actually needed them? There was no point in engaging in this charade unless they were watching, ready to report what I'd come here to do.

Dickhead licked his lips. "Do you know how long it's been since I've seen a filthy little minx such as yourself?"

At one time, men like Dickhead might have feigned a gentlemanly attitude for at least a few minutes, long enough to try to lure me into a false sense of security. In the world of the Great Nightmare, where there was no one who'd hear me scream, he didn't even bother with that performance. As far as he was concerned, a *filthy little minx* such as myself was virtually defenseless here, ready for the taking. Sure, I might have a bow slung over my shoulder, but what were the chances I'd use it?

He waggled his eyebrows. "Why don't you shuffle over to that alley, darling, pull up that dress of yours? Can't imagine you'd be showing everything off like that if you didn't want it, am I right? You're gagging for it."

When I glanced at the skies again, my chest tightened. Still no sentinels. How long would I have to endure him?

"Don't speak much, do you? Last girl I tried to pull was a little freckled thing, not very nice. Had to punch her, but she still got away from me. You'll be nice to me though, won't you?"

Rage simmered. *Freckled thing.* He was talking about Katie. My fingers twitched, desperate to pull one of the weapons from my back. I just needed an audience first.

My gaze darted over his shoulder. There, just behind him, a large-eyed sentinel drifted from behind a street corner. When I glanced at the skies, I found another floating overhead.

Fucking finally.

I pulled the bow off my back, nocking an arrow. When I aimed it at him, he paled.

"I'm not sure I can aim very well," I lied loud enough that the sentinels could hear me. I had to appear ruthless while also under-playing my actual skills. "I could fire a warning shot, but I'm not quite sure it would miss you. I think the lesson here, my friend, is that you need to keep your hands to yourself."

"You're not really going to shoot me with that thing, are you? It's not my fault women like you walk around, frothing at the gash…"

My arrow hit its mark in his thigh. "Whoops! I was trying to do a warning shot but the thing slipped. How do you even use this…"

I loosed the second, taking out his other thigh. His shrieks rent the air.

"Oh dear." I frowned at my bow. "They just sort of go where they want, don't they? I think I'll use something less confusing."

The sentinel soared overhead serenely, taking it all in.

I reached into the quiver on my back, pulling out my baton.

As he hunched over screaming, I slammed the baton into the side of his head. *Once. Twice.* The bag of potatoes fell to the sidewalk.

I needed it to look brutal, bloody. *Three times.* And Dickhead's broken nose didn't disappoint. It was the second time I'd broken it. Blood spewed from his nose, spattering over my arms, and he fell to the pavement, unconscious.

My whole body was shaking, but I slowed my breathing, trying to project calm. I could still see his chest rising and falling.

I swallowed hard, staring down at him. What would happen if I let him recover? He'd keep tormenting my friends, maybe try to assault Katie again. He'd steal their food. He'd probably kill them.

In the world of the Great Nightmare, mercy didn't make any sense.

There was a time when I'd have considered it a great moral crime to execute an unconscious man. It wasn't self-defense; he wasn't attacking. He was simply lying there, bleeding.

But there was nothing to stop him from carrying on in the same way when he woke up. No one was getting put in jail, no one was getting rehabilitated by a team of well-meaning psychologists. In the Great Nightmare, we could kill the monsters or let them kill us.

I slipped the bloodied baton back into my quiver. Then I pulled my knife from its holster. I brought it down hard into his heart. When it pierced his flesh, a thin stream of blood trickled from his lips, and his chest stilled. I swallowed hard.

My first kill.

I stood in the darkening street, and a cold sweat prickled over my body. *Calm, Ruby. Stay calm.* Neither death nor shadows would rattle a succubus. I was supposed to be a creature of the night.

I stared at the blood pooling below the body. Soon the hounds would arrive.

CHAPTER 19

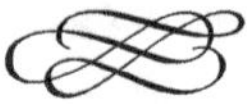

Standing over Dickhead's corpse, the shadows were thickening and growing around me. Icy fear surged through my veins. I lowered the quiver from my back, then pulled out a handkerchief. Carefully, I wiped the blood from my arms.

Here was the thing about angels. They didn't need to plan any more massacres or plagues. All they had to do was peel away the veneer of civilization, and we'd do it ourselves.

I glanced at the sky. The last rays of sunlight had nearly disappeared. In January, that put the time at around four-thirty. *Nearly time.*

Without looking back at the corpse staining Brick Lane, I strode down the narrow, winding lane, whistling cheerfully to myself. *Angela Death*—my succubus character—might not be great with a bow and arrow, but she certainly wouldn't be rattled by a human death.

Two more sentinels drifted overhead, eyeing me carefully. Clearly, the brutal succubus had attracted their attention. I'd achieved at least one of my goals so far, but this evening wasn't over. And it wasn't about to get any easier.

By the time I reached the end of Brick Lane, the sun had disappeared behind the buildings, the sky now a deep indigo. Goosebumps rose over my skin, and I wished desperately for a lantern or a candle.

I crossed to Bishopsgate, heading toward Liverpool Street Station. When I crossed the London dragon marker—the statues that demarcated the old city lines—I heard the first hounds, howling in the distance.

The moon shone brightly tonight, streaming over the ruined city. An icy shiver ran up my spine, but I kept strutting over the sidewalk—just a glamorous succubus out for a walk in an apocalyptic city, impervious to the cold, or the night, or the creatures that would tear the flesh from my bones.

After two blocks, I saw them—the three members of The Institute I'd been expecting. They stood below a net. Flickering torches lit its powerful ropes. Despite the impending chaos, I felt a flood of relief at the soothing signs of light.

I caught a glimpse of the ruby-red eyes of one of Kratos's hounds inside the net. The beast hung suspended between two derelict lampposts. Despite its terrifying howls, I almost felt sorry for the creature.

I kept my pace steady as one of the Watchers pointed a gun at the net. All three men wore masks, their faces completely obscured.

I glanced at the sky again, taking comfort in the sight of the sentinels floating beneath the moonlight. Our brutal, choreographed dance was all going according to plan, every step in the right place—so far. And just as we'd planned, the sentinels were our audience.

Something bright glinted in the corner of my vision, a flare of copper light, and my breath caught in my throat. *Kratos is coming already.*

My pulse began to race. If he came within two hundred yards of us, I had a feeling we'd all be dead within moments, with a flick of his wrist.

This part of the performance was just for the sentinels. We wanted them to report everything to Kratos. We just didn't want him to be here for all of it.

I sped up my pace, moving closer to the trio of Watchers.

The one with the gun shouted into the air. "If the Hunter wants his dog back, he'd better meet our demands!"

I readied my bow, squinting at the Watchers. If I freed the hound while they stood nearby, the beast would tear them to pieces. I had to deal with them first. My gaze flicked to the sentinels, a horde of them hovering above us.

Then I took aim at the Watchers, unleashing a furious volley of arrows. I purposefully allowed many of them to go wide, cheerfully calling out, *"Whoops!"*

But some of the arrows pierced their arms, their stomachs and chests. Their screams pierced the silence—faked, of course. They'd come prepared with armor under their leather clothes. Unbeknownst to the sentinels, the arrows simply sank into their armor, leaving their flesh untouched. I was careful to avoid their heads.

Still, the blows I was about to deliver wouldn't be as painless—nor the one I was going to receive.

From further down Bishopsgate, the coppery light grew brighter, and Yasmin's words echoed in my mind. *You will shine like a beacon in the shadows.* Kratos was moving closer.

I forced myself to tear my gaze from him, eyes on the Watchers again. *Stay focused on your performance, Ruby.* Just as I was closing in on them, headlights flashed. A battered old taxicab screeched around the corner—right on cue. It slammed to a halt in front of the Watchers, who began frantically hobbling toward it, feigning pain.

I pulled my baton from my quiver, sprinting over to the Watchers. Just as the last Watcher was getting to the taxi, I reached him and brought my baton down hard on his back. "Human vermin!" I shouted.

The Watcher fell to his knees, arrows jutting from his body. From above, the sentinels observed my performance.

My gaze flicked to the copper light, where Kratos now appeared, his horse's hooves pounding furiously over the pavement. His outstretched wings seemed to glow with divine light, so beautiful I wanted to bathe in it. Around him, his hounds bayed, as adrenaline burned through my nerve endings. For just a moment, I nearly forgot my mission.

But my performance wasn't done. I had to make sure the angels would never associate me with the Watchers.

I refocused, slamming the baton into the Watcher's arm, his jaw, silencing the part of my mind that begged for mercy.

The Watcher fell forward, his limp body slumped over the car seat.

One of the others leaned forward, grabbing my arm. "Take it easy. That's good enough."

Genuine fear tinged his voice, but I needed this to look real if I was going to survive. Blocking out the civilized part of my mind, I slammed the baton down hard again into the Watcher's shoulder blade. I wasn't fae anymore—Angela Death was a demon of shadows. The crack of bone didn't even make me wince. *Angela Death was born to punish humans.*

I lifted the baton again to bring it down into his arm.

I didn't even see the Watcher pull a gun. I just heard the sharp report of gunfire, and pain slamming into my shoulder. I fell back hard on the pavement.

It took a few terrifying moments for the pain to register.

From the sidewalk, I heard the Watchers slam the door, then the sound of tires screeching over the pavement. At least they'd gotten away safely—apart from the one I'd nearly beaten to death.

When the pain registered at last, the agony stole the breath from my lungs. They'd shot me in the shoulder—just like we'd planned. It hurt even more than they'd described.

Still, four-thousand-year-old succubi didn't crumple in the face of pain. Gritting my teeth, I pushed myself up on my elbows. Kratos's gleaming white horse hammered the pavement, racing closer. Moonlight glinted over his coppery wings.

At the sight of him, my heart slammed against my ribs. He was heading right for me. Just before he reached the trapped hound, he reared his horse to a sharp halt. The horse snorted, steam rising from its nostrils.

Surrounded by his hounds, Kratos stared at me, his amber eyes boring into mine. He wasn't making a move for his hound yet; he was still trying to figure out what the hell was going on.

Slowly, blocking out the pain, I rose. Agony ripped my shoulder apart as I stood. "Those humans think they can mess with immortals like us." I laced my voice with ancient arrogance, keeping it steady as I spoke. "I wanted to teach them a lesson."

I nodded at the net. "I'd shoot him down, but I haven't got very good aim." *Bullshit.*

Gracefully, Kratos jumped off his horse. He stalked toward me, golden light radiating around him. As he drew nearer, warmth pooled off his body. Part of me wanted to shoot him right then and there, but he'd survive it, and I'd lose any chance of helping Hazel or anyone else.

He held out his hand. "Give me your bow."

I handed over my bow and a few arrows, watching as Kratos aimed at the rope that connected the netting to the streetlamp. He unleashed one arrow, then another, with perfect precision, until they'd ripped through the rope.

The hound dropped to the sidewalk, yelping and snarling, then freed himself from the netting. He turned to us, slowly padding closer, his red eyes on me.

I sucked in short, sharp breaths, trying to manage my agony and fear. When the hound reached me, he sniffed my hand, his ears flattening on his head. He snarled.

Did he remember my scent from weeks ago? Maybe he remembered his master commanding him to leave me alive.

When I looked at Kratos again, he was still staring at me. "Tell me exactly what you saw. How did Culloch end up in that net?"

I pretended that blood wasn't roaring in my ears, that my heart wasn't threatening to gallop out of my chest. "Culloch? Is that your hound's name?"

Culloch began to lick the blood off my arm, his tongue hot on my skin. Inwardly, I shuddered.

"Yes. Why did you risk your safety to help him?" Kratos asked sharply. Around him, his hounds snarled, teeth bared.

I shoved my fear deep below the surface. "Risk myself? Should I be afraid of *humans*? What's next? Should I cower in a ditch when I see a horde of rats? Anyway, I prefer hounds to humans, as it happens."

"You did take a risk. They shot you," he pointed out.

I narrowed my eyes at him, touching my shoulder. "This? I'm immortal. I'll outlive them, just like I've outlived generations of humans. We have a new landscape now. While the humans suffer, eating rats and living in filth, I will flourish once again. They will worship me again, or they can die in a hailstorm of arrows." I smiled coyly. "As soon as I learn how to aim. Maybe you could teach me."

For just a moment, his eyes flared with a golden light. I could only imagine that my haughtiness was enticing him, stoking his urge to conquer me.

Then his amber gaze flicked to one of the sentinels. Immediately, the creature swooped down, hovering about ten feet away. Kratos crossed to him, leaning in close to hear what the creature had to impart.

With any luck, the story would be just as we'd planned: the sloppy but ruthless murder of Dickhead, the attack on the Watchers. A succubus with limited fighting skills who wanted to kill humans as badly as the angels did.

At last, the sentinel drifted away, and Kratos turned back to me. As he walked closer, a faint smile curled his lips. "How long have you been in London? A few weeks? And already you're breaking men's bones."

I sighed. "They got what was coming to them."

When he took another step closer, his power thrummed over my bare skin, hot and soothing. In fact, I could have sworn it was taking some of the pain away from my shoulder.

He narrowed his eyes. "I've seen you before, haven't I, succubus? You were dressed like an angel." He let his eyes linger over my body. "You were taking your clothes off on stage, if I recall."

I smiled, compelled to move closer to his soothing light. "Oh, I remember. In fact, I was hoping I'd run into you when I came to London."

He raised his eyebrows. "Oh really?"

"You were there when the dragons arrived. They took my sister." He had been there when it had happened. I'd told him about it. I swallowed hard, mentally working overtime to transmute my rage and grief into something less threatening, like *sass.* "There aren't many of us left, you know. I thought you might know where the dragons took their women."

He gazed down at me. "Succubi are wildly protective of their sisters, aren't they?"

"We're an endangered species. Human males, demon males—they see something pretty, and they want to kill it. You know how it goes."

"Oh believe me, I know."

Well that's... scary. "So I'd like to find those dragons of yours, slaughter them, and get my sister back."

"What makes you think your sister is still alive? And what makes you think they're *my* dragons?"

I choked down my anger. My objective was to get him to trust me, not to lose my shit.

I folded my arms, trying to block out the pain screaming through my shoulder. "I just know." That was a lie. I had no idea. I just had to believe it, or I'd lose my fucking mind.

He shrugged. "I don't control the dragons. They came out of their caves when I arrived, sent by another force. And I think my presence lured them, too. They're attracted to conquest. That's all."

"Conquest." The word sounded oddly seductive on his tongue, and I watched his body tense when I repeated it, eyes flaring with gold.

He had to know more than he was letting on. Right?

Mentally, I tried to balance my different objectives. I couldn't push him about the dragons when I was trying to get an invitation to Death Angel Palace. I needed to keep the big picture in mind. The big picture was... I blinked, my thoughts cloudy. In fact, the pain and the blood loss were starting to get to me.

Maybe this was good. Maybe my vulnerability was an asset right now.

I clutched my shoulder. "I don't feel so well." The first honest thing I'd said.

He moved closer to me, his magic pulsing over my body, and I faltered.

Deftly, Kratos swept his arm around me, steadying me against him.

My heart pounded against his chest, and he made a noise like a low, pleased growl. His body radiated warmth and the scent of cedar smoke. If I hadn't known what a monster he was, I'd have actually found this comforting.

Gently, he touched my shoulder, his fingertips leaching away my pain. "You're bleeding heavily. You need treatment."

"Those vermin shot me," I said into his chest. "I don't suppose you could help me hunt *them* down, since you're going to be no help at all with the dragons." Through my cloudy thoughts, I remembered to pout for the full effect.

"I'm going to take you somewhere safe."

Perfect. "As long as there's a warm bath."

"What's your name?"

"Ruby." I tightened my fingers around the rich, expensive fabric of his shirt. "When I dance, I'm Angela."

"Ruby, I'm going to take you with me." Gently, he stroked his fingertips over my cheek. As he did, a strange, relaxing warmth pooled through my body, and I melted into his embrace. "I just can't allow you to see how we get there."

A cloud of calm enveloped me, until I could no longer remember who I was or the specifics of my mission. I only knew that powerful arms had tightened around me, and as the sound of great wings beat the air, the cold January winds bit at my face.

CHAPTER 20

I woke surrounded by the smell of cedar smoke, my limbs bare under silky sheets. I didn't want to open my eyes yet, afraid of what I might see. I'd been dreaming of four black suns in the sky and an empty throne of black thorns. The images had filled me with a cold sense of dread. Four suns? Why had I dreamt of that?

Shadows pooled around me, chilling my skin. No one would know that a supposed succubus was scared of the dark.

Slowly, I forced myself to pry my eyes open, and a wave of fear slammed into me as I discovered the night surrounding me like a funeral pall. As my eyes slowly adjusted, I slowed my breathing a little. Faint streams of moonlight filtered into the room through tall windows. Frantically, I looked for a lantern or a candle—and I found one, lying next to my bed by a box of matches.

With shaking hands, I struck a match, immediately breathing easier at the sight of the guttering flame. I lit the candle, then held the brass candleholder out to investigate my surroundings.

I found myself in a canopied bed. I swung my legs over the side, wincing at the throbbing pain in my shoulder, and stepped onto a cold flagstone floor, shivering at the chill in the room.

A red-hued tapestry covered one of the stone walls, its embroidered image depicting images of war and victory, golden trumpets held aloft. Just to the right of the tapestry stood an arched oak door. I crossed to it, trying the doorknob—but I'd been locked inside. So that was a great start. Bit of a fire hazard.

To my right, tall windows stretched high above my head—two stories high, in fact. No one had hung up curtains in here.

From my vantage point, I could see movement in the woods outside—something white moving between the trees, something glowing with gold. It took me a moment to recognize that it was Kratos, riding through his woods with the pack of hounds surrounding him. The sight of the ghostly hunt sent a shiver of fear through my bones.

I moved away from the window, carrying the candle around the circumference of the room. A great stone fireplace stood empty in one wall. I'd be asking if someone could light that in the future, so I didn't have to wake up gripped by abject terror.

Behind the canopied bed was a stone wall, bare except for an oak wardrobe, a full-length mirror, and an arched doorway. *That* would be a daytime exploration. I was already creeped out enough in this place.

I peered up. Vaulted wooden ceilings soared above me, and a balcony divided the room into two stories. Without more light, I couldn't quite see what was up there.

Still, despite the eerie shadows, a sense of victory whispered through me. *I'm in. I made it into the palace.*

Now that I'd gotten a look at the room, I thought I should inspect my own body. I sat on the edge of the bed, using the candle to illuminate myself. Just as I'd hoped, faint tendrils of charcoal glamour still curled off my body. My glamour had maintained, even while I was asleep. That was good news.

Somebody had treated my gunshot wound, and a bandage now covered the hole, tinged with blood underneath. Pain still throbbed through my shoulder.

I blinked with the sudden realization that if I'd ended up in this skimpy nightgown, *someone* had changed my clothes while I slept.

Kratos? Had Kratos undressed me? In fact, not only was I in a different outfit, but I smelled different—my hair and skin scented of roses and poppies. Someone had *bathed* me. What the hell? And moreover, what had happened to the knife of Nyxobian silver that had been strapped to my thigh?

My jaw clenched tightly at the violation. And making matters worse, a sentinel drifted past the window in the moonlight, gleaming eyes locked on me.

I crawled back into the bed, sliding the candle across the bedside table. Feeling exposed, I pulled the crimson blankets tighter around me. *What have I gotten myself into?*

As I clutched the blanket around me, the locked oak door unlatched and creaked open.

A tall, stooped man stood in the doorway, his black hair falling over a high forehead. His pale skin practically gleamed in the light of his lantern. To my complete surprise, he was wearing a pink sweatshirt featuring the grinning image of a gray cat.

He smiled shyly at me. "I saw a light coming from under your door, so I knew you were awake. You slept for a full day, did you know that?" he chirped.

I stared at him as he crossed into the room. Who the hell was this?

"You look better," he continued. "I mean, you're not hemorrhaging blood anymore." He cleared his throat. "Just so you know, it wasn't me who dressed and bathed you. It was one of the female maids. Kratos said if I did anything untoward, he would gouge out my eyeballs and feed them to the crows." He huffed a laugh. "He has the funniest turns of phrase. Not that I would do anything untoward anyway."

I raised my eyebrows, lowering my voice to the sophisticated timbre of a succubus. "Who are you, exactly?"

"Oh! Right. I'm Elan. I serve the angels. I'm a..." he held his hand to his mouth to whisper conspiratorially. "I'm a fae."

"Is that a secret of some sort?"

He wrinkled his nose. "Well, Adonis might skin me alive if he ever remembered that I existed, so..." He blinked at the moonlight. "You know, sometimes being forgettable has its perks."

I was beginning to get the impression that Elan might be an excellent source of information. "And who is Adonis?"

His dark eyes widened. "Oh, you don't know? He's the one with the dark blue wings." His eyes crinkled as he smiled. "He really loves death. I saw him vaporize a shadow demon a few days ago. Just blood and entrails everywhere—" He stopped himself short. "Sorry, you probably don't want to hear this. It was actually pretty disturbing, now that I think about it."

Oh, wonderful. So Adonis could vaporize people, and he particularly hated the fae. I should be probing for more information, dizziness clouded my head, and I had a sudden urge to change the subject. In any case, if I could keep Elan friendly, maybe I could learn a lot from him.

"I like your sweatshirt," I said.

He grinned. "Thanks. It's the original internet cat. He's dead." His smile faded, and he sort of winced. "I'm not good with people."

My stomach rumbled, and I clutched it. "I know it's the middle of the night, but I don't suppose you have anything to eat around here? I slept for a full day, so I'm positively famished." A succubus had no problem ordering servants around.

He nodded enthusiastically. "One moment." He hurried out of the room, the door whooshing shut behind him.

At least Elan seemed harmless, and was a relief to be around another fae—even if he had no idea I was just like him.

Elan returned a moment later, his shoulders hunched but a smile on his face. "Food will arrive soon." He pointed to the arched doorway inset into the wall behind the bed—the room I'd been too scared to explore. "You'll find the bathroom just there if you need it. Everything will be provided for you here."

I'd been hoping the arched doorway might lead to a "secret documents with dragon maps" room, but I supposed that was unrealistic.

"We even have a bar in the Tower of Wrath for when... for when you are allowed to leave your room."

"Wonderful. Tell me, Elan, since I'm a new guest here. What are the angels like?" I asked.

Elan rubbed his forehead. "I'm not sure if I can say. I'm not sure if it would anger them." He spoke in a furious whisper. "All I can tell you is that they are celestial creatures untainted by our bestial trappings."

Before I could finish rolling my eyes, a female servant pushed through the door with a tray of steaming food. The air filled with the scent of fresh bread, and my mouth watered in anticipation.

The girl's dark hair framed a long face, and she smiled nervously. As she slid the food onto the bedside table, her hands shook. Human, this one. The angels seemed like they hated humans, but I supposed they needed someone to serve them.

As she leaned in closer to me, arranging the food on the tray, she whispered so quietly I nearly missed it, "I hid your things."

Relief flickered through me. Maybe she'd kept my knife safe.

As the girl slowly backed out of the room, I turned to the tray. There before me was a feast that far outshone anything Yasmin had been able to provide while trying to fatten me up. For a moment, I stared at it as if in a dream.

Warm bread lay next to slabs of bacon, the steam curling into the air. Roast potatoes sat beside them. Two hard-boiled eggs had been sliced and seasoned. And for dessert, sugared almonds and a bowl of fruit and custard.

I have died and gone to heaven. Suddenly, infiltrating the home of the death angels seemed like the best decision I'd ever made.

Elan raised his eyebrows. "Is it to your liking?"

"Elan..." I breathed. "This looks amazing." I began shoveling bacon and potatoes into my mouth.

He grinned. "I oversee the cooking here. I think it's the only reason they allow a fae to remain in Hotemet Castle. I've been a chef in homes such as this since the twelfth century."

Hotemet Castle. It has a name. For a long moment, I didn't speak, too focused on the food before me. The rich, savory flavors melted in my mouth, enrapturing me so much that I hardly noticed Elan filling a wineglass.

I closed my eyes, losing myself in the pure pleasure of the food. "This is why the fae remained on Earth," I muttered.

"What?" Elan asked sharply.

I opened my eyes, jolted from my reverie. "Your race. You're angels who chose to stay on Earth because you loved the earthly pleasures, the food and the dance. Isn't that right? You stayed on Earth so you could make delicacies like this."

"Of course. We each have our own particular skill. Mine is cooking."

I tore into a buttery piece of fresh bread. "You said the angels allow you to stay here because of your cooking. They eat, then? The angels?"

He nodded.

I honestly didn't know the first thing about them, but apparently angels on Earth had fully corporeal bodies.

I arched an eyebrow as I chewed. Maybe they'd become like us, then. *The fallen*—angels lured in and trapped by the temptations of Earth.

Probably best to keep that particular heresy to myself.

Elan straightened. "I'm a high fae. I believe the angels view us as superior. If I were a feral fae..." He mimicked a "throat-slitting" gesture, his eyes widening.

Wonderful. I sipped my wine. "Why? What have they got against those animals? They seem to like hounds, why not the feral fae?"

"They are abominations." He looked at me gravely. "A hound is simply a hound. A feral fae is an angel in the body of a true beast."

"Right. I forgot about that. Elan," I asked. "Why did they tell you I was here?"

"Kratos said you saved his hound. He says that he owes you Culloch's life, and that we're supposed to take good care of you." His throat bobbed. "I can't promise everyone else will be as welcoming as I am."

"And who do I need to look out for, can you tell me that?"

A heavy silence filled the room, and Elan looked around himself nervously. I speared a flaky potato and brought it to my mouth, waiting for Elan's answer. I had the feeling he wanted to help me, but these people scared the shit out of him.

After a moment, he took a few nervous steps closer, then pressed his hand to one side of his mouth. He mouthed a word that looked something like *Johnny.*

That couldn't be right.

I cleared my throat, whispering, "Did you say 'Johnny'?"

He lifted a finger, shushing me, then nodded.

"And who is he?" I asked.

Elan stole a quick glance at the window, and in the darkened skies outside, I saw the gleaming of a sentinel drifting by. A chill rippled over my skin.

When the sentinel had passed, Elan turned to me and mimicked flying wings with his arms.

An angel? So there was an angel here named Johnny. Seemed awfully modern.

Elan bowed his head. "I have to go now."

He cast another nervous glance at the window. "Have a good night, then. You'll want to rest more. They'll all want to speak to you in the morning."

Goosebumps rose on my skin. All of them: Kratos, Johnny—and Adonis.

As he walked to the door, I called out, "Elan. Tomorrow, do you think we could keep the fire lit? It's dark and drafty in here."

"Sure. Sleep well."

When he closed the door, I almost regretted his departure—maybe it was his unassuming personality, or maybe it was the lantern he'd carried with him.

All I knew was I'd have to permanently perform here. An angel's interest could be explained by only one thing. I was supposed to be seductive and alluring. It would be a dangerous line to walk—luring them in just enough, without pulling them in too far. I wasn't going to sleep with Kratos, but I had to keep his interest just enough for him to want me around.

I couldn't let them know what I really was. A fallen angel in the body of a feral beast. An abomination.

CHAPTER 21

I woke to ruddy sunlight streaming through my window. I rubbed my eyes, blinking. At the sight of daylight, relief bloomed in my chest.

While I'd slept, a servant had left a tray on my bed—coffee and pain au chocolate.

May the gods bless you, Elan. Earthly gods, Old Gods, all of them.

Based on the fact that steam was rising from the coffeepot and the pastries, the tray hadn't been in here long. I poured myself some milky coffee, then dipped a pastry into it.

I could imagine my sister Hazel here, her long limbs tangled in the bedsheets, messy hair falling in her eyes as she chomped the pastries, crumbs falling over her nightgown. When I closed my eyes, I could almost hear her voice, hear her snarling with frustration as her computer crashed or laughing at some weird animal video online.

I had to find her. And on top of that, I had to do what I could to make the world safe for her.

I'd gotten about halfway through the pain au chocolate when the door opened, and Kratos strode into the room. In the morning light, he looked resplendent in his crimson and gold brocade clothing, even if his wings weren't making an appearance. Maybe he only brought them out for killing.

With the covers pulled up around my shoulders, I summoned the haughty demeanor of a succubus. "Hello, Kratos. May I introduce you to the wonderful earthly custom of knocking before entering a room?"

He bowed his head curtly. "Welcome to my home. Since you saved Culloch's life, it is only fair that I allow you to recover here. You will have all the food you desire." He gestured at the balcony above us, which I could now see was lined with rows of books. "You'll even find books to entertain you."

"The room is sufficient," I said haughtily. "But why keep the door locked? I'm not a prisoner, am I?"

He narrowed his golden eyes. "You do realize that your lodgings would be far inferior if I'd left you in the streets." Under his smooth voice lay a steely threat.

My first instinct was to pull the blankets up even tighter over my chest, to scream at him to leave, then to lock the door. But he wouldn't keep me around here very long if I didn't tempt him the way a succubus was supposed to.

I let the sheets drop and arched my back. "Like I said, the room is lovely."

For a moment, his gaze slid down my body, and I realized just how much of me was showing—in the pale pink nightie, most of my cleavage was on display, my skin peering through the lace fabric. I let the strap of the nightgown fall, exposing just a little more of the curve of my breast.

I sensed his gaze mentally stripping the rest of my meager clothing off, and I had no doubt whatsoever as to what he was thinking about. Despite myself, my cheeks flushed at the way he was looking at me.

"Oops," I said, pulling up the strap again.

The open-mouthed expression on his face told me that I now had the upper hand. His gaze locked on my breasts, and golden light beamed from his body.

I slipped my legs over the side of the bed, making sure he had a view of my skin all the way up to my thighs. Then I leaned back on my hands. "Nice of you to come visit me."

For a moment, he seemed to have lost the ability to speak, his fists clenched tightly, eyebrows drawn together as if a brutal battle raged in his mind.

After a long pause, he spoke in a husky voice. "We haven't had many female visitors here," he said, as if by way of explanation. "I lived in isolation for a long time."

I cocked my head, keeping my back arched. "That sounds lonely."

He took a step closer, apparently entranced by my body. "We have a mission, and I should not let myself become distracted by earthly temptations, or I'll become one of the fallen."

So he *hadn't* spent much time around women. Were angels even allowed to touch women, or was I his forbidden fruit? Whatever the case—given the way he was undressing me with his eyes and probably thinking about touching my body—I had the impression that the urge to fall nearly overwhelmed him.

I hated him more than anything. And yet, weirdly, the thought of him lusting after me didn't bother me like it should.

"Well, I wouldn't want to tempt you away from your mission." *Seduce him and make him trust you, Ruby.* I toyed with the hem of my nightgown, pulling it up just a tad to expose more leg. "How is your hound? Recovering from the attack?"

"He is fine, thank you for asking." His powerful voice rumbled over my skin. "The other angels will want to meet you, of course. They don't trust outsiders and demons."

I smiled coyly. "And you trust demons?"

His eyes wandered down to my chest again. "Perhaps 'trust' isn't the right word. You intrigue me."

Based on your eye contact, I don't have to wonder too much which part of me intrigues you. "Where are we, exactly?"

"Hotemet Castle. Outside London. It's been hidden through magic for thousands of years."

"Will I be able to look around? I'd like to see what sort of a place I'm living in."

With what looked like considerable effort, he raised his gaze to mine. "Perhaps I could give you a guided tour."

Of course. He wasn't going to leave me to wander around unsupervised to search for his secret apocalyptic plans. He wanted to see me naked—that didn't mean he trusted me.

A flicker of movement in the window caught my eye, and I watched as another sentinel drifted by, eyes locked on me.

I yawned lazily, feigning relaxation. I half wondered if I should let the strap of my nightgown fall lower. His restraint—the fact that he didn't want to become fallen—suggested that he wouldn't be too eager to jump into bed with me.

"Kratos," I purred. "Tell me what *fallen* means? I don't understand your kind so well."

"When angels fall, we become like the beasts. Like the fae. It would destroy our mission."

Destroy his mission. That sounded like something worth exploring.

I sipped my coffee, still aware that his gaze was devouring me. "So you haven't spent much time around female company?"

"I was raised to remain separate from humans and demons—to think only of my purpose."

"And what purpose is that?"

His gaze shuttered. "Like I said. You intrigue me, but it doesn't mean that I trust you." His fists clenched again, knuckles whitening.

"Mmm. Well, Kratos, I'm sure we will get to know each other better." Was it possible that this ancient warrior angel was a full-blown virgin?

"I've gotten to know humans mostly through books," he said. "Demons, too. I've learned about the strange mixtures of brilliance and depravity among both species." His eyes flashed with an intense light. "I must say, some moral standards are lacking in human history, at least as much as among the demons."

Tell him what he wants to hear, Ruby. Tell him what a succubus would say. "Oh, don't lump the succubi in with the humans. Human culture is riddled with hypocrisy. Look at the literature. A girl tries to have a little fun for once, and she's stuck wearing a scarlet letter *A* for the rest of her life, or throwing herself under a Russian train. Men are allowed to do what they want. I know you angels aren't big on pleasure, but surely even you can see that humans are irrational."

I was playing a role, but those sentiments were pure Ruby. Humans could be so stupid about how they viewed pleasure. They lived for a mere eighty years and wasted most of that time feeling bad about all the things that made them feel good.

That's what civilization meant to some humans. Self-denial.

Kratos's eyes glinted in the morning light, and he took another step closer. "Tell me more about your experience of humans."

"Humans are not supposed to kill other humans. Unless, of course, one of their leaders has demanded it, or if their victim is evil enough, or if someone stepped on their lawn, or was the wrong color or religion." I let out a long, weary sigh. "I think the Earth is due for a reckoning, don't you?" I smiled wickedly, letting my nightgown strap fall once again. "Burn it all. Let's start again. That's why you're here, isn't it?"

For a moment, an icy silence fell over the room. I felt as if an electrical current buzzed over my skin, raising the hair on the back of my neck.

After another moment, golden light glinted in Kratos's eyes. "I like the way you think."

So far, this was working out nicely. Maybe it was time to step it up another notch. I'd seen the uncontrolled lust in his eyes, knew that he wanted me. Could I actually bring myself to undress in front of this virgin, even if I hated him? Could I lure him to fall?

I rose from the bed, wincing at the pain in my shoulder. "I think I'll get dressed now."

His body seemed to glow brighter. "I'll leave while you dress, of course."

For a man who slaughtered people with dogs, he really was a gentleman.

"You don't have to—"

My sentence was interrupted by the opening of the door, and my stomach tightened.

The angel who strode into the room was not what I'd been expecting. Slate-gray wings swooped behind him, the color a dull contrast to his electric-blue mohawk. He gripped a half-empty bottle of vodka, and he wore tight, ripped jeans riddled with safety pins and a torn black T-shirt with a skull that read *Eat the Rich.*

Given his scrawny physique, maybe he needed to expand his diet. His bony elbows and legs made him look about a month away from starvation. Come to think of it, there probably weren't many rich people around since the apocalypse had taken root. But since this dude's wings were out, was he about to slaughter someone?

All I knew was, this angel must be Johnny.

The punk frowned at me. "Ah. And here we have one of your best strategic decisions. Bringing a demon into the angels' castle for no reason whatsoever, apart from her admittedly perky breasts and shapely legs. Which, all things considered, will probably tempt us to become fallen. Do I have that all about right?"

Kratos cut him a vicious glare. "Silence, Johnny."

Well, well, well. I'd come here looking for divisions within the angels' forces. Had I stumbled into a little one already?

I didn't really like Johnny's eyes on me, so I slid back into the bed and pulled the covers over myself. "I was actually hoping to dress before meeting the entire castle."

Johnny chewed a piece of gum. "Too late now, I guess. I'm Johnny Savage."

"I'm Ruby. I also go by *Angela Death.*"

Johnny blew a bubble, letting it pop in front of his face. "How old are you, anyway?"

This was one of the biggest distortions of reality I had to contend with. The succubi were ancient. "Four thousand years, roughly." Only about… oh… three thousand, nine hundred and seventy-six years off my real age. "And how old are you, Johnny?"

He nodded at Kratos. "Not half as old as this ancient bastard. I was born in 1961, came of age in the seventies."

My eyebrows rose. I had no idea some of the angels were so *young.* Were they born, just like fae and humans were? Did they procreate?

Johnny grinned. "Nineteen seventies were the best time in the history of the world."

Kratos's gaze flicked to him. "Be honest, Johnny. You really don't know anything about the history of the world."

Johnny shrugged, popping his gum. "Can't argue with that." Suddenly, his blue eyes sharpened, his jaw stilling. An icy chill fell over the room, and he took a few slow steps closer to me.

As he did, a wild hunger began to grip my stomach, and I had the strangest feeling that Johnny was causing it. I clutched my gut, practically drooling.

"Kratos." Johnny's eyes narrowed on me. "How much do you know about this demoness, exactly? What if she's here to find out things about us, pass it on to the humans so they can resist us? Wouldn't want dangerous types in here, would we? Unsavory types?"

"I know she's not working with The Institute, because I watched them shoot her, and I watched her beat one of them within an inch of his life." Kratos arched an eyebrow. "Something on your mind, Johnny?"

Johnny cocked his head. "Maybe I did a little research with the sentinels. Maybe I unearthed a few things about a vindictive and maniacal demoness slaughtering people willy-nilly."

I raised my hand. "I'm right here, you know."

Kratos's body glowed with gold light. "Care to share?"

Johnny curled his lip in a sneer. "The day you brought her here, she murdered a man in cold blood. Beat him half to death, stabbed him. Shot him with an arrow or two. Watched him die in the street. I just wanted to be sure you were aware of what sort of person you picked up off the street, though of course, if you're bringing home stray demons, you might not be too particular."

I opened my eyes wide, as though I'd been caught. As though I hadn't set this all up to prove that I didn't care about humans.

Kratos blinked. "I don't understand your objection. You love killing people." He turned away from Johnny, quirking a smile at me. "Burn it all to the ground. Start again, right, Ruby?"

I smiled. "Exactly."

Johnny crossed his arms. "She might try to slit my throat in my sleep. Wouldn't kill me, but it would be unpleasant. How do you know she's not some sort of a Trojan horse?"

I blinked. "Do you expect an army to burst out of my chest at any moment?"

"Not a literal horse." Johnny scowled. "It's like… a metaphor. And anyway, why do I think this has more to do with how she looks than anything else? She'll distract us from our mission."

The idiot was on to something, because that's exactly what I had planned, along with thwarting their mission entirely. Once I figured out what the hell it was.

Kratos remained silent, but I could almost feel the tension rolling off him, and something about it terrified me at a primal level. "Do you really think I would let anything distract me from my mission? I know what happens if we fail."

I don't. But maybe that can be objective number one.

Johnny scratched his cheek. "Nah. Of course I don't think you'll forget our goals. Just be careful."

Kratos's jaw tensed. "I have work to do. Don't harass my guest."

And with that, he strode out of the room.

Johnny pointed a long, bony finger at me. "I'll be watching you, succubus. And Adonis will too."

As Johnny let the door slam behind him, another sentinel floated by, eyes wide.

Oh believe me, Johnny, I know never to relax here.

Someone must have drugged my tea, because I slept more in those two days than I'd slept in the past few weeks put together. Curled up in the silky sheets, with light beaming through the tall, open windows, I'd dreamt of those four black suns darkening the sky. Sometimes I dreamt of a black, thorny throne towering above me, its beauty luring me in and sharp spikes warning me away at the same time. Each time I woke up, the pain in my shoulder had subsided a little more.

As the thick fog of sleep began to clear, I stared out the window at the reddening sunlight. I'd woken at sunset. In the forest, I caught a glimpse of Kratos and his hounds moving between the trees—those flashes of ivory, gold, and red. I shuddered at the sight.

I was pretty sure that, two days in a row, I'd missed my early morning summons from Yasmin. I could only hope she hadn't spent too much time lingering in reflections until the sentinels spied her.

Tracing my fingertips over my bandage, I tested my wound. I could hardly feel the ache in my shoulder at all. When I peeked under the bandage, I found the wound almost closed up. Fae, like demons, healed fast, but some magic had been at work here too, knitting veins and tendons together until I barely had a scar.

When the sun drifted lower behind the oak boughs, energy buzzed through my body, and I sat up in bed. Now that I'd recovered, it would be time to set to work learning about this place, even as I waited for my guided tour with the warrior-virgin.

For now, I remained locked in my room. As soon as I had earned enough trust, I needed to investigate that magical forest and find out what the gods were trying to tell us. I mean, assuming Yasmin wasn't completely full of shit—which, quite frankly, was a big assumption.

But while locked in here, I supposed I could start with the vast library around me. Kratos had said he'd learned about the human race through books. Now I'd find out what he thought of them.

As requested, a fire had been burning in the fireplace day and night since my first night here.

Dressed in my rose-pink nightgown, I stood, stretching my arms over my head. Even with the shadows lengthening over the wintry ground outside, the fire warmed the room.

First on the agenda, I wanted to learn what I could about this luxurious prison.

I started with the vast tapestry across from my bed—the one I stared at every time I opened my eyes. In the light of day, I'd a better view of it. Vibrant gold, blue, and red threads depicted a battle scene, one in which a man sat atop a white horse, his head gleaming with a golden halo of light, gripping an enormous golden sword.

Kratos really wanted me to worship him, didn't he? I had a feeling he'd put me in a room specifically designed to glorify his exploits through the medium of needlework.

Honestly. Apparently, even angelic men craved phallic symbols to feel good about themselves. Nothing particularly illuminating there.

Time to move on to the upper story. The book selection would give me a window into Kratos's mind.

I crossed to the spiral stairwell—a set of narrow, winding steps that led up to the books. On the balcony level, the air cooled. Shelves of dusty books spanned the three walls of the mezzanine floor. I crossed to the side above the canopied bed, where I found row after row of books about war.

Given the tapestry on the wall, I supposed it wasn't surprising. The dude was into war. The books began with the ancient Greek section: the histories of the Peloponnesian war and the Persian expedition. I scrolled past tomes about Napoleon, Sun Tzu, Genghis Khan, Hannibal and Scipio, and Caesar.

The war books gave way to books about leadership strategy and philosophy: Machiavelli, Thomas More, Hume, Aquinas, Kant, Plato, Nietzsche.

Boy, these angels really knew how to have fun. I didn't suppose I'd find any beach romances in here to pass the time.

On the next wall—the one above the fireplace—I found Greek tragedies that blended into shelves of epic poems: the Iliad, the Odyssey, Beowulf, Gilgamesh, Metamorphoses, and so on. Shakespeare lined these shelves, too—mostly the tragedies, but *The Tempest* was there as well. I snatched it off the shelf—I liked a little magic in my books, a little escapism, and this could make for some bedtime reading.

On the final wall, I found the tragedies. Not the Shakespearean tragedies; the *real* tragedies.

Here I found the history books chronicling some of the worst events in human history. The Ephesian Vespers Massacre, the Massacre of Thessaloniki, the Crusades, preventable famines, Byzantine massacres, the European invasion of the Americas—and on and on until I got to the world wars and the thick tomes about the Holocaust. My throat tightened.

Okay. So *this* was what Kratos had learned about humans. Obviously, he didn't have a very rosy view of humanity, and after reading the titles on the spines of all these books, I had to admit my feelings about the human race had soured a bit as well. No wonder he preferred his hounds.

I hadn't learned anything about dragons, but at least I'd gathered insight into Kratos's mindset: war and conquest, and the heart of a warrior, coupled with complete and utter disgust at the entire history of humanity.

Slightly depressed, I descended the stairs, clutching *The Tempest* under my arm. When I glanced out the window, I glimpsed a sentinel drifting past.

I let out a long breath. *Well, I could always explain that I was looking for a good beach romance.*

A chill had crept over my skin, and I wanted desperately to settle into a warm bath. Padding across the bare flagstones, I headed for the bathroom. A silver tub stood in the center of a stone room, right in front of another tall window that overlooked the forest.

On the opposite wall, I eyed another tapestry of Kratos, this time standing proudly with his sword. In fact, he was standing proudly on another man, whose ugly features were contorted in pain. A nice soothing image of violent domination to accompany my relaxing bath.

I turned on the steaming water, and as the tub filled, I decided to do a slight bit of redecorating in the bathroom so as to be ready for Yasmin's communications.

A gilded mirror hung on one wall. In one corner of the bathroom, an alcove was inset into the walls. This is where I found the toilet and a wooden hamper containing fresh towels. If I stood in the alcove, the sentinels couldn't see me. Seemed like a perfect place for the mirror if Yasmin would be flickering into the room.

I pulled the towels from the hamper, dropping one by the bath. Then, when the view was free of sentinels, I crossed to the gilded mirror. I hoisted it off the wall and carried it to the alcove, where I rested it on the empty hamper.

Now I had a little communication center, assuming I could get Yasmin over here.

I peered out of the alcove. As another sentinel drifted past the window, I shuddered at the idea that they'd be watching me in the bath. Still, I supposed the watchful eyes of the sentinels weren't the worst thing in the world. I had a feeling the sentinels had no real blood running through their veins, and they'd feel nothing at the sight of me naked. Not that I knew for sure.

Unlike Kratos.

As the bath filled up, I pulled off my nightgown and underwear. Slowly, I slipped into the steaming water. After a few minutes, I was working up a lather over my body with the rose-and-poppy-scented soap.

As the sentinels drifted past, staring at me in the bath, I began to measure the intervals. If I was going to hide anything from their view, I'd need to know exactly how much time I had between their drive-by viewings.

By my calculations, I had between four and six minutes. That was it. Not a ton of time to stage a coup against lethal, immortal beings, but I'd do what I could.

For just a moment, I closed my eyes, trying to imagine the angel named Adonis. Mostly, I remembered he'd been terrifying. As I breathed in the rose-scented air, his image blazed in my mind. Golden skin, gray-blue eyes with silver flecks, that dark sweep of hair…

Then a vision of Kratos burned in my mind, his body glowing with gold. By the way he'd devoured me with his gaze, I knew he lusted after me. I hated him, and I planned to kill him—but for some reason, I didn't mind the thought of him fantasizing about me. I needed to find out exactly what the angels had meant about becoming *fallen*. If seducing him meant I could destroy his mission—would I actually do it?

I opened my eyes, finding my skin flushed in the hot water.

I leaned over the side of the tub, snatching the copy of *The Tempest* off the floor.

I thumbed through it, frowning at the damp smudges my fingerprints left. My gaze swept over the word *library,* and I read a bit of dialogue:

> *Me, poor man, my library*
> *Was dukedom large enough.*

If only that were enough for Kratos. If only he didn't feel the need to conquer the Earth.

As I sank deeper into the bath, the steam enveloped me, easing my mind—until a familiar power rippled over my skin.

Slowly, I turned my head to find Kratos looming in the doorway, as if I'd lured him here with my thoughts.

CHAPTER 23

I dropped the book on the floor. My first impulse was to scream at him to leave, but that is not what a seductive succubus would do. Instead, I schooled my features to calm. I even sat up a little in the bath—high enough to give him a view of the suds on the tops of my breasts.

He stood there with a sort of slack-jawed look on his face, his eyes burning into me. He really *had* been isolated, hadn't he?

"Can I help you with something?" I asked. Soap slowly dripped down my arm, pooling on the stone floor.

Kratos was supposed to be the terrifying angel of death. And yet, with the stunned look on his face, I felt like the one in control.

"I should have knocked. I'm not used to…" A muscle clenched in his jaw, and he turned around, his shoulders tense. He spoke with his back to me. "I just came to check on you, and when I didn't see you in the bedroom… How is your shoulder?"

"I'm fine. Just doing a bit of reading in the bath."

A pulse of golden light brightened the air around him. Through his finely cut clothes, I could see tension rippling through every one of his chiseled muscles. "If you're feeling better, I thought you might want a tour of the castle."

Why yes, actually. That's exactly what I want. I want to find out every-thing I can about you people so I can kill you.

"Are you going to show me around yourself?" I asked.

"I plan to give you the aerial tour."

Interesting. And unnerving. I rose from the bathtub, watching him glow brighter at the sound of water dripping from my body into the bath.

"I'll just get dressed," I said.

"I'll wait outside." He strode out of the room, his golden aura trailing behind him.

It seemed I'd be flying in the arms of a death angel tonight.

* * *

WHILE I'D STOOD WRAPPED in a towel, Elan had bustled into the room wearing a sweater knitted with the image of a grumpy cat. He'd laid out carefully selected clothing for me—black leather pants, a cream-colored blouse, and a fitted, berry-blue coat to keep me warm in the January air.

I left the coat unbuttoned and kept the blouse wide open at the collar. I didn't want to get too close to the murderous psycho, but so far, my cleavage had been my best leverage over him.

As soon as I finished dressing, I pulled open the door to find Kratos standing in the dim hallway, torchlight dancing over the chiseled planes of his face.

"I like the way you decorated the bedroom." I smiled coquettishly. "Lots of images of you killing people."

He began walking, his footsteps echoing off the walls. "It's what I do best. It's my gift and my curse."

Interesting. "Why your curse?"

"I was born to conquer. Killing is my sacred duty, and I'm compelled to do it. But of course, it comes with isolation."

A lot to pick apart there. Starting with: "What do you mean you're compelled to kill?"

He cut me a sharp look. "It's not important."

Oh but it is, Kratos. It's the most important thing in the world.

I trailed my fingertips along the cold stone walls, thinking of what he'd said about isolation. Of course he couldn't get too close to anyone if his job was to kill them all—even if he longed for contact.

As we walked on, I glanced outside. Here, the narrow windows overlooked the forest.

He took a sharp left into a winding stairwell, and we began climbing the stairs.

"What were you reading in there?" he asked.

"*The Tempest.* Or at least, I'd started it when an angel interrupted me."

"I don't suppose a succubus would be interested in the war books."

"I'll get to them." Here in the stairwell, a draft rippled over my skin. "But since you've learned about humans mostly from books, don't you think you should expand your collection beyond all the death, maybe? Try some romances."

"It's not just death books. I've made it a point to learn about human history. Some brilliant thinkers: Kant, Descartes. They understood duty for a higher purpose."

"Duty for a higher purpose..." I repeated. *You mean like being compelled to kill.* "And what is your sacred duty, exactly, besides hunting people?"

"To restore the Earth's natural balance. Long ago, when humans lived among the other beasts, there was a natural balance. Humans lived with a sort of peace in their minds before divine knowledge poisoned them. Their species are savages infected by a brilliance they cannot handle, that becomes a destructive force."

I sighed. "I think maybe the savagery has gotten worse since you unleashed all the death."

"I'm hardly responsible for *all* the death. In any case, the changes to civilization have only brought the brutality out into the open. The confines of human society offer their own brutality. If one group of men is given complete control over another group of men, they treat them worse than dogs. *That* is human nature. They are wild animals the gods mistakenly imbued with angelic cognition."

He had a point. I thought of an experiment I'd learned about in one of my college psychology classes, when college students had imprisoned their classmates under controlled conditions. It had turned out even worse than you might imagine.

Still, Kratos had only learned about humans from books. He didn't know the people that I did—people like Alex, who always tried to cheer everyone up, who gave Katie his extra food when she was feeling sick.

But I couldn't tell him about Alex, could I? I couldn't tell him anything real.

I still needed to understand his mental state. "So *that's* why you're compelled to kill."

"No, that's not why," he said quietly. "If I don't kill, agony pierces my body, and I will become fallen—warped into a demonic form and cast into an eternal hell on Earth."

Oh. Shit. "Well, I'm not gonna lie. That doesn't sound wonderful."

If that was the outcome, perhaps tempting him to fall would be a no-go, even if I could bring myself to do it. But I had to wonder—was it possible that, if he'd gotten laid once in his long life, this particular angel would be out of the game? I couldn't let myself think about that right now, or I'd end up trying to push him down the endless staircase.

By the time we finally reached the top of the stairs, my thighs were burning. Given how long we'd been walking, I thought we must be halfway to the heavens already.

Kratos pushed through a doorway, and I followed him outside onto the tower wall. Here, a cold wind whipped over the parapet, blowing strands of red hair into my face. To my right, the forest spread out before us, a vast expanse of trees. On the other side of the tower walls, I had a view of the courtyard—a cheery sward of grass with a bloodied wooden block that I was pretty sure had been used for executions. One stark, dark-stone tower stood in the center of it all.

The soaring walls connected six towers, with the seventh in the middle. At the top of the central tower sat an enormous hall of domed glass. In the darkness, I couldn't quite see inside of it.

I pointed at it. "What's that Tower called?"

"The Tower of Silence. And that domed room is the Celestial Room, the crown jewel of my castle. I often spend time in there, staring at the stars and thinking of conquest."

Ahhh, Kratos... definitely fun at parties.

Halfway across the tower's high wall, Kratos stopped walking and turned to me.

"I promised you a guided tour. I thought I'd begin with a view of the grounds and the castle from above."

A shadow passed above us, and I glanced up at a sentinel swooping through the skies.

"Will they be watching us?" I asked.

"No, not when I'm here." Without warning, Kratos crossed toward me and scooped me up in his arms.

Cautiously, I wrapped my arms around his neck. He held me close to his enormous chest, his body warming mine.

His eyes glowed golden in the night. "Are you cold?"

"You're warming me up." I hated the guy, but it was the truth.

Within moments, he'd lifted me into the air. The frigid winter winds rushed over my skin as we swooped over the parapet. Instinctively, I curled in closer to Kratos.

For a moment, I closed my eyes, feeling nothing but the wind and Kratos's heartbeat and his muscled arms enveloping me. Since the dragons had come—since I'd watched them drag humans into the skies, then drop them to the earth—I hadn't been great with heights. As much as I loathed everything about the angels, his warm, woodsy scent was oddly soothing.

Clearly, death came in some beautiful disguises.

"You're missing it all with your eyes closed," he pointed out.

After a few seconds, I felt brave enough to open my eyes.

I peered over the side of Kratos's arm. Stretching below us, loomed the seven towers, each reaching hundreds of feet into the air. Outside the ring of towers stood timber-frame stables. "How many horses do you keep in there?"

"One for each of the angels," said Kratos. "And three more. You wouldn't like riding them. They're difficult."

We swooped lower over the battlements, heading for the forest. As my keen fae eyes adjusted in the silvery moonlight, I could make out a riot of vibrant colors in the oak and ash trees, their leaves tinged shades of dark umber and rich gold.

"Seven towers seem a bit much for three angels, don't you think?" I asked.

"We like our space," he said simply.

There was a time when you would've been able to see London's lights glittering in the near distance. Now only a canopy of stars burned brightly around us.

"This is how it once was." His deep voice rumbled through his chest into mine. "Don't you remember? For hundreds of years of my memories, only starlight lit the skies. The only noise at night was the rustling of leaves, the scattering of animals through the woods. We lived in peace."

So Kratos was one of those beings who liked to be alone with his thoughts. I counted myself among the opposite. Before the Great Nightmare, I'd liked to have music blaring, the TV on, small talk with a neighbor.

And yet I couldn't deny the allure of the quiet midnight beauty out here, over the darkened forest.

With my arms clamped around his neck, we soared lower over a grove of ash trees. From here, I could hear the wind whispering through their boughs like an ancient song.

Was it possible that Kratos had a point? Humans craved knowledge, but as soon as Adam and Eve ate from that tree, they learned a terrible truth about themselves. As soon as they had language, they learned that all things died, and that they would too. After that, they could never feel peaceful in the silence again.

Kratos soared in a large arc over the forest, and as he did, his body glowed with a deeper, richer light. His fingers tightened around my thighs, around my ribcage, and I knew that, right now, a war was raging in his mind. He so badly wanted to give in to those "earthly temptations," to carry me down to land and let his hands explore the rest of my body.

But that whole *eternal hell* thing obviously put him off.

When he met my gaze again, his eyes burned brightly. He was born to conquer—and he wanted to conquer *me,* was desperate to loose the leash he kept on himself.

An unwelcome flush spreading over my skin, for reasons I didn't even want to think about.

I had to lure him to fall, to abandon his mission. What would he do if I strode into his room in the Tower of Silence and just took off my clothes?

Morality—like he'd been going on about before—sometimes meant making sacrifices for the greater good. I'd seduce him away from his stupid sacred duty while looking for the key to the angels' deaths in the forest. Then I'd kill them all.

As I pondered this, his gaze shuttered, muscles tensing again. I was quickly getting the impression that if he let himself fantasize too much—dwell on earthly pleasures—he'd mentally punish himself immediately afterwards.

Kratos swooped around in a wide arc, heading back for the castle, as the wind whipped my hair around my face. This had been useful, but not enough. I wanted more. I wanted to learn everything I could about these angels—everything they were willing to tell me.

I studied his face again—the dark eyebrows and eyelashes framing amber eyes, the hint of golden stubble, the moonlight silvering his features. Women must have thrown themselves at him over the years, and he'd somehow resisted it all.

"How long have you been on Earth, Kratos?" *How long have you been keeping this tight leash on yourself?* "I never knew we had angels among us."

"I didn't have wings until recently, but I've been alive over a thousand years."

"So… how did it work? You came to Earth from the heavens a thousand years ago?"

He swooped lower over the tower's edge, landing gracefully on the stone wall. Gently, he put me down on the walkway. As soon as I pulled away from him, I regretted the lack of warmth. I hugged myself, pulling my coat tighter.

Kratos looked down at me, and an unearthly, celestial light dazzled in his eyes. "I was born in Denmark, the son of a Viking king. My father taught me how to navigate by the stars. He taught me how to live off the land. I'll never forget the smell of the brine in the air, the feel of the wind in my hair. I was free then."

Surprise washed over me. "You were born to human parents?"

He nodded. "Human parents, yes, but they knew what I was." The frigid winds whipped at his pale golden strands of hair. "My father even tested it and had my brother split my skull open with an axe to determine my immortality. I recovered, obviously."

I grimaced. "So the halcyon days weren't all open seas and briny air."

"No, but I learned about duty. I learned I was meant for something more than the human world around me. My father taught me about conquest—until other humans slaughtered him in battle. I was there. I watched them smash his head to pieces."

And thus began his hatred of humans. "I'm sorry."

"When I found the humans who did it, I ripped their lungs and spines from their bodies."

My stomach dropped. "Any reasonable person would do the same." Worried he could hear the sarcasm in my tone, I followed up with, "Nothing is more important than family."

Something sparked in his eyes, and he took another step closer. He spread out his gleaming copper wings, forming a protective shield around me, blocking the wind. "And what about your family? You said you miss your sister."

Through all of my lies, he'd managed to home in on one simple truth.

"Yes," I said softly. "I miss her."

"Nothing is more important than family," he repeated.

I smiled up at him innocently. *That's right. And I'm here to destroy you, so my sister can return to a safer world.*

CHAPTER 24

The first hazy rays of morning sun bled into my room, waking me from my deep sleep. I'd been dreaming of the four black suns again, looming over the Earth.

But I had to clear the cobwebs from my mind quickly. Today, I had to make sure I was in the right place when Yasmin called. I lit a candle at the side of the bed, then snatched it up to investigate our communication portal. Yasmin could appear anywhere in this place—and with any luck, it wouldn't happen when the sentinels were watching.

I snatched an almond croissant from a tray on the bedside table, chomping into it with enthusiasm.

As I crossed the chilly flagstone floor in my bare feet, I wished desperately for a warm bathrobe and slippers. How quickly we got used to luxury. I'd only just arrived here, and already I'd moved on from appreciating the bed and food to desiring specific clothing items.

With one eye on the window for sentinels, I scurried around the room, searching for signs of movement in the reflective surfaces while stuffing my face with the pastry. According to my calculations, I only had about one minute left before another sentinel appeared.

So when Yasmin's dark eyes and hair shimmered into view in a mirror hanging on one of the walls—directly across from the windows—my heart leapt into my throat. As quickly as I could, I used the candle to signal *no*, to tell Yasmin to bugger off for a few minutes.

Could I get her into the bathroom—the spot with the mirror the sentinels couldn't see? Maybe the scryers could actually find my exact location.

After a few more false starts in candlestick holders and the side of the coffeepot, I finally met Yasmin's reflection in the bathroom mirror, tucked safely into the alcove.

I signaled with the candle five times and watched her shimmering face smile with relief.

She held up a handwritten sign: *Thank you for your work.* Then she leaned down, scribbling again. She held up a second sign that said, *Alert us at the first sign of danger to London.*

She waited a moment to see if I would signal that I needed to meet right away. When I didn't, her image shimmered away, leaving me faced with the charming sight of my flaky, crumb-spattered nightgown.

It all seemed a bit pointless, but at least I knew I had a slight life-line here.

Just as I was crossing back into the bedroom, a knock interrupted the silence. So I had a morning visitor.

"I'm not dressed yet!" I called out.

Of course, no one here actually cared if I was dressed or not, and the door edged open.

Relief loosened my chest as the dark-haired servant poked her head in the room. "Sorry to interrupt you, miss. Madam. Your... highness..."

Your highness? "I'm a succubus, not a royal. Just go with Ruby. And what is your name?"

"Susie. Just Susie." She scurried into the room. "I'm here to deliver a message. The Dark Lord desires to meet you tonight." She pointed to the oak wardrobe by the bed. "You can find a suitable dress in there, and I assume you've discovered the bath—"

I held up my hands. "Back up a second. The *Dark Lord?*"

She nodded, fear etched on her pale features.

"Adonis?" Just a guess.

"Yes." She wrung her hands, looking out the window. A sentinel drifted past, watching us. When the creature disappeared from view again, Susie met my gaze steadily. "You'll also find your... other things in there." She cleared her throat. "You'll want to look *sharp* tonight."

Sharp... sharp like a knife? The emphasis on the word hadn't gone unnoticed.

Understanding began to dawn. She'd hidden my weapons—maybe the arrows, maybe the knife. And what's more, she seemed to think I needed to come armed to my little meeting with the Dark Lord tonight.

* * *

I SPENT the day reading books and searching the room from top to bottom. The door to my room remained locked, and I was picking up absolutely no intel in here. On the plus side, I'd quickly discovered my Nyxobian knife hidden in the wardrobe. I couldn't spend much time examining it, since the sentinels were always just a few minutes away from swooping by, but I'd found it hidden under a panel, and its presence made me feel a *lot* better.

I was under no illusions. I was here as a prisoner of sorts. Granted, my prison had silky bedsheets and the most amazing food I'd ever tasted, but it was a prison nonetheless.

I crossed to the window, pressing my palms against the cold panes. Outside lay a dark forest of oak, hazel, elder, and ash trees—the boughs strangely verdant for January. Overhead, a flock of crows swarmed from the trees, cawing wildly.

As a sentinel floated past, awkwardly close to the window, I jumped back, before pressing my nose against the glass again.

Yasmin had told me that the Old Gods would provide. She seemed to believe that the key to our salvation lay in the woods around the castle. I couldn't really tell if she knew what she was talking about, or if she was just a mom desperate for a solution to safeguard her child's life. But in any case, I had to get out into those woods when I could.

In the distance, between two ash trees, a creature slipped between the trunks. I squinted, using my fae senses to pick it out. Was that a… a *boar?* Since when had wild boars returned to the English forests?

Of course, someone like Kratos was a born hunter. I could imagine him galloping on horseback through the forest in search of his prey.

I traced my finger over an aged window pane. Where would I find that Devil's Bane Yasmin had promised me? According to her, that was the key to human survival.

If I was going to find it, I needed Kratos to trust me so that I could snatch a moment of freedom.

I mean, assuming I made it out of my evening with the Dark Lord alive. Best not to dwell on that particular terror right now. Might as well lose myself in books until I had to face him.

After grabbing another pastry, I climbed a ladder to the balcony, where Kratos's old books lined the walls.

I spent the next few hours on the balcony, poring over a book about the history of Tudor prostitutes, looking up only when Susie brought my lunch into the room. I spent the day reading in the firelit room, while working my way through roast chicken and bread pudding.

When the sun began to dip behind the trees, casting long shadows like bony fingers over the grassy earth, a cold chill rippled over my body. *Almost time to meet with the Dark Lord.*

I blew out a long breath. *Best get on with it.* I slammed my book shut. My march down the stairs toward the wardrobe felt only a little like a final death march.

Sucking in a deep breath, I flung open the wardrobe I'd searched earlier. Here, a row of stunning dresses in jewel-like colors greeted me—a few more in black, midnight blue, and ivory. Just as I'd done before, I ran my fingertips over the fabric—the most delicate silk I'd ever touched.

I scanned the lower shelf of the wardrobe, where I'd found my quiver earlier, next to a pile of neatly folded underwear.

I cast a quick glance behind me and waited for a sentinel to float by.

I didn't suppose Kratos would ever trust me enough to afford me the luxury of curtains? No, that was probably ridiculous.

After another minute, the wide-eyed sentinel drifted past. *Four to six minutes.* I began counting.

Once he was out of view, I dropped down, the flagstones biting into my knees. Carefully, I ran my fingers around the lower shelf until I felt a break in the smooth wood. *Here we go.* Slowly, I slid my fingernails into the gap, pulling up a small panel of wood, exposing the small hollow in the bottom of the wardrobe.

I slid my hand inside, feeling around the gap until my fingertips brushed metal. *Bingo.* I reached for the hilt, then pulled out the knife Yasmin had given me. For just a moment, the Nyxobian silver glinted in the light. And next to it—helpfully—Susie had left my thigh holster.

Kratos had seen the bow and arrow and had probably ordered them taken from me. But the only person who knew about the knife was the woman who'd undressed me. If she worked for The Institute, I was pretty sure Yasmin would have mentioned it, but maybe she just hated the angels as much as I did.

I tucked the knife and holster into a corner of the shelf and cast another quick look back at the window.

I'd let the sentinel catch me dressing like a normal succubus—a harmless, non-assassin sort of demon.

Let's see… what dress should I choose to meet the Dark Lord, the terrifying predator who hated my entire race? Perhaps a nice midnight blue. Maybe if my dress matched his wings and his eyes, he'd be less inclined to rip me in half with a flick of his wrist.

I pulled the dress off the hanger, my breath catching at its beauty. Once, I'd lived among shining, beautiful things, danced in the most stunning gowns and beaded costumes. I stroked my fingertips over the sheer, sleeveless dress, and the silky fabric shimmered. Would it be opaque enough to hide the knife? I'd find out.

I pulled the blue gown over my head, wincing for a moment at the dull pain in my shoulder, still a little sore from the gunshot. As I lowered my arms, the silk slid luxuriously over my bare skin, skimming over my thighs and down to my ankles. Now *this* was a dress fit for an ancient succubus.

A deep slit ran all the way up the right leg, ending just below my hips. The front of the gown plunged to my waistline, the narrow fabric exposing the curves of my breasts. There, the fabric was layered just enough to be opaque.

Given the way the thin fabric was layered, I could conceal the knife on my left thigh.

I glanced in the mirror, smiling at what I saw there. My crimson hair tumbled over my shoulder, its vibrancy a sharp contrast to the dark gown.

While I waited for the sentinels to drift past again, I put on shimmering makeup, a hint of rose on my cheeks, a bit of black eyeliner. *Nothing threatening here.*

Then—immediately after the sentinels swept past the window—I lunged for the knife, strapping it around my thigh.

Granted, by the time I had a chance to reach under my skirts and pull it out, Adonis could slice my ribcage in two with a single breath, but...

Again, best not to dwell on these things.

I'd just have to watch him very carefully, to try to understand him, to predict his actions. I had to know what he might do *before* he acted.

A knock sounded on the door, and my pulse began to race. *Already?*

I slipped into a pair of heels, then hurried toward the door.

To my surprise, I found Kratos standing there, his amber eyes gleaming in the gloom of the castle hall.

He towered over me in the doorway, his coppery wings sweeping down gracefully from his shoulder blades. He was dressed for the Hunt tonight. His clothes were finely cut in a deep maroon color, showcasing his powerful body. A sword hung at his hips, and coils of golden light glowed from his wings. He looked so godlike, the sight of him almost made my breath leave my lungs.

That's how they get you, these angels. With their beauty, their allure, and… well, the whole omnipotent thing.

His bright gaze swept slowly up and down my body, and as it did, his jaw tightened, his muscles tensing. Handsome and sophisticated as he looked, everything about his tightly coiled muscles suggested a raw brutality under his restraint. This was a man born to conquer. "That is what you're wearing to meet Adonis?"

Maybe Kratos couldn't touch me, but he didn't want another man conquering his territory.

I just shrugged. "Someone left a bunch of dresses for me in the wardrobe. I liked this color."

He met my gaze again, eyes flaming copper. "It suits you, of course."

I took a step closer, making sure he had a good view of my cleavage, and I let the tendrils of glamoured charcoal magic writhe around my body, mingling with his gold and copper.

His gaze seemed to devour me. By the way he was clenching his fists, I had the impression that he was restraining himself from just pulling the blue dress off me right now. "I want to watch you dance again," he said, his voice husky.

Not a request—a demand. My stomach tumbled. It had been one thing to perform in New York for a whole crowd. There, I'd been in complete control. My performance, my rules. Here in Hotemet Castle, I was a rabbit among a pack of wolves.

"You know, it's been a while since I've danced," I said. "Will you be joining us for dinner?" As soon as the words were out of my mouth, I was startled to realize I wanted him there. I didn't trust a single one of these angelic assholes—including Kratos—but at least I knew he wanted me alive.

"I won't be there." His expression darkened, and at his shift in mood, a cold draft chased over my skin. "Adonis wanted to meet you alone. And anyway, I hunt at this time."

Of course. Kratos wouldn't be in Hotemet Castle at all during the night because he'd be out killing people. I swallowed hard at the sharp reminder of what Kratos truly was—a hunter of humans. And yet I was completely dependent on him.

I smiled sweetly at him. "Well, that's a shame. Hey, do you think I'll be able to leave this room at any point soon? I'm going to start feeling a little cooped up in here. If I'm going to dance well, I'll need to get a little exercise."

"Of course." Kratos's body glowed. "I'll unlock the door. You can explore the forest outside. I wouldn't keep you prisoner."

Liar. "Just the forest outside? I'd heard there was a bar in here somewhere."

"Yes," he added. "Feel free to look around the Tower of Wrath. Just don't go beyond it."

I blinked. "That's the name of this tower? Have you ever thought of maybe rebranding it?"

"No."

I bit my lip. "What are the other towers called, out of curiosity?"

"You have no reason to visit them."

Not my question, but okay. From the aerial tour, I knew walls linked all the towers, and I could sneak around if I needed to.

"No problem, Kratos. I'll stick to the Tower of Wrath and the woods. I'll try not to get lost."

"Oh, you won't be able to wander too far in the forest. You'll find it has a way of keeping you close to Hotemet Castle."

Ah, there we are. The prison.

I flashed him my most charming smile. "Well, enjoy your night. But tell me, Kratos. Why do you hunt every night?"

Standing this close, the heat pulsed off his body onto my skin. His amber eyes darkened to copper, and a violent, primal magic coiled off his body, snaking over my skin. "I'm compelled to do it. If I don't hunt, I burn from the inside out. And if I don't kill, a far worse predator than I will stalk the Earth."

I swallowed hard. "Oh?"

"The Heavenly Host. They make sure we do our jobs. They're the ones who sent the dragons that day. When the dragons crawled from their caves and castles to steal women and burn cities, they were following the commands of the Heavenly Host."

Gold. This information was pure gold. "And who are they?" *And how do I find them?*

His warm cedar scent curled around me. "Angels, in the heavens." He touched his chest as if something pained him. "I must go now."

I didn't want him going out there, hunting my friends. I wanted to beg him to leave Whitechapel alone. Instead, I just stalled. "Kratos, do you always catch your prey?"

He smiled faintly. "Not always. I can't always have the things I desire."

He turned to leave before stopping himself again and fixing his keen gaze on me. "One of my servants will fetch you when it's time to meet Adonis. But take care. Don't let him get too close to you."

Sweet earthly gods, even Kratos is warning me. A shiver snaked over my skin. "Why?"

"You can't trust him."

You don't say.

"Don't worry. I haven't survived for thousands of years by being an idiot." *More accurately, I haven't survived for thousands of years at all.*

Kratos nodded, then strode off down the hallway. I stepped back into the room, closing the door behind me. With my back against it, I took deep, slow breaths.

He wanted to meet you alone. Did I detect a bit of a hierarchy here in Hotemet Castle? At the bottom of the pile were the outsiders—the human, demon, and fae rabble in the streets, like I'd been a week ago. I was pretty sure the angels thought of them as little more than vermin.

Above them were the castle's servants, human and demon alike. Of the angels, Johnny was the youngest, which might suggest the least power. At top of the hierarchy of terror sat Adonis, my dinner date.

Oh—and let's not forget the Heavenly Host. Whoever the hell they were.

As I waited, my back to the door, I tried to steady my nerves.

Already, I'd gathered information I could report back to Yasmin when the time came. The angels were compelled to kill by forces greater than themselves, and they could fall from grace. Tension lived in this hierarchy. Did that mean there was a chance of fracturing a fragile alliance?

A loud knock on the door interrupted my thoughts, and I nearly jumped out of my skin.

When I pulled open the door, I found Elan standing in the torchlit hallway, dressed in a powder-blue sweatshirt featuring a cartoon cat on a rainbow. The incongruous sight eased some of my nerves. I was beginning to feel a strange, protective surge of warmth every time I saw him. He didn't belong in this place, and for that I loved him.

Elan grinned. "Hello. I've been sent to bring you to dinner. I see you're dressed already. Wonderful." He tapped his fingertips together, his smile fading. "I will bring you most of the way to Adonis's dining room, but not the whole way, if that's all right with you." He grimaced a little. "I prefer that he never looks at me, because if he doesn't remember me, then he won't kill me."

"Does he often kill arbitrarily?"

Elan gave a little shrug, frowning. "Well, maybe a bit more than average."

"This should be a fun night. Can't wait."

Abruptly, he turned and strode down the arched hallway, his shoulders hunched. Torchlight wavered over the stones. In the hall—the one I hadn't yet been able to explore—narrow windows over-looked the forest. Outside, faint lights seemed to twinkle among the boughs.

"Kratos said I could explore the tower and the forest," I ventured.

"That should keep you plenty occupied."

"And what will I find in this tower?" As much as I could, I needed to make a mental map of the place.

"You'll find a banquet hall that we never use, the bar I mentioned, the bakehouse and kitchen, and the granary."

None of that sounded particularly interesting, and I had no idea why Elan thought it would keep me occupied.

I was hoping for something like a "secret documents room," though I guess if it was a secret, he wouldn't come right out with it. "There's no library in here?"

"No, but your room is stocked with enough books for a lifetime."

I frowned. "If it's mostly food-related, why is it called the Tower of Wrath?"

Elan huffed a laugh. "Oh, that. They're a little bleak with the names. You'll be dining in the Tower of Ash tonight."

"Can't wait." I traced my fingertips over the cold stone walls. "So, Elan. Any advice for me about this dinner? Why exactly does the Dark Lord want to meet me?"

He smiled. "Oh, I wouldn't know something like that. I just prepared the food. But… I imagine he will be deciding if you seem like a threat or not."

"Does Adonis make the final decisions, then?"

Elan smiled nervously. "I couldn't tell you. If there is one thing I learned from growing up enslaved by a race of psychotic mountain trolls, it's that you never speak about your superiors out of turn, or they might nail one of your best friends to a blackthorn tree."

I cringed. Useless. Gods-damned useless. "Okay. Just take me to dinner, then, Elan."

He smiled pleasantly. "Just note that you should call him Dark Lord, not Adonis, and he kills quickly with his mind. And I think he can read your thoughts and has mind control powers. Oh! I almost forgot. I made strawberry pudding."

"Great! That should take the edge off all the death and terror."

We passed through a doorway, the arch above marked with a skull and crossbones. This, presumably, was the charming entrance to the Tower of Ash. We took a left down a short hall. At the end of the hall, a short set of stairs led up to arched wooden doors. Two human servants flanked the doors.

Elan turned to me with a small bow. "Well, this is where I leave you, so... I hope the food is good. Stay safe." He slunk back into the shadows.

I brushed my fingertips against my thigh, taking comfort in the faint feel of the knife strapped there.

I turned to the doors, sweeping my gaze over the servants who lingered there.

There was something... *off* about them, but I couldn't quite put my finger on it. They looked ordinary enough—thirty-year-old men, one of them with a bit of a paunch and stubble over his ruddy face. They wore simple brown clothing and gray caps.

So why did my gut tell me they weren't human?

When they pulled open the doors, my pulse raced. Slowly, I stepped up the stairs into the doorway.

On a dais at the end of the hall sat Adonis, midnight magic curling off his body. His inky wings swooped over either side of a black, thorny throne. *Lovely.* Hadn't I dreamt about that? A shiver crawled up my spine.

All I knew was, he was putting on a full show of intimidation this evening.

Amusement glinted in his icy eyes. He looked relaxed, slouching on one elbow as he stared at me.

In the most treacherous hollows of my mind, a voice whispered, *There he is. The most beautiful man you've ever seen.* Was that a bit of his angelic mind control or my own thoughts?

A sly smile curled Adonis's lips. "Come in, succubus."

And here I was, granted an audience with the Dark Lord himself.

"My name is Ruby," I corrected him as I crossed over the stone floor, my eyes sweeping over the oak table lining the center of the room. "Not *Succubus.*"

A vaulted ceiling—bony, like a ribcage—soared high above us. My heels clacked over the stone floor as I walked closer to him, closer to the end of the long table where food had been set.

I eyed him, pretty sure he'd staged it this way on purpose. He could sit relaxed on his throne while I stood on the ground gazing up at him. And just as I had with Kratos, and in my dream, I wanted to fall to my knees in front of him, to worship him. Maybe *this* was angelic mind control—or just something that happened naturally with these monsters?

In an effort to resist the urge to drop to my knees, I tore my eyes away from him and surveyed the space. In this banquet hall, moonlight poured through the narrow, sharply peaked windows, and warm light glowed from candles in iron chandeliers. Weapons lined one of the stone walls—battleaxes, swords, crossbows—charming decor, really, in the Tower of Ash.

The smell of roasted meat curled into the air. On this side of the long table, a feast had been set with roast duck, bread, fruit, and a steaming stew. Elan had done well.

The doors slammed behind me, trapping me inside with an echoing boom. I whirled to find another row of servants blocking my exit.

The human servants stood in front of the door and the far wall, dressed in simple brown clothing and black caps. Some were male, some female. A curly-haired brunette woman's eyes were wide open, as if she were terrified. I couldn't see anything remarkable about the servants—except—*something* was off. Was it the woman's fear? Or was that a normal human reaction to being in the presence of a terrifying predator?

Adonis rose from his throne, slowly prowling closer to me. He hadn't yet invited me to sit, content to let me linger awkwardly by the food I so badly wanted to devour.

So I stood by the table while the dark angel stalked lazily around me, sizing me up, shadows cloaking his powerful body. Unlike Kratos, he moved with a languid ease, every movement imbued with pure sensuality. Adonis didn't seem like a virgin. Why hadn't he fallen?

If Kratos was born to conquer, Adonis was born to lure people to their deaths.

The candlelight gleamed in his eyes. "That color suits you. In fact, I think Hotemet Castle will suit you. No redcaps for you to brawl with, but we have our own sort of rabble here in case you choose to pick a fight."

I put my hands on my hips, trying to act at ease. "And who would that be?"

"The humans, the demons…" He was sizing me up with his eyes, inky tendrils of night pulsing off his broad shoulders as he prowled around me. "I'd wager Kratos thinks of you as some sort of a prize."

I blocked out the low, erotic timbre of his voice, the silkiness of his tone that seemed to wrap itself around my body.

"You make me sound like a possession," I said.

Amusement danced in his eyes. "A possession, or prisoner. But what a lovely prisoner you are." Smoothly, he leaned in close, and I could smell the intoxicating scent of myrrh on him. His power stroked my skin like a lover's caress, and goosebumps rose on my chest.

Then he whispered something that sent an icy tendril of fear coiling around my ribs. "But did you really think I wouldn't notice the knife, my beauty?"

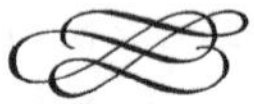

CHAPTER 26

My breath hitched, but I couldn't show fear at any cost.

I clenched my jaw. "Did you really think I'd show up in an angel's lair unarmed? You must think I'm stupid."

He stepped away from me, his cold eyes twinkling. "You know what really interests me, Ruby? Your heart rate sped up when I moved close to you. Tell me, was that fear, or do I make your heart race for a more interesting reason?"

I swallowed hard. I knew his game. He liked to play with people. I couldn't let him catch me off guard.

I narrowed my eyes. "Did you know that heart rates speed up for anger, too? Your astounding arrogance irritates me."

Careful, Ruby. Don't push it too far. I saw what he'd done to the redcap who'd insulted him.

"It's just that your cheeks flushed, and your blood began to race." He frowned. "Strange. I've never known a succubus to blush so easily."

I focused on trying to keep my breathing steady and blocking out the sensual allure of his voice, his movements.

"You're wondering if you can tempt an angel to fall," he purred. "I'm wondering what I'd need to do to get you out of that flimsy dress. I could compel you to do it, I suppose..."

His words sent a dark heat racing through my blood. I wasn't sure what to make of it all, but a succubus didn't suffer insolence from anyone, and I had to play my part well.

Biting down my fear, I raised my hand to slap him. He caught my wrist easily. Slowly, he leaned in to me a second time, his ancient power thrumming over my exposed skin, sending my blood racing.

In a deep voice, he whispered, "Careful, darling. You don't know who you're playing with." So close, his breath warmed the shell of my ear, and his hand on my wrist sent a jolt of electricity racing through my nerves.

He dropped my hand, stepping away. "Relax. I was just curious to see how you'd react."

In the V of his shirt collar, I caught a glimpse of the lethal-looking tattoos that snaked over his skin.

I took a deep breath to steady my nerves. I needed to find out exactly what powers he had in his arsenal. If he could read people's minds, I was screwed. If he could read people's minds and compel them to act, I was particularly screwed. "Why do you need to test me?" I asked. "I thought angels like you could just read minds and control bodies."

He smiled slyly. "Is that what you've heard?"

"Is it true?"

His smile faded. "Not entirely. I can sense things. Emotions. I can't hear your thoughts."

Thank the gods. "And can you compel people to do what you want?"

He shrugged. "If I tried really hard, but what fun would that be? Better to watch people scramble around desperately of their own free will."

"So is that why you've come to Earth—to watch humans and demons scramble around desperately while they try to survive?"

"Ruby, it almost sounds like you disapprove." Candlelight danced over the masculine planes of his face as he towered over me. "It's time for a purification. Wouldn't you agree?"

I would put this knife through your twisted heart right now, if I could.

Still, I had to put on a good show. "I suppose. When I was born, fewer than a hundred million people lived on the Earth." The words of a succubus tasted bitter on my tongue. "That's when humans knew how much they needed us, their gods, their demons. That's when they worshipped us in temples, when they quaked in fear. Now they live crammed together like rats, forgetting all about us."

So, this was going well. Adonis liked to toy with people, and he could potentially compel me to do whatever he wanted. Worse, it seemed he could see straight through my dress to everything underneath—the knife, my black lace underwear. I might as well be sitting here naked before him. In fact, when I glanced down at myself, I saw that the moonlight streaming into the room gave the dress a translucent quality.

Thanks, Susie. If you want someone to conceal a weapon on their body, make sure you give them a choice of fabrics a bit thicker than tissue paper.

Adonis nodded at the curly-haired woman, who scuttled over and pulled out a chair for me. As she moved, I was finally able to put my finger on what it was that unsettled me about the humans. It wasn't just the woman's fear.

They were *glamoured*, and I was the only one here who'd know. Only a fae who'd spent years honing the fine art of glamour would notice the faint shimmer of that particular magic. Even another fae, like Elan, would be clueless.

As I took a seat at the table, I looked at the servants a little more closely. Were they fae, like me?

Maybe not. Another fae could have glamoured them. They could be anything.

Right now, I had no idea what it meant, but I knew better than to share my observations with the Dark Lord. It was a small mercy he couldn't simply pluck the thoughts from my skull.

I picked up my glass of wine. "Why have you invited me to dinner?"

Adonis sat across from me, leaning back in his chair. As he did, shadows slid through his eyes. "It's important to know whom you're living with, wouldn't you agree? And I'm not entirely sure you are who you say you are."

Shit. The room chilled around me, and shadows seemed to slide over my skin.

Adonis leaned closer, studying me like he was trying to read a book. "In fact, I'm pretty damned certain you're not who you pretend to be, Ruby."

He reached for me, gently stroking my cheek, his touch feather-light. His dark magic thrummed through my chest, his eyes burning like stars. "I can feel your loneliness. Your grief. I can feel the guilt that threatens to crush you." Intensity laced his words. "You play a part, Ruby, and it's not the real you."

I swallowed hard. Why did I get the feeling that he wasn't just talking about me? I pulled his hand from my cheek, still gripping it lightly, and took a wild stab in the dark. "I'm not the only one, though, am I? What do *you* feel guilty for?"

He ripped his hand from mine as if I'd burned him.

Bingo. I'd hit a mark, and I pushed on. "Did you kill someone you regret killing? Are you capable of love, Dark Lord?"

For a brief instant, his mask slipped, and I caught a glimpse of something else there—an expression that looked acutely agonized. For just a moment, a look of intense vulnerability gleamed in his eyes.

Then he breathed in deeply, his lips curling in another sly smile as he composed himself. "I feel guilty for nothing. And like I said, I just wanted to learn more about who we've invited into our castle."

A flicker of movement in the corner of my eye caught my attention. A black, scaly thing was creeping in the shadows. Shuddering, I pointed at it with my fork. "What exactly is that creature?"

He turned to look. "Ah. Drakon. My pet. Careful you don't get on his bad side. I understand shadow demons don't react well to fire."

"You have a pet dragon. Of course." I shuddered. I *hated* dragons.

"Merely a dragonile. He won't get any larger than he is now."

Adonis nodded at the female servant, and her footsteps echoed off the ceiling as she crossed to us. She began serving food onto our plates: slices of duck and roast potatoes. Her face had entirely drained of color.

As she poured Adonis's wine, her hands were shaking so hard she spilled some of it onto the table.

"I'm so sorry," she stammered, clutching the bottle tightly.

"Relax," he said quietly.

The servant slunk away, and I picked up my own wineglass to gulp it. I still didn't quite understand why he'd wanted me here alone.

"So you've invited me here to find out if I'm a threat," I ventured.

He met my gaze. "Oh, I'm not afraid of you, Ruby. But the rabble out there must be controlled. How do I know you're not here to tell them our secrets?"

I curled my lip, just as a succubus would. "Humans? Do you really think I would conspire with humans? I feed from them. They worship me. I don't treat them as equals. And you must know that succubi are solitary demons. We always have been."

"Mmm. Perhaps." He pulled a single grape from a bunch on the table.

His raw, dark power skimmed over my bare skin, sending my pulse racing.

Act normal, Ruby. I cut into the roast duck, taking a bite. The rich meat seemed to melt on my tongue, and I practically moaned. Even sitting across from the death angel, a fae like me couldn't ignore true pleasure. Then I washed it down with a sip of the red wine.

"So tell me, Dark Lord, if you're worried I might pass on information to the rabble outside, does that imply that you're afraid of *them?*"

A hint of disdain shone on his features. "Afraid, no. They're an inconvenience. Humans and demons are working against us. Their very existence is at stake, and they don't even understand how much worse it could be. The humans don't concern me at all. They break so easily. But the demons—in high enough numbers—they're harder to ignore."

Now this was interesting. "And you think the demons may be coming for you?"

He shrugged. "They're annoyed that we've been killing their food. And the earthly gods, of course, are furious. We're stealing souls from them."

I let the fruity wine roll over my tongue. "The *gods*." I injected a bit of venom into my voice. "Do they honestly still believe they can return to the heavens if only they collect enough souls?"

He smirked. "You and I both know they'll never be released from their torment. They gave the Angelic language to the humans, and they must pay the price. Forever."

"Is that why you've come to Earth?" I probed. "Still pissed off that humans are abusing your Angelic language?"

The faint smile had left his lips. "Something like that."

Don't push too hard, Ruby.

"Nyxobas is raising an army of demons," he continued. "Along with the fire goddess. It seems the threat of angels is the one thing that can unite the gods of shadow and light."

I swallowed another mouthful of duck. "Maybe my calculations are a bit off, but if you've got several gods raising armies against you, and… How many angels are there on earth? Is it just the three of you?"

"As far as you know."

I swallowed hard. I knew from Yasmin that there weren't many angels on Earth—that London was their central headquarters. But I couldn't give away that knowledge. "Well, I haven't seen many angels. Aren't you a bit outnumbered?"

He leaned back in his chair, unperturbed. "They'd have a hard time getting beyond our defenses, and they don't know how to kill us."

"And what about the Heavenly Host? That sounds like an army."

"I don't know where you heard that term."

I kept my tone bored, my expression disinterested. "From Kratos. I wasn't really listening. It just sounded like an army of angels or something."

He sipped his wine lazily, pinning me with his gaze. "The Heavenly Host are far worse than we are. That's all you need to know. If they come to Earth, the ground will rumble with the shifting of mountains;

the sun will turn black, and the rivers will turn to blood. Meteors will rain down on the Earth. So you'd better hope that we do our jobs here, and that you never have to learn anything more about them."

A shudder danced up my spine, and I snatched my wine from the table. "And what exactly are the chances they will wind up here on Earth?"

He shrugged. "As long as Kratos, Johnny, and I can achieve our goals, they won't come to Earth at all."

Oh. Shit. So… if I believed this angel, they were actually killing a smaller number of people to save a greater number of people? Was that really possible?

Adonis twirled his wineglass. "I can see I've rattled you. You've lived for thousands of years, and you're reluctant to depart from all those centuries of pleasure with a final death."

"No one wants to die."

For just a moment, I caught a flash of that agonized look again before he composed his features. "Is that quite so? In any case, the most pressing issue right now is your allegiance. Considering you're a shadow demon of the night realm, and considering we are under the threat of attack by the night god, I need to hear from you what you think of him. And Ruby, I can tell if you're lying."

I believed that he could tell if I was lying. Luckily, I didn't need to lie. "I have no allegiance to Nyxobas whatsoever, and no connections to other shadow demons."

He studied me for a moment, the candlelight glinting in his stormy eyes. "And why is that?"

I'd have to be careful to phrase my words in a way that I knew to be the truth. "Shadow demons never accepted the succubi. Succubi are the outcasts of the night realm. Nyxobas, the night god, is an ascetic. Even his own son and grandson—the incubi—are considered whores. And that's one of the reasons succubi are in perpetual danger."

"Ruby." The faint smile on his lips was heartbreakingly beautiful and terrifying at the same time. "If you don't cross me, I'll protect you."

I didn't believe him for a second.

Gripping my wineglass, I tapped the edge of it thoughtfully. "If shadow demons attacked, I'd be as much a target as you." That was the truth.

So Adonis had interrogated me, and now crucial questions whirled through my mind. *Where do you come from? What have you been doing all this time on Earth?* And most important of all—the one question that rang loudest and clearest above the rest—*why must all of this happen?*

Out of the river of questions, I chose one carefully. "You said you've been living on Earth for thousands of years. Like me. Where were you born?"

"Afeka," he said simply.

I blinked. I had a sense this was an ancient name for a city, but I couldn't ask where. After all, I was supposed to be a four-thousand-year-old succubus from Mesopotamia, and I had a hunch Afeka was somewhere in that vicinity. "Afeka," I repeated. "A beautiful place."

He cocked his head. "You know it?"

"Of course. Beautiful blue skies."

It was as safe a bet as any. Every city had a sky above it, and only the British Isles had really shitty skies.

I cursed myself for not having stumbled into an easier disguise. A vampire, perhaps, born in the nineties, wouldn't be too much of a stretch.

"In my garden in Afeka—" he began, but stopped short. "Anyway, that was a long time ago."

I was going to press on, to ask another question, but a whoosh of air and the glint of metal rushing past my head stopped me short.

With a lighting-fast reflex, Adonis's hand shot into the air, and he caught the hilt of a knife. I recognized the pale gleam of Nyxobian silver.

His eyes turned to black, but before he could react, ropes of dark magic coiled around him.

I whipped my head around at the humans—who, of course, no longer looked human. Not even the curly-haired woman.

They'd dropped their glamour, revealing themselves as four towering, brutish shadow demons.

Among them, a horned demon with ivory-white skin shot a stream of shadowy magic at Adonis.

His eyes, two inky black pools, met mine. "Succubus…" he hissed. "Whore."

CHAPTER 27

$\mathcal{W}$rapped in shadow magic, Adonis still managed to look unfazed. "If there was ever a good time to reach between your thighs, succubus, it's now."

I was already one step ahead of him, grabbing for my knife. Adrenaline blazed through my nerve endings. Just as I pulled it from its holster, a wave of icy shadow magic slammed into me, knocking me to the ground. Shadowy tendrils coiled around me, the texture like slick vines, coiling around my calves, my thighs, my waist…

But Nyxobian silver could cut through anything.

I sliced through the magic, the blade sliding easily through the shadow coils, taking care not to cut my skin. When I reached my calves, the horned demon lunged for me. His enormous body pressed on top of me, fangs glinting in the candlelight, and he pinned my wrists to the ground.

There was something deeply unholy about his skin, the color of sour milk.

When he leaned in closer to me, the scent of rot wafted around us. "Whore," he growled. "Traitor. You're supposed to be one of us. I can't wait to hear your screams when I pull your body apart, piece by piece."

I gritted my teeth. "I don't take kindly to my meals being interrupted."

He nudged his leg between my knees, making it clear that he wanted to dominate me completely, and revulsion rose in my throat. Still, I gripped hard onto the knife in my hand, refusing to let go even though it seemed as if he was about to crush my bones into dust.

I couldn't lift my wrist high enough to stab him. What weapons did I have at my disposal?

Glamour—that was it.

Fucking glamour.

And yet... as long as Adonis couldn't see me from this angle, I could use it. I searched for Adonis. Where he lay below the table, he didn't have a view of me.

As the shadow demon leaned in closer, I tried to focus, tried to block out the fact that he was extending a long, thick tongue to lick my neck.

I closed my eyes, summoning my glamour—I only needed it for a second—just a quick flash to get him to release his grip on me. While he pressed his knee further between my thighs, magic tingled over my body as the glamour took hold.

"Oh shadow demon..." I cooed.

He looked into my face, shock registering on his features. He was staring at a mirror image of his own face, but one haggard and worn by age, his cheekbones gaunt. His milky skin paled even further.

The shock of it forced him to relax his grip on my wrists, just enough for me to yank my knife hand free. I let the disguise drop, then slammed my knife into the demon's back, plunging it straight through to his heart. His hot blood spurted onto me, and I pushed his enormous body off of me with a grunt.

Dripping in demon blood, I rose, ready for the next attack. But when I stood, the room had gone completely silent. A dark, electrical magic crackled in the air, sparking over my skin. Adonis stood on his dais, where shadows seemed to spill around him like ink through water.

For a moment, I wondered if he could have seen my little glamour trick, but his arctic gaze was on the other side of the room. I followed his line of sight. There, I found the rest of the humans and demons—or at least what was left of them. Each had been torn in two at the chest, each exsanguinating in glistening pools of gore.

I swallowed down my revulsion. When I glanced at Adonis again, his eyes were on me. Unlike me, the man had not a single drop of blood on him. "There may be more coming."

"You didn't have any idea that demons had infiltrated your servants?"

"No. A *fae* must have glamoured them." The way he said the word "fae" sent icy fingers of dread up my spine. "And the humans clearly helped them. Our response will be swift and brutal. We're not done killing tonight."

I swallowed hard, trying to stay in character. "When this is all over, I'd like a warm—"

Frantic shouting in the hallway stopped me short.

Johnny burst into the room, his gray wings trailing behind him. He practically stumbled over the corpses at his feet.

"Adonis!" he bellowed, unnecessarily loudly, considering we were the only ones in here. "The servants are attacking all over the place. There's a stream of them climbing up from the lower levels now. Filthy fucking shadow demons." His lip curled and he stalked toward me. "Funny that this happened after we let a shadow demon into our midst, isn't it? Not ha-ha funny, but *weird* funny—"

"Where are they?" Adonis interrupted him.

"Headed for the Great Hall, but they'll be up here next. They're searching for us."

Adonis shot me a sharp look. "You'll want to lock yourself in your room. Don't let anyone in."

"No thanks."

First of all, demons could get through locks, and I'd be a sitting duck in my room. Second, I wanted to find out what the hell was going on in here.

I crossed to the wall of weapons, heading straight for a bow and a quiver of arrows. The bow looked heavier than fae craftsmanship, but

I'd be able to use it all the same. And when I looked into the quiver, I found the arrowheads coated with the unmistakable pale gleam of Nyxobian silver.

"I'm not sitting there waiting for them to find me," I declared. "And I'm not relying on you two to keep me safe. I may not be great with a bow and arrow—" *Lie.* "But it's better than waiting to be clawed to death by misogynistic shadow demons."

I slung the quiver over my back, then pulled the bow off the wall.

Johnny's gaze bored into me, his bony fingers twitching. "You're going to trust her with that?"

Adonis was pulling a broadsword off the wall. "Trust her? No. Fear her? Also no. I doubt she can even use it. Let's go."

Jerk.

I slid the knife back into its holster on my thigh, wishing it were just a tad more accessible.

Johnny snatched a sword for himself, and I followed the two of them into the hall. They moved so fluidly and swiftly, I struggled to keep up.

Blood roared in my ears as I walked behind them down a winding stairwell, clutching my bow. I knew what a horde of shadow demons would do to a woman they saw as a traitor. They'd sniff me out in my room and corner me. Even if I turned into my fae form or glamoured myself as an ogre, I'd be seen as a collaborator. A traitor. They'd torture me to death, and I'd never find Hazel.

Thing was, I couldn't let these angels know what I was really capable of. I'd have to kill quietly and protect myself in the shadows— and if it got really bad, I could always run. Harder to kill a moving target, anyway, than one cornered in her bedroom.

Our footsteps echoed off the stone walls in the stairwell. Fear thrummed through my body. Yasmin had conveniently failed to warn me I might be under threat from both sides, from demons as well as angels.

Adonis stormed through a doorway into a narrow hall. Here, half a dozen demons seemed to slither from the shadows, horns and fangs gleaming. Among the demons, some humans brandished swords and knives, weapons they must have raided from an armory. Shadow magic coiled through the air around us, its slithery texture different from the dark, electric crackle of Adonis's magic.

A demon with a leathery body roared, and I nocked my first arrow. He lifted his hand to shoot a stream of shadow magic at me, and I loosed my shot.

Then I ducked. I watched as the arrow slammed into his shoulder, and the stream of shadow magic spooled above me, missing me narrowly.

I couldn't shoot to kill, because that would give away my skill. I could only shoot to injure, and I'd have to count on the angels to finish the job. Plus, I'd have to let a bunch of these arrows go wide.

I watched Adonis, his sword almost an extension of his body. He didn't need it, but I understood why he used it. He moved with a thrilling grace, a brutal and elegant waltz of blows and parries. Blood streaked his blade.

Watching him, I knew he felt about fighting the way I'd once felt about dancing.

I nocked a few more arrows, unleashing them all over the place. "How do you use this thing?" A few of them struck the shadow demons in limbs and hands; others simply clattered to the floor.

Johnny and Adonis were already leaping into action, swords raised. By injuring the shadow demons, I was making their fight significantly easier.

Not that Johnny seemed to care. "She's bloody useless!" he bellowed.

I let an arrow hit him in the leg. "Whoops! Sorry!"

Johnny hardly seemed to notice the arrow, which was... unnerving.

From the shadows, a silver-haired vampire ran for me, his fangs shining in the dim light. I pulled another arrow from my quiver, then unloaded it into his neck, taking care to let a few more arrows go wide.

Only hawthorn wood killed vampires, but the arrow would slow him down. He fell to the ground, clutching at his throat.

All around me, the demons roared, shadow magic spilling into the air. I held back in the doorway, letting my arrows fly willy-nilly into demon limbs and clatter over the floor.

After a minute, we'd nearly cleared the hallway, apart from the vampire, who was struggling to his feet again. Adonis leaned down, punching his fist into the vampire's chest in a small explosion of blood. He ripped out the vamp's heart, tossing it to the side. As he did, the vampire's body crumpled to ash.

I choked down the urge to puke right there.

Already, Adonis and Johnny were marching on, swords ready. I pulled another arrow from the quiver while the two angels in front of me turned into a tall, arched doorway. They stopped abruptly.

I peered between their wings. Here, in the Great Hall, shadow magic cloaked the air, so cold and powerful it had snuffed out the lights.

Things were about to get *really* bad.

CHAPTER 28

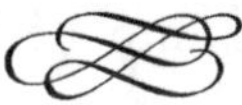

Slowly, my eyes adjusted to the darkness—a fae trait, one honed from thousands of years of living in forests. We stood at the threshold of a bare hall, with tall, empty alcoves lining the stone walls. Candles burned in chandeliers above, but the billowing shadow magic dampened their glow.

A glint of silver told me there were demons in here already.

Within moments, the angels moved into the hall, swords slicing through the air. Here, clouded in shadow magic, I could hardly see any targets.

I listened to the sound of metal clanging on wood, and then the sounds of gurgling and grunting echoing off the high ceiling. I had no doubt what had happened—Adonis had dropped his sword and was now vaporizing demons with his angel magic.

The more he killed, the easier it was for me to see.

Red eyes gleamed in the dark, telling me where the demons were. Once again, I aimed for their limbs, my task here to weaken them only. But there were so many of them…

"Succubus…" one of them hissed.

If I were a real succubus, I'd be able to see through the shadow magic. Instead, all I knew was that the shadow demons were closing in around me. I pulled the knife from its holster. Here, in close combat, I needed a close-range weapon, and I might need to actually kill now.

I channeled some of my inner feral fae—not so much that I'd lose control, but just enough that I could fight with ruthless abandon.

With a cold thrill, ancient battle fury began to race through my blood, my instincts taking over. I lost myself in a whirlwind of flashing movements, of blade into flesh and bone. In my fight for survival, the darkness seemed to slowly lift as my most primal instincts took over.

Stay in control, Ruby. If I let the full fury of a feral fae take hold, it was all over. The shadow demons *and* the angels would team up to kill me.

Swiftly, I plunged my knife into another heart, and an icy silence reigned around me.

The haze of battle fury cleared from my mind, and the shadow magic had thinned all around me. A pile of demonic bodies lay at my feet, blood oozing over the floor.

Across the Great Hall, Adonis flicked his wrist at a silver-scaled warrior, severing the creature's body in two.

Johnny still gripped his sword, which he was using to decapitate a human male.

More demons were slipping through a doorway at the far end of the Great Hall, heading for Adonis. And while he was slaughtering them with his terrifying angelic magic, a human crept up behind him. This human was practically large enough to be an ogre, and he held a broadsword in his enormous hands.

I dropped my knife, snatching my bow from the bloodied floor. I nocked another arrow, lining it up to fire at the human.

If he struck Adonis, that Nyxobian silver would slice right through his skull. Yasmin didn't think the angel could die that way—he'd have some way to recover, maybe return in another form. But at the very least, a severed brainstem had to be a bit of a setback. Which was exactly what I wanted.

Should I let it happen?

My heartbeat roared in my ears, my sights locked on the human as he raised his sword above Adonis's head.

Then, in blur of dark magic, Adonis slashed his fingertips in an arc. The human's throat exploded, and blood sprayed over the stone hall as the man's body crumpled to the ground. I lowered my bow, a cold sweat tingling over my skin.

Chewing gum, Johnny pulled his sword from another human's body.

And that was the last of the attackers.

I dropped my bow, snatching my knife from the ground. I slid it into my holster—I'd be keeping this Nyxobian silver as close to me as possible.

When I looked up again, I saw that the angels were staring at me. Shadows curled around Adonis, and his pale eyes blazed. His predator's gaze was now locked on me.

Covered in spatters of blood, Adonis stalked across the hall, heading straight for me. I took a step back, my stomach swooping with fear.

Had he known—had he seen me hesitate? I thought he'd been preoccupied with all of his own killing, but based on the murderous look he was giving me right now, he might have caught a glimpse of my whole thought process—the thoughts that had included *maybe it would be better if someone put a sword in his head.*

I took another step back, realizing I'd backed myself into an alcove, a knife in my hand.

Adonis's eyes swirled with shadows, his dark wings spread behind him. For once, he didn't look at ease, and the sight of him angry terrified me.

Adonis boxed me into the alcove, his midnight wings forming a sort of cage around me as they spread out, their feathers shot through with streaks of silver.

"You could have taken that shot," he said, his voice low. "You hesitated."

"I'm not very good with a bow and arrow. You must have noticed."

"But you didn't even try."

I swallowed hard. "You're immortal. Relax," I parroted his words from earlier. "I just wanted to see how you'd react."

For just an instant, I thought I saw a smile flicker across his lips. Then he scanned the demon bodies that littered on the floor, the ones I'd slaughtered with the knife. "Did you kill all these demons?"

"Maybe a few of them? I'm not really sure." I widened my eyes. "Everything was scary and confusing."

From behind Adonis, a voice boomed over the hall. "Adonis!"

Adonis lowered his wings, and the unmistakable gleam of Kratos's gold magic warmed the room.

Kratos stood in the center of the Great Hall among the fallen bodies of our attackers. He looked every inch the warrior in his gold and crimson brocade.

"What happened here? Why are you standing so close to Ruby?" A steely threat of violence laced his voice.

Adonis swept his gaze to Kratos. "Back so soon from your little hunt?"

"The heart of the castle called me back."

Johnny wiped the blood off his face on the back of his sleeve. "I'll tell you what happened here, Kratos. We let a shadow demon live with us, and then a horde of other shadow demons attacked us. From within the castle. I can't be the only one connecting the dots here, can I?" he bellowed. "You can't deny the facts, Kratos."

"The facts, Johnny," I began, "are that these glamoured servants were in your midst before I got here. The shadow demons disguised themselves as humans, blending in with the real humans. You let them live among you before I even got here. Connect those dots." *Asshole.*

"She has a point," said Adonis smoothly. "In any case, she seemed to be killing the shadow demons this evening, or at least trying to in her own inept way."

I looked down at the blood coating my bare arms, now desperate to get into a warm bath.

I was pretty sure I'd walked the line well enough—protecting myself while still convincing them I was a harmless little succubus, confused by weapons. Let them think I posed no threat at all.

I stretched my arms lazily over my head and yawned. "All that death made me tired. I'll be turning in for the night."

I wouldn't be sleeping any time soon. Demons and humans had rebelled against the angels in Hotemet Castle, and that meant the angels would be planning a fast retribution. As soon as I got the chance, I'd be sneaking out of my room to listen in on what the angels were planning.

This was exactly why I'd been sent here in the first place.

CHAPTER 29

*I*n my bedroom, I glanced at the window, waiting for the sentinel to pass. Standing here in the dark, cold fear slid through my bones. I *really* wanted the lights on.

Still, I'd needed the darkness to disguise my actions tonight.

With the sentinels watching, I'd dressed in my little nightgown. I'd snuffed out the fire, and I'd crawled into bed. When the sentinels weren't in view, I'd bunched up the duvet and sheets. Good enough to approximate a sleeping form.

Unfortunately, as I stood huddled in the corner of the chilly bedroom, waiting for the coast to clear, fear was ripping my mind apart. I could hardly think through the rising panic.

At last, I saw the ghostly form of a sentinel move past. It was time to slip into the hallway.

My blood thundered through my veins as I listened at the door, trying to ignore the feeling that the shadows were closing in around me.

When I heard silence in the hallway—no footsteps or chatter—I turned the doorknob, all the while keeping a running tally in my mind of how many minutes had passed since the sentinel's appearance.

Given the speed at which they moved, I calculated that I had about two minutes and thirty seconds to get to the next hiding spot.

I moved swiftly through the hall, relieved to be in the warm torch-light again. As I moved, I counted the seconds. When I thought it was time for a sentinel's appearance, I backed up against the wall, waiting until the thing passed.

Tonight, I'd donned a specific type of glamour—one that didn't disguise me as another being, but just made people less likely to notice me—a glamour of unobtrusiveness. But as well as it worked on humans, I wasn't sure the sentinels would be fooled.

When the coast was clear, I darted over to the stairwell, yanking open the door. I breathed a sigh of relief. In the stairwell, there were no windows to give me away. Candlelight flickered over the rough stones.

The view of the castle that Kratos had shown me had given me an overall picture of the place, but I still didn't know where to find a secret meeting between angels.

My plan was to head for the parapet, to use the high view to look for lit rooms around the castle. I'd have to move fast, keeping to the shadows in order to escape the notice of the sentinels.

As I climbed the stairs, I shivered in my stupid skimpy nightgown. After about ten twisting levels, my thigh muscles began to burn. At least I was getting a workout here.

At the top of the stairs, I pushed through the door into the frigid night air, the wind biting into my skin. Immediately, I ducked behind the edge of the parapet, sticking as close as I could to the shadows. My teeth chattered, the shadows closed in around me. The air left my lungs. Tonight, clouds covered the moon and stars, and the darkness would swallow me whole.

I closed my eyes, slowing my breathing until I had control again. I cast a quick glance overhead, relieved to find the sky clear of sentinels.

From my crouched position, I peered over the edge of the parapet, and I caught a glimpse of a light burning warmly in a room. No—two rooms were lit up in the castle, in the same hall—six stories down and one tower over. I counted the windows, trying to approximate the number of doors I'd need to move past in the Tower of Ash.

The rest of the castle looked pretty dark. This seemed as good a guess as any.

Keeping low and in the shadows, I crept back to the door, desperate to be in the light again. As soon as I pried the door open, the torchlight of the stairwell washed over me like a soothing bath. Shivering, I rubbed my arms, trying to warm up.

I walked down the chilly castle stairs, running my fingers over the wall. I wasn't sure how hard it would be to overhear the angels' plan. Under normal circumstances, I'd glamour myself as a servant to linger in the background as they talked, but I doubted they'd be planning their revenge in front of any servants tonight, considering the problem in question was a servant rebellion.

As I walked down the stairs, my mind roamed to Susie and Elan. They hadn't been involved, had they? Worry tightened my chest. I hoped not. I actually liked those two. Maybe I could find a way to check on them after this.

When I'd climbed down six stories, I listened carefully at the door for sounds of movement in the hall. Silence greeted me, and I pushed through into the corridor. From there, I moved swiftly from one obscure point to another, dodging the prying eyes of the sentinels.

At last, I reached the skull and crossbones that marked the Tower of Ash. I crossed through the arched doorway. Mercifully, there weren't as many windows in this hall—just a few arrow slits.

I glanced at a painting that hung on the wall. The gold-leaf paint mixed with vibrant reds made it look like a medieval image—they were the type of hues used for saints' iconography. But I'd never seen a medieval image like this. Above the gold-leaf landscape, a black sun rose over a river of blood. A shiver danced up my spine as I realized it was the exact sort of bleak imagery Adonis had been talking about. *If the Heavenly Host come to Earth...*

Shuddering, I moved on, scanning some of the other paintings that adorned the stone walls under the vaulted ceiling. Some depicted midnight skies and burning stars, while others showed fig trees and mountains under a fiery night sky.

As I walked, I counted to the tenth door, approximating where I thought I'd seen the candles burning. I crept over to the door, pausing outside. As luck would have it, the door was slightly open. A dim light burned in the room.

I pressed even closer, feeling a cold sweat break out over my skin. What exactly would the angels do to me if they found me out here spying on them?

I pressed my ear closer, listening for the sound of voices. I heard nothing. If Johnny were involved in a meeting, his irritating voice would boom right through the oak, right through the stones of these walls.

Time to move on.

I was pretty sure the next candlelit room would be four doors away. And already, as I began to move closer, I could hear Johnny's booming tone. *Bingo.* I flicked a quick glance at the arrow slits in the wall. Unfortunately, this door stood right across from one of them. I'd have to watch for sentinels.

I pressed my back against the wall next to the narrow window, and from the corner of my eye, I watched for movement. As soon as a sentinel drifted past, I scurried over to the door, pressing my ear against the wood. I began my count, tracking the interval while listening in at the same time.

"Why can't we just kill them all?" It was Johnny's voice, penetrating the oak door.

"That's not our mission," said Kratos. "We are supposed to purify. Not incinerate all life."

"And that's what you're doing with your hounds?" asked Johnny. "Purifying?"

"They only kill the evil humans. It's what they were born for."

Sure, Kratos. Keep telling yourself that.

"The sentinels tell me," said Kratos, "that this mission might be linked to The Institute—humans who live within the Tower, hiding like cowards behind walls while the rest of their brethren suffer."

A flicker of anger smoldered in my chest. Was this really linked to The Institute? Maybe Yasmin could have clued me in that this might be coming.

"We slaughter those in the Tower," said Kratos. "That's where it ends. They have some sort of magical wards protecting the place, but Adonis has the power to break through them."

"Oh really?" asked Johnny. "Is he going to do some killing for once? I could go with him and do something a bit creative, you know? I've been wanting to design a plague."

"Let's keep it simple and precise. Adonis can break through the wards and spread death through the Tower, kill The Institute within a day. I don't know why he hasn't done it already, to be honest."

"He doesn't need to, does he? He's not like us," Johnny shot back. "He's not cursed yet. That's why he hasn't even bothered showing up here."

"He's a soldier. He'll do what he needs to do. The entire Tower will be dead within moments. He knows what could happen if he doesn't."

My mouth went dry as I thought of Yasmin's child, the one she'd been working so hard to keep alive with her herbs.

The interval between sentinels was almost up now, and I rushed over to the wall again, crouching below the window.

"Fine," boomed Johnny. "Speak to the Dark Lord, then." His voice began moving closer, and my pulse raced.

Their meeting was coming to a close, which meant I had to get the hell out of here.

As I began to rush down the hallway, I heard heavy footsteps moving closer. My heart leapt into my throat. Frantically, I tried opening the nearest door.

Locked.

Two doors down, I knew where to find an open room.

I moved at full fae speed, pushing through the door into a candlelit bedroom, and I shut the door behind me.

As I did, the air left my lungs.

There, Adonis sat on his bed. And given the way his icy gaze was locked on me, that *glamour of unobtrusiveness* did not work so well on angels.

CHAPTER 30

donis sat shirtless on the edge of his bed, his wings not in view tonight. A small relief—he wasn't in slaughter mode. Still, his icy gray eyes pierced me to my very core. "I hadn't realized you enjoyed our dinner so much."

His voice wrapped around me like silk, so seductive that I nearly forgot I found myself in a completely horrific situation.

In the hallway behind me, I heard Johnny's footsteps echo off the stones as he walked past. At least I'd avoided his notice.

Adonis's pale gaze swept over my clothing—the nightgown that hung only to my upper thighs. "I must say that I approve of the outfit you chose."

I looked down at my nightgown, mortified to find that not only were my legs on display, but the cold castle air had fully engaged my headlights. Once again, I felt completely naked before Adonis.

And some insane, perverse part of me *liked* that thought. Must be part of his angel magic, I guessed. *Bastard.*

Adonis's gaze dipped to my chest, and for just a moment, his jaw opened slightly. He clutched tightly to the blankets on his bed, knuckles whitening. Then he composed himself again, his expression clearing. "I'm surprised you're not terrified to be in my presence."

"Scared? Me? Don't be ridiculous," I said airily. *Think of something to say, Ruby. Act casual.* "So what's the deal with your wings? Sometimes you have them, sometimes you don't. Do they rip through your clothes when they appear?"

The corner of his mouth twitched. "No. They're formed of magical energy, and they don't behave like normal matter. I take it you've come here, then, to ask about my shirt ripping off my body." For the first time, I noticed a pendant around his neck, glinting in the candlelight.

"Just making conversation." I waved a dismissive hand. "So this is a nice place you've got here," I added casually, surveying his bedroom —the bookshelf lining the wall, the painting of red flowers by a riverside. What did Adonis's books tell me about him? Not much. Apart from the painting and some candles in thorny iron sconces, the only thing of note in his room was the bookshelf—mostly empty. On its oak shelves lay a few poetry books, some ancient tomes in dead languages, and a book with silver lettering called *Bringer of Light.*

Interesting.

"So glad you approve, succubus."

"I thought you'd have more skulls or something."

He let out a low chuckle that rumbled through places I shouldn't be thinking about right now, and my chest warmed.

"I keep those in my summer cottage," he said.

Something shifted in the shadows, and I caught a glimpse of Drakon—larger than I'd realized before, nearly the size of a golden retriever. The dragonile was covered in black scales, with thin wings that swooped off his back and a long, spiked tail. He strutted over to Adonis, rubbing against his legs, and the angel stroked his scaly head. Drakon snorted appreciatively, his yellow eyes closing.

How did I explain why I was here, dressed like this? Maybe I could just avoid the whole topic altogether. "Nice pet."

"He keeps me company and only occasionally lights things on fire. But you still haven't explained why you're here."

I guess not. I swallowed hard, forcing a calm smile onto my face.

"Afeka," I said abruptly. "I was just remembering a visit to Afeka years ago."

He rose from his bed, shifting past Drakon and prowling closer.

As he moved with predatory grace, my eyes trailed over the thorny, brutal tattoos on his chest, some of them with the spiked, leafy patterns of hemlock. That seemed appropriate. Poison hemlock was a beautiful flowering plant, deceptively lethal, as if it were designed to enchant a person to their death. And that's what Adonis was—poison hemlock.

Among his tattoos were words written in a language I didn't understand—an ancient language that a real succubus *would* understand.

More surprising than the tattoos were the vicious-looking scars around his heart and marring the skin of his wrists. He looked as if he'd been stabbed repeatedly over the years. How many times over would this man be dead if he'd been mortal?

Kratos's words rang in my mind: *he's a soldier.* And he had the body of a powerful warrior, powerfully muscled and scarred.

Now that he'd moved closer to me, I got a better view of the pendant around his neck. It looked like resin encasing something crimson—droplets of blood, perhaps.

He arched an eyebrow. "You came here, half dressed, to talk about Afeka?"

I glanced at his windows, the heavy curtains pulled closed. We were alone in here, hidden from view. A strange, magnetic force pulled me toward him, as if some insane part of me wanted his powerful arms around me.

This close to Adonis, the scent of myrrh slipped over my body, and a draft chilled my skin through the silky fabric. I tried to look relaxed as I rested against his door, but I felt aware of every single inch of exposed skin in the frigid castle room. I was completely vulnerable before him, and the thought was disturbingly thrilling.

My pulse was racing. "It's just, I remembered stopping by Afeka once, and the food was amazing." *Think of something universal, Ruby.*

What did all cultures have? "The fruit, I remember the fruit being particularly succulent."

"Mmmm." His voice was almost a growl, and he took another step closer. "I see. You came here to talk about succulent fruit."

In the dim candlelight, flecks of silver gleamed in his eyes as he studied me with an intense curiosity.

My heart thundered harder against my ribs. I swallowed hard, acutely aware of the power that pulsed through every inch of his thickly corded muscles. His skin was a perfect bronze color—definitely Middle Eastern, I thought.

"Olive oil," I said abruptly.

Amusement glinted in his eyes, and I was pretty sure even Drakon was looking at me like I was full of shit. *Olive oil?* Idiot.

"If you're so desperate to get your hands on me, Ruby, you can just ask. Are you wondering if I can fall, and if you can tempt me?"

I sighed, trying to bluff again. "You know, in my four thousand years, I'm not sure I've ever met a man who loves himself more."

"Of course you haven't. You never met a man who deserved it more."

I flicked a strand of hair out of my eyes. "Look, I couldn't sleep. That's all. Succubi are creatures of the night. I saw a light on, and I figured someone was up. I honestly didn't even know you were going to be in here when I pushed through the door. I was hoping for one of the servants." And that was the truth. "I mean, one of the ones we didn't kill tonight. Instead, I find myself face to face with the Archangel of Narcissism. My mistake."

He shook his head slowly, a dark smile playing about his lips. "No, Ruby. I don't believe in mistakes like that. Something draws you to me, doesn't it?"

"Maybe the gravitational pull of your massive ego. I'm not sure anything could withstand its force."

He stood close to me now, his eyes blazing like moonlight. "I know you're not exactly who you say you are. I know you didn't come here to talk to me about Afeka, or fruit, or olive oil. I know you're hiding things, and loneliness pierces you to the core. I know the dark scares you." Gently, he pushed a strand of hair out of my eyes, and the brush of his fingertips against my skin sent a shiver racing through my veins. "But I know it draws you in, too. The sweet release of the shadows. You want it."

His words had my heart practically galloping out of my chest. How much did he suspect about me, this man who could slaughter a city with a flick of his wrist? His powerful magic thrummed over my body, vibrating like an ancient, exotic song.

"And what else do you think I'm hiding?" I asked, keeping my voice low and steady.

His gaze roamed lower over my body. Heat prickled over my skin as I felt him studying me, taking in my curves, my exposed skin.

"I don't know who you are." His voice was husky as he lowered his face to mine, leaning in so close that his breath warmed my neck. "I think I might enjoy finding out."

Gently, as if testing my reaction, he ran a fingertip over my hipbone, tracing the silk. His light touch sent liquid fire swooping through me.

My pulse raced out of control, and I was sure he could hear my heart beating wildly.

Poison hemlock, I reminded myself. *Don't get lured in.*

"Like I said..." My breath was coming embarrassingly fast. Surely he could hear the heaving breaths, right? That I sounded like I'd run a marathon? "I came here by accident. I was looking for someone else."

"Wait." He pulled his hands away from me. Suddenly, his eyes sharpened, and it took me a moment to realize what he was listening to. With my acute fae hearing, I could make out the sound of a door creaking open down the hall.

When the corner of his lips twitched, I knew he was about to do something *really* irritating.

As the sound of footsteps moved down the hallway, Adonis pushed even closer against me, his powerful body warming mine.

Then he opened the door.

I nearly fell out of his room.

There—walking down the hallway—was Kratos.

At the sight of me standing next to a shirtless Adonis and wearing a nightgown that barely covered my ass, Kratos's eyes began to glow a strange and terrifying gold. His copper wings shimmered into view behind him, like he was ready to rip the two of us to pieces.

Tension rippled through his body, a powerful pulse of magic spilled off him. "What is going on here?" An icy chill laced his voice.

"Kratos," said Adonis with a smile. "I thought I heard you."

Kratos's eyes burned into me. "Why is Ruby in your room?"

Adonis leaned against the doorframe, his stance completely at ease. "You know that I had dinner with her tonight. I asked her to pay me a visit after, and she was happy to oblige. She's just been entertaining me."

Heat warmed my cheeks. Adonis wasn't just fucking with me—he was fucking with Kratos, too. And yet I couldn't exactly argue with his account, given that I had no better explanation. *No, no, that's not what happened. I was actually just spying on you to try to figure out how to kill you, so I'll just be on my way...*

Adonis had seen right through my bullshit excuse about Afeka, and my next excuse about looking for servants, and he knew I had nothing to counter his story.

I shrugged. "I thought it would be rude to turn down one of my hosts, but after literally a minute in the Dark Lord's room listening to him talk about how much he loves himself, I believe it's time for me to return to my own."

I stepped into the cold hallway.

Adonis's icy eyes glinted with silver. "I'm sure we'll be seeing each other again soon enough, Ruby."

"Stay away from her." The threat of violence laced Kratos's voice, but his eyes were still on me. "I'll walk Ruby back to her room."

Adonis closed the door, and I walked next to Kratos through the hall. No point in hiding from the sentinels now—the jig was up.

We walked in silence. Never before had I really understood the meaning of the phrase "walk of shame," but as I strutted through the Tower of Ash in my underthings, it seemed to suit my mood perfectly.

It was Kratos who broke the silence. "I told you to stay in the Tower of Wrath."

"True," I sighed. "But Adonis asked me to leave it. I wasn't quite sure which of you I was supposed to listen to. Is there some sort of hierarchy here?"

He cut me a sharp look. "No."

"Why is it that you want me to stay in the Tower of Wrath?" I prodded.

"You're safest there. We're safest with you there."

Ah, the whole fallen thing.

Even though I'd been caught—even though I'd had a disturbing run-in with Adonis—it had been worth it. Tonight, I'd learned the angels planned to attack the Tower, and this was why I'd come here. I could warn Yasmin in advance, give them a chance to evacuate.

Tomorrow, I'd slip out into the forest to find the mulberry grove.

As we walked, a cold fury rippled off Kratos's body. This was the downside of my mission. Until I found out more information, I was completely dependent on Kratos's approval—where I could explore, if I could persuade him to search for Hazel—in fact, if I could stay here at all. If I pissed him off too much, he'd drop me back in my old VD rookery.

What had Yasmin's advice been with the angels? *Charm them. Seduce them.*

She hadn't known about this whole "fallen" thing, that they'd be resistant to my seduction.

Kratos turned to look at me, studying me closely. "What would make you happy?" he asked.

Killing all of you so the world can return to normal. "Dancing," I said impulsively.

"Maybe I can arrange for that. I could find you a place to dance."

He seemed willing to please me. I should be using that. "What would make me truly happy," I said, "is reuniting with my younger sister. You really don't know where the dragons took their conquests?"

"I could try to find her."

My heart thrummed in my chest.

I thought of Hazel—just fourteen when I'd last seen her. Those who'd captured her wouldn't care that she still had nightmares and needed soothing in the middle of the night, that she had to eat snacks all the time or her sugar dropped and she got crazy. They wouldn't care that she made the most shockingly morbid jokes in her sweet, high-pitched voice, that she stayed up late into the night reading fantasy books with a flashlight. The dragons would not care one bit. Only I cared.

Genuine tears pricked my eyes. "Could you do that? Could you find her?"

"I could at least try. Like you said, there aren't many succubi around."

And then all my hope flitted away like a burning moth. *A succubus.* Of course. He'd be looking for the younger sister of a succubus, not a fae.

Still, I clung to the elusive tendrils of this idea with every fiber of my being.

Maybe Yasmin could find a way to get word to Hazel, give her a warning to glamour herself, just a subtle hint of dark magic that only an angel would notice.

I now had two pressing reasons to get to Yasmin tomorrow—to save my sister and to save everyone sheltering in the Tower.

As we approached my room, I looked at Kratos, beaming with genuine gratitude. "That would definitely make me happy."

Kratos opened the door to my room, leaving me to step into the dark alone. Gently, he closed the door behind me, and I scrambled to light a candle. Exhaling, I watched the tiny flame dance.

Mentally, I reviewed everything that had just happened. What were Adonis's motives—and why was he so eager to upset Kratos? There was a crack here, a weakness in the angels' alliance. Adonis wanted to unsettle Kratos, though I didn't know why.

In the words of the Dark Lord, *I planned to make it my mission to find out.*

CHAPTER 31

I didn't have to worry about an alarm. The morning sunlight streaming through the bare windows was enough to wake me from even the deepest of sleeps.

Yasmin's mirror call was arriving just after dawn, so the morning light was a blessing. Today—more than ever—it was crucial that I made contact with her.

I jumped out of bed, crossing the cold flagstone floor to the bathroom. There, I stood in front of the gilt-frame mirror and lit a candle.

When Yasmin's blurry face appeared in the mirror, I held up the candle close to the glass. Then I held my palm in front of the flame to shield it, giving Yasmin the *one, two, three* signal.

Yasmin leaned over, scribbling something on a piece of paper. Through the reflection, she held up a sign that read, "Six hours. Meet in the cave." Then her image shimmered away.

A lump rose in my throat. *Six hours?* We weren't that far from London—couldn't she get here faster? I needed to tell her that this was a desperate situation, that she needed to get here right away. But I had only a candle to get the message across. As I racked my brain for what I could remember of Morse code, the connection cut out.

I swallowed hard. How long would the angels wait before exacting their revenge?

They were relying on Adonis for the slaughter. Maybe I could find a way to keep him occupied for now. Another trip to his room to talk about Afeka and fruit and tempt him to touch my nightgown? But if I pissed off Kratos too much, he'd never find my sister for me.

I crossed into the chilly bedroom, goosebumps covering my skin.

I pulled open the wardrobe, snatching out the only bits of warm and comfortable clothing in there—a pair of leather leggings and a long black sweater. At my request, Susie had found a pair of boots for me, and I pulled them on over my leggings.

While I waited for Yasmin to show up, I'd go on another fact-finding mission. Kratos had said I could explore the Tower of Wrath and the forest outside. Besides following Adonis, the forest seemed like item number one on my spy agenda for the day. I needed to find the mulberry grove, and while I was at it, I needed to stumble on the key to saving Earth from the angels.

At least according to Yasmin, the super reliable woman who'd failed to warn me about the great Winter Servant Uprising.

First, I'd start with an early-morning visit to Adonis's room. And this time, I had to make certain no one would catch me.

I slipped out the door, one eye on the windows for sentinels.

* * *

TWENTY MINUTES LATER, I was back in my room, none the wiser. On the one hand, my mission to the Tower of Ash had been a success, considering no one had caught me. On the other, I was left with a deep sense of unease, because Adonis hadn't been in his room, and I had no idea where to find him. Had he already left for London?

I had to go out and do a bit of exploring, looking for ways to kill these angels.

I slipped into my berry-blue coat, then looped my quiver over my shoulder. If I found any poisonous plants, I'd hide them in there.

I pulled open the door to my room and was immediately greeted by the sight of Susie carrying a breakfast tray. Relief flickered through me—she was alive. "Morning," I said blandly.

"Ruby. I've got pastry and coffee. Won't you be eating this morning?"

"You are amazing, Susie. Glad to see you made it through the slaughter." I pouted. "I don't suppose you've seen the angels this morning, have you? I was looking for a bit of company."

"No, I haven't seen them. They weren't in their rooms."

"So where would they be?"

Her expression was stony. "I couldn't say."

She wasn't going to divulge anything to me.

Disappointment washed over me. Okay. Time for plan B.

"Speaking of finding a little company, where would I find the bar in this place?" I plastered my most bored expression on my face, pretending not to care. "Did that fellow Elan make it through last night's massacre alive? I was hoping the two of you would join me in the bar later today. I don't like to drink alone."

"He's fine. Yes—we can show you the bar around lunch time."

"Wonderful." *Because I want to get you wasted so you'll actually help me.*

I snatched a warm croissant off the tray. Then I eyed the coffee. What were the chances I could walk without spilling it all over myself? Moderate, if I used my fae powers. I pulled a steaming cup of coffee from the tray.

"I'll just leave the rest in your room!" she called after me as I walked down the hall. "I'll see you later."

I sipped the coffee as I walked, and it warmed me in the chilly stairwell. Where would I find the angels, and what exactly was going on between them? If I got Elan and Susie drunk enough, I was hoping they'd spill some angel secrets.

By the time I reached the bottom of the stairs, I'd finished my coffee, and I rested the cup in a little stone alcove near the door. Thick iron bars locked the oak door from the inside—an obvious fire hazard, but I'd let it slide. What really bothered me was the iron itself. Angels were the only supernatural creatures on Earth unperturbed by iron. To the rest of us—especially the fae—it sapped our magic and burned our skin. The more magic we used, the worse it felt—and unfortunately for me, I was perpetually disguising myself with glamour.

Never in my life had I wanted a pair of gloves more.

Instead, I shoved the croissant in my mouth to hold it, then pulled down the sleeves of my sweater so they covered my fingertips. Gingerly, I touched the metal. Through the fabric of my sweater, the iron seared my skin as it burned off the magic. I winced as the smell of burnt wool curled into the air. And was that—burnt flesh?

Maybe this wasn't such a good idea with the glamour still on.

I stepped back into the shadows of the stairwell, soothing my pain with the comfort of eating a flaky, buttery croissant. As I ate, I listened carefully for the sound of footsteps from above. My sharp fae senses told me I was totally alone in here.

I closed my eyes, tuning in to the magical glamour that skimmed and shimmered over my skin. I always wore some level of glamour to hide my true fae side. The magic was second nature to me, such that I almost forgot its presence. It was like the medieval scientists had said about the music of the heavenly spheres—you'd never notice it until the music stopped.

I willed the glamour to drop, feeling uncomfortably naked without it. Now, if anyone saw me, they would see my true fae side—white-gold hair, silver eyes, skin that faintly glimmered with gold, slightly pointed ears. At the first sign of danger, my canines would come out.

Magic-free, I approached the door again. This time, when I put my shielded hands on the iron, I was able to hold them there long enough to slide the iron bar free. It dropped to the stone floor with a loud clang.

Before yanking open the door, I summoned my glamour, my hair returning to cherry red, my eyes to the deep black of a succubus.

I pushed through the heavy oak door into the milky morning sunlight, so clear and white that it burned my eyes. Based on the position of the sun, I knew to head north, where Yasmin had said I'd find the mulberry grove.

Today, a glorious thaw pervaded the winter air. I took a right, following the curve of the castle wall until I reached the north side. Here, mossy elm trees reached for the skies, their leaves tinged ginger and dandelion yellow.

From there, I crossed to a path within the elm trees. My feet crunched over the fallen leaves as I walked, imagining seeing Hazel again. Here, under a canopy of honey and amber leaves, calm and peace imbued me for the first time in over a year. The forests were the true homes of the fae, the reason why, millennia ago, we'd chosen to stay on Earth instead of returning to the heavens with the other angels. We knew what delights lived among the oaks and moss, in the marigolds and wild poppies, in the acorn stews and drinks made of nectar. We knew what delights came from dancing naked in a myrtle grove. The fae were angels who loved the Earth.

The forest felt particularly *alive* to me today. For the fae, spring began February first. I hadn't been able to keep track of the date, but I was pretty sure January was coming to a close soon. If that was the case, I'd better lock myself up. On Eimmal, the first day of spring, I'd be going a bit nuts.

As I walked through the woods, the wind whispered over my skin, toying with my crimson hair. If only I could bring Hazel here, if only we could find a way to live in the forest like our ancestors had. Maybe we could carve out a life for ourselves in the world of the Great Nightmare, assuming none of this got any worse. We could build ourselves a cottage with a fireplace, eat the food the forest gave us. It was the best I could hope for, and it seemed like a dream.

Could Kratos really find her? *Would* he really find her?

As I walked deeper into the forest, my path met a burbling stream, and I began to walk parallel to the water. This meant I'd be able to orient myself more easily.

With the sound of water rushing beside me, I lost myself in a fantasy—one in which Hazel and I stewed venison and made berry pies in our cozy little cottage. In the old fae tradition, I could easily make a bow from the hickory or yew trees that grew around me, and I could hunt without any problem.

I scanned the trees and plants, looking for signs of the Old Gods. I needed Devil's Bane, and whatever else they were willing to give me.

How would I recognize a gift from the Old Gods? If the gods wanted me to find this key to angelic destruction, I hoped they would make it obvious. The forest equivalent of a flashing neon sign.

After about two miles of trekking, I spotted a cluster of purple flowering plants. *Devil's Bane.* Like hemlock, the plants were as beautiful as they were deadly.

As far as I knew, these plants were highly poisonous, so I checked my hands for cuts, regretting once again my lack of gloves. Ripping them out by the stems, I shoved them into my quiver. I filled the thing halfway, then moved on.

Yasmin had been right about the Devil's Bane, at least.

The spring's allure washed over me, and I had to work to stay focused. All my instincts were telling me to drop my glamour, strip off my clothes, and run naked through the woods until heat flushed my chest. I *definitely* had to ignore those instincts.

I must've covered several miles before I reached the mulberry grove, and despite my best efforts, I'd seen few signs of godlike intervention along the way. Still, I found the meeting spot. When I returned later, I'd know the fastest way to get there. Follow the river, veer to the right when the trees grew so tall and thick they nearly blocked out the sun, and ignore the desire to flee naked through the woods like a wild person.

As I returned to the fortress, my quiver full of poison, dread crawled over me. Was any of this really enough to stop the angels from completing their mission?

CHAPTER 32

*I*n the bar, shadows danced over empty stone alcoves. From iron chandeliers above, candlelight lit the room.

I leaned on the oak countertop, nursing my whisky. Elan, Susie, and I were the only ones in here. Turned out the barman had been a secret vampire, slaughtered yesterday along with the rest. Still, we'd managed to scrounge up some bread and cheese for sandwiches, and I'd pulled a few bottles from behind the bar to serve Susie and Elan.

After spending the past few hours searching in vain for Adonis, I frankly needed the drink.

And I needed the servants to talk. The drunker they got, the more likely they were to spill secrets.

Apart from the free booze, the best thing about the bar was the lack of windows. Not a single sentinel could report what I was up to in here.

Eyeing Elan's empty glass, I snatched the bottle of whisky from the countertop and refilled his cup. Top of my agenda was finding out what Adonis was up to, and what was going on between him and Kratos.

"Thank you." His forehead crinkled. "I'm not really sure if I should be drinking that much while still on the clock. I usually just have an ale and a liver sandwich at lunchtime."

I stared at him. "Half your colleagues died yesterday. I don't think anyone is going to judge you. And even if they did, no one is going to fire you, because you two are the only ones left to bring them food."

Elan had been restrained in his drinking and wasn't nearly drunk enough. Susie had *not* been restrained, but she'd surprised me by how well she could hold her liquor. She'd downed at least five shots of whisky already, yet her speech sounded normal, her eyes alert. Who would've thought a quiet, mousy girl could hold her liquor like that?

Obviously, Elan would have to be my target.

I just had to get him to drink more.

I smiled at him. "You know, there's an old succubus tradition, the day after a massacre."

"Oh?" asked Elan.

"Basically, you purify your grief with sacred alcohol. It helps rid the air of all the mourning spirits. Helps them move on to the spirit realm. It's actually very important."

Elan wrinkled his nose. "I'm not really grieving. Is that bad? I didn't like most of my colleagues."

Dark, Elan. Dark.

He gripped his glass, shadows wavering over his gaunt face. "They said I looked like a necromancer's greatest regret."

I filled his glass. "Okay, forget that then. There's another old succubus tradition where you celebrate the deaths of your enemies. Or your... coworkers that you marginally tolerated. Anyway, the point is, when a lot of people die, a bit of whisky is warranted. What do you think, Susie? Take the edge off all the death?"

I knew Susie was game. This girl loved her whisky.

Susie shoved her glass across the bar. "I would never pass up an opportunity to learn about another culture. Like you said, let's drink to the memories of the coworkers we vaguely tolerated."

I filled her glass. *Good old peer pressure should do the trick.* I raised my eyebrows at Elan, who looked unsure.

"What's the matter, Elan?" I asked.

"It's just that, you know. I'm a fae. And Eimmal is in two days."

My stomach dropped. *Two days.* Sooner than I'd thought. No wonder I'd been getting high off the forest.

I still hadn't worked out the logistics of Eimmal. Normally, I'd spent the day dancing in a stupor in a remote forest or—last year—locked up in a hospital room, courtesy of Alex. What was I supposed to do here? I'd have to lock myself in my room that day, maybe feign sickness. Maybe I could even bar my own door with iron.

Masking my thoughts, I simply smiled at Elan. "A bit feral, are you, Elan? I thought you were a *high* fae."

"Maybe a bit feral." He scratched his cheek, frowning. "To tell the truth, I don't know my exact lineage, as I was left next to a pile of dog carcasses in Houndsditch as a baby. I do always feel a *bit* loopy around Eimmal."

You and me both, buddy.

Elan's face paled. "Don't tell the Dark Lord."

I tapped the side of my glass. "That's right. He hates the fae, especially the feral kind. Abominations. Well, I won't judge you, Elan. Let's take the edge off that panic, shall we?" I topped up his glass even more. "It isn't Eimmal yet. You have more time."

He chewed his lip. "I suppose I don't want to be left out."

"Exactly." Now I just had to distract them from the fact that I wasn't about to drink any of this. "Bottoms up!"

I brought the whisky to my lips and mimed drinking it. While their eyes were closed as they knocked back their shots, I dumped my pour onto the floor.

I wiped my hand across my mouth. "Now that is good stuff." How to segue to what really interested me… "So is this bar just for the servants, then? Or do the angels ever drink in here?"

Elan shrugged. "Just Johnny sometimes. Saunters in, puts his feet on the table, makes everyone nervous. He drinks straight vodka."

I cocked my head. "So the angels can't have sex, but they are allowed to indulge in alcohol."

"Seems that way," said Elan.

In the mirror behind the bar, I caught Susie's shudder. The angels terrified her.

I refilled our glasses. I couldn't seem too eager for information, or I'd scare them away. "Seems a waste of a good bar if the angels won't use it and half the servants are dead."

I lifted my glass, signaling that it was time to drink again. Once again, while their eyes were shut, I emptied it out over the side of my leg.

"Kratos and Adonis wouldn't set foot in here." Susie stared at the bottles of liquor lined up before the mirror. "Johnny is the only one who likes slumming."

Good to know. "Does he get drunk? *Can* angels get drunk?" I whispered conspiratorially.

Elan nodded, refilling his own glass. "Once, he got trashed and tried to unleash a famine, except he couldn't find his way out of the castle. He starved one of Kratos's hounds instead by accident. And he lit his curtains on fire. Pretty sure Kratos would have murdered him, except I don't think angels can actually kill each other."

Definitely good to know. "Oh well. He seems nice enough to me. In fact, he's been quite welcoming to me since I arrived." I smiled at Elan. "Would you mind bringing him a gift from me? A few bottles of vodka. As many as you can find, in fact."

Elan smiled. "Of course."

Let's see how long Kratos would tolerate a trashed angel in his midst.

Susie turned her gaze on me, her eyes suddenly sharp. "Speaking of slumming, I wouldn't have expected someone like you to spend time in here, either. An ancient succubus such as yourself."

Clever Susie. "I simply don't have much to *do* here. The angels—I'm sure they have other important things they need to be doing with their time." I refilled the glasses again. "Mind you, I have no idea *what* they do with their time. Do you know, Elan? I was hoping to track them down today, only I'm not supposed to leave this tower."

Elan emptied his glass without even waiting for us, then leaned over the edge of the bar, his eyelids drooping slightly. "Not sure what

Kratos does during the day. At night, of course, he hunts. Nasty habit," he muttered before looking shocked and blinking his eyes as if suddenly alert. "Of course, he has many wonderful qualities."

"Oh?" I prompted.

Susie's glass was now empty. I was pretty sure they were no longer paying attention to what I was drinking. "The dogs," she said simply.

"The dogs," I repeated.

Elan was reaching for the bottle now, his face beaming. The effects of Eimmal were already getting to him. "Yeah. He is very kind to his dogs. Raises them from a young age. Nurses the sick ones. They're like his children, really. I remember when Culloch was having a hard time growing. Couldn't drink milk from his mum. So Kratos soaked cloth in milk and dripped it into the puppy's mouth until the little thing began to thrive. He did it all himself."

I bit my lip. Hard to reconcile this puppy-nurse image with the angel of death who slaughtered humans in the streets.

"And the trees," said Susie abruptly.

What shot was she on now? Eight? Nine?

"The trees." I repeated her confusing fragment.

"Into nature, isn't he." Elan's accent had been changing slightly with every shot, becoming more London, less posh. Apparently, I wasn't the only one here pretending. "Tends to the gardens outside, the trees in the forest."

My eyebrows shot up. "Why?"

Elan waved a hand. "You know, it's his whole philosophy."

I had no idea what he was talking about. "Right." I refilled my glass, then the others. "The whole nature thing."

Elan pointed at me. "Exactly. See? You know. Rampant human expansion has destroyed the Earth, and he's helping to restore it to its original thingamajig, tending to plants. You get the idea."

"Original natural state," added Susie, taking pains to enunciate clearly. "The way the angels intended it. Everything in the proper balance."

"Right." I pretended to sip my drink. "He mentioned that."

"Hence," Elan lifted a finger, "gardening. Coppicing. That sort of thing."

I casually drummed my fingertips on the counter. "And what do the others do with their free time?"

Elan leaned on his fist. "Johnny plays pinball and drinks caffeine. And the Dark Lord… I sometimes see him in the yew grove, from my window. He's hard to see. Shadows seem to follow him."

I'd noticed that about him.

I traced my fingertip over the rim of my glass. "Any idea what he's doing today?"

Elan's forehead crinkled with the effort of thinking about it. "Bit of retribution, I imagine. Only I don't think he's left yet. I saw him heading toward the yew grove not that long ago. I hid from him under a pile of leaves."

I clutched my glass tighter.

The yew grove would be my next stop, though I hadn't found one yet. "Yews! I do love a good yew tree." That was the truth—fae used yews for making weapons. "Succubi burn the bark as a perfume." *I'm just totally making stuff up here.* "Where exactly is the grove?"

Elan pointed to the wall, his eyelids heavy. "Somewhere out that way."

Susie pointed to another wall. "No, that way. By the oaks."

Elan glowered. "Whole forest is full of oaks. That's not a useful description."

Maybe I'd gone a bit too far with the whisky.

Susie met my gaze. "Can you imagine what it would be like to be human, like me?" She clutched her glass tightly, and I saw the same fear in her eyes that I'd seen when Elan had mentioned Adonis.

I really wanted to get back to the yew grove conversation.

"Human? Not really." I tossed my hair over my shoulder. Susie and I were probably about the same age, but she didn't know that. "I can't imagine such a short lifespan. It must be… terrifying."

She lowered her voice to a whisper. "Bad enough before this lot came. When your bones got old and crushed and full of dirt, then you died and turned into a ghost. Now death is all around us."

I swallowed hard. Definitely too much whisky.

"Something about that sentiment reminds me of Adonis, but I can't quite—" I began.

Susie lifted a finger to her lips. "Shhhh… don't speak of him. He exudes death like a god." She blinked, then reached for the bottle again. "Death wears a pretty face."

Annnnd I was pretty sure I'd gotten all the information I could get out of these two. I slid my glass across the bar, regaining my haughty succubus composure. "Well, it's been lovely slumming with you two, but I think I'm going to get some fresh air. Kratos has the right idea. A return to nature's original thingamajig."

* * *

I PULLED my coat tight around me as I walked through the forest. This time, I'd come armed with my Nyxobian blade—and now the blade had been coated with Devil's Bane. I'd just have to be very careful not to nick myself with it, or it would be exactly like Susie had said—my bones would get crushed and full of dirt and I'd turn into a ghost.

Before leaving to hunt for the Hunt, I'd swung by the bar one more time to ask about the yews again. There, I'd found Susie and Elan leaning over the counter while Elan forlornly chanted an old fae song. Neither of them had been able to tell me where to find the yews.

So I was on my own. If I remembered correctly, yews had the charming nickname "trees of the dead," so I supposed that explained Adonis's interest. After all, he exuded death like a god. I just hoped he would not be exuding it all over the Tower of London before I got the chance to warn Yasmin.

I glanced up at the sunlight slanting through the boughs, unnerved by the sentinels swooping overhead, watching me. Yasmin's plan had been for me to glamour myself as a fox and meet her in a cave, where the sentinels wouldn't be able to see us. I hoped she had a bit more of a plan than that, because the sentinels were watching *everything*.

After two hours of walking through the forest, the shadows grew long, climbing like spindly fingers over the dirt and moss. I tried to ignore the enticing allure of Eimmal that whispered through the boughs.

Based on my calculations, I didn't have long until it was time to meet Yasmin, but I'd failed to find Adonis or the yews. It had been several hours now, several hours of wandering through oaks and hazels while my stomach rumbled and briars scratched at my legs. I picked some blackberries as I walked and nibbled on acorns, feeling more connected to the old fae ways than ever.

As my mouth filled with the taste of berry juice, it occurred to me that berries shouldn't be growing in January. But maybe it was like Yasmin had said—the Old Gods would provide, if we just paid attention.

I grabbed another handful of berries from a low blackberry bush. As I shoved them into my mouth, a flutter of movement in the corner of my eye caught my attention. When I looked up into the branches, I caught sight of a magpie, its wings shimmering an iridescent blue. My pulse began to race. Before she died, my mother had told Hazel and me stories about magpies while we lay curled around her in bed. According to her, they were messengers of sorts, creatures who would bring news.

> One for sorrow
> Two for joy
> Three for a girl
> Four for a boy
> Five for young
> Six for old
> Seven for a secret never to be told

Humans thought a single magpie was bad luck. That was only because it meant that a fae might be nearby, ready to strike them down with an arrow or seduce them away from their lives.

I'd never paid much attention to signs before, and once I hadn't believed in the old fae ways. Then again, I'd never before seen blackberries growing in January.

My footsteps crunched over the deadfall as I quickened my pace, trying to keep up with the magpie. I glanced at the sky, and as soon as it was clear of sentinels, I launched into a full-blown, fae-style sprint, feeling the forest wind whip over my skin.

I skidded to a halt when a shimmer of silver caught my eye.

As I caught my breath, I looked up into the boughs, where a silver branch of an ancient, gnarled rowan tree gleamed in the honeyed sunlight. I'd never seen a rowan tree anywhere near this large—and I'd definitely never seen one with a silver branch.

If anything was a sign from the gods, *this* was.

Surrounding the single rowan tree was a grove of knotted and twisted yews. At their bases grew Devil's Bane.

Had I found the yew grove that Adonis visited?

Something cold and ancient snaked over my skin, and goosebumps rose on my neck, my arms. Shadows claimed the air around me, darkening the sun.

From one of the yews, a flock of ravens burst into the air.

And then, from behind me, a deep voice. "Are you looking for something, Ruby?"

I whirled to find Adonis standing behind me, cloaked in shadows. He smiled slowly. "Is it just me, or do you run awfully fast for a succubus?"

CHAPTER 33

$\mathcal{A}$t his words, cold fear slid through my bones.

From the dark tendrils of magic that snaked and curled around him, his pale eyes pierced the shadows, rooting me in place.

Don't let him rattle you, Ruby.

I crossed my arms. "*Do* I run fast for a succubus? I don't know many, considering men like you killed them all."

Amusement glinted in his eyes. "Men like me? There are no men like me. I'm a god on Earth."

Despite my fear, I rolled my eyes. "You've got to be kidding me."

"Have you seen anything that suggests otherwise?"

I examined my nails, hoping to convey boredom, even if my heart was slamming against my ribs like a war hammer. Could he hear it?

"Whether or not you're a god," I continued, "I *am* talking about men like you. You're all the same, aren't you? You see something you love, and you want to destroy the very thing that draws you in."

I leaned down, gingerly plucking a violet corncockle from the undergrowth, careful not to mix it up with the Devil's Bane. I crushed it in my fist until purple juice ran between my fingers. "You see a virginal woman, and you want to defile her. You see a beautiful woman, and you want to cover her up. You see a powerful woman,

221

and you want to take her down a notch. So yes—I mean 'men like you.' I've lived for thousands of years, and you're all the same."

He cocked his head, the rest of his body so preternaturally still it raised my hackles. Given the shadows whirling in his eyes, I had the sense that I'd struck a nerve again.

"I've lived for thousands of years," he said in a low voice. "And I know when a warrior holds back in a fight. I know better than anyone what it means to restrain your power, to clamp down on your most primal instincts. I know that when the demons attacked, you weren't fighting at your full capacity. You've wanted to appear weak to us, when you are not."

He didn't ask why. He just let the accusation hang in the air.

My mind whirled as I tried to plan my next course of action. I wanted to interrogate Adonis about what his plans were, if he'd been to the Tower already, if there was anything I could do to stop it.

Instead, I let out a long sigh. "Well, I wanted to see what you pretty little angels could do, if you could actually fight with all those feathers weighing you down."

He cocked an eyebrow. "And?"

I shrugged. "And I was impressed."

He straightened. "Of course you were. I've been slaughtering for eons."

I adopted a breezy tone, while inside, my blood raced through my veins. "Is that what you were doing today, also? Slaughtering? I heard a rumor that you spent time in the bar. Or was that Johnny? I get all of you confused."

I knew very well he hadn't been in the bar today.

"Maybe I was killing today. Maybe I was resting. What difference does it make to you?"

My heart clenched. "It's just that I heard you were getting revenge on the humans, and I thought it sounded delicious."

The oaky breeze toyed with my hair, blowing it in front of my face. Adonis took another step closer, brushing the strand out of my eyes. "If only I couldn't hear your frantic heartbeat, I might believe that you're truly as calm as you pretend."

His words curled around my ribs like smoke. This close, his powerful beauty hit me like a fist. With Eimmal looming, I couldn't be near him without wanting to touch him.

Talk about clamping down on your most primal instincts.

Adonis's gaze flicked to the yew grove. "I'll leave you now to—whatever you were doing here."

I swallowed hard. "Just out for a walk." I'd lost the conviction in my voice.

As he turned and slipped into the darkening forest, shadows whirling around him, I simply stared after him.

* * *

MY FOOTSTEPS CRACKLED over the leaves and twigs. So Adonis was on to me, my cover had been somewhat blown, and yet I had no idea what he planned to do about it.

And what exactly was *his* interest in the yew grove—the one that happened to have a silver branch, a gift from the Old Gods?

I quickened my pace through the woods, desperately hoping I hadn't been too late to save those in the Tower.

The sunlight slanted through the branches, flecking the ground with gold. I kept my eye on the trees' long shadows, which told me how to stay headed north, and how much more time I had. As I walked swiftly, I mentally ran through Yasmin's instructions to me.

Hellebore and cockle weeds by the mulberry grove.

While the shadows grew longer around me, I spotted them.

No wonder Yasmin had recruited me. Not only was glamour important, but only a fae would know what the hell all these plants were.

I glanced up at the sky through the trees, catching sight of a sentinel flying overhead, eyes on me. The chilly wind whispered over my skin, and I waited for the creature to pass.

When the skies above me were clear of all movement, I summoned a powerful glamour. Magic rushed and buzzed over my skin as I cloaked myself in the form of a fox.

I wasn't a shifter. When glamoured, I still moved like myself, still had the same speed, same gait, same body. But to anyone who happened to observe me, I'd look like a little red fox. A glamour was like an illusory bubble around me.

Unlike my succubus guise—a subtle shift—this extreme glamour took effort. Already, my muscles burned. On top of the physical strain, remembering how to keep up the appearance of a four-legged creature was taking up most of my mental energy.

Still, I kept walking, moving northward through the forest until, at last, I reached a dark cave, carved into a rocky surface. Pine trees flanked the cave's mouth, just as Yasmin had said. I ran inside, and under the cover of the cave, I dropped the exhausting fox glamour.

As I did, the sound of a striking match echoed off the cave walls, and a burst of flame illuminated Yasmin's handsome features. She'd dressed in simple black clothing, a bow and arrow slung over her back.

I loosed a sigh of relief. "You're alive."

"Why wouldn't I be?"

"Humans and demons attacked the castle last night. The angels are blaming a nefarious organization known as The Institute. They're sending Adonis to kill you all. I'm surprised he hasn't done it already. Apparently, he has the power to break through your wards."

Her face paled in the warm candlelight. "When is he coming?"

"I don't know. I just saw Adonis in the woods, and I couldn't get him to tell me anything. Also, I'm pretty sure he and Johnny are on to me."

She was already pushing to move past me. "I need to get back."

"Hang on. You just got here. I have questions."

"I don't have time for questions. I need to warn the others. And while I'm doing that, I need you to distract Adonis. Keep him here. Do whatever it takes, do you understand me?"

I clamped my hands on my hips. "Adonis is on to me. Everything I do, every time I see him, he tells me that he thinks I'm hiding some-thing and that I'm not who I say I am. Everyone here is *terrified* of him, and I don't even want to know what these angels will do to me if they learn I'm spying for you."

She clenched her jaw. "Do whatever it takes. You need to find Adonis *now.*"

"Why didn't you tell me about the planned attack?"

"We had a servant uprising planned half a year ago, but we lost contact with that cell two months ago, and we haven't been able to find them through scrying. I thought they were all dead. I had no idea they were still planning to attack."

"So you failed to tell me about all your agents dying in the castle. And by the way—why did it take you so long to get here?"

Her eyes flashed. "I had things I needed to take care of. No one else is willing to make this journey anymore, and I can't just run out of the Tower on short notice."

I stared at her, my irritation rising. I was risking my ass to help her, and she was only feeding me crumbs of information.

Still, I realized why she was so desperate to get home—the little girl I'd met when I'd stayed in the Tower. "You want to get back to your daughter, don't you?"

Her expression softened. "She's only three. Every night before she goes to sleep, she asks me if I'll protect her. I tell her I will. What else can I say? I don't know if I can, but I will do everything in my power to try. We both watched her father die, torn to pieces by dragons in front of us, and I couldn't do a single thing about it." She wrung her hands together. "She was having an asthma attack this morning. I couldn't get out of there until her lungs sounded clearer. No one else can look after her like I can."

I nodded. "Okay. Evacuate the Tower, and I'll try to keep Adonis from leaving before the night is over." I shivered at the thought. "But I need you to do something else for me. I need you to contact my sister, Hazel. Tell her she needs to glamour herself as a succubus. Kratos is sending people to look for her, and he has no idea she's a fae."

"Are you sure you want me to risk it?"

"It's the only chance I have."

She started for the cave entrance, but I grabbed her arm. "Wait.

The angels suspect me now, all of them except Kratos. Is there an exit plan for me? How am I getting out of here if they turn on me?"

"I sent you here because you're resourceful. I trust you to figure it out. Listen to what the Old Gods are trying to tell you."

Are you kidding me? "I haven't found anything but the Devil's Bane."

"There must be something else."

I shook my head. "I found a silver bough in the forest, in a yew grove. That's it. It doesn't look like it comes with instructions about how to use it to kill angels."

Her eyes brightened. "A silver bough. Now that is worth investigating. It's a gift from the Old Gods. I'm sure of it."

"Okay, I'll investigate." I grabbed her arm. "Before you run out there, let me check for sentinels. A woman wandering around with a crossbow isn't exactly inconspicuous, and Adonis has seen me around here already."

"Fine."

I summoned my fox glamour once again, magic flickering and sparking over my skin. Fully disguised, I crept from the cave. An icy rain had begun to fall over the forest.

When I scanned the skies, I spotted a murmuration of sentinels swarming by the forest's edge.

Shit. Clearly, they'd seen Yasmin. And they were waiting for her.

I stepped back into the cave, dropping the glamour again. "They saw you. They're curious about you. And they're probably going to follow you back to the Tower, reporting to the angels the whole time. You don't want their eyes on your daughter, and you don't want them connecting us when they realize someone screwed up the angels' attack plans."

Her eyes looked frantic. "I can't stay here."

I held out my hands like I was calming a wild animal. "I understand. But we need to get them out of the way. I need a few of your arrows."

"What do you plan on doing?" she asked doubtfully, but she was already pulling a handful of arrows from her quiver. "Shooting all the sentinels?"

"Just wait here."

I glamoured myself as a fox again, disguising everything to outside observers—the arrows, my bright red hair—and stepped out into the rainy forest.

The Old Gods will give us everything we need.

Standing before one of the pine trees, I reached for my sweater, tearing a fat strip off the bottom. I ripped this strip into more pieces. I wrapped each of the arrow tips in wool, fighting hard to think clearly through the mental fog in my brain. Then I lay them gently on the ground.

I reached for the knife strapped to my thigh. Fighting through the glamour-fog, I began hacking away at the bark on the tree, penetrating the pine wood with the blade until, at last, a thick stream of sap began to trickle out. Shivering in the chilly rain, I carefully slid my blade back into its holster.

Dizzy from the glamour, I snatched the arrows from the forest floor. Now a sharp pain pierced my temples. Dark dots swam in my vision as I dabbed the arrowheads into the pine sap, trying to maintain my focus. I needed to get this done before I passed out in front of the cave.

At last, with each arrowhead coated in pine sap, I hustled back into the cave, grunting at the searing pain in my head. I dropped the glamour immediately, then hunched over on my knees while the pain and dizziness subsided. I clutched the bunch of arrows tightly.

"Care to fill me in on what you're doing?" asked Yasmin.

"Like I said, I'm going to create a diversion. I need the bow and your matches."

As she handed me the bow and matchbox, the idea of the *Old Gods* burbled in the back of my mind. We had everything we needed here in the forest, didn't we? Food, weapons.

And pine sap, as it happened, was extremely flammable.

With the weapons in hand, I crossed to the cave's mouth, then scanned the skies. The sentinels still swarmed by the very northern edge of the forest, waiting for Yasmin.

I stepped back into the cave, then ignited the arrows, letting them burn on the rocky floor. I nocked the first arrow and loosed it to the south. I watched it soar at least two hundred yards into the air before arcing downward again.

With all the fallen leaves blanketing the ground, it shouldn't take long for the deadfall to ignite at least a little. But the icy rain would ensure nothing spread too far.

From the cover of the cave, I loaded up the next arrow, then unleashed it into the air. That one slammed against my forearm, bruising it badly. I grimaced, regretting my lack of arm guards.

Then I refocused on my task. One after another, I loosed the arrows into the same spot. After the fourth arrow, the sentinels took notice.

I watched their pattern shift, their movements growing sharper. In the distance, where the arrows had hit, smoke curled into the air as some of the leaves ignited.

From my spot in the cave, I watched the sentinels soar overhead toward the thin tendrils of smoke until, at last, the entire swarm had cleared the northern tree line.

"Go." I handed Yasmin her bow again. "Fast, before they come back."

She pulled the bow from me. "Thank you. Just—please find a way to keep Adonis here."

"I will. *Go.*"

She launched out of the cave in a swift sprint, the desperate rush of a mom determined to get back to her little girl.

CHAPTER 34

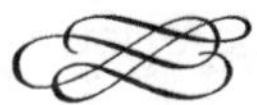

Glamoured as a fox, I trudged back to the castle, my body burning with the strange fatigue of a magic drain. I didn't want the sentinels reporting that I'd been anywhere near the bow-and-arrow attack.

And I definitely didn't want them to see what I was about to do next.

Like Yasmin had said, I was resourceful. Already, I was planning my escape from Hotemet.

Moving swiftly, I raced past the spot where I'd started the fire. Ankle-high flames burned and hissed over the ground.

Already, Elan, Susie, and two other servants were out there trying to douse the flames. Unsurprisingly, Elan wavered on his feet, his eyes dazed as he gripped a bucket, and Susie was tripping over her own feet. As I watched them scrambling with buckets of water, I felt a twinge of guilt for dragging them out here.

Still, the icy rain was soaking everything around us. The fire wouldn't last long.

With the bubble of glamour around me, I hurried toward the yew grove. When I arrived, I pulled out my knife to begin carving a sapling. I wouldn't get far now, not when the magic was draining all of my resources, but I needed to make a start on it.

Tomorrow, the angels would know that someone had warned the humans. They'd know that I'd been out lurking in the forest, and that a human woman had been spotted marching into the woods with a crossbow. Adonis knew that I'd been lying through my teeth. It wouldn't take much for them to piece it all together.

I had to lay the groundwork for my own escape.

When I couldn't take any more of the glamour, I buried the beginnings of my bow and started back toward the castle.

Now my muscles burned, and pain ripped through my skull. A few times, my eyes drifted closed, and images flashed in my mind—Hazel and me, dressing up in boas and sequined gowns to take photos of ourselves, Marcus's sleepy eyes as he lay next to me in bed, my parents drinking coffee as they read the Sunday papers. And each time my mind cleared, the truth shocked me once again. Those days were over.

By the time I neared the fortress, the cold rain had soaked completely through my clothes, and the chill penetrated right down to my bones.

At the forest's edge, I peered through the branches once again. When the iron-gray skies looked clear of sentinels, I ran across the clearing toward an arched doorway in the wall of the Tower of Wrath, my head searing with pain.

Only when I'd safely sheltered in the alcove did I drop the glamour. With chattering teeth, I pushed through the door, glancing nervously at the iron bar still on the ground.

My mind seemed to whirl with shadows. Desperate to get back to my room, back to the warmth, I pulled off my sodden jacket.

Climbing the stairs, I leaned against the wall, trying to focus my mind, but I'd burnt myself out. I had a vague sense that I couldn't let anyone see me now—that I could barely keep the succubus glamour together. Apart from that, it was hard to grasp onto a clear thought.

My footsteps echoed off the walls, and I tried to count the floors until I got to my own, five stories up.

When I thought I'd reached five, I pulled open the door to peer into the hall. It looked right to me—same creepy shadows, same empty alcoves.

Clutching my soaked jacket, I took a right toward my bedroom, so tired I could hardly tear my eyes off the floor, could hardly stand up on my own.

So tired I nearly missed the inky shadows that always seemed to curl around Adonis.

He stood before the door. Slowly, I dragged my gaze up to meet his frigid stare. His midnight wings, streaked with silver, swooped majestically behind him.

"It looks like you've had a rough afternoon. Something happen to your sweater?"

I leaned against the wall for support. The good news was, if he was here, it meant he wasn't off killing Yasmin's three-year-old daughter.

"I got lost." I couldn't stop my damned teeth from chattering, and I could hardly keep my succubus glamour on. I *needed* to get back into my room.

A wave of silky magic from his body rippled over my skin. "And you ripped apart your sweater to find your way home. It all makes perfect sense."

His lethally beautiful smile sent shivers through my blood. "It seems there was a bit of a commotion in the forest. Several flaming arrows ignited a few oaks. You wouldn't know anything about that, would you?"

I struggled to summon a coherent thought, to find my way out of this mess. I needed to get into that hot bath to warm up a little, and then I needed about fifteen hours of uninterrupted sleep. "Probably a stray human. Lots of people have learned to use arrows since the Great Nightmare began. No guns around here, are there?"

His eyes grew darker. "The Great Nightmare? Is that what you call it? It almost sounds like you don't approve."

I had about thirty seconds before I lost all ability to glamour myself. "Would you kindly get out of the way? I'm freezing and I need a bath."

"Of course. I wouldn't dream of standing in your way."

With his hands in his pockets, he stalked away, draped in shadows.

I opened the door to my room, practically falling inside. Stumbling forward, I didn't even make it to the bath. Instead, I collapsed on the bed, pulling the heavy covers around my freezing body.

* * *

I woke when sunlight streamed through the windows. I still wore the damp, ragged sweater from the day before. Pain throbbed in my arm, and I lifted my sleeve to find a brutal purple bruise spread out over my forearm. I pulled down my sleeve quickly. I couldn't let anyone see that.

The smell of pastry made my stomach rumble. Next to me, Susie had laid out a tray of steaming food on my bedside table.

It unnerved me that Susie came in here while I was sleeping, but I couldn't complain too much about hot coffee and pastries.

I sat up, snatching a warm croissant off the tray, and washed it down with hot, milky coffee.

One hot bath later, I stood in front of the bathroom mirror, my muscles tensed as I waited to see if Yasmin had survived the night. As soon as her face flickered into the reflection, I heaved a sigh of relief.

Yasmin held up a sign that said, "Thank you. We evacuated," and another that said "Message sent to Hazel."

My heart began to race with euphoria. If they'd sent a message to Hazel, that meant they'd found her. And if they'd found her, it meant she was still alive. *Thank the gods.*

Now I just needed to wait to see if Kratos would make good on his word.

Yasmin's image shimmered away. I had no idea where The Institute hid now, but of course Yasmin wouldn't tell me. If I knew, it meant the angels could torture me into confessing it. Not my favorite thing to think about.

As I crossed back into the bedroom, my mind burned with images of a reunion with Hazel. Would she throw her arms around my neck and cry? Would she ask to sleep in my bed with me?

I pulled open the wardrobe. I'd pretty much run out of clean sensible clothes, so I grabbed one of the flimsy gowns instead—a long, shimmering blue dress with a plunging neckline and fitted sleeves. Appropriate for the castle atmosphere, not so appropriate for ass-kicking, but with any luck that would not be on the agenda today.

When the sentinels weren't looking, I strapped the knife to my thigh. Now that it had been dipped in Devil's Bane, I took care not to nick my own skin. If I did, I'd be facing an agonizing death instead of a reunion with my sister.

A loud knock on the door interrupted my thoughts, and I crossed the room to open it. When I did, I found Elan standing in the hallway in one of his knitted cat sweaters.

"Morning, Elan. How are you?"

He stood hunched, his fingers steepled. "Bit of a headache from yesterday."

"Drink some water. You'll be fine."

He smiled. "I have my own hangover remedy. I drink the blood from two feuding crows. Anyway, umm…" He tapped his fingertips together. "Johnny is agitated about something, and he wants to see you on the parapet. He seems a little murderous."

My mouth went dry. Oh good. One of the insane angels would like to throw me to my death this morning. "I'll just grab my croissant."

* * *

With my coat draped over my shoulders, I trailed after Elan, croissant flakes flying all over me. "Any idea what this is about?"

"You know, he didn't want to tell me. Just, it's probably not a good idea to get too close to him. Physically or emotionally…"

I followed Elan into the stairwell. "Fortunately, emotional closeness with Johnny wasn't high on my agenda today."

As we walked up the stairs, a strange, giddy power rippled through my blood. *Eimmal.* That's why I wasn't quite as scared as I should be.

"Elan, my little feral fae. What do you plan to do to safeguard yourself tomorrow?"

"I'll probably ask Susie to tie me to a chair, just to be on the safe side," he said cheerfully. "It's how I spent my formative years in the troll encampment anyway, so I really don't mind. Bit of nostalgia."

I frowned. I didn't suppose I could ask Susie to do the same for me without arousing some serious suspicion. Maybe I could lock myself in the wardrobe for the day, free from the prying eyes of sentinels or angels.

After our long ascent, we reached the top floor at last, and Elan pushed through the door into the icy air.

Pearly winter light washed over the parapet, and the scent of early spring filled me with a wild giddiness.

Johnny leaned against one of the stone walls, his gaunt form and gray wings reminding me more than ever of a vulture. He wore a tattered, safety-pinned T-shirt that read *Destroy.* His bright blue mohawk stood out sharply against the gray castle walls. A bow and quiver lay at his feet.

What fresh hell is this?

A sneer curled his lip. "Ruby."

"Good morning, Johnny."

"I heard the rumors. You killed a human man before you came here, is that right?"

"We've been over this. He deserved it. Is there anything else, or can I get back to my coffee?"

"And you want me to believe you don't really care about humans." His breath reeked of vodka, and his words were slightly slurred. "You want us to believe you have nothing to do with a human organization like The Institute. That about right?"

I clenched my fists. Maybe the gift of vodka had backfired a bit, because I now found myself faced with a trashed and angry angel. "That's entirely right."

"It's just that it seems a bit funny to me. We were about to go on a bit of a rampage, you see. Or at least Adonis was. Had a bit of slaughtering to do with the humans." He picked up the bow from the ground. "But by the time he got to the Tower—poof! Everyone was gone. How do you think that happened, then? How did they know we were coming, succubus?"

He stumbled closer to me, and wild hunger bloomed in my gut. I clutched my belly, trying to ignore the gnawing emptiness.

From the corner of my eye, I saw Elan skulking away, hoping no one would notice him.

I crossed my arms. "I don't know, Johnny. Maybe they figured they'd attacked the angels, and they needed to move out before you came for them. Just a thought."

"Yeah, or maybe the sudden information leaks have to do with the new presence of the street demon we just let into the castle. How about that?"

I leaned on the parapet. Inside, adrenaline was surging through my nerve endings, but I blinked lazily in the morning sunlight as though none of this concerned me. "That's an interesting theory. Tell me, Johnny, does thinking strain your brain? I feel like it physically hurts when you do it."

"You know what else is an interesting theory? The one that says you were living in London in one of the rookeries with a bunch of humans, eating rats. I've been querying the sentinels, asking them about everything they might know, every ginger tart they've seen in the past year. They tell me a little skinny redhead was living among the filth. That wouldn't happen to be you, would it?"

I shot him my most imperious stare. "Do I look like someone who would live among filthy humans?"

"Let's find out. Because it just so happens I found those humans." A smile twisted his lips. "Why don't you take a peek into the courtyard?"

All at once, the spring giddiness rushed from my body, replaced instead with panic clawing up my spine. Where was Kratos? And what the hell did Johnny have in mind?

I crossed to the other side of the parapet, and when I peered over the edge, my stomach dropped.

There, in the courtyard, three humans stood on a gallows. Katie, Lucy, and Alex stared up at me, eyes wide, mouths gagged. Thick nooses had been tied around their necks.

I swallowed hard. *This is not good.*

"You tried to convince us you're no good with a bow and arrow," he continued. "But I'm going to give you a little test, succubus. I'm going to hang these three humans, who you say you don't know. If you truly don't care about humans, you can watch them choke to death at the end of a rope. If you're so shit with a bow and arrow, there will be nothing you can do about it anyway."

Panic sunk its claws into my heart. *Oh. Shit.*

CHAPTER 35

Johnny took another step closer to me. With him standing so near, raw hunger seemed to eat at me from the inside out—a void that could never be filled. I wanted to get away from him.

Instinctively, I took a step back.

A million thoughts raced through my mind as I considered my options. I had the knife of Nyxobian silver strapped to my thigh. If I went full fae and acted swiftly enough, I could pull the knife from its sheath. I could slit Johnny's throat, poisoning him with the Devil's Bane. He'd be unconscious for a while.

But that would leave us seriously screwed, wouldn't it? How would I get my three friends out of here before the other two angels descended and killed us all?

I tried to push away my whirling emotions and think rationally. What was my ethical obligation here?

It was like the old moral test—a man is tied to one branch of a train track, and five are on the other branch. The train is headed for the group of five. Do you pull the lever and switch the train's trajectory?

There was supposed to be a right answer, I thought. You were supposed to kill the one guy, saving the five. Never mind that I wanted more information. What if the five people were Nazis, or had painful terminal illnesses? You weren't supposed to think about that. It was supposed to be a numbers game—kill the one to save the many.

And right now, before me, I had a numbers game. Three human lives for the lives of the many I could potentially help by collaborating with The Institute.

By this point, all the euphoria of Eimmal had rushed right out of my system, and fear gnawed at my ribs.

"Are you ready to watch them die?" asked Johnny. "Don't worry. Their necks won't snap, so you'll get to watch them suffocate slowly. A miserable death, really."

"I really don't care," I said hollowly, my hands shaking.

Johnny handed me the bow and the quiver of arrows, and I worked to still the shaking in my hands as I took them from him.

"Put the quiver on," he ordered.

My legs were shaking as I followed his instructions, sliding the quiver onto my back.

Sacrifice them for the greater good, I told myself. *You can save many more lives if you don't blow your cover here.*

I just couldn't stop myself from thinking about how much we'd been through together—the cold, starving nights, the gangs, our little shared garden. Our nights of keeping sane by telling stories around the fireplace. We were survivors—all of us.

"Let the show begin!" shouted Johnny. He flicked his wrist, and the trapdoor descended from the bottom of the gallows.

My heart thundered in my chest.

He'd lowered the trapdoor just enough so that they were choking slowly, their tiptoes straining against the wood below them.

Weakness shook my legs. It wasn't just a numbers game, was it? It was stupid to pretend emotions played no part in moral decisions. I wasn't a machine.

Fury raced through my body, and I nocked an arrow, my arm still searing from where I'd injured it yesterday. I loosed the arrow, and it struck Alex's rope. I shot off my arrows rapid-fire, and after three hits to his rope, the thing snapped. Alex fell through the trap-door. I was already reaching for the next arrow, unleashing a rapid volley until Katie, then Lucy fell through the trapdoor to the earth below.

I lowered my bow, turning to look at Johnny.

I'd just completely blown my cover, and the punk angel now glared down at me.

"Well, well, well. The succubus cares about humans."

I racked my mind for a way to get out of this that would still be in character. Trembling all over, I cocked a hip. "Listen, Johnny. It's been a long time since I've fed from humans, and I didn't see any reason to waste perfectly good resources. The human male looked tempting."

He snarled, "Explain to me your sudden prowess with the bow."

I shrugged. "I've had four thousand years to practice. So I held back a bit in our demon battle. I just wanted to see what you flying vultures were capable of."

Johnny snarled, stepping closer until his tall form loomed over me, leaving me in shadow. "Thing is, love, I really don't believe you, do I? I can see it in your eyes. You're lying."

Adonis yesterday, Johnny today.

I was well and truly fucked at this point. If I made it off this parapet alive, I'd sneak out of here and find my way back to the rook-eries as soon as I could.

My stomach tightened. *But then I'd never see Hazel again.*

A shadow swooped above us, and I glanced up at Adonis's form soaring lower, his midnight wings gleaming in the morning sunlight.

Oh sweet earthly gods. My morning wasn't about to get any better, was it? Johnny already thought I was guilty—and Adonis was about to confirm it.

My heart thundered as the Dark Lord landed. I glanced over the parapet one more time at my human friends, watching them scramble out from under the gallows, arms tied behind their backs. This must have been terrifying for them.

Adonis's footsteps turned my head.

A smile ghosted across his beautiful features. "Please don't tell me you decided to have a slaughter party without inviting me. Honestly, I'm insulted."

Johnny's eyes were positively murderous. "I have a little theory about our street demon."

Adonis leaned against the parapet, folding his arms. "Oh? Indulge me."

"I think she's the very ginger tart the sentinels saw wandering around East London. Mind you, they said she wasn't a succubus, and she was a bit skinnier, but what the hell do they know?"

I offered a sympathetic grimace. "He's been at the vodka."

Johnny pointed at the courtyard. "And I think she was living with those humans down there—the ones she just saved with her considerable aim. And what's more, I think she's the reason all the humans evacuated the Tower yesterday. You wouldn't by any chance have seen her wandering about the woods yesterday, would you?"

Adonis's pale eyes slid to me, and an icy shiver ran over my skin. This wasn't turning out well for me.

He seemed to be studying me, assessing me. "Mmm. No. In fact, before my visit to the Tower, I was in my room all day. As it happens, Ruby was with me. You know, Kratos wasn't lying about her dancing."

Johnny and I both stared at him.

What the hell? He was covering for me?

"She was with you?" Johnny repeated. "The whole day?"

His lips curled in a wicked smile. "Did you know that a succubus can get herself into positions I've never seen another creature achieve?"

I nearly decked him, but I held back.

"Kratos won't like that," Johnny slurred. "He resents the fact that you can't fall yet."

Adonis shrugged slowly. "Probably best you don't tell him about what I was up to."

Johnny scratched his head. "Why did she save the humans, then?"

Adonis shrugged again. "Demons get annoyed when we kill their food. Let me take care of the humans."

Johnny didn't look like he was ready to let this go. "And her sudden skill with the bow and arrow? How do you explain that?"

Adonis blinked. "Johnny, of course she's always been skilled." He spoke slowly, as if Johnny were a particularly dull child. "A demon's not going to give away her gifts around the angels unless she needs to, is she? Any skilled warrior would have done the same."

I just stared at him. What exactly did he have planned here?

Johnny shot me a sharp look. "Just because you were stripping in front of the Dark Lord yesterday, don't think this leaves you in the clear. Maybe you're not guilty of this particular leak, but I don't trust you."

"Your opinion is noted. Can I keep the bow?"

"No." He snatched it from my hands, then stalked off, gray wings trailing behind him.

Adonis was still leaning against the parapet, his powerful magic humming over my body, curling luxuriously over my skin. His expression suggested this whole thing was hilarious to him.

I tapped the stone, trying to mentally block out the plight of my friends still bound and gagged in the courtyard below. I needed to stop Adonis from executing them. "I was stripping for you yesterday, was I?"

He cocked his head. "I could see your hands shaking from above. Even high in the air, your fear washed over my skin. I thrive on terror, did you know that? It feeds me. Yours tasted exquisite."

I swallowed hard. There wasn't much left I could say at this point. I dropped the act. "What do you want? Why did you help me?"

"I'd ask you to tell me the truth, but I suspect you'd sooner eat your own entrails."

An icy wind whipped over the stone walls, toying with his dark hair, and his gray-blue eyes glinted in the bright light. "You want me to let your human friends live? Come to my room tonight after dinner."

My mouth went dry. "For what? I'm not stripping for you. That's not the kind of dancing I do…" I bit my lip. "Well, that's part of it, but not like you think."

He shook his head slowly. "Is that any way to treat someone who just helped you?"

"*Why* did you help me?" All I knew was that he had something sinister planned. "And what are you going to do with them?"

"Because now you owe me, and I'll get them somewhere safe."

"But what do you want from me?"

His gaze raked over my body in a sensual caress. "Maybe you were right. Maybe men like me like to have control over beautiful things."

I shivered, hugging myself tightly. What the hell had I gotten myself into?

That heartbreakingly beautiful smile curled his lips again. "I was told you can dance. I want to see it. And I don't think you have much choice, do you? Unless you want me to kill your friends." He stalked off with that infuriating, languid ease.

An icy shudder rippled up my spine. Two out of three angels now suspected me of betrayal.

Now I had two projects for today: make myself a burlesque costume for some sort of performance for the Dark Lord; and finish carving my bow and arrows from the yew grove. I had a terrible feeling I'd be needing them soon.

CHAPTER 36

*I*n the yew grove, I scaled the rowan—an ancient, gnarled tree with a single silver branch at the top. A gift from the Old Gods.

From a window, I'd watched as Adonis had led my friends out into the forest. Was it stupid to hope that Adonis would keep his word? I hadn't wanted to seem too desperate by demanding details from him.

I grunted as I pulled my way to the top of the tree, using the rowan's knots and branches. As I hoisted myself up, the wound in my arm burned. The archery wound hurt like a bitch, but at least Yasmin had gotten out okay.

And now I was working on that gleaming silver branch. This could be the key to the angels' downfall, right here in the yew grove. Maybe Adonis had even been trying to protect it.

I winced as I hoisted myself higher.

I had one guess as to what I was supposed to do with a silver branch—and it happened to be something I was very good at. I needed to make it into weapons, and then use them to kill the angels.

Weirdly enough, I felt a flicker of guilt at the idea of killing Kratos, and even Adonis. Must be some sort of Stockholm syndrome taking effect.

I reached the top—the rowan branch that blended into silver at the end. I peered down from the boughs at the wintry ground below, dizzy from the height. My pulse began to race. One false move and my skull would smash against the cold earth.

Straddling it, I shimmied along the branch until the rowan's bark smoothed over to silver. Here, the tree was about eight inches in diameter—not thick enough for me to feel well-supported. And definitely not thick enough for me to feel great about taking one hand off the branch to reach for my knife.

Still, it's not like I had access to a ladder or a cherry picker in Hotemet Castle.

Clenching my teeth hard, I reached down for the knife strapped to my thigh.

My plan was simply to sever the branch here and see what I could do to fashion it into arrows, knives—anything that could be used to kill. But as soon as I brought the knife down to the branch's surface, the tree's ancient magic began seeping into my body, and light whirled around me.

Even with just the tip of my knife in the tree's branch, my body began to tremble with an overwhelming power. This was a magic so ancient, it had bloomed and grown before language. I wanted to taste it, to touch it, to bathe in it. But as I slipped my knife deeper into the branch, it started to overwhelm me, snapping and buzzing through my body in a riot of power until I could hardly remember my name.

Light. Light all around me. The branch blazed with a blinding force —a divine magic, sublime and terrifying.

With my knife sticking into the branch, I was tapping into a raw source of magic, both dreadful and breathtaking. *I'm not ready, not ready.*

The power awestruck me. With the stupefying display of blinding light around me, the Old Gods were delivering a message in their own wordless way.

Stop. This way, madness lies.

I pulled my knife from the tree branch, and the light around me dulled. I sucked in a few shaking breaths, my entire body trembling.

Whatever the Old Gods wanted me to do with the silver branch, hacking it off with a knife of Nyxobian silver wasn't it.

Okay. Okay. I'll leave you alone for now.

I slid my knife back into its holster and slowly began shimmying my way back along the branch, my body still vibrating with that strange power.

I still had weapons to finish from the yews, and as long as I dipped them in Devil's Bane, I could use them to disable the angels.

But soon enough, I needed to find out exactly what I was supposed to do with the silver branch.

* * *

I'D SPENT the rest of the afternoon carving my ordinary yew weapons in the forest. When I'd finished, I'd laced the tips with Devil's Bane, ready to pierce an angel's flesh. Then I'd buried them in the woods, keeping them safe from prying castle eyes.

Kratos had invited me to join him for dinner, and I'd dressed in a distractingly low-cut gown—crimson and gold, his favorite colors.

What exactly did I want to distract him from? For one thing, there was the fact that I'd spent all day trying to develop weapons that could kill him, and for another, there was my evening dance date with Adonis.

Across from him at the dinner table, I took a long sip of wine. I couldn't drink too much, but I needed to calm my nerves tonight. At least my stomach had been lined with a sumptuous meal.

Kratos's copper eyes burned into me, as though he could read my secrets. After a while, a distracting gown wouldn't be enough to hide what I really was. Still, he looked relaxed in his wooden chair, his wings not in appearance tonight. He wore finely cut clothing in a deep red fabric, golden rings glinting on his fingers.

As he studied me, his body radiated light. "Don't worry, Ruby. We'll find a way to hunt down the demons and humans connected to the attack. You'll be safe here."

I forced a smile, lifting my glass. *For the love of the gods, just leave them alone.* "I'm sure they're not much of a threat. They seemed so easily killed."

If he wanted to know who the real threat was, it was his dinner guest.

A muscle twitched in Kratos's jaw. "The attackers never should have gotten so close to you."

I sipped my wine slowly. "Do you have any leads on where The Institute went?"

His fingers tightened around his wineglass. "Not yet. But we'll find them."

"What about my sister?"

"I'm sorry. We haven't been able to find her. My men are still looking."

I tried to push away the disappointment. At least I knew she was alive.

I leaned back in my chair, my belly full of venison pie. It was only a matter of time before Johnny tried to poison Kratos against me, and that meant I had to get in there first. Right now I had an important seed to plant with Kratos.

I sighed deeply, pushing my glass away. "I probably shouldn't have too much to drink. I hardly touch the stuff."

"Oh?"

"Well, in times like this, when we're under attack by demons, you need to keep your wits about you, don't you? The earthly gods will exploit any weaknesses they can find."

He frowned. "Funny that you mention that. I found Johnny passed out among three empty bottles of vodka in one of the hallways today."

I raised my eyebrows as if surprised. "Well, I'm not suggesting that's how The Institute knew you were coming…"

"What do you think happened?" he asked.

I shrugged. "All I know is that the earthly gods, like Nyxobas, can take many forms, and it wouldn't be difficult for one of them to pry secrets out of a drunken angel. Of course, it could have been *anything,* and I don't want to blame Johnny."

Kratos nodded gravely. "I need to keep him away from the alcohol."

"It's not a bad idea. With magic as powerful as he has, he could be a danger to himself, you know."

Kratos pushed his wineglass away. "Enough of this bleak discussion." He stood, holding out his hand to me. "Before I leave for my hunt, I have something I want to show you."

With my hand in his, he led me into the hall. Kratos was the one powerful being here who still trusted me, and I had to do everything I could to keep him intrigued with me. As we walked, I let my arm brush against him, and his gaze slowly slid to mine. The expression on his face was purely carnal. This angel wanted to fall *bad*.

He led me through the torchlit corridor until we arrived at a set of oak doors inset into the wall. He pulled open a door, revealing an expansive room with a wooden floor, a mirrored wall—and a bar across the mirror.

A strange flicker warmed my chest. He'd built a *dance studio* in his castle for me.

Was he actually, genuinely, being kind to me? How did I reconcile this with the fact that he was a murderous maniac?

Maybe it was the fact that Eimmal was coming up the next day, the fae spring fever beginning to heat my blood, but I suddenly felt an uncontrollable urge to dance. My body seemed to strain against the confines of my clothes. What sort of wild temptations would torment Kratos if he watched me engage in my favorite activity, my body glowing with pleasure?

I smiled at him. "Thank you, Kratos."

Maybe I had just thought of a good way to keep him distracted from his apocalyptic hobbies.

I ran my fingertips up his arm, watching his body tense. "Soon, I want you to watch me dance."

* * *

IN THE CANDLELIGHT, I threaded a needle with white string. I'd be keeping tonight's activities under wraps.

Already, I'd blown out the candles in the bedroom and snuffed out the fire, which of course had scared the shit out of me. I'd placed Fake Ruby in the bedclothes to confuse the sentinels.

Then I'd hidden myself in the toilet alcove where the sentinels couldn't see me, and I'd begun working on my costume in the candlelight. For tonight's performance, I had no sequins or proper wigs. Just a sewing kit I'd gotten from Susie, and the makeup that I'd brought with me in my quiver.

I curled another loop of white fabric, then pinned it down to the silky base. Carefully, I began sewing the loop shut. When I finished, I'd have something approximating a wig—except one made from fabric. It was the best I could do.

When I used to dance on the stage, I'd been in control. Some people called burlesque stripping—and yes, taking your clothes off was part of the act. But *stripping* usually meant something else—a business transaction where the dancer has to please individual customers.

When I put on a burlesque show, it was like any other performance—I controlled the production, the stage. The audience was full of both men and women, and I didn't get too close to any of them. Didn't matter if any particular individual was happy with the act. As long as people kept buying tickets night after night, I got paid.

I kind of thought of it as art. I chose the music, the costumes, the dance routine. It *might* be sexy, it might be funny, it might be aggressive—or it could be downright disturbing. I had an act about a repressed Victorian woman with hysteria, one about President Lincoln, and one about Harry Potter. I even had a Mario Kart act.

A few times in Massachusetts, I'd performed a routine about the Salem witch trials: sexy Cotton Mather dancing to a Tom Waits song —*Dead and Lovely.*

For this private show? I was still sewing my costume exactly the way *I* wanted it, even if I only had sliced-up dresses to work with. So even though I was about to perform for one man, alone in his room—

a man who'd said he wanted to control something beautiful—I still felt like I was running the show.

On Eimmal eve, I actually *needed* to dance, and a powerful desire to move my body pulsed through me.

Already, my skin was heating with excitement, my heart racing faster. In just twelve hours, I'd devolve into a completely wild beast. Tonight, hopefully, I could keep things under control in Adonis's room.

On top of the urge to dance, I was kind of looking forward to the fact that Adonis was getting my Cotton Mather routine. *You want to watch me dance? How sexy do you find a Puritan judge?*

Tonight, I didn't have any pasties or tassels, and I didn't want them. I wore a long black gown, with a shorter black dress under it. Even though my neckline plunged, I'd fashioned a white Puritan collar to go around the top. And under both of those, I wore the poison-tipped knife strapped to my thigh.

I sewed another loop shut, straining my eyes in the dim candle-light. The only other thing I'd need tonight would be music. I hadn't told Susie why I needed it, but from Johnny's collection, she'd rummaged up a cassette player. Tonight, I'd be dancing to Tears for Fears' *Mad World.*

With the last curling white loop sewn, I pulled the wig on over my red hair, tucking in the crimson strands. I smiled at myself in the reflection. Despite the weirdness of the evening, for the first time in forever, I actually *wanted* to dance.

I grabbed my cassette player and my witch-trial victim off the floor—a broom, with a severe Puritan face taped to the front. I called my drawing *Goody Brown*—a generic victim of Cotton Mather.

I grinned. "All right, Goody Brown. Ye olde show must go on."

As I crossed into the darkened bedroom, a wave of fear slammed into me, and I hurried through it. *Still afraid of the stupid dark.*

With one eye on the windows for sentinels, I tucked myself into the corner by the door, my heart beating hard. I focused on the light I could see—the moonlight washing over the room, gleaming off candlesticks, highlighting the floor. I steadied my breathing.

After a few painful minutes, the sentinel passed. With a racing pulse, I pulled open the door to the hallway.

Moving swiftly, I skulked through the drafty hallway, taking care to hide from the sentinels' prying eyes. As I moved, anticipation lit up my body.

Tonight, on Eimmal eve, the air vibrated with an ancient magic. Maybe it was the power of the Old Gods, skimming and humming over my skin. Already, I was feeling the call to reconnect with the earth, to lose myself in the soil and moss, the hellebore and blackthorn. Eimmal was a day to binge on euphoria.

As I stalked through the corridor, my silk gown skimmed luxuriously against my legs. I hummed the Tears for Fears song to myself, my heart pounding rhythmically to the tune.

Given the excitement in my blood tonight, I *definitely* had to lock myself away tomorrow, or I'd end up running through the woods covered in nothing but hemlock boughs and a smile.

By the time I reached Adonis's room in the Tower of Ash, I could practically smell the vernal power curling through the air.

I knocked on Adonis's door.

He opened it a moment later. Even without his wings in appearance, the full force of his heartbreaking beauty hit me like a hurricane wind. Candlelight danced over the striking planes of his face, gilding him. It had to be Eimmal heightening his allure, bringing out the silver flecks in his stormy eyes.

Right?

This close to Adonis, the magic in the air felt different—deadly and seductive at the same time.

Something like amusement twinkled in his deep eyes. "Beautiful wig," he purred, then glanced at my broom Puritan. "You didn't mention you'd be bringing a friend."

"You want to let me in before the sentinels see me?"

He opened the door wider. "Right, I nearly forgot. You're a prisoner here."

Shadows swarmed in the air around him, sending a lick of fear up my spine. In his presence, some of that vernal giddiness subsided, and the hair rose on the back of my neck. When I stepped into the room, the door seemed to close by itself behind me.

I glanced nervously at the windows, the curtains drawn back.

"The sentinels will see me in here," I pointed out.

"I can't imagine why they'd be interested."

I glared at him. "Kratos told me not to come here. I wasn't supposed to leave my tower." *And Kratos is the only person here who trusts and protects me.*

His eyes blazed. "Don't worry, little succubus. I told you I'd keep you safe."

Like hell he would.

CHAPTER 37

*A*donis sat on his bed, leaning back on his hands. "Well? I can't wait to see what you have in store for me. It's not every day I have a succubus dressed as a Puritan in my room. And I'd *love* to see what you have planned for that broom."

I glared at him. "I'm dressed as Cotton Mather, to be specific. One of the figures in the witch trials."

He nodded. "I'm familiar with his death work."

"Tell me, Adonis. Are you particularly interested in burlesque, or do you just like exerting control over people?"

"Mostly the latter, and it's particularly delicious to exert control over a succubus. Plus, it will annoy Kratos." A tinge of venom underscored his voice.

Now *that* was an interesting admission. "Why would you want to annoy Kratos?"

"Come now, Ruby. When you've lived for as long as we have, you find ways to amuse yourself."

He wasn't telling me the whole story, but I couldn't trust a thing he said anyway.

Best get this night over with.

I leaned down, pressing *play* on the cassette player. As soon as the drum machine started, the rhythmic spirit of Eimmal pulsed through my body.

I grabbed my broom Puritan off the floor, launching into the dance. The music filled me, rumbling through my blood. Soon every step was falling into the right place, every movement imbued with a perfect surety as I twirled over the flagstones.

As my body twisted and writhed to the music, I lost myself in the role of Cotton Mather and his forbidden love—a sinful prisoner in one of his cells. Cotton, you see, was tormented by lust for his witch captive, even though the fusty old pervert wouldn't admit it to himself.

Unacknowledged desires happened to be my favorite theme.

As I stroked the broom, my only regret was that I hadn't adopted the role of the prisoner. Call me crazy, but I kind of related to her a lot right now.

In fact, I didn't want to be Cotton, didn't want the wig on anymore. I pulled it off, shaking out my red hair. The collar came off next.

To the pulsing rhythms, I threw myself into the dance, filled with a sense of pure, powerful freedom I hadn't felt in years. I was fully *fae* again, a creature of the soil and moss, honeysuckles and apples, and the darker things too: an arrow through the air, teeth piercing flesh, a necklace made of bones. A heart pounding like a war drum.

A thrill rippled through me as I stretched my leg high into the air, giving a full view of upper thigh—the one without a knife strapped to it.

And as Adonis watched, the ancient power of the fae lit up my body. This is what it meant to be fae—to be me.

Humans could be stupid about the human body. They wanted women covered up; they valued virginity. I had no idea why. Their lives were so short, and they had no idea how to enjoy them.

As I danced, my movements felt precise, every footfall landing in the right place, every sinuous twist of my arms exactly the way nature intended it. Slowly, I ran my fingertips down my ribcage, my hips swaying languidly to the music.

Time for the long dress to come off.

I shouldn't have looked at him as I peeled off my long gown, but his gaze drew mine like a magnet.

He was a monster, and I should have hated him looking at me. And yet, for some reason, I didn't mind his eyes on me. It was weird, but in his beautiful features, I found an expression I'd never seen on him before. It wasn't his usual wry amusement, wasn't boredom or disdain. Instead, I saw intense curiosity.

If I wasn't mistaken, I saw lust there, too. In fact, he was gripping the edge of his bed with an alarming ferocity, and his inky magic coiled sensually around his body.

See, Adonis? You're not the only pretty thing around.

What was he thinking about right now? As I twisted my hips, I had a strong suspicion that he was envisioning exactly what I looked like under the black fabric that hugged my body.

Poison hemlock, I reminded myself. I *definitely* had to stay away from him tomorrow, or I'd end up dead.

Under the powerful thrum of his magic whispering over my skin, I'd become *Angela Death* again.

At last, the song ended with me lying on the cold flagstones. And yet, I hadn't wanted it to end. I wanted to keep dancing into spring, until Kratos found my sister and brought her back to me, until we could run off into the woods together.

My heart hammered hard against my ribs. I blinked to clear my thoughts, then sat up.

From his spot on the bed, Adonis stared down at me.

I curled my knees into my chest. "I danced for you. Am I done now? Have I met the demands of your bargain?"

"Quite beautifully."

A thin sheen of sweat covered my body as I looked up at him. I'm not sure what compelled me to ask the question, but the next words out of my mouth were, "What happens if you fall?"

"I don't think you'd like the results," he said. "Not only would I become a demon, but the Heavenly Host would come to Earth to finish our jobs for us."

Oh. Shit. So luring the angels to their fall *wasn't* an option?

Adonis leaned back on his bed. "Lucky for me, my curse hasn't taken effect yet. Kratos has spent his whole life under its control. I do believe the sight of you undressed would drive him completely mad, but you'd be stupid to tempt him unless you want to destroy every living creature on Earth."

I swallowed hard. It was a good thing I was learning about this now—assuming Adonis was telling the truth.

"If Kratos fell, the entire Earth would be destroyed?" I repeated.

"So you'd best keep your dresses on around him."

A cold breeze shivered over my skin, bringing with it the first glimmers of spring. My skin heated, and a thrill bloomed in my chest, making it hard for me to focus. I needed to keep my senses clear tonight.

I rose from the floor and crossed to his windows, the magic of the dance still soaring through my blood. I pulled the curtains shut. Since Adonis seemed willing to talk right now, I had before me an opportunity to learn more about these angels.

Leaning against the windows, I crossed my arms. "And you can't fall at all until, what... some curse takes effect?"

"Yes."

"I can't imagine what you'd be like after a fall. You seem evil enough already."

His body had gone eerily, inhumanly still. He reminded me of a beautiful statue of Lucifer I once saw.

"What have you seen me do that's so evil?" he asked.

I opened my mouth to list his litany of offenses—but I didn't have much. Mostly, it was the fact that he terrified everyone, and what he'd done to the redcaps. Though maybe they deserved it. "It's not what I've seen you do. I've heard that you spread death across the world, that you're an angel of the apocalypse. And that you hate the fae in particular." The last words were out of my mouth before I could stop them.

He stood, lazily prowling closer to me. As he closed in on me, the scent of myrrh coiled around me, raising goosebumps on my skin.

"Why would you care if I hate the fae?"

I shrugged. "Just curious about whatever trauma you might have. When you're as old as we are, you have to find some way to amuse yourself. Surely you know that."

A smile ghosted over his beautiful lips for just a moment before the air thinned around us. When he spoke again, his voice was a low rumble. "Because, my little succubus, they can't control themselves. They're beasts with divine powers. Abominations."

My breath was coming faster. "Control is a big thing for you, isn't it?"

His eyes burned like stars. "Of myself, yes. Without it, the world falls apart."

Okay, that sounded… ominous.

My breath hitched in my throat. "Why?"

"Tell me who those humans were. The ones that I let live."

I made my expression blank. "I have no idea."

He shook his head slowly. "Is that any way to repay my generosity? I saved the lives of your friends, and you lie to me." He shrugged, an elegant gesture. "I don't suppose I could persuade you to tell me one true thing about yourself."

He could, actually. "I'm looking forward to when Kratos brings my sister back. She was taken by the dragons."

He snorted. "And you actually think he'd do that?"

Fear gripped my heart. "Why wouldn't he?"

"Because your sister's absence means you need him. You're dependent on him, and he likes that. He doesn't know you're pretending to be something you're not."

A heavy silence hung in the air.

As he took another step closer, he narrowed his eyes, studying me closely. "Did you know that I'm something of an expert in pain?"

I swallowed hard. "I had that impression."

"I can see it in your eyes. And when you danced, too. The way you moved your arms—it was graceful and sensual, but they didn't move quite the same."

He reached for one of my wrists, gently lifting my sleeve. His touch sent a thrilling shiver through my body. It took me a moment to realize what he was exposing—the deep, purple bruise on the inside of my arm. The one I'd gotten from shooting arrows.

Oops.

He pinned me with his gaze. Then, shockingly gently, he raised my wrist to his lips. He pressed his warm, sensual mouth to my bruise. Heat raced through my body as Adonis's silky magic whispered around me, and his kiss pulled the pain from my arm, his tongue flicking against my skin.

His lips moved against my exposed forearm, and a shock of euphoria raced through my body, tempting me into the wild abandon of spring. Ecstasy washed over me. I tilted back my head as he worked his tongue over my skin. Liquid heat pooled in my core, and suddenly I felt too hot, too constrained by my dress, the desperation to pull off all my clothes nearly overtaking me.

Slowly, he pulled away from me, silver light sparking his eyes as he appraised my healed arm.

"There," he said huskily. "That's all better now."

The bruise had disappeared, but my knees felt weak. What would his mouth feel like on mine?

He smiled lazily. "I won't bother asking why you had an archery injury."

I couldn't remember how to put a coherent sentence together, so I just stared at him.

As I did, something slammed into the room, wood splintering all around us.

Kratos stood in the doorway, amber light radiating from his body, his eyes burning like the sun.

CHAPTER 38

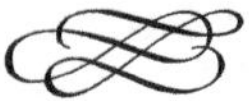

Slowly, I took a step away from Adonis. I scrambled for something to say. I needed Kratos on my side to get Hazel back, even if Adonis didn't think it was going to happen.

I blinked innocently. "I hurt my wrist falling down the stairs. Adonis told me he could heal it."

"I saw you dancing through my window," said Kratos.

Why did I have the sudden suspicion that Adonis had planned it all this way—that he'd known Kratos was still here, that he'd wanted Kratos to see me?

Rage rippled through my body, but I schooled my features to calm. "He had a price for the healing, of course."

Kratos's gaze burned into Adonis. "Ruby." His voice was terrifyingly calm. "Please get back to your room."

As I passed first Adonis, then Kratos, words whispered in my mind. *You're a prisoner here.*

* * *

I'M NOT sure what had happened after I left Adonis's room; I only knew that I'd woken on Eimmal morning with a wild fury pulsing through my blood. I'd hardly been able to focus on my morning call with Yasmin, though it's not like she had anything helpful to convey to me anyway.

Today of all days, I needed to stay away from the angels. A distant song floated through the early spring air, the rhythms beating through my body.

I rose from my bed, practically overcome by the desire to pull off my nightgown and run outside.

When a pounding noise filled the room, for a moment I wasn't quite sure if it was the beating of my own heart or someone come to visit me.

Knock knock knock.

Barefoot, I crossed to the door. "Who is it?"

"Kratos." His voice boomed through the oak.

Shit. I needed to avoid him today. "I'm not feeling very well, Kratos. I'm going to stay in here today."

"I have some important news about your sister."

I yanked the door open immediately to find Kratos standing in the hall, dressed in his usual shades of maroon and gold. A powerful wave of Eimmal magic washed through me, and I had to fight the urge to run my hands over his chest. I gritted my teeth, biting down hard.

"What's the news?" I asked, unable to hide my desperation.

"I found her."

My eyes widened. "You found Hazel?"

"An envoy is bringing a succubus from a dragon lair in Scotland. She should be here by the end of the day."

Joy bloomed in my chest, so wildly that I nearly threw my arms around his neck. Adonis had been wrong. Kratos *had* been looking for her.

"Are you serious?" I asked in a whisper.

"From what I hear, she's quite the handful."

I frowned. "That doesn't sound like her."

"Long black curly hair, six inches taller than you, same porcelain skin. Demanded books for the journey."

I grinned. *Hazel.* "That's her." Euphoria raced through me, and I had to restrain myself from grabbing Kratos and embracing him. "She'll really be here tonight?"

"It seems that way."

Oh hell. If past experience could be relied on, Hazel wasn't quite as vulnerable to the effects of Eimmal as I was. She was just born with better restraint. But even so—keeping on the succubus mask wouldn't be easy for her. This was literally the worst day of the year for this transportation to happen.

Still, knowing that she was alive and headed for me filled me with a radiant joy. "Thank you, Kratos. I won't forget this," I said evenly, trying to keep my cool. "That does make me feel better."

Concern glinted in his eyes. "If you're not feeling well, should I send a healer for you?"

I shook my head. "I'll be fine. I just want to stay alone today. Please tell the servants to leave the food outside my door." *Because my door will be barred with iron.*

"Of course."

A sharp thrill snaked through my body as I closed the door.

Today, I'd be keeping the windows and doors shut—starting now.

I crossed to the wardrobe, where I pulled out a pair of gloves. I'd use them to pick up the iron bar for the door. Yesterday, I'd set the stage for my self-imposed imprisonment. I'd stolen an iron bar from a castle door, and in the cover of terrifying darkness, I'd nailed pieces of wood to the door to form—

I didn't know the word, and my mind began racing. *Latches? Loops? Bar holes! Iron bar hole thingies.*

I closed my eyes hard, trying to focus. *Holes for sticking things into. The lady part of the door.*

Shit. Eimmal had just started, and I was already losing it. I needed to quiet my thoughts.

I had the iron bar *brackets. I'll go with brackets.*

I slid the bar into the brackets, trying to tune in only to the sound of iron against wood, to the feel of the metal burning my skin through the leather gloves. Language was a prison of my own making—sensations would be my savior. I winced at the feel of the iron singeing my skin.

With the door barred, I needed to make sure I couldn't open it again. *Get rid of the gloves, Ruby.*

I crossed to the window, cranking it open just a fraction. As soon as I did, the Eimmal air slammed into me. My skull whirled with images of bonfires and hawthorn, a moonlit forest hunt, fingernails digging into dirt, heat swirling through bodies and that primal thrusting...

Drop the gloves, Ruby. Drop the damned gloves.

Trembling, I unclenched my fingers, watching the leather gloves flutter to the wintry earth like plucked moth wings.

I raised my eyes to the forest outside, and its song *called* to me.

I breathed in deeply, trailing my fingertips down the front of my body...

A wide-eyed sentinel drifted past my window, snapping me out of it.

Cold bath. Get in a cold bath.

I slammed the window shut, then rushed to the bathroom, where I turned on the cold water, filling the tub.

I pulled off my clothes, stepping into the frigid water as the bath filled, shivers rippling over my skin.

The icy water helped me think clearly again, strategically. Hazel was coming back tonight. Once she was here, once I could safely protect her in my room, maybe we could figure out together exactly what I was supposed to do with that silver branch.

There had to be *some* way to harness its power. Maybe using a Nyxobian blade was an anathema to the Old Gods. Nyxobas, after all, was an invasive god.

I settled deeper into my unpleasant, icy bath. This was good. This was working out well for me so far. As long as I kept myself locked in here behind the iron bar, with the windows locked and no fresh air in the room, maybe I could keep my sanity.

A banging noise from the bedroom had me jumping out of my skin. Someone was *pounding* on my door.

Johnny, maybe? It sounded like the pounding of a madman.

I rose from the bath, icy water dripping from my body, and grabbed a towel to dry myself off. "Hang on a minute!" I shouted.

"Let me in!" It was Elan's voice.

Wasn't he supposed to be tied up today?

I crossed the cold floor, clenching my jaw. "Not today, Elan. I'm not feeling well." *And I don't want to turn feral like you.*

A heavier banging shook the door, until the wood began to splinter. "Ruby! Let me in!"

I winced. What if he was actually in trouble? I didn't have an easy way to get the door open without my gloves, but—

Before I could hatch any sort of a plan, the top of the oak door splintered and shattered, and Elan's grinning face beamed at me from the other side. He reached over the top half off the door, forcefully sliding the iron bar through the brackets. As he did, the scent of burning flesh filled the air, and he yelped until it clanged to the floor.

What the fuck...

Wearing a tattered and stained cartoon cat sweatshirt, Elan beamed at me again as he pushed through the destroyed door. "Ruby!" He glanced down at his smoking hands. "That really hurt, but something drew me here."

I knew what it was. Usually on Eimmal, I felt the same wild desperation to be around other fae. I didn't want Elan to leave, even though this was the worst possible thing that could happen right now.

Well, there go all my best laid plans. I clutched my towel tighter. "I thought you were supposed to be chained up for the day."

"I broke the chains." He raised his hands to the ceiling. "Today is the first day of spring! And the gods are more powerful here. They're all around us, in the forest, the trees." He lowered his voice to a whisper. "The Old Gods."

Of course. I clenched my jaw, trying to keep control of myself. So *this* was why this Eimmal felt even more powerful than previous years.

"Elan," I said evenly. "I'm going into the bathroom to get dressed, and when I come out, I want you to be gone. And I want you to find a way to bar the door again, because I don't need your crazy fae ass busting in here again."

He went pale and nodded vigorously. "Of course. I don't know what drew me here. When I lived as a prisoner in the troll encampment, I always needed to be around other fae. No idea what compelled me to find a succubus. You must be an honorary fae."

Uncontrolled giddiness bubbled through my blood, and I crossed to the wardrobe. I violently yanked a dress off the hanger while Elan continued to babble about trolls. I took an extra moment to snatch my knife from the wardrobe too. *I will hunt with my hands today.*

In the bathroom, I strapped the knife to my thigh. Then, I pulled an emerald green gown over my naked body, luxuriating in the feel of the thin, silky fabric on my bare skin. I couldn't run around naked today, but maybe going commando would be a small concession to the old ways.

As the hem of my dress touched the stone floor, a wave of fresh air wafted into the room. It smelled of rowan trees and honeysuckle, and it smelled of joy.

Oh hell no.

I rushed into the bedroom, where Elan stood next to an open window, his eyes closed. "Don't you smell them? The Old Gods?"

Primal desire rumbled through my bones. The forest outside was calling to me.

He opened his dark eyes again, and they sparked with light. He pointed a bony finger at me. "You..." he breathed. "I know you're not a fae. But you're an honorary fae."

I lifted a finger to my lips. *Shhhhh...*

Elan lifted a finger to his own lips. *Shhhhh...*

I had to feel my bare feet in the soil, in the streams, had to feel the rowan bark against my skin, the flower petals and leaves brushing against my fingertips... had to feel the thrill of the hunt in the forest.

Even a fae doesn't live forever. It's a sin to deny oneself.

Elan stepped into the hall, beckoning me to go with him. "Honorary fae," he whispered.

Barefoot, we ran down the stone steps until Elan slammed into the barred door. Once again, he singed his skin pulling away the iron bar, but today, I knew he didn't feel any pain.

Today, we were blood and moss, earth and claws, creatures who'd gnaw on bones in a marshland.

And with the song of the forest thrumming through our bodies, we rushed out into the open air.

CHAPTER 39

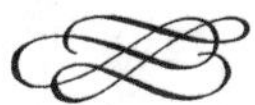

I spent hours running through the depths of the forest. When the sun fell lower behind the trees and the shadows stretched over the rich soil, my head began to clear a little.

Blood and berry juices stained my fingertips, and I paused by the stream to wash them off. As I did, I realized my mouth tasted faintly of blood, too. Was it my own?

I honestly had no idea. Either I'd been eating raw animals, or I'd bitten my tongue.

I winced. Hopefully I hadn't bitten Elan. Sometime during the day, I'd lost track of him, maybe around the time we'd chased a stag into a cave.

At the base of a hawthorn tree, I washed out my mouth with the clear spring water. When I finished, I looked down at my body, relieved to find that, throughout all the chaos, I'd managed to keep my succubus glamour intact, and the charcoal magic still shimmered around my body. At some point, I'd obviously jumped *into* the stream, because my wet dress now clung to my body.

Still, I couldn't feel the cold. Only that I was alive.

I'd made it through the day without revealing myself to the angels, without running into any of them—I hoped. And now I just had to wait until Hazel arrived here at the castle.

Maybe I could go inside and sit in a cold bath until the last waves of Eimmal dissipated from my body.

Another hot wave of euphoria rippled over my skin, and I dug my fingertips into the muddy earth by the stream, my mind spinning. I had the strangest desire to rub the mud all over myself…

Hastily, I plunged my hands into the cold water again. *Think strategically, Ruby. Get back to the castle. Clean up your room. Get everything in order for Hazel's arrival.*

My memory was hazy, but—had Elan broken the door this morning?

I forced myself up, my body dripping with icy spring water.

Half in a daze, I began walking back to the castle, my feet crunching over leaves.

I was as prepared as I could be if suspicion continued to turn against me—weapons buried, tipped with poison. Seeds of doubt planted between Johnny and Kratos. I knew how to channel right into the power of the Old Gods, if only I was willing to risk my sanity. Which—let's face it—after today didn't seem like a super valuable commodity.

Even as I tried to think clearly, incoherent thoughts swarmed my mind as I stumbled toward the castle.

A sea of peat, a throne of blackthorn, bluebells beneath my fingertips, a stream flowing with wine...

I pulled open the oak door, then dragged myself up the stone stairs.

Lichen-covered bones, the beating heart of a stag...

I clenched my fists tighter, piercing my own skin. Maybe once inside, I could look out the window for signs of Elan.

When I reached my floor, I crossed into the hallway. As soon as I turned left, I glimpsed the destruction from earlier today—the shattered door, the splintered wood.

Well, there was a good chance Johnny had been drinking today. I could always blame him.

But as I crossed the threshold into my room, I saw an unmistakable swirl of inky magic and midnight wings gilded with amber flecks of dying sunlight.

Adonis was leaning against one of the bedposts in my room, his arms folded, a faint smile on his lips. "Interesting day, Ruby? I happened to walk past your room, and I saw the door smashed. Then I caught sight of you walking outside the fortress, barefoot and drenched. If I asked the sentinels what you were up to today, what would they tell me?"

Oh hell. Here we go.

I wasn't ready to see one of the angels yet, and the force of his heartbreaking beauty slammed into me. I stared at his golden skin, the stormy gray eyes that faded to midnight blue... I'd never seen anyone so beautiful in my life.

Snap out of it, Ruby, you idiot. I wasn't going to stand here and moon over one of these egomaniacal vultures.

As he walked closer to me, a seductive smile playing about his lips, I clenched my fists so tightly that I'm pretty sure my palms started bleeding.

So close to me, his magic electrified my body, making my back arch. I hated this effect he had on me, and as I stood there barefoot, naked apart from my drenched green gown, I felt gloriously naked before him.

Scavenger. Bird of prey. "Carrion bird," I said out loud, without really meaning to.

"Did you call me a carrion bird?" He shook his head slowly. "Oh, my lovely Ruby. And I thought we were getting along so nicely last night when you danced for me." His forehead crinkled. "Was I wrong to think that you liked the feel of my mouth on your skin?"

His words sparked a vivid memory, and an unwelcome, warm thrill rushed through my veins. Despite myself, a hot flush spread over my chest.

Before, when I'd been with Elan, I'd simply felt wild, maybe a little violent. Ready for a hunt.

Now—alone with Adonis's seductive magic—my body trembled

with anticipation for something else, every inch of my skin ripe and full as a rowan berry.

"I felt nothing," I managed. I took a step away from him, backing up against the stone wall.

Surprise flickered across his features. "Is something worrying you, Ruby?"

"No." It was a lie. Everything about him entranced and terrified me at the same time. As his magic rippled over me, I felt as awestruck as I had with my knife stuck into the silver rowan branch.

Staring at him, I shivered, goosebumps rising over my skin.

His gaze moved slowly over my body. "Why have you bathed in a river in February? You're freezing."

We'd left the window open earlier, and the forest wind rippled over my skin, cooling some of my fevered blood. I still couldn't think of what I needed to say to Adonis.

He took another step closer to me, folding his dark wings around me in a sort of protective barrier from the February gale that rushed into the room. His seductive magic coiled around me like a dangerous caress, making my body strain against the silk I wore.

"Are you going to tell me who you really are?" he asked quietly.

I stared at his throat, where a vein pulsed in his neck, drawing my eye. So much death and life all in one creature.

He gazed down at me, his stormy eyes entrancing me. "What were you doing out there, barefoot and barely dressed?" he asked in a deep whisper.

The scent of myrrh curled around me, and his warmth pulsed over my body. What did I want from him? I couldn't think clearly right now. I could only think of pulling off my dress and running my hands over him.

The feel of silk against my bare skin had never tortured me so much.

Slowly, his hands slid over the wet silk of my gown, thumbs pressing gently in the hollows of my hips.

It was Eimmal, and I should be naked. I bit down hard on that impulse—but not the one to pull him closer to me, to press my body against his until his heartbeat pounded against my skin.

Poison hemlock, I told myself. And then, *but just one taste won't kill me.*

I stood on my tiptoes, my body sliding against his as I made myself as tall as possible. Then I reached out and cupped my hand around the back of his neck. His eyes remained completely transfixed on mine, as if he were trying to read a book in a language he couldn't quite understand.

At the feel of his skin beneath my hand, a fresh wave of euphoria rushed through my body. His veins beat beneath my skin in an entrancing rhythm. Silver flared in his stormy eyes.

Vulture, I tried to tell myself. *Poison hemlock.* But I could no longer quite remember what the words meant, or why they mattered. Or, in fact, why words mattered at all.

I pulled him down to my level and kissed his neck, first lightly, then hungrily, my tongue moving over the pulsing vein in his neck. I needed to taste him, to feel the warmth of his naked body against mine, to feel his mouth all over me.

Poison hemlock! Somewhere in the darkest recesses of my mind, the words rang like a death knell.

I pulled my mouth away from his throat, but I couldn't quite bring myself to take my hands off him.

His eyes burned, and his midnight wings still curled around me. Dark magic whirled around us, shielding us from the sentinels' view.

"You shouldn't have stopped." The sensual timbre of his voice was more of a command than the words themselves.

From my hips, he trailed his fingertips up my ribs to the strap of my gown. Despite myself, despite what I knew about him, I ached for him to pull it off me. As if hearing my thoughts, he slipped his finger-tips under the silk strap. Slowly, he pulled it down, and the cool forest air kissed my bare skin, peaking my breasts. *Yes. This is what I want on Eimmal.*

My neck arched in a silent invitation. When I closed my eyes, his mouth warmed my neck. His tongue flicked over my skin, then a hint of teeth brushed against the most vulnerable part of my body until I practically moaned.

As he slowly moved his mouth lower over my skin, wild lust pooled between my legs. *More.*

One of his hands moved down, pulling up the hem of my dress, fingertips brushing against my thighs. They skimmed over my knife holster, but he didn't seem to mind. In fact, the feel of the knife elicited a low growl from him. As his mouth moved over my breast, his other hand was traveling up my leg, fingers moving lazily—so painfully slowly. Torturing me, he brushed his fingertips up the inside of my thigh, lifting my dress higher.

I'd gone without underwear today and should be stopping him. Instead, I practically moaned as the cool, February breeze whispered over the bare skin under my dress.

He was taking his time with me, and these slow movements of his were a strange sort of torture. I needed more from him, needed him to kiss me *hard.*

I gripped him by the collar of his shirt, pulling his mouth up to mine. I pressed my lips against him, kissing him with wild abandon, my tongue brushing against his. He'd lifted my dress now, his hand cupping under my thigh, and I hooked a leg around him, pulling him closer to me.

As he claimed my mouth, I lost all sense of time and place, my body beaming with pure ecstasy.

I am blood and moss, earth and claws, a creature who runs naked through the forest, berry juices running down my chin...

A jolt went through my body as I felt myself changing... fading.

Oh hell.

I pushed Adonis away, and his eyes went wide with shock. A lock of my hair blew in front of my face in the chilly breeze.

With horror, I realized it had faded to a pale gold. My eyes would be silver, my canines sharpened, ears pointed.

No.

I'd dropped my glamour. *All* of it.

"Ruby." His voice was a deep rasp.

Horror clawed at me. I'd just blown my own cover—with the one angel who hated feral fae.

Frantically, I pulled up the hem of my gown to break into a sprint. With the glamour dropped, I could move at full speed, and my legs carried me fast out the door.

I nearly froze in the hallway—there, at the other end of the corridor, stood Johnny, gaping at me, the feral fae running around the angels' castle.

That made two angels I needed to take care of.

Run, Ruby. Run for your weapons.

At the full speed of an unglamoured fae, I raced into the stairwell, pounding down the stairs. I moved like the wind, a blur of speed, until I was out in the forest air again.

My feet hammered the damp soil. My pale hair whipped around my head as I ran, at one with the spring air.

Get to the weapons.

I wasn't holding back anymore. I was going to fight with the full force of my power, and I knew exactly where I needed to go. I was going to draw angel blood today.

I reached the buried weapons within moments and dropped to my knees. My body blazing with adrenaline, I clawed in the dirt, digging up the soil until I reached my buried bow and arrows.

As I slung the quiver over my back, the shadow of wings swooped over me.

I looked up at the angel coming in for a landing nearby—gray wings and a scrawny physique. Johnny had come for me.

I nocked one of my poison-tipped arrows, getting ready to aim.

But as I did, Johnny flung out his arms, and utter darkness fell over the forest.

CHAPTER 40

My hands trembled, still gripping my bow and arrow. My heart pounded so loudly I was certain Johnny could hear it, could track me by the sound.

"Oh, Ruby!" he called out into the void.

Panic whirled in my mind like wild spirits, and I rose on trembling legs.

Darkness, shadows all around me. Utter and complete blindness.

Terror pulled me under. I began running blindly, my hands extended to feel for trees. When I slammed into a tree trunk, Johnny's laughter rang across the forest, sending icy shivers through my blood.

He was going to toy with me until I died.

I stopped running, trying to slow my breathing until I could come up with a plan. Hard to think when blood was roaring in my ears, drowning out my thoughts, when the darkness was all around me…

But a fae didn't need vision the way humans did. I breathed in deeply, trying to tune in to my sense of smell. Floating on the wind were the scents of the trees, the groves—yews, elders, hawthorns— and a single rowan.

If I could tap in to that power, the power of the Old Gods, maybe I could ignite a light in the shadows, enough to see where Johnny was, enough to look out for Adonis.

A sharp, shrill noise pierced the air—the cry of a magpie.

I ran, following the scent of the rowan, the sharp cries of the magpie. My shoulder slammed into a tree trunk, and I winced with pain. I tried running with my arms out in front.

"Ruby, darling!" Johnny shouted. "Do you have any idea how ridiculous you look? I could end this now, only I don't want to."

Tree branches and blackthorn clawed at my skin, but I tuned in only to the sound of the magpie shrieking overhead. The Old Gods were calling to me, leading me. I had to believe it, because I had nothing else left.

My feet sank into the damp earth as I ran.

Just as the sound of the magpie grew more distant, I caught a glimpse of a faint silver glow.

The rowan branch.

Yasmin's words rang in my mind. *In order to be our beacon, you'll have to descend into the shadows.*

With my pulse pounding hard, I ran for the tree. Wild relief flooded me as I reached the rowan trunk, and I looped the bow over my shoulder to free my hands.

"Ruby!" Johnny's voice was overhead now, circling me. "Trying to sow divisions with me and Kratos, were you? Trying to make him think I had a bit of a drinking problem?"

Even as he was shouting at me, his words were slurred.

I pushed out his taunts, focusing on grasping for the knots and branches to hoist myself up the tree.

Laughter echoed around me. "Little beast. Do you really think climbing a tree will keep you safe? I'm not one of Kratos's hounds."

I was pretty sure Johnny could kill me with a flick of his wrist if he wanted to. The only thing keeping me alive right now was the fact that he was enjoying watching me scramble and stumble blindly.

Could he really not see the glowing silver branch?

I played up my helplessness, yelping and pretending to grasp wildly for branches, pretending to miss.

"Awww, dear Ruby." His voice boomed. "I'm tempted to watch you starve out on that tree branch, feel the talons of famine sinking into your pretty little body. Your sister is supposed to return tonight, isn't she? And how shall I kill her? Slowly, I think, and with as much pain and indignity as possible. Bit like you, clinging to this tree branch."

Oh, you're going down, Johnny. I reached the silver branch, then began shuffling along the bough, my blood pounding through my veins.

"Is it weird that I'm getting turned on watching you straddle that branch?" Johnny boomed.

With my pulse racing, I edged along until I reached the glowing silver. Johnny hadn't mentioned it, hadn't said a damned thing about it. At this point, I could only imagine that he couldn't see it at all.

I used my thigh muscles to clutch tightly to the branch, because I'd need both my hands for what was about to happen.

Before I reached for the knife strapped to my thigh, I took mental stock of my weapons. In my right hand, I held the bow. From the quiver, I pulled out an arrow, shoving that into my right hand as well, taking care to make my movements look as clumsy as possible, minimizing the appearance of a real threat.

"What's the plan, Ruby? Shoot me blindly?"

With my left hand, I reached for the knife at my thigh. I'd only have one shot.

Moving at the speed of a fae, I yanked the knife from its holster and jammed it into the tree branch.

I am a child of the forest, of the Old Gods, and I command the light.

As I did, intense, ancient power blazed through me, and a burst of pearly light bloomed around me, illuminating Johnny flying just above me.

I was ready with my arrow.

I had just enough time to catch the look of utter surprise on Johnny's face before I loosed the arrow, right for his heart.

It struck its mark in the center of his chest, and his jaw dropped, wings drooping. Horror contorted his features, and a thin stream of blood dripped from the corner of his mouth.

The power of the ancient gods still flowed through my body, and I felt their vengeance, their wrath.

The Old Gods screamed through my veins as I watched Johnny clutch his chest.

A sly smile curled my lips. "Is it weird that I enjoy watching you suffer?"

Johnny fell to the earth, gray wings trailing behind him. I pulled my knife from the silver bough, still feeling the gods' power thrumming wildly through my bones. The sound of wind and rivers roared in my ears, electrifying my body.

As pure, silvery light continued to blaze around me, the forest soil welcomed my bare feet with a lover's embrace.

My gaze flicked to Johnny, who writhed on the mossy earth, eyes bulging.

I nocked another arrow, my pale hair blowing around my face. "You were never supposed to be here, Johnny. The Old Gods want you to leave."

With the music of the forest pounding in my ears, I shot him again and again, until arrows protruded from his body like St. Sebastian.

I stood over him, a primal power skimming the length of my body. He began to convulse, a red foam pooling at his lips. I had a vague sense that night was falling around us, but that silvery light still bloomed in the air.

Ruby the beast had taken down an angel—with the help of the Old Gods.

When he stopped twitching, and his pupils paled to a milky white, I began digging, claws in the dirt, flinging soil with abandon.

The sounds of the forest grew louder around me, the colors brighter, until I was no longer sure I could separate myself from the gods—wasn't sure where I ended and they began.

As I buried Johnny deep in the forest's soil, my mind whirled with burning lights, the cries of the magpies. The magic inside me was sparking too hot, so intense that I felt at risk of burning out, of turning into a husk of a creature.

By the time I finished covering his pale, scrawny body with the last handful of dirt, my body was trembling, desperate for a reprieve from the gods' magic. I fell onto the mossy soil above him, breathing in the rich scent of the earth.

CHAPTER 41

I woke to the scent of myrrh, to the feel of shadows whispering over my skin, to powerful arms carrying me over the earth.

I opened my eyes, staring in horror at Adonis, his features silvered in the moonlight.

My body tensed. *Where are my weapons?*

"Relax," he said softly. "I'm not going to hurt you."

My head was pressed against his muscled chest, and I could hear his heart beating against my ear. "You're reassuring me? I just took down an angel. You should be scared of me." Pretty tough talk from someone who couldn't reach her weapons right now.

I knew my glamour had dropped completely, but I didn't feel completely feral anymore. Some of the wildness had faded.

"I was watching," said Adonis.

"Why didn't you stop it?"

"I didn't want to. I've been working against Johnny, against Kratos."

"You have?"

"Why do you think I wanted Kratos to see you in my room? You've

277

been utterly distracting him from his mission, and his jealousy threw him completely off course."

I blinked, my thoughts hazy. Now that my secrets were all out in the open, I could ask what I really wanted to know. "What happened to my friends? The humans you saved?"

"They're safe. I set them up in a cottage outside of London."

I tried to make sense of what he was saying. "Why would you do that?"

"You risked your life for them. I thought their lives must be worth preserving for some reason."

My eyes were drifting closed as I leaned against his chest, but I still had so many questions. "I don't understand. Why are you working against the other angels?"

"To end the Great Nightmare. I've been searching for someone like you."

A million questions raced through my mind. "What? Why? What do you mean someone like me?"

As the words tumbled out of my mouth, I winced at the pain in my shoulder.

"Shhhh." His magic kissed my skin, soothing some of the pain away like a delicious salve. "Before we go back into the castle, you need to glamour yourself as a succubus again. Kratos can't know that you're a... *fae.*"

He said the word with such contempt that I still had no doubt he hated my kind. "Why were you searching for a fae if you hate our kind?"

He shook his head, his pale eyes gleaming in the night. "I wasn't searching for a fae. I was searching for the Bringer of Light."

"And what does that mean?"

"It means you can help lift the shadow of darkness from the world." He met my gaze, his stormy eyes blazing. "You need to glamour yourself now, Ruby."

"Fine." With the last vestiges of my magic, I summoned my succubus glamour.

And then, with the sound of Adonis's heart and the feel of his body lulling me, my eyes began drifting closed once more. Before I fell asleep, my last thoughts were of Hazel.

* * *

I woke to ruddy sunlight filtering into the room and the smell of cedar. I felt warm and protected in here, even if the ghosts of the Old Gods still whispered in my mind.

I blinked in the light, and when my eyes adjusted, I saw Kratos, sitting in a chair like a king on a throne. Warm firelight wavered over his tan skin and sparked in his amber eyes.

Coppery light beamed from his body. "The succubus awakens. Nearly in time for dinner."

I blinked at him. I'd slept for a whole day, but at least I felt sane again. "Is Hazel here?"

"First things first. I leave the castle for a day, and all hell breaks loose. What happened to Johnny?"

I glanced at the door to my room, still smashed to pieces. "He must have been drunk yesterday. In a rage about something. Did you two have a fight?" I asked, all innocence.

"Something like that."

"He said I was trying to poison your mind against him. He broke down my door, chased me through the woods. And then... he just disappeared."

Kratos nodded slowly. "That's exactly what Adonis said."

"Well, it's the truth." I sat up in bed, my head still swimming. "Where is Hazel?"

He stood. "I'll leave you two alone."

As soon as he crossed out of the room, a tall, lithe succubus entered, dressed from head to toe in black leather.

Hazel?

My jaw dropped at the sight of her—the porcelain skin, black curly hair, eyes dark as the night sky. In an instant, I was out of the bed, folding my arms around her, breathing in her familiar smell. Tears pricked my eyes.

"Easy, sister. I'm not used to all this carrying on." Still, her features were beaming, a grin lighting up her face.

I gaped at her, tears streaming down my face. "Are you *okay?* What happened to you? I haven't seen you since… since…" Since the day I watched dragons slaughter Marcus and rip you from the Earth.

She crossed to the edge of my bed, kicking off her shoes, and sat cross-legged on the blanket. In her leather clothes and with her height, she didn't look fourteen anymore.

Of course, she *wasn't* fourteen anymore. She was sixteen, I had to remind myself.

"I was living with a horde of dragons in a Scottish castle." She bit her lip. "They were terrifying at first, but they kind of grew on me. They like having women and girls around, but they didn't touch us or anything. They just like hoarding things. What have *you* been doing? I thought you were in New York this whole time. How did you get here?"

"We'll get to that." I blinked. "So you lived with a whole bunch of other women and dragons in a castle?"

She nodded. "The food was quite good there. Dragon shifters are very into fine cheeses. And there was gold everywhere."

None of this was what I had been expecting, but my stomach rumbled at the mention of fine cheeses.

Already, I was heading for the wardrobe to get dressed. "Hazel, we have a lot to catch up on, and I'm taking you to breakfast. I mean, dinner."

"Where exactly are we going?"

"To the bar." I frowned at her as I pulled on a dress. "You don't seem nearly as traumatized as I was expecting. Considering we had a whole apocalypse and everything."

She shrugged. "Maybe the Earth needed a reckoning. Maybe it was time for a purification."

What. The. Hell. Was she saying this for the benefit of people who might be listening, or did she really believe that?

"Purification," I repeated.

"Keep the humans in balance," she said lightly. "Is there alcohol in this bar? Because the dragons let me drink whisky."

As I grabbed her hand, I scowled at her. "You are sixteen, and you are about to find that the dragons and I do not have the same rules."

She rubbed my arm gently. "Sweet sister. You don't get to make the rules now."

I bit down on an angry retort. We'd only just reunited, so I wasn't going to start arguing with her. Plus, I had to accept the fact that we'd been separated for nearly two years now, and a lot had changed. Maybe people grew up fast in the world of the Great Nightmare.

Hell, I'd never killed anyone before all this started, and last night I'd gloated over the body of a convulsing angel.

As I led her into the bar, I grinned to find Elan sitting at the counter over a glass of whisky. Bruises and scratches marred his pale skin.

"Elan!"

"Ruby!" He grinned, pointing at me. "You know, for a demon, you really got into the spirit of Eimmal. I'm always impressed with someone willing to throw themselves into new cultures with such abandon."

I took a deep breath. "I can't say I'll be doing the same next year. Took me a while to get the dirt out of my nails."

"Anyway, I'm glad to see you've recovered from Johnny's drunken attack."

So the rumors had spread around the castle already. "Not only have I recovered, but I've got my little succubus sister with me. Elan, meet Hazel."

Elan lifted his whisky glass. "To the succubi! Creatures of ancient terror and seductive legend, mothers of all demons..." He trailed off, frowning. "That's a bit much, isn't it?"

I was already behind the bar, pulling out bread for sandwiches. "Hazel, apparently, has been living in a castle with amazing food."

She beamed, "And I learned how to ride on the back of a dragon."

I smiled uneasily. "Great."

"What have you been doing?" She gestured at the empty bar. "Have you been in Hotemet Castle the whole time?"

I glanced at the arched doorway, catching a glimpse of an angel with dark wings and stormy gray eyes drifting past. Was it really true —that Adonis and I were on the same side after all? The fact that I was standing here, still breathing, suggested it was.

Adonis was working against the other angels, and that meant I had a *lot* of questions to ask him as soon as I could get him alone.

"Helloooo!" Hazel waved her hand in front of my face. "Did you hear me? Have you been here the whole time?"

"No, not the whole time."

We had a lot to catch up on, a million stories to swap, but I didn't want to tell her all of them—didn't want to tell her about the things I'd done, or the starvation that had gnawed at my ribs. I'd be leaving out the rats, and the murder of Dickhead. The raw, overwhelming terror.

I'd put on a show. I'd stick to the funny stories—Elan's cat sweatshirts, a jaunt through the night sky with an angel, my accidental entrance into Adonis's bedroom.

In the world of the Great Nightmare, only our stories kept us sane, and as we sat in the warm light of the bar, I'd be telling her only the ones I wanted her to hear.

BLACK OPS FAE - BOOK TWO

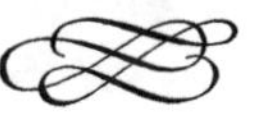

CHAPTER 1

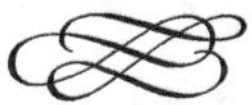

In the forest outside Hotemet Castle, I nursed a small, silver flask. In the amber morning light, Hazel and Elan walked by my side.

Just three fae out for a walk among the oaks. Two of us pretending to be demons.

I scanned the forest, my chest tightening as I thought of Johnny. I'd buried his scrawny angel ass in a shallow grave out here, but angels were immortal. I had no idea how long it would take him to recover. At any minute, he could come bounding out of the soil, hunting for me with murder on his mind.

I'd just be keeping that particular image to myself for now. No reason to spoil our evening stroll.

"I like it here." Hazel chomped into the cheese and onion pasty she'd snagged from the kitchen, the crumbs flaking over her black clothes. "We get to go outside and talk to each other and stuff."

Elan frowned. "And you couldn't in the dragon lair?"

"Nope." Hazel's mop of black curls tumbled over her shoulders. Like me, she was glamoured as a succubus, which meant that wisps of shimmering magic lifted from her body in steamy tendrils.

Warm light washed over Elan's pale skin and gaunt features. He grabbed the flask, taking a sip of Irish coffee—spiked with just the right amount of scotch.

Don't judge. Things had been stressful lately.

Another spray of crumbs over Hazel's clothes. "And the dragon food wasn't this good," she said through a mouthful of pie. "They ate a lot of sheep. Not flavored or anything. Just sheep they caught and then roasted in their fire-breath."

I finished the last bite of my own pie. "I guess that would make sense." I *really* didn't want to talk about dragon shifters, or think about them, or know what I might find on their menu. "Since they're giant, disgusting lizard people."

In her leather outfit, Hazel looked so much older than the last time I'd seen her—older than a sixteen-year-old should look, and I was pretty sure she'd spiked her own flask of coffee with the scotch.

But considering she'd spent a year among the dragons, I supposed a few changes were to be expected.

Our feet crunched over leaves and twigs as we walked.

Smiling, Hazel nudged Elan with her elbow. "You know what you remind me of? A starving egret."

"Hazel!" I snapped. The dragons certainly hadn't taught her any manners.

Hazel widened her dark eyes. "What? It's not an insult. It's just because of the paleness, and the thinness, and the haunted look in his eyes. As if he'd spent years in captivity eating frogs."

"A hundred forty-seven years," he confirmed. "Working in troll mines. Frogs were an infrequent delicacy." He scratched his cheek. "From what I understand, some people like the haunted bird look."

"There are all kinds of people," Hazel agreed and sipped her coffee.

Elan took another swig from the flask, then wiped the back of his sleeve across his mouth. "I should probably get back to my cooking duties before one of the angels vaporizes me. I've been asked to roast a pig for lunch. Kratos's favorite." He turned, stalking off through the forest without another word.

And at last, I was alone with my sister. Considering we'd only reunited yesterday, we still had a lot to talk about.

As soon as Elan was completely out of earshot, I grabbed my sister's arm. "Hazel. I need to fill you in on a few things."

"Let me guess," she whispered. "You're pretending to be a succubus so the angels will let you stay in the nice castle with the nice food."

Honestly. How shallow did she think I was? "Not exactly. I mean, I'm not complaining about the food, but I'm here as a spy. I'm working with the Institute to stop them from wrecking the earth any more than they already have."

"Why the hell would you do that?"

My jaw dropped open. "Because they kill people, Hazel, in case that's escaped your notice. Please don't tell me that you're fine with that."

She pursed her lips, shrugging. "It doesn't matter if I'm fine with it. It's happening, and we can either adapt to the new world, or starve like peasants in the dirt. Those are our options."

Anger flared. She'd become a bit jaded in the past two years, but maybe living among fire-breathing reptiles did that to a girl.

"I'm not adapting," I whispered. "I'm fighting them. You should be, too." I scanned the forest again, my heart thudding at the idea that Johnny could be lurking out here somewhere.

Hazel arched an eyebrow, whispering back, "And how do you plan to fight them?"

I took a sip of my coffee. "With information. And a little faith."

After everything that had happened recently, I'd become a believer in the Old Gods. The angels were powerful and terrifying—yes—but there were older beings, ones who'd been born native to the earth itself. And in the past couple of weeks, I'd started to believe they were providing us with everything we needed to combat the angels.

Hazel sneered. "Faith. Right."

"Yasmin was right to believe in them."

"Who?"

"My handler from the Institute. I'll arrange for us to meet soon.

Anyway, she told me when we needed something, the Old Gods provided. And watch this." I scanned the skies for sentinels, making sure none were in view. Then, I stood still, lifting my hand in front of my face. Since I'd jammed a knife into the silver tree branch yesterday —mainlining the power of the Old Gods—some of their magic continued to live inside me. I'd stayed up late last night, summoning a faint glow around my fingertips.

I concentrated, trying to bring up that beautiful light.

Hazel loosed a sigh. "Am I supposed to keep watching you stare at your fingers?"

"Hang on." After a few moments, the tips of my fingers started to gleam with incandescent light.

"Hmmm…" said Hazel. "What does it do?"

"I'm not sure yet. This is just the beginning. But it's something, right?" I let the glow die out on my fingertips.

Hazel looked unimpressed. "Or—instead of fighting the heavenly horde with your glowing hands—we could just stay in the luxurious castle. A servant brought me breakfast this morning, and then I had a hot bath. I have a brilliant idea. How about we don't mess it up? Do you know that every time you try to change something, you have the distinct possibility of making it worse?"

I shook my head. "It can't get any worse. And anyway, I don't have a lot of choice at this point. Apart from the fact that the angels are psychopaths, Johnny is lying out here in the dirt somewhere. Still alive. He knows I'm a fae, that I've been lying the whole time. I shot him with a poison-tipped arrow. When he wakes up, he's going to remember that I was the one who put him in the ground. If I don't find a way to end his life for good, I won't be drinking any wine or having any baths, because I'll be dead, or possibly locked in a torture room for eternity. And you will be too. Understand?"

For the first time, she looked rattled. "Maybe he won't wake up for years. Maybe he won't remember."

"That's a risky dream to pin your hopes on."

She sipped her coffee, her gaze never leaving mine. "Between now and then, we have time to charm the other angels. We'll take care of this whole…shooting and burying situation you created."

"Don't take this the wrong way, but I'm not sure charming people is in your skill set."

She glowered at me. "What makes you say that?"

"You just met Elan a day ago and you already called him a starving, haunted egret."

"He didn't seem to mind. Anyway, the dragons liked being mildly insulted. I was their favorite."

I *definitely* needed more whiskey in this coffee. "You're telling me you *charmed* the dragons. After what they did…" I let the sentence trail off, didn't want to give life to that particular horror with words.

Her jaw tightened. "Yeah, I got on their good side. How do you think I survived? How do you think I was able to control them? It doesn't matter if I *liked* them, Ruby. What mattered was that they liked me. That meant they protected me, gave me food and a place to sleep. All I had to do was entertain them and keep them happy."

I gritted my teeth. "Did they know you were fifteen?"

She glared at me. "Yes, and I didn't entertain them like that. I told them jokes, told them stories, filled their drinks. I flirted." She scowled. "Oh, don't look so shocked. You and I are the same. I lived among the dragons, pretending to be someone else. You lived in a castle, pretending to be someone else. And it doesn't matter if we liked it, or if other people would approve. Dragons and angels will do what they want. Our job was to survive."

"We can do more than just survive. We can fight them."

"We can't. I remember, Ruby. I remember when dragons killed our parents. I remember when they ripped Marcus apart. He was trying to save us, and—"

I held up a hand, cutting her off. "Let's not think about that, Hazel. You're right that we need to survive, but it's not going to happen by dwelling on all the terrible things that ever happened to us."

Something dangerous sparked in her eyes. "And ignoring all the terrible things will get you killed. Don't underestimate the forces working against you if you try to cross the angels. No one is looking after us, Ruby. We need to look after ourselves, and we can do that by pleasing the people in power."

"I will look after you. We just need to return to our roots. If we can end the Great Nightmare, we'll have a normal life. A cottage in the woods, with a fireplace, venison that I hunt, and…I don't know… root vegetables. Just like our ancestors. We can even bring along the haunted egret if you like. In any case, we don't belong among the angels *or* the dragons. We belong among our kind, and I'm going to do whatever I can to protect the only family I have left."

Her jaw dropped. "Are you out of your mind? Root vegetables and fireplaces? How do you expect to achieve this domestic dream?"

I loosed a long breath. The answer sounded ridiculous, even to me. And yet, I was starting to have faith in something older than the angels themselves. "The Old Gods are helping us. They've always been here—we just never knew about them. They're the reason why I was able to put Johnny in the ground in the first place."

She arched an eyebrow. "Sounds like bullshit. And even if the Old Gods are real, everything has a price. You realize that, don't you? *Everyone* has a price."

"So cynical for sixteen." As we walked, I fixed my gaze on hers intently. "Hazel. What I'm about to tell you is important, and you *have* to keep this to yourself, do you understand?"

She nodded. "I can keep a secret."

"Not all the angels are on the same side," I whispered. "Adonis says he's working against the others. I don't really understand why, and I don't trust him, either, but there are fractures in their alliance. He is the only one here who knows what I really am. I don't know what his motives are, but he let me live."

Hazel ran her fingertips along the leaves of a nearby shrub. "Now that is interesting."

My jaw tightened. I wasn't sure she was getting the severity of the situation. "Hazel. If Johnny wakes up—*when* Johnny wakes up, I'm going to need to leave here, fast. In fact, a smart person would probably leave *before* he wakes up. And you'll need to come with me, because he'll blow your cover, too."

She shot me a sharp look. "Maybe. Or maybe I stay here and use my own skills to keep Johnny and Kratos from coming after you. Then I can continue to eat Elan's food, because let's not overlook the fact that I just ate a pie for the first time in two years."

"That's wonderful. And your plan is to charm Johnny enough so that he won't care that I'm a lying fae spy who wants to kill him."

"Maybe charm isn't the right word. I'm good at confusing people."

"You don't say."

She grabbed my arm. "I'm not joking. I can *persuade* people, just by talking. Like, I confuse them, and then they forget what they were angry about, or they forget what they want me to do. How do you think I explained to the dragons why I was suddenly a succubus?"

"You confused them." I narrowed my eyes, an idea sparking in my mind. "Little sister, you just might have inherited the ancient fae skill of befuddlement."

Hazel smiled. "See? Our problem is solved. We can stay here with the pies and the fireplaces, and we won't end up out on our asses trying to hunt rabbits in the woods. I'll just befuddle them."

I shook my head. "No, Hazel. This isn't just about us. Look, we're going to dinner tonight with the remaining angels. If you really do have these powers of befuddlement, I could use your help. Kratos has asked both of us to dinner tonight, but he wants to keep me as far as possible from Adonis. I'm not supposed to go into Adonis's corridor, or leave my tower, or walk anywhere near the Dark Lord."

"A gilded cage."

"Pretty much. But we can see Kratos. Any chance you can persuade Kratos to invite Adonis to this dinner? And then find a way to get us alone?"

"Easy." She studied me closely. "And of course you'd like to get him alone. I caught a glimpse of him in the courtyard. Looks like a god."

"It's not like that. I need him for information, but I don't trust him as far as I can throw him. He hates the fae as much as he loves himself. Whatever his motives are, they're not altruistic. If I had to guess, he's angling for even more power than he already has."

"So stick with him, then. In this world, when power dynamics shift, you'd better make sure you're on the winning side." She snatched my spiked coffee and took a sip.

I didn't even try to stop her. Right now, I was pretty sure "little Hazel"—the one who'd once crawled into my bed to stave off nightmares about closet monsters—was well and truly gone.

In this world, maybe a loss of innocence wasn't the worst thing.

CHAPTER 2

I spun across the dance floor, my body thrilling at its own movements. Kratos had installed this studio for me, with a wooden floor and everything. I was only now getting to use it for the first time. Truthfully, a fae preferred to dance outside, but since he didn't know my true nature, the wooden floors would have to do.

That morning, I'd taken a quick mirror call from Yasmin—just a few flashes of the candle to signal to my handler from the Institute that I was in no immediate danger. Then, I'd quickly found my way to the dance studio.

As I moved, arching my back in an arabesque, a thin sheen of sweat spread over my body. *Gods* it felt good to dance again, and now that Hazel had returned to me, I could finally truly enjoy myself for once. I glimpsed myself in the mirror as I danced.

Twirling, a familiar ecstasy rippled through my ribs. This was what I was born to do. And ever since I'd connected to the Old Gods in the forest outside—since I'd harnessed their light—I felt connected to the earth, to my body, more than ever.

Closing my eyes, I twirled, a smile lighting up my face—until I spun right into a powerful chest that felt a lot like a wall of steel.

I opened my eyes, finding myself face-to-face with a muscled chest dressed in a finely cut crimson shirt, and the sweep of coppery wings. Then, I looked up into the chiseled face of Kratos, his eyes blazing like sunlight as he stared down at me. A vein throbbed in his neck.

From somewhere behind him, one of his ivory hounds growled, as if sensing the tension in the room. As if *I* were a threat to *him*. The creature padded over, his claws clicking against the hardwood floor, and stood next to his master. Kratos reached down, giving the hound an affectionate pat.

"Culloch, I'm fine. You can go away."

With a low whine, Culloch turned and padded in the other direction.

Kratos's golden stare turned on me again, and energy crackled between us. Suddenly, I felt intensely aware of the sheer amount of skin I had pressed against him, seeing as I was only dressed in a leotard.

"Good afternoon," I said sweetly. "I was wondering how you were doing." I knew he was going out tonight to kill, to hunt humans, and I still smiled at him. Maybe Hazel and I *were* more alike than I was admitting, pretending to be people we weren't. "Thank you for bringing my sister back."

A muscle twitched in his jaw as his gaze swept over my body. "I want you to be happy."

"I am. This dance studio is everything I want. Dancing and Hazel, who you found for me." A sharp pang of guilt coiled through me. He was standing here telling me that he wanted me to be happy, while I'd come here to find a way to destroy him. I'd already taken down one angel—at least temporarily—and maybe Kratos would be next.

Of course I needed to stop them. What the hell was I feeling guilty for? They'd destroyed New York, London, one city after another. They hunted people and sowed death and destruction across the world. I had no loyalty to his kind, and I could never forget that.

"You belong here." His voice was a low murmur that warmed my skin.

Every word of his seemed like a command, so powerful that I

wanted to obey. And sometimes, when he looked down at me with his golden eyes, like he was doing right now, I had to fight the urge to fall to my knees before him. Something about his raw magic compelled me to bend to his will, to worship him. The wooden floor called to me, urging me downward to kneel in supplication. My legs practically shook as I resisted him.

Kratos's gaze swept lower over my body, and his muscles visibly tensed. He wasn't allowed to touch me—not *really* touch me. He'd been cursed for his whole life, and that meant that if he gave into earthly temptations, he'd fall. He'd turn into a demon, all leathery wings and horns.

And yet, he seemed entranced by my throat right now. Without entirely realizing what I was doing, I tilted my head back.

"Must you dance in something so revealing?" Tension laced his voice.

I swallowed hard. If I tempted Kratos to fall, the consequences would be terrible for everyone, but I wouldn't let it go that far.

I just needed to distract him enough that he kept his mind off slaughtering everyone, but not so tempted that he'd actually fall. If he did, the terrifying archangels known as the Heavenly Host would fly to earth to finish off the last of the living.

"Maybe you could take the night off hunting," I suggested. "Stay here to watch me dance."

His golden eyes darkened to a deep umber. "I can't skip the hunt. The curse compels me to do it." He ran his fingertips over his chest. "When I don't act as the curse commands me to, I burn from the inside out." He closed his eyes, breathing in deeply as if some strange sort of ecstasy were overtaking his body. "But sometimes I wonder if it would be worth it to burn." He opened his eyes again, trailing his gaze over my body, and I had the disconcerting feeling that he could see right through my leotard to the bare skin beneath, to the freckle just below my left breast.

Maybe I shouldn't get too close to Kratos—maybe an angel tempted to fall was too much of a dangerous thing.

Now seemed as good a time as any to dig for information, now that Kratos seemed completely entranced by my body. "And Adonis is the only one of you who isn't cursed?" I still didn't understand these angels.

For just a moment, a cold fire flashed in Kratos's eyes, and his coppery wings spread out behind him. "You need to stay away from Adonis." His voice was almost a growl. From his back, his hound snarled in warning.

I reached up to touch Kratos's cheek as if soothing him. "What do you think will happen if I don't?" I asked, widening my eyes innocently.

He was looking at me the way a predator sizes up his prey. Instinctively, I took a step away from him, backing up into the wall.

But Kratos moved with me. In the next instant, his hands were around my waist, then lower, sliding down over my hips. I gasped as his fingers tightened possessively.

He leaned in, his breath warming the shell of my ear. "If I weren't cursed, I'd be pulling that scrap of clothing off you right now and…" He stopped himself, fighting with his impulses.

I was certainly doing my job of distracting him. His fingers moved up my body, until his powerful hands curled around my biceps, pinning me to the wall. Something wild and untamed blazed in his eyes.

"Are you trying to tempt me to fall?" he asked, his voice a growl.

No, that would be bad. I shook my head. "I don't know what you're talking about."

He was breathing deeply, his golden magic burning from his body like sunlight. "I see you walking around the castle, the way you sway your hips, the way your clothing hugs your body. You want to turn me into a demon, like you. Maybe I want to know what that feels like. I want to know what *you* feel like."

I clenched my jaw, suddenly realizing what a dangerous game I'd been playing. "I think you should let me go now. Get a cold shower in."

"You're making me insane, Ruby." His voice was a snarl, and it rumbled over my skin.

Despite myself, my back was arching into him.

"Ruby." My name sounded like a command on his tongue, and once again I had to fight that overpowering urge to drop to my knees, to pull off my clothes like I knew he wanted me to.

My body was trembling now, and sweat dampened my skin again, this time for another reason. I raised my hands to push on his powerful chest, but it was like trying to shove an oak tree. "This is a bad idea."

He tightened his grip on my arms, and in the next moment, his mouth was on my neck, teeth grazing my skin. He growled as his tongue replaced his teeth. He was kissing me—*hard* and possessively, as though he were claiming his territory—and he really shouldn't have been. I tried pushing against him, my hips bucking, but he had me pinned.

One of his hands slid up my back, and I heard the tear of fabric as he ripped my leotard. Cold air whispered over my skin, peaking my breasts as he tugged it down.

"Stop." I slammed my fists against his chest. "Stop!"

The words seemed to hit him like a slap to his face, and he stared at me, stunned. I gripped the top of my leotard, holding it up to cover myself. From behind him, Culloch was snarling.

My breath was coming rapidly, my cheeks flushed. *I can't stay here.*

At the sound of footsteps, I realized another presence had entered the room—this one draped in shadowy magic.

Adonis crossed the wooden floor smoothly, as though moving through water. His dark magic trembled up my spine. "Get away from her, Kratos. Now." An unmistakable threat of violence laced his tone, a ruthlessness under his perfect exterior.

Kratos growled, almost inaudibly, but took a step away from me.

As he did, Adonis's cold rage seemed to disappear like smoke on the wind.

Adonis shoved his hands into his pockets, completely at ease now, a wicked smile on his lips. "Has it occurred to you that maybe having a succubus in your home is a bad idea?"

Kratos clenched his fists, his eyes still locked on me. "I'm fine. I just need to hunt soon. That's all."

"Let's go, then." Adonis's tone brooked no argument.

Gripping my leotard, I stared after the two angels as they left the room, and dread began to bloom in my chest. I *definitely* needed to end this as soon as I could.

CHAPTER 3

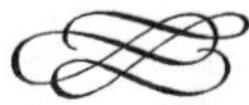

Until tonight, I'd never been in the Celestial Room—the crowning jewel on top of the Tower of Silence. Nor had I ever sat below an enormous glass dome, with a canopy of stars twinkling above me.

It might have even been relaxing, if it weren't for the sentinels drifting above us, their dark eyes glinting with suspicion.

Below the dome, I sat at a round table with Kratos and Hazel. Red candles burned in iron candelabras, casting a wavering light over the flagstone floor. It wasn't the coziest place I'd ever been, but it had a certain stark elegance. Perfect for an angel, I guess.

I took a sip of my Bordeaux, trying to ignore their ever watchful eyes. If it hadn't been for the whole apocalypse issue, maybe Hazel would have a point about how we should just stay here enjoying the food, luxuriating in our silk dresses.

Kratos leaned over the table, refilling Hazel's wineglass. Considering we were supposed to be thousand-year-old succubi, I couldn't exactly point out that she was only sixteen. And Hazel certainly wasn't turning it down.

"Cheers!" Hazel beamed, lifting her glass. "To the angels and their amazing castle!"

Kratos lifted his glass, his rings glinting in the candlelight. "I never imagined I'd be dining with *two* ancient succubi."

Well, that's because you aren't.

His golden eyes slid to me. I still hadn't quite gotten used to the look of them—the eerie gold that faded to a burnt umber around the edges. Everything about him blazed with an inner golden light—and yet, according to Adonis, *I* was supposed to be the Bringer of Light. Whatever that was.

I'd already eaten at least half a roast quail, plus a good amount of potatoes, and Adonis still hadn't made an appearance. Had Hazel been able to persuade him to join us, or had she overestimated her befuddlement powers?

Kratos's gaze was slowly lingering over my sheer, pewter-gray dress. I watched his body tense, glowing brighter with that honeyed light. "I must get you some more concealing clothing."

He sounded almost angry this time. Clearly, my wardrobe was straining his ability to keep a leash on himself.

"You don't like my dress?" I asked.

His gaze was locked completely on me, as if Hazel weren't in the room at all. "I'm starting to wonder if it might be worth it to wear the wings of a demon."

I bit my lip. "I can almost picture you as a demon. Maybe some horns."

Hazel cleared her throat. "You guys remember that I'm here, right?"

When Kratos glanced at her, he looked almost surprised to find that she was still there. Then, his brow furrowed. "Did you ask me to invite Adonis to dinner earlier?"

Hazel widened her eyes and blinked. "When I spoke to you in the forest's edge? No, we talked about the sparrows and the rowan trees, and I wondered about poisonous plants and you said there were many in the woods, and then you thought of Adonis and inviting him to dinner. That was, of course, before your thoughts turned to my sister's body and how she would look completely naked in a rainstorm. But the point is, you wanted to invite Adonis because you're the same, really, and your fates are the same, like a pair of oaks grown intertwined. Can I have more wine?"

Now *that* was befuddlement.

Kratos simply nodded at her, a faint line between his brows. Before Kratos could answer, the sound of footfalls echoed off the stone floor outside the room.

Adonis pushed through the oak door, a sly smile curling his sensual lips. As usual, he wore finely cut, dark clothes, and shadows seemed to cloak his body. Dark tendrils of midnight magic swept into the room, rushing over my skin like a night breeze. "Sorry that I'm late."

"You really didn't need to come at all," said Kratos sharply.

Adonis arched an eyebrow as he pulled out his chair. "You did invite me."

Kratos leaned back in his chair, sipping his wine. "For the life of me, I can't remember why."

"For my scintillating company." A smile ghosted over his sensuous lips. "Obviously."

Kratos winced, nearly dropping his wineglass, and clutched his chest.

"Okay there?" I asked.

"I must go hunting soon." Kratos's eyes burned deep gold. "You should return to your tower."

Kratos really didn't want me anywhere near Adonis, did he?

"Kratos," Hazel chirped. "Golden one. Can I walk you outside? I just want to see where you keep the hounds, and I was saying earlier that I had a burning desire to see the hounds, and I thought you might want to take me to them now, and to fulfill your heart's desire by going to the hounds *now*, and you really just wanted to hunt and feel that sweet release in your chest like a great explosion of joy." She rose, her chair scraping over the floor, and beamed a smile at Kratos. "Shall we go?"

Brilliant. My sister was a brilliant manipulator.

Kratos frowned, confusion clouding his features. "Right. Hunting." He rubbed his chest, wincing for a moment. "I need to go."

"Of course you do," said Hazel. She strode out of the room, and Kratos trailed after her.

At the threshold, he turned back to me, his body flashing amber. A corona of light beamed around his head, and his copper wings appeared behind him, cascading down his back. "You'll want to get back to your room, Ruby."

As he turned and left, my stomach dropped. That was right. I couldn't forget that I was a prisoner here.

When I glanced at Adonis, amusement was dancing in his pale eyes.

"He seems awfully eager to keep us apart," I said.

Adonis picked up his wineglass. "Of course he is. I'm a monster."

A shiver danced up my neck. Sometimes, his beauty had a cruelly mocking edge to it.

I took a long sip of my wine and glanced around the room, taking care that no servants lurked in the shadows. "If you're a monster, why are you working against the other death angels?"

"Their vision is limited. They're slaves to the commands of the Heavenly Host. They don't want what I want."

"And what do you want?"

His masculine scent wrapped itself around me, bringing with it promises of dangerous pleasure. "To rebel against those who seek to control us. To maintain my free will, to drag the gods from the heavens, and make them suffer, just a little." The ice in his eyes hardened. "To put them in their place."

"And you need a Bringer of Light to achieve…your rebellion?"

"Precisely. Powerful as I am, I can't kill the other angels. Funny, isn't it? You're a fae from nowhere, but only the Bringer of Light can stop them."

"What exactly is a Bringer of Light?"

He leaned closer, his dark magic curling around his powerful body. "Someone who can control the magic of the Old Gods. A power grew in the rowan branch. I couldn't see it like you could, but I could feel it. When you fought Johnny, I watched you harness that power. You're a vessel, Ruby."

"I see. And you want to use me, but you haven't explained what I need to do."

In his eyes, I saw nothing but the cold, staggering arrogance of an ancient god. "It's quite simple, Ruby." The candlelight flickered over the chiseled planes of his face. "As the Bringer of Light, I want you to serve me. I don't want to rule on earth. Worship from humans is hardly an achievement. I want to rule the celestial realm. You can help me achieve that."

"How? And what's in it for me?"

A wicked smile. "What's in it for you, my little feral fae? You get to live."

CHAPTER 4

y chest tightened. Of course, he'd keep his cards close to his chest. Bringer of Light—whatever that was—obviously came with some serious power, and he wasn't going to give me access to it without keeping complete control.

"You want me to *help* you gain even more power than you already have?"

Adonis's magic moved in menacing whorls around him. "Yes."

"Call me crazy, but I'm not sure I'm keen to give more power to a monster."

The air thinned around me. "You're surrounded by monsters. You just have to decide which ones are your allies." An easy smile, a predator toying with his prey. "I must say I find it interesting that you were perfectly happy to kiss a monster on Eimmal. I heard your heart speeding up, felt your blood racing. I saw the look in your eyes, how much you wanted me. Tell me, Ruby. Does death lure you in?"

I tightened my grip on my wineglass. "No. The spring fever affects me that way because I'm fae. I kissed you because you were there. That's it. I would have preferred Kratos." I wasn't sure why I added that, except I thought it would help to keep Adonis at a distance.

Adonis's eyes hardened like chunks of ice, and a cold draft whispered over my skin. "Is that right?" His powerful, shadowy magic slid through to my bones, making my body shiver. "Then you're a wise one, Ruby. And you're right to think me a monster. I've killed scores of humans. I've spread plagues over continents. When I lived among the fae, I helped them kill for fun." His eyes gleamed with a terrifying intensity, and his magic coiled around my ribs. "I killed my own parents, Ruby. That is what I am."

The hair on the back of my neck stood on end, and I swallowed hard. "Wonderful. Sounds like a promising partnership. Why the hell should I choose you as an ally?"

"Because I'm the only one here who knows the truth about you. Kratos's reaction to your deception is an unknown. And what's more, if I rule the celestial realm, I won't be here. We both have the same goal, don't we? Get me away from this world."

"You make fair points."

"You don't have the first clue how to fight the Heavenly Host, or even what you're looking for. I suppose I could fill you in on a few details, except that I don't trust you at all."

The wheels began to turn in my mind. He had a book in his room —*Bringer of Light.* If I could steal that from him, maybe I could learn this information on my own. Then I wouldn't have to rely on a death angel.

"So in this partnership of ours, you're not going to tell me what we're looking for, or where we're going, or anything remotely useful."

He traced his fingertips over his wineglass. "What would be the fun in that? Besides, I don't need you running off to the Institute with every little morsel of information I give you. And I don't need you turning your powers on me."

Bastard was holding all the damn cards. "Hazel will never come with us if we can't tell her where we're going."

A cruel smile. "And what makes you think I have a use for your sister?"

My fingers tightened into fists. "I'm not leaving without her. You need me, and I'm not going without her."

"You do realize I can compel you to act. The fun I could have with a beauty like you." His sensual voice promised excruciating temptation.

I sucked in a sharp breath. "But you never have compelled me. How do I know you're not bluffing?"

Adonis's eyes flashed with a pale light, and I felt his magic ripple over my skin in a dangerous caress. The hair rose on the back of my neck, and an invasive power crawled through my blood, wrapping itself around my bones like a vine. Against my will, I felt my arm rise, my fingers reaching out for Adonis's face.

I couldn't control my voice anymore, but if I could, I'd be screaming at him. His intoxicating magic gripped me against my will. He had complete control over my body. I stared, entranced, as my fingertips stroked down his smooth cheek. He closed his eyes, breathing in deeply.

As soon as the magic loosened its grip on my body, I yanked my hand from his cheek. Snatching my wineglass from the table, I flung the contents in his face.

"Don't ever do that again," I snarled.

He leaned back in his chair, wine dripping from his skin in red rivulets. That infuriating, amused smile curled his lips as he dabbed the wine from his cheeks. "You did ask for a demonstration."

Once again, he had a point, but that didn't negate the primal outrage I felt at being controlled by an outside force. I tried to still the shaking in my body. I had nothing to threaten him with, no power of my own to stop him. Just my own impotent fury. "Promise me one thing. If you rule the celestial realm, will you be able to stay the fuck away from our world? Because angels like you don't belong here. This is our world. The demons, the fae, the humans. And we want it back."

Adonis seemed completely unperturbed. Bored, even. He held my gaze for a long moment, shadows pooling in the air around him. "Johnny could wake at any moment, and when he does, you'll be faced with not one, but two angels you've betrayed. I'm your only way out of here."

True. I refilled my glass, not answering him.

"Here's what you need to know for now," he continued. "We're going to my castle first. I have some informants there who can tell us about our next move. But if you think I'm going to tell you where to find *that,* you may as well dig yourself a shallow grave next to Johnny's."

I raised my eyebrows. "You have your own castle?"

"Where do you think I've been living all these years?" He rose from his chair, his pale gaze sweeping over me. "Get your things ready to leave quickly. Whether you like it or not, it's me and you against the world."

I shuddered, and his footsteps echoed off the high ceiling as he stalked out of the room.

Screwed. Adonis had all the power here, and I was truly and completely screwed.

Unless, of course, I could steal that book from his room and learn a few things of my own.

* * *

I LURKED outside Adonis's door, my ear pressed to the wood. I heard nothing inside his room. I sniffed the air—I couldn't smell his exotic scent, either.

Darkness had fallen outside, and only a few guttering candles lit the hallway. My pulse raced as I thought of sneaking around inside his room without his permission. What would he do to me if he found me?

I grabbed one of the candles from the sconces. Best if I got in and out of there fast, before I had the chance to find out.

Slowly, I turned the doorknob, opening the door into darkness.

I loosed a sigh of relief when I found the room empty. With a slow, careful movement, I shut the door behind me. Adonis had closed his curtains, and shadows seemed to climb the walls. I glanced at Adonis's bed, wondering for just a moment if he ever entertained women there, what it would be like to give in to his seductive power...

None of my business.

I crossed to the bookshelf, and a spark of hope lit in my chest when I spied the thin, black volume, *Bringer of Light* etched on the spine.

I pulled it from the shelf, holding the candle above it. I opened it with one hand, turning to the first page—a hand-drawn picture of light beaming from a tree branch.

That was when I felt something else in the room—a seductive, exotic presence that whispered over my skin. I froze at the sensation of breath warming the back of my neck, fingertips skimming my hips.

"Ruby, my darling," Adonis purred in my ear. "Did you think you could steal from the Dark Lord?" His voice was a dangerous caress.

Goose bumps rose on my skin. Of *course* he caught me. But how did he sneak up on me so quietly? My pulse raced, breath speeding up at the feel of his body's warmth behind mine.

I snapped the book shut, speaking to him over my shoulder, my heart pattering like a frightened animal. "I just wanted a little more information. Since you won't just tell me things."

"No one steals from me. But I suppose I have to let you live." His fingertips skimmed my hips again, a subtle promise of tormenting pleasure. "I can think of one way you can make it up to me."

Heat swooped through my belly. I pivoted, shoving the book at him. "You can keep your book. I'll find out the truth, one way or another."

Adonis plucked the book from my fingertips. "Honestly, this one doesn't contain anything useful anyway. You need to know Phoenician and cuneiform for that."

"Whatever." I stalked out of the room.

A part of me wanted to give in to the torturous pleasure he promised, but I'd never submit to the seductive allure of a monstrous angel of death.

CHAPTER 5

$\mathcal{A}$ howling noise woke me from my sleep—something inhuman that chilled me to my marrow.

I glanced quickly at Hazel, who snored gently by my side.

But that ragged keening kept winding through the air, piercing ice in my blood. I pushed off my blankets and crossed to the window. I pressed my hands against the cold panes, jumping as a sentinel drifted past, dark eyes wide, soaking in everything.

Even as a creature rent the night air with its cries, the sentinels were watching me. The only creatures the sentinels didn't watch were the angels.

I swallowed hard. Johnny couldn't have risen already, could he? It had only been a few days. Granted, I had no idea how long poisoned angels stayed unconscious. It wasn't like there were reference books for this kind of thing, and if there were, Adonis would probably just yank them from my hands.

I focused my vision, summoning my keen fae senses to search through the dark for signs of movement in the trees, but I could see nothing outside.

As I pressed my hands against the glass, a flock of ravens burst from the trees, squawking as they swooped away from the forest.

They soared over the castle walls. More birds followed—crows, swallows—desperate and writhing murmurations that fled the dark forest in a chaotic panic.

Johnny. He was waking. I could feel it like a deep, gnawing hunger between my ribs, an emptiness I could never fill. I'd had the same feeling before, when I'd gotten too close to him on the castle parapet.

Adonis was right. These angels never belonged on earth.

A chill rippled over my skin at the sight of gray mist curling from the trees.

"Hazel," I said quietly.

"Mmmm." She rolled over, pulling the sheets tighter around her shoulders.

"Hazel," I said a little louder.

This time, she sat bolt upright.

My mouth had gone dry. "I think Johnny is waking already. We have to get out of here."

She rubbed her eyes, yawning. "Why?"

"Because he's going to tell everyone what I did." I spoke in a harsh whisper. "He's going to tell Kratos that I'm a fake, that I'm trying to kill them all."

Hazel blinked, suddenly becoming more alert. "Oh, right. I thought we had more time."

"So did I."

Her dark eyes were wide, skin pale, and her forehead furrowed. "Is that him? That terrible howling sound?"

"I think so. Doesn't sound happy, does he?"

In an instant, Hazel was by my side, hands pressed against the glass. Our breaths fogged the window as we stared outside. When a sentinel swooped past, my heart leapt. Would they report us—the two succubi with their faces pressed up against the window—as we waited for the angel to crawl from his shallow grave in the woods?

That hunger in my gut intensified, and I clutched my stomach. I'd never be full, never satisfied. My soul itself was starving, desperate for life. It was Johnny's strange magic—ripping through the air like a tornado.

Kratos made me want to fall to my knees and submit to his power, while Adonis lured me toward either death or seduction—I wasn't sure which. Johnny, on the other hand, filled me with an agonizing hunger.

Hazel pressed her palms to the window, and I could have sworn her cheeks looked thinner. "I'm starving," she said listlessly. "Do you know what it feels like to starve?"

Dear sister. I've fought men over scraps of rat meat.

"Not really," I lied. Through the confusion of hunger, I tried to scramble up a plan. Maybe we could pack what clothing we had, grab a few things from the kitchen—some bread, cheese, butter, a bit of meat...

Hazel's eyes had taken on a haunted look. "I want to stay where the food is." She shook her head. "We can't leave. We'll starve out there."

"Hazel. Our minds are being clouded by Johnny's magic. We'll bring food with us."

Bread, cheese, the pastries, lamb, venison, fruit... My mouth watered, and a wild hunger tore through me. How could we leave all this behind?

As we gaped out the window, dusty gray magic swirled from the trees, a sickly light tingeing the fog. And from the mist, a figure emerged—punctuated like a black hole against it. An angel stalked from the forest, his wings ragged, body gaunt and hunched.

My stomach dropped.

Definitely Johnny.

Frantically, I pushed all thoughts of starvation out of my mind, trying to focus. I ran for the wardrobe and yanked open the wooden doors. Unfortunately, these clothes weren't made for survival—they were made only for strutting around a castle, looking pretty. I had two sets of leather leggings, a sweater, and one jacket, plus a pair of boots. The rest was a useless collection of flimsy dresses.

Fast as I could, I dressed in the warm clothes. As I scrambled to put them on, I tossed a pair of leggings at Hazel.

With my sweater and my jacket on, I snatched my poison-tipped knife sheathed in its holster from the wardrobe and tied it around my waist.

Hazel still stared at the window, her body shaking. Didn't she realize what was going to happen here? I didn't even want to think about how they'd execute us. Kratos had tolerated me because he thought I was a succubus. I didn't think he'd tolerate betrayal. He demanded loyalty—worship, even.

My mind whirled in a fog of hunger, and I was dimly aware of Hazel babbling on about food—

Another sharp pang of famine ripped through my stomach, and I doubled over. In the hollows of my mind, images flashed of a woman starving, her ribs protruding through her back. A vulture circled overhead.

My fingernails were digging into my flesh, and I glanced at Hazel. *We have to get out of here.* I was ready to wrestle those leggings onto her slender body.

"Hazel," I said through gritted teeth. "Get dressed, or I'm going to have to kill you and eat your corpse."

"I'm going to the kitchen," Hazel declared.

In the next moment, she was rushing for the door.

I took off after her, our footsteps echoing down the corridor. She slammed through the door to the stairwell.

We didn't get very far when Hazel doubled over, clutching her stomach. She leaned against the stairwell wall for support. "It's killing me."

Only one thought could drown out the oppressive hunger, and only one thing terrified me more right now. It was the sound of the heavy footfalls coming up the stairwell.

"He's coming," I whispered. He'd chosen this tower—the Tower of Wrath—the one where I slept. He was coming to kill me.

I pulled the knife from its sheath and stepped back up the stairwell. "Hazel," I whispered, grabbing her by the arm. "He's coming for us." She only seemed to care about one thing right now, so I'd have to focus on that. "That feeling of hunger that's ripping you apart—it's coming from Johnny. We have to get away from him."

We'd have to find another way out—another stairwell.

She nodded listlessly, seeming to listen to me for once.

Quietly, I pulled her back up the stairwell, backing away from Johnny. Gray magic, tinged with that pale green light, climbed toward us.

Shaking with hunger and exertion, I backed through the stairwell door—and into a powerful body. Slowly, I turned, looking up into Adonis's pale eyes. His midnight wings cascaded behind him.

Bizarrely—I actually felt relieved to see him.

"Johnny's coming," I whispered. My whole body was trembling. Pretty sure I was just a few minutes from passing out.

Adonis grabbed me by the biceps to steady me. "Johnny's magic is affecting you. He's not able to control it right now."

He touched my shoulder, and a soothing sensation rippled through my core, assuaging some of the hunger.

"Can you get us out of here?" I asked.

Adonis nodded, but the starvation kept intensifying. A tortured scream from Hazel ripped through the quiet castle. I knew what she was feeling—that death hovered over her like a bird of prey.

Adonis let go of me, then swooped down to scoop up Hazel. She wrapped her arms around his neck. Just as we began to move, the stairwell door slammed open, and Johnny's giant figure loomed in the doorway.

CHAPTER 6

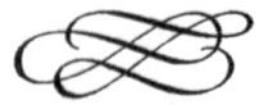

Dirt covered his face, and streaks of green smudged the side of his mouth, as if he'd been eating moss and grass. His shirt hung ragged and torn over his bony frame, and his blue Mohawk hung limp and dirty over his skull.

There, in his chest, an open wound gaped through his clothing. Where his heart should've been was instead a ravaged, corrupted hole. Right where I'd stabbed him.

The three of us—Adonis, Hazel, and I—stared at him, waiting to see what he would do.

Johnny reached for the wound, tracing his fingertips over it. Then, he smeared the blood down the front of his torso. His eyes were locked on me as he moved, wide and staring.

I clutched my stomach, leaning on Adonis for support. The closer I stayed to Adonis, the more his magic seemed to protect me from Johnny's, soothing that crippling hunger.

Johnny pointed a bony, blood-covered finger at me, and his jaw dropped.

Adonis cleared his throat. "Johnny. Wonderful to see you again. You look well."

As if this situation weren't terrible enough, I felt the presence of a third angel moving closer—this one beaming with gold.

Kratos strode toward us, his coppery wings radiating light. "Johnny," he boomed. "I thought I felt your presence. What the hell is going on here?"

Johnny just kept staring at me, pointing with his bloodied finger.

Adonis broke the silence. "It seems our favorite drunken angel has returned to us after one of his benders. No idea what happened to him, except that he seems to have had a brush with Devil's Bane. I'd hazard a guess that he doesn't remember the full story either. A tankard of vodka or two will do that to you."

Kratos narrowed his eyes. "Why are the succubi clinging to you like that?"

Adonis shrugged. "Johnny's famine magic is ripping their minds apart right now. Mine helps to soothe their pain."

"Johnny," Kratos said evenly. "Control yourself."

Johnny continued to glare at me, hatred burning in his eyes. Yet he wasn't saying anything, and his silence unnerved me.

He grunted, rubbing the wound on his chest again. His pale lips opened and closed. Maybe that Devil's Bane had gone straight to his mind, because he didn't seem to be firing on all cylinders anymore.

Without another word, he lunged for me, his eyes shot through with incendiary red. The next thing I knew, his hands were around my throat. I reached for the knife at my thigh—poison-tipped. If I poisoned him in front of Kratos, the jig would be up. Wouldn't take a genius to figure out who'd been messing around with Devil's Bane.

Through the blood roaring in my ears, I could hear my sister screaming my name.

My heart slammed against my ribs, my lungs burning as Johnny squeezed. Frantic, I lifted the knife—

Fortunately for me, I didn't have to make the call about whether or not to stab him, because Adonis was ripping Johnny away from me by his withered, blue mohawk.

"Subdue yourself," snarled Adonis, still gripping Johnny by the hair.

For a moment, Johnny seemed to grow calmer, some of the fire in his eyes dulling, even if his gaze was still locked on me. He took deep, ragged breaths, and a thin stream of drool slid from his lips.

Slowly, Adonis let go of Johnny's hair.

Then, like a wild beast, Johnny howled and whirled on Adonis.

Midnight feathers scattered into the air, and I watched with horror as Johnny tore a brutal rip in the top of Adonis's wing. The sound of a wing tearing is something I don't think I'll ever forget—the shredding of tendon and bones.

Adonis roared, and the temperature around us plunged, shadows swallowing up the light. With a feral snarl, Adonis rushed at Johnny. It took only a few moments for Adonis to snap the punk angel's neck, and the crack of bone echoed off the stone walls.

Kratos looked down at Johnny's crumpled, filthy body on the flag-stones, his expression betraying nothing. "I've come to expect dramatic entrances from Johnny, but this one has surpassed my wildest dreams."

Adonis grimaced with pain. His hand hovered protectively near his wounded wing, but he didn't seem to want to touch it. A bit of bone jutted from the top of it, and streams of crimson blood trailed down his dark feathers.

I swallowed hard. "That looks like it hurts."

"I'll live."

Kratos's gaze slid from me to Adonis and back again. "Anyone care to tell me what the fuck is going on here?"

Hazel stepped closer to him, blinking her dark eyes innocently. "Johnny was drinking again. He reeks of vodka. Must have been quite a bender, and he found himself—yourself—tangled in the forest's brambles, unable to remember what got him there. When he tried to think back, it's all a foggy mist of vodka, moss, and the elder roots that pulled you deep into the earth, deep until the secrets are forgotten and questions plague you no more."

Kratos cocked his head, mesmerized by Hazel's rambling, as though she'd just uttered the wisest jumble of sentences in the history of the world. Fortunately for me, I seemed immune to her skills. And given the way Adonis was frowning at her, I had a feeling he was too.

Another set of footsteps echoed down the hall as Elan approached, his arms full of pastries and an entire baked ham. Some sort of custard coated his cat sweater and was smeared over his cheeks.

His eyes were on Johnny. "He returned! Is he all right?" Crumbs rained from his mouth as he spoke.

Hazel rushed over to the lanky fae. She grasped for the baked ham, while Elan clung to it, dropping all of the other food in his arms.

"Adonis," Kratos said sharply. "Can you stifle Johnny's magic? It's still creating chaos in here."

Still shielding his wing protectively, Adonis whispered something under his breath. His dark magic swooped around Hazel and me, soothing some of our gnawing hunger.

Kratos stared after him. "I'm going to find some stronger servants to drag Johnny back into his room until he recovers." He glared at Elan. "Share your food with the succubi, and see that they get back to their room." He stalked away, a golden glow in the gloom.

With Adonis's magic whispering over my body, some of the raw pain of famine began to bleed out of me, even if my stomach still rumbled.

While Elan and Hazel scooped food from the floor, I raised my eyebrows at Adonis. "How long will that take to heal?"

He looked positively murderous. "I won't be flying anytime soon."

"Thanks for pulling Johnny off me. I thought of stabbing him, but…" I glanced at Elan, unwilling to continue the conversation about poison-tipped weapons in front of him.

"Come." Adonis nodded at my bedroom, then quietly slipped into the fire-lit room.

While Elan and Hazel continued to gnaw on food in the hallway, I followed Adonis. He stood on the flagstones, and warm firelight wavered over his perfect features. The door closed softly behind me.

"How long until Johnny blows my cover?" I asked quietly.

"When Johnny wakes, his mind will be addled. He was already

confused from being underground for days, and the poisons are probably still working their way through his brain. When I snapped his neck, I bought you more time. But he's immortal, and he'll recover eventually. You can't stay here any longer."

I swallowed hard. How could I trust Adonis? Everything he did was self-serving. Not to mention that I'd seen him vaporize people.

Kratos—for all his faults—had reunited me with my sister. He'd done it because he actually seemed to care for me on some level.

But what would Kratos do once he learned that I'd been lying to him this whole time?

I heaved a deep sigh, stuck in an impossible situation. "I'll go with you. But I want to take my sister."

The door creaked as Hazel opened it, and she crossed to my side. She'd chomped halfway through the ham already. "I heard that. And I'm staying here," she declared.

Irritation sparked. "Don't be ridiculous. I'm not leaving you here."

Adonis folded his arms, wincing just a bit at the movement. "She should stay here until Johnny shows the first signs of recovery."

"What are you talking about?" My voice came out a little too harshly.

Adonis stared at me. "If Johnny recovers within days, your sister can keep him confused for as long as possible. She has a remarkable skill."

Grease smeared Hazel's lips, and she wiped it off with the back of her hand. "Yeah. See? I have a purpose here."

I cocked my hip. "I really don't see how that's safe."

Hazel fixed her dark eyes on me. "I'm staying, Ruby. You go do what you can, and I have my own part to play here. You have to trust me. I survived the dragons, and I can survive the angels."

Adonis smirked. "See? She'll be fine here. Useful, in fact."

I clenched my jaw, pointing at my sister. "At the first sign of danger, you need to flee, okay? I don't care how hungry you are."

She nodded. "I'm going to keep a bag packed with food and clothing at all times, ready to go. Don't forget that I can summon dragons if I need to, so like, it's really not a big deal."

I frowned. "You can?"

"I told you. I charmed them." She pulled a gold dragon's tooth pendant from her shirt. "Right before I left, Uthyr the Harvester of Souls gave me this. Says he'll come for me when I need him. He's actually quite nice once you get to know him."

Well. I didn't see that coming.

I turned to Adonis. "What are you going to tell Kratos? He doesn't want me anywhere near you."

Adonis was already heading for the door. "You pack your things for tomorrow morning, and you leave the rest to me. Meet me outside the Tower of Wrath after the sun rises tomorrow morning."

The door closed with a final click, and his footsteps echoed off the hallway outside.

The farther he moved from me, the more that gnawing hunger began to return, and I pulled the ham from my sister's reluctant hands. "Tomorrow morning, I need you to make contact with Yasmin, from the Institute of the Watchers. I told you the signal, right? She'll let you know where to meet her. Tell her everything. Johnny came back, he could recover his memory, and Adonis is taking me—somewhere. Tell her that he plans to rule the celestial realm, I'm the Bringer of Light, and that's all I know."

"And how will you and I communicate when you're away?"

"We won't. That's why I didn't want to separate from you in the first place."

She crawled into the bed, pulling up the covers around her. "Such a worrier. What's the worst that could happen?"

My mouth dropped open. "The world could literally end and all living things could die?"

She blinked. "I have faith in you, Ruby. You'll figure something out."

A memory clawed at the recesses of my mind—a dark pool of glistening blood and gore on the pavement. *If I couldn't save Marcus... I* slammed an iron door over the memory. No point dwelling on the past.

A fae believed in beauty, in pleasure—dark thoughts were wasted moments.

After a final bite of ham, I crawled into bed next to my sister, listening to her breaths as they grew heavier.

CHAPTER 7

With the morning rays streaming into our room, I shoved my meager, useless clothing into a backpack. My chest ached at the thought of leaving Hazel again—but maybe she was right. I had to trust that she was smart enough to survive. And considering she could apparently summon a dragon at will—as well as befuddle anyone around her—I had to admit she had her own set of protections in place.

Dressed in my warmest clothes—my berry-blue wool coat from the night before, my leather leggings—I crossed to the bed. Rolling over, Hazel blinked sleep away. For just a moment, I caught a glimpse of my sister as she had been—the little twelve-year-old who'd cried when a boy at school dumped milk onto her backpack.

She smiled sleepily. "Ruby. You're dressed already."

"I have to go. I can't tell you where I'm going, because I don't know. Only that I'm going to Adonis's castle, and that we're looking for…something."

Hazel rubbed her eyes. "I'll keep Johnny and Kratos off your case."

"Just keep yourself safe. And check in with Yasmin to tell her what we know. Remember—use the candle to summon her. She'll want to meet you by the cave at the northern edge of the forest, near the mulberry grove. Find it as soon as you can."

She nodded. "Got it."

It was no wonder Adonis was keeping me in the dark. I took all the information I had straight to the Institute.

I pushed through the door into the frigid hallway. Every step away from my sister felt like a growling hollow in my chest, and I blinked away my tears.

Still, I had to do this. We couldn't stay here. There was only one way out of this situation alive, and that involved stopping the apocalypse itself. Unfortunately for me, I had to rely on one of the angels of death himself to get what I wanted.

I traced my fingertips down the cold stones as I descended the stairs. What made me a Bringer of Light? Yasmin had said something like "you can be our beacon, but first you must descend into the shadows." Maybe she meant it literally.

At the bottom of the stairs, I used my gloved hands to pull the iron bar from the door. I pushed outside into the frigid February air, and the sunlight dazzled my eyes for a moment. When they adjusted, I gaped at the slightly terrifying sight of two angels on horseback, their wings on full display.

Kratos sat on top of his powerful white horse. Sunlight streamed over his copper wings, blazing off his head like a crown of light. He wore his battle gear, and given the rigid set of his shoulders, he looked as if he were about to rip Adonis's heart out.

Adonis didn't look any more approachable. His midnight wings swooped out from a dark cloak, and he and his pale eyes blazed from within a dark cowl. His left wing hung at an awkward angle. I winced at the sight. I guess now I knew where to attack an angel. An angel could rise from the dead in just a few days, but a wing injury seemed like it could lay them out for weeks.

A sheathed sword glinted on his back, the hilt studded with red gems. His horse was a color I'd never seen before—a sort of purple-gray, like a fading bruise, with eyes of pure white and a silver mane. A large, black satchel hung off his saddle.

Another saddled stallion stood to Adonis's side, his fur a murky blue-green, like seawater. A gleaming, silver star shone from his forehead, and his mane flowed over his shoulders, the creamy color of seafoam. Clearly, these were not ordinary horses. In fact, they were creepy as hell.

As I drank in the scene, it took me a moment to realize both angels were glaring down at me.

"What?" I asked.

Kratos's hands gripped his horse's reins rigidly, looking like he was about to snap the leather through sheer force of will. "Adonis tells me that you're not safe here. He tells me that Johnny is coming for you. Something about his drunken escapades, a fixation on you."

"Is it any wonder?" A half smile curled Adonis's lips. "Succubi were created to tempt. Johnny is fighting his urge to fall, and Ruby is making it hard for him."

Kratos's golden eyes studied me. "Is this true, Ruby? Has Johnny been coming after you?"

I shot him my most innocent, baleful expression. "Yes. You saw him last night, pointing at me. He seems to blame me for something. Whatever got him into that state he was in. But I think Adonis is right. He's scared that I'll tempt him to fall, and he hates me for it."

Kratos's jaw tensed. "I should be the one to take her from here. You can't even fly."

I wished that Kratos had been the one to discover my secret, and that he and I were the ones going off together. He might be a monster, but he was a monster who'd returned my sister to me. That was worth *something*.

"I don't need to fly." Adonis's voice was pure ice.

Kratos grimaced, stroking his chest. He clearly hadn't been hunting enough to keep the pain away. "With that crippled wing of yours, you won't be able to disguise yourself. An angel traveling through the countryside will attract every vengeful demon in the country."

"Since when have I let a hostile demon get anywhere near me?" asked Adonis. "In any case, you won't be able to take her anywhere,

Kratos. You're as tempted as Johnny is. I *saw* you with her, ripping her clothes off. If I leave the two of you alone for ten minutes, the Heavenly Host will tear the rest of the world to shreds. And besides. You need to hunt."

Kratos's wings spread out behind him, and for just a moment, hot fury glinted in his eyes. After a heavy silence, he asked, "Where are you taking her?"

"I have to return to my castle. A shadow demon rebellion has been brewing nearby. It will give you and Johnny enough time to get control of yourselves, and if you still want her, I'll return her."

Kratos glared down at me. "Fine. Go with him. You'll be back here as soon as I get control of Johnny."

He didn't give me any choice in the matter. I was his to command, apparently. I no longer felt quite as guilty about plotting against him.

Adonis nodded at the seafoam horse. "I hope you can ride."

I nodded. One of the many fae gifts my parents had given to me— not that I was particularly practiced at it. "Kind of."

Kratos met my gaze evenly. "If you need me, write my name on a piece of paper and burn it. I will hear the summons and come for you."

Like a magical text message. "Thanks, Kratos."

Without another word, Kratos reared his horse and galloped off into the forest. I had a disturbing feeling he'd be exceptionally savage on his hunt tonight.

Adonis peered down at me. "Do you need any help mounting Nuckelavee?"

I frowned. That name seemed somehow familiar. "Nuckelavee? Isn't that...a demonic horse monster?"

Adonis shrugged. "He's not as bad as people make him out to be."

Wonderful. "No, I can mount him fine." *I think.*

I crossed to the horse. I knew this was insane, but I could have sworn the thing narrowed his dark eyes at me as I approached. I stroked his mane, and the creature snorted, steam rising from his nostrils. He jerked his head away, not wanting anything to do with me.

Shit. Well, charming a horse couldn't be any harder than charming humans, could it?

I stroked his mane again, trying to conjure my inner horse-whisperer. "We're going to be friends," I whispered.

He snorted again, then reared on his hind legs.

"Nuckelavee!" Adonis barked. "Stop it."

I grabbed the stallion's reins, trying to gain control of the situation. Clearly I wasn't getting anywhere with charm. I scrambled to slide my left foot into the stirrup, clutching the saddle as if my life depended on it. With a loud, ungraceful grunt, I swung my right leg over the saddle.

Nuckelavee took off in a gallop.

As the stallion carried me away from Hotemet Castle—away from my sister—I felt more alone than ever before. I'd only just reunited with Hazel, and maybe she wasn't even quite the sister I remembered.

Still, she was all I had left at this point. Since the Great Nightmare had begun, every separation had the overwhelming potential to be permanent.

Three hours into our journey, I wanted to die. The word *uncle* rang in my head like a curse. My thighs were not coping so well with the situation. In fact, they'd been trembling and screaming for the past hour, and I'd started to look forward to Nuckelavee's little grass-eating detours.

Still, my pride stopped me from calling out to Adonis. When I used to play Mercy as a kid, grappling with older boys who twisted my arms behind my back, I was never the first to cry *uncle*. I wasn't about to start giving in now.

Leaning into the wind as he rode, Adonis seemed completely impervious to exertion, silver-flecked wings sparking with sunlight. He was supposed to be the one who was injured. Why did this seem so easy for him?

He hadn't been one for conversation so far, which gave me nothing to think about but my shrieking thighs. I clenched tighter onto the reins, willing myself not to fall off.

"What's your horse's name?" I called up to him as we rode through yet another windswept, grassy field.

Adonis slowed his pace, turning back to look at me. "Thanatos."

I frowned, pulling on Nuckelavee's reins until he slowed to a trot.

Good. I'd stalled our pace. "Thanatos. Doesn't that mean *death*? Like, a Greek god of death?"

"Yes." He slowed his horse to a trot by my side.

Circling above us, Adonis's pet, Drakon, screeched, piercing the quiet countryside. The black-scaled dragonile's cries slid through my bones, and I shuddered. Given that Drakon's larger, dragon-shifter counterparts had killed my parents *and* my boyfriend, I didn't have particularly warm feelings about demonic, reptilian creatures.

I blocked out the dragonile's cries and heaved a sigh of relief at our slowed pace. Maybe I could keep Adonis talking about his favorite topic, which I imagined to be himself.

I nudged Nuckelavee onto a patch of clover, and he wandered to the right. "Can't control this thing," I said. "I think he needs a snack, and we can just have a little chitchat for a minute."

"A chitchat," Adonis repeated with no inflection.

I needed a snack. Didn't Adonis know that the fae needed to eat?

He reared his horse to a halt by my side. "I can help you control Nuckelavee if—"

Distract him. "So you named your horse after a Greek god of death?"

"Not exactly." The wind toyed with his cloak.

"Care to elaborate? How did Thanatos get his name, then?"

"Thanatos is my true name, and my horse and I are inextricably linked. He appeared when I was born."

My mouth went dry, and I swallowed hard. "So…you're a literal god of death."

"Archangels. Gods. Humans use these words interchangeably." A nearly imperceptible shrug. "I suppose 'god' suits me, but I don't like to brag."

I snorted. "What do you mean your horse—"

A squirrel scampered across the field nearby, and Nuckelavee jerked me toward it in a chase. Pain screamed in my thighs. I grimaced, struggling to rear my horse to a halt again, when Nuckelavee stopped and began munching on a dandelion.

"We should go," said Adonis.

"Hang on." I caught my breath. "The horse needs to rest. You can't run these beasts into the ground. Anyway, I don't think you've explained your death-god thing to me well enough. What does it mean?"

"It means that I'm incredibly powerful and destined to kill. You already know this."

Lovely. At least I'd found a way to stall him. "Can you escape your destiny? Who makes the rules, anyway?"

"It's a very interesting question, Ruby. One probably best left to philosophers and people who like to hear themselves speak."

"I took a psychology class in high school. Have you ever heard of the Thanatos drive?"

"What *are* you talking about?"

"Humans aren't just driven to live, or to procreate, apparently. That's Eros." I chewed my lip. "Wait, is Eros a real god, too?"

"He's a demon." Adonis arched an eyebrow. "He's awful. Thousands of years old and he acts like an eighteen-year-old. What was your point exactly?"

"Humans have a Thanatos drive. They're attracted to death. It's why they smoke, start wars, drive fast cars... Why they drink themselves into comas."

He nodded slowly. "Humans crave oblivion as much as they fear it. They crave release."

"Why?"

His eyes pierced me, his dark magic curling around him in sharp whorls. "So they can have some peace and quiet, I should imagine. It's an idea I empathize with at the moment."

I blinked, watching as Adonis took off at a gallop. Of course, he just expected me to follow. I gritted my teeth, spurring Nuckelavee on. Pain shot through my thighs, and I groaned.

After another five minutes of cantering, I glimpsed an iron-gray river cutting through the field. Willow trees lined its banks, and an old stone bridge spanned the rushing water.

How *good* it would feel to rest against the trunks of one of those glorious trees, or the stone bridge. How much I wanted to drink some water and lie down in the grass…

Desperation screamed in my mind.

"Adonis!" I bellowed, blood roaring in my ears. "Uncle! Uncle! Uncle!"

He halted Thanatos, his eyes wide as he turned around to look at me. "Why on earth are you shouting the word *uncle*?"

"I'm done!" I shouted. "I don't care anymore. I'm tired. This is ridiculous. You win!"

He cocked his head, his dark magic swirling around his horns, his leathery wings. "What do I win?"

I swallowed hard. I wasn't sure exactly why I was so angry, except that I hadn't wanted to admit defeat, and now I'd done it. Humiliatingly, I felt tears sting my eyes, and I blinked them away.

A shadow swooped over my head, and I glanced up to catch sight of Drakon soaring in lazy arcs above us. He opened his throat, breathing a hot burst of fire into the air.

I cleared my throat, taking care to speak with a steady voice, the voice of reason. "We need to rest. I can't keep riding."

"You should have just said so."

I lifted my chin. "I'm saying it now."

A small smile curled the corner of his lips. "What does *uncle* mean?"

I swallowed hard. "It's an American game. It's not important."

He nodded at one of the trees. "Let's rest under there."

I nodded, so grateful the tears nearly started again, but I clenched my jaw until I had control of myself again.

Under the naked boughs of a willow tree, I dismounted from Nuckelavee, slowly sliding down his enormous side. I walked hunched over, my legs trembling.

Adonis frowned at me with concern. "You look as if you can hardly walk," he said quietly. His pale eyes stood out sharply below the straight, black lines of his eyebrows.

"Not all creatures are made to gallop on horses for hours at a time.

I'm stronger than a human. Not as strong as a death god. Plus, you're part horse or something, as we established."

"I didn't say that."

I pointed to his twisted wing. "How does that feel?"

"I can hardly feel it now." He nodded at a large rock on the river's edge. "Sit down. I'll help you."

Pain ripped through my legs as I lowered myself to the rock. "Help me how?"

Without a word, he sat next to me on the rock. "I can take your pain away if you let me."

I blinked at him. "And are you concerned about my comfort? I thought we established that you're a monster."

"I can't have you slowing me down with a broken body." A slight edge tinged his voice.

Bone-deep pain screamed up my legs, my hips. "Fine. Whatever you need to do."

With a smooth movement, he brushed his fingertips over my knees. Shadows seemed to thicken around him, and his magic wrapped around me, both soothing and electrifying at the same time. Warmth streamed from his fingertips, swirling into places I had no business thinking about right now. As he touched my legs, he pulled the pain from me.

But at the same time, his agonizingly light touch filled me with a hot ache. I wanted more of him.

"That's helping," I whispered, disturbed by my own body's reaction to him.

Slowly, he traced his fingertips farther up my thighs, his warm, silky magic penetrating my body. I stared at the dark swoop of his eyelashes, such a stark contrast to his pale eyes. I fought the impulse to kiss his skin, to press my breasts against him. *Sweet release.* I hoped he didn't notice the subtle arch of my back, or my pulse racing. I hoped he didn't hear my heart slamming against my ribs. Molten heat pooled in my belly, and my mouth opened, ready to be kissed.

As he soothed my pain, his face moved closer to mine, his breath warming my cheek. Up close, I had the chance to study the perfect, golden smoothness of his skin, the perfect, straight eyebrows. I remembered the thrilling rush of heat when my tongue had brushed against his...

Then, he pulled away, and the loss of his touch felt like a cold, sharp shock to my system. I almost grabbed his hand and put it on my thigh again, before I regained some composure.

Get a grip, Ruby. He has this effect on every woman he meets. The thought annoyed me. How easy it was for him to seduce, and how little it probably meant to him.

"Better?" he asked, completely unruffled by what might have been one of the most erotic encounters of my life. If he could do that to me by just touching my thighs, what would it feel like—

"Ruby?"

I blinked at him, trying to remember how to form a sentence. "What?"

"Does your leg feel better?"

I sucked in a deep, steadying breath. "Oh, that. Yes. It's better."

I narrowed my eyes at his wing. The wound had opened again, and a bright stream of blood spilled down the front.

"Isn't there something we can do for your wing?" I asked quietly.

"Not unless you have healing powers like I do."

"If you're a god of death," I asked, "why do you have the power to heal?"

"Because death is an analgesic."

I frowned. "This doesn't have any side effects, does it? Like necrosis?"

He smiled slowly, pulling his hands away. "No. You'll be fine."

The pain had completely left my body, replaced instead with a warm, tingling excitement. I could get addicted to his touch, like a drug fiend craving opiates.

Pretty sure the last thing I needed was to let Adonis's seductive beauty lure me in. I'd be keeping my Thanatos drive well and truly suppressed.

CHAPTER 9

I stared out over the wildflower-dappled field. "I might not have healing powers, but I'm supposed to be the Bringer of Light, right? And the Old Gods will provide. All we need to do is tune in to their beauty."

"Is that right?" I heard a faintly mocking tone in his voice.

"They've given me what I needed so far: poison, sap from the trees to light my arrows, the power of light." I sat up straight. "Let me try it."

I closed my eyes, focusing on the sounds around me—the rustling of the wind through the grasses, the gentle lapping and splashing of the river. A faint whispering floated on the breeze, the words unintelligible. A vibrating power seemed to move up my feet, up my limbs, lighting my body from the inside out. Something faintly floral wafted through the air—an unusual scent for February.

I opened my eyes, scanning the tall grasses around me, until I spotted a faint smudge of yellow in the distance. "There," I said.

"What?"

"They're giving us a remedy." I rose on my newly healed legs. I bit my lip. "I don't suppose you have any bandages though?"

He nodded at Thanatos. "You can find a blanket in the satchel. Tear a strip off it."

I crossed to his enormous, bruise-colored horse, who reared back his head, snorting as I approached. Gingerly, I stroked his silver mane until he quieted. Then, I reached into the leather satchel, pulling out a blanket. I ripped a strip from it, then stuffed the rest of the blanket back into the satchel.

With the bandage ready, I hurried over to a patch of white and yellow wildflowers blooming among the grasses.

When I was a kid, my mom took me out on long treks into the New England forests. We'd walk through the forests, her pale hair gleaming in chinks of streaming sunlight, her hiking boots and jeans muddied. She always wore long sleeves, even in summer. She had some kind of brutal scar she didn't want anyone to see. An attack from a wild beast that had disfigured her—a reptile, probably. She'd never tell me the whole story.

In any case, those long nature walks were my salvation.

I smiled, then plucked a handful of the weeds and stroked my fingertips over the delicate, fern-like leaves. I remembered Mom's voice as she told me yarrow was a styptic—a substance that can staunch bleeding.

I stripped the leaves from the stem, piling them into one of my palms. Then, I closed my eyes and held my palm up to the sunlight. Warmth blazed from my palm, the sun's rays using my hand as a brazier, and an herbal smell filled the air. When I opened my eyes again, the leaves had been heated, dried to a crisp.

I grinned. Maybe I didn't know what the hell it meant, but I felt blessed by the Old Gods. This was the way of the ancient fae—live in the moment; merge with the beauty around you.

I scanned the earth for moss until my gaze landed on a bright green patch among the rocks and grasses nearby. I knelt down next to it and pried off a cool, damp chunk.

Clutching my handfuls of moss and dried yarrow, I crossed back to Adonis. When I reached him, I plopped down next to him on the rock.

He was studying me with an intense curiosity. "Communing with the Old Gods, I suppose?"

I opened my palm. "I have my own healing treatment for that shattered wing of yours."

"Is this really necessary?"

"It will heal a lot faster than if you just rely on your own magic. And what if it heals all crooked?"

"I must admit. I want to know what your hands would feel like on my wings."

My cheeks flushed. "What, is that some kind of sex thing for angels?"

A slow shrug.

"I'll try to forget I just learned that." I examined his midnight blue wings, cascading gracefully over the back of the rock. Streaks of blood pooled from the jagged break at the top.

"So I'm supposed to trust the healing skills of a deceitful, feral fae?" A seductive purr softened the harshness of his words.

"Yes. I know you hate the fae, but we have our own set of skills." Carefully, I laid out the moss and crushed herbs on my makeshift bandage. "I spent my formative years with my mom, learning about the trees, the plants, the herbs. We found a broken sparrow once, and she taught me to treat and set his wing."

A wicked smile. "And you think I'm like a broken sparrow."

"Same idea. You're just bigger." Gently, I ran my fingertips over the top of his wing.

Adonis inhaled sharply, his wing twitching, pupils dilating.

"Did that hurt already?"

"No. But wings are a sensitive area. I don't normally let anyone touch them."

"It's a closed fracture," I said. "I think the open break has begun to set itself already. This will help with the tears in your skin and muscle."

"How ever did I survive four thousand years without you?"

I leaned in closer to him and began pressing the dried yarrow against his wing, his feathers soft and silky against my fingertips. As I pressed the herbs against him, he gasped faintly, and his lids lowered.

I couldn't quite tell if he was enjoying this or hating it, but I tried not to think about it either way.

"Yarrow will staunch the bleeding and clean the wound," I said quietly. I picked up the moss from the rock and gently held it over the broken wing's surface. "And this will help pack the wound." Holding the moss in place, I reached for the bandage.

Carefully, I tied it over the top of his wing, pressing the moss and yarrow to his feathers. He winced slightly, but as I threaded it gently around his muscle and bone, through the curtain of midnight feathers, his stormy eyes were locked intently on my face. I was pressing in close to him to reach his back, and his body radiated warmth.

I sat back on the rock, admiring my work. He drank me in with his gaze.

"There. Good as new." I took a deep breath. "See? Fae skills can be useful. We're not *just* beasts."

A twitch of his lip. "You didn't grow up around them, did you?"

I shook my head. "My parents left the fae realm long before I was born." I swallowed hard. "What did you mean when you said you lived among the fae, helping them kill for fun?"

Any trace of a smile disappeared from his face. "They're savage and driven to dominate."

My wild antics obviously didn't do much to dispel that notion—not that he'd seemed to mind at the time.

"If they were so savage, why did you help them kill?"

"I told you. I was born to kill." He definitely wasn't smiling now. In fact, his voice had a despairing edge.

"But why the fae in particular—if you hate us so much?"

Sharp tendrils of his magic cut at the air, and he pulled his gaze away from me.

I heaved a sigh. "Fine. Don't elaborate. I wouldn't expect you to. We can get on with the journey now that you've healed my legs." My stomach grumbled loudly.

Adonis scowled. "You should have told me you were hungry."

I rubbed my belly. "I didn't feel the hunger until now. Now that my legs are no longer screaming at me."

He cocked his head, studying me like a curious child would a dying insect. "And why didn't you tell me you were tired?"

My jaw tightened. "Because I didn't want you to know. You don't tell me things, and I don't tell you things. That's our relationship."

He quirked an eyebrow. "I see. I thought you were big on chatter." He stood and crossed to his horse. He rummaged in his leather pack for a moment, then pulled out some packages wrapped in brown paper. He pulled out a flask too.

The rock felt frozen beneath my bum, and I pulled my coat a little tighter around me. "Do you feel hunger?"

"No. But sometimes, I eat for pleasure. I understand your kind need sustenance."

I began unwrapping the food he'd brought: a package of bread, one of chorizo, and one of cheese. My mouth watered, and I had to restrain myself from throwing my arms around Adonis's neck to thank him for understanding the concept of "needing sustenance."

I gingerly broke off a small piece of chorizo, before I gave up on manners and just started gnawing on it like a wild animal. When I took a break from the chorizo to build myself a hasty cheese sandwich, Drakon ambled over and snatched the sausage from the ground.

I grumbled through my mouthful of sandwich. "That was mine."

When I finished eating, crumbs littered my blue coat. "Sorry. Did you want any?"

Adonis's eyes were wide. "I honestly didn't know the fae got *quite* that hungry."

"Older fae can control it better."

"And how old are you?"

I cleared my throat. "Not as old as I'd pretended to be."

"*How old?*"

"Twenty-five."

His eyes snapped open. "Sweet heavenly gods. You were just born."

I folded my arms. "Johnny isn't that much older than me. Born in the seventies." I squinted in the sunlight. "How does it work, exactly? Why are you all such different ages?"

He sipped from his flask. "Johnny, Kratos, and I—we're different than other archangels."

"Different how?"

"The Heavenly Host is made up of ten archangels. Like us, they're nearly impossible to kill. But they're heavenly beings. Johnny, Kratos, and I—we're archangels who were born on earth."

I frowned. "And your parents were…what exactly?"

"My father was an archangel. My mother was a human."

Surprise flickered through me. "So you're…half human."

"There's nothing human about me. An archangel is defined by his soul."

"Right." His mother would have died thousands of years ago, but his father? I couldn't quite believe he was telling me all this, and I had a burning desire to know more about him. About all of this.

"Did your father return to the heavens?" I asked.

His gaze shuttered, and something about the raw look in his eyes told me not to push anymore on this question. I'd touched a nerve somehow. Still, I *needed* to know more. Needed to know how and why all this had happened.

"Why did it start?" I asked. "The Great Nightmare?"

"Once the wars started between humans, demons, the fae—the Heavenly Host decided it was time for a purification. Since the fall, they've just been waiting for the right moment to unleash us. And you all gave it to them with your infighting."

"I see." I swallowed hard. "Why does Johnny make me feel so…*hungry* when he stands near me?"

Adonis's keen eyes searched me. "He's an angel of famine."

"Famine," I repeated. "And you're…death."

"Is that what you feel when I stand near you?"

Not exactly. But I wasn't going to tell him that standing near him made me yearn for the excruciating pleasure I knew he could give me. That he made my blood heat, my breasts strain against my clothes until I wanted to pull them off.

Nope, no way I was saying that. The archangel's ego was oppressive enough as it was. Instead, I said, "Something like that. Shadows seem to cling to you. You give off a bit of a death vibe."

I almost thought I saw a flicker of disappointment in his pale eyes. He sipped his flask before handing it to me. "And what do you feel when you're near Kratos?"

My throat tightened. *Like I want to fall to my knees.* "He exudes dominance. Like he was born to conquer."

"And there you have it."

My pulse raced as a glimmer of understanding began to spark in my mind. "Death, Famine, Conquest..." My stomach clenched as I pieced it all together. "Your horse."

Adonis's pale, gray eyes pierced me. I shivered, and he widened his wings, shielding me from the wintry winds that whipped at my hair and skin. The feathered tip of one wing brushed against my skin, and I shivered.

"I thought it was a human myth," I said hollowly.

"You thought what was a human myth?"

"The four horsemen of the apocalypse."

CHAPTER 10

"*I* prefer angel to horseman," he said, "but either is fine."

My throat had gone dry. "So that means there's one more. War, right?"

A hint of mockery in his smile. "I think your young mind has learned all it can handle at this point."

The wind rushed over the river, carrying with it the scent of early wisteria shoots.

I didn't understand him, or the archangels, or the horsemen. Adonis was a dark and foreign power. I only knew that in the sound of the wind rustling the leaves, I felt the Old Gods calling me.

"And your purpose on earth is to kill in massive numbers." I hugged my knees to my chest. "I don't know what you have planned for me, Adonis, but I happen to believe that the good guys always win in the end. Even if you have to go through several years of hell and death to get there."

Shadows slid through his eyes. "And you're sure you know who the good guys are?"

A shiver danced up my neck. "Not exactly. But I think the Old Gods are the good guys. I felt them in the forest outside Hotemet Castle. I feel them out here, even, whispering on the February wind,

339

mingling with the early scents of spring. And I felt them on Eimmal, when their power flowed through my body like an ancient river. They're looking after the fae, the humans."

"Don't mistake them for benevolent gods. Nature gives as much as it takes. Death is as much a part of nature as life. Have you ever seen a starving grizzly take down a deer? Or watched smallpox spread through a village? That is nature as much as the pretty flowers you enjoy sniffing."

I bit my lip. "Fine. Nature is full of terrible things, but we don't need to focus on it, do we? Is the world a terrible place or a beautiful place? The answer to that is a choice. Our lives and our souls are our stories. That's where truth lies. And I want to tell the stories of love and happiness, not chaos and death."

Adonis was studying me closely. "And what are your personal stories of love, Ruby?"

The word *love* on his tongue was a sensual caress that licked up my spine, but I pushed the temptation out of my mind. "Not the kind you'd want to hear. They're not about seduction and pleasure, they're about knowing someone so well they become a part of you." A flicker in my mind, a pile of ash on the ground. I slammed my mental door down. "Before your archangel friends started destroying the world, I had that kind of love."

"What was his name?"

I didn't want to say Marcus's name in front of him. In fact, I didn't want to think about him at all, now. Because whenever I did, vicious images clawed at the back of my skull. Loss gnawed at me from the inside out. Those last, agonizing moments—

I clamped my eyes shut. "I don't want to think about this anymore. Like I said—our souls are our stories, and I want to focus on the good ones."

"But when you cut out the blood and the death and all the monstrous things that scare you, you'll start to forget the people you've lost. And you'll lose yourself, too."

My fists tightened. "Is that right?"

The breeze toyed with his dark hair, and his exotic scent wrapped around me. "There's no light without darkness, no good without evil, no meaning without death. The seeds of destruction grow in the gardens of paradise."

I scowled. "Did you just make that saying up? That is a super depressing aphorism."

"It's an old archangel saying."

"I think I preferred it when you were just making vaguely suggestive comments about touching my thighs."

His brow furrowed. "I've made no comments about touching your thighs. Would you like me to?"

He hadn't? Flustered, I rose. At that moment, I realized that my bladder was completely full. "This has been a fascinating philosophical discussion, but I'm going to the other side of the bridge. Give me a few minutes."

"Why are you going to the other side of the bridge?"

I frowned. "I need to pee, if you must know. And I'd rather not do it in front of one of the horsemen of the apocalypse. Don't come anywhere near there."

"I'll try to restrain myself."

With my arms folded, I walked briskly over the river bank, heading for the stone bridge. My mind whirled with everything I'd learned today. Strangely, instead of being overwhelmed, I felt energized. Sure, things died, nature was harsh. I'd signed up as a partner of the horseman of death. But the Old Gods thrived all around me, and I had the sense that they wanted to lure me into their realm, that they'd be on my side when I needed them.

I snuck behind the bridge, shielding myself from Adonis's view on the other side of a stony wall. After checking around me for any signs of life, I pulled down my leather leggings and underwear. I crouched on the sloping river's edge, taking care not to pee on my own shoes or pants. The wind nipped at my bare bum.

When I'd finished, I quickly pulled up my pants. In the shadows of the bridge, I took a moment to readjust the holster on my thigh. As I did, a splashing sound in the water behind me turned my head.

My heart stopped. There, in the steely, frigid river waters, stood a black hound, the size of our horses. Mist whirled around him, chilling me to the bone. His eyes blazed like hot, red coals, and his lips curled back from his teeth in a terrifying snarl. I reached for the knife at my thigh.

As I did, the creature began to shift, twisting silently in the ghostly mist—until he transformed into three humanoid forms. They looked massive, their hulking bodies dripping with water.

One of them sniffed the air, water streaming from his dark hair in rivulets over his pale skin. Tight, black clothing clung to his body, and claws grew from his fingertips. "You look like a succubus," he growled. "You smell even more delicious than a succubus, though. What are you?"

Since the Great Nightmare had begun, demons seemed to have free reign to terrorize smaller creatures as much as they wanted. My hand twitched at my knife. Should I simply stay and fight, or scream for Adonis at this point? I didn't suppose these were friendly demons.

"What do you want?" I asked quietly.

"Food and fucking," the three identical demons said in unison. "You showed us your naked arse, and it looked good to us."

My stomach turned. *Oh, gross.*

"No thanks." I took a step back, pointing my knife at them. "I don't want to have to hurt—"

One of the demons silenced me with a sharp slash of his arm. I mean he *literally* silenced me, stealing my voice. I opened my mouth, trying to shout, and no sound came out. A jolt of fear gripped me.

As I readied my knife, one of the demons lunged for me. Heart pounding, I sharpened my senses and gripped the hilt. When the demon reached me, I was ready for him. I darted forward at the full speed of a fae, driving my knife between two of his ribs.

He clutched his chest, gurgling, and I let him slump to the ground. To my horror, two more enormous hounds emerged from the churning river waters, eyes blazing red.

In the mists, the black hounds transformed into more hulking, red-eyed demons.

"Bitch!" one of them hissed. "I will tear your flesh from your bones!"

I opened my mouth again to shout, but only a whisper wheezed from my throat. My legs shaking, I turned to run. I only got a few feet before rough hands were dragging me back over the rocks, into the water. I opened my mouth to scream for Adonis, and a rush of air puffed out.

I kicked one of them hard in the shins with the heel of my boot, and he loosened his grip on me just enough that I could wrench my knife arm free. With a clumsy gesture, I managed to nick his skin before more rough, powerful arms began dragging me under the water. One of them shoved my head into the icy river. Still, I clung on to that poison-tipped knife with everything in my power. I held my breath.

He released my head for just a moment, allowing me to suck in a frigid breath.

"You need to learn some manners," one of the demons barked. "Give a blessing to the river god." He rammed my head under the surface again.

I kicked and bucked fruitlessly. *Air. Sweet, heavenly gods, I need air.* After what seemed an eternity, my lungs started to burn, and panic ripped through my body.

At last, I tore my arm free and brought the knife down hard into the shin of one of the demons. I flailed, getting my head above water just long enough to draw a breath. That was when I felt the light burning dimly in my body, a warm glow of primordial power.

With a burst of wild energy, I wrenched free from the demons' grasp. I sucked in a sharp breath, desperate to sprint away from them. But I knew I needed to face them. If I turned my back to these hounds, they'd just pull me under again. I whirled, my blade ready, glowing with the light of the Old Gods.

As the first demon reached me, I slashed my blade across his throat, severing his jugular. Blood sprayed.

How many of them *were* there now? My heart hammered against my ribs, and I took another step back on the muddy shore, clutching my knife.

Five. Five enormous demons still standing, all gunning for my blood. Even with the power of the Old Gods…

Just as another one of these demons was running for me, Adonis's magic skimmed over my skin, snaking around the demons' bodies. Trembling, I stepped away from them. Tendrils of dark magic curled in a wild dance around them, freezing the demons in place.

Their jaws dropped, their expressions slackening. Abruptly, with jerking movements, they turned in the water, stumbling toward the bridge.

My entire body was shaking, blazing with light, with energy, with battle fury. But I just stood there, gaping at the Dark Lord's magic. So *this* was what Adonis's mind control powers looked like. A terrible sort of awe bloomed in my chest. This was the power of a death god.

I glanced back at him, standing just a few feet away from me. His silver-streaked, midnight wings swooped behind him, and his eyes gleamed like stars. He loomed above the riverbed, murmuring in an ancient language, shadows cloaking his powerful body. The sight of him sent an icy lick of dread racing up my spine.

Through the rushing water, the small demon horde trudged closer to the bridge, moving faster now. I cleared my throat, finding I could vocalize again.

My stomach jolted when the first red-eyed demon began bashing his head against the sleek stone of the bridge. More followed, slamming their heads against the rocks. I winced at the sound of cracking bone, the grunts and strangled cries that came from the demons, bashing their own skulls in. Blood and gore sprayed across the bridge's rocky surface.

Bile rose in my throat. He *did* tell me he was born to kill. And I'd wanted to kill the demons, too. Just maybe not with the same disturbing, bone-chilling brutality.

I stared grimly at the scene before me, cringing at the agonized snarls and shrieks, and my fingers tightened into fists.

Did I really want to give Adonis more power? What if he was lying about returning to the celestial realm, and just wanted to weaken the other archangels so he could assume complete control over the earth?

I found it hard to believe he wanted to take off into the heavens. I couldn't imagine him as an incorporeal being, just floating around. He was blood and bone, lust and violence, primal seduction—as bestial and full of cravings as I was.

I clenched my jaw. I'd go along with him for now to learn what I could from him, but I wasn't about to start trusting him.

When the last of the demons had slumped, bloodied and broken, into the churning river, I loosed a long breath.

"That was an interesting execution method," I said quietly.

Adonis's pale gray eyes had darkened to the color of iron. "Sometimes I like to get creative." He took a deep, shuddering breath, then winced, turning away from me. It almost looked like he was in pain. "Are you all right?"

"I'm fine. Just cold."

As he began walking back to the horses, I followed after him. Drakon circled slowly overhead, plumes of smoke curling from his mouth.

"Does that sort of magic drain your energy?" My teeth chattered from the freezing water.

"Yes, but sometimes it's worth it."

I hugged my coat tighter. "Why? What was it about these demons in particular that provoked your rage?"

"I sensed what they wanted to do to you. I could practically hear their thoughts. It was repulsive, and they needed to answer for it."

I arched an eyebrow. Once again, I reminded myself never to get on his bad side.

CHAPTER 11

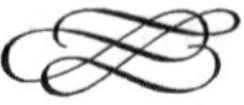

$\mathcal{A}$donis's magic had worked its way into my body, providing a sort of painkiller as we rode farther north through darkening fields. I'd changed into dry clothes, though I had to wait for my coat to dry before I'd feel warm again.

Neither Thanatos nor Nuckelavee showed any signs of tiring, and we were able to take them at a gallop for part of the way.

As the sun set, long shadows climbed over the fields. By the time darkness had fallen, we'd reached the north of England.

Darkness still terrified me. Now, we had only the thin moonlight to light our way, casting a dull glow over the rocky, undulating fields. My grip tightened on the reins. If a cloud went over the moon, I'd be at risk of a humiliating panic attack.

I strained my eyes, making out the short grasses that grew among the rocky hills. Was this what I'd heard was called the moors?

Farther ahead on the path, moonlight dimly illuminated a grove of sycamore trees that stood out starkly against the flat landscape.

Even if my thighs had recovered somewhat, tiredness had sapped my energy, and my eyes started to drift closed. Under the cloak of darkness, an icy chill had fallen over me, and the February wind stung my skin. When, exactly, were we stopping? And where were we going to sleep?

My teeth chattered. I'd already admitted weakness once today. Might as well run with it.

"Adonis!" I called out.

He whirled, and Thanatos's eerie eyes gleamed in the darkness.

"Are you all right?" His voice carried over the moors.

"Fine. I just thought… Maybe we could sleep soon. I'm about to fall off Nuckelavee, and I think the beast is heartless enough to trample me to death. There's a grove of sycamores over there that can shield us in the wind. Maybe we can make a fire pit."

"Fine. But no fire. We don't want to attract attention."

Gods damn it.

I clenched my teeth, unwilling to admit the truth—that under the shadows of night-dark sycamores, I'd be left alone with my own fears. Not to mention the fact that I was going to freeze to death.

"It's freezing."

"I'll make sure you're warm." A taunting, dangerous invitation delivered in a sensuous timbre. "The fae live for pleasure. Isn't that right?"

"Pretty good pickup line, Adonis, but watching you force men to bash their heads into rocks didn't really get me in the mood."

Cruelty hardened his beautiful features once more, but he didn't reply.

We trotted over to the grove, and I shivered in my coat. In a small clearing in the center of the trees, I pulled Nuckelavee to a halt beside Thanatos. I dismounted, practically falling off the stallion's side. When my feet reached the earth, I considered just throwing myself on the frozen ground to fall into a deep sleep.

Instead, I eased myself down against a sycamore trunk, watching Adonis as he pulled something out of his bag. A blanket, it looked like —thick and woolen. I rubbed my arms for warmth, my breath forming clouds around my face.

"I don't suppose you have more than one of those blankets? Since I didn't know we were traveling all the way across the country, I had no idea I needed to pack a duvet or anything."

He handed me the dark blue blanket. "I don't need it. I'm going to be keeping watch for hostile demons. Or for Johnny."

"You think he might come after us?"

"If he recovers his memory, he will definitely come for you. And that would ruin my plans, wouldn't it?"

I swallowed hard, suddenly intensely relieved that Adonis would be staying up. "You don't need sleep?"

"Sometimes." He sat, leaning against a tree trunk. "Not as much as you."

I lay on the blanket, then folded one half over myself, curling into a ball. I lay my cheek on the soft wool, hugging the blanket tightly.

In the shadows of the sycamore grove, my heart was beating hard against my ribs, and the darkness felt as if it were closing in on me. And in the shadows, those sharp, pointed memories—the dragon's teeth in Marcus's chest—

Sharp teeth piercing an arm—

I pulled the blanket tighter around my shoulders, trying to stave off the feeling that I was standing at the edge of a void. If I fell in, my soul would rip apart.

"I can hear your heart pounding."

My eyes snapped open, and I met Adonis's curious gaze.

"It's nothing." I loosed a slow breath. There was no way in hell I was telling him I was scared of the dark. "I just get a bit nervous being outside at night with demons roaming around."

"You'll be fine, Ruby," he said quietly. "I'm the most dangerous creature for thousands of miles. And I'm on your side. Just relax."

Somehow, I found that reassuring, and I tuned in to the strangely soothing feel of his magic, which kissed my cheeks like a night breeze.

Now, when I closed my eyes, a vivid memory lit up the hollows of my mind: I lay in a field, my arms spread out to the sides. White puffs of dandelions dappled the tall grasses, and from my spot on the ground, Hazel toddled over to me. She must have been two, and smears of chocolate ice cream streaked her chin and lips. She straddled my tummy, knocking the breath out of me, then reached for a white puff of dandelion by my side. She plucked it from the ground.

"Make a wish!" she commanded, holding it to her mouth. Her dark curls framed her chubby cheeks.

"You're supposed to make the wish," I said quietly.

"Make a wish!" she shouted again, this time angrier, cheeks reddening.

I'd given in. I always gave in to her.

"I wish that you'd find another place to sit because you're crushing my stomach."

She touched the dandelion to her mouth, then blew. The filaments caught in the breeze, and some of the fluff stuck to her chocolate-streaked cheeks.

Slowly, sleep claimed my mind, and with it, the sun-drenched park of my memory receded, replaced by frozen, windswept fields. I dreamt of a barren landscape, and icicles gleaming from tree branches.

As I slept, I was dimly aware of the cold air piercing me to my bones, of shivering and teeth chattering. At least, until a blanket of warmth covered me, and my dreams shifted. A river rushed from a cavern, flowing over a cliff. It smelled of melted mountain water. At the base of the waterfall, banks bloomed with tall grasses and crimson flowers. The scent of myrrh trees coiled around my body.

When I woke in the dazzling, ruddy sunrise, Adonis was nowhere near me. He leaned against a sycamore trunk, watching as the sun streaked the sky with lurid shades of orange.

I rubbed the sleep from my eyes, then slowly sat up. Adonis had covered me in his black cloak during the night. Maybe it was the smell of myrrh, but I had the strangest feeling that I'd been dreaming of something from his memories.

The full power of his icy eyes fell on me. "You're awake. We have a whole day's riding ahead of us. I hope your legs hold up today."

I didn't want to take his warm cloak off my body. "How's your wing?"

"It's healing quickly. In a few more days, it will be good as new."

"Good." I rose slowly, my body groaning, and I handed Adonis his cloak. "Thanks for the extra warmth."

"The sound of your teeth chattering was driving me insane."

I scooped up the blanket from the earth, crossed to Thanatos, and tucked it into Adonis's leather satchel. The horse snorted, steam rising from his enormous nostrils. Then, he nuzzled my face. I smiled. It seemed Thanatos liked me better than Nuckelavee.

"Any chance you could tell me how much farther we have to go?" I asked.

"We'll be riding until nightfall, assuming we can keep the same pace as yesterday."

I suppressed a groan. Adonis's healing magic had been helpful, but it wasn't a panacea. I leaned over, rubbing my thighs. "Sure. All day riding again. No problem."

He wrapped his dark cloak around him, and the shadows seemed to thicken in the air surrounding him. "This time, tell me when you're falling apart instead of randomly screaming *uncle*, will you?"

CHAPTER 12

My pride took a serious hit that day. By sunset, Adonis's magical attempts to soothe my muscles were no longer working, and I'd completely given up.

A cold rain had begun hammering down on us as we traveled, completely drenching my clothes. When the cold had me shivering uncontrollably in my saddle, Adonis had reared Thanatos to a halt. In the icy downpour, he'd pulled the saddle off Thanatos, loaded his satchel onto Nuckelavee, and scooped me onto his horse with him.

Now, I rode wrapped in his powerful arms, with his soothing magic pulsing through my muscles. Drakon soared above us, occasionally igniting the dark air with sharp bursts of fire.

Nuckelavee cantered on beside us, completely compliant, with only the help of Adonis's orders.

Adonis's body kept me warm, his feathered wings shielding me from some of the wind and rain. As we rode into the night, I hated myself slightly for the disturbing thrill that surged through my body whenever his arms brushed against my sides, just skimming my breasts...

Don't fall for his charms, Ruby. He seduced every woman he met.

Plus, that whole thing about him being a god of death, born to kill. It made sense that someone like him thought of nature as brutal and cruel—a paradise sown with seeds of destruction. The world around us was a mirror, reflecting our own souls back at us. And Adonis's was savage.

When we got to his castle, I'd be doing a bit of spying. Mainly, I needed to find out all the things Adonis was unwilling to tell me, starting with—what the hell was a Bringer of Light, and why did he need me?

Exhausted, I leaned back against his muscled chest, and the feel of his warm body against mine sent my pulse racing. I could have sworn I heard a low growl rise from his throat as I did.

Still, the movements of the horse began lulling me into a sense of calm, along with the slow rhythm of his pounding heart at my back. As I leaned into him, I breathed in his soothing smell. My eyes began to drift closed.

After only another minute, his deep voice pierced the silence. "We're here, Ruby."

I opened my eyes. There, in the darkness, a castle loomed above us. It towered over the edge of a cliff, its dark stone walls gleaming with rain in the faint light. Shadows claimed the space beyond the cliff, but the sound of waves crashing against rocks filled the air. I ran my tongue over my lips, tasting salt.

"When we get inside, I'll find a room for you." His voice was a soft murmur in my ear.

"Where are we, exactly? And what time is it?"

"Scotland, and late," he said quietly. "Everyone will be asleep."

"Everyone?"

"You'll meet them tomorrow."

Adonis led Thanatos over the rocky terrain toward his castle. Rain slid down my skin, between my breasts. Still, Adonis's warmth kept me from freezing.

As we moved closer to the gatehouse, I caught sight of the carvings in the walls—the skulls and gargoyles—haunted, human-like faces whose mouths and eyes gaped in horror.

Looks cozy.

My breath caught in my throat at the sight of the castle looming above us, the peaks and towers majestic against the dark night sky. At our approach, the heavy portcullis began to creak open. The gate's iron teeth speared the air, giving the entrance the appearance of a wild beast. The gatehouse's narrow windows gaped out onto the rocky landscape like empty eyes.

When the gate had groaned fully open, it revealed a towering, arched hall, lit by the dancing flames of torches. The horses' hooves echoed off a vaulted ceiling high above us. Vines climbed the walls, blooming with blood-red flowers.

The hall gave way to the open air—a wide outdoor passageway between towering gothic structures.

As I dismounted from Thanatos, a movement in the shadows caught my eyes. Cloaked in a cowl, a figure glided over the stones. I caught the faintest hint of bone-white skin under his hood. Creepy.

Adonis slid off his horse, and pulled our leather bags off. He handed over the reins, and the cloaked man led the two horses away, their hooves clopping over the stones. Adonis handed me my sodden bag, and I clung to it.

I surveyed the walls around me, each one carved with leering or agonized gargoyle faces. This place was built to intimidate, but I'd already lived through one horseman's castle. I didn't scare that easily.

Wordlessly, Adonis stalked to a second arched doorway, expecting me to follow him. We crossed a stony courtyard. Here, a statue loomed over the center of the courtyard—a beautiful man sitting on a pedestal, his wings arched and demonic. He looked down at the ground, and a stone snake coiled up his leg.

Drakon landed on the ground by the statue's feet. He hissed, and a flame shot from his mouth at the statue's base.

"Lucifer," I said quietly.

"Also known as Azazeyl."

"He's beautiful." I paused at the statue, frowning. "Who was he, exactly?"

"He introduced humans to the magical language. He was an

archangel, and when he plummeted to earth, he fractured into the seven earthly gods. Then with him, a horde of angels fell, transforming into demons."

I hugged my sodden coat tighter. "Why do you have a statue of him?"

"The other horsemen think it's to remind us of our mission—to correct the great original sin. I have no interest in doing that. I admire him."

"Why?"

"Because he rebelled against those who would control us," he said with a touch of awe. "He broke the rules."

Like the snake at the statue's base, Drakon began scaling the statue, crawling up the stone in a slinking motion. He seemed quite at home there, almost as if the marble god were a long-lost lover.

Apparently done with our conversation, Adonis moved on toward one of the towers that loomed over us. As we neared it, an oak door swung open on its own.

I followed him into a hall—a vast, stony atrium. From here, a wide stairway led up to a second floor. Wordlessly, Adonis led me up the stairs.

Vaulted stone ceilings arched above us like ribs, and my footsteps echoed off a stone floor. Faintly, my fae senses tuned in to the distinct scent of old parchment and leather. *Bingo.* Somewhere around here, I'd find a library. Maybe the Dark Lord had one or two books about the Bringer of Light on his shelves.

He wasn't big on filling me in on things like what we were doing, or why we'd come here. Or what, specifically, a Light Bringer was going to do. He didn't seem to feel the need to tell me how I'd help him rule the heavens, or why he wanted to return there if he had such contempt for the celestial angels in the first place.

I was still a spy, though, wasn't I? I didn't need to wait for the information to come to me. I went out and found it.

At the top of a stairwell, Adonis led me down a long mezzanine. To my left, sculptures of twisting and thorny vines snaked over the walls. In the hallway's guttering candlelight, the sculptures looked half alive.

"Nice place you have here," I said. "Real homey."

"It suits me."

He paused at an oak door, and pushed it open to reveal a cavernous bedroom. Here, pale light shone through steeply peaked windows onto an ornate, tiled floor, inlaid with rubies. A canopied bed stood on a dais, the blankets a deep crimson. Black, thorny vines climbed the stone walls, and poison hemlock grew among them. A dark, arched doorway led to another room—the bathroom, probably. Candles hung in chandeliers high above us, but none of them were lit.

I swallowed hard. When I said before that I was no longer easily intimidated by creepy spaces, I was vastly overestimating myself.

"You'll be comfortable here," he said.

"You must be misreading my facial expression."

"What's the problem?"

I glanced at the marble fireplace, as gaping and empty as the gargoyles' eyes. "It's cold. Do you think we could get a fire going?"

He studied me, his eyes gleaming like stars in the shadowy room. "That's right," he said softly. He crossed to me, his hands in his pockets. "I'd nearly forgotten that you were scared of the dark."

I bristled. "How did you know that?"

"I can feel it." His eyes gleamed in the dim light. "You said darkness surrounds me. Do I scare you, Ruby?"

I wasn't sure what to say to him, so I thought I'd just go with the truth. "Yes. You were born to scare, weren't you?" *Born to seduce, too, but let's not get into that.* I turned, meeting his gaze head on. "But you don't scare me all the time."

Sometimes, he made me feel calm.

He snapped his fingers, and firelight burst into the empty fireplace. "That will keep you warm."

With another flick of his wrist, curtains fell over the windows. At least in Adonis's home I'd have some privacy from the ever-watchful eyes of the sentinels.

"You can hang all your wet clothes by the fire to dry. I don't have anything for you to sleep in, I'm afraid."

"I'll sleep naked."

His eyes widened, body tensing.

"As long as no one randomly barges in here, it's fine."

He paused, eyeing me for a moment before heading for the door. "Get some rest. Tomorrow, you meet my friends."

Or, I could find out more about all of you while you sleep.

CHAPTER 13

Pressing my ear against the door, I waited until I heard a nearby door open and close. To my surprise, the sound had been nearby. In this enormous castle, Adonis had put me in a bedroom right next to his.

Keeping an eye on me, I supposed. Still, unlike at Hotemet Castle, no one had explicitly told me to stay in my room, nor had I heard a lock click to trap me in here.

Before crossing into the hallway, I pulled off my boots so I could move more quietly. I slipped off my sodden jacket and laid it out by the fire. Then, I slowly opened the door.

Creeping into the hallway, I peered over the balcony's ledge to the stony floor below.

I searched for signs of movement around me, any flickers in the shadows.

A complete and eerie silence had fallen over the castle, and I could hear only my own breathing. I sharpened my fae senses, until the sights and lights dazzled me.

As I did, I homed in on a particular smell—one both deeply familiar and enticing. The smell of old books, luring me closer like a siren song. Books were my home, my refuge.

More importantly, a library might have crucial information.

I moved silently over the balcony floor, drawn in by the smell of paper and leather, until I reached an open archway. I'd found the library.

I just didn't want to walk into the darkness, exactly.

I pulled a torch from its iron bracket on the wall, and its light wavered around me as I stepped into the library.

Moonlight poured through a towering window onto vast walls of old books that reached to the ceiling. I let out a long breath. In Hotemet Castle, Kratos's book choices had given me a window into his mind. Would I learn anything about Adonis here?

I crossed to one of the walls lined with oak shelves, each one crammed with old tomes. Spindly ladders led up to the higher shelves.

I held the torch in front of a bookshelf, and some of the lettering on the spines glinted in silver and gold. I couldn't read it, unfortunately. The languages looked ancient and unfamiliar. One of them, I was pretty sure, was the angular markings of the Phoenician alphabet. What secrets were contained in these old books?

I moved on from there, eager to get to the books I could actually understand. It took me a few minutes of wandering around the bookshelves before I arrived at anything written in English. Bafflingly, they seemed to be books about gardening. Ancient catalogs of trees, herbs, some of flowers.

What did that tell me about Adonis? I could hardly see him tooling around in a garden, crouching down in a pair of rubber boots to do the weeding, but maybe he was into it.

I moved on again, this time to books of poetry—romantic poets like Coleridge and Shelley, Shakespeare, modern poets, ancient epic poems like *The Epic of Gilgamesh*…

So far, Adonis's book choices were a complete surprise. I hadn't expected a death god to be into gardening and poetry, but I supposed I didn't know much about death gods.

In any case, I was no closer to learning about the Bringer of Light. I didn't suppose there was a *Bringer of Light for Dummies* book around here…

Still, I wasn't in a rush. In this forbidding castle, I actually felt like I belonged here. When I was a kid, I'd spent hours curled up in an alcove in my parents' old library, reading books about faraway places. I used to like the books that scared me—the ones about ghosts and haunted castles—and then I'd see monsters in the corner of my room when I tried to sleep at night. I'd call to my mom over and over again, asking for protections, for spells and charms. Over time, she started hiding the scary books, but they called to me.

I crossed to a dark corner of the library along the far wall, then slid my torch into an empty sconce. These books were in an altogether different alphabet—one with squat, sharp marks that looked millennia old. As I scanned the shelves, one book caught my eye, the lettering on the spine seeming to gleam brighter than the rest.

I pulled it from the shelf, and cracked open the spine to the faded parchment pages. Gently, I leafed through it. I scanned text, then drawings of angelic destruction—winged beings lighting fires, sending curls of dark magic streaming from their fingertips while piles of skeletons lay beneath them. Each one had his own horse. Halfway through the book, I found a picture—a simple, stylized drawing of a woman standing in a grove of trees, her hair painted the color of straw. Golden light beamed from her head.

The Bringer of Light?

A few pages more, and I found the woman again, this time accepting glittering blue jewels from vines that grew up around her.

"The Old Gods," I whispered.

I flipped another page. Now, the woman held the gems aloft, and a pale blue light radiated from them, forming a shield over her. And just above the shield, tiny winged angels flew for the heavens—

A screeching noise turned my head, and I jumped, slamming the book shut.

There, Drakon stood in the middle of the stone floor, his beady eyes on me. He hissed, and a stream of fire blazed from his mouth.

I hissed back at him, now feeling completely justified in my hatred of him.

I brought my finger to my lips. *Shhhhhh.* "I will give you..." What the hell did dragoniles eat? "I will give you rabbits if you keep quiet. Just shut the fuck up, okay?"

Drakon ignored my warning, stepping closer as he screeched again.

"Chickens," I whispered. My heart began to sink.

Let's hope Adonis and these friends of his weren't too precious about their library.

Just as I was shoving the book back onto the shelf, a figure appeared in the doorway—a rather terrifying figure, I might add.

A demon.

She must have been six feet tall—shockingly gorgeous and pale as ivory. A short, white dress hugged her curvy body, ending just below her ass, and her dark hair writhed around her head like snakes. A crescent-moon tattoo stood out on her forehead, and her red lips curled back in a vicious snarl. She lifted her clawed fingertips, and I braced myself for an attack.

I snatched my torch from the wall, holding it out as if I were about to fend off a wild beast with fire.

"Tanit." Adonis's deep voice pierced the silence. "Call off the attack. I brought her here."

Tanit hissed at me. "*This* is the Bringer of Light? She smells like the bottom of a swamp."

I glanced down at my mud-spattered, rain-soaked clothing. "We've had a very long journey, and I haven't had the benefit of a bath yet."

Tanit growled. "You're telling me we can't kill her and feed her to Drakon?"

"No."

Her nose crinkled. "Fine. Well, I'm going to insist that she leave all her filthy, rain-soaked clothes outside her door. She smells of moss and grass and dank forests, and I want the filth burned."

I frowned. "And what am I supposed to wear?"

She cocked a hip. "I'll have the servants bring her some of mine."

"I could just wash my clothes," I suggested. "Clothes are meant to be cleaned and reused indefinitely."

"They *what*?" She widened her eyes, her expression pure frustration. "We're going to burn your things. I'll give you new ones. Just be happy I'm not suggesting running *you* through the flames."

Adonis's eyes narrowed. "Simmer down, Tanit. She's on our side." He raised his eyebrows. "Ruby, Tanit doesn't often offer to give people things. This is her version of being a welcoming host." Smooth as silk, he prowled closer to me, his hands in his pockets. "And now we get to the part where you tell us what you're doing in here."

"I can't sleep without reading before bed."

"I see. And you like to read cuneiform?"

Casually, I sauntered back to the English poetry section and pulled a copy of *Don Juan* off the shelf. "I must have gotten mixed up. My mistake." I smiled at Tanit. "My name is Ruby. Pleased to meet you."

Her eyes flashed with silver. "Okay."

Through the window, the first honeyed light of morning began to warm the sky, tingeing it with pink.

Was it really that late?

"You were searching for information," said Adonis.

"That's what happens when you withhold it. People search for it on their own. So you could tell me exactly what we're hunting for, and why you've brought me here. Or I can use my own methods."

"Sophisticated methods like failing to read ancient languages."

"What are the blue gemstones?" I asked.

A sigh slid from him. "Tomorrow, when you wake, I'll explain what you need to know. Go to sleep now, and dream of all your beautiful love stories." He spoke with a soothing, lover's purr, and nothing had ever sounded more convincing than his suggestion. He was out of the room so swiftly, I hardly noticed him leave.

Morning sunlight began warming the room with coral, washing over the towering stacks of books. I'd never felt so tired in my life, and the stare Tanit was giving me urged me to move quickly.

As I crossed back to my room, I couldn't get the image of the gleaming blue stones out of my mind. Adonis said his destiny was to kill. Were the stones my destiny?

Just as I opened my door, Tanit pushed past me, glaring. She snatched my bag from the floor, yanking out my damp clothes. "This is all going in the fire."

She pulled out my sheathed knife and holster, examining it before letting it fall to the floor with a clang.

Then, she glared at me expectantly. "The rest. Take off the rest."

I was too tired to argue, and I wasn't particularly self-conscious—as long as Adonis wasn't around. I stripped off in front of her.

"All of it," she barked. "I'll leave new clothes outside your door."

"When?"

No answer.

She left with everything but my knife, leaving me damp and naked in the room. Good thing I wasn't attached to any of the clothes.

Miserable as she was, when she left my room, a deep sense of loss bloomed in my chest—complete isolation. I crawled nude under the warm covers, loneliness eating at me.

Somehow, traveling with Adonis, he'd masked my loneliness. Now, as I lay naked and alone, isolation slid through my blood like a poison.

I pulled the covers tight around me. When I closed my eyes, I dreamt of a thorny throne on a craggy cliffside, and the desolation of that image pierced me to the bone.

CHAPTER 14

Naked, I stumbled out of the bathroom, still completely disoriented from a heavy sleep. In fact, I'd managed to sleep through the whole day.

A fire still burned in the marble fireplace, warming the bedroom. Its orange light wavered over the walls, overgrown with flowering vines. I closed my eyes, and for just a moment, my mind wandered back to a happier time, when I'd gone with Hazel and Marcus to the Museum of Natural History in New York. Then, further back, to my mother and father curled up next to each other on a sofa, reading books. I'd always crawl in between them, splitting them up so their attention could be on me.

When I opened my eyes again, the loneliness of my current situation hit me like a fist.

Not to mention the fact that I'd ended up in a creepy death angel castle completely naked. I shuddered, rubbing my arms.

At least I'd have fresh clothes waiting for me outside the door, just as Tanit had promised.

I rose from the bed, crossing over the cold stone floor. Goose bumps rose over my bare skin, and the chilly air peaked my breasts.

Slowly, I pried the door open, looking down expectantly for a fresh stash of clothes.

A cold stone floor greeted me.

Of *course* she hadn't brought any new clothes back. Why had I trusted the crazy-eyed demoness in the first place?

I slammed the door closed again, and a draft whispered over my skin. *Should have hung on to a few items there, Ruby.*

I opened the door, then poked my head out, looking for signs of movement in the hallway. Nothing except the shadows dancing over the stone walls, the flagstone floor. I couldn't hear anything moving in the castle either.

Well, I wasn't about to just strut around the death castle bare-ass naked. I crossed back to the bed, pulled off a soft crimson blanket, and wrapped it around my naked skin.

Here, naked in the quiet castle, with only a blanket covering my body, I felt completely vulnerable. A desperation for human contact speared me, sharp as talons piercing my ribs. Inexplicably, I wanted to see Adonis. After our journey together, maybe he was the closest thing I had to a friend in this place. Or maybe he was just the most likely to find me some clothes.

I scanned both directions in the hallway. Barefoot, I crept over to the first door and pressed my ear against the wood.

As I did, the sounds coming from inside raised the hair on the back of my neck. I let my keen fae hearing sharpen, listening closely to the sound of a stifled moan. Then, a grunt.

Was Adonis torturing someone, or screwing someone? Or a little of both—a mixture of pain and pleasure? Was it *Tanit*?

Not that I cared. Whether or not he and Tanit were screwing had nothing to do with me. Clearly, I should turn around and leave this situation alone, and yet...

I needed to know. What if those weren't noises of pleasure I was hearing? What if he was peeling someone's skin off? I needed to know what kind of death god I was dealing with here.

Pulling my blanket tight around me, I knelt on the cold ground. Then, I leaned forward, peering through Adonis's keyhole. My pulse raced as I caught a glimpse of him. He stood, shirtless, his back to me. His midnight wings spread out behind him, their feathers flecked with silver. My eyes roamed over his smooth skin, his thickly corded arms.

This is intrusive, and I shouldn't be here.

And yet, I couldn't seem to tear my eyes away.

His powerful back arched, and dark shadows appeared around his neck, his wrists—like thorny manacles of magic. Something about them looked so *invasive*—a toxic magic that didn't belong here.

Still, Adonis's exotic scent seemed to lure me in. Despite the shackles around him, something about the arch of his back screamed of ecstasy. Pure, carnal pleasure.

I felt myself reaching for his door, stroking my fingertips over the wood. I hated myself a little for spying on Adonis, but—

Then I noticed the stream of blood, pooling on the floor. I gasped, and my hand flew to my mouth, knocking the doorknob just slightly.

Adonis whirled, giving me a view of the blood streaming from his chest, the shallow wound, the knife in his hand.

What the hell was he doing? *Cutting* himself?

My jaw dropped, and I stumbled to my feet, clutching tightly to my blanket as if my life depended on it.

The door swung open, and Adonis's gaze pierced me to the core, cold with fury.

"What are you doing?" he asked, venom lacing his voice. Already, his chest had begun to heal a little, though a thin stream of blood still dripped over the savage tattoos on his chest.

"What are *you* doing?" I shot back.

"Not staring through someone's keyhole, for a start." His arctic tone cooled my body. His dark hair seemed to stand out sharply against his golden complexion, his black eyelashes stark against his pale eyes.

"I didn't have anything to wear. Your friend Tanit never returned after she burned my other clothes. I thought you could help. I heard something that sounded like pain..." *Or pleasure.* "And I just wanted to look before I knocked. For all I knew, you were torturing a human or something." I could feel my cheeks reddening. "I have to know who I'm dealing with here."

For the first time, he seemed to notice the blanket wrapped around me. Then, he cut a sharp gaze over my shoulder. "Come in." He opened the door wider.

I surveyed Adonis's bedroom—a circular space adorned with faded tapestries: a night sky, a dark-winged angel. On one tapestry, red flowers blossomed by a river's edge. And on the expanses of stone wall, actual blood-red flowers bloomed on vines.

A tall window in his room cast silver light over a large bed, the blankets and sheets charcoal gray. Below his towering window, a few fernlike plants climbed the wall. On a small, oak table lay a dark cloth and a bandage. He dropped the bloodied knife on the table. A small pool of blood glistened on the floor. Did he get some kind of pleasure from self-harm?

"Look," I started. "I'm not judging. I just… Do you do that for fun?"

"Do I stab myself in the heart for fun? Are you joking?"

My jaw dropped. He'd actually *stabbed* himself in the heart?

I swallowed hard, the soft blanket skimming against my body as I walked deeper into his room. "Okay. So—why did you stab yourself in the heart?"

I'd seen his scars before—his chest, his wrists, the knotted ridges marring his perfect skin. I'd assumed they were battle scars—not self-inflicted.

He met my gaze, and a preternatural stillness came over him—a stillness more animal than angel. It unnerved me when creatures did that. The hair rose on the nape of my neck.

"No one else knows," he said, his tone edged with steel. "You can't tell anyone."

I pulled the blanket tighter around me. "I won't tell anyone."

He grabbed the dark cloth off the table, swiping some of the blood off his muscled chest. "You know that Kratos and Johnny have been cursed. It's because their apocalyptic seals have broken, and they can no longer resist their destiny. They must kill. For a horseman, the curse is applied when the apocalyptic seal is broken. The breaking of a seal feels like an ecstatic state. An overwhelming euphoria. And once you give in to euphoria, it's all over. Your fate controls you."

"And you use pain to stop the euphoria?"

"Exactly."

I shuddered. What a miserable existence. No wonder he wanted out. "I saw something around your neck and your wrists...like manacles."

He raised his eyebrows. "You can see them?"

"Was that the seal?"

He traced a fingertip over his throat, staring at me contemplatively. "I thought only angels could see it, but yes, that's the curse emerging. I guess a Light Bringer gets the privilege of witnessing that particular magic."

"How long have you been doing this for?" I asked quietly.

Only a slow, subtle shrug interrupted that animal stillness. "A few centuries."

I grimaced. "No wonder you want to rule the heavens instead of the earth. Let me treat it, at least."

"With what, exactly?"

"With the gifts from the Old Gods." I crossed to the fernlike plants that grew under his window, but something caught my eye. Adonis's sword lay against the wall, its hilt studded with red stones formed to look like flowers. I ran my fingertips over them.

"Do you like her?" asked Adonis. "Ninkasi has been with me for thousands of years."

"It's beautiful."

"*She*. She's beautiful," he corrected me. "And you plan to heal me with her?"

I frowned. "No, I told you. The Old Gods give us what we need. And right now, we need something to take care of that bleeding." I crouched down, clutching the blanket with one hand. "Even in the lair of a horseman, they give us what we need."

I snatched a handful of the yarrow that clung to the wall. As I stood, I held up the herbs to the moonlight streaming through the window. I closed my eyes, and a warm, soothing light washed over my hand. An herbal scent curled into the air.

When I opened my eyes again, a handful of dried yarrow lay crushed in my fist.

As I walked back to Adonis, my gaze flicked to Drakon by the fire, his reptilian tail flopping up and down against the stone floor.

Adonis studied me. "The magic of the Old Gods really is fascinating to watch."

"Maybe it's in my destiny to become a healer."

I surveyed the laden table, where a bandage lay. The tricky part would be fixing him up with one hand, but I could probably manage with his help.

"Lay out the bandage flat," I commanded.

"Quite commanding for a naked fae, aren't you?" Amusement danced in his eyes. He spread it out, the ends draping off the table.

Carefully, I offloaded the dried plants into the center of the bandage. Then, I slid my fingers under the bandage, scooping up the fabric and the dried plants together with one hand.

With a swift movement, I pressed the herbs against his heart.

This close to him, the smell of myrrh wrapped around me, sweeping over my neck, my chest. I looked up into his eyes—at the gray that blended to midnight blue, at the flecks of silver. His magic whispered over my body, stroking my bare shoulders, my hips, skimming up my thighs. The look he was giving me penetrated me to my core, and sent a dark heat racing through my blood.

I couldn't think around him, could hardly remember how coherent ideas worked. It took me a moment to realize that I'd just been standing there, pressing a bandage full of dried plants against his chest, gaping at him.

"Do you need help?" he asked in a velvety voice that curled my toes.

I swallowed hard. "I just need to tie the bandage around your back."

He arched a perfect eyebrow. "Is that right?"

Already, his wound seemed to be healing—probably some of his own magic at work.

Without another word, I tightened the bandage with both hands, then reached around his back to try to tie it—only, I could hardly reach around the width of him, and—

A cold gust of air swept over my bare skin, tightening my nipples.

Oh god, the *blanket.*

It took me a long, horrified moment to realize that I'd ended up completely naked, my breasts just inches from his muscled physique.

I dropped the bandage.

Adonis's jaw had dropped, his attention completely rapt as he stared at me. His arm muscles twitched, eyes burning with pale light.

The cool of the castle's drafty air raised goose bumps on my arms. A low growl escaped his throat. His expression shifted—no longer remote, angelic serenity, it was now pure carnal lust. He looked like he was about to throw me on his bed right then and there.

At the sound of his growl, at the promise of his hands on my body, heat shot through me. My chest flushed.

Finally, I mustered the presence of mind to bend down, snatch the blanket off the floor, and hastily wrap it around myself. "Sorry," I mumbled.

Words seemed to have deserted him.

Distraction. Distraction. Let's pretend like nothing happened. I nodded at his chest wound, trying to think of something to say. "You know, it looks better already. The bleeding has stopped. Maybe it doesn't need the bandage."

After a moment, Adonis broke his silence. He crossed his arms with a wicked smile. "Never apologize for appearing naked before me. And certainly don't wear that blanket on my account. I prefer you without it."

Heat prickled over me, and I pulled my blanket tighter. "Can you ask your ill-tempered demon friend for those clothes now?"

"I'll send Drakon for her."

I shivered. "I don't suppose you have a shower in here, while I'm waiting. My room had a bathroom but no shower."

"Bath is in there." He pointed to an arched doorway, and I nodded, scurrying away from him with the blanket clutched tightly around me.

As I crossed into his bathroom, Adonis purred instructions to Drakon in an ancient language. Phoenician? Sumerian? I had no idea, but the angel probably knew more languages than I could count.

In his bathroom—a round, domed space—candles burned in iron sconces. A circular stone bathtub stood by one of the walls. Next to it, dry towels lay folded in a stony alcove, along with a few bars of soap.

I turned on the tap, and warm water rushed from the faucet, steam rising into the air. When I dropped the blanket once again, the castle's drafty air whispered over me. I stepped into the hot bathwater, watching it redden my legs, and slipped down into its welcoming embrace.

I rubbed the anemone-scented soap over my skin, cleaning my neck, my chest. I couldn't quite get Adonis's carnal expression out of my mind, or the promise of what might have happened if I hadn't pulled that blanket around me again.

He was Adonis—a creature known for his beauty. Of course I reacted that way to him.

Before the Great Nightmare had begun, Marcus and I had the perfect relationship. There were no questions, no mysteries. When he was upset, he told me, and he told me why. I knew that blood-hunger made him cranky, that sometimes his own snoring woke him up, that —despite being a vampire—clowns terrified him.

Adonis was the opposite. All mystery. Granted, I'd been learning a little more about him—that he hurt himself to stop the curse from setting in, that he dreamt of a great rebellion against the angels who controlled him. But he kept most of his secrets buried deep. What was that strange necklace he wore around his neck? What were those intense flashes of pain I sometimes saw in his eyes? What was his whole history with the fae?

I couldn't deny the allure of the unknown. Maybe there was a strange sort of power in that mystery, of things unspoken and unnamed. But danger lay there too.

A clicking sound on the floor pulled me from my thoughts, and I turned to see Drakon prancing into the room, tail slicing through the air. He clutched a bundle of clothing in his teeth. He dropped it on the floor, then cocked his head to stare at me, tail thumping expectantly.

I glared at him. "Off you go, hellspawn." So I might smell a bit like reptilian spit, but at least I wouldn't have to walk around naked under a blanket.

I stepped out of the bathtub, water dripping down my body—keenly aware that Adonis's bathroom had no door, that he could pop his head in at any moment. Not that he'd see anything new at this point.

I grabbed one of the towels from the alcove and quickly dried myself off. Frowning, I eyed the clothing on the floor—an extremely short black dress, some thigh-high boots. Tanit, it appeared, had enjoyed the 1960s. Not exactly my style, but I wasn't afraid of a little dark glamor.

Surprisingly, the boots fit well enough, and the dress hugged my body.

I wasn't about to ask her for underwear. Maybe one of those magic books in the library could summon some into existence.

When I crossed out of the bathroom, I found Adonis waiting for me, leaning casually against the doorframe, hands in his pockets. A dark, fitted shirt now stretched across his broad chest. His bleeding must have stopped quickly, because his shirt looked completely dry.

A sensual smile. "You do look amazing, though I preferred the previous outfit. When you're ready, Drakon will show you to dinner. Kur is desperate to meet the Bringer of Light."

Drakon. My favorite little monster.

Without another word, Adonis slipped into the hallway. But my mind wasn't on this new person—my mind was on the memory of Adonis's face when his pale gaze had roamed over my naked body.

CHAPTER 15

Through Adonis's windows, silver moonlight washed over the horizon. Just as in my room, I had a view of the slate-gray ocean, and the waves breaking on the jagged cliffs below.

Like its owner, the entire castle was breathtakingly beautiful. But it wasn't the peaceful, gentle beauty of the forests. It had an edge of terror, of brutality. I didn't belong in a place like this. I belonged in a simple cottage in the woods—just Hazel and me, and whatever the Old Gods would provide for us.

My stomach rumbled as I crossed the room. When I opened the door, Drakon was waiting outside, his head cocked. His tail cut through the air. Then, he rose and rubbed against my legs, scales sliding along my boots. I shuddered, suppressing my bile.

Of course Adonis couldn't choose a cute little puppy as a pet. Or a kitten. No, he wanted a red-eyed hellbeast with scales.

"No need to get too friendly there, Drakon. Care to show me where the others are?"

Drakon's claws clicked over the floor as he prowled along the balcony, until we arrived at the wide, curving stairwell that led to the lower level.

I followed him through a vaulted hallway. Windows on my left overlooked the dark, churning sea. To my right, arches opened into the wider marble hall. Stained-glass windows in the panes were decorated with pictures of red flowers, white butterflies, and upside-down torches.

Through the colored panes of glass, I had a view of the sea.

Apparently, Drakon was growing frustrated with my pace, because he began to weave in between my feet, nearly tripping me as I walked.

As I moved farther down the hall, the scent of garlic and roast meat curled into the air, and my mouth watered. If Hazel had known we were headed for more delicious food, maybe she would have come with me.

At last, the arched corridor opened into an enormous stone hall.

There, I found Adonis sitting at a long, oak table near two demons. Tanit stood in a dark alcove, sipping from a silver goblet. She wore a short red dress and shiny thigh-high boots.

At the table near Adonis sat a male demon—this one in a throne-like chair, his feet resting on the tabletop. The demon's long, black hair flowed over his broad shoulders, and a few delicate green scales lined the tawny skin of his cheekbones and the backs of his hands. His pure-black eyes locked on me.

Light burned from iron lanterns hung high above us, bathing the room in amber. Drakon scurried over to Adonis, crawling into his lap. The Dark Lord stroked his pet's black, scaly skin.

Here, in his own castle, Adonis seemed a little different—no longer staging the situation to intimidate, no longer seating himself on a dais or in a spiky throne.

Adonis's gray eyes pierced me, and his wings draped over the sides of his chair. He lifted his chalice. "Ruby. You've joined us, fully clothed." He nodded at the male demon. "May I introduce you to Kur."

Kur nodded, his inky eyes on me. "You're the one who woke everyone up last night." His voice was gruff. "Lucky for you, Adonis informed us we're not to kill you. Apparently he likes the way you look, and something about saving the world."

"Sorry. I was just looking for a book," I muttered.

Tanit examined me through narrowed eyes. "This one is really supposed to defeat the Heavenly Host?"

Adonis nodded at an empty chair next to him, already pulled out. "Join us."

Servants had laid the table with food—a bowl of apples and herbs, roasted with leeks. Browned chicken legs, covered in a delicate sauce that smelled of garlic and lemon, bread with mint leaves and olives, and salads. It looked very different from the meat-heavy pies I'd had in Kratos's castle.

I plopped down in the chair, serving myself apples and chicken. "So you all know about this plan, I take it? I'm hoping you'll fill me in."

Kur knocked back a long swig from his cup, then wiped the back of his sleeve across his mouth. "Ruby. I assume Adonis has told you of his plans to rule the celestial realm. But what are you hoping to get out of all this? What do you want?"

"Right now, I want this chicken, and then to work my way through the rest of the food. Beyond that, I want things to go back to the way they were. At least, as much as they can. I just want a simple home with my sister, free from demons and angels and everything else that might try to kill us. I want my human friends to be safe." My gaze slid to Adonis as I cut into the chicken. "I want the horsemen and dragons to leave us alone so normal people can rebuild civilization from the rubble. That's about it."

"You want a normal life," Adonis said quietly.

I helped myself to a bit of wine. "Simple pleasures are the reason that life is worth living, aren't they? Sunlight, good food, good company. I don't need to rule the heavens."

Adonis traced his fingertips over his wineglass. "You sound like a human."

I shrugged. "Or like a fae. Pleasure is the purpose of our lives."

Adonis's eyes flashed. "You might find that a bit empty after a while," he said. "Or at least you would if you'd lived as long as I have."

Tanit slowly walked closer, swaying her hips, her dark eyes locked on me. "How much time have you spent among humans?"

I speared another apple in the bowl. "I have more in common with humans than I do with demons or angels. Or even the fae. I just want what we all want—happiness."

I caught a faint glimmer of a ruby-red drop on Tanit's lips. I was pretty sure she was drinking blood.

"Happiness," she hissed.

"Now, how exactly are we going to defeat this Heavenly Host I've heard so much about?" I asked.

Adonis leaned closer, his intense eyes piercing me to my marrow. "Here's the first thing you need to understand, Ruby. You're not ordinary. You never will be. You've spent your life pretending to be a human, hiding your true nature. If you want to defeat the Heavenly Host, you'll need to stop running from yourself. If you're divided from yourself, the power of the Old Gods could tear you apart."

"I don't even know what that means." A dark memory flickered in the back of my mind—dragons, ripping Marcus to shreds in front of me. If I'd been a hero like I was supposed to be, why couldn't I have saved him? My stomach clenched, and I pushed the thoughts away, strangling the life out of them.

I shook my head. "Anyway, I've been harnessing their magic already."

Kur folded his hands behind his head. "Listen, Ruby. Adonis tells me that you're our only hope. I've never known him to be wrong. But if he is, and if you fail, every living creature on earth will probably end up dead, slaughtered by the Heavenly Host. They'll just kill everything and start again. Earth will become a bone garden. Your fault."

My mouth went dry. "You guys really suck at pep talks, you know that?"

CHAPTER 16

"*L*ook," said Adonis. "Assuming you can handle the power, our task is simple. We need the Stones of Zohar."

I remembered what I'd seen in the book. "Blue gems by any chance? That form a shield?"

Kur had resorted to simply drinking straight out of a wine bottle, which right now didn't seem like the worst idea. "Exactly. Only a Bringer of Light can wield them. They'll help you channel the power of the Old Gods. Your kind are the ancient and powerful enemies of the Heavenly Host. As long as you're not…divided from yourself or whatever Adonis was talking about. He's got some abstract sayings."

I nodded. "Garden of paradise and that kind of thing." At last, they were filling me in. "I need some concrete specifics. What's the power like?"

"We don't have a ton of specifics," said Kur. "We know in the right hands, the stones can repel the Heavenly Host. They can create a shield of some kind. And you can use them to fight the other horsemen."

"Okay," I said. "And where do we get them?"

Tanit smirked. "You're not the only spy, darling. While you were running around in the woods outside Hotemet Castle, I was discovering the location of the Stones of Zohar."

"She has yet to tell me," said Adonis with a hint of irritation.

Frankly, I was surprised Adonis didn't just threaten to vaporize her or something.

Tanit smiled. "Sadeckrav Castle. Aereus has been securely protecting them, just in case any errant Bringers of Light surfaced to find them."

I raised my eyebrows. "The horseman of war, right?"

"Yes," said Tanit. "He's wildly paranoid. He won't admit that he has them, and no one knows where he's keeping them. But my sources tell me he plundered them centuries ago, and he's always kept them close by. They terrify him."

Adonis tapped the edge of his glass. "He's unhinged. But I think speaking to him is on our agenda anyway."

"Why?" asked Kur. "He's a lunatic."

Adonis leaned forward. "True. But he's a lunatic we'll need on our side. If Johnny remembers what Ruby did to him, he and Kratos will be coming for us. And they could turn the horseman of war against us. We need to get to him first, to convince him that Kratos and Johnny are at risk of rebelling against the Heavenly Host. A lunatic ally is better than no ally at all."

"Sounds promising," I said. "What can you tell me about him? What are his weaknesses?"

Tanit knocked back a sip of her "wine." "Weaknesses? Not sure that he has any."

"Everyone has a weakness," Adonis replied.

"What does he love?" I asked.

"Himself," said Adonis emphatically. "That's it."

I nodded. "So he has an ego problem. Even more than the rest of you angels?"

Adonis glared at me. "Yes."

"Where is this castle?" I asked.

"France." Kur was frowning at Adonis's injured wing. "I'm not sure our angel of death will make it there just yet."

"It's nearly healed," Adonis growled.

I practically drained my wine. "So let me get this straight. We need to get some gemstones from the horseman of war, whose only weakness is his ego. And I need to use them to destroy the other horsemen, as well as the immortal, incorporeal celestial archangels known as the Heavenly Host. If I don't, every living being on earth will die, and it will be my fault."

"That about sums it up," said Tanit. "The dirty fae catches on quickly."

Adonis twirled his wineglass. "I wouldn't put it quite that way…"

I took a deep breath. "I don't want to come off like I have trust issues, but how do I know any of this is true? I'm supposed to put my faith in the word of one horseman and two shadow demons I've only just met. One of whom burned my underwear."

Kur nearly spit out his wine. "She did what?"

Tanit's forehead crinkled. "What's the purpose of underwear, anyway? I've never understood that."

Adonis let out a long sigh. "Since you're so interested in reading material, Ruby, perhaps a reference book would help. I take it you were looking for one last night."

"I guess it would be better than nothing."

Adonis stared at Tanit, who grimaced. "I'll get the books."

I speared a bit of chicken on my fork. "Tell me more about the Heavenly Host."

"Pricks," growled Kur. "Bodiless, ancient pricks. They're still angry that Azazeyl gave their precious Angelic language to humans a hundred thousand years ago. And for some reason, Adonis wants to be their god."

Adonis folded his hands behind his head. "A hundred thousand years of torment hasn't been enough for them. Not great at moving on, the Heavenly Host. They need someone new to lead them."

"How many of them are there?"

Kur finally pulled his feet off the table. "A hundred million angels."

My fists tightened. "A hundred what now?"

Adonis leaned closer. "Relax. We don't need to kill all of them. We just need to weaken the ten archangels, and repel them from the earth. The Stones of Zohar can help us do that. Without the archangels leading them, the rest of the angels will be trapped in the celestial realm."

I narrowed my eyes. "And then you just swoop in and take control up there. There are ten archangels and one of you. Do you really fancy your chances?"

"Against ten weakened, sickly archangels? I don't have any doubt." Adonis lifted his wineglass. "Leave this festering hole to the demons, the fae, and the humans, and I'll rule the hordes in the heavens."

"Festering hole. Cheers, mate. That's my home you're talking about." Kur snatched another bottle of wine off the table and uncorked it with his teeth. He spat the cork onto the floor. "You did promise us you'd come back regularly, or I'd never agree to help you in the first place."

I raised my eyebrows. "So you two are close, then? I hadn't expected…" I wriggled uncomfortably in my chair. "Well, I never expected Adonis to have any friends, to be honest."

A warm smile from Adonis. "I fell in with some shadow demons a few thousand years ago. Ancient protectors of the succubi."

Kur's eyes had taken on a slightly glazed look. "If Adonis hadn't already told me you were a fake, you might have had the rare pleasure of watching me drop to my knees when you walked in the room."

I looked down at my arms, half surprised to find I was still wearing the succubus glamour. "Oh, right. I can take this off now, I suppose."

Kur shook his head. "Best not to. Adonis hates the fae. I hate humans. Succubi are about the only thing we can agree on."

At the mention of Adonis's fae-hatred, my stomach flipped. Did he hate me, under all his flirtatiousness? It didn't seem that way.

Tanit broke the awkward silence by gliding back into the room, clutching two books to her chest. She moved with a disturbingly fluid motion, as though she were hovering just slightly off the floor. "One in cuneiform, and one in English so the young fae can read it."

She dropped them on the table next to my plate with a loud thud. "There. Your literary proof."

I stroked my fingertips over the black, leather-bound book on top, its surface etched in silver lettering: *The Bringer of Light.*

"This is the one I saw in your room."

Kur rolled his eyes. "Of course you were in his bedroom."

"It wasn't like that," I said sharply, cracking open the book. "I was dressed as a puritan witch judge."

I turned the book's yellowed pages, taking care not to rip them. The book was written in English, but it seemed to be Middle English. Still, as I scanned the text, I could figure out its meaning. The first section gave an account of everything I already knew—Azazeyl's fall from heaven, his soul fracturing into seven pieces that became the seven earthly gods. Nyxobas, god of night. Emerazel, god of fire, and so on. Each god tormented by their punishment.

I turned the page, my pulse racing at an illustration of Azazeyl falling from the skies. Pain creased his beautiful features, and the wind appeared to tear at his wings.

When I turned the page again, I found an image of Nyxobas, god of night. His cowl cloaked his features. The artist had painted a midnight sky with silver stars around him. Just a picture of him was enough to fill me with a sense of dread—as if a void were beginning to eat at me from the inside out.

Shuddering, I turned the pages until I got to a chapter about the Heavenly Host. Just as Kur had said, the text mentioned a hundred million angels, organized into cohorts and legions. An archangel commanded each legion.

Okay. Demons and angels, we'd covered that part. Where did I come in?

I continued leafing through, landing on a page where the text was adorned with images of leaves, beside a picture of a tree whose gnarls seemed to form a sort of face. Silver light glowed around the tree— and a single, silver branch gleamed in the candlelight.

Of course. This represented the Old Gods. A quick scan of the text confirmed everything Yasmin had told me—the Old Gods had grown with life on earth, and were native to this world. They sought to free us from the scourge of the earthly gods, from the angels and demons who tried to control us. In times of crisis, they gave us what we needed through the earth itself.

A loud, exaggerated yawn from across the table interrupted my thoughts momentarily, and I looked up to find Tanit staring at me. "Is this really how long it takes a fae to read?"

Sighing, I returned to the text. And that brought me to the final section—the one about the Bringer of Light. Here, the artist had painted an image of a silver-haired creature, her body incandescent. Blue gems gleamed from her forehead like rays of light.

My pulse began to race. I was supposed to be one of these godlike creatures? I was good with harvesting herbs and moss from the ground, but this seemed a bit much. I sucked in a sharp breath, focusing intently on the text.

Here, I found an account of the Stones of Zohar—gemstones mined from a watery grotto.

According to the book, Bringers of Light were born every few hundred years, and they served the Old Gods. A Bringer of Light, united with the gems, would have the power to fight angels, to reclaim the earth for the Old Gods.

Of course, it didn't give any details beyond that.

As I closed the book, a cloud of dust rose in the air. "Okay, I guess the story checks out in the old book. When do we leave?"

"As soon as my wing heals," said Adonis. "We just need to hope for two things. One, that Johnny fails to recover his memory anytime soon."

"And the other?" I prompted.

Adonis's eyes flashed with a pale light. "Well, let's just hope that none of the celestial angels manage to figure out who you are before we get to Sadeckrav Castle."

Tanit smiled. "We wouldn't want your pretty fae face splattered all over the earth."

CHAPTER 17

*A*donis's powerful, dark wings practically trailed against the ground as he walked by my side over the rocky outcrop that overlooked the ocean. I pulled my coat tight around myself, tasting salt on my lips.

"So glad we managed to convince you," said Adonis. "I'd hate for the fate of the world to sink into an abyss just because of your trust issues."

"Yes, I'm on board."

The scent of brine floated on the wind, and along with it, Adonis's deliciously exotic scent slipped around my skin.

"You're going to be undercover again," he said. "But you're used to that."

"What's my role?"

"We had to go with something realistic. Kur sent word to Aereus, explaining that I've tamed a succubus concubine for my pleasure," he purred. "Obviously, it was the most logical thing to do."

I glared at him. "*Tamed?*"

"Taming a succubus is a common angelic fantasy. It's how you were able to beguile Kratos so easily."

"Right. That was the only option, I'm sure. Are you going to tell me why you're so desperate to go to the celestial realms? You've never lived there before. Why so eager to divest yourself of a human body?"

When he met my gaze, I found something unexpected there—just the faintest hint of vulnerability in his gray eyes. "I've been here long enough. I've done all I can on earth."

"I suppose it wouldn't be super awesome to have to stab yourself in the heart all the time."

"You're certainly catching on."

The marine winds toyed with my crimson hair. "It seems like you spent your time among shadow demons over the centuries. When did you join up with the other horsemen?"

"We didn't find each other until just before the Great Nightmare began. I've spent most of the centuries hiding my wings, disguising myself as a demon. I fought alongside Tanit and Kur in more wars than I can count."

Below us, the waves crashed hard against the rocky shore, and mist dampened my skin. "So you spent centuries pretending to be someone you're not."

"Something you're familiar with, isn't it?" His voice twined softly around me.

"I guess. You're not complaining about my disguise, are you? You hate the fae."

He studied me carefully. "Not all of them."

I walked by his side, our footsteps crunching over the gravel path. The path wound sinuously around the cliff's edge, wrapping around the ancient, gothic castle itself.

I folded my arms. "And what makes us worse than demons?"

"Demons lose control because they can't help it. The fae worship chaos, seek it out. I spent too much time among them."

"Why?"

"Let's just say my particular skill set appealed to them—death and pleasure." A haunted edge tinged his voice, and I knew he was only giving me part of the story—a sanitized version.

"Your kind are fascinating, I'll admit," he continued in his deep, alluring timbre. "The fae are as beautiful as you are brutal."

His description startled me. In fact, it was exactly how I'd describe him. "Beautiful?"

A slow, heartbreaking smile. "Yes." He paused, running a fingertip over my cherry-red hair. "Where's the real Ruby under all this?"

Warmth spread between my ribs. "I'm not sure you want to see the real Ruby. It's not just glamour that hides me. Glamour is an illusion—the hair color, the eye color, the ears. But you know the fae also shift. That's an actual, physical change. My canines grow, and my muscles become stronger, swifter. Some older fae stay in that state all the time. But a young fae like me—we don't keep control so well."

"Show me." A seductive plea and a command. "I want to see you under there."

A dark heat thrummed through my blood. I never shifted completely, not unless I went feral, and yet here, in the forlorn salty air, I found myself wanting to do as he said. "Like I said. It's not easy to control."

Amusement curled his beautiful lips. "I think I'll be able to handle it."

Why was it so hard to say no to him? Maybe because he'd spent thousands of years honing the skill of getting what he wanted. He used his voice, his beauty as a weapon.

I closed my eyes, letting the glamour fade with a sharp tingling over my skin. The sea air wrapped around me.

I opened my eyes, knowing that Adonis would be staring into pools of silver. Pale-gold hair whipped in front of my face. Still, I wasn't shifting. Who knew what would happen if I went feral with Adonis again?

Adonis reached out to brush my hair from my face, and the feather-light touch of his fingertips stroked against my skin, ice-cold and fire-hot at the same time. "But that's still not the real you, is it?"

"Just because I have a feral side doesn't mean it's the real me. Maybe this is the real me. Or my human glamour. Maybe it's Angela Death, the succubus, dressed in sequins on a stage. Maybe my disguises are the real me."

Without my glamour, I felt completely exposed before him, like I'd walked into his room naked, submitting myself to his judgment. I closed my eyes again, summoning my human glamour, hiding my ears, my inhuman hair, as the magic whispered over my skin.

I opened my eyes again, catching a flicker of disappointment in his gaze. I cocked my hip. "That's enough of that. I'm not a performing monkey. And anyway, I'm not as convinced as you are that you'd be able to handle me when I'm feral."

He peered down at me with a wicked smile. "Oh, but I would love to try." With his hands in his pockets, he moved deeper into the garden, and I followed. "Do you like it here?"

It honestly surprised me that he cared what I thought, like he was looking for my approval. "I do. It's a little bleak, admittedly." I gestured at the dark, craggy shoreline below us. "How long have you lived here? It's elegant, but it's…unforgiving."

"Nearly a thousand years, I suppose. But it has its own strange beauty." His eyes drank me in, the corner of his perfect mouth quirked in a smile. "Like the fae. Do you want to see?"

"How could I resist that description?"

The path twisted around the castle's walls, and thorny shrubs crawled over the path around us. A vast canopy of stars spread out above us.

Adonis met my gaze. "Kur was wrong. You don't need to disguise your fae side around me."

He led me toward a crumbling stone wall.

"I lived among humans for my whole life. It's just an old habit, I suppose. I've always glamoured myself."

He pushed open an old, creaking gate. In the darkness, the silver seemed to burn brightly in his eyes. "But there's more to it than that, isn't there?"

"I'm not sure what you mean." As we moved through the gateway, I cast my gaze over an enormous, untamed garden, the plants and flowers silvered in the moonlight.

A jagged tree grew in the center of the garden. A stream ran past it, burbling out of the ground. It had carved a sinuous path through the plants. On the far edge of the walled garden, the stream poured under a low archway, cascading off the cliff's edge to the rocks below.

Myrrh trees grew by the riverbanks. Blood-red flowers dappled the grasses—poppies maybe—growing among blue and white anemones. The air smelled of wild thyme and marjoram.

One of the ancient walls had partially eroded, giving way to a view of the ocean. Moonlight glinted off the water.

My breath caught in my throat. "This is your private garden? It's beautiful."

"This is where I spent many of my days when I wasn't off getting tangled up in shadow demon wars. Reading. Writing. Drinking with Tanit and Kur, hosting visitors from the shadow realms."

Tall wildflowers brushed against my fingertips, featherlight. "Why would you fight with shadow demons? You're not one of them. Why would you be loyal to Nyxobas?"

"The god of night?" He snorted. "I have no loyalty to him."

I nodded slowly, my gaze trailing over the perfect planes of his face. "So what were you fighting for, then?"

"For my friends. They saved me when I escaped the fae realm. And I saved them, whenever I could." Adonis's exotic scent mingled with the heady perfume of the wildflowers.

"Let me see if I understand this correctly. You have close friends who you love, who you've been with for thousands of years. You have this gorgeous garden, where you read books, drink with your friends. I'm going to wager you've seduced a few beautiful women in your time. I know it must suck—like, seriously suck—to have to stab yourself in the heart. But isn't there another way? Do you really want to give all this up to float around in heaven?"

"The thing is, Ruby, angels were never meant to walk the earth."

I'd said the same thing many times over the past year and a half, but I still felt the impulse to argue with him.

He froze abruptly, staring up at the sky, and an icy chill rippled over my skin as the temperature seemed to freeze around me.

"Speaking of angels going where they don't belong..." Ice chilled his voice. "You need to get inside."

donis's voice had changed, became commanding. No longer was it the sexual purr of a lover, but the voice of a general.

I narrowed my eyes at the sky, but I could see nothing among the stars. "Can you at least tell me what's happening?"

"It seems some of the angels have found us. Not the archangels, but still a nuisance. Hide in my room. There's a secret passage behind the garden tapestry."

My heart began to hammer. "Are you going to fight a whole horde of angels?"

"Oh, you don't need to worry about me. Go."

I hurried back to the castle door, my fingertips brushing over the holster at my thigh. I still had the knife, though I wasn't sure how much good it would do me in a fight against a legion of angels. How many angels were we talking here, exactly?

I sprinted through an open archway to the courtyard. Distantly, the sound of trumpets pierced the air, and the noise rumbled through my gut.

I raced up the stairs to Adonis's room and flung open the door. I scanned the room, searching among the old, faded hangings for one that looked like a garden. The tapestry of blood-red flowers hung just across from his bed.

First, I rushed over to the window. I peered through the glass, catching sight of a small horde of angels racing toward the earth, bodies glowing with golden light. If I narrowed my eyes, I could make out the swords glinting in their hands.

My mouth went dry. Were all these angels really after me? Being a spy was one thing, but I didn't have much supernatural war experience.

Adrenaline burned through my veins. I hurried over to the tapestry, then pulled it aside. Just as Adonis had said, a door stood inset in the wall. I pushed it open into a dark, narrow passageway. For just a moment, I froze, my heart thumping hard.

Complete darkness in here.

Which was worse? An angelic horde hell-bent on my death, or a dark hallway? Clearly, the hallway was the better option.

With my heart slamming against my ribs, I began to run. I had no idea where I was going, just that it was away from the angel horde.

Dread coiled around my heart. If these angels knew I was here, did that mean it was all over? Did they all know? I couldn't hide from them forever.

I raced through the bowels of the castle, my fingers tracing the damp walls as a guide. At last, the passageway gave way to a wider hall, and the sound of screeching echoed off a high ceiling. I still couldn't see anything, and my blood began to roar in my ears. It sounded like I'd run into hell itself—and for all I knew, I had.

Air whooshed over my head as something swooped lower. A leathery wing brushed against my forehead. No—not leathery—scaly.

My heart threatened to gallop out of my chest, and the darkness felt as if it were closing in around me. The otherworldly shrieks echoed in my own skull. I pulled the knife from its holster. I'd never wished more for a flashlight, a match, anything.

In the darkness, images began to ignite in my mind—the dragons diving for us on the day the world had ended, their screams rending the air. Hazel, clutched tightly in a demonic talon.

And the one image I couldn't face—the one I'd been hiding from. Marcus, trying to save us, climbing onto the dragon's back. I knew what was coming next.

I crouched on the ground, clamping my hands over my ears. "No!" I whispered.

Another scaly wing brushed against me, a scrape of talons against my shoulders. Dragons were going to rip me to shreds, just like they'd done to Marcus.

A sharp, painful certainty coiled through my chest. Adonis had sent me right into my own personal hell, and I couldn't even see the way out.

I fell deeper, lost in the hell of my own memory. If I let the iron door break open on my memories, they'd consume me. Or else, the dragons would.

A flicker—just a flicker of the blood that had stained the pavement, and I felt as if my mind would rip apart.

I couldn't save him. I didn't save him.

When I opened my eyes, my breathing started to slow again. Strangely, light was blooming around me, radiating from my own body over the cave. Apparently, some of the Old Gods' power had stuck with me since I'd plunged that knife into the silver branch. My terror must have sparked it.

I swallowed hard, staring at the domed, stony cave. It wasn't some kind of hellish dungeon. It seemed to be a rookery for dragoniles, and they swooped in wide arcs below the ceiling. My breath caught at the beauty of them—stunning shades of violet, gold, and blue, their scales faintly iridescent.

I looked down at my own body, beaming with radiant light, then I gaped at the illuminated ceiling, the dragoniles. They seemed to delight in my light, unleashing cheerful squawks.

"A Bringer of Light." A deep voice echoed off the ceiling, slicing through the reptilian squawks.

Slowly, I turned around, my pulse racing.

There in the entryway stood an angel, dressed for battle. His sword hung strapped behind his back, and his golden wings spread out behind him. Long, blond hair hung over his powerful shoulders, and a smug smile twisted his lips. "I smelled your magic when you unleashed your light. I smelled the magic of the Old Gods. Animals, the lot of you. I raced here at the speed of the wind so that I might have the honor of putting you to death."

I tightened my grip on the knife, ancient battle fury pulsing through my blood. I'd have to kill this one before he called the others. "A celestial angel. I've heard about your kind. Is it true that if you're not an archangel, you're mortal on earth?"

For just a moment, his smile faltered. "Now why would the horseman of death be hiding one of your kind?" He rushed for me, fast as lightning. Just as I began to lift my knife, he pressed his sword against my throat. "Drop your knife. And tell me what you're doing with Adonis."

Stall, Ruby. Stall. I swallowed hard. "He's imprisoned me here. Something about not wanting me to mess up his apocalypse. I don't know what he's talking about."

He pressed the blade harder. "Drop your knife."

I let go, and it clanged to the floor. One way or another, I needed to get it back. Poison still laced its blade. He'd be dead in seconds. But given the way his sword was pressed against my neck, I'd need one *hell* of a distraction to get my hands on it again.

The dragoniles screeched above me, their wings beating the air.

The angel stared down at me, his eyes burning with a bright, heavenly fire. "You're telling me that Adonis is keeping you prisoner? Why wouldn't he simply kill you? You're a threat to the entire angelic race."

Think fast, Ruby.

"He thinks there are more of us." I needed to keep myself alive, through talking. "Adonis thinks I might know where these Bringers of Light are, just that the memories are buried deep in my subconscious or something. I have no idea what he's talking about, but he's definitely not on my side." I widened my eyes, letting my body tremble a bit. Truth be told—with an angel pressing a blade into your throat, it wasn't really that hard to fake fear. "He's awful to me. He keeps torturing me."

The angel's eyes flashed brighter, and one of his hands found its way to my waist. That last bit apparently fascinated him. "Torturing you? Tell me." His lips twitched.

Did I detect a hint of desire in his words, in his eyes? Fae were experts in pleasure, and I do believe I'd found this angel's weakness. Here on earth, angels were not only mortal, but vulnerable to primal desires—just like the beasts. And this one was a sadistic perv.

I thought I'd found my distraction. I let my lip tremble. "You want me to tell you how he hurt me?"

"Oh yes."

I swallowed hard. I didn't have any visible scars, so I'd have to get creative. "He locks me in here, knowing that I'm scared of the dark, that I'm scared of dragons." I widened my eyes, all innocence. "He uses his mind control on me and forces me to hold my head underwater until my lungs burn, or to contort my body in painful positions for hours. I've never felt so helpless. I've never felt such excruciating pain."

The angel licked his lips, his wings spreading out wider behind him. "What else does he make you do?"

"Sick, depraved things that I can't even speak about. And the pain. The *pain*. I can't bear it anymore. Can you get me out of here?"

The angel's fingers tightened on my waist. Oh, he liked that idea. Sicko. "Tell me more."

"He uses his angelic mind control powers to make me choke myself until my lungs burn."

"I want to watch you hurt yourself," he rasped.

I shot a quick glance at the knife on the floor. Pervy Angel still had a sword at my throat, and I wasn't able to reach for it. "I'm afraid he's broken me completely. But it's no use. I still can't remember anything about the Old Gods."

The angel's eyes burned with desire. He wanted what Adonis had. Right now, he'd give anything for that power of mind control.

He gripped the back of my neck, forcing his blade deeper into my skin. I winced at the sharp pain, and a trickle of blood ran down my throat. He kicked the knife away from me, and it spun across the floor with a scraping noise.

My blood roared in my ears. I wasn't getting to that damn knife this way.

Still, maybe there was another way out of this.

Angels could fall. All I needed was for him to give in completely to earthly desires, to lust and the thrill of power.

Lucky for me, this creep had telegraphed his weakness.

CHAPTER 19

"Please," I whimpered. "I'll do anything you want."

If a horseman fell, it would summon all the archangels from heaven. I could only hope that the fall of a regular, mortal angel like this perv would go fairly unnoticed.

He snarled. "I want you to hurt yourself."

Honestly. Couldn't he have had a nicer desire? Maybe massages with oil, long walks on the beach? Of course it had to be something like forcing women to hurt themselves to exert complete sadistic domination.

Demons got a bad rap. I was increasingly certain angels were worse.

"Hurt myself how?" I asked.

"You can start by falling to your knees."

Ugh. Males. Always the same.

I widened my eyes, trying to look shocked as I dropped to my knees. The cold stone bit into my skin.

A smile split his features, and something new appeared in his eyes—his golden irises darkened to black.

"Yes," he growled. "Good. Now pull off your dress."

Oh, you've got to be kidding me. Could I take out his knees and rush for the knife on the ground? Not likely. He looked incredibly powerful.

I pulled down just the top of my gown, giving him a view of my shoulders. Given that I'd still never gotten any underthings, that was as far as the dress was going. In any case, I didn't think nudity was the important part. It was terror and humiliation that excited him.

"I'd never shown another man my shoulders until Adonis kidnapped me," I pleaded.

A rumbling noise rose from his chest.

I let the fear shine in my eyes. "But I'll do anything to save my life."

His features were changing, teeth sharpening. Ash began to rain from the ceiling, coating our bodies, the floor.

The dragoniles circled above, their wings whipping at the air. Reptilian screeches echoed off the walls. They could sense a change falling over the room.

"Touch my sword," he said, a quaver in his ragged voice. "Run your fingertips along the blade until they bleed. Hurt yourself, succubus."

Bile rose in my throat, pure disgust. Ash began to coat me, falling on my dress, my bare shoulders. And the cold floor chilled my knees.

He was changing, though, horns growing from his forehead.

I reached up for the sword, running my fingertips over the blade. The steel sliced into my skin, drawing blood that ran down my palms, my wrists.

"Yes!" The angel roared, his wings spreading out behind him. His feathers were beginning to darken, the pale gold now tinged with the faintest charcoal gray. "How does it feel?"

"Painful," I whimpered. *Like your transformation is about to be.*

Above, the dragoniles swarmed faster. The light created by my body began to dim, but the dragoniles punctuated the darkening air with hot blasts of fire from their jaws.

So *this* was what it was like to watch an angel fall.

The angel gazed down at me. "You're mine," he growled. His body had begun shaking, convulsing.

Slowly, I rose, and he lowered his sword, his expression completely rapt. I suppressed the bile rising in my throat, my complete and utter disgust, and stared in mock horror at the blood on my hands. It wasn't a deep cut, but I played it up.

He moaned, and I fought down more nausea. I glanced at him, smiling darkly as I watched the transformation at work.

Now I had him exactly where I wanted him.

Blood-red streaks speared the black of his pupils, and claws sprouted from his hands. Two gleaming, ivory horns emerged from his head, and his wings began to shrink, the feathers shifting and smoothing into sleek leather.

As they did, pain began to contort his features. An agonized groan rose from his throat, and he fell to his knees. He clawed at his shoulders where his wings were changing shape, becoming more pointed and angular. His back arched, and his mouth opened. Golden light poured from his open jaw, racing for the ceiling, and his body twitched and jerked like a dying man on the gallows.

I couldn't say I felt sorry for him.

I ran for the knife, snatching it off the stony ground. Overhead, the dragoniles flew more frantically, swooping lower over the transforming angel, over me. I crossed the floor, and brought the knife down hard into his back.

The demon's body jerked one last time, then fell still, slumping on the ground. The bursting flames of the dragoniles cast blasts of warm light over the growing pool of blood. I pulled my knife from his back, catching my breath.

Too bad my victory was short-lived. A golden light brightened the air behind me, and I whipped around. There in the doorway to the dragoniles' rookery stood four angels, their wrathful eyes locked on me.

At the front of the group stood an angel with silvery-white hair, his wings the color of pearls. "We felt your power, Bringer of Light. And here we find you. Covered in blood, gleaming like a beacon." His deep voice echoed off the ceiling, and he pointed to the fallen angel on the stone floor. "You lured him to his doom."

I gripped my knife. How could I take out four angels with one knife?

"Didn't take much," I said. "He was awfully eager to fall."

Pearly Angel drew his sword. He stalked toward me, his footsteps echoing off the walls and ceiling through the cacophony of dragonile squawks.

My palms sweated over the knife's hilt, and I clutched it tighter. If only I had control over this light, I'd be in a much safer position right now. To be honest, the Old Gods were screwing me over a bit by giving me uncontrollable powers. Right now, this magical light only served to paint a glowing target on me. A giant neon arrow to enemy number one of the angelic horde.

I summoned a glamour to cover myself, but this time a sharp sting pierced my skin. *What the hell?* Maybe fae magic and Old Gods' magic didn't mix so well.

"Light?" I asked, playing dumb. "I don't know what you're talking about." Not a brilliant strategy. Just the best one I had right now.

Pearly shook his head, and firelight glinted over his sword as he prowled closer. "Little Light Bringer. You can't hide it from us now. We feel it. We've seen it."

Another angel, one with curly ginger hair, stalked closer, by Pearly's side. "Imagine this, Afriel. We come here to check on Death, who hasn't been slaughtering like he should. And instead we find something much more interesting."

Afriel cocked his head, gripping his sword in both hands. "His seal should have broken once the terror began. Does this creature have anything to do with that?"

Ginger's eyes blazed with cold light. "Don't move too quickly, Afriel. She might have honed her powers."

Fear shone in Afriel's features. "We need to kill her now, before she brings us all down." He stepped over the demon's body. "Look what she did to Xapham, the filthy little minx."

"So you didn't come for me, then?" I asked.

This was the first good news I'd had this evening. If by some miracle I made it out of here, none of the other celestial angels knew about me.

It was just the whole "getting out of here" part that I couldn't quite work out yet. I could throw my knife and take out one of the angels immediately. But then I'd be all out of knives.

I'd have to lure them closer until they were in range. It was my only hope.

The dragoniles swooped over my head, squawking wildly. Their fiery breath singed the air, burning strands of my hair. The situation seemed increasingly disastrous, like I might not have a way out of it alive...

As the specter of death crept over me, a cold, primal rage began to roil within me. My hunter's instincts took over.

I can hear your mortal hearts beating, angels. I want to pierce them.

Oh shit oh shit oh shit. Feral Ruby was about to come out, and if she did, I'd lose control completely. Feral Ruby didn't necessarily make the best decisions.

Afriel raised his sword. "You are quite the serendipitous discovery."

My glamour began to fade.

Then, as fury erupted in my blood, I began to shift, my ears changing shape, canines lengthening. Ancient power burned through my body, ready to explode.

"Come on, then," I snarled. A wild energy ripped through me. My pale hair whipped around my face as my body glowed brighter.

Afriel rushed for me, probably expecting me to run from him. But the hunter's instinct raged strong in me, and I surprised him by rushing for him, too, until I was pressed up close to his body. The sound of his heart seemed to echo in my own blood.

This close, he couldn't strike me with his sword.

Go in for the kill. Instinct propelled my knife into his chest, finding its mark between two of his ribs. I thrust the blade up higher—right into his heart. He dropped his sword, and with a lightning-fast reflex, I snatched it from the stony ground.

Pure, primal instinct overtook my body until I felt at one with the stones beneath me. *I am blood, moss, bones, and earth, a creature of the damp caves. I am the feet pounding the leaves as you run from me. I am the rhythmic terror of your blood roaring in your ears.*

My heartbeat slammed against my ribs like a war drum as I gripped the sword in my hands. From the corner of my eye, I glimpsed movement, another sword, metal. A threat.

Thrust. Kill. Draw blood.

Move away from the threat. I dodged back, eyes landing on the ginger one—the pulsing vein in his neck. Life—so much life pulsing in that body. I licked my canines.

Time to end it.

I needed to sink my teeth into those hot veins. To hear him scream.

I snarled, no longer able to remember how to speak. I'd make my message clear enough.

I rushed at the speed of storm wind toward my prey. Primal fear glinted in his eyes, and my sword found its mark in his chest. My lips curled with a dark smile at the feel of shattering bone, the tearing of veins.

Blood soaked my sword, spraying over my body. *Glorious. I am home.*

CHAPTER 20

$\mathcal{A}$bove me, the dragoniles pierced the air with their strange, primordial song, and it called to me, stirring my blood. Why had I hated the dragoniles so much? We were alike, these creatures and me. The beating hearts of beasts, driven to break, to kill—to drink the blood of our enemies.

With the angel's sword in my hand, I moved across the blood on the floor like a dancer, whirling and ducking, fighting the next threat. When I pivoted again, I found the next angel coming for me, black hair streaming behind him. *Kill.*

My sword clashed with the angel's, sparks lighting up the dark air. Another angel pressed in on me—and my twisted, bestial heart started to panic, a rabbit cornered by wolves.

From above, a black dragonile scorched the air with his fiery breath, singeing the angels.

Just enough to give me an advantage.

Smiling, I whirled my sword through the air, cutting into the angel's sword arm, thrilling at the destruction. How would he like the feel of mortality?

Blood-soaked soil, thunder rumbling over the horizon, lightning searing my blood.

I swung my sword again, hacking into his other arm, sword through bone, through flesh—

Fear flashed in his eyes, and he screamed, "Get away from me!" His terror sang through my blood like an aria.

Dimly, I wondered where the beautiful one was—the man with the blue-gray eyes and the broken wing. But he wasn't here.

I was here, and I wanted blood. I hacked through one of the angel's wings, creating a masterpiece of blood-stained feathers.

"Evil flee from me!" he shrieked.

At his words, an image—a distant memory seared in my mind like a brand: sharp, monstrous teeth, sinking into pale flesh, blood streaming onto the pavement.

I stumbled away from him as if I'd been burned. As I did, a blur of white moved for me—another threat. I gritted my teeth, swinging for him in a haze of steel and red. Our swords clashed, and his eyes blazed with silver light. He pressed in on me, his golden hair streaming behind him.

Kill. Prey.

He was the strongest among them, and my muscles burned, my sword faltering. My legs began to shake, blood pumping hard as his steel clashed against mine.

Kill.

A single thrust, and my stolen sword plunged into his heart. His pale eyes widened, a stream of blood dripping from his lips.

I pulled my sword from his body, and he slumped to the floor.

Light blazed from my chest, and the disturbing memory faded from my mind. Even with the din of the dragoniles howling around me, a sort of peace had overcome me.

Blood and gore glistened in the dim light of my body. The screams of the dragoniles hummed deliciously over my skin—wild beasts, the lot of us.

I'd left one alive, hadn't I? He'd escaped while I'd been fighting the last angel. An injured one had run from the rookery, his arms and shattered wing hanging off him. The hunter in me wanted to chase him down, to finish him off, but I'd probably lost my chance.

I glanced at the doorway—waiting for more angels to come through—*hoping* for more angels to arrive. I needed more to kill.

For just a moment I faltered, horrified at my own thoughts. Free from the risk of death, some of the feral rage began to slowly seep out of my body. It cast a silver glow around the dragoniles, one of them circling the air protectively above me. Drakon.

Footsteps pounded in the hallway outside the rookery, and I readied my sword, my eyes on the hallway.

Before anyone had a chance to arrive, a figure rushed into the room in a blaze of silver light. A silhouette of dark wings spread over the hall, and my feral bloodlust exploded once again.

Kill. Dominate. Devour. A bestial growl rose from my throat, mingling with the wild symphony of dragonile shrieks. My canines lengthened, and I rushed for the angel, sword ready to slash through flesh—

His hand shot out, grabbing my wrist.

My heart began to slow at the feel of soothing, myrrh-scented magic.

In the silvered light glowing from my body, I looked up into a pair of stunning, gray eyes that faded to a midnight blue around the edges. I couldn't remember who he was, just that he was the most beautiful man I'd ever seen.

He squeezed my wrist harder, until I dropped the sword.

"Well, well, well," the angel purred. "*This* is interesting."

Feral Ruby still didn't quite have the power of speech, and another snarl escaped my throat, my lip curling.

He searched my face, like he was trying to interpret primitive scratches clawed into a tree. "Ruby." His voice wrapped around me like silk, and his grip softened on my wrist until it almost felt good. "Not your enemy."

Some of the battle fury raging through my nerves began to go quiet. The battle drum pounding in my ears began to still.

"Not an enemy," I repeated.

Footsteps echoed off the walls and ceiling, and I turned to see the two demons—the male and the female. Couldn't remember their names.

The male's mouth dropped open, and leathery wings spread out behind him. *"This* is the Bringer of Light?"

The female folded her arms, and her eyes blazed. "Is it just me, or is she covered in blood and ash, and surrounded by dead bodies?"

The large male nodded. "I'd honestly expected something a little more...civilized."

The demoness's hair writhed around her head, and she pointed at the fallen one. "Is that a dead demon?"

The beautiful angel searched my eyes, his expression probing. Gently, he ran a thumb over my wrist, and his soothing magic wrapped around me, pulling the fear, the violence from me.

Adonis. I breathed in his smell, and my gaze roamed over his broken wing, the place where I'd healed him.

"Are you in there, Ruby?" he asked softly. "Are you hurt?"

I nodded, finally remembering how to speak. "Yeah. It's me." My voice sounded too quiet, too tame for what had just happened. "I'm not hurt."

Slowly, the bloodlust drained from me completely, and Adonis released his grip on my wrist.

I looked down at my body, at the glowing silver light. It illuminated the stark spatters of blood all over my dress, although it was starting to dim.

Vaguely, I was aware of how I looked to Adonis, of the horror he must have felt at my appearance. Feral, bestial, covered in the blood of angels.

Why did I care what he thought, anyway?

I took a step away from him, surveying the damage, and swallowed hard. "So, you probably want me to explain this."

Tanit licked her fangs. "We slaughtered the angels outside. Or rather, Adonis did most of the work, while we watched on—"

"I killed plenty," Kur interjected.

"And then we heard the dragoniles calling us," added Adonis.

"How many angels were there?" I asked.

"Twenty," said Adonis. "It may take a while for the Heavenly Host to even notice that they've failed to return."

"The angels weren't coming here for me," I began. "They were here to check on you, Adonis. They want to know why your curse hasn't taken hold, even after the apocalypse has started."

Adonis stroked his fingertips across his chest. "Little messenger angels. Well, they're all dead now, so I don't imagine the message will get through."

Tanit nudged the dead demon with her foot. "Can we get back to what the fuck happened in here?"

I surveyed the carnage around me. "Oh. The bodies. Well, the fallen one over there was the first to arrive, and he said he could smell the magic of the light bringer." I looked down at the incandescent light that radiated from my body. "It just sort of came out when I panicked. And I used his demonic transformation process to kill him."

Adonis's eyes flashed with a cold light. "How exactly did he come to fall?"

I curled my lip. "Weird torture fetish. I indulged it a bit until he lost control."

Adonis's eyes flashed with anger, and the air seemed to thin around us.

"Four other angels followed," I continued. "They could all smell my light magic. And then I went a bit feral, and slaughtered them in a brutal bloodbath. So that about sums it up."

Kur smiled at me, his dark eyes glinting. "Oh, I like her."

"You killed all of them?" asked Adonis.

I shook my head. "One of them got away, but I'm not sure he'll live. His arms and one of his wings were in tatters."

Dark magic whirled around Adonis. "Seems the magic of the Old Gods still fills your body. That's the good news. The bad news is that we now have another problem on our hands. We're racing against Johnny's recovery, and against discovery by the Heavenly Host."

I looked down at my body, at the silver light pooling from my skin.

Adonis nodded at the demon's body. "You've glossed over a thing or two. What do you mean, a torture fetish?"

Somehow, it felt undignified to go into it, but I supposed it was stupid to cling on to dignity when coated with a sticky mixture of blood and ash. "He wanted me to kneel on the ground, pull off the top of my dress, and cut myself on his sword. He really wasn't a very nice angel."

Adonis's gray eyes darkened, and his wings spread out behind him.

Kur scrubbed his hand over his mouth. "Oh, this will be interesting."

Violence glinted in Adonis's eyes. "He will suffer a painful death."

I blinked. "Pretty sure he's dead already."

"He isn't." Adonis's voice was pure ice. "I'd know."

Dark tendrils of his magic spread out around the room, and a claw-sharp filament of magic caressed my cheek.

As his power roiled around us, the demon on the floor began to twitch and moan. Slowly, he pushed himself up to his knees, his black eyes landing on me. He roared, the sound echoing off the hall. Just as he began to run for me, Adonis cut his wrist through the air. With that one sudden motion, he severed the demon's body in half at the waist.

The creature unleashed a half-strangled scream, refusing to die.

I closed my eyes, trying to block out the last of his shrieks as he bled out on the floor.

Glad I wasn't the only ruthless killer in here.

"Now he's dead," Adonis said quietly.

The stench of blood curled into my nose, sickly sweet. Dark, unwelcome memories prodded at the depths of my mind. An old memory—brutal, monstrous teeth sinking into a pale arm, blood staining the pavement—

My eyes snapped open again, and I took a deep, shaky breath. "Well. This night turned out well, didn't it?" I smeared some of the blood off my arms, watching as it dripped onto the floor.

The sound of the dragoniles screeching still echoed wildly around us.

"You may want to wash the blood off." Among the chaos of reptilian screams, Adonis's voice sounded oddly soothing.

"Brilliant idea." I was already heading for the door. "I need to get away from that horrific screaming."

Tanit's lips curled. "What's the matter, little flower? Can't handle a little blood?"

"Leave her alone, Tanit," said Adonis.

Kur waved at the carnage all over the floor. "Doesn't look like she's afraid of a bit of blood. We could have used her at the Battle of Plataea. She could have fended off half the Greeks where they'd trapped us."

Ignoring them, I crossed over the blood-slicked floor to the doorway, my entire body shaking. "Bath time for Ruby."

"Don't take too long," Kur cautioned. "We need to leave here as soon as we can in case that surviving angel manages to pass along a message."

Ten minutes ago, when I'd been feral, a strange sort of calm had quieted my mind. But now, dark memories roiled just below the surface, and a lick of dread danced up my spine.

The Heavenly Host might be coming for me. As archangels, they wouldn't be quite so easy to kill—at least, not without the Stones of Zohar.

I had no idea what might happen now, only that there was no going back.

CHAPTER 21

*I*n Adonis's bathtub, I scrubbed a bar of soap over my skin. It smelled faintly of anemones, and formed a pink foam over my forearms. It felt good to clean the stench of death off myself.

We had two ticking time bombs on our hands now—Johnny, and the injured angel who could be limping his way back to the celestial realm.

In the bath, some of the battle fury began to seep out of my body, and the shaking in my legs went still. But when I closed my eyes, my mind flashed with images of the fight—the angelic sword slicing into flesh, through bones. When I'd fought the angels, I'd wanted more death, more blood. I'd wanted to hear the crush of bones under my sword's steel, to feel the hot rush of their blood in my mouth.

Adonis seemed strangely fascinated by the fae, but he also thought we were savage beasts, driven by the worst, basest impulses. That we worshipped a lack of control. After he'd seen me dripping with angelic blood and gore, I doubt his opinion had changed on that front.

Reddened suds dripped off my arm. Maybe the Old Gods were sparking something in me—a complete rebellion at the presence of angels on earth. They didn't belong here—not the horsemen, nor the angels. The earth belonged to the gods of nature, not these nightmarish, heavenly creatures.

I rinsed off the pink, bloody foam in the bathwater. My jaw clenched as a dim memory flickered in my mind—sharp, bestial teeth ripping into flesh. As I ran the soap over my legs, my mind whirled with images of blood that turned to something darker—blood dripping down a pale arm, streaming over the pavement. Dragons, maybe. I was remembering a dragon attack.

No wonder Drakon unnerved me.

I clamped down hard on the unwelcome memory, gripping the soap so hard my fingernails dug into it.

This was no time to lose myself in haunting memories—I might have an angelic horde coming for me. I rose from the warm bathwater, letting the suds drip off my skin. As I unplugged the drain, goose bumps rose over my body.

The shock of the cold castle air pulled me from my dark thoughts, and I stepped from the bath. I grabbed a towel and dried myself off.

In the stone alcove, I had a fresh set of clothes laid out, courtesy of Tanit—a wool dress that looked like it would fall just below my ass, and wool stockings that would reach up to mid-thigh. And apart from the boots, that was it. I'd asked for something warm, and that was what she'd brought me. At least she'd found something made of thick material.

Freshly dried, and smelling of anemones, I pulled on the woolen stockings, the fabric rough against my bare skin. The dark dress hugged my body, sleeves reaching down to my wrists. I pulled on the thigh-high boots, then slipped my sheathed knife into one of them— the leather loops making a perfect holster. I'd reapplied the Devil's Bane poison to its blade.

My heels clacked over the floor as I crossed into Adonis's room.

Tanit and Kur sat on the edge of the bed.

Tanit leaned back. "Oh, the feral one is here. Ruby, did you manage to civilize yourself in there with a bit of soap?"

Adonis paced the stony floor. His sword—Ninkasi—hung over his back, ready for battle. His icy gaze met mine. "Tell us about the angel who got away. How bad were his injuries?"

I closed my eyes, shuddering as I remembered the flashes of savagery from our battle. "I think I cut into both of his arms, but I didn't take them off completely. I don't think he can use them. I sliced into one of his wings. He'd have a damn hard time flying, and if he were human, he'd bleed out. I'm not sure how mortal angels heal."

Adonis stroked his chin. "Drakon and I followed his trail of blood while you were bathing. It ends just at the edge of the cliff face. Either he plunged to his death in the ocean—or he managed to fly off to report what he saw."

Tanit's eyes burned into me. "He was half dead, his arms hanging off, wings severed, and you let him get away? Why?"

My jaw tightened. "It was four against one. And I started with a knife against their swords. I think I managed fairly well, to be honest."

Tanit rose from the bed, her predatory eyes locked on me. "I don't think the numbers were the problem, though, were they? Did you feel mercy for that angel fucker?" She laced the word *mercy* with disdain.

I shook my head. "No. Not mercy."

Adonis's midnight wings spread out wider as he assumed more command over the room. "This is hardly the time to nitpick a battle."

Tanit's dark eyes shone. "We're going all the way to France to search for the Stones of Zohar, just to hand them over to someone who can't handle the bloodshed."

Adonis raised his hand to silence her. "That's enough."

I sucked in a deep breath. "I can handle the bloodshed. I just go a little crazy when my fae side takes over, and it's hard to think clearly."

"I thoroughly approve of your crazy side," said Kur in his deep, rumbling voice.

Tanit wasn't letting this go. "It's not the craziness that I object to." She took another step closer. "With the Stones of Zohar, you'll be wielding an overwhelming power. You'll need to be able to control it, which means you can't be afraid of it. You can't be afraid of killing people."

"She'll be fine," said Adonis sharply. He handed me a leather bag, stuffed with Tanit's clothing. "Or at least, she's our best option."

"A ringing endorsement. Is someone going to tell me how we can get to this castle?"

"We'll be flying," said Tanit. "Only, you don't have wings like we all do, so Kur will have to carry you."

Adonis shot them an irritated glare. "I'll carry her."

"With that shattered wing of yours?" Tanit protested.

Adonis ran his fingertips over his feathers. "It's nearly healed."

"Don't worry," said Kur. "If he drops you, I'll do my best to catch you."

* * *

HIGH ABOVE THE ROCKY LANDSCAPE, Adonis pulled me in close. The February winds whipped over my skin, chilling me, and I nestled my head in closer to Adonis's warmth.

His heart pounded through his clothing, and his wings rhythmically beat the air. One of his arms was wrapped around my lower back, the other beneath my knees. His large hand curled around my thigh, practically encircling it. I clutched my little bag of clothes.

Something about his smell and the feel of his magic soothed my muscles, washing away all the violent images that had burned in my skull earlier.

A vault of stars arched over us, and my red hair whipped into my face. I brushed it out of my eyes. Stretching out far below us lay the vast, darkened wasteland of the post-apocalyptic UK. Every now and then, flashes of bonfires pierced the darkness, a few cities punctuated by flickering candles in windows. Those were probably the demon enclaves, since they now felt free to roam over the land unperturbed. Vampire cities, valkyrie havens, shifter dens...

I shot a nervous glance at Adonis's injured wing. "Do you really think it was a good idea to take me instead of Kur?"

Our gazes met. "Do you know that most women would give their right arm to fly with me?"

"Do you usually require that kind of a sacrifice?"

He ignored my comment.

A burst of flame punctuated the darkness, and my gaze flicked to Drakon. He soared above us, occasionally belching fire.

"Why *did* you want to take me instead of Kur? You've told me that you hate feral fae. And you've just seen a feral fae at her worst. Half naked, covered in blood and gore. Why insist on sticking close to me?"

"You don't seem like the other feral fae I've known. Violent, yes, but I can hardly object to that." His voice was smooth as a lover's caress. "Maybe I like it a little."

Was that a spark of warmth I felt in my chest? No—of course it wasn't. I didn't care what he thought.

"I wasn't raised among the fae. My parents taught me some of the old fae ways, but not the brutal parts, I guess." I tried to ignore the fact that the brutality just seemed to come naturally to me. "My mother taught me to carve weapons from trees, to live off what the forest provided us."

"What did they do?"

"They were spies among the Institute. Their work was dangerous, and my mother made sure I'd be able to look after Hazel if anything happened to them." That was my job, my destiny. "Except..."

"Except we came into your world, and the dragon-shifters, too."

"You know, none of the tree carving or berry picking came in very handy when faced with a hundred-foot-tall reptile." I didn't tell him how completely powerless I'd felt, but given the way he pulled me closer to his hard, masculine body, I thought he could sense it. "And I just want to get back to that old dream—the one about living in the forest off berries and venison. That probably sounds stupid to someone whose goal is to be worshipped by celestial angels."

"It doesn't sound stupid at all."

Drakon screeched at the night sky, and a chill rippled over my skin.

"I'm just glad I got my sister back." At the thought of Hazel, my mind wandered to Kratos. Sure—he was a monster. But monsters surrounded me at this point—and he was a monster who'd returned

Hazel to me. Would the Stones of Zohar drive him from the earth? Maybe Adonis wanted to enslave him.

I knew angels didn't belong on earth—that they had to leave. And yet still, the question prodded at the back of my mind.

"What will happen to Kratos if the Stones of Zohar return him to the heavens?" I asked.

Adonis's body tensed, and he lowered his head so his breath warmed the side of my face. "Why are you worried about Kratos?"

"I just want to know what will happen to him. He found Hazel for me. I know he's a horseman, and he's at risk of falling, and he is forced to kill scores of people...but he did something kind for me. I owe him."

"Is that right?" Adonis's velvety voice had a hint of steel in it.

I frowned. "Yes. I mean, he searched for her, and he brought her to me, just because she was important to me. He even made me a dance studio."

He stared evenly at the night sky in front of us, his enormous wings rhythmically beating the air. "I see."

"Is there something you're not telling me?" My teeth chattered.

Instead of answering my question, he pulled me in closer to his chest. "You're freezing, aren't you? I can feel your body shivering." The sensuous tone of his voice slipped around me like silk.

One of his hands curled around my leg—the gap between my dress and my stockings. Slowly, the tip of his forefinger began a lazy stroke up my inner thigh. At his touch, a liquid heat slowly unfurled in my body, pooling around my belly, my ribs.

He kept his glacial eyes on the night air ahead of us, as if he were only half aware of what he was doing. I, on the other hand, was completely aware of every minute shift of his fingers, and my world narrowed to his light touch.

A slow, lazy stroke up and down my bare inner thigh, eliciting an ache in my belly. Another slow, gentle stroke. Sparks ignited up my spine, and my back began to arch. His plan to warm me up was work-ing, and my body heated with every gentle stroke.

I pulled myself in closer to him, my breasts pressing against him, and he met my gaze. Once more, that carnal look burned in his eyes, and his fingers moved higher up my bare thigh.

I hated myself for it, but I desperately wanted to know what it felt like to kiss him. *Stay in control, Ruby.* He was born to kill and seduce.

If this went any further, at some point he'd realize that I wasn't wearing any underwear. And yet—who was I to stop him?

My breath came faster in my throat.

"You interest me, fae." Then, an unexpected question. "Why a succubus? You hide yourself as a human to blend into their world, but of all the demons, you chose succubus to mask yourself."

Again, that fingertip moved lazily along my skin, his eyes fixed straight ahead as if he was completely unaware of it. Did he realize that with every slow caress, a dark heat arced through my blood? I let my gaze trail over his full mouth, trying to remember how words worked.

At last, I cleared my throat. "Fae males like to dominate the females. To some degree, the same is true for angels, demons, humans… It's kind of a male thing."

Amusement glinted in his eyes. "Is that right?"

"There was one exception. Succubi ruled over men long ago. Shadow demons, human males—they all used to worship the demonesses of the night."

"Mmmm." His deep purr licked up my nape. "You envision yourself dominating men. I must admit. The image has a certain appeal."

"I mean, I don't dwell on it." Could he hear how fast my heart was beating right now?

The tip of his forefinger continued to trace lazy, exquisite strokes on my thigh, and warmth pooled in my core. I wanted to feel his lips against mine, his tongue licking my body.

"Do you feel warmer now, Ruby?" The way my name sounded on his tongue—instead of *succubus* or *fae*—sent a throbbing ache through my belly.

I liked being up here with him, feeling his arms around me.

I swallowed hard. "Yes. Warmer," I managed.

He lowered his face to mine. "This is why I didn't want Kur to take you." His voice was a purr against my neck, a dangerous invitation.

I had to stop myself from kissing his neck. What would he do if I pressed my lips against his throat, against that pulsing vein in his neck? I tried to imagine how hard it would be to wrap my legs around him from this angle.

It was a strange sort of torture, flying with him hundreds of feet in the air, desperate now to feel my body pressed against his masculine form. My gaze dipped to his sensuous mouth—the subtle curl of his full lips.

Another slow, lazy swoop up my inner thigh, and I let out a low moan. His body called to me, an inexorable magnetic pull. Tightening my arms around him, I moved my lips closer to his neck, an ache throbbing between my legs. His hand slid higher still. A cold rush of air—

Then, I slammed down the iron door on my desire. "Stop with the hands," I said.

I wasn't on this mission to enjoy myself, and definitely not to enjoy the pleasures of a dark angel of seduction.

My body went rigid, and I tugged down my dress. "I mean, I'm warm enough now, thanks."

A low, nearly imperceptible growl in protest. Maybe he tried to hide it, but Adonis had his own conflicts—his perfect masculine beauty masking a primal side.

The combination was disturbingly tempting.

<h1 style="text-align:center">CHAPTER 22</h1>

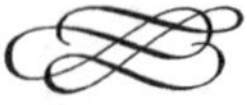

As we soared over the English Channel, icy wind bit into my skin. Adonis was no longer using his seduction power to warm me, and I was starting to regret it deeply. Particularly when a light, freezing rain began to fall, drenching my clothes.

Drakon circled around us, igniting the dark air with his fiery breath.

"I told you about myself," I said. "Now you tell me about yourself, then. You're Death, supposedly. You can kill with a flick of your wrist, and you have. But you have a problem with the savagery of the fae."

"Some creatures deserve violent deaths. Others don't. The fae don't discriminate in their ecstatic states."

"Ah. So you've got a moral code."

"Morality," he said. "Shockingly, it's quite important to angels. Sacrificing the few to save the many, brutally punishing those who deserve it. And do you know what? The second bit is my favorite part."

"Of course it is." I shivered. "I'd hate to be the recipient of one of your morally righteous punishments."

"I don't see that happening."

"Any idea how far we have to go?" I asked.

"Another hour, maybe."

I glanced down over the dark, churning sea, and it sparkled faintly in the moonlight. If Adonis decided to drop me for any reason, I'd freeze to death quickly. Maybe I should minimize the "Are we there yet?" questions.

"Close your eyes," he said quietly. "I'll wake you when we're over Paris."

I'd never sleep here, hundreds of feet in the air. Freezing, and with wildly sexual thoughts blazing in my mind.

Still, as I leaned against his powerful chest, the rhythmic beating of his heart lulled me into relaxation, and his soothing magic whispered over me. Slowly, sleep began to claim my mind, and I dreamt of a river carving through a wild garden dappled with red flowers.

* * *

A GENTLE NUDGING on my side woke me again, and my breath caught in my throat as I stared down at Paris. Or at least, what was left of Paris.

The Eiffel Tower still stood sharply in the dark landscape, silvered in the light of night.

While I'd been sleeping, rain had soaked my body, and I clamped down on my chattering teeth.

As we flew deeper into the city, warm lights burned in the ruins of Paris's buildings—rookeries, just like the ones that had sheltered me in London. Around us, pale creatures flew through the air on gossamer wings. As one of them swooped close to us, I caught a glimpse of his face. His eyes were milky white, and curly gold hair spilled from his scalp. The creatures looked eerily like children, but with haunted expressions, mouths gaping slightly open.

"What are they?" I asked.

"Cherubs. They're Aereus's version of the sentinels. They watch everyone, report to him."

"So Aereus will know the moment we arrive."

"Oh, he'll definitely know."

Adonis's wings beat the air rhythmically, then flattened out as he began to take us lower. The night air kissed my damp skin.

At last, we got to the center of Paris, where a vast palace stretched out below us—an expanse of ornate honey-colored buildings, joined together in a rectangular shape. A ruined garden spread out before the palace—all dead plants and broken statues.

In the center of a sandstone courtyard between the palace buildings, light blazed from within an enormous, glass pyramid.

"The Louvre," I said. "We're going to the Louvre?"

"Aereus always admired it. And when he got the chance, he made it his own."

"How enterprising."

"I should warn you that Aereus has his own effect on people."

"I think I can guess. Johnny, angel of famine, makes people hungry, Kratos the Conqueror makes us want to submit. You make people..." I swallowed hard, wishing I hadn't begun that sentence. "Yearn for things." *Vague. Good.* "And the angel of war will probably bring out my violent side."

A wry smile. "Not that it appears to take much in your case." His breath was warm against my ear. "Do you remember the role you're supposed to play?"

"Submissive succubus lover, her wild side tamed by the sexual prowess of the great and mighty love god Adonis."

"You've actually elaborated a bit there, not that I object to the description. It sounds entirely realistic."

I didn't think he could see the roll of my eyes in the darkness. "Just one of these days I'd like a spy scenario where I get to be the all-powerful Empress, and a beautiful man has to cater to my every whim."

A wicked smile. "Depending on your whims, I'm sure we could arrange something."

At his words, that heat surged again in my blood.

We seemed to pick up speed as Adonis carried us lower toward the Louvre, and the wind rushed over us. We glided to a smooth landing in the courtyard beyond the pyramid, swooping down gently before a towering set of doors. Drakon screeched to a halt beside us.

A line of milky-eyed cherubs stood before the doors, their bodies glowing like starlight in the dark.

Adonis wrapped his arms around me, his wings surrounding me like a shield.

"Aereus is expecting us," Adonis said in his commanding voice.

"The Dark Lord," the cherubs spoke in unison. "Welcome to Sadeckrav Castle."

A gentle thudding behind us turned my head. Kur and Tanit landed, their leathery wings folding behind them.

Eyes wide and gleaming, the cherubs glided to the side, and the front doors creaked open with a groan into a vast hall with an arched ceiling. Marble columns and alcoves lined the walls.

I'd been to the Louvre before—long ago, on a trip with my parents. And I didn't remember it quite this way. Aereus had definitely made it his own.

Torches burned in brackets along the stone walls. Statues of a war god—Aereus, presumably—stood over a marble floor.

Without Adonis's arms around me, a chill had spread through my body, and my teeth chattered. My wet hair felt positively icy on the back of my neck.

From a shadowy hallway, five humans emerged, each with an iron collar around their neck, each dressed in a simple gray tunic.

I bit my lip. Considering they weren't chained to anything, the iron collar served no practical purpose. Maybe they were chained up when they slept, or maybe Aereus just wanted to give them a harsh reminder of their servitude.

Four cherubs glided around us, their wide eyes peering up at us. "Dark Lord," they said in unison. "We understand you have arrived to discuss important matters with our master. You must rest now. The human servants will take you and your lover to your room. Please, follow them."

Eerie little buggers.

The humans stared at Adonis, their eyes wide with terror. Two of them stepped forward—the two largest men, one bearded and over six feet tall, the other a younger man, his body lean. They trembled as they stared at Adonis.

Nervously, they beckoned us down another expansive hallway, lined with stately columns. The other humans beckoned Tanit and Kur in the opposite direction, splitting us up.

My high-heeled boots echoed off the stone walls as we walked, and I summoned more of the charcoal glamour of a succubus to waft off my body in tendrils. Drakon's claw-tipped feet clicked over the floor behind us.

The path that the cherubs took led us past long, winding marble halls, the walls festooned with paintings of deeply unnerving battle scenes. Swords cutting off heads, blood spattering battlefields—*Saturn Devouring His Son,* the god's eyes wide with insane bloodlust. I shivered, maybe from the icy rain, or maybe the decor.

At the end of a long hall, the cherubs paused at a door that swung open, revealing a small room with a simple bed in the center of a stone floor. White sheets, a few pillows—literally no other furniture in the whole room apart from a claw-foot bathtub. The place didn't have windows, just a few iron sconces protruding from the sandstone walls.

After all that grandeur, I'd been expecting something more luxurious than this. Aereus, clearly, was trying to make a point.

Adonis turned to the cherubs, his eyes darkening, and the candles wavered in their sconces, nearly snuffing out.

"*This,*" he hissed, "is the room Aereus wants me to stay in?"

The bearded man shrank away from Adonis. "He thought you might be comfortable here. With your friend."

An eerie, animal stillness had overtaken Adonis's body, only faint whispers of his magic moving in the air around him. Nothing, I was coming to realize, was more dangerous or terrifying than the quiet stillness of an angel.

CHAPTER 23

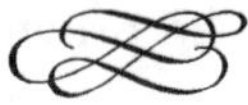

"*A*ereus has done this on purpose, to prove a point," said Adonis. His lip curled in a snarl, then with a lightning-fast movement, he had the bearded man pinned up against the wall.

Drakon spread his wings and hissed, a stream of fire pouring from his mouth in the direction of the humans.

Sweet earthly gods, all this over a room?

"Relax, Adonis," I snapped, before changing my tone to be sweetly seductive. "This will be perfect for us. No distractions, just a bed and a bath to keep us occupied."

Adonis didn't appear to be listening to me, his hands wrapped around his victim's collar. Instead, he leaned in closer to the man. "I want you to go back to Aereus and tell him that this is perfect for me, and that I love it." Despite the gentleness of his words, icy rage poisoned his tone.

He dropped the man in a heap on the floor. The other servant seemed to have slunk into the shadows, probably hoping Adonis would forget he existed.

Within a moment, both humans had scrambled off, their footsteps scuttling over the floor as they ran. Adonis slammed the door.

When he turned back to me, his expression was one of complete serenity, his body entirely at ease.

I cocked my hip, trying to calm the chattering of my teeth. The flight's rainstorm still chilled me to the bone. "Did you really just violently assault someone over the furniture?"

Surprise flickered in Adonis's eyes. "He's fine, isn't he? And I don't care about the furniture, but the other horsemen expect me to act in a certain way. I'm supposed to be the Lord of Death, and all that." His movements smooth and easy, he prowled closer to me. "Surely you understand playing a role, Ruby."

I nodded. "I get it." I sat on the edge of the bed, desperate to pull off my boots and crawl under the covers. "So who gets the bed?"

"Plenty of room for both of us."

I swallowed hard, then lowered my voice to a whisper. "We're not really lovers, Adonis. We're just going to play the part."

Behind him, his wings shimmered away—the first time in days I saw him without them.

He pulled off his shirt, giving me a view of his chiseled chest. The network of scars over his heart interrupted the sharp lines of his tattoos. Already, he was sliding between the bedsheets. He leaned back on his hands, eyeing me as I stood there hugging myself.

"Can you turn around?" I asked, shivering. "I want to change out of my ice-cold dress."

"I have seen you naked before. In fact, the image is seared deeply into my fondest memories."

"Close your eyes," I barked.

He did as he was told, and I pulled off my drenched dress, my skin frigid and puckered in the cold air. I rifled through the leather bag until I found one of Tanit's dry dresses, and I slipped it on over my naked body. Then, I snatched the sheathed knife from the bag.

I hugged myself, my teeth still chattering. "So where am I supposed to sleep, now?"

Adonis opened his eyes again, and his gaze roamed over me as if imagining what he'd missed. "If you don't want to sleep next to a godlike being, that's your choice. There's always the floor, or the bathtub."

I shivered, and the warmth of the bed called to me.

Adonis cocked his head. "But I can see that you're freezing. You'll need me to warm you."

I tightened my fingers into fists until the nails pierced my skin. "Fine. I hope you're okay with sleeping with the torches lit," I added. "Because I'm still not into the whole darkness thing." I shoved the knife under the pillow. "And if you do anything I don't want you to, I have a poison-tipped blade under my pillow."

"Of course," he purred. "I'll only do things you want me to."

Don't fall for his charms, Ruby. He was like this with all women, of course. Definitely the kind of guy you couldn't trust. The kind who kept secrets, who never told you what he really felt about you. The kind who'd leave the earth to rule the heavens at the first chance he got. Typical.

Still shivering, I crawled into bed next to him, trying not to look at his perfect body. I was painfully aware of the fact that I was still going commando. I'd have to make sure my dress didn't shift too much during the night.

In any case, I definitely wasn't going to dwell on his smooth, tan skin, his powerful arms, or that perfect mouth that could torture me with excruciating pleasure.

I cleared my throat. *Shut down those thoughts.* "Since we're here for a reason, and that reason is to spy on Aereus, maybe it's time we figure out a specific plan. What else do I need to know about him?"

"Aereus is competitive with me."

"Hence the room." I lay down stiffly, keeping my eyes trained on the ceiling. Every one of my muscles was tensed.

"He's furious that my curse hasn't set in, that I inspire more fear than he does. He will want to steal you from me like the spoils of war."

Adonis leaned on his elbow, looking over at me. I tried to ignore that his searing gaze was roaming over my shoulders. I pulled the sheet tighter around me, clutching hard to it.

"That explains how I can capture his interest. Maybe he'll want me alone." Already, the gears were turning in my mind, and I started to envision myself functioning as a honey trap. "Any clue at all where he might be keeping these Stones of Zohar?"

"No. As you've seen, the palace itself is enormous. But they're so powerful, so valuable to him, that I'd guess he keeps them close to him, locked up safely in his bedroom or his office of war."

I took a deep breath. "I can probably contrive to get into either of those."

A troubled expression crossed Adonis's beautiful features. "He's dangerous—not just for who he is, but for what he can inspire in you. He'll draw your violent thoughts from you like nectar from a flower. He can sense inner conflict—and he can exploit it. I want to keep a line of communication open with you if you're alone with him."

"How exactly?"

"If you allow it, I can link our minds, so I'll be able to hear your thoughts."

My jaw dropped. "You must be joking."

"You can control it to some degree, but I'll be able to hear if you're in danger."

"I'm guessing it's not reciprocal. You'd never agree to me hearing your thoughts."

"It doesn't need to be reciprocal. I don't need you to save me. In any case, it's only temporary."

"I haven't agreed to anything."

Adonis's dark eyebrows furrowed. He reached for me, tracing his fingertips over my collarbone. His touch left a trail of tingling heat. "Goose bumps. You're still freezing."

He ran his fingertips over my skin, and his magic began to whisper through my blood, warming me and soothing me at the same time. Even from that light touch, my back began to arch, my breath speeding up. I knew a flush had spread over my chest, giving away my real desires, even if I wanted to keep them hidden.

He leaned in close, his breath warming my neck. I felt as if my body were straining against the dress. I wanted him to touch and tease me with his fingertips, to let them roam over my thighs again. *I knew this was a bad idea.*

Slowly, his fingertips trailed over the neckline of my dress, gently tugging it down.

"I want to see all of you," he rasped, inching down my dress.

I arched my back, a silent invitation, and he tugged the fabric down to expose my breasts. The look on his face as he took me in was positively *starved*, like he'd emerged from a famine to find a succulent feast before him. He kissed my throat, his mouth searing, teasing me with a hint of teeth, and I felt my legs opening. I groaned.

I wanted him, *needed* him to touch me, so badly I was practically shaking. One of his hands moved up the inside of my thigh, and liquid heat pooled in my core, between my legs. Already, my hips were rocking, anticipating his touch moving higher…

From a corner of the room, Drakon let out a growl, and my body jolted. I pulled away from Adonis, pulling my dress up again.

What was I doing? This was all wrong. He was a power-hungry, maniacal death angel. I slammed down the iron door on my desires, and elbowed him away from me.

"This isn't a good idea." Granted, my body was screaming at me in rebellion, but I wasn't going to let him lure me in.

Adonis rolled over, disappointment etched across his gorgeous features. "Is there a reason a pleasure-loving fae would deny herself what she wants?"

I pulled the sheets up around me, my body suddenly freezing at the loss of body heat. "How about the fact that you've straight up told me you're evil?"

Candlelight danced over his skin, and he closed his eyes, inhaling deeply. As he breathed in, he pulled the light from the room, dimming the torches to a low burn—just enough to keep me comfortable.

My body still buzzed with the excitement of his touch. *Forget about how good that felt. Think of something vile.* I pressed my fingernails into the back of my hand, summoning instead images of blood and violence, of Saturn ripping the head off his child. And when I slept, I dreamt of blood spreading through a field of white anemones, staining them red.

CHAPTER 24

"I may not be entirely objective, but I do feel the bath would be better with two people in it," said Adonis.

"Oh, really?" I splashed the soap off my skin.

Wingless, Adonis sat in a chair facing the other direction. Drakon had been banished to the hallway.

"There are delicate parts of your body I could attend to better than you can." The sensual promise in his voice made my pulse race. "You can trust me on this."

At his words, a flush spread through my body. "I can manage."

I tried not to imagine his hand sliding gently between my legs, exploring my body, and I fought the burning ache. I tried not to imagine the sweet release of giving in to him completely.

"Stop distracting me," I said. "I have to meet the horseman of war. Alone, of course."

Adonis snatched a silver flask off the bed and unscrewed it while keeping his eyes straight ahead. Despite trying to tempt me with his words, he was acting like a perfect gentleman. "He's trying to send me another message. He wants to show that he can take what's mine."

"What's *yours?*"

"As far as Aereus knows, you're my succubus—a demoness I've

claimed as my own. We've come here, purporting to seek his help, and he'll want to use it as an opportunity to put me in my place. It enrages him that I remained un-cursed."

"When I'm finished with him, should I meet you back here?"

"If you learn anything—or even if you don't—go to Tanit's room and wait for me there."

Honestly, I didn't want to ever leave this bath—especially not to meet yet another possessive, domineering horseman. The warm water licked at my bare breasts, and I found myself staring at Adonis's powerful back, imagining running my fingertips over his chiseled shoulder blades.

I loosed a long sigh. Yep, I wanted to stay in here forever, thinking about how Adonis's fingers had felt on my body. Almost unconsciously, I began tracing the path his fingers had taken up my leg, staring at the back of his shoulders.

Adonis folded his arms behind his head. "I want to hear your thoughts when you're with him."

I froze. "Oh. That again?"

"If I leave my mark on you, it will allow me to hear your thoughts. Not every single thought—not all the filthy thoughts I'm sure you're having about me right now while you wash yourself and stare at my back."

I cleared my throat. "Don't be ridiculous. I'm not sure why everyone thinks Aereus is the one with the ego. Wasn't Adonis the legendary figure who got trapped mooning over his own image in a lake? Is that who you're named after? It's fitting."

"That was Narcissus," he said sharply. "Not even close."

"Anyway—you want to read my thoughts?"

"I can link us. You'll be able to feel me, a little. And I'll be able to hear if you're in trouble. You can scream for me in your mind."

"So...is this a permanent thing, or what?"

"Only if you want it to be. In any case, it's the only way you should go in there on your own. You don't know what he's capable of. He's quite fond of torture. Mental. Physical. All kinds."

I cringed. "Give me a minute to think about it. I'm not looking forward to meeting him, but going alone is probably for the best. All that I know about him is that his ego is his greatest weakness, and if I can flatter it, I might be able to get him to talk. If you're there, you'll suck up all the attention in the room like a black hole of narcissism and ruin it all."

I stepped out of the bath, and water dripped off my skin onto the stone floor. I grabbed the towel to dry myself off, and scrubbed at my hair.

On the bed, I'd laid out one of Tanit's outfits—a short, silver dress with long sleeves. And by the dress, my most important item: the poison-tipped knife.

Adonis sipped from his flask. "Can I turn around now?"

"Not yet. I'm completely wet and naked."

A bit cruel, maybe, but I enjoyed watching his entire body tense, fingers tightening around his flask.

I pulled the dress over my freshly cleaned body, completely bare under the luxurious fabric that fell midway down my thighs.

I pulled on the thigh-high boots, then slipped the sheathed knife down the side of one of them. "You can turn around now."

Adonis rose from his chair, and a deep curiosity burned in his pale eyes when he turned to me. He prowled closer. "Do you agree to what I asked?"

I crossed my arms. I'd hardly make a very good spy if I let someone I didn't trust invade my thoughts. "The whole mind-intrusion thing. Not a fan. Couldn't I just wear a wire?"

He shrugged, a smooth gesture. "I'm not familiar with that technology. But I can tell you that you're about to meet with one of the most dangerous beings who has ever walked the earth, and it might be wise to have an even more lethal ally backing you up."

"Yeah. Not really into it. How about I just call for you?"

"His rooms are often sealed so screams can't escape." Adonis's eyes darkened. "I once watched him trap two human women in his torture room for hours. Just for his own amusement. When he emerged, not a single piece of them was recognizable. He radiated joy that day."

I swallowed hard.

I leaned against the wall, still trying to gauge how much I trusted this self-professed dangerous being. He'd held back from telling me the truth about things. He wanted an insane amount of power for himself.

But—I didn't get the sense that he'd lied to me. And more—he was asking permission, when he really didn't need to. We'd already established that he could control my mind if he wanted to, yet he never did it. "It's definitely temporary?"

Another step closer, and he was standing right next to me, so close now that his magic slipped over my skin, kissing my bare thighs.

"Just temporary," he confirmed.

I let out a long breath. In this world, maybe I had to pick and choose which monsters I wanted to trust. The lesser of two evils, as it were. "Fine. Do what you need to do. And if I find out it's not like you described, I'm carving the thing off."

Without another word, he slipped his fingers into the sleeve of my dress and gently pulled it off my shoulder. Goose bumps rose over my skin, and I gasped at the feel of his fingertips on me.

"What are you doing?" I asked.

"I need to leave my mark on you, in a place where no one will see it. It won't hurt." His voice skimmed over my body, lighting me on fire. "Much."

I nodded mutely, the power of speech deserting me.

Adonis leaned down closer, and in the next moment, his mouth was on my shoulder, his kiss searing me. Involuntarily, my back arched into him, and liquid heat swooped through my core. Pure ecstasy lit up my body, until I was only dimly aware of my leg hooking around his to pull him closer, or of my fingers threading through his thick hair. His tongue flicked over my skin, then a hint of teeth. I moaned lightly.

Visions burned in my mind of Adonis pulling my dress all the way up, of his hands and tongue exploring my body. Wild heat arced through me.

Then, a sharp pain scalded my flesh below his mouth, snapping me out of my fantasies.

"Ow!" I clenched my fingers tight.

Slowly, Adonis pulled his face from my neck, his eyes burning with desire. It was at that point I realized that I hadn't threaded my fingers through his hair, but through his soft, midnight feathers, and I'd entirely wrapped my leg around his, sliding my foot higher until my dress rode up, practically to my hips.

"You're piercing my wings with your fingernails." Despite the complaint, an erotic tone suffused his voice. "Although I guess I kind of like it."

Reluctant as I was, I unwrapped my leg from Adonis and pulled my fingers from his wings. "Sorry."

When I looked down at the place where he'd marked me, I found a small, black tattoo—a perfect circle with a sort of dash in the center.

"That's your mark?" I asked. "What is it?"

"Theta. The eighth letter of the Greek alphabet."

"Okay, but...why?"

His arms loosened around me, but his eyes remained locked on the mark on my shoulder. "Thanatos. Death. It's what I am. It's who I am."

I pulled up the shoulder of my dress. "I like the name Adonis better."

A faint smile played over his lips. "So do I."

"And now you can hear my thoughts?"

"Unless you're capable of guarding them from me, I'll hear your thoughts. Particularly if you shout."

Oh sweet heavenly gods. Had he just heard...? "Were you privy to my thoughts just a moment ago?"

That slow, seductive smile. "I didn't need to hear your thoughts to know what you were thinking."

A thin sheen of sweat had risen over my body. "Right." I smoothed out my dress. "Let's just forget about that, okay? That was some sort of magic, obviously, when you left the mark."

Adonis just looked at me, that infuriating smile on his perfect lips.

"I have to go." I moved quickly for the door, trying to gather my thoughts. In the hall, cherubs glided over the marble floor, heads cocked, white eyes on me.

Focus, Ruby. Adonis's mouth on my neck had just ripped the world right out from under my feet, but I had another horseman to meet, and I needed to keep my wits about me if I was going to have any hope of manipulating him.

* * *

I stood before Aereus, in a large hall with a dais that towered high above me. Golden wings swooped from his back over his throne, the feathers blending to a deep maroon at the tips. A crown of chestnut-gold hair shone from his head, lit up from behind by a stained-glass window. Sunlight streamed in from the windows, gleaming over his golden breastplate. The room smelled of roasting meat.

Aereus studied me intently, tapping the armrests contemplatively.

The longer he stared at me, the more my muscles tensed. In fact, as my gaze slid over the humans lining the side of the hall, I picked out a ruddy-faced man with dark eyes. Something about him sparked my rage, and for a single, dizzying instant, I envisioned myself ripping open his rib cage and pulling his still-beating heart from his chest...

Simmer down, Ruby. Already, Aereus's power was beginning to affect my mind—and the way he was watching me, I was pretty sure he was doing it on purpose, testing the results. Above him, the stained-glass window depicted another image of Saturn devouring his son. A god so ruthlessly driven by power that he was willing to consume his own living child to preserve his throne.

Seemed to be a favorite motif for Aereus.

I licked my lips, desperate to taste blood there.

"Tell me about why you've come." His commanding voice boomed over the hall.

Why was he asking me and not Adonis? Maybe he didn't trust Adonis. I could start planting the seeds of our plan now, anyway. "You

429

know, the Dark Lord hasn't really discussed his plans with me, but it was something about Johnny and Kratos rebelling against the Heavenly Host. Johnny ripped Adonis's wing—I know that much. Oh! And something about Kratos starting to fall? Does that sound right?"

Aereus's primal snarl slid through my bones. "Fall? Kratos?"

I shrugged, feeling minuscule before him. "Adonis thought they were angry about their curses, that they might rebel against the archangels in heaven. Whatever you call them. And he thought they could be coming for you."

As soon as Johnny and Kratos descended from the skies above the Louvre, Aereus would know. And with any luck, he'd be on our side when we had to face them.

Blood-red veins glinted in Aereus's eyes. "Coming for me?"

Fury rippled off him, stirring my rage once more, until my mind swam with visions of teeth tearing at flesh.

This was a dangerous game for a feral fae. A succubus had more control than I did—pure seduction and elegance. A bit of soul-stealing through sex, but relatively blood-free. But a feral fae in the presence of the horseman of war? Not a great situation.

Aereus cocked his head, moving for the first time in minutes. "You look hungry, Succubus. Do any of the humans appeal to you?"

The feral snarl that escaped my throat echoed through the hall. "I feed from human males, and there are plenty in here. But none particularly strikes my fancy."

A faint accent tinged his words as he spoke. "I'd heard that Adonis had managed to tame a succubus, but I wasn't sure I believed it. I suppose some think Adonis is the most adept seducer in the world, but frankly, I find it hard to believe. Death surrounds him."

It was quickly becoming clear that despite his angelic demigod status, despite ruling over a medieval palace with chained humans at his beck and call, despite all of his powers—this man's ego was in need of some serious stroking.

All alike. You men are all alike.

Another white-hot burst of rage tore through me, and for just a moment I envisioned myself with immeasurable strength, ripping the arrogant angel from his throne, hurling him to the ground, and crushing my boot into his neck. My mouth watered.

Aereus begs for his life as I thrust a blade between his ribs...

"You look as though you've become lost in a fantasy." Aereus's voice boomed over the hall.

"It's hard not to fantasize in the presence of greatness." I shrugged, looking down at the marble floor—a succubus who could be overwhelmed by the right godlike presence. "I can feed from humans, but they don't excite me the way real power does." I lifted my eyes to his in an invitation.

A satisfied smile spread across Aereus's chiseled features. "So it's not Adonis who excites you in particular."

Slowly, I ran my fingertip over the front of my chest, tracing the curve of my breast. "It seems to me like your palace is bigger than his." While volcanic rage surged inside me, I schooled my features—coy, compliant on the outside. I needed him to bring me into his inner sanctum, to find out where he kept his most important objects.

I bit my lip, swaying my hips slightly from side to side. "Where do you rule from, Aereus? When you want to summon a war between the humans, when you want to drive them to destroy each other—do you make your decisions from here? From that throne?"

He shook his head, and a phantom wind skimmed over my skin, dry and hot as the desert air.

"Not from here, no."

Tuning in to my glamour, I focused on the tendrils of dark magic emanating from my body. I sent them spiraling through the air toward Aereus. "Can you show me your war room?"

He studied me for an uncomfortably long time before nodding curtly at a guard behind me.

When he rose from his throne, his body cast a long shadow over the floor.

Wordlessly, he descended from the dais. With each footstep, the floor trembled as if he were an actual giant. Just after he passed me, he cast an impatient look over his shoulder. "I'll take you to my war room. But first, a detour through my garden."

"A *garden?*" Given the whole *war god* thing, I'd been expecting something a little more brutal from him than gardening.

As if reading my thoughts, Aereus replied, "It's not as tame as it seems at first. In fact, it's how I control my servants."

My throat went dry. I really didn't want to be anywhere near this angel or his garden.

CHAPTER 25

I followed Aereus through a heavy door, and I squinted in the bright light outside. It took my eyes a few moments to adjust.

At first, the garden's wild beauty struck me. It wasn't the stark, elegant beauty of Adonis's garden, but a vibrant riot of color—roses in shades of violet and pumpkin, cherry-red, deep amber, mulberry, and indigo. I breathed in the heavy floral scent.

Sunlight gleamed off the golden sheen of Aereus's wings, sparking over the reddened tips of his feathers like fire. His brutal magic sizzled up my spine, bringing with it images of death—a bleak forest of soldiers impaled on spikes, their bodies casting long shadows over desert sands. The vision dissipated from my mind as quickly as it had arrived.

His footsteps crunched over a winding path, and he led me deeper into the garden. Patterns in the mosaic path stretched out far ahead of us—images of swords and crowns, Greek letters and wild animals.

I'd suggested I wanted to see his place of power. So why had he taken me to a rose garden—and what did he mean that he used it to control his servants?

Only after a few minutes did I notice the dark gleam of barbed iron in the garden. I swallowed hard. Only one reason for barbed iron, as far as I knew.

In the depths of the garden, Aereus led me to a spiked, iron wheel, its surface stained rust-red. *Not rust.* My stomach dropped.

Aereus stood before it, a merciless smile on his face. "I was born in the Roman Empire. I once watched a man broken on the wheel. A vision I never forgot. The power a man can exert over another is thrilling."

The blood draining from my head almost left me dizzy. "You must have been a soldier."

"I helped to defeat Hannibal. I razed Carthage."

Desert air skimmed through my hair, and I twirled a lock of it around my fingertips. "I can only imagine how the armies of Carthage would have trembled before you." I blocked out the fury roiling in my chest. "And do you use this wheel for anything now?"

"It's how I keep my human servants in line. They don't wear chains, but they know not to rise up against me. They wouldn't dare. Sometimes, I kill their loved ones instead of them."

I plastered a serene smile onto my face. "How thrilling. You must be like a god to them."

His eyes flashed with a fiery light. "I am a god to them. I'm a god to your kind, too."

Bile rose in my throat. Never before had I felt it so strongly, the sense that these angels had to get away from us. I'd do anything to rip them from the surface of the earth.

As my thoughts raged, a silky-smooth presence caressed the depths of my mind. Was it Adonis?

I'm fine, I mentally telegraphed to him. *Just disturbed. Deeply fucking disturbed.*

As we walked the garden's winding path, we turned a corner, and my stomach dropped. Across from a row of wild roses, a line of guards stood. Their spears glinted in the sunlight. Instead of human forms, they had the bodies of enormous scorpions, with sharply pointed tails that curved over their heads. They stared at me through inky pools.

Masking my fear, I pointed to them. "What are they for?"

"Ah. They guard the poison garden. I grow a collection of dangerous plants here—extremely toxic. The guards simply ensure that no one dies accidentally."

"I see. How kind of you to look after your servants."

As if he gave a flying fuck. If I had to guess, Aereus couldn't stop the Old Gods from growing Devil's Bane in his garden. He didn't want any humans getting their hands on it, trying to destroy him. In fact, I could just about feel the warm glow of the Old Gods around me.

We moved farther along the path, and I ran my fingertips over the rose petals. The closer I looked, the more I found signs of death within this garden—iron devices with jagged rows of teeth jutting from the earth, designed to tear at flesh, to crush bodies. Among the flowers, bones—human, demon maybe—protruded from the soil.

Now, when I studied the mosaic on the ground, I realized the patterns were formed from teeth—human and animal, some painted black to create the designs.

I tried to choke down my disgust, but a wave of rage unfurled in me. I closed my eyes, pretending to breathe in the scent of his garden. Inwardly, I was envisioning myself strapping Aereus to the iron wheel and smashing his limbs with one of those spiked iron mallets. I'd crush *his* bones. I'd thrill at his screams. I'd rid the earth of this angelic scourge...

Easy, Ruby.

Once again, Adonis's presence stroked the depths of my mind like a lover's caress.

I'm fine, I screamed at him, unable to keep the wrath from my mental communications. *You angelic fuck.*

Taking a deep breath, I refocused on the garden around me. I was supposed to be charming the angel, not envisioning his gruesome demise.

I just...honestly had no idea how to relate to a two-thousand-year-old, omnipotent sadist.

"Those were the good days, weren't they?" I ventured. "The Roman Empire's glorious expanse over Europe, Asia, Africa…"

"My legions brought the Roman eagles over the farthest corners of the earth."

Aereus pivoted over the bony mosaic path, leading me farther into the garden, where someone had created sculptures from human bones, each one pierced with iron spikes. Roses climbed some of the sculptures. A strange, perverse sort of beauty in this garden of death.

Who had these bones belonged to? Servants who'd displeased Aereus? I could pull the knife from my boot now, ram it into his neck…

Charm him, Ruby.

What was it Adonis had said? His depressing angelic aphorism? Something about seeds…

I moved closer to Aereus, then flashed him my most charming smile. "This reminds me of a saying. The seeds of destruction grow within the gardens of paradise."

Aereus stopped walking, then turned to look at me. The wind toyed with his red cape, his hair. "So you know that expression? It's an angelic concept that I take very seriously." He gestured around him, pride beaming from his features. "That saying inspired all this. Glorious, isn't it?"

"It's good that you angels have come to earth to teach us. When you're done purifying the earth, we can begin again, creating a true paradise from the glorious destruction you've wrought."

"I was born for this. Born for war. Born to rule as an archangel on earth, just as the Heavenly Host rule as archangels in the celestial realm."

At the mention of them, a shudder danced up my spine, and I glanced at the cloudless skies. Had that injured angel made it back to them, or had he bled out before he had the chance?

Would the terrifying archangels be coming for me soon?

Whatever the case, I didn't have much time to screw around admiring Aereus's plants. I *needed* those stones as soon as I could get my hands on them—even if I didn't quite know what they did, or how to use them, or any of those somewhat important details.

I plucked a red rose, then began pulling the petals off one by one, hoping to enchant him. "So this is your beautiful paradise. Will you show me from where else you rule your kingdom? The real destruction? I want to know where you keep your most powerful, dangerous treasures. I want to *touch* them."

CHAPTER 26

I followed after him, heels clacking on the marble floor. In the large hall, sunlight streamed through the windows onto walls painted the color of dried blood.

As we reached the imposing oak doors, they creaked open of their own accord. I walked behind Aereus in the hallway, and his essence crackled over my skin. A hot current of rage roiled under the surface of my mind. How could the humans let themselves cower in here as slaves? Why didn't they work together, rise up against their oppressors? If they worked together, they could find the Devil's Bane, poison him again and again.

They scurried and shuffled in the shadows, hoping to remain unnoticed. A woman, her filthy hair hanging in tangles over her shoulders, hurried past us, her eyes downcast. She carried a bundle of rags in a basket.

Simpletons. Every human we passed was potential prey. How easy it would be to sink my feral teeth into their necks. How easy to punch my fists through their chests, snapping their ribs, to rub their blood over my bare skin...

A gentle, soothing presence licked at the hollows of my mind —*Adonis?* Apparently he could feel my rage.

I mentally cursed myself. It had been Aereus's magic clouding my mind. I didn't hate these humans. I hated *him*. But the horseman of war provoked a will to dominate the weak.

The iron collars around their necks probably served to dampen some of their rage. But as humans, they wouldn't be as vulnerable to fury as a feral fae.

Aereus shot me a sharp look as we walked. "Ruby. Is that a violent side I can sense?"

Put on a good show, Ruby. Always put on a good show.

I flashed him a sweet smile. "I think your powerful presence might affect me a little."

He smirked. "Does the Dark Lord affect you?"

"Not the same way you do. You're a god of war, the beginning and the end. War has shaped all of history, hasn't it? The reason why angels fell to earth in the first place, the explanation for nearly every advancement in human history. War. Nothing is more powerful."

Aereus's approval was a low rumble that trembled through my gut. When he spoke again, his voice echoed off the high ceiling, off the marble columns surrounding us. "Tell me why you think Kratos might fall." In the bright light of the hall, blood-red streaks shone in Aereus's eyes. "He's lived for nine hundred years without falling. Why now?"

I shrugged. "I think he's developed a taste for succubi."

"I can understand his temptation. And Johnny—he really attacked the Dark Lord?"

"I saw it happen. He looked crazed, like he'd lost the ability to speak. He'd been on a drunken bender, maybe poisoned himself with something. Mud and grass covered his body. There was something distinctly wrong with him."

"It's good that you came here to tell me. Only I can help you."

Flatter his ego. "I don't think Adonis wanted to admit it, but he was worried he couldn't handle them on his own."

"Fool." Aereus snorted. "He'd never admit something like that."

At the end of a glass-ceilinged hall, Aereus led me to an iron door. I balked at the sight of it. Touching the iron would drain my energy completely.

Aereus stroked his enormous fingertips over the iron surface, and his body glowed with a golden light. He whispered in the Angelic language.

Angelic was the language of magic—passed down from one generation to the next. In fact, it was the ancient language of fae and demons alike. I'd studied it, like I was supposed to, but I wasn't fluent.

Adonis would be, though.

Mentally, I repeated each syllable as loudly as I could so Adonis would hear it.

When Aereus finished the spell, the iron door groaned open, revealing a dim, windowless room. Torches burned in some of the alcoves, and a long table stretched across the center of the stone floor. Weapons hung from brackets in the walls.

Across the table, stacks of papers lay scattered, and my gaze wandered over them. The writing looked like Angelic, which meant I had no idea what it said.

The moment I stepped inside, the door slid shut behind us, scraping over the floor. At this point, I was pretty relieved about the mark Adonis had left on my shoulder, because I'd never be able to get out of here on my own if I needed to. Even if I went feral and pulled the knife from under my dress, the iron door would stop me.

The single mercy of the closed iron door was that the murderous rage clouding my mind seemed to have dissipated a little. Apparently, Aereus's magic mostly affected how I felt about weaker creatures, people I could dominate.

Aereus stood at the head of the table, staring at me. The torchlight wavered over his breastplate and his red-tipped wings.

I traced my fingertips over the wooden table in the center of the room. "This is thrilling."

Violent energy pulsed from his body, and he took a step closer to me, his armor gleaming in the warm light. "Your little succubus body reacts to me, doesn't it? You feel my power."

I feel like I want to tear your eyes out, if that's what you mean. "Yes, I can feel it."

"That's because you're at war within yourself."

He lumbered closer, then ran a meaty finger down the front of my chest. Inwardly, I shuddered, but I tried to hide my disgust.

"I sense your turmoil, Ruby. Deep in your chest."

I stared at him, trying to control my own aggression. What the fuck was he talking about?

Aereus closed his eyes, breathing in the air. Then, he gripped my shoulders. "You want something, but you deny yourself. Guilt eats at you, doesn't it? You left someone behind. What was his name?"

Stop intruding in my mind. I didn't want this monster talking about Marcus, or thinking about Marcus. He had no right to invade my memories.

He gripped my shoulders tighter. "You're scared of someone. Scared of a monster that you can't get rid of."

Now I had no idea what he was talking about, and I slipped away from his grasp. I schooled my features into a perfect mask of calm. "We're not here to talk about me," I said serenely. "I'm not interesting, Aereus. I want to know about *you*."

That seemed to do the trick, and he arched a golden eyebrow at me. "Of course you do."

I sat coyly on the edge of the table. "What happens in here?"

"Since the Great Nightmare has begun, I've started wars on three continents. I've inspired bloodlust across the globe. I've recreated the conquests of Alexander the Great, riding into Persia and India. For the past year, I've planned my bloodshed from here."

He crossed to an alcove, where a chalice glowed with golden light, and he plucked it from its resting spot. "Do you know what this is?"

"Some sort of magical chalice?"

"Azazeyl, the fallen angel, drank from this the night before the angels expelled him from the heavens. The night before he fractured into seven gods. No angel was ever more powerful, more beautiful— no one ever more tormented." A dark satisfaction dripped off his words.

"Amazing," I breathed, eyes wide. "What other ancient treasures do you keep in this room?"

Aereus crossed to the wall of weapons, lovingly stroking a long spear. I tried not to think of the phallic implications as he caressed it.

"The sarisa belonging to Alexander the Great, the weapon of his Diadochi army. Conquest has imbued this weapon with power."

This was all fascinating, and at one point I'd have been thrilled to find myself standing before Alexander the Great's spear. Now, I could think about only one thing—how to rid the earth of the angelic scourge.

Ignoring the fury that surged in my blood, I sauntered over to him. "Alexander the Great was amazing, I'm sure. But no one could rival an angel for skill in war."

His body glowed with fiery light, and I fought the urge to turn and run from him, or to grab Alexander's spear right off the wall and ram it through his body. "I was born to create war."

I cocked my head. Time to test his reaction. "And nothing can stop you, right? There's nothing on earth with the power to stop an angel from his quest."

He crossed to me, and a sharp pang of dread pierced my chest. I didn't want him too close to me. "Nothing," he repeated—but his tone lacked conviction.

For just a moment, his eyes flicked to a darkened corner of the war room. He was thinking about something there.

And that was exactly where I needed to look when I returned later.

Aereus moved closer, boxing me in where I sat on the table, and planted his hands on either side of my hips. "Tell me how war thrills you."

My gaze darted to the door. This would be a great time to get the hell out of here, if I didn't have a giant angelic asshole breathing down my neck.

Put on a good show, Ruby. "I can feel the power in this room, all around us. Once, I fed off the worship of humans, and I remember that feeling. It's coming back to me now."

His wrathful power intensified, choking me like a fist at my throat. Even though I'd never be able to take him in a fight, my mind began to burn with images of his bloody demise.

"In the old days," he began, "I took what I wanted. I'd have you bent over the table right now, that little dress up around your waist. I'd show you what you're missing with Adonis."

For just a moment, Aereus's eyes began to darken—the first hint of a fall. Then, he gripped the oak table so hard it began to splinter.

Swiftly, I slipped off the table, ducking under his arm.

"From what I understand, you can't get too close to me, can you?" I said. "Or you'll be at risk, just like Kratos. And I know you have the power to resist that temptation." I began traipsing over to the corner of the room—the place where I'd seen him looking.

There, a wooden bookshelf stood, crammed with faded texts.

Books? I'd been hoping for a box of some kind—something that might contain stones.

"I can't get too close to you," he roared. "But Adonis can, can't he?"

I turned to face him, backing up against the wall.

This topic *clearly* pissed him off.

"Only temporarily," I said. "I'm sure his curse will torment him soon enough."

Aereus's lip curled. "I've been cursed for five centuries." Rage dripped from his voice. "What good is war without the spoils?"

It took me a moment to understand what he meant—*women* were "the spoils."

Once again, I had to bite down on a searing flash of rage that threatened to overtake me.

Okay. *How do I get out of this situation?*

I touched my chest, feigning horror. "Five centuries of abstaining! How terrible. No reason to sabotage your success now, though, is there? Perhaps you should get back to ruling your palace."

I started to make a move for the door, when Aereus lunged for me, pressing his hands to the wall on either side of my head. Veins bulged in his thickly corded arms.

"I want what Adonis has. I can't touch you. But I can see you. I want you to take off your dress."

I clenched my jaw. I could let my feral side come out, inflicting some serious damage with my poison-tipped knife. But that would disrupt the entire mission. I'd come here for the Stones of Zohar.

This seemed like a good time to use that mental link I had with Adonis.

"Adonis!" I screamed within my mind. *"This would be a good time to interrupt!"*

I needed to stall. I took a deep breath. "Oh my, your arms are very strong, aren't they?" The words tasted like poison on my tongue, because I could think of nothing but ramming my knife into his stupid, fat neck, right into his throbbing jugular.

"Yes," he growled. "Strong. Take off your dress. Let me see Adonis's prized possession."

Before I could get another word out, the sound of shearing metal pierced the air as the iron door twisted away from the frame.

I let out a slow, relieved breath as Adonis strode into the room, bathed in light, his midnight wings trailing behind him. As soon as he stepped inside the space, my muscles began to relax a little, and Aereus released me.

Adonis shoved his hands in his pockets, completely at ease, as if he'd just happened upon us at a picnic.

His eyes shone with amusement. "Ah. There you are. I thought I felt a current of primitive, mindless rage spilling through the door, and I knew it must be my old friend Aereus."

"He was just showing me his war room," I explained hastily, as if we'd been caught unawares. "It's all completely innocent."

Aereus's entire body had tensed, and he unleashed a wild roar that trembled through my bones. "You broke my door."

Adonis blinked. "That? It didn't seem to have a doorknob, so I found my own way in. I suppose it's not there to guard against other angels."

I'd mentally telegraphed the spell to Adonis, and I was sure he could have used it. But that would have given away our mental link.

"Now I'd like my succubus back." This time, Adonis injected venom into his voice.

I needed to satisfy Aereus's primitive ego to smooth things over.

"Did you know that Aereus has caused thousands of wars?" I cooed.

Adonis's eyes shone with icy rage, and shadows thickened around him. "Get back to our room, Ruby."

I smoothed out my dress, crossing over the floor as if I'd been chastened.

The moment I stepped into the hallway, the roars of wrathful angels rumbled over the hallway, and the walls shook with the sounds of divine bodies slamming against marble.

CHAPTER 27

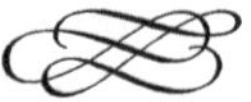

I stood in Tanit's room, waiting for Adonis and his demon friends to arrive. The eerie cherubs had guided me here—just as Adonis had suggested—but I'd found it empty. I could only hope Aereus hadn't broken Adonis on one of his iron-spiked garden features.

From the expansive bedroom, I stared out over the Jardin des Tuileries, at the charred stumps of trees and the frozen earth. Aereus had put all his efforts into his death garden, completely neglecting the world outside the Louvre.

Outside, a group of cherubs drifted past the window, heads cocked. As I'd moved around the castle, I'd tried to study the cherubs' movements. Sometimes, they glided together in groups, speaking in unison. It was as if they shared some kind of mental connection. If I had to glamour myself as a cherub, I'd never be able to work as a synchronized drone among their numbers. They seemed to patrol the same paths within the Louvre, their movements predictable and unified, the product of a shared mind.

But occasionally, a taller cherub with silver-streaked hair would float by on her own. The taller ones seemed to move about more freely, taking on some sort of supervisory roles. I never heard them speak, but their pale eyes held a keen intelligence I didn't see in the smaller cherubs.

Behind me, the door creaked, and Adonis crossed into the room. Tanit and Kur followed close behind him.

At the sight of Adonis unharmed, my chest unclenched a little. "How exactly did that situation resolve?" I asked. "It sounded like you were both breaking the walls with each other's bodies. I'm surprised your wings are intact."

Adonis rubbed his chin, narrowing his eyes at me. "Of course my wings are intact. I can hold my own in a fight. One scuffle with Johnny and everyone's acting like I'm broken. I'm an immortal who's lived for—"

"For four thousand years, since the Amorite conquest of Ur," Tanit chimed in. "We know."

A few bruises marred Adonis's skin, but he seemed to be healing quickly. "As to how I resolved things with Aereus, after we battered each other senseless for a while, I simply told him that we needed his help to keep Kratos in check." Adonis leaned against the wall, folding his arms. "He seemed to like the idea of being needed. Pathetic, really."

His pale eyes stood out sharply in the room's dim light.

Tanit and Kur dropped into large armchairs on the other side of the room, their bodies illuminated with the twinkling light of a chandelier. Tanit had definitely landed herself a better room than ours.

"It's a good thing we're not being kicked out," Tanit said, eyeing me sharply. "So far, you've only found a bookshelf. Is that right?"

"An important bookshelf," I corrected. "Why keep a bookshelf in a war room? Aereus is obviously not a reader. He's more of a 'sticking sharp things in people' type than an intellectual."

Kur leaned back in his chair. "I see it didn't take you long to work out that Aereus is an idiot."

"I need to get back into the war room," I said. "When I asked if anything could stop him, his eyes definitely went to the bookshelf. He was thinking about it, and it made him nervous. Maybe there's something hidden within the books."

"Maybe," said Kur without much conviction.

"You're not going back in." Adonis's inky magic tinged the air around him. "I already regret leaving you alone with Aereus in that room. He's worse than Kratos. This time, I'll go on my own."

I crossed my arms. "And how will you get in there discreetly? You can't even glamour yourself."

Adonis tilted back his head. "I have other skills. Aereus has invited us to dinner tonight to discuss the fallen angel problem. I just need you all to keep him distracted, while I use shadows to cloak myself. As long as he's with you, I know that he won't be surprising me in his war room."

Kur threaded his fingers behind his head. "I could challenge him to a wrestling match. I've noticed he likes throwing men around."

"A wrestling match," I repeated. "At this dinner party."

Kur sneered. "Nothing can keep him occupied like a chance to prove his physical prowess."

"That's a start," I said. "And maybe Tanit can flirt with him. I already took one for the team earlier, and I'm not eager to revisit it."

Adonis smirked. "Let him think that you both belong to me, and that he has a glimmer of a chance of stealing you from me."

Tanit hissed, her eyes flashing with blue light. "I belong to no one."

"We all know that," Adonis soothed. "But you can play the part. Let Aereus think he's stealing something from me."

I paced the room, the cogs turning in my mind. "If we both moon over him and ask him about all his glorious war stories, we'll have his attention completely rapt." I met Adonis's gaze. "All you have to do is return with the stones, without anyone noticing."

* * *

WE SAT at a long banquet table laden with food, my stomach already full of shortcrust pie and fruit. Torches lined the stone walls, and below them, a row of human guards stood pressed against the walls, their faces gaunt and scared.

I cast a nervous glance at the ceiling.

You know how sometimes people use the "sword of Damocles" as a metaphor, a threat of an impending demise hanging right over your head?

Tonight, we had literal swords hanging over heads as we ate. On the high ceiling above us hung an assortment of weapons—battle-axes, broadswords, maces—all of them dangling from iron chains that I could only hope had been forged with care.

The dinner hadn't begun until ten p.m., which had given me plenty of time to search the entire palace from top to bottom, glamoured as a cherub. I'd found no stones, no references to stones—just a crapload of violent art festooning the walls. The hours glamoured as a cherub had cost me—sapping my energy with magical effort. Now, fatigue burned through my body.

So I sat at dinner, with my most charming smile on my face, trying to block out our utter failure so far.

A human female, her neck ringed with an iron collar, refilled my glass of wine.

Tanit sat on the other side of Adonis, candlelight gleaming in her dark eyes. "So glad Adonis took me with him on this trip." Her tone-less inflection suggested otherwise. "You know, being the lover of the angel of death doesn't always come with many travel opportunities."

Aereus's lip curled as he gripped his copper chalice. His hand clenched, bending the metal in his fist. "Two lovers? You have two?"

Adonis flashed a satisfied smile. "Why not? Might as well enjoy myself until my seal is broken."

Okay. We didn't want to go too far down this path or we'd end up with shattered walls, broken angel bodies, and no allies.

I took a final bite of my pie. "I'm just so glad you're agreeing to help us. If the other horsemen come for us, I'm not sure what we would do. But with you two working together, you can simply unite against them, imprison them until they come to their senses."

Aereus leaned back in his chair, surveying us. "Then you should stay here. Sadeckrav Castle has superior magical fortifications to your humble pile of rocks, Adonis. We'll figure out a way to capture them, to weaken them with..." His gaze darted around the room, uneasy. He didn't want anyone to know about Devil's Bane. "We'll weaken them, until the mortification of their bodies reminds them of their mission here on earth."

"Good," said Adonis. "All your iron toys will come in handy."

Aereus smiled. "Yes. We will make them submit. No one must rebel against the mission of the horsemen. You and I both know that. The heavenly horde rule as archangels in the heavens, while we may rule as archangels on the earth."

Adonis lifted his glass. "As it was meant to be."

Tanit leaned in to Adonis, then stroked her hand up his thigh. "You two are both so *strong.*"

I narrowed my eyes. She didn't need to go *quite* that far with her hands to prove that she was his lover—Aereus had already bought that story.

Not that I cared.

I glanced at Kur, giving him a quick nod. Time to get this show on the road, so Adonis could make his discreet exit.

CHAPTER 28

*K*ur spread out his arms, flexing his muscles within his leather clothing. "I've heard you're known for your wrestling ability, Aereus... Is it true?"

Adonis lifted his wineglass, staring at the wine as he sloshed it in the chalice. "You know, I do think Aereus may have spread those rumors himself."

Gods below. He just couldn't help himself, could he?

Aereus gripped the edge of the table, face reddening. "Just as you spread the rumors about your legendary seduction abilities?"

The easy smile never left Adonis's features. "Is that what you tell yourself?"

Aereus's snarl told me he didn't believe his own claims. His anger curled off him, rippling over my skin. Unconsciously, I'd started gripping my knife, ready to plunge it into something. No one else seemed quite as affected by Aereus's magic as I was. But then again, none of them were feral.

The horseman of war's face had become dead serious, flecks of red burning in his eyes.

Kur cleared his throat. "Wrestling. How about it?"

Aereus turned to him. "No one has ever beaten me in a wrestling match."

Kur cracked his knuckles. "Really? *No* one?"

"No one." Aereus's tone brooked no argument. "Do you doubt me?"

Kur leaned back in his chair. "It's just that I've never lost a wrestling match, either. And I've wrestled some of the high lords of the shadow kingdom."

Aereus's lip curled in a snarl. "But you've never wrestled the horseman of war, have you." His chair scraped across the floor as he rose, and he marched into the center of the hall. "It's not often that I have a formidable challenger, though a shadow demon could never win against an angel such as myself. These two shadow demonesses have probably never witnessed prowess such as mine. We'll wrestle now. Let's find out how long you can last."

Kur rose from his chair. "Do you think now is the best time for this?"

"Right now." Aereus held out his arms to either side. "Servants!" he barked.

Instantly, two male servants hurried over to him, pulling off his brocade coat. The swiftness with which they executed this maneuver suggested that this was something Aereus did often.

Kur strode into the center of the floor and held out his own arms. Another set of servants pulled his coat from him. Then, the angel and the demon pulled off their shirts, tossing them on the ground.

Kur's body rippled with muscles, lines of green scales glinting in the torchlight. Still, Aereus had at least a foot on him. The horseman's skin was a deep gold, his muscles thick as oak trunks.

In unison, they paced to opposite ends of the hall, then pivoted to face each other.

Tension sparked in the air as they glared at each other, and Aereus's magic hummed across the room. The hot, arid feel of his magic sparked an ancient wrath that burned within my ribs, stoking embers of rage. I gripped the chair, restraining myself from running into the wrestling match to try my own mettle. They'd crush me—I knew that. But the stupid part of me wanted to fight.

In fact, I was beginning to think that angels' magic gave me a bit of a death wish.

"You know the rules, don't you, Kur?" asked the angel. "When I throw you to the ground, I will be declared the winner."

"Likewise." Kur's grin was cocky. "If I throw you to the ground, I win. I'm ready for it."

In the next moment, they ran for each other, feet pounding over the stone floor. They collapsed into each other with the force of hurricane winds, arms grasping for each other's shoulders.

As they began to grapple with each other, eyes blazing with aggressive intent, violent impulses gripped my body. Aereus's power was overwhelming me. My gaze darted to one of the human servants who stood pressed against the wall. My muscles tensed, thighs clenching, lip curling in a snarl. It would be so easy to break her neck...

Adonis brushed his fingertips over my knee, soothing some of the rage out of my system. I hadn't even noticed as he'd slipped next to me. He really *could* move discreetly within the shadows. In the depths of my mind, his silky presence brushed against my thoughts, and his magic swept over my body like a balm. My muscles began to relax, thighs unclenching.

I nodded at him, letting him know it was okay for him to go now while Aereus was completely distracted.

As I looked at him, he seemed to fade away before my eyes, shadows cloaking him. I felt his presence move from me—disappear, really. Only someone who'd already been paying attention—like me— would notice the departure at all.

Kur slammed Aereus into a wall, and the entire building trembled. The horseman of war roared like an injured beast.

I tightened my fingers on the chair. *Please tell me Kur understands that he has to let the angel win this.*

They threw each other into the walls, cracking stone. Clanking metal filled the air. I glanced at the ceiling, where the weapons jostled violently in their chains, banging together.

I nudged Tanit, then pointed at the ceiling. "I think we need to move."

"Good point." She reacted swiftly, and in the next moment, she'd taken shelter in a doorframe.

In another second, I was by her side, crammed into the arched doorway.

The angel and the demon gripped each other's shoulders, grunting and straining, fingers digging into flesh. Groaning, Kur pulled Aereus's neck down into a headlock, trying to dominate him.

I leaned into Tanit, whispering, "Kur knows he needs to lose, right?"

Tanit cocked her head. "Demons can be irrational when it comes to domination."

"Wonderful," I muttered. Maybe a bit of a reminder was in order.

"Aereus seems to be winning!" I shouted, despite all evidence to the contrary. "How thrilling to see an angel dominate a demon!" I punctuated each word carefully.

The interjection actually seemed to work, because in the next moment, Kur released his grip around the angel's neck. Then, Aereus was able to grip the shadow demon by the shoulders.

With a wild roar, Aereus threw Kur onto the ground. The crack of demon bone against stone echoed through the hall.

Victorious, Aereus lifted his arms above his head, his muscled body glistening with sweat. "Victory is mine once again! The angel of war reigns supreme!"

I suppressed the urge to roll my eyes, instead forcing myself to clap. Honestly. I'd never expected ancient angels to act like such children.

Kur pushed himself off the ground with a groan. As I crossed back to the table, still clapping, Kur shot me a withering look that spoke of his resentment. Even if we'd all agreed to the plan ahead of time, it killed him inside to let Aereus win.

Without uttering a word, Kur collected his shirt and jacket from the human servants, sullenly dressing himself.

Still shirtless, Aereus dropped into his chair, breathing heavily. Sweat slid down his chest.

One of us would need to get up close to him, to block his line of vision. I gave Tanit a nudge.

I was pretty sure her groan was audible only to me as she rose from her chair. "In the shadow kingdom, the high lords never told us about the angels." She sat before him at the edge of the table, her dress riding up. Given what she'd said about underwear earlier, I was pretty sure Aereus's eyes wouldn't be leaving her body anytime soon.

She ran a fingertip over his bare chest. "I never knew you had inspired so many heroes in human history. Genghis Khan, Alexander the Great..."

"You see, my little shadow demonesses? Your males can't compete with me."

"Amazing," said Tanit, a little too deadpan. "Such power. Tell me about the wars you've fought."

Aereus stared up at her, transfixed, and began to launch into the tales of his historic exploits. With every word, a little more of that primal rage began to seethe in my blood. Now that Adonis had left the room, I had no one here to calm me. I gripped my wineglass tightly, taking out my anger on its stem, until a smooth presence kissed my skin once again.

It took me a moment to realize Adonis had already returned, shadows darkening the air around him. My clenched thighs and fingers began to relax once more. I met his gaze, and he shook his head—nearly imperceptibly. But it was enough to tell me that our plan hadn't worked.

My heart sank. Our death warrants may have been signed, and we were no closer to protecting ourselves from the archangel onslaught.

ordlessly, two cherubs led us back to our room, while I restrained myself from asking what, exactly, Adonis had seen in the war room.

At last, when we reached our room, I rushed inside and closed the door hard behind us.

I gripped Adonis's arm. "You gave me a head shake. What did the head shake mean? Please tell me there is a chance the head shake meant 'I found the stones and everything is fine.'"

"Unsurprisingly, the head shake meant 'no.' I did not find the stones. Just a book I already have, and Aereus's relics."

I wasn't letting this go. I'd been *certain* something lay hidden there. "What's in this book?"

His steely eyes betrayed nothing. "It's about the Bringer of Light. When you caught Aereus looking at the bookshelf, it's likely what he was thinking about was this text. But the book doesn't contain any information we don't already have."

I studied his chiseled features, so beautiful I could hardly think clearly around him. "I need specifics. What do we already know, exactly?"

"It's merely a description of the stones' origin."

"Please tell me you took it with you."

"I didn't need to take it. I have my own copy. I bring it with me wherever I go, searching for clues in its text."

I thrust out my hand. "Show me."

A dark power rippled off his body. He wasn't used to being ordered around. "You won't be able to read it, but if you must see it…"

He turned away and lifted up the mattress. He pulled out a thin, dark volume—one with no lettering on the front. "I don't think you'll discover anything I haven't already."

I took it from him and sat on the bed. The spine cracked as I opened it, and I began scanning the yellowed pages. I couldn't read the text, wasn't even entirely sure if it was Greek or Phoenician, but luckily for me, it came with pictures. Images of vines coiled around the edges of the pages, and artists had depicted page after page of flowering plants, each one labeled in that ancient language.

"What does it say?" I asked.

"It gives an account of the Old Gods, of the gifts they provide to combat the angels. The Devil's Bane that grows where archangels walk the earth, the sacred rowan tree that channels the power of the Old Gods. And the Stones of Zohar, mined from gleaming blue gemstones."

I turned another brittle page, uncovering an image of a grotto—one I was sure I'd seen before. A river carved through a rocky landscape, its banks dappled with blood-red anemones. I'd seen it in a dream, I thought, when I'd flown in Adonis's arms.

"This looks familiar."

"Does it?" Surprise tinged his voice.

"I've dreamt it." I studied the gentle curve of the river, the myrrh trees growing by its banks. "And it's not just that I dreamt it. The garden outside your castle is a version of this place. The red flowers, the river carving through the center."

"It's where I was born."

"Afeka. Right. Why is your birthplace in a book about the Stones of Zohar?"

Adonis leaned in to me, pointing to the cave. "Some say this cave is the entrance to the underworld, the realm of the Old Gods. I was born in their presence, surrounded by the stones that could kill me."

"Right…the seeds of destruction thing."

"This cave is where life mingles with death. It's where Aereus found the stones in the first place."

I traced my fingertips over the picture. "I didn't know the Old Gods had anything to do with an underworld."

Adonis's magic caressed my body. "That's the first thing you need to know about gods. All gods rule the realms of the dead. All gods demand sacrifices for their gifts. Even the Old Gods."

Frankly, that didn't sound ideal. I was about to reap a metric ton of power from the Old Gods. "A sacrifice. And what sacrifice will they demand from me for using their stones?"

He considered it, a concerned look in his eyes. "I honestly can't tell you that. I think they'll want you to change, to become something new. That's how the gods of nature work, isn't it? They sacrifice the old to make way for the new. Death gives rise to new life."

Among the plants by the mouth of the cave, the artist had painted a few shimmering blue stones.

I pointed at them. "This must be them. The Stones of Zohar."

"I remember them," he said quietly. "The color of the sky over Afeka."

I breathed in his exotic scent of myrrh. When an angel like him looks at a garden—he sees a place of death. No wonder Aereus's garden had unsettled me so much. From an ancient immortal's perspective, it was already dying.

My gaze trailed over Adonis's breathtaking, masculine features— then lower, over the pendant he wore at his throat. I touched it, gripping it gently between two fingers. He nearly flinched at my touch. Candlelight glinted off the amber.

"What is this?"

For just a moment, a sharp flash of pain lit his gray-blue eyes, then his gaze shuttered. An easy smile replaced the brief look of pain. "Just something I've kept with me a long time."

And there it was again. Adonis keeping secrets from me, even if he could hear some of my own thoughts.

459

CHAPTER 30

Curled up in bed, I'd given in to sleep, to the bone-deep
tiredness that gripped my body. In my dreams, I'd wandered
through the grotto from the pictures in the book, surrounded by the
sound of a rushing river echoing off stone walls.

A hand at my throat woke me, powerful arms pinning me to the
bed—one encircling my neck, the other gripping my wrists.

My eyes snapped open with shock, and I looked up into Adonis's
eyes—not icy blue, but the cold hardness of obsidian. His midnight
wings spread out behind him, ready to fight, and his magic thrummed
over my skin.

For a moment, fear gripped my heart. What the hell was he doing?
Instead of his soothing presence whispering through my mind, I felt
claws of rage, of panic.

"Adonis," I whispered.

His powerful body completely pinned me down, one of his legs
pressed between mine. His hand enclosed my throat—but he wasn't
pressing down. All I knew was that he had complete control here, and
I had no idea what was going on.

I searched his eyes, expecting to find rage. Instead, I found only confusion. He hadn't fully woken yet, and his breath sounded ragged in his throat. He'd been dreaming of something terrible.

Within my mind, I called to him. *Adonis. Now would be a good time to help me.* With my hands pinned, I couldn't gently jostle him to wake him. Instead, I stroked one of my legs up the back of his. Slowly, I felt those claws of rage begin to recede, replaced by a soothing calm.

"Adonis," I whispered again.

He blinked, his muscles relaxing, and his eyes began to focus, returning to pale gray-blue. He pulled his hand from my throat, searching my neck. Gently his fingertips brushed over my skin. "Ruby?" he rasped. "Did I hurt you?"

"I'm fine," I said. "You were having a nightmare. I think."

Frowning, he glanced at my wrists before pulling his hand away from them. He rolled onto his side, propping up his head to peer down at me. "I was dreaming of the fae."

I swallowed hard. That made sense. He was in bed with a fae. "Not a good dream, I take it."

He shifted, sitting up in bed, his wings disappearing from view. Dim torchlight danced over the savage scars on his chest. He stared at the bed, looking lost in his thoughts. "More of a memory."

He'd shifted his body away from me, and the loss of the heat from his skin made me want to press up against him again. "Of what?"

His magic sliced the air around us in vicious swirls. "About when the fae king imprisoned me when I was young."

My throat tightened. "What happened?"

A deep, searing pain flashed in his eyes for a moment, before he masked it again. "After my parents died, the fae captured me. The king gave me as a gift to his consort. She used to say she wanted to surround herself with beautiful things." His voice had a sharp edge to it. "Most of the time, King Oberon kept me imprisoned within an oak grove. He used a certain magical enchantment to trap me there, and Devil's Bane to weaken me."

I tightened my hand on his, just a little. "Fae magic. Devil's Bane. Was that really enough to trap someone like you there? You're a god of death."

He searched my face, as if he might find the answer there. Then, his familiar charming smile curled his lips. "Maybe I wasn't always the powerful being you see before you today."

"What happened to you there?"

"At night, I slept outside on a bed of moss. When King Oberon brought humans to his realm, he'd command me to enchant the air, so the women were out of control with lust. They used me as an agent in their lurid rituals. They worship euphoria, ecstatic states. It doesn't sound so terrible, does it?"

Silver flecks, like starlight, shone in his gray-blue eyes. I almost thought I could get lost in those arctic depths. "Except there's a dark side to that ecstasy." His fingers flexed on the bedsheets. "The violent, primal side of ecstatic states. The fae euphoria."

Seemingly lost in his thoughts, he reached for me, brushing his fingertips over my hips, stroking up and down. "Sometimes, the fae turned on each other in their frenzy. But they mostly went after human females. They dragged women into their forested palace, seduced them in their frenzied states. Fae males like to dominate women."

"Yep. And that would be why my parents left the realm."

"Some fae feed from humans, just like vampires. Except instead of blood, they draw power from heightened human emotions. Ecstatic or devastated states. The humans' frenzy fed King Oberon's magical ability. The hunt filled him with power."

A cold shudder danced up my neck. "What do you mean 'the hunt'?"

He idly traced over my hip, lost in his own memories. "Another form of fae entertainment. They'd let human females loose in the forests, pretending to free them. The women would run, naked, thinking they'd been given a chance at freedom, thinking they could get home again. King Oberon drank in their terror. His body glowed with power. The fae males would work themselves up into an ecstatic, feral frenzy. Their eyes would gleam with silver, their canines would lengthen. Claws and horns would sprout from their bodies."

Shadows darkened his eyes, and his voice had taken on a haunted tone.

I swallowed hard. "And the women were the prey."

"Exactly. Their deaths were brutal, savage. The fae would tear them limb from limb. They'd feast on the women like beasts."

My stomach turned. "You obviously don't approve of the fae. You have your own moral code—punish the wicked and all that. So why stay with them? Why take part? You're a death god. You could have survived the Devil's Bane."

He didn't answer.

Compelled by a sharp need to touch him, I ran my fingers over the savage scars on his chest.

Ice glinted in his eyes. "I am the single most lethal creature to have ever walked the earth. I was never meant to be here. I can kill just by thinking, just by feeling. It's in my nature. It's what I am. When given the chance to slaughter the unworthy, I enjoy it. My captivity kept me from killing in greater numbers."

My fingers froze. "Do you actually kill people just for fun?"

"Not anymore. That was a long time ago." His features softened as he looked at me. "I was like you, once. In love with beauty. Every now and then I remember that feeling. I get glimmers of it, and it makes me feel alive again."

"When?"

"When I look at the color of your skin, the flush on your cheeks, the heat in your eyes after I kissed you. The perfect, tempting shape of your body when you dropped your blanket in my room. The dirt smudged on your skin when you were a feral fae, caught up in passion."

At his words, my blood heated, and I pressed in closer to him, until my skin skimmed against his. Finally, I was getting some of the real Adonis, the truth behind his facade. I reached for his face, stroking it.

"Show me you—without the glamour," he rasped. "Show me all of you. When I kissed you on Eimmal...I haven't felt so alive in centuries."

"You hate the fae, but you're drawn to us."

He shook his head slowly. "I'm not drawn to the fae. Just to you."

I sucked in a deep breath, letting the glamour fade completely. My pale hair tumbled over my shoulders, and I took a deep breath, waiting to see his reaction. I felt completely exposed before him.

It was at that point I realized how close our bodies were—my dress riding up under the sheets, my bare thigh brushing against his leg. My pulse raced, heat flaming through my body. Adonis seemed to notice, too, because his breath grew heavier, eyes burning like starlight. He reached for the neckline of my dress, tracing his fingertips under the hem. At his touch, pleasure rippled over my skin.

My mind flashed with an image of Adonis pinning me down again —except this time, in my fevered mind, he was kissing me hard, my legs wrapped around his waist.

"Intense emotions still fascinate me." The unexpected gentleness of his touch made me want to moan. Glacially slow, he began to tug down the neckline of my dress, studying the vivid flush on my chest.

I hooked my leg around his. I wanted to feel his hands gripping me, to feel his mouth pressed hard against mine. Instead, he was teasing me, silver glinting in his eyes.

I threaded my fingers into his dark hair.

With a slow, graceful gesture, he eased down the top of my dress to expose my shoulder, where his mark stood out starkly on my pale skin. He lowered his mouth to the mark, then ran his tongue over it, sparking a wave of wild heat arcing through my blood. Slowly, his mouth moved farther up my neck. Now, his fingers were gripping my hip possessively. Wild, liquid fire surged through my core, and I felt my back arching, my legs falling open.

Moving like honey over ice, he slid the collar of my dress down just a little farther, exposing only the tops of my breasts. My nipples hardened, my breasts swelling and straining against the fabric. I'd told myself I'd never let him seduce me, but right now, I didn't really care. I just wanted him to keep touching me.

His mouth moved lower, heating my skin, his tongue now swirling around my nipple. I wanted his mouth on mine.

"Adonis," I moaned.

He was drawing this out, stirring me to a peak of desire until I forgot how words worked.

Another slow tug at the top of my dress, this time a little more forceful as he kissed me deeply. He pulled down the front of my dress until my breasts slipped out. Adonis let out a low growl, his eyes raking over my body. He was still keeping a leash on himself, still restrained, and the kisses he brushed over my breasts were agonizingly light, even as his hands grew more possessive on my body.

I moaned, rubbing my hips into him. Of course Adonis would turn pleasure into a strange sort of torture, until my mind and body screamed for him.

It was at this point I realized that his wings had appeared again behind him. I ran my fingertips over the feathers at the apex, and his muscles tightened. Now, he pulled down the front of my dress roughly, practically ripping it. A hint of teeth on my breasts, an exquisite torture. Another growl from deep within his throat.

I whispered his name.

He reached my mouth, pressing his lips against mine in a searing kiss. I moaned into his mouth, my tongue brushing his.

"Yes, Ruby?" His voice was a low, deep sigh.

I tried to find the words to tell him what I wanted, about the desperate ache that had spread through my body.

He reached down, his fingertips circling around to my inner thigh. As he traced upward, raw desire throbbed in my core. I stroked his wings again, and his body tensed against me, fingers gripping my thigh more possessively before releasing it again.

I couldn't take the teasing anymore—I wanted him to move faster. I pulled off my dress entirely, and the cool castle air kissed my skin. I wanted him to look at me—all of me—and I let my knee fall open in an invitation. For a moment, he leaned back, staring at me, torchlight dancing over the powerful planes of his torso. His potent magic licked at my body, caressing parts of me that burned to be touched.

Just as I was sure he was about to unleash the restraints he'd been keeping on himself, a sharp, piercing cry ripped through the air in the distance.

A reptilian cry.

The warlike scream of a full-sized dragon.

And all the heat warming my body chilled to ice.

CHAPTER 31

Within moments, alarms were sounding within the Louvre, and I had my dress back on. The voices of the cherubs penetrated the door, chanting in unison about a dragon.

Of all the things we'd anticipated—archangels from the Heavenly Host, the descent of the other horsemen—I hadn't expected dragons to attack.

Adonis was out of the bed in a flash, already pulling on his clothes. "I need to find out what's happening."

"I'm coming with you." My heart was still pounding hard now, but for a different reason.

Gods below. Talk about a bad moment to interrupt.

I grabbed my boots from the floor.

Maybe the interruption was for the best, anyway. Adonis wouldn't be on earth for much longer. What was the point in falling into his seductive trap now, when he had to go? I zipped up my boots, trying to think clearly. Adonis and I agreed firmly on one point—angels didn't belong here. Nothing could happen between us.

Adonis pulled open the door, his sword slung around his back, and I hurried after him. Cherubs bustled through the hallway, and among their eerie whispers, I heard a few words repeated: *Dragon... Jardin des Tuileries... Succubus.*

I swallowed hard. Dragon. Succubus. *Hazel?*

Adonis strode quickly through the hall, and I hurried to keep up. When we reached the entrance, Aereus was standing in the center of an atrium, his wings and body glowing with golden light. Like Adonis, he'd dressed for battle.

"Any idea what's going on?" I asked.

Aereus's eyes burned with gold and red fire as he spoke to me. "Any idea why your sister has come to join us?

* * *

When the large, oak doors groaned open, I was greeted by a sight I didn't think I'd ever forget—my younger sister, mounted on a golden-scaled dragon whose wings shimmered in the silver light of the moon.

Hazel gripped the dragon's neck, her dark hair tumbling over her shoulders. A flush brightened her cheeks, and her eyes sparkled.

I stared at the dragon, my mind swarming with unwelcome memories. A dragon—clamping Marcus in its jaws, its teeth piercing his flesh, ripping him to shreds. Blood streamed over the pavement... My chest clenched, until I took a slow, steady breath.

Hazel flicked her hair over her shoulder. "Adonis. Ruby. I hope you don't mind the interruption."

Aereus stepped forward, his body towering over me. "No one told me you were coming."

Emitting a deep rumble, the golden dragon lowered his head, and Hazel slid off.

My heart thudded hard. Please tell me she had some kind of plan here, that she hadn't just shown up on a dragon for the hell of it.

As soon as she slipped off the dragon's neck, the beast began to shift, with a snapping of bones and sinews that pierced the night air, until a man stood before us, his large body covered in gold armor. I shuddered, still repulsed by dragon shifters.

"Hazel," said Adonis. "You've come as a messenger, haven't you? To give us news about Johnny and Kratos."

Hazel crossed to us, her gaze on Aereus, features totally placid. "Exactly. I remained in Hotemet Castle, and Adonis told me I was supposed to let him know if Johnny or Kratos seemed as if they were going to fall." The night air whipped at her dark hair. "They've started to change, I think."

"Change *how?*" Aereus demanded.

She blinked at him, her features serene, and I knew she was about to enchant him. "They look different, like when you're staring at the water's warm surface on a hot summer day, and the lake looks black as iron, and the steam wafts off it, and you think you can see your past in it, you think you can see your mom's face, right? And you remember how sometimes she made you so mad but you couldn't do anything about it, and the steam curls around you. All those times you wanted things but you couldn't have them. And that's how you know the angels are going to fall, that their heavy, leaden wings are pulling them to the earth. That's why you need me here, Aereus. To fix things."

Aereus stared at her, his fiery eyes glazed over. "I see. Yes..." He blinked. "I can see why you'd think they were falling. I'm glad you've come to warn us."

She looked back at the starry sky. "You might want to set up some of your creepy cherubs to watch the clouds in case they show up anytime soon."

Aereus nodded dumbly.

Apparently, this little teenage fae was capable of manipulating one of the most lethal creatures to ever walk the earth's surface, and it didn't even seem to take much effort on her part.

"It flickers in and out," she added with a slight shrug. "Sometimes they get control of themselves. I just thought you should know."

Aereus beckoned her closer to him. "Another succubus. No wonder Kratos has been unable to control himself."

Mentally, a war raged in my mind. *She's sixteen, you creep. Back the fuck off.* But we were supposed to be ancient.

Adonis shot me a pointed look—no doubt he could feel my roiling anger. "Thank you for letting us know, Hazel. Now, you must be tired after your journey. You can sleep in our room."

Aereus's lip curled. "Oh, that's how it is, is it? One succubus isn't enough for you?"

Adonis's icy gaze slid to the horseman of war, but he said nothing.

Gross. Still, I could see why Adonis had made the suggestion. Hazel had obviously come here for a reason, and we needed to know what it was. We needed to speak with her alone. Now.

Aereus glared at Adonis, his magic tingeing the air around him with gold. "Sleep for a few hours. But in the morning, we must make a move against the other horsemen. We'll drag their imperiled souls here and pierce their bodies until they see the truth again. Until they once more understand that we must give up the temptations of the flesh in order to rule as gods on earth."

Adonis's eyes sparked with a cold light, shadows shifting and darkening around him. "Horsemen were born to make sacrifices." A hint of regret suffused his words, and I knew that he believed it, even if the rest of this was a sham.

Aereus's lip curled. "Kratos will feel his sacrifices in his flesh."

I swallowed hard, thinking of Kratos. Our ruse would never get that far, so I shouldn't be worrying about it. But the idea of this maniacal horseman of war torturing Kratos with his iron instruments made me feel sick.

Adonis nodded. "In the morning, then," he said quietly. He strode back into the palace, his night-dark magic trailing behind him. He moved swiftly, with the gait of a soldier, his footfalls clacking over the floor.

On the walk back to our room, the cherubs eyed Hazel, whispering among themselves. I bit down hard on the impulse to turn to Hazel, to demand to know what the hell was going on right now. At last, we reached our door, and I shoved it open.

Hazel plopped herself down on the bed, surveying the rumpled sheets. "You both sleep in this? Cozy."

I opened my mouth and closed it again. "Hazel. What are you

doing here? You just… You summoned a dragon?"

She flicked her hair behind her shoulders. "Uthyr? I was one of his favorites. Like I said. I charmed them." She lifted the pendant from her neck—a dragon's tooth. "Remember? Uthyr gave me this to summon him if I ever really needed him."

Adonis leaned against a wall, his arms folded. "What's been happening at Hotemet Castle?"

Hazel sucked in a deep breath, and my stomach clenched. She hadn't come with good news.

"Johnny has slowly recovered his memories," she said. "He knows Ruby tried to kill him. He knows that she's not really a succubus, which means he knows I'm not really a succubus. Hence, I had to get the fuck out of there. What else? Oh yeah. He's on his way here to kill you."

My jaw dropped. "And what about Kratos?"

She screwed her mouth to one side, eyes narrowing as she thought about it for a moment. "I'm not entirely sure what his plan is, but he was angry enough to go on a bit of a rampage. He started breaking things and lighting things on fire. I befuddled them just long enough so that I could get out of there, but it wasn't a *great* situation, per se."

Shimmering, midnight magic burst from Adonis's body, and his wings emerged behind him, spreading out. "Did they follow you, Hazel?"

She shook her head. "I don't think so. If they'd been anywhere nearby, Uthyr would have smelled them."

Adonis snatched his sword, Ninkasi, from beside the bed.

"What are you doing?" I asked.

The air around us hummed with his magic, making my pulse race. "I'm going to search for them, and I'll stop them if they're on their way. I need to find out if they're coming for you. While I'm gone, find Tanit and Kur. Tell them what's going on. Tell them I'll be back as soon as I know anything."

I didn't want him to leave, for some reason, but I just said, "Come back to us soon."

He was out the door without another word.

CHAPTER 32

When he left, Hazel dropped down on our bed, exhausted.

I started to pace the stone floor. "Did you hear anything about their plans?"

She shook her head. "Something about archangels. Heavenly something."

A chill rippled through my blood. "The Heavenly Host?"

She pointed at me. "That's it. Johnny wanted to speak to them. To tell them Adonis was rebelling."

Even if that injured angel hadn't made it back to the Heavenly Host, Johnny could drag them here at any moment to destroy me.

I clenched my fists. "Did Kratos try to stop him?"

"Why do you think Kratos would want to stop Johnny? I think they're on the same side."

My chest tightened. "I don't know. He's a psychopath, yes. He left me stranded there after dragons ripped Marcus to shreds." The memory pierced my chest. "But then he did a kind thing for us. He brought you back to me."

She scrunched up her features. "Huh? Kratos?"

"Yes, Kratos. I told him I was looking for my sister, and he sent out a search party for a succubus in the dragon lairs. He didn't stop until he found you."

Her brow furrowed. "No, that's not what happened. First of all, do you know how much effort it takes an archangel like them to find anyone they want?"

I crossed my arms, wearing the floor thin with my pacing. "Not really, no."

"It took Adonis a few hours to find me. He's the one who turned up in the dragon's lair. When he did, he sent word to Hotemet Castle to say I was coming. Apparently Kratos took credit for it."

Surprise knocked the wind out of me. "Adonis reunited us?" I shook my head. "He never told me. Kratos didn't specifically tell me that he'd found you, but he certainly implied it."

"Oh. I thought you knew."

When I cast my mind back to Hotemet Castle, I remembered telling Adonis about Hazel, that I wanted her back. Adonis had said Kratos would never find her for me—that he'd want to keep me dependent on him. The next morning, my sister had been found. And it had been Adonis's doing.

For most of the time I'd known him, I'd been positive Adonis only ever acted for self-interested reasons. He'd done nothing to convince me otherwise, never mentioned that he'd been the one to find Hazel. Clearly, I wasn't the only one playing a part, pretending to be someone I wasn't.

My heart thudded hard, and I tried to focus on the problem at hand. Now, we had two potential problems headed our way: two horsemen, and the Heavenly Host. Still no gleaming blue gemstones.

I crossed to the bed and slid my hand under my pillow, snatching my knife and the holster. I slipped the sheathed knife into my boot. "Okay. First things first. I need to find Tanit and Kur and tell them what's going on."

"And what is going on? What's our plan? Run? Hide?"

I swallowed hard. "I don't know. Maybe I can speak to Aereus again. Find out what he knows."

"We have a dragon. I can take you anywhere you want. We could leave now, let the archangels sort all this out between them, and we charm whoever wins."

I scowled at her. "I'm not leaving without Adonis. And anyway. It's like you said. An archangel can find us if they want to."

* * *

WITH MY ARMS FOLDED, I continued my pacing in Tanit's room while the two demons stared at me.

Tanit's dark hair snaked around her head. "So the Heavenly Host know that you're the Bringer of Light, but they don't necessarily know that Adonis is working with you. He could be oblivious, for all they know."

"I think so."

Tanit cocked her head at Kur. "We could simply hand the fae over, if we must. We could say that we found her out, and Adonis had no idea, and the archangels can do with her what they like."

I paused, glaring at her. "I'm right here, you know. I can hear you."

She looked between Kur and me, reading our expressions. "What? I'm not saying it's a good idea. I'm just saying it's an option. We should consider all options. That's what brainstorming is, right?"

Kur shot her a sharp look. "Let's not sacrifice the little fae just yet. I have a feeling Adonis may not be thrilled about that particular option."

I bit my lip, desperation building in my system. "I'm going to talk to Aereus again. I'm going to see if I can get him to drop any kind of information about the stones, whatever it takes." A quiet panic had begun to race through my veins. I'd torture the bastard on his own instruments if I had to. "At least give me a few more hours before you throw me to the wolves."

"Be careful!" Kur called out as I yanked open the door.

I walked through the stone halls, closing my eyes and trying to tune in to the Old Gods around me. As a Bringer of Light, would I be able to sense the stones? I ran my fingertips over the stone walls, inhaling deeply. A faint smell of roses tinged the air, the bloom of Devil's Bane... Was that them?

I followed the lure of roses until the smell of roasting meat began to overpower me, and a primal violence churned in my gut. That meant only one thing. Aereus.

When I opened my eyes again, I found him towering over me, his eyes blazing with flames. His fire-tipped wings spread out behind him.

"Ruby," he growled. "A little black crow just delivered the most interesting message to me." He grabbed me by the ribs, lifting me from the ground, and his fingers tightened over my bones. "He tells me you're the Bringer of Light. Tell me. Does Adonis know?"

Sweet earthly gods, Hazel needed to get out of here. Fast.

Hot rage—Aereus's magic—sparked through my nerves. I wanted his revolting hands off of me. For just a moment, I envisioned my thumbs plunging into his eye sockets, blinding him.

"No. Adonis doesn't know," I managed to say evenly.

With a roar, he yanked me from the wall, then threw me through an open doorway. I landed hard on the stone floor, and pain shot through my bones.

From my prone position on the floor, I flicked my tongue over my lengthening canines, blood roaring in my ears. I couldn't let my feral instincts take over completely or I'd never find out what I needed to know.

The sound of a slamming door echoed off the walls.

Aereus stood above me, staring down, and his immense body blazed with fiery light. "No one will hear you scream in here. Your friends won't be able to find you."

It was just as Adonis had said. Aereus liked to isolate his victims.

I began pushing myself up on my elbows. We were in a stark room —one with stone walls and iron chains and brackets inset into the walls. Sharp, iron instruments lay in the corner on the floor, tipped with old blood. Fear pounded into me like a fist when I looked behind me—a wooden table stood in the center of the room. Torture tools jutted from its surface, and crimson stained the wood.

My heart slammed against my ribs. If any one of those iron instruments pierced my flesh, there'd be no way out of here. The iron would work its way into my blood like a poison.

Before I could reach for the knife in my boot, Aereus lifted me by the neck. He slammed me into the wall, holding me aloft so my legs kicked futilely at him.

"I knew there was something inside you," he said. "A woman at war with herself. A woman fighting not to remember the truth, what she really is."

He closed his eyes, a deep growl rumbling from his throat.

Pain shot through my neck, and my lungs burned. Violent impulses gripped my mind, and in its dark recesses, blood ran down a pale arm, pooling on the pavement.

I kicked him hard in the crotch, but it didn't seem to faze him. My throat, my lungs were on fire.

I closed my eyes, screaming through the mental link to Adonis. *Adonis. Now. I need you here now.* How far was he? Could he get here before Aereus tore me to pieces?

Aereus pulled down the shoulder of my dress, exposing Adonis's mark. He snarled hungrily at the sight of exposed flesh, pressing his enormous body into me. "So Adonis protects you, does he? Does he know what you really are? Does he know what you could do, my little poison flower? You could destroy us all."

Aereus pulled me away from the wall for just a moment before slamming the back of my head into the stone. Pain splintered my skull, and the urge to go feral nearly overpowered me.

One of Aereus's meaty hands was on my waist, moving up toward my breasts, and I choked down bile.

"Why isn't he coming for you now?" he hissed. "Adonis. Why isn't he here, when I'm taking what's his? He should be pulling me off of you."

He squeezed one of my breasts. Fury exploded in my mind. I kicked at Aereus, my glamour fading fast. He was choking me again, squeezing the life out of me. Mentally, I screamed for Adonis.

Aereus's fingers dug into my flesh, his eyes darkening. "If Adonis isn't coming for you now, then it means he's nowhere near us, is he? And you're at war with yourself still." Aereus pressed in closer, his magic overwhelming me. "A woman who thinks she enjoys pleasure, but she denies herself what she truly wants. A woman who won't let herself give in, won't let herself remember all the things she's done."

Adonis's image ignited in my mind, the memory of his fingers on my skin. Would my last thoughts be of the angel of death?

CHAPTER 33

osing air. Can't breathe.

"What scares you the most, Bringer of Light, is that something terrible will happen to your sister. That you'll be all alone in the world, trapped at the edge of the dark, dark void. And there, you have to face the real monster, don't you? There, you'd have to face yourself."

I kicked him hard in the groin again, and he dropped me for a moment.

I sucked in a sharp, rough breath. "Don't you dare touch my sister."

A powerful backhanded smack cracked my skull, and I fell to the floor, my head throbbing.

"I'll tell you what's going to happen, Ruby." His voice was low, controlled. He pressed his boot into my neck, cutting off my air again. At least my hands were free now.

I reached for my boot, inching my leg up, closer to my hand. Aereus wasn't paying attention to my hands, focused instead on my reddening face.

"I'm going to kill you in the most painful way possible," he growled. "I'm going to delight in the sound of your screams as I break you on my iron wheel. I will revel in the beauty of your blood feeding my roses. Before you die, I want you to know that when I kill Hazel, I'll take even longer to rip her body apart."

Teeth in flesh, breaking bones. I'm not Ruby anymore. I'm your worst nightmare. I ripped the knife from my boot, then drew it across the back of his ankle. Just enough—just enough to weaken him, not enough to knock him out.

His eyes widened at the feel of Devil's Bane entering his blood. Then, he stumbled away from me, eyes bulging. Frantic, I gasped for air, my breath ragged in my throat from my position on the floor.

"Poison!" he roared. His boot slammed into my ribs, and I felt the crack of bone.

Maybe I hadn't given him quite enough poison. Slowly, I pushed myself up onto my elbows again, gripping the knife. Aereus stumbled toward me, stepping on my wrist.

I screamed with pain, dropping the knife. I rolled away from him, agony splintering my ribs where he'd kicked me.

Get up, Ruby. I forced myself to my knees, then rose, my eyes locked on the horseman of war.

He'd snatched an iron tool off the table—a sharp, claw-like thing. I couldn't let it anywhere near me. He looked a little unsteady on his feet, but he wasn't going down yet.

"You're not going to touch my sister," I hissed as a volcanic fury erupted in my mind.

Kill. Rip out his throat. Bathe in his blood.

My canines pricked at my tongue, and I darted across the room for my knife. Without realizing what I was doing, I found myself lifting the blade to my lips. I licked Aereus's blood off the knife. Devil's Bane didn't hurt the fae.

Ambrosia, rich and sweet as honey. I wanted more.

My gut tightened. *Stay in control. Get from him the information that you need.*

My prey staggered back, the iron tool gripped in his hands as the poison slowly took effect.

"I will make you submit." He lunged for me, and I sidestepped.

A vicious smile curled my lips as I started to feel in control. I lunged for him, fast as the wind through the trees, and nicked his skin again, then leapt away from him.

He grunted, fear glinting in his eyes, and he clutched his arm where I'd cut him. "How did you learn about Devil's Bane?" A thin line of spit trickled from his mouth, and he dropped the iron tool.

Earthy fog began to cloud my mind, and I tried to think clearly. I needed something from this beast… I needed…

Roaring, he flicked his wrist. A wave of hot, arid magic slammed me into the wall.

The blow sent a shock of adrenaline snapping through my nerve endings, and a bubble of clarity illuminated my mind for a moment. I threw my knife, and it landed in his shoulder. He howled.

This horseman could withstand a lot more Devil's Bane than the skinny one. I rushed for him, snatching my knife from his shoulder again.

Think, Ruby. Don't let the beast take over completely.

I scrambled to remember how words worked. "Tell me," I rasped. Something other than blood that I needed from him. "Tell me."

He staggered back, his features slackened. "Of course someone who looks like you would conceal a festering monster inside. The seeds of destruction grow in the gardens of paradise, do they not?"

"Garden!" I shouted, though I wasn't sure why. The rational part of my mind was fighting for control. I bit down hard on the powerful urge to hurl my knife into his heart and just end it all.

He kept stumbling away—running from me, and my hunter's instincts were kicking in. *Kill the prey.*

I prowled after him, my sights locked on his slumping shoulders, his weakening body.

My prey grabbed another tool from the table—a sharp iron knife. The fucker wasn't giving up easily.

Mustering all the restraint I could, I grabbed a blade from the table, wincing at the feel of iron burning my skin.

"Garden." The word tumbled out of my mouth again. With lethal precision, I hurled the iron spike at my prey. It pierced his wrist, and he dropped his weapon.

I slammed my boot into his chest—hard—and he grunted. He'd tried to break me, hadn't he?

Fury erupted in my blood, and I kicked him harder this time—right in the ribs. He flew into the wall—not far from the chains.

Rip him to pieces. Drink his blood.

In the next second, I had my knife pressed against his throat. My lips curled back from my teeth. I needed to use words, couldn't remember them. I snarled.

"Knife," I managed to grunt. "Poison. More."

Good. Threat conveyed.

That damned peaty haze clouded my mind, the scent of dirt and moss. What was it I needed here? What did I need except this creature's blood and pain, and the glorious fresh meat filling my mouth, and the feel of fingers clawing into the dirt? What did I need apart from the beautiful, dark-winged man with the pale eyes?

Yes…him… I needed him to tear my clothes off and run his tongue over my body, needed him to grab me hard by the hips and fill me... Needed my fingers in the dirt, hands and knees on the ground before him.

I clenched my jaw tight. I couldn't think straight through the haze in my mind.

My prey rallied, punching me hard in the cheek, and I groaned, nearly dropping my knife.

A wild snarl tore from my throat. I gripped my knife tighter, swinging wildly to nick him again. I pierced his skin through his clothes, right below his elbow. He bellowed like an injured animal. And with that, my knife was at his throat once more, pressing harder this time.

Capture your prey. Then toy with it.

Without entirely realizing what I was doing, I found myself chaining the creature's arms to the walls with one hand. I kept the poisoned blade pressed against his throat, while my other hand snapped the cuffs around him.

He hissed at me, more bestial than angelic. In my feral state, I delighted in the fear in his eyes—this powerful man at my mercy. Fear rippled off him, so intense I could practically smell it. Fear was something even Feral Ruby understood.

No wonder he kept such fierce control over everyone. No wonder he tortured them, kept them terrified. They scared the shit out of him.

He was screaming at me, but I tuned out his cries, stepping back to look at my conquest.

That thing I needed from him… That thing that wasn't blood.

I closed my eyes, trying to clear the haze, but his words were drowning out my own thoughts.

"You don't know where the stones are, Ruby," he roared. "And without them, you can't kill me. I don't know where Adonis is. But I do know who is flying fast for my castle. The Heavenly Host."

I stared at the trickle of blood oozing from the nick in his throat, trying to make meaning out of his words.

"Flying fast," I repeated.

A sharp, panicked laugh escaped his throat. He rasped, the poison seeping deeper into his bloodstream. "You're not really there, are you, Ruby? Does Adonis know he's been fucking an animal?" He sniffed the air. "Can't say I wouldn't mind trying it myself, in your case, though I'd hate myself after."

I clamped my eyes shut, trying to gain control. The pig was right about one thing—I wasn't myself right now. I needed the roaring of my primal side to go quiet.

"Garden," I snarled, still unsure why I was saying the word. There was something I wanted to get at—an important idea of some kind.

Another little bubble of clarity began to penetrate the peaty haze in my skull.

I surveyed my victim. Feral Ruby had done well. If I hadn't poisoned the fucker, he'd be able to break right out of those iron chains. But the Devil's Bane had weakened him severely, and he was barely hanging on.

What had he said? I couldn't kill him without the stones.

Right. The stones. If the gods-damned Heavenly Host were actually on their way right now, I needed to find out where the stones were, and I needed to make the blue shield. Just like I'd seen in the pictures.

I stepped back from Aereus, marching over to the iron tools on the torture table. They would hiss and sting when I picked them up, but they wouldn't poison me unless I nicked my own skin. I walked down the line of torture instruments. Slowly, the power of speech began returning to my mind.

I stared at a two-pronged iron instrument. "Sharp," I said.

"What are you planning on doing?" Aereus bellowed. "The Heavenly Host are on their way. If you hurt me, your death will be agonizing. They'll keep you alive for centuries, torturing you until there's nothing left of your mind or soul." He was threatening me, but raw fear tinged his voice, and it warmed my heart.

A little more of the haze dissipated in my mind. "Which sharp thing?" I asked.

"You're not thinking clearly." His desperation reverberated around me.

"I want to hurt you."

"You can't hurt an archangel. It's against the rules of nature. We reign supreme over your kind. We are gods. You're a filthy beast who scrambles and fucks and feeds in the dirt."

I pulled the edge of my sleeve over my hand so I could pick up a three-pronged instrument, like a tiny devil's pitchfork. "This one."

Just enough haze in my mind right now that I could be brutal, but not so much that I'd forget what I was doing.

"What do you want?" he screamed.

I cocked my head. "No one can hear you in here. You told me that. No one will find you."

"Don't hurt me." He sagged in his iron chains. "What do you want from me?"

"Tell me where the stones are."

"You must be out of your fucking mind if you think I would tell you that."

I was looking into his eyes as I thrust the iron into his side, between his ribs. His scream rent the air. "I need to know. Now."

Aereus heaved a sob. "The seeds of destruction grow in the

gardens of paradise. Heavenly Host, please come for me now, your humble servant. I need to rule as a god on earth!"

Garden.

That was why I'd been saying the word over and over. Aereus, as he'd told me, took that aphorism very seriously. And I was his destruction, wasn't I? I'd lay his plans to waste.

He shook his head. "You can't use them. You'll destroy everything. You'll kill—"

I was out the door before he had the chance to finish his sentence.

CHAPTER 34

With the shield of glamour around me—a cherub's form —I prowled through the hall. I ignored the bruised, battered pain that throbbed along my ribs.

I'd disguised myself as one of the taller cherubs—the ones without predictable movements. With any luck, I could go where I wanted without rousing suspicion.

I moved swiftly through the hallway, heading for Aereus's garden. When I caught a glimpse of myself in a statue's armor, I shuddered at the sight of the milky eyes staring out from the face of a haunted child, silver streaks in my hair. The appearance of a gossamer white dress trailed behind me. A cold shiver rippled over my skin.

I moved on, gliding gracefully over the marble floor, past empty alcoves and into an arched hall. I wasn't sure what had once hung on these walls, but now they all featured war gods—Saturn, Mars, some of Zeus hurling lightning bolts from his fist.

My muscles began to ache as I moved, my ribs and neck bruised where Aereus had attacked me. This glamour, so different from my real appearance, drained my energy. My head swam.

When I turned the corner into the next hall, my throat tightened.

A group of cherubs swarmed past a statue of Aereus atop his horse. Would they notice anything strange about me?

I kept my eyes straight ahead, the way I'd seen the taller cherubs behave.

The others passed me without comment.

At last, I found myself in the hall that led to the garden.

The idea of spending any more time in the torture garden filled me with dread, but I pushed through the door anyway. Cold air greeted my skin.

Outside, moonlight washed over the plants, the shards of bone. My footsteps crunched over the mosaic bones beneath my feet.

As I moved deeper into the vegetation, I tried to tune into the feel of the Old Gods. I closed my eyes, envisioning their blinding light—that pure warmth that had filled my body.

I slipped past the iron wheel, where Aereus delighted in torturing his victims.

With my eyes closed, I could feel the plants around me, and my fingertips skimmed over their leaves, thorns, petals, summoning that inner light I'd managed to capture once or twice before...

A dull, warm glow moved up my chest. The power of the Old Gods —still, it wasn't telling me where to find the stones.

A faint movement caught my eye—a bobbing tail—and my gaze flicked to the line of scorpion guards in one corner of the garden.

Bingo. Of course Aereus would guard the stones, and of course they'd be among the thorny, poisonous plants. I already knew he didn't give a flying fuck whether or not his servants poisoned themselves. He'd want to keep people from discovering the gems that could ruin his plans.

I moved closer to the scorpions, trying my best to go unnoticed— just a simple haunted-eyed cherub, out for my nightly patrol.

My gaze landed on the flowering, purple plants behind the guards. Devil's Bane—just as I'd thought.

I took another step closer, trying to peer through the thick, arachnid bodies of the scorpion guards at the plants behind them.

One of them grunted, moving forward. He gripped his spear and snarled. Still, I didn't think he saw me. Maybe he smelled me. After another moment, his body seemed to relax again.

My throat had gone dry. I *needed* to see what lay behind them without arousing suspicion, to find out if the stones were here.

I glided from the shadows—a cherub, nothing more. The scorpions didn't seem to notice me.

One more step closer, and—just soil. Disappointment coiled through me until—faintly—the soil began to shift, trembling. Light warmed my chest, and I stared as the unmistakable gleam of blue stones emerged from the soil, drawn by my presence. A wild euphoria bloomed in my chest. I ached to touch them, to harness their power. As soon as my eyes locked on them, I could feel them calling to me, demanding that I pluck them, that I feel their magic. They wanted something from me as much as I wanted something from them.

I could go feral at this moment and possibly slaughter the guards. But then—I'd never remember what I was doing here in the first place, and there'd be no point.

Adonis! I mentally screamed at him. *I found them. If you can hear me, I need your help.*

As I glided away from the scorpions, a pale, pearly light in the night sky pulled my attention. My heart slammed hard against my ribs. Focusing my keen fae vision, I made out the outline of powerful, feathery wings. I stared, my pulse racing, as ten gleaming archangels loomed brighter above us. And at their forefront, a scrawny, gray-winged angel. The horseman of famine.

My heart stopped.

The Heavenly Host were coming for me now—and Johnny was leading the charge.

Panic sank its talons into my heart, and I clamped my eyes shut. *Adonis!* I screamed through the mental link. *They're coming. The Heavenly Host are coming for us—now.*

Where the hell was he?

My gaze flicked back to the line of scorpion men. I didn't have any more time to waste. I had to kill them now, and I had to get my hands on the stones.

My hand twitched at my thigh, and I sank back into the shadows again to let my glamour fade.

I'd have to go just a little feral, and I'd have to catch the guards unaware.

Under the boughs of a sycamore, I let myself fade just a bit—a little of my primal side to give me extra strength.

My canines began to grow in my mouth, my body buzzing with wild energy. I breathed in the scent of Aereus's violent power all around me, and it electrified my wild fae body even more. *Keep a leash on it, Ruby. Stay in control.*

In the shadows, I yanked my knife from its holster, breathing fast. Scanning the guards, I made a quick calculation—kill the small one on the right, steal his sword, use it to slaughter the rest. Do it all as quickly as I could, without letting too much of the primal side take over.

A small swarm of cherubs moved along the mosaic path toward me, their murmuring growing louder. They'd noticed something amiss here—that I wasn't one of them.

And they were about to notice something *very* amiss when I dropped my glamour. My gaze flicked to the skies.

It didn't matter. I had no more time to waste.

With a primal growl, I launched myself at the first of the scorpions. I lunged through the air, slashing my blade across his throat before he had a chance to react. Blood sprayed over me before my feet hit the ground. When I landed, I yanked the guard's sword off his fallen body.

Whirling, my blade crashed into the next guard's, the metal sparking in the shadows.

The scorpion roared, his tail pressing closer to me, and I lunged away from him.

Rip apart the enemy. Put him in the dirt.

As my sword clashed against his in a violent waltz, I wanted to taste his blood, to feel his veins and tendons ripping in my teeth. My sword arced through the air, an extension of my body, and the glory of battle fury trembled along my bones. I was made for this.

I drove my blade into his neck, then drew it out to kill again.

Dimly, I was dimly aware of another presence nearby—one forged of night and ancient power. One that I needed like plants needed water.

I couldn't remember his name—the beautiful one with the wings. For just a moment, my gaze flicked to him and I watched as he sliced his fingertips through the air in a brutal gesture.

The three remaining scorpions split down the middle, their severed bodies slumping to the dark earth.

I snarled. They'd been *mine.*

I moved toward the angel—the arrogance of him—didn't belong on earth—an abomination. His icy, alluring eyes designed to seduce, to confuse... Growling, I gripped my sword, ready to swing it into this abomination.

But he was speaking to me—pulling me out of my feral rage.

"Ruby," he said, his voice calming as a blanket of night.

A calm, soothing magic washed over me, relaxing the tension in my muscles. I lowered my sword. Slowly, my canines began to recede, and my gaze flicked to the sky again.

The Heavenly Host were pressing down on us, bodies blazing with light. "They're here." My voice trembled.

"Get the stones," Adonis said gravely. "This is our last chance."

Right. I rushed over the bodies of the scorpion guards, snatching the blue gemstones. Dirt covered their glittering surfaces from their burial underground. They *wanted* me to have them, to possess them. But what, exactly, was I supposed to do with them?

The sound of a door creaking open pulled my attention away. I had only a moment to register Aereus's presence before a brutal force knocked me into the air—a magic that burned my skin and smelled of arid desert winds. My body slammed down hard on the bony path, and I dropped the plant from my hands.

"Why have you killed my guards?" Aereus roared. "I told you the Heavenly Host would arrive!"

Another horseman—Adonis couldn't kill him. He could only try to slow him down—although given how he'd withstood the poison, that wouldn't be an easy task.

Adonis had drawn his sword, ready to fight Aereus.

The pale light burned brighter above us, washing over my skin—so pure and perfect I didn't want to fight them. No, I wanted to bathe in their glory....

The sound of steel against steel pulled my attention back to the earth, my gaze landing on the two horsemen battling each other. Adonis's dark magic whirled around his body.

"You're after the Stones of Zohar," Aereus seethed, his sword cutting sharp arcs through the air. "I buried them deeply, but they rose in the presence of a Light Bringer. Why would you bring her here? You know what she can do to us."

Adonis grunted, meeting Aereus's blows.

I scrambled over the path, searching for the fallen plant, its leaves encrusted with gemstones.

"You know what they'll do to us!" Aereus bellowed.

There—among the bloodied soil—a glimmer of blue, the azure of the skies above Afeka. I reached for it, when another blast of hot, arid magic slammed into me with the force of a train.

My body shattered against a stone wall, ribs cracking. Pain splintered my entire body, and I groaned.

Adonis's roar sent a lick of fear racing up my neck. He viciously swung his sword through the air. He pressed in on Aereus with an increased ferocity—looking more feral than angelic.

The agony of my broken bones clouded my mind. I was on my knees, fingers on the mosaic path of teeth, blood streaming from my mouth. I rasped for breath, pain ravaging my body.

Gritting my teeth, crawling over the bony path, my mind so gripped by agony that my thoughts were no longer making sense... I could only stare at the teeth beneath my fingers, and wonder who they'd come from, if they'd died in this garden. Would I join them?

I shuffled along the ground, now only dimly aware of the angels moving closer.

If I died here, what sort of a disturbing design would they form with my teeth?

Blood dripped from my mouth onto the path. Adonis's magic rippled over me, soothing the pain just a little. *I have to get to the stones.*

I glanced up to see him carving his sword through one of Aereus's red-tipped wings, and the howl Aereus unleashed pierced me to the bone.

Another inch forward over the teeth, crawling toward the glittering blue gems, and pain ripped through my chest, my legs.

Tentatively, I looked up to the skies, at the gleaming angelic horde, now only a hundred feet in the air, and my heart skipped a beat.

They're almost upon us.

I pulled myself a little farther along the path, still staring at the sky—staring, in fact, as a golden dragon soared through the air just below the angelic horde. I blinked at the sight of a female form riding on top of the dragon's neck, her black hair trailing behind her in the night sky.

Hazel?

Uthyr carved a sharp arc below the angels, then arched his back to breathe a hot stream of fire at the oncoming horde.

Idiot—what was she doing? They'd *kill* her. She was buying me time, and I couldn't waste it.

I grabbed the stones, and my body surged with warmth and light. My forehead tingled, and I fought the bizarre urge to press the stones against it.

I felt powerful arms around me—Adonis's arms cradling me, his magic soothing my body. Already, he was healing my bones with his power, numbing the pain. I inhaled deeply, able to breathe a little easier now. Adonis closed his fist around mine, enclosing the stones.

"Now," he whispered. "Use their power now."

I clutched them tightly, closing my eyes. I wasn't sure what I was supposed to do with them—but considering I couldn't move my body, I didn't have many options right now anyway.

They tingled in my fist, then a cold, soothing magic whispered over my skin. Light seemed to ignite me from the inside, blazing through my blood, ancient and pure. The power of the Old Gods flowed through me, my back arching with the intensity. The stones wanted something from me, as if they had their own consciousness.

Their desire whispered through my blood. They wanted me to protect the earth—then to return them home.

Pure strength infused my bones and muscles, and my eyes snapped open. I looked up into Adonis's eyes, and the voice of the Old Gods whispered to me.

He doesn't belong here. They don't belong here. Rid the earth of their presence, and bring the stones home.

Another part of me rebelled at the thought, wanted him here, but the gleaming light burned out those protests.

Still cradling me, Adonis pushed my hair out of my eyes. "Now," he whispered. "They're here. You can't stop—no matter what happens."

At his words, a spark of dread flickered through me. He knew something that he wasn't telling me.

"If what happens?" I asked firmly.

His eyes flashed. "*Now.*"

My gaze flicked to the skies, where the eleven archangels raced for us—for this garden.

Power snaked and rippled along my spine, and I flung out my arms. Light beamed from my ribs, burning with a white-hot intensity.

The angels froze in midair, and a dome of blue light arced over the earth. I closed my eyes, my skull whirling with images of caves and rivers, of oaks overgrown with ivy, sunlight burning through the leaves.

The power snapped and buzzed through my lungs, and lower, through my belly. I gave in to it. Among the blazing sunlight, something darker lurked in the power of the Old Gods, too. The wolf taking down the stag, the plants growing from corpse-enriched soil.

My body a vessel for their power. And the stones were calling to me, too, urging me on. The Old Gods wanted them back, needed them returned to their original home.

It was always meant to be this way.

My body trembled, stones gripped tightly in my fist, until I felt as if my ribs might explode with a pure, wild ecstasy.

A crash pulled me from my reverie.

When I opened my eyes again, I stared up at the sky, my breath clouding around my head in the chilly air.

Beyond the dome of blue light, a horde of angels raced away from the earth. Fleeing—from my power. The glow around them seemed to weaken. Clouds began to roll along the horizon. But where was Johnny? He wasn't among them. Almost as if he'd just fallen from the sky.

It took me a moment to realize that I'd ended up hovering in midair, that my feet hung a meter above the ground.

When I looked down, my heart leapt into my throat.

Adonis lay on the path, his body completely still.

I dropped the stones, falling back to earth. The power of the gems had completely healed my body, but it seemed to have the opposite effect on Adonis.

Fat drops of icy rain began falling from the sky, chilling my skin.

I pressed my hand over his chest, feeling for a heartbeat. For a moment, I felt nothing. Then—a faint pulse, just below his scars.

His pale eyes opened, and I slid my arm under his neck, cradling his head. "Adonis?"

The rain picked up, hammering us harder now.

Adonis met my gaze, his eyes flaming with intensity for just a moment. "You made me want to stay here longer. I need to know the real Ruby. But angels don't belong on earth."

My throat had gone dry, heart slamming hard. This didn't feel right. "What's happening? Are you going to be okay?"

He shook his head, almost imperceptibly, and his eyes began to close. Even close to death, he looked perfect—a god of beauty.

"The stones will carry me to the underworld." He spoke in a whisper. "It's where the horsemen belong. But I want to see you..." His words died out on his tongue.

He'd known.

All this time, he'd known what the stones would do to him—and he'd wanted me to use them anyway.

Sacrifice the few to save the many.

Sadness and a rising panic washed over me.

I'd freed the earth from the scourge of the horsemen, but when I looked at Adonis, grief pressed down on me all the same, suffocating me like heavy dirt. I pressed my hand over his heart again, desperate to feel a beat pulsing beneath my palm.

This time, I felt only the stillness of a grave.

CHAPTER 35

I tried to calm my panicked thoughts, to think of a solution.

My hand shook on Adonis's still chest, and I scanned the garden. Aereus lay on the mosaic path—not far from me. His torn wing had stopped pumping blood, and his heart no longer beat.

Dread slammed into my chest like a fist. I'd just killed them all. I'd killed the horsemen, and as insane as it was—I wanted to take it back. At least for this one.

I'd been so focused on Adonis, I hadn't even noticed that Hazel had landed nearby until I began frantically searching the garden, desperate for some answers. Desperate for a way to undo this.

Hazel's dragon had flattened half the garden, crushing trees beneath it. Rain battered Hazel as she slid off the creature.

Bursts of white streamed from the castle windows, racing for the sky, and it took me a moment to realize the cherubs were fleeing, soaring for the heavens in a mass exodus. The burst of power from the Old Gods had sent them racing away from us.

I pulled Adonis's body in close, embracing his head and his chest as though I could revive him with my body heat. A wave of sorrow washed over me.

This wasn't how it was supposed to end.

"What happened?" Hazel shouted.

I held him close to my heart. "I don't know! I used the stones." I heaved a sob. "They made a shield, just like they were supposed to. They wanted something from me. To be returned home, I think. The Heavenly Host took off, just like they were supposed to." Sorrow slammed into me. "But it killed the horsemen."

Hazel stared down at Adonis, her brow furrowed. "I think you're right."

His body felt cold as ice in my arms.

The shock was a fist in my throat. "I didn't know this would happen."

Deep in my chest, I felt something breaking, and I leaned over Adonis's body, grasping for the stones again, my hand shaking. He looked still and perfect as a god carved of marble.

Maybe I could fix this; maybe the Old Gods would revive him. The Old Gods provided, right?

I gripped the stones tightly in my hands, holding them over his chest—his scarred heart where he'd stabbed himself again and again, stopping his own seal from breaking. It was only now that I was beginning to understand the fuller picture of him, a man who viewed his role as one of sacrifice.

As I held the Stones of Zohar, light flowed through me—a dazzling summer light that tinged the air with honey. I put my hand on Adonis's chest, trying to channel the light into him, to stream it right into his heart...

A thin ray of blue light flowed into his ribs, and for just a moment, his back arched. But all I could feel through the stone's magic was a deep yearning to return home. The light dulled again, and Adonis's body went still.

Above me, the sound of rhythmic wings beat the air. Tanit and Kur were diving for the earth, rain hammering their bodies.

"What the hell happened?" Tanit shrieked.

Grief wrapped around me. The stones hadn't revived him— Adonis's body lay still in my lap, and my mind raced. He'd known, hadn't he? This had been his plan all along. He'd been talking about a sacrifice—all gods demand sacrifices. Maybe a part of him had wanted out of this endless cycle of euphoria and pain. Reliving the same self-inflicted wounds over and over.

Kur kneeled next to me, placing his hand over Adonis's heart. Inky magic coiled from his body, winding around Adonis.

I tuned out the driving rain and the wind, tuned out Tanit's frantic screaming and the painful thoughts hammering at the back of my skull.

I gripped the stones in my hands, closing my eyes. Their power ignited my blood with the pure, buttery light of spring rays filtering through oak leaves, illuminating dust motes in the air with their brilliance. I held Adonis's head, trying to channel that power into him.

I had to look up at the sky—couldn't bring myself to look at the ground. Teeth ripping apart an arm, a woman screaming. Whose teeth were they? I couldn't look at the blood staining the pavement...

The light called to me, the piercing light from above.

"Ruby!" Tanit screamed, ripping me from the vision. Her face wore a haunted, ravaged expression, rain pouring down her features in rivulets. "It's no use. That's not doing anything. He didn't tell us this would happen, but obviously this was his plan. This was his sacrifice. The Great Nightmare is over, and Adonis thought he had to go with it."

"I know. He said he was going to the underworld or something..." I mumbled. I clutched tighter to the stones. *No.* This wasn't how it was supposed to end. The good guys were supposed to win in the end, not die in the soil of a torture garden.

My mind whirled, searching for answers. I tuned out Hazel, tuned out Tanit's crying. I did my best to tune out Kur's rampage, vaguely aware that he'd moved away from us, that he was ripping things from the ground—the iron, the spikes, glass breaking, tearing through the garden like a furious god.

I stared down at Adonis, tracing my fingers over his chest again. A faint spark of hope lit in my mind. This death wasn't the result of dragons or fire. Adonis's death came from magic. And magic could always be undone, right?

If this was supposed to be a gift from the Old Gods, it was a gift I wanted to return.

I wanted to know *exactly* what Adonis had known. I wanted to know everything about the Stones of Zohar and the Bringer of Light.

I wiped the back of my hand across my face to clear away the rain and tears.

Nearby, Kur was ripping human bones from the garden.

"Kur!" I shouted. "I need your help!"

"With what?" he snarled, flashing a hint of sharp teeth.

"Can you read Phoenician?"

Stark pain shone from his dark eyes. "What the fuck does that have to do with anything?"

"I need you to help me learn everything that Adonis knew about the Bringer of Light. About the Old Gods," I shouted. "This isn't where his story ends. I'm sure of it."

CHAPTER 36

I slammed through the door into the bedroom where we'd been staying. Behind me, Kur carried Adonis's body into the room. Hazel sauntered in behind the two demons. At our arrival, Drakon yelped, fluttering his wings frantically.

My heart thundered against my ribs as I scrambled to find the book—tucked under the mattress, just where Adonis had left it. I pulled it out, and Kur laid Adonis's body on the bed. Panicking, Drakon crawled over to his master, curling up on his body, wings fluttering.

Kur sat down on the edge of the bed, ignoring the chaos behind him. I handed the book to him, and he began paging through it, muttering to himself in an ancient language. "And Adonis read this?"

"He's had it with him this whole time. He said he had it memorized. It's the same one that Kratos keeps in his war room. He only told me part of it—he left out the bit about how the stones would kill the horsemen. He said he wanted to rule the celestial realm. Same thing he told you." I shivered, my teeth chattering. I'd wanted to rid the earth of archangels, but this didn't feel like a victory.

Kur gripped the book hard. "This book explains that the Bringer of Light can harness the magic of the Old Gods to repel archangels from the earth. And her magic will kill all the living horsemen of the apocalypse."

Cold dread slid through my bones. Adonis had wanted me to act as his executioner. All along I'd thought he could lure me to my death through seduction, but I had it wrong. He'd been drawn to me precisely because he knew I could kill him.

Tanit tugged at her hair. "Of course he didn't tell us this. We would have stopped him."

There was a lot he hadn't told them. He hadn't mentioned how he kept the seal from opening. I'd been so sure that Adonis was only looking out for himself, that I'd failed to see the truth—Adonis had found a way to keep himself from slaughtering, to beat his curse.

There was still so much he hadn't told me, too.

"His story isn't finished," I said again, more forcefully. Adrenaline and wild desperation surged. "I'm sure of it."

Hazel leaned against the wall, her arms folded. "I told you we should have left things as they were."

Fury bloomed in my chest. "Shut up, Hazel. I'm trying to think." As it was, I could hardly hear my own thoughts over Tanit's sobbing.

"What did he mean his soul was going to the underworld? Is it…is it the one he told me about? Where he was born?"

Kur nodded slowly. "The Old Gods have claimed the souls of the horsemen. This book is written by one of their followers, lauding the defeat of the horsemen. Praising the work of the *Bringer of Light*." Contempt dripped from his words. "As you might imagine, there are no instructions on how to fix it."

I closed my eyes, wracking my brain for everything I'd learned about the Old Gods. The poisonous herbs that grew where horsemen tread, the power I'd felt surging through the silver bough, so raw and overwhelming it had almost driven me insane. The Stones of Zohar, mined from the grotto where Adonis had been born. The entrance to the underworld...

"Afeka," I whispered. "The stones want to be returned to Afeka."

Kur looked up from the book. "What?"

I stared at him. "His soul is in the underworld, where the stones come from, right? And I could feel the stones' desire to return there. They want to go back to Afeka." As soon as I said the word, the stones pulsed in my hand, as if affirming what I was saying. "Any idea where it is, exactly?"

"Lebanon," said Kur.

I nodded. "The Old Gods reside there. Maybe I can make a trade."

Hazel's expression was bleak. "Didn't Adonis warn you that every god wants a sacrifice? I don't think they're into making trades."

I glanced at Adonis, at his pendant that stood out like blood droplets against his tan skin. "The Old Gods want their magic rocks back. I can feel it, even now. Maybe they'll give us just one soul in return."

Hazel's expression was dark. "Or maybe they'll just kill you and take the stones."

Tanit pointed at Adonis, tears streaking her cheeks. "You need to fix this." Her voice was low, cold. "He thinks it was his job to sacrifice himself. It's why he stayed with the feral fae so long."

"I don't understand."

Fury seemed to ripple off Kur's powerful body. "Only the fae could keep his powers in check. Before he could control them himself, his emotions could spread waves of death around him—plagues, earth-quakes, a frost on the crops. Just by feeling intensely—by growing angry or loving another person—death rippled off of him. Only the fae knew how to contain it, with their close connection to the Old Gods."

I felt the bone-deep chill of his words. He'd never wanted to kill, but death simply coiled out of him uncontrolled. I could hardly imagine the guilt, the stark isolation that must have plagued him all those years.

"Over time," Kur continued, "Adonis learned to control it better. He grew into his powers, the way a fae learns to control her hunger. He wanted to keep the world from his destruction." Sharp whorls of magic spilled from Kur's golden body. "Same reason he carved himself up every time the seal started to break open."

"You knew about that?" I asked.

"Of course I knew. I've known for centuries. Adonis always thought he needed to suffer in silence."

I wrung my hands. "He and Kratos both said the same thing. Sacrifice the few to save the many. That was their angelic sense of morality." I choked back the tears that threatened to rush out. I had to keep my thoughts clear. "I guess the horsemen were the sacrifices here. But I'm not going to let it end this way."

Kur met my gaze, his eyes suddenly piercing, body tense. "Do everything you can to fix this. Do you understand, *Bringer of Light?*"

I met his gaze evenly. "I understand. I am the Bringer of Light. And I'm giving back the gift the gods have granted me."

* * *

IN AEREUS'S garden of death, I stared up at Uthyr's cold, reptilian eyes. His dragon form made my entire body tense. For just a moment, my mind flashed with the image of the dragon attack, the sharp teeth piercing bone, flames searing flesh. This thing was a ruthless monster.

I swallowed hard. At least, I thought he was a ruthless monster. Maybe I wasn't always the best at figuring out who the monsters were.

I closed my eyes, mastering my fears. Dragon or not, I had to get to Afeka.

With a noise in his throat like a deep rattle, Uthyr lowered his chin to the muddy earth. I looped my leg over the dragon's scaly neck, half terrified by the power in this creature's muscled back. Then I slid over his body until I found a spot on his spine where I could get a good grip on his scales.

Hazel climbed on in front of me, looking at ease on her perch. The creature's blood pumped below me, his muscles twitching.

What I hadn't expected was for Kur to climb on behind me, sliding over the dragon's hide like it was second nature to him. And given Kur's scales, maybe it was.

I turned to look at him. "You're coming?"

"I'm going to make sure you two fae don't fuck this up. Besides. It's a long way back to Afeka, and you'll both freeze to death without me. Probably fall asleep and slide off the damn dragon."

"Thanks for your vote of confidence."

My stomach lurched as Uthyr lifted off, his powerful wings thumping in the air to keep us a few feet above ground.

From the garden, Tanit lifted Adonis's body, like a supplicant offering up a sacrifice. Uthyr grabbed Adonis in his talons.

As we took flight into the stormy sky, I gripped hard to Uthyr's scales, using my thighs to hold tightly to the beast. The rain hammered against my skin, and Uthyr's wings stirred the air around us.

I tried to peer beyond Hazel, then beyond Uthyr's enormous haunches to catch a glimpse of Adonis, but it was no use from my vantage point.

Kur's powerful arms curved around me, keeping me in place. With the rain pounding in my face, I could hardly see where we were going, but the speed of flight thrilled me all the same.

I'd actually done what I'd first set out to do—I'd defeated the horsemen. I'd slain them all, driven the archangels from the earth. A shimmering, blue sphere still glimmered around the earth's surface, protecting us from the archangels' onslaught.

The Great Nightmare was over. Right?

It didn't feel like a victory. I couldn't let it end this way, not without trying to save Adonis, too. If his soul remained in the underworld of the Old Gods, I had to imagine he was trapped in some sort of hell.

The freezing rain made my teeth chatter. I slumped back into Kur, and he steadied me on the dragon's back.

"You two fae will get tired fast," he said. "We have a long way to go."

"Do you know where we're going?" I asked.

"Afeka is my home, too. It will take us almost a full day to get there."

Thank the gods Kur had come with us, because he wasn't wrong when he said we'd probably fall off this thing. If there was one lesson

I'd learned from riding Nuckelavee, it was that about three or four hours in, my thighs would be on fire.

Hazel's dark hair whipped into my face as we flew through the air.

"I don't suppose you have any of that magic that Adonis had? The kind that stops your muscles from hurting?"

"I have my own magic," said Kur. "I'm a demon of the night, and I'm going to put you to sleep."

I clutched tighter to Uthyr's scales. "Not sure that's a great idea, Kur. I'm kind of holding on for my life here."

"I'm not going to let you fall." As soon as the words were out of his mouth, a soothing, starlight-tinged calm swept over me, curling around my sister. Her slim body slumped into me, and Kur's muscled arms wrapped around me, holding me in place.

I sank deeply into a dreamless sleep.

* * *

I woke to the sun's rays warming my skin. When I opened my eyes, we were soaring over a rocky terrain, the land tinged with stunning shades of blue and green. A turquoise river carved through the land below. Despite everything that had happened, hope stirred within me.

"We're here," Kur said quietly.

I prodded Hazel in the ribs, and she jolted awake with a snort. "What?"

I leaned in closer. "Tell your dragon to bring us down. This is Afeka."

Hazel bent toward Uthyr's ear, whispering something to him. Uthyr's glimmering, membranous wings shot out, and he arced lower over the rushing river.

The wind whipped through my hair as Uthyr took us down to the river's bank. Around us, red anemones bloomed in tall grasses, and I breathed in the humid air of Adonis's birthplace. The dragon circled a few times above the grotto, where water rushed from a cave mouth over a rocky cliff face. It pooled below, a cerulean blue in the bright sun.

Uthyr swooped lower, aiming for a rocky cliffside above the river. Before he reached the ground, he hovered near the earth, his heavy wings pounding the air.

"What's he doing?" I asked.

"He's setting down Adonis," said Hazel.

At least he was being careful. A moment later, Uthyr gracefully landed on the path next to Adonis. Kur slid off the beast first, then helped us down. Fatigue ate at my muscles as I slipped off Uthyr's scales. If Kur's magic hadn't been here to soothe my body, I'd be lying on the ground right now, or possibly dead.

I crossed to Adonis, his body peaceful and perfect, his dark lashes stark against his golden skin. I crouched down, touching the smooth skin of his cheek.

"Do you know what you're doing here?" asked Hazel.

I shook my head. "No idea. I only know I'm taking these stones into the underworld, and I'm going to try to make a trade for Adonis's soul."

I rose, and the Stones of Zohar thrummed faintly through the leather satchel on my back, already urging me onward. I felt their power driving me, compelling me to move past the rows of myrrh trees. Here, everything smelled like Adonis.

Kur crouched down, lifting Adonis's body off the rocky earth. "We're both going to find him. I'm coming in there with you."

I squinted in the sunlight. "I'm not sure the Old Gods want demons in their realm."

"I'm coming," he said with a growl.

A vernal breeze whispered over me as my footsteps crunched over the path. The grotto was the entrance to the underworld, but I felt life pulsing from it.

Kur trod behind me. As I walked along the cliff's edge, the turquoise water in the gorge below seemed to shift in color. I swallowed hard, watching it redden to the deep crimson of blood. A shiver rippled up my spine.

I wasn't entirely sure what that was about, but I wouldn't say the blood river seemed like a *good* omen.

As we walked on to the cave's mouth, distant cries skimmed past us—agonized cries. A woman weeping, a man's tormented screams.

Again—not a particularly welcoming omen in my book. I glanced at Kur, but he hadn't seemed to notice any of it.

At the cave's mouth, I paused, running my fingers over the arched, rocky wall by my side. I cast a nervous glance at the river of blood, dread pooling in my gut.

Awfully dark in there. So far, everything I'd seen of the Old Gods had been beautiful and full of life. The herbs growing in the forest, the gleaming silver bough, the scent of spring. Here, at the mouth of the underworld, I faced uncharted territory. Depths I really didn't want to plumb.

Pushing aside my fears, I reached into the leather satchel and pulled out the Stones of Zohar. I'd brought them back to their original home. My forehead tingled at the sight of them, and again I fought the overwhelming impulse to press them against my head.

They glowed in my hand, casting a dull blue light over the cave's interior.

Would the gods accept this as an exchange for Adonis's soul? I had no idea. Bartering with the gods for souls was, frankly, completely unfamiliar terrain.

I'd think of it as a sacrifice. That was what Adonis would say. All gods required sacrifices, and that was what I'd come to offer.

Distantly, those faint, agonized cries floated on the mountain wind. The cries didn't sound fully present, exactly. More like an echo, a memory of something from long ago.

My footsteps echoed off the cave walls. Fear began raking its talons through my chest, raising the hair on the back of my neck.

Something from my past flashed in my mind— blood running down a pale arm, streaming onto the pavement. Teeth piercing the flesh... A woman screaming, a look of horror... Something I didn't want to think about.

Why did that memory keep haunting me? The dragon attack, maybe, of Marcus. No, it was something else, something with a woman. Whatever it was, the memory was a piercing staccato hammering at the inside of my skull, hot and crimson.

I slammed down the iron door. *Not now.*

As I moved deeper into the cave, Aereus's words began whispering around me. *There, you'd have to face the real monster.*

The light from the Stones of Zohar began to dim, now a faint glow. They cast a dull light over the glistening rocks around me, and icy water began running over my feet, growing higher and higher with every step. I tried not to think about the fact that it had looked bright red, or that I might be bathing in the blood of the undead. Where were the Old Gods in here? How far did I have to go?

I whirled around, alarmed to find that Kur was nowhere around me. My throat went dry.

"Kur?" My voice echoed off the stone walls. "Kur?" I called out more urgently.

No response.

Shadows smothered the stone's light completely. *Darkness. Darkness all around me.*

Icy fear raked its claws through my heart as slick, tight vines began snaking around my limbs, rooting me in place. Like a python, they climbed around me, threatening to suffocate me.

They dragged me under the water's surface.

CHAPTER 37

$\mathcal{A}$s the vines pulled me under, I managed to cling to the stones. Holding my breath, I clutched them to my chest. My lungs burned. After a few moments, the waters receded again, the vines loosening on my limbs. I kicked until my head rose above the water, and I sucked in a ragged breath.

What the fuck is going on?

I scrambled for a foothold to stop the rushing river from carrying me with it, kicking and bucking until my tiptoes skimmed over the river bottom.

Stable ground. Thank the gods.

I gripped the stones tightly in my palm as the water rushed over my body. Music pulsed around me—a low, rumbling bass noise that trembled along my bones. Darkness closed in, and all I could see was the thick glistening of the rocks overhead.

Slowly the water receded, and the ground sloped upward. Another presence lurked in here, a female presence. The stones began to glow faintly again, casting a dim, blue light over a figure looming above me in a throne made of glinting rock.

A cloak of moss hung over her, and the scent of peaty soil curled off her. I couldn't quite see her, but for a moment, when the light of the stones flashed a little brighter, I had a sense of thin, wispy skin, like layered spiderwebs.

A voice echoed in my mind. *Bringer of Light.*

I cleared my throat. "I'm looking for Adonis."

Archangels should never roam the earth, the voice boomed.

I clutched the stones tightly to my chest.

A wispy huff of laughter. *Archangels should never walk the earth, Bringer of Light. His soul will remain here, with the other horsemen. See him if you must. You won't be leaving here, either. You're descended from the Old Gods, Ruby.*

Long ago, the Old Gods mated with the fae, creating a race of Light Bringers. You belong among us, now.

A wispy substance skimmed over my skin. "I'm part…Old God?"

The goddess pulled off her hood, and white light beamed through her translucent skin. From the shadows, more glowing beings emerged. Their naked bodies blazed with light, skin as thin as shed snakeskin.

You belong with us, Bringer of Light, my child. You may serve me here forever.

She reached for me, and I took a step back. *Oh, hell no.* Okay, so —*this* was the sacrifice. And it was one I wasn't willing to make.

The stones began to heat in my hands, held tight against my heart. Once again, I felt an overwhelming urge to press them against my forehead like a salve on a wound.

The goddess rose from her throne. Thin threads of silver hair curled over her shoulders, and her eyes shone like moonlight glinting off water. A cloak of moss draped over her shoulders, and a wreath of hawthorn encircled her head. Her lips looked parched, skin dry and flaky despite the damp air.

Give the stones to me. Within my mind, her voice had a sharper edge. Desperate, almost. *I must drink from them.*

Was she out of her ancient, mossy mind? I wasn't giving over the stones just so she could trap me here.

I clutched them tighter to my chest, unwilling to part with them. At least, not until I regained some control over the situation. "Yeah,

I'm not staying here with the army of the glowing, so we'll need a different plan. How about I give you these stones, and you give me Adonis's soul, and then I'll be on my way."

Rage blazed from the goddess's eyes, and she took another step closer. *I protected you. And now you want to bargain with me, for what's rightfully mine?*

When she stepped closer, I could see indentations in her skull—indentations that perfectly matched the size of the stones. She'd worn them once, a crown of sorts. These stones had once been a part of her, and they'd been stolen. Another step closer, her hands grasping for them—and my own skull ached to feel them pressed against it.

She heaved in a raspy breath. *I've been trapped here for a thousand years, unable to leave without my powers. Give them back to me.*

My utility to her was starting to become clear. She'd needed me to bring them to her. A messenger, working for her.

A lump rose in my throat, and I shook my head. I'd rid the earth of the horsemen. I'd protected it from archangels who wanted to slaughter us all. Was I about to undo that spell—just for one man? Adonis would never approve of it. A small sacrifice to save the larger numbers. But I needed a different kind of morality. I needed good to triumph over evil. I needed the heroes to live.

One last chance. "I want to leave here, and I want to take Adonis with me."

She snarled, long canines protruding. Claws emerged from the tips of her hands—long and curled, the color of aged tree bark.

The goddess was going a bit feral before me, and I took a step back from her in the icy water. My skull ached for the stones like a parched throat aches for water.

I could do it. I could use the stones' power for myself…

Snarling, the goddess lunged for me. I darted back, pressing the stones against my forehead, and my skin soaked them up.

My own voice echoed in my skull. *Gods don't run from themselves, Ruby.*

All at once, the rock around me seemed to fall away, and I was standing in the park in New York. Blood spattered the ground near my feet. I recognized this scene. This was the day the world ended, the day the Great Nightmare had begun.

I didn't want to look up. I knew what I'd see there—the dragon ripping Marcus to shreds. An unseen force gripped my chin, forcing me to lift my head.

Before me, a shadow loomed over Marcus, and the reptilian stench of ancient caves and rock dust pooled in the air. I whirled, just in time to see the dragon lunge.

I screamed a warning, but it was too late.

My world tilted as the dragon clamped Marcus in its jaws, teeth piercing his flesh. Blood streamed over the pavement, glistening in the afternoon light. My chest clenched with pure, raw panic.

Screaming, I leapt into the air, trying to get a grip on the dragon, but it was too tall for me, and my fingers slipped off its scales. *I can't protect him.* I slammed back down onto the ground, knocking the back of my head on the pavement.

With Marcus's body clamped in his jaws, the dragon shook his head back and forth, red streaming from his teeth.

Frantic, I hurled my knife at the dragon's eye. Somehow, I managed to hit it just at the edge of the iris, even as it flailed its head around.

I tried to slam the iron door down on the memory, tried to fight my way out of this hell, but there was no escape.

The dragon tossed Marcus into the air. Blood poured from his chest, his ribs. *It's too late.*

I screamed, not hearing my own voice.

I couldn't look down, couldn't stare at what the dragon was doing to Marcus. I had to bury those thoughts, lock them up in a mental coffin—but it wasn't working now. I had to see it, had to look at what had happened. The dragon had ripped through his ribs, his spine. His blood pooled over the pavement...

Until nothing was left of him but a pile of ash.

Ruby. Who do you believe the real monster is?

I started shaking my head, unwilling to make meaning from this. I heaved a sob. "I don't know what you mean."

The world around me fell away again. For just a moment, I glimpsed the dragons—a flash of blonde hair and flailing limbs. Teeth ripping at her flesh, her pale arms...

The image faded as soon as it had come, leaving me in the dark. I sucked in a sharp breath. Is that what I'd been imagining all this time? I hadn't been there when dragons had killed my parents—long before the Great Nightmare had begun. It wasn't a memory. And yet this image of blood on the pavement kept hammering at my skull, the piercing, red-hot staccato...

From the darkness, light bloomed around me. My mother towered over me. She was gripping my arm, trying to pull me into the house. She looked scared. *Why* was it so important to her that I stay inside?

Her blonde hair flowed over her shoulders, and I wanted to pull her outside. Spring blossomed in the air around us—the fae spring. February. Eimmal.

My canines lengthened, and a feral growl tore from my throat. *Hunt. Kill. Stop the heart.*

"Ruby!" my mom screamed, frantically tugging on my arm. "You need to get inside the house!"

Light shone brightly off the house's metal siding.

Her words began to blur into the red mist in my mind, lost in a haze of moss and peat, until I only knew that she was prey. My teeth sank into her arm, hot blood pulsing in my mouth, flesh tearing...

Blood streaming over the pavement.

It wasn't until strong arms pulled me off her that I saw what I'd done, that I heard my dad screaming my name. That I saw the horrified look in my parents' faces, as they realized what I was. *A monster.* They weren't as feral as I was.

The image faded, leaving me again in the dank cave. The stones had disappeared from my fingers, but their light seemed to pulse through my blood. A deep, throbbing rhythm thrummed around me.

Vines slithered from the ground, curling around my feet, my ankles—then penetrating my skin. Sharp pain splintered my body, shooting up my bones. My ribs, my skull fractured with the pain, and a flash of sunlight blinded me—burning away the image of blood staining the pavement. At last, the vines receded again, freeing my body. I gasped with relief.

Ancient, primal power surged in my veins. I opened my eyes again, and pale blue light blazed from within my skin. I wasn't alone anymore. Around me, shimmering forms moved—just wisps of scintillating outlines—shoulders and hair and fingers that glimmered like phosphorescence in the ocean.

The souls of the underworld—each with their own scent.

I licked my canines, my hunter's instincts propelling me forward through the dank cave. I'd come here for Adonis, and I was going to find him. Already, the *theta* on my shoulder tingled, as if summoning me closer.

I broke into a sprint, running through the shallow waters as they rose around me. I followed the alluring scent of myrrh. Light blazed from the gleaming crown around my head.

Gods rule the realms of the dead.

In the far recesses of the cave, I found them—the four horsemen, lurking together—each one distinct by his smell, his aura. Four horsemen, their forms translucent. Adonis's blue eyes shone in the darkness. His eyes widened in surprise.

I homed in on Adonis, grabbing him by the hand, and pulled him closer to me—and his hand felt like pure warmth within mine. Light flowed from my body around his soul, wrapping us closer. "You're coming with me."

Those deep, blue eyes burned into me, shock written all over them.

Water rushed higher and higher around me, covering my body and surging over my skin. I lost my grip on Adonis, completely submerged in the icy waters--until at last, my head breached the surface. The water receded around me, and I pushed myself to my feet, frantically looking around for Adonis.

And there—at the cave's mouth—he stood with sunlight silhouetting his body. Alive again.

His back arched. Around his neck, snaked thorny vines—his seal, opening before my eyes.

Instinct kicked in, and I rushed for him and stroked the vines of magic with the tip of my finger, scraping it across the thorns. Blue light glowed from my fingertips. A sharp jolt of ecstasy surged into my body—life and death melding together.

The seal dissipated beneath my fingertips.

Adonis staggered back from me, his hand at his throat. A grimace contorted his features.

Then, he stared at me, his jaw open.

I touched my forehead, feeling the smooth stones that had become a part of my skin.

I cleared my throat. "I, um... I stole the goddess's magic rocks."

"You *stole* them." He blinked, as if awakening from a dream.

"I had to. It was the only way to get you back. Plus, she wanted me to stay here with a bunch of creepy Light Bringers to serve her or something."

He grabbed me by the hand. "I want to get you out of here."

I glanced behind me, relieved to see that no gods or Bringers of Light were following me.

"You've stolen the goddess's power," he said. "Now you have the power of a goddess. Do you understand that?"

Primal magic—the kind I had when feral—coursed through my veins. But I didn't feel feral anymore. I simply felt powerful.

"This magic feels native to me." River water rushed over my ankles. "I guess it is. The goddess said the Bringers of Light descended from the Old Gods."

Before we crossed out of the cave's mouth into the beaming sunlight, Adonis turned to me. Gently, he stroked the stones set into my forehead. "You found me in the underworld, and you pulled the curse off me. Why did you do it?"

I knew what he wanted. He was looking for some kind of well-reasoned, rational explanation about morality. Maybe some sort of plan. But I didn't have that, so I had to go with the truth.

"Because you're one of the good guys, and I didn't want you to die." I wrapped my arms around him, breathing in his smell. His heart pounded against my ear, full of life, and joy sparked in my chest. "You're not supposed to die yet."

His hand stroked up my back. "Ruby. You pulled out their souls with mine."

"Whose?"

"The three other horsemen. I felt their souls depart with me. The other horsemen aren't going to let this end here."

My body tensed. *Well, shit.* "I pulled your curse from you, didn't I? I'll free the other horsemen, too." My thoughts began to race. "And we'll just have to get them on our side. Five of us against ten celestial angels. They're not great odds, but...well, we've got a dragon." I could feel the words tumbling off my tongue, nearly nonsensical.

Adonis pulled away from me, his pale eyes beaming intensely in the dim light. "Our four deaths could have ended this all."

I shook my head. "I'm supposed to let you die to save the world. I know that. A few deaths to spare millions, or however many are left on this earth. But what if those aren't the only options? What if we change the rules?"

He stroked a fingertip down my cheek. "Do you know what happened when the last magical being tried changing the rules?" He leaned in, whispering into my ear. "He fell."

My stomach tightened. *Lucifer. Azazeyl.* It hadn't turned out well. In fact, it had led to millennia of death and destruction. "Admittedly, it's not the best precedent. But can we not dwell on the negative right now? I just hauled your ass out of eternal cave hell, and I have some brand new magical powers I need to try out."

When we stepped out of the cave into the beaming sunlight, Adonis gaped at the river in front of us. Kur and Hazel were already rushing toward us, but Adonis seemed lost in his own world. He bent down and plucked a red flower from the ground, studying it, the expression on his face one of remorse.

The flower's crimson color perfectly matched the red pendant around his neck. *So that's what he'd been wearing...*

It was only then I realized Hazel was clutching my arm and screaming into my face.

"Ruby! What is going on with your head?" she shrieked.

"I stole the Stones of Zohar. They seem to have formed a crown on my head."

Her jaw dropped. "So what does it mean?"

I bit my lip. "I don't really know yet, Hazel." I stared at my hands, at the glowing light that tinged my fingertips. "I think we're going to find out."

CHAPTER 38

I lay back against the trunk of the myrrh tree in Adonis's garden, listening to the burbling of the spring. Sunlight washed over me, warming my skin.

A small, barren patch of earth stretched out from the tree to the stream, and I leaned over it, breathing in the scent of the rich soil. What could I do with this little patch of dirt?

I closed my eyes, summoning the warm power that pooled in my skull, then tingled down my spine. It settled between my ribs before streaming on through my arms, my fingertips… It smelled of moss, of damp leaves and wildflowers, and I felt as if I'd always had it within me.

When I opened my eyes again, light streamed from my fingertips over the damp earth. As I stared at the ground, tiny green shoots sprouted, curled like miniature ferns. I loosed a long breath, staring as they grew under the rays of blue light. As I gaped at them, the buds began to unfurl into crimson blossoms that trembled in the light.

When they'd opened fully, I let my light fade. I brushed my fingertips over the petals, smiling at what I'd created. I'd been toying with my powers for a few days, and this was the best result so far. Some kind of magical photosynthesis, I guessed. An antidote to the vast wastelands created by the Great Nightmare.

Gentle footfalls sounded behind me, and I turned to see Drakon padding over to me, his tail swishing behind him. When he reached me, he rubbed against my skin, his scales slick and slightly oily. I stroked his head. His eyes closed, and he nestled his head against me. Then, he crawled into my lap, crushing my legs with his weight, claws piercing my clothes.

"Ooof, Drakon."

He attempted to curl up in a ball on my lap, prodding at me with his claws. Apparently, Drakon hadn't figured out yet that there would be no way he'd fit on me, or that his scaly, clawed body on my lap felt extremely uncomfortable.

I nudged him off onto the grass, and he reluctantly prowled off me, then curled up into a ball by my side.

I smiled at him. Once, he'd disturbed me—a demonic reptilian beast from hell. Now, I was starting to like the guy. In fact—maybe I felt a strange kinship with him. We both had our bestial sides.

"My two favorite creatures." Adonis's smooth voice wrapped around me.

The sunlight washed over his deep, golden skin, and my eyes roamed over the finely cut clothes that hugged his masculine form.

Just the sight of him made my heart race. "Want to join us?"

"Sitting in the dirt?"

"It's more fun than you'd think."

A smile ghosted over his lips, and he sat by my side, his arm brushing mine as we looked out over the stream. "What have you been doing out here?"

I shrugged. "Nothing amazing. Just creating new life from my fingertips."

He cocked his head. "Testing your new goddess powers?"

"If a desperate need to garden arises, I'm your guy." I glanced at the sky, at the shimmering blue shield above us. "Any news on the other horsemen?"

Adonis squinted in the bright sunlight. "We've received a message from Kratos. He wants to come speak to us."

My shoulders tensed. "About what?"

"He wants to form an alliance. He wants his curse removed."

"What's going on with Johnny and Aereus?"

"Drakon located them. They're both in Sadeckrav Castle. If I had to guess, they're forming an alliance of their own, and they plan to kill us."

I swallowed hard. "They still want to rule the earth as gods."

"Can you imagine Aereus wanting anything else?"

"Conquest and Death against Famine and War. I like our odds."

The red pendant at his neck glinted in the sunlight, and I reached over to touch it. "This is one of the flowers from Afeka, isn't it?"

"Yes. It's nearly as old as I am."

"Why do you wear it?"

His expression darkened for just a moment, and he stared at the rushing water. Sparks of sunlight glinted off its surface. "I lived with my mother in Afeka when I was younger. She knew what I was—the horseman of death. But she thought she could keep me from my fate through love."

"She sounds like an amazing mom."

"She taught me to love living things. She taught me to identify plants, to grow flowers. She kept me away from humans, so I wouldn't hurt them. We lived in isolation—near humans, but never among them. Then the fae came for me. They attacked everyone in the nearby city, burning, slaughtering until they got to us."

He met my gaze, and my chest tightened at the raw pain glinting in his eyes.

"I fought them off," he continued. "I killed most of them, trying to protect my mother. But they stabbed her in the side." His voice sounded hollow. "She might have lived. If a real healer had been looking after her, she *would* have lived. But I tried healing her myself. I thought I could do it."

I swallowed hard. "What happened?"

"Sometimes, if powerful emotions overcome me, I unleash death.

I've changed, but…when I was young, I couldn't control it. I pressed her side, trying to staunch the bleeding. She was telling me to run, I think. Her blood covered my fingers, staining the flowers around her. She kept saying I should run, but—I was fifteen and she was the only person I knew." He didn't meet my gaze, just stared at the red flowers around us. "It was just us. She was the only person I knew. Where was I supposed to run to?"

A lump rose in my throat. "I can't imagine how scared you must have been."

"I was trying to help her. I was thinking about living on my own—just living forever in isolation. Then I felt the wave of darkness roll off me—that sweet release that soothed my nerves, like a blanket of night, like dreams sweeping over the horizon." His shoulders sagged, as if the weight of his unseen wings were dragging him to the earth. "I killed her. And everyone around us for miles. A vast landscape of death. That's what I was created to do."

I reached out, touching his arm. "It wasn't your fault."

"Her blood spilled over the white flowers, staining them red. They've been that color since then." He loosed a long, slow sigh. "I turned myself over to the fae who'd hunted me, the ones who served the Old Gods. I thought they could control me. Until one day, I realized I didn't need them anymore. I'd learned to control myself. You cannot imagine how much I enjoyed killing those fae, though…" He touched his necklace. "I've always kept this with me, one of the flowers stained red."

"It's a reminder of your mother, but—it seems like some sort of penance. Like you feel guilty."

"Of course I feel guilty. This is a reminder of why I needed to die. It's why I belong in the underworld. I am Death incarnate, and the archangels should have never put me here."

I slid my arm into the crook of his elbow. "But you are here, and I want you here. And you've changed. You've gained control over your power. We're not just one thing, Adonis. You're not just Death. Every one of us has many facets."

He turned his head toward mine, his face so close that his breath warmed my skin.

When I met his gaze, I felt a jolt of electricity rush through me. "I want you to teach me about all the plants your mom taught you. And we can grow them all."

"I can't think of anything I'd like to do more."

"What do you think will happen next?"

He plucked a red flower from the river bank and twirled it between his fingers. "We fight. And we rebuild."

ROGUE FAE - BOOK THREE

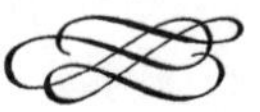

CHAPTER 1

donis handed me a canteen of water. Sunlight filtered through the laurel leaves, sparking in his pale eyes. Above us, Drakon—his dragonile—swooped between the tree branches.

"See?" Adonis said. "I remember things about you. You need to drink water to stay alive. I may have even packed you and Hazel sandwiches."

I took the canteen gratefully from him. "Your understanding of biology astounds me." I cocked my head. "What did you put in the sandwiches?"

"Bread with strawberries and butter. And a little pepper."

I quirked a smile. Adonis had no idea how food worked. "That is weird as hell, but it sounds strangely delicious." Much like him, in fact.

It was sweet of him, anyway. Unfortunately, we weren't alone, or I might have kissed him right then.

Muriel, an angel friend of his we'd just met this morning, was staring right at us. "I'm just concerned that Ruby and Hazel are slowing us down." She delivered this declaration to my sister and me in a sickly sweet tone, batting her eyelids.

Adonis shot her a sharp look. "Don't be ridiculous, Muriel. We're making good time."

I glared at her. Ostentatious diamonds glittered from her wrists and from her blond curls. They were probably real, but her smile was fake as dollar-store rhinestones. Everything about her annoyed me, to the point where I nearly forgot about the fact that we were probably on our way to be slaughtered.

Adonis had arranged to meet the Horseman of Conquest to discuss an alliance. Kratos had chosen the location. Did I trust him? Hell no, I didn't trust him. Hence, I'd brought my bow and arrows with me.

I had a strong feeling Kratos had set a trap for us. And yet, Adonis seemed to think this meeting was our only chance to win in a war against the two evil horsemen. The ones who were just about ready to cleanse the rest of the earth of every human, fae, and demon.

I screwed the top back on the canteen. "Let's just keep going, shall we?"

Muriel cast an irritated glance over her shoulder. "No offense, but I don't think we need the fae. Sometimes powerful forces take on dead weight, and that's bad for everyone. We all know animals get overtired easily."

Adonis halted his march over the forest floor, and I nearly ran into his back. At the look he was giving Muriel, a chill rippled over my skin. Even *he* was about to lose it with his old friend.

"Sorry." She blew me a kiss. "I forgot the fae can be sensitive about being called animals. But people should just accept what they are, right? Just like I've accepted that I'm divine. Right, my darlings?"

Muriel had a way of unleashing the most brutal commentary with kisses and terms of endearment that made my skin crawl.

Hazel seemed amazingly unperturbed by Muriel's attitude. She ignored the insults, lazily threading a string of leaves together as she walked.

Clenching my jaw, I started marching again, and the others moved along with me. Even though I was trying to keep my cool, the gemstones in my forehead were heating up, ready to claim some angel life.

"Just so we're clear," I snarled. "I've infiltrated the fortresses of two horsemen. I stole the gemstones from Aereus *and* the Old Gods, blocked the Heavenly Host from the earth with a magic blue shield, and I rescued Adonis from the underworld. And I'm the Bringer of Light."

"I don't even know what that is." She wrinkled her nose. "And the Heavenly Host broke through that crappy shield you made, then disappeared somewhere on earth, so, I'm not super impressed with your powers." She sighed, flicking her eyes to the heavens like a martyr. "Look, there's no reason to get upset with me, sweetie. I dedicate my life to helping people. I ask for nothing in return."

Annoying as she was, she had a point about the Heavenly Host. The shield I'd created to block the angels from the earth had only been temporary. Now, we were on borrowed time before the angels destroyed the rest of the earth, and all of my attempts to create new shields had failed miserably.

Ever since I'd stolen the gemstones, I'd had the feeling that the Old Gods didn't really want me using their powers. Believe me, I'd been trying to master my new skills over the past few days. My life—maybe everyone's life—depended on it. But each time I tried to summon the magic of the Old Gods, it seemed like the magic would kill me. I'd actually spent an entire week in an empty field outside Adonis's castle trying to conjure a new shield, and each time my magic intensified, it had felt as if my body was about to blow apart with the force of their rage, and I could no longer focus. Since I'd stolen the gemstones, I'd completely lost control of the magic.

If I had to guess, the Old Gods didn't take to kindly to thievery. And worse, I thought they might want me dead now, but I kept that last part to myself. I was supposed to be the earth's only hope. It wouldn't do any good to extinguish hope, right? I'd just have to work at my powers, until they didn't kill me.

"Let's just keep going, shall we?" I snapped. "We don't want to be late for Kratos's slaughter party." I'd only known Muriel for a few hours, but already I wanted to fling her into the gorge.

Still, as much as I'd like to see her perfect body tumble down the rugged slope—slamming against every jagged rock on the way—she had a purpose here. Muriel was a bridge between Kratos and Adonis. In fact, she'd known them both for a thousand years or so. She was supposed to function as some sort of mediator in our negotiations. If either Kratos or Adonis tried to pull any shit, Muriel would use her angel powers to keep them in line.

Apparently, they both trusted her, even though she was clearly an asshole.

"How long have you two known each other, anyway?" My voice sounded a little too sharp as I glared at her.

"For centuries, sweetie. Adonis was there to help me when I nearly fell from grace."

"Oh?" At last, Muriel was starting to seem interesting.

"Centuries ago," she said. "In London. A wickedly beautiful incubus seduced me. Only Adonis's magic was able to pull me back from eternal ruination." She shuddered. "I'd started to grow horns. Like a demon. Revolting."

These angels and their abstinence. It really was a sad waste of life.

A languid sigh escaped Muriel. "Such young creatures, these two little fae."

"How old are you, anyway?" asked Hazel.

Muriel stretched her arms over her head. "Older than Adonis. I was there when Eve ate the fruit in the Garden of Eden."

Hazel scrunched her nose. "Wait—the Garden of Eden is real? I thought that was just a myth, like alligators who live in sewers and plants that give you rashes."

"Plants can give you rashes." I scowled at the leaves in her grip. "Hazel, that's poison ivy."

"Whoops." She dropped them on the ground, wiping her hands on her jeans.

"And the Garden of Eden was real," Adonis added. "Only it wasn't an apple that Eve ate. It was a grape."

Hazel frowned. "Well, grapes don't grow on trees, so there are holes in your story already."

Muriel stared at her nails. "I don't see what was so great about the Garden, anyway. Nature's boring."

Another reason why Muriel was dumb as rocks. Right now, we were walking through a sylvan paradise, and she couldn't even see it. Edible mushrooms grew along the forest floor, and ripe hawthorn berries and rose hips grew from the shrubs around us. Drakon swooped through the cherry trees above us, his teeth stained with the fruit. There was a banquet here for those who knew where to look. Forget Eden. *This* was Paradise—nature was the church of the gods.

My gaze flicked to the left of the path, where chinks of sunlight flecked a simple cottage. It looked like it had just been built since the Great Nightmare began.

Smoke curled from the chimney, rising between the gnarled boughs of an oak. Through the window, I caught a glimpse of a woman stirring something in a pot over a fireplace. Soup, I imagined. When she tucked a strand of her platinum hair behind her ear, I realized her ears were pointed. A fae—just like me. I stared as a fae male came up behind her, planting a kiss on her cheek.

That's what I'm missing. Living out here in nature like the fae were supposed to. A simple life, surrounded by the paradise of nature.

"A little fae cottage," said Muriel. "How quaint. Until they go feral and eat each other."

I blocked her out, already envisioning my life in a cottage like that. I'd hunt deer and drink ice-cold water from a forest stream…. Adonis would wear nothing but a fig leaf. At night, we would sit in front of the fire sipping home brews, eating soup. Then, he'd push me up against an oak tree, grab my thighs, and—

"Ruby," said Hazel. "You're about to walk into a tree."

My eyes snapped open, and I stopped short of a laurel trunk. "I know what I'm doing," I muttered.

"What were you thinking about?" asked Hazel.

I cleared my throat. "Nothing. Just the upcoming meeting with Kratos. I was thinking about our best strategy."

Ugh. Weird that the vision had been so potent. I was beginning to suspect that the stones I'd stolen from the Old Gods might be messing with my head a little. These days, my fantasies—my phantom life— sometimes seemed more vibrant than the real world.

Or—it was possibly the fact that Adonis and I had been separated for a week after I saved him from the underworld, and now I couldn't stop staring at his muscled body. For a full week, he'd been away, trying to make contact with Kratos.

"Are you nervous for this meeting?" asked Hazel. "What if it's an ambush? What if Kratos is just luring us into a trap?"

"I certainly don't trust Kratos. But we have Adonis on our side, and if it comes down to an angel battle, I like his odds."

As I looked at Adonis's perfect body, it occurred to me that maybe the problem with temptation in the Garden of Eden had nothing to do with Eve. From my perspective, everything was the angels' fault. If had to guess, Azazeyl—the angel who tempted Eve—was a stone-cold hottie. And when she ate the grapes he offered her, Paradise was lost. Not her fault, even though it did ruin everything for everyone.

Azazeyl cursed humanity with the ability to speak—and with language came neurosis. Adam and Eve were no longer simply cavorting through the plants and screwing up against oak trees. After the fall, they were thinking about things like *What is death, and what happens to your soul when you die? Does Adam always have to chew with his mouth open? Is there more to life than fig leaves and fruit trees? And is Azazeyl ever coming back here or did I weird him out when I tried to compliment his abs?*

If it weren't for the angels, Adam and Eve and the rest of humanity would have happily stayed in their paradise, neurosis-free.

Angels had screwed up everything.

And now, I'd be relying on these same angels to fix the whole apocalypse they started.

Muriel turned to frown at me. "I've always wondered if the fae take baths or if you just lick yourselves clean like dogs?"

I picked up a clump of earth from the ground and hurled it at Muriel, eliciting a shriek when it hit her white gown.

"That's cats, dipshit," I shouted.

Since the world's fate depended on it, it was a good thing I had a natural rapport with these angels.

CHAPTER 2

The cave's entrance didn't look like much—a four-foot-tall hole that opened from the side of a vine-covered rock. Tree roots grew around it, and Adonis had to crouch to fit through the opening.

Muriel followed right behind him, close enough to be all up in his metaphorical fig leaves.

I crawled on my hands and knees into the cave. After a few feet, the passage opened up enough that I could stand.

Muriel spoke a few words in Angelic, and a glowing orb appeared above her, casting warm light over smooth stone walls.

"What is this place?" asked Hazel.

"Once, these caves were used by the Templars," said Adonis. "They built them as a place to worship the gods in secret. If the Inquisition had found these temples, they would have burned the Templars."

"Like they did in France," added Muriel.

My eyes roamed over the carvings on the walls—the Angelic script and alchemical symbols—stars, kings, two men riding a horse.

As we walked deeper into the caves, the walls became rougher and the pictures more primitive. The carvings changed—no longer words, but now thorny vines and gnarled boughs of trees, the lines increasingly crude and violent. Somehow, it seemed like we were walking back in time.

In these ancient caverns, a shiver rippled over me. Kratos had chosen an isolated place for this meeting point.

"You're sure he doesn't want to trap us here?" I whispered.

"We had to take a risk," said Adonis. "He insisted on meeting on his terms."

"Sure," I said. "That doesn't sound suspicious at all."

"I thought you had goddess powers," said Muriel.

"Yep." *It's just that they'll kill me, so I'm not eager to use them.*

"Anyway," Muriel continued. "If I know anything about Kratos, it's that he's serious about having the horseman curse removed. The man has been desperate to make love to a woman for thousands of years. Only you can make that happen."

"What an honor," I said. "I'm like a cosmic wingman."

At last, the tunnel opened into a large cavern, and my heart sped up at the sight of Kratos. He stood alone, his coppery wings swooping behind him. Always, at the first sight of Kratos, I had the strongest urge to drop to my knees, his power of conquest washing over me. I wanted to lower my eyes, to sink to the ground. Still, I fought the urge, forcing myself to keep his gaze.

The candlelight wavered over his masculine features, his eyes blazing like sunlight.

It took me a moment to realize that someone else had come with him—Elan, the fae servant from his castle. Elan smiled at me, nervously tugging on the hem of his cat sweater. I smiled back at him. With tension thick in the air, it felt good to see a friendly face.

"Kratos," said Adonis. His dark magic whipped around him with an air of menace. I had to wonder if he did that on purpose, like a cat raising his hackles to seem more threatening. "I received your missive."

"Do you have news about Aereus and Johnny?" asked Kratos.

Adonis shook his head. "Only that they've joined forces at Sadeckrav Castle. Are you committed to joining an alliance with us?

As allies, we might be able to combat the other horsemen while Ruby fights the Heavenly Host. As soon as we find them."

Kratos stared at me. "Remove the curse from me, and I'm on your side."

I tried not to think about the fact that if I pulled his curse off him, the first thing he'd be doing was trying to get laid. That was his own business.

I took a step closer to him, letting my gaze become unfocused until I could see the dark magic of the curse writhing around his neck. "Are you ready for this?"

"I'm stiff with anticipation."

I narrowed my eyes. Was it just me, or was that a double entendre?

"I'm ready to thrust myself deeply into my new life," he continued. "Until I reach the fulfillment I've always been seeking."

He *had* to be doing this on purpose. He looked dead serious, though.

I pushed those thoughts out of my mind and stared at the magic swirling around his neck. With the curse removed, Kratos would no longer have to follow the demands of the Heavenly Host—to hunt humans, to force them into submission. He'd no longer have to worry about falling from grace if he indulged in pleasure.

In short, I had the power to free him completely.

The stones in my forehead began to warm, and the ancient power of the Old Gods began to thrum over my body as I prepared to pull the curse off him.

Except—another, otherworldly power was mingling with my own. A deep, uncontrolled rage built in my chest, making it hard for me to focus. My stomach growled as hunger joined in with fury, starvation and wrath mingling together into primal hangriness.

This meant only one thing. Aereus and Johnny—our enemies— were nearby.

I should've known Kratos would betray us.

I whirled around, meeting Adonis's gaze. "They're here. The others."

Already, Adonis was pulling the sword from his scabbard, the blade glinting in the torchlight. I unslung my bow, nocking an arrow, my grip tense on the bowstring.

Except, as I lifted my bow, my skull filled with a cacophony of voices—angelic voices that echoed inside my mind, confusing my own thoughts. I couldn't remember what I needed to do. The arrow clattered harmlessly on the ground.

From one of the tunnels behind Kratos, angels rushed into the cavern, swords raised. Each of them was chanting in their infernal Angelic language. As they did, rock began to rain from the ceiling. The ground shifted and jerked beneath my feet, and the carvings on the walls seemed to come to life, snapping through the air.

Angelic was the language of creation, and they were using it to mess with us, big time.

Chaos rampaged through my skull until I could no longer hear my own thoughts. Flanking me, Adonis and Kratos were adding their own Angelic chants, bending the universe to their wills. Unfortunately, they were bending my mind with it. Drakon swooped above us, his screeches reverberating in the cavern, adding to the tumult.

For a moment, we were horribly outnumbered. Then, a low growl rumbled across the cavern, and darkness fell. Adonis's dark magic whispered around us, and shadows consumed the cave.

Shouts rang out and light sparked as angels tried to fight the darkness. I dropped to my knees, my hands over my ears, dimly aware of the sounds of clashing swords clanging above the Angelic clatter. Something slithered against my skin, and I opened my eyes to find vines from the walls—come to life and curling around my body like pythons.

The stones in my forehead began to warm up. The magic of the Old Gods simmered in my body, giving me a little strength. I just couldn't let them overwhelm me.... For just a moment, the chaos in my skull went quiet as the light inside me built. *Sweet relief.*

Then, with a burst of strength, I ripped the vines off me. My canines began to lengthen, hands twisting, becoming claws, adrenaline racing through my veins. Feral Ruby was coming out to play, and she was angry as hell.

An angel was upon me, his perfect features twisted in hate, wings spread wide. His sword arced down. I shifted sideways, fast as a snake. I let out a bestial snarl as I pulled my dagger from my belt, thrusting, moving with the blade. It plunged into the angel's belly. His eyes widened in surprise and fear. When I pulled out the dagger, I felt it scrape the angel's ribs. He fell, his wings twisted and broken underneath. He struggled to raise his sword, blood trickling from his lips. I licked my dagger's blade, then kicked him in the face. He gasped, the sword dropping to the ground.

A wild roar escaped my throat, and I snatched his sword from the ground. The next thing I knew, I was carving my blade through the vines that had trapped another fae—an important one. My sister? Instinct compelled me to free her. The hacked vines dropped from her limbs, and I watched her run away from me.

I tried to think clearly through the haze of my mind, and I whirled to look for my enemy. Wrath consumed me, and I wanted blood. My sword clashed with an angel's, and the music of the Old Gods whispered through my blood, urging me to slaughter the invasive species. *Drive the angels from the earth. Reclaim it for us.*

Somewhere, under the fog of fury, the real Ruby screamed. She wasn't quite in control anymore.

CHAPTER 3

J scanned the cavern. Among the chaos of warring angels, I was looking for my prey—one of the leaders. It took a moment until my gaze landed on the starving one—the one who filled my gut with a gnawing sense of emptiness. The Horseman of Famine.

His eyes widened at the sight of me. Scared. Good. My hunter's instincts roared at the smell of his fear. I needed to cut my way through the other enemies in order to get to him.

I pushed my way through the throng. The angels surrounded me, but they didn't fight well in the cramped space of the cavern. They tried to swing their swords, to spread their wings, impossible moves when bodies are squeezed and mashed together. This was a place to fight dirty. To claw, and bite, and scratch. To fight like a beast. Perfect for me.

I left the sword behind me, carving with the knife. Somewhere along the way, I found a jagged rock, dripping blood. Not mine.

Someone was laughing hysterically. Me, I thought. *The death of angels brings me joy.*

Or was it … *The Angel of Death brings me joy…?* I wasn't sure which thought made sense.

The Old Gods' light beamed from my ribs, blazing over the cavern. Their magic wanted me to reclaim Paradise. *Kill them all....*

Only problem was, the light magic wanted to drive me from the earth, too. As the magic built inside me, I could feel it tearing cracks in me. It was splintering my ribs, power rising in a wild crescendo. My body was going to explode.

The Horseman of Famine lifted a bow and arrow, but his hands were shaking too much to aim it properly. My magic was affecting him. He shrieked, smoke rising from his starved body. He was trying to save himself, screaming something at me.

Still, I couldn't hear him over the screaming in my own mind. This wasn't right. A creature like me—a beast—was never meant to use divine magic, and it would kill me to use it.

An arrow pierced my flesh, and the sharp stab of pain snapped me out of my haze.

With the agony, the Old Gods' magic began to dim, and I clutched my chest. Even with the pain gripping my body, I was relieved to be free of that powerful force. That shit did *not* feel right.

Johnny loosed another arrow, but I knocked it off its trajectory with a surge of light magic. Instead of hitting me in the heart, it struck me in the shoulder.

I slammed against the rocky earth. Agony rippled down my body. I gritted my teeth, trying to block out the pain. And yet the pain was doing its job, sharpening my mind further as I lay on the ground, clutching my shoulder. I tightened my jaw. Now, the whole situation was crystal clear to me, and it was not ideal.

Johnny was aiming another arrow at me. If it hit my heart, I'd die. I tried to summon the concentration to unleash another surge of light magic, but the fucker had used iron-tipped arrows, and the metal sapped my powers, poisoning my blood. Our eyes met, and I saw death.

A shriek pierced the air, and Drakon swooped down, knocking Johnny off his perch. I grunted with agony and tore one of the arrows from my body, nearly fainting from the pain. But I couldn't have the iron poisoning my body further. Blood gushed from the open wound. From the ground, I glanced around frantically, looking for my lover.

There!

He was standing up, searching for me. My movements were sluggish, I was dizzy from pain. I couldn't hide, couldn't rush to him. At any second—

Just then, I felt a tingle on the back of my neck. Adonis's dark magic whispered over my skin, soothing the pain. The shadows became thicker around me, giving me cover from the arrows. Shaking, I pushed up onto my hands and knees, sucking in ragged breaths. I crawled away from Johnny.

A burst of light flashed in the cave—one of the angels fighting back against Adonis's shadows. A volley of arrows soared overhead before darkness fell again. Like an animal crawling off to die, I dragged myself into a dark corner of the cave. Pebbles bit into my palms and knees until I leaned against a wall.

Johnny's voice echoed off the cave—Cockney-tinged Angelic spells—and Adonis's dark magic dissipated like smoke.

Raw pain arced through my body once more. I fell back against the wall. Flames rose all around the cave—the angels trying to smoke us out.

In the dancing light of the fire, I could see Adonis locked in a swordfight with Aereus, but I couldn't see my sister through the flames.

"Hazel!" I shouted.

I tried yanking the remaining arrow out of my shoulder, but my hands were shaking too badly. *I can't stand up.*

"Hazel!" I shrieked, panic rising. I couldn't find her.

Flames rose around me, illuminating the cave, and high-pitched screams echoed off the cavern walls. In the smoky haze, I blinked at the sight of an angelic mob pulling Muriel though the dirt—her body beaten, bloodied. A broken bone jutted from her chest, and her head lolled. If she was human, she'd be dead.

I could hear Kratos roaring with fury, glimpsed him briefly slicing his sword through an angel.

Through the chaos of blood and flames, I caught another glimpse of Adonis. His sword clashed with Aereus's. I gasped as I caught sight of Johnny—an arrow trained on Adonis from behind.

"Adonis!" I shouted, trying to move across the cave.

I tried standing, but a stray arrow slammed me in the leg. I screamed, certain my femur was splintering.

When I looked up again, Johnny had already unleashed an arrow, piercing Adonis's heart. Drakon's shrieks were ear-splitting, as if he could feel his master's pain. Horror slammed into me. We were losing.

Get up, Ruby. Godsdamn it, get up.

Pain shot through my body, but I pushed myself up. This wasn't happening. I couldn't let them take Adonis from here. The Devil's Bane on Johnny's arrow had already worked its way into his system, blood staining his clothes, his eyes losing focus.

I shuffled forward, determined to get to him. Aereus—Horseman of War—lifted Adonis from under his shoulders and began dragging Death's body from the cavern. The poison-tipped arrow protruded from Adonis's chest.

I let out a scream of anger and bloodlust, and rushed after them, but a cluster of angels blocked my way. No, not a cluster. A legion. I would plow through them all. I would.

Someone grabbed my wrist. Snarling, I raised my dagger, about to thrust it into the bastard's neck.

"Ruby!" Kratos roared at me. "We're pulling back!"

"No!"

"Your sister needs you." He waved at her. Hazel was lying on the ground, blinking, confused, blood running from her temple.

Tears of frustration blurred my vision as I hurried to her, helping her stand.

"Through there!" Kratos shouted at me, pointing to a side cavern.

I began to shuffle in the direction of the opening, stumbling, Hazel groaning with pain. A group of angels detached from the host, rushing for us. There were at least a dozen. I was dizzy, weak, desperate.

Kratos raised his sword, his wings spread wide, and lunged at them. The Horseman of Conquest laid waste around him, his sword carving through wings, limbs, and bodies. I turned away, pulling Hazel through the small opening.

And then—darkness.

* * *

WHEN I WOKE, an angel stood over me, his head haloed by the moon. It took me a moment to realize it was Kratos. Anger slammed into me. The bastard had betrayed us.

Hadn't he?

I pushed myself up onto my elbows, and my chest felt like it was fracturing. It took me a moment to realize the screaming I heard was my own.

Kratos held up a hand. "Easy there. I only took the arrows out a few hours ago."

I clutched my collarbone. Kratos might have pulled the arrows out, but the iron had worked its way into my bloodstream. I felt like I'd been run over by a train. "What's happening, you traitorous fuck?" I gasped. "Where's Hazel?"

"Calm down. She's sleeping." He nodded to his right. "She's fine."

Wincing, I turned my head. She lay in the dirt, curled up by a bonfire. Her chest slowly rose and fell. Elan slept next to her, his gentle snores floating through the air.

"I'm not the enemy," said Kratos.

Maybe. Unlikely.

I'd seen the other angels drag Adonis and Muriel out. What had become of them? A sharp pang of protectiveness welled in my chest. Adonis was the Angel of Death, but I still wanted to keep him safe, and I'd failed. If anyone hurt him, I'd smash their heads into the rocky earth. And right now, Kratos seemed like enemy number one. Probably.

I clenched my jaw. I wasn't exactly in a position to fight right now, but it didn't stop the fury. "You led us into a trap. Johnny and Aereus took Adonis, didn't they?"

His eyes gleamed in the darkness. "I have no idea where they came from. If I'd planned this, do you really think you'd still be here? You were their target. It's why they brought iron. You're the only one who can kill them. The capture of Adonis is just a way to get to you."

None of this made sense. "So how did the other horsemen know about this specific location, then? They knew exactly where we were." As much as I hated Muriel, I didn't think she'd been the leak. I'd seen them drag her battered body out of the place.

"I don't know," said Kratos. "Spies, probably. Watching your movements."

I shook my head. "We took a secure route here. I didn't see any sentinels or cherubs, and believe me, I'm conditioned to notice them."

"I traveled underground, so they wouldn't have seen me."

I glared at him. I was almost certain he'd betrayed us, but I wasn't going to get him to admit it right now. I needed to keep a level head. "Where's Drakon?"

"I have no idea." He didn't really seem to care, either.

Blocking out the sharp pain, I scanned my surroundings. We had camped out in an oak grove. Of the six of us who'd met in the cavern, only four remained. I had a hard time believing either Hazel or Elan had given up our location, which meant Kratos was just playing along with this charade, concealing his real plans.

For now, I'd keep my suspicions to myself. If I was going to uncover the truth, I'd need Kratos to let down his guard.

A wave of dizziness and nausea washed over me, and my head fell back against the earth. The last thing I saw before I lost consciousness again was a faint gleam of moonlight silvering Kratos's unearthly copper wings.

CHAPTER 4

$\mathcal{I}$ woke in a four-poster bed, moonlight streaming through the windows. I had vague memories of a journey: the scent of cedar wrapped around me, wings rhythmically beating the air as the wind rushed over my body. I'd been flying in Kratos's arms.

Pain still pierced my body. I wanted nothing more than to lie flat on the pillows, minimizing the pain, but I needed to figure out what was going on. When I was a kid, I'd competed in gymnastics tournaments. My dad had been a little intense about it—the only parent screaming on the sidelines. Now, whenever I had to push myself, his voice boomed in my head. *Don't get complacent, Ruby.*

Grimacing, I pushed myself up to look around me. Stone room, tapestries glorifying war, the four-poster bed—I was back in Kratos's castle.

One of the tall, peaked windows was open, and wisteria vines had climbed through it, spreading across the floor like an outstretched hand reaching for me. I lifted my arm, and the vine seemed to strain for me. For the first time, I felt as if I could *hear* the music of the vines—a faint humming. The sound of the spirit that lived within it.

I strained my eyes in the dim light, examining the rest of the room.

Faint, golden light glowed around the doorknob. Angelic magic. If I had to guess, Kratos had locked me in here.

I clutched my chest. This was the first time I'd been here without Adonis, and his absence felt like a hole between my ribs.

Could he still hear my thoughts? I had no idea, and I'd never been able to hear back from him. I breathed deeply, trying to think calmly.

Adonis? I'm going to come for you. Wherever you are.

That was assuming I could get past Kratos and get out of here. What the hell was his plan? Maybe he wanted to take the Bringer of Light out of the equation and join forces with the Heavenly Host. Maybe I was supposed to be his first sexual conquest after I pulled the curse from him.

I had no idea. Whatever the case, I had to get out of here. I might have to kill Kratos, break Hazel free from her imprisonment, and get us the hell out of Hotemet. Find my way to Adonis.

But before I could piece together anything resembling a coherent plan, the doorknob began to turn.

The door creaked open, and my body tensed.

When Hazel's crown of wild black hair poked into the room, I loosed a breath.

"What the hell is going on?" I whispered.

Hazel didn't look particularly concerned about anything. In fact, she was holding a tray of steaming food. My stomach rumbled. Already, my gaze was roaming over the roast chicken and mashed potatoes.

"I'm bringing you dinner," said Hazel. "Thought you'd be hungry."

"Yeah I am, but … why am I locked in this room? And why don't you seem concerned about it?"

"What do you mean?"

"I can see the magic on the door."

Hazel glanced at the golden light pulsing around the doorknob. "Oh, that? It's not locking you in. It's keeping out anyone but me and him. He doesn't want Johnny coming in to pick your bones out of your body."

I grimaced. "Does everyone know about this bone picking thing?"

Despite the topic of conversation, my muscles began to relax. I still didn't trust Kratos, but at least he hadn't trapped me in here against my will. At least, not this time.

I tried to sit up completely, but the ache in my chest had me flat on the pillows again within seconds. "Hazel. This is serious."

"What?"

"I'm gonna need you to feed me that chicken," I said. "And the mashed potatoes, too."

"Ugh, fine."

I heard the sound of a knife scraping against the plate. The next moment, a speared piece of chicken hovered above my mouth. I chewed it thoughtfully, trying to figure out what the hell had happened to us in the Templar cave. A silence fell over the room.

Hazel wouldn't have leaked the info, would she? I mean—she'd said some things about how we were better off being ruled by the horsemen. After her time with the dragons, she'd come back a totally different person than she used to be. Hazel thought that you should always choose the winning side of a war, no matter what the costs. But she wouldn't have turned on her own sister.

Right?

"Are you worried about Adonis?" she asked.

"Yes. I know he won't die. I'm the only one who can kill him. But I don't want to think about what Aereus the Angel of Torture might be doing with him." In my current state, I wouldn't be able to rescue him, and I didn't want to lose my mind imagining the worst. "I'm going to get him as soon as I can."

"I don't think that will be anytime soon."

Was I the only one who saw the danger we were in? Every day that we let pass was another day the Heavenly Host could come out of hiding and slaughter the rest of the earth's inhabitants. And we didn't even know where to find them. "We don't have much time to fuck around, Hazel. I don't know what the angelic horde is planning, but it's not going to be pretty."

Hazel shoveled a forkful of mashed potatoes into my mouth, and I studied her. Her blasé attitude was a little concerning.

What if Kratos and Hazel were working together? Maybe they were both lying to me, keeping me here until they could take over the world, along with Famine and War.

Ugh. Speaking of losing my mind, I would probably drive myself nuts imagining all the possible scenarios that might destroy the world.

I needed to keep a clear head and speak to Yasmin. It had been far too long since I'd gotten in touch with my handler from the Institute. We could exchange information, and she could help me figure out exactly how to ferret out the leak. Maybe the Institute even had some information I could use.

As soon as I physically could, I'd haul my broken body out of bed and find a way to contact her. I wasn't going to get complacent here in my comfortable bed.

* * *

Night had fallen in the garden.

A beautiful man approached me—completely naked. His hair hung to his shoulders, and moonlight washed over his perfect body. I recognized him from somewhere—from the statue at Adonis's castle. Azazeyl, the original fallen angel.

He handed me a grape, and I ate it. The sweet, tangy juice burst in my mouth, and as it did, chaos erupted in my mind. My own voice echoed off the inside of my skull—screaming about death, until I no longer knew who I was or what I was doing here. The world collapsed into chaos around me.

My own scream ripped me from my sleep.

I gasped, trying to sit up, but my body still wasn't quite there yet. I'd come a little too close to dying from an iron arrow to the heart, and my mind wasn't letting me forget it. The door slammed open, and I lifted my head just enough to see Kratos rush into the room in a blur of copper.

"What's happening?" he demanded.

To a thousand-year-old horseman of the apocalypse, "I had a bad dream" probably sounded a bit lame. "Just, uh … just the pain from the arrow wounds. I rolled on my ribs funny."

A brusque nod. "Oh."

I narrowed my eyes at him. The timing of the ambush had been interesting. The other horsemen had busted in right before I could remove his curse—almost as if he was still working with the Heavenly Host, still committed to completing his sacred duty.

"Do you still want your curse removed?" I asked.

He sat at the edge of my bed, his weight compressing the mattress.

"Of course. But we will wait until you've had a chance to heal. The iron still courses through your blood."

How convenient. "Actually, I think I'm on the mend. I want to find Adonis as soon as I can." I could hardly sit up, but these were minor details.

Kratos frowned. "You're in no condition to travel. In any case, Adonis will be fine. The other horsemen can't kill him, and they'll want to use him."

"For what, exactly?"

"To trade for you and Hazel."

My chest tightened. "They want Hazel, too?"

"She's from the same bloodline as you. If you can harness the power of the Old Gods, so can she. But Adonis will be fine. I'm sure they'll torture him within an inch of his life, but—"

"Exactly why we're going after him as soon as we can."

"You can hardly move, Ruby."

Convenient, again. Angels had brought language to the earth. And along with language came the ability to lie.

Blocking out the pain, I forced myself up onto my elbows. "We're running out of time. There's a horde of angels who want to slaughter us and everything else on earth, and you don't seem particularly bothered about it. You know, I never saw who knocked me out." Just a hint of an accusation tinged my voice.

His eyes flared with gold. "What are you implying?"

"It's just interesting that my injuries mean that you have to keep the curse, just like the Heavenly Host would want, and we can't go after Adonis." I'd planned to play it cool, but in the dead of night, with the pain wracking my body, I was kind of failing at that.

"If you want to pull the curse from me now instead of in the morning, be my guest."

I gritted my teeth, forcing myself to sit up as agony danced up my spine. "It doesn't hurt that much," I said defensively.

Kratos touched his heart—maybe unconsciously reminded of his own pain. His heart hurt when he didn't hunt humans like he was supposed to.

If I took his curse away, all that would change.

"How does this work, exactly?" he asked.

"I just need to see the curse around your throat. It looks like black vines. Then, I'll pull them from you."

He arched his neck, and I let my eyes linger over his throat. The stones in my forehead began to warm up, and I stared as the ropes of dark, thorny magic began to writhe around his skin. The invasive magic of the heavens.

Instinctively, I reached for them. I stroked the magic vines with the tip of my finger, scraping it across the thorns. Blue light beamed from my fingertips. At the touch, a powerful jolt of ecstasy raced through my hand, arcing up my arm and blazing into my chest.

I gasped, my back arching as euphoria surged. This magic wasn't splitting my body apart. Instead, it was doing something entirely different and somewhat mortifying to my body. There was something sexual about this magic, and my body warmed, thighs clenching under the sheets.

My eyes opened. I stared at Kratos's neck, watching the seal dissipate like dark smoke. I was panting, a thin sheen of sweat on my body.

Kratos's body had gone rigid, his back arched, and golden light radiated from his chest. His fiery gaze met mine, and I tried to ignore what this meant—Kratos could now bone with impunity.

He closed his eyes again, as if in prayer. "Your magic fingertips have stroked me to perfection."

"You're doing that on purpose, aren't you?"

He didn't answer, seemingly lost in his own thoughts. His eyes were still closed, hand on his heart—the very part of his body that had tormented him for a thousand years.

After a few moments, he met my gaze again with a reverent look. "Free," he said quietly. He looked down at his chest, his brow furrowed. "After a thousand years, I control my fate now. I will kill only when I want to. The things that I've done…."

His voice trailed off.

I almost felt bad for the guy. Unless he had betrayed us, and then I wanted him to die a painful death.

"It's over now," I said quietly. "You're free. Like you said."

The back of my neck throbbed, and I rubbed it. The blast of magic from the Old Gods had dulled some of my pain, but it hadn't healed me completely. Only Adonis seemed to have that power.

I studied Kratos closely. Maybe he'd wanted the curse pulled from him, but I still didn't trust him.

"How much time?" I asked.

"Till what?"

"How much time do you think we have until we all die?"

"That's anyone's guess. None of us knows what the Heavenly Host are doing, or where they are."

"Well, someone is going to have to find out."

CHAPTER 5

Three days. That was all it had taken for me to heal—at least enough so that I could haul my broken ass out of bed. My ribs and shoulder still hurt like hell, but I could put one foot in front of another.

I might have the power of the Old Gods, but I wasn't immortal. The fae had long lives, but we were still mortal creatures. And damned if I hadn't felt that mortality when the iron arrows had slammed into me. Still, I was pretty sure the gemstones were helping me recover faster.

Last night, Drakon had arrived at Hotemet, carrying a piece of stone Kratos had identified. A sand-colored chunk of Sadeckrav Castle.

Assuming we could trust this form of primitive communication, we needed to take a little trip across the English Channel. It seemed Adonis was in the torture palace, just like I'd feared. But I needed a plan before I rushed over the English Channel to France. I didn't want to screw up this rescue.

With the morning sun filtering through the leaves, I followed the winding path through the forest, moving as quickly as my battered body would take me. I hadn't seen a single sentinel out here this morning. Had they deserted Kratos since I removed the curse from his neck, ripping away his apocalyptic seal? Whatever the case, it definitely made it easier to move around without them.

My feet crunched over the leaves, and the crisp February air felt cool against my skin. That morning, I'd summoned Yasmin through a few flicks of the candle in the bathroom mirror. I hadn't spoken to her in weeks, but if anyone could help me develop a plan to rescue Adonis, it was her.

As I walked, I closed my eyes. I tried to block out the rising panic—that little, niggling fear that the Heavenly Host would murder the world's entire population at any moment. I tried to tune out the dark visions of the torments Adonis might be enduring. Panic was the enemy of strategy.

I breathed in the scent of oaks. As I did, my mind flooded again with images of Eden—grape vines curling up a fig tree, a gleaming blue river winding between thorny shrubs—a crooked cottage, where Adonis sat by a roaring fireplace....

I opened my eyes, stunned for a moment to find this vision alive around me—the fig trees standing where oaks had been, purple thistle instead of deadfall, a rushing azure river. A cottage stood among the trees.

Holy shit. The gemstones seemed to have intensified my powers of glamouring. I'd created the illusion of Paradise. As I stared at the vision around me, euphoria rippled over my body.

I blinked, and the illusion disappeared before my eyes. I hadn't even realized it was possible to glamour the world around me. I'd glamoured other people before—sentient beings. Never objects, and definitely not an entire landscape.

I stared down at my fingertips. So, I could now create an illusion out of thin air. I concentrated on the space above my fingertips, trying to conjure the illusion of a butterfly. Warm magic flickered over my forehead, tingling along my arms. For just a moment, something winged and pumpkin-orange burst into the air, before the illusion shattered.

I clenched my fists, no longer sure if I was creating illusions or just straight up hallucinating.

I bit my lip, remembering what I'd seen that morning. When I'd woken, light was streaming through the windows—and along with it, the vines from outside the castle had worked their way into the room, snaking over the floor toward my bed. I kept feeling as if the forest were straining for me.

Unless, of course, I was just losing my mind. Maybe a fae like me was never meant for this godlike power. Maybe it would make me insane.

I hugged myself, walking along the winding path again. As I moved deeper into the woods, my thoughts kept returning to that perfect Garden of Eden, and I was sure I could hear the song of the Old Gods whispering through the back of my mind.

"Eden…" I whispered to myself. "The perfect paradise."

I clenched my fists until my fingernails bit into my palms. You know what else was the enemy of strategy? Fantasizing about damn gardens. *Stay focused, Ruby.*

When I reached the grove of mulberry trees—overgrown with hellebore and cockle weeds—I knew I was nearly at the meeting spot. And when I spotted the mouth of the pine-flanked cave that was our meeting point, I sped up my pace. Yasmin and I had to make a plan, *stat*.

I crossed into the dank cavern, where I found the her—the Queen of Poisons.

Yasmin's dark eyes were wide in the dim light. "Well, well. It's been a while, Agent Hudole." She stared at the stones in my forehead. "What in the gods' names are those things in your head?"

I touched them gently. "Yeah. I guess we didn't get to update you about this yet. I stole these from one of the Old Gods, who I found in a cave in Lebanon when I was trying to raise one of the horsemen from the dead. And now they're in my forehead, and I think they might be messing with my thoughts a little."

Her eyes widened. "You did *what?*"

"I accidentally raised the horsemen from the dead after stealing gemstones from the gods," I repeated, trying to act blasé. "I think you'll agree this situation could have happened to anyone."

Something like rage tightened her features. "Slow down. The horsemen were dead? And you brought them back?"

How did I explain to her that I couldn't just let Adonis die, that if she knew him like I did, she'd save him, too?

I traced my fingertips across the gemstones. "Look, the horsemen are at war with each other, and Adonis might be our only hope. Problem is, he's been abducted, and now the odds are against us. He and I were ambushed, and I'm going to need your help to get him back." My gaze flicked to the skies. "Look, we don't have a ton of time. The Heavenly Host are somewhere on earth, and we're all gonna die, like, any second, so...."

"You want to save the Horseman of Death. I'm not even sure what to say to you."

I let out a sigh. This was a hard sell, and I hadn't prepared well enough. "Adonis has been working against the other horsemen. His seal was never broken, and his curse never took hold. For thousands of years, he staved off the power of the curse by hurting himself. With the magic of the Old Gods, I was able to pull it from him. We *need* him to fight the other angels, or we don't stand a chance. The Heavenly Host are mortal on earth. Once we know where they are, he can kill them all in an instant."

"And what makes you think he would do that?"

"He's the one who helped me get the stones. He sacrificed his life so I could rid the earth of the horsemen. He's only here because I brought him back."

From there, we stood there in the cave for what seemed an eternity, arguing over Adonis until she reluctantly conceded I might have a point, that he *might* be a key to our survival.

"Maybe I will keep an open mind." Yasmin's dark eyes were fixed on me intently. "But don't rule anyone out as a leak. Hazel, Kratos, the fae boy—they're all suspects. Feed them false information, and see what they do with it. Find out which of them passes it on to the other angels. If you allow them to keep passing on information, we don't have a chance in hell of defeating the destructive angels."

"Like leaking a fake plan of attack?"

She shrugged. "That could work. Get your enemy to show up to a specific location. You'll know who leaked the information when you know where they show up."

Seemed simple enough. "Maybe I can do this at the same time I'm rescuing Adonis."

Yasmin crossed her arms. "When you go to Sadeckrav, I'm going with you. There's no way I'm letting you make decisions on your own at this point. Not with the stakes this high. I just need to find someone to look after my daughter, and we'll head off together. I want to make sure you don't cock it up this time."

I raised my eyebrows, not entirely sure I liked her tone. "You've lost a bit of faith in me, haven't you?"

"Like you said, we don't have time to mess around. The Heavenly Host have come to earth, and it's only a matter of time before they slaughter each and every one of us. And apart from your terrible decision-making, I'm not sure you're handling your new powers well."

"What makes you say that?"

"I saw you muttering to yourself as you approached me."

I crossed my arms. Okay, maybe I was losing my mind. "Right, come with me if you want. But what's important is that I want to get back to Adonis as soon as we can."

"Don't rule out Adonis as the traitor, either."

"What? No. He was captured, along with an asshole angel named Muriel."

She shrugged. "It could have been a ruse on his part. Maybe he and Muriel were in on it. What if you were the real target, and the plan simply failed?"

My throat tightened at the idea. I didn't want to argue the point too much. It would just make me seem biased. "Fine. Maybe it was Adonis. Any chance you have any good news to share? I could really use some right now."

"Perhaps. While the angels have been fighting amongst themselves, things have changed in the human cities. Humans have been organizing themselves into armies. They've formed a resistance. Your former rookery in Whitechapel is one of the command centers. While the Hunter no longer patrols the streets, they want to take the opportunity to rise up against the angels."

My eyebrows shot up. I'd been desperate to know what happened to Alex and my other rookery-mates. "Do you know who's involved?"

Yasmin nodded. "I've identified the leaders, but they don't trust the Institute. I'm working on making inroads."

I took a deep breath. "That Whitechapel rookery you mentioned."

"Yeah?"

"If you can find a man named Alex living among the resistance, I want to know how he's doing. And his friends, too." Adonis had taken them to a safe house out of the city after Johnny had nearly killed them, but it was possible they'd found their way back.

"I'll find out what I can, but they don't trust outsiders like me. The Institute has a bad reputation since we barred the Tower doors to most of London's population. Plus, people are more spooked than ever in the past few weeks."

I frowned. "Now? Why now? The Hunter is gone."

"People are afraid of what they don't understand. And right now, there's a new puzzle haunting London's streets."

"What's that?"

"Humans are dying, just like they have been for over a year now. Starvation, disease. Except now, their bodies are going missing. They're buried and dug up again. And no one knows why."

A cold shiver rippled over my spine. I had no idea what that meant, either, but it didn't sound wonderful. If I had to guess, humans might be eating the dead, and I was superstitious enough to believe that was a line that should never be crossed without inviting the wrath of the gods.

CHAPTER 6

oonlight washed over the darkened landscape. I stood before the window of my room, staring at an unlit candle.

To an outside observer, it may not have seemed the best use of time given our current, desperate situation, but I needed to test my new powers to see if I could use them. I wanted to create the illusion of a flame. I squinted my eyes, failing to spark anything before me.

A cool breeze filtered in through the open windows, rippling over my silk dress and raising goosebumps on my skin. The wild symphony of the Old Gods sang in the back of my mind.

I closed my eyes, imagining a flame dancing at the tip of the wick. When I opened them again, a spark of light burst into the air before dying out again.

Almost.

I still had time to work on this skill—assuming it had been real.

But right now, I had to speak to Hazel.

I pulled open the door, crossing into the hallway. I had a good idea where I could find my sister. As much as I'd tried to keep her away from the bar, it had become her favorite haunt.

I hated the idea of lying to Hazel, but I supposed Yasmin was right. I had to suspect everyone.

As expected, I found her sitting in the bar's shadows, nursing a bright blue cocktail by herself. She leaned back in her wooden bench, raising her glass. "Sister. You look better."

"Well, I was in bed for three days." I frowned at her cocktail. "Are you just helping yourself in here?"

She took a sip of the disturbingly fluorescent drink, ignoring my question. "Since you've recovered, does that mean we're going after Adonis?"

"I have a plan. But I'll need your reptilian friend to give us a ride to Sadeckrav Castle."

And here was the lie. A lie was no different to any other performance, right? *Put on a good show, Ruby.*

"And then what?" she asked.

"You can't tell *anyone* this. But Yasmin is connecting us with a demonic assassin named Balam. He's going to arrive, cloaked in darkness, at the Porte de Richelieu at the Louvre. He'll slaughter everyone in his path until he gets to Adonis."

"Just one demon?" she asked.

"He's a legendary assassin. That's all it will take."

"What kind of demon?"

She was asking for an awful lot of details, here. "An alû demon. He'll be completely stealthy."

"Interesting." She lifted her cocktail glass. "You want to stay for a drink? I call this the Apocalyptic Julep. It's three parts whiskey, one part vodka, some of the blue alcohol, and some other number of parts of that green stuff."

I gagged. "Midori?"

"I guess. What the fuck is a julep, anyway?"

"Not *that.*" I rose. As soon as I got the chance, I was going to throw all this alcohol away. But first—I had to move on to my second lie. "I can't stay for a drink. I need to get ready for our trip. Find Uthyr, and let him know we need to get to France."

* * *

I FOUND Elan in the kitchens, rolling out pastry dough on the countertop. Flour covered his sweatshirt, which featured a cartoon cat hanging from a tree and the words *Hang in There!*

Really, there was no way in hell Elan was a double agent, but I had to dot all my i's and cross all my t's.

A steaming Cornish pasty lay on the table, and my mouth watered. "Mind if I grab this?"

"Go for it." Elan's cheeks had their characteristic ruddy glow.

I bit into the rich beef and potato filling. *For the love of the gods, we can't lose Elan.*

"I need your help, Elan."

Shock lit up his features. "Mine?"

I nodded. "I want to get Adonis back from Sadeckrav Castle, and I'm gonna need a team."

"You want me to be part of your team?"

"I need people I can trust." I glanced furtively around me. "The truth is, I don't trust Kratos, and I want someone to keep an eye on him. Do you think you can do that?"

"Of course."

And here comes my next lie.

"Good. We're taking a flight on Uthyr tomorrow. Yasmin has hooked us up with a legendary shadow demon assassin. He'll be glamoured as an angel guard, and he'll waltz right into Aereus's main entrance." I bit my lip. "Just please don't tell anyone else of the plan. Not even Hazel or Kratos. I'm not sure I can trust them."

He smiled, his cheeks dimpling. "I'm honored to be part of your team."

* * *

BEFORE I EVEN GOT TO the Celestial Room in the Tower of Silence, the rich smell of cedar wafted through the halls, curling around my body. Goosebumps rose on my skin, and I wasn't sure if it was from the drafty castle air that skimmed over my silky dress, or the raw power I often felt emanating from Kratos whenever I got anywhere near him.

On the top floor of the Tower of Silence, two armored guards stood before a heavy wooden door. Without a word, they shifted aside, and the doors swung open.

Under a large glass dome, Kratos moved over the floor, carving his sword through the air. He was shirtless, and silver light washed over his chiseled muscles. A faint sheen of sweat covered his body, and he seemed to be fighting invisible attackers with a level of viciousness usually reserved for virgin night at the vampire ball.

Unless he lost his mind completely, I had a feeling that once he finally found his way out of his castle, the man would have no problems finding someone to stroke him to perfection.

Perfection ... a perfect paradise....

For a moment, the hollows of my mind flashed with vivid images —a cottage in a garden by a river's edge, the leaves outside tinged with autumn gold. Adonis, sat at table before a roaring fire, with a bowl of soup in his lap.

Paradise.

Distracted, I stumbled. My phantom life—the one with the cottage and the soup—had somehow seemed more real than what was actually going on now. I blinked, and it took me a moment to realize I was still in the Celestial Room, with a shirtless horseman of the apocalypse. These gemstones were really fucking with me.

Kratos stared at me, lowering his sword. His body looked rigid with tension. "Are you all right?"

I clenched my jaw. "Yes, why?"

"You don't seem yourself." He lifted his sword again for another brutal slash through the air.

"Neither do you. Working off a little tension, are we?"

Slash. "I have a lot on my mind right now. What's your excuse?"

I brushed my fingertips over the gemstones in my forehead. "Just getting used to my new powers, I think. They can overwhelm my thoughts." I wasn't about to tell him about my new ability to conjure illusions out of thin air, but it was obvious something had changed about me. "I have to resist their influence, I think."

In fact, I had to resist my own intense fantasies.

He lowered his sword, but his knuckles had gone white on the hilt. "Resisting urges is something that I understand well."

True—a thousand years of abstinence couldn't have been easy. "How did you manage it?"

He closed the distance between us, his golden eyes piercing in the darkness. "When the temptations of the flesh began to lure me in, when a beautiful woman's body and her scent drew me closer, I would remember my mother's death. It killed my ardor."

It *did* sound like a mood killer. "What happened to your mother?"

"She was a Viking warrior. A shield maiden. She was captured during a raid in Britain and burned to death for witchcraft. I was only eleven. It wasn't a fast death, either." His eyes took on a faraway look. "But her dreams for me were clear—that I fulfill my destiny when the time came." He met my eyes again, his gaze sharpening. "I'm afraid I would have disappointed her."

I didn't say what I was really thinking—that it was a cruel thing for her to ask, and she sounded like a shitty mother.

He closed his eyes, running his hand over his heart. "When I thought I might give in to the temptations of the flesh, I thought of her dying body. I thought of the curse that the Heavenly Host placed on humans—the curse of anticipating mortality. My mother knew she was going to die, and thinking of that killed my cravings."

So Kratos could be a bit of a downer. And clearly, he was having something of a hard time adjusting to his new, curseless life. Was he regretting it?

I cocked my head. "And after all those years resisting temptations, what made you change your mind? Why did you want the curse removed?"

"Because I never asked for this. My destiny will be my choice. I am Conquest, and I control my fate. Not the memory of my mother. Not the Heavenly Host. No one but me."

Reasonable. Unfortunately, I wasn't sure his method would work for me. If I summoned my worst memories, they'd drive me insane: my mother's torn arm after I'd savaged her in one of my feral states; Marcus being slaughtered before my eyes; Adonis, after I'd killed him. I was already fighting madness as it was.

He looked me over slowly. "You've made a rather amazing recovery."

"I have. And I'm ready to go after Adonis now."

Slash. "I haven't come up with a plan yet. Like I said. I've been distracted."

And also, you don't really care that much if Adonis is tortured within an inch of his life. "What if I have a plan?"

Slash. "You? What's your plan?"

"The Institute is on our side. I've met with one of their agents. She's offered sending us an assassin, who I will glamour as a cherub. He's going to sneak right in to the Porte des Lions entrance. Just— don't tell anyone else. I'm not sure I can trust anyone. Not even Hazel."

He pivoted, his sword carving a ferocious arc. "And when do you plan to travel?"

"Tomorrow. I want you to come."

"Fine." A hint of anger laced his tone.

The stones in my forehead began to heat up. *Rid the earth of the angels...*

I clamped down on the voice in my mind, but the sentiment remained. If Kratos betrayed us, I would use my new powers to end him, fast.

CHAPTER 7

I wrapped my arms tightly around Kratos's neck, while strands of my red hair whipped in front of my eyes. As we soared over the English Channel, the briny scent of the sea whispered through the air. I carried my bow and arrow on my back, and a poison-tipped knife at my belt. I hardly went anywhere without my weapons these days.

Just above our flight path, Uthyr carried Elan, Yasmin, and Hazel on his back.

Yasmin had insisted that everyone come. If we found out one of them was a traitor, she wanted them dealt with. Fast.

Except—no matter what Hazel might have done, I wouldn't let anyone touch her.

Exhausted, I blinked my eyes, fighting to stay awake. Last night, I'd spent hours in one of Kratos's libraries with the curtains closed. I'd needed time to practice my new illusion-conjuring skills. Instead of sleeping, I'd managed to summon a menagerie of creatures inspired by the medieval books and tapestries I'd found: cats with weirdly human faces, men with arrows up their butts, medieval rabbits who stood on their hind legs and wielded swords, knights fighting giant snails....

I'd learned two things. One, medieval artists were into some weird shit.

And two, the key to creating illusions was to turn off my thoughts. I had to summon the images vividly in my mind's eye. Then, they'd simply appear around me. But if any amount of chatter started flowing in my mind, it ruined the whole thing. The illusion would pop like a bubble before me. Basically, I had to get all Zen.

After a night of practice, I was *pretty* sure I'd be able to summon the illusions I needed.

"Can you glamour all of us?" Kratos's voice was low in my ear. "At least make us less noticeable?"

I nodded. It was time to go into stealth mode. I closed my eyes, summoning a glamour of unobtrusiveness.

By the time we reached Paris, it felt like we'd been flying for days. In synch with the dragon, we swooped lower over the city.

I gazed below at an encampment in one of Paris's parks. Tangerine rays of light slanted over a park dotted with tents and fire pits. Small gardens for growing food spread below me, and children wandered among them. I watched a dark-haired toddler sitting by his mother stuff his face with what might be mashed potatoes. Here, even among all the death of the Great Nightmare, life was thriving. And if we didn't stop the horsemen, all this would turn to ash.

* * *

We stood in the Jardin des Tuileries among the dead trees, staring at the Louvre. Outside the main entrances to the old palace, a few cherubs milled around with angelic soldiers.

Now, all I had to do was create my illusions and find out if one of my team had passed on the information to Aereus.

I met Yasmin's gaze, and she nodded curtly. She was the only one here I hadn't lied to, the only one who actually knew what was about to happen.

I stared at the palace before us—the pale golden stone, ruddied by the setting sun. *Adonis, I'm coming for you.*

What had Aereus done to him in his palace? I couldn't think about the torture garden, the Catherine wheel—

Stop.

I swallowed hard. I needed my mind to go quiet if I was going to get this to work.

Hazel nudged me. "Where is the assassin?" she whispered.

I shot her a fierce look. "Shhhh."

Adonis, are you here? I felt a warm, tingling tug on my shoulder—the exact place where Adonis had marked me. He was here. Even if I couldn't hear him now, I could feel him.

Let your mind go quiet, Ruby.

I took a deep breath, focusing on stilling the chatter in my brain. I closed my eyes, imagining Eden before the fall—before language ruined everything for everyone.

Sunlight streamed through the fig trees, and a deep blue river rushed through it all. My back arched as my body surged with a power older than words. *Paradise.*

And in my mind's eye, I conjured the three assassins—a wisp of darkness at the Porte de Richelieu for Hazel, a cherub at the Porte des Lions for Kratos. And for Elan, an angelic soldier marching for the main entrance.

I opened my eyes again and smiled as I watched my creations crossing the stone piazza. Slowly, I scanned the others in my group— each of them watching the entrance I'd told them about.

As my glamour worked, my body surged with a song of ancient magic, my skin tingling. I stared as one of the entrances burst open, giving away our informant. Dozens of angels streamed out, swords drawn, to surround my illusion, and shock slammed into me.

They'd been expecting him. I made him turn and run, sprinting away from them, and they followed the illusion in hot pursuit. A stream of angel soldiers rushed out of the Louvre, following him.

And now I knew that Elan was our traitor. Rage ignited in my mind, and I whirled on him, teeth bared.

"What in the gods' names is going on?" asked Kratos.

I could feel myself going feral, about to rip Elan to pieces. "What's going on," I said, "is that I was testing you all to see who was leaking info. And Elan is the one feeding information to the other horsemen. Isn't that right, Elan?"

I felt a sharp shove from the side. "You were testing me, too?" said Hazel. "Asshole. You should have known better."

Elan stumbled back, trembling in his cat sweater, his eyes wide. I *nearly* felt sorry for him—apart from the fact that he was responsible for Adonis's capture.

"So, Elan—"

Before I could finish my sentence, Kratos rushed for him, lifting the wiry fae by his neck. "Explain yourself, fae."

Elan emitted only a choking sound, his face turning red.

"He can't speak while you're strangling him," I pointed out.

Kratos let him drop to the ground, and Elan looked up at Kratos, his entire body shaking.

"Adonis always hated me," Elan stammered, meeting my gaze. "He hates the fae. He'll always hate the fae. Don't you realize that? He thinks we're animals. He'll never—"

I hardly even saw the gesture Kratos made—just a subtle flick of his wrist was all it took to sever Elan's head from his body.

I grimaced at the sight of his body collapsing to the stones, blood pooling around him.

Kratos turned back to me. "I thought we'd heard enough."

Hazel crossed her arms. "Okay, jerk. Now you know who the leak was, and that it wasn't me, which you should have already known. So what's the actual plan?"

Sunlight glinted off Kratos's armor. "You're the Bringer of Light. You're supposed to be able to defeat the Heavenly Host. You blocked them from the earth one time. Can't you do it again?"

I shook my head. Not without dying, so … I was holding off on that for now. "In theory, yes. Except—every time I try to use powerful magic, I go feral. I lose control, forget what I'm doing. My teeth come out. The Old Gods take over my mind completely, and I can't control the magic."

Kratos looked unimpressed. "I think I can manage you, Ruby. You need to at least try."

I didn't want to explain all of it. That if I used the magic of the Old Gods to its full extent, it would kill me. News like that would just extinguish all hope.

But maybe it was worth one more shot.

I swallowed hard. "Okay, here goes. If I start to lose my shit, pain can snap me out of it." I closed my eyes, tuning in to the faint sound of the Old Gods' song. I felt the gemstones in my forehead warm up, and ancient magic vibrated over my body.

My mind flashed with images—the Garden of Eden, feet sinking into the dirt, vines curving around naked flesh. My canines began to lengthen, yearning for blood. Angelic blood.

Kill the angels....

A peaty haze clouded my mind, and I whirled, my gaze landing on the copper one. *A bringer of death should not walk the earth....*

My nostrils flared, my body begging to explode with light. The power of the Old Gods was going to rip me apart, and I craved life.

In the next heartbeat, my canines were at Kratos's throat, piercing flesh, the sweet rush of blood—

A sharp smack to the side of my head snapped me out of it. Delicious angel blood dripped from my lips, and I wiped the back of my hand over my mouth.

My body was shaking. Yep, the Old Gods wanted the angels dead, but they wanted me dead, too. Probably because I'd stolen the gemstones from them in the first place. "Sorry. I'm afraid I still need to refine this a bit."

Kratos had clamped his fingers over his neck wound. "Interesting. The Bringer of Light has a bit of a biting problem."

Yasmin stepped forward, the wind toying with her hair. "It's fine. We have a plan B that may at least buy us some time. Ruby needs to create a serious decoy, so we can sneak in another entrance." Her dark eyebrows drew together. "How many demon soldiers can you conjure at once?"

"As many as we want. I just need to let my mind go blank."

"Shouldn't be hard," Hazel grumbled. "Since you've got literal rocks in your head."

"I get it. You're mad at me. Let's move on." I focused on Kratos. "You've been here before. Once we get inside, any idea where we need to go? The torture garden? A dungeon, maybe?"

"Aereus created a dungeon in the lower level," said Kratos. "It's protected by wraithlike creatures called the *dames blanches*. We'll need to be very careful with them."

I blinked, mentally translating. "The white ladies?"

"What are they going to do?" asked Hazel. "Throw pumpkin spice lattes at us? Strangle us with yoga pants?"

"Are they going to make us listen to Taylor Swift?" I knew this was serious, but I couldn't stop myself.

"They're more dangerous than they sound." Kratos looked annoyed. "They're part fae, part phantom, and they can drive a person mad."

"How do we defeat them?" I asked.

"I have no idea," Kratos said. "But I can tell you that when we go in there, we're going to create chaos. If we get separated, we'll meet back here."

A tug pulled at my shoulder—the mark from Adonis. I brushed my fingers over the spot, the theta Adonis had marked me with. "I can feel him here. He's pulling me toward him. I might be able to use our link to find him. Hang on."

I turned to my companions, inspecting the glamour. I'd already shielded us with a glamour of unobtrusiveness, but it wasn't foolproof. They were still visible if you knew where to look.

"I'm making us into angels before we go in there." I closed my eyes, summoning my magic. The glamour tingled down the length of my arm, and when I opened my eyes again, I was standing with three other winged, white-clad angels.

I breathed in deeply. "Okay. Let me focus. When I say 'go,' we run for the Porte de Richelieu." I closed my eyes, tuning in to the subtle feel of the breeze on my skin, the gentle, cool mist dotting my face. My skin buzzed and hummed with the magic of the Old Gods.

I turned down the chatter in my mind, summoning a vision of a wispy, black smoke that writhed and curled before the glass pyramid in the piazza.

Then, from within the dark tendrils of smoke, a demonic horde began to emerge, as if slipping through a wormhole. Horns, armor, black eyes, and shadowy magic whipping around their bodies, slashing through the air. Even though I knew they weren't real, a chill rippled up my spine at the sight of them.

The doors to the main entrance slammed open, and angels streamed out to fight their illusory enemy. I stroked the strap over my chest, my bow bringing me comfort. I had a feeling I'd be using it soon.

"Now!" I said.

In our angelic disguises, we broke into a run across the piazza.

CHAPTER 8

At any moment, the angelic hordes would realize they were fighting phantoms, and they'd be scanning the palace for invaders.

"We have to move quickly," I rasped as I ran.

We'd slipped through the Porte de Richelieu unnoticed, our feet pounding the floor as we raced through the marble palace halls. Chaos whirled around us, a river of angels flowing through the halls toward the main entrance, where my phantom demons attacked.

As we moved, I felt the tug on my shoulder, a sort of certainty that spurred me onward. The theta linked me to Adonis, guiding me through the palace.

"Left," I called out.

Fleeing through the marble halls, I felt the inexorable pull to Adonis, as if his dark magic had coiled itself around my collarbone. I just had to follow his lead.

We moved swiftly through a hall of medieval Catholic art—the walls lined with statues of saints and ancient wooden confessional booths.

We raced down a marble stairwell, moving into the medieval foundations. Lantern light flickered over rough sandstone.

Even from here, I could hear the shouts of the angels as they streamed back into the Louvre, looking for their real attackers. Right now, the only thing keeping us from their notice was our angelic glamour.

Almost there, Adonis. On the lower level, I could feel his magic even more powerfully. In this ancient part of the palace, our footfalls echoed off the stone ceilings, and we kicked up dust as we ran.

But as we rounded a corner though the tunnels, a sharp, searing pain bit into my skin—my arms, my neck and face. I ground to a halt, and my own screams echoed off the halls, mingling with Hazel's and Yasmin's.

"What's wrong with you?" barked Kratos. "Stop screaming."

Whatever it was, he was fine.

I stared down at my arms, watching the glamour shimmer away until only my own clothing remained, coated in deep gray powder. My heart leapt into my throat.

"Iron dust!" I shouted. It was burning away the magical glamour with a startling pain. As an angel, only Kratos was unaffected.

My heart slammed against my ribs. Now, nothing shielded us from Aereus and his angelic horde if they should happen to search the lower levels. We were exposed.

"We have to keep moving," said Yasmin.

Kratos began to chant in Angelic, to try to draw the iron off our bodies, but more of it kept pouring from the ceilings.

As his Angelic words echoed around us, wispy white creatures crept out of the stones—gaunt women with long, white hair and haunted green eyes. They smelled of ancient riverbeds, like damp sediment and algae. Their appearance sent a tendril of fear coiling through my gut.

One look into their oily eyes rooted me in place. Now, even Kratos had frozen. My pulse raced out of control. What would Aereus do to us if he found us here? We'd be ripped to shreds in his torture garden —slowly. Perhaps over a period of centuries. Adonis would remain imprisoned forever. Oh, and the rest of the earth would die. Not ideal, really.

Still, the *dames blanches* transfixed me.

Fuck. Balls. We need to keep going.

My heart jumped into my throat as one of them crept near me, slipping her arm around my body. They looked like wraiths, but the touch of her tangible flesh against my skin told me they weren't. This woman was as solid as I was, and a stroke of her cold fingertips against the back of my neck sent an icy lick of fear racing up my spine. She hissed as she touched me, as though the contact pained her, and yet she didn't stop.

My mind whirled with brutal images of Aereus and his Catherine wheel—his sharp, iron instruments that could tear flesh from bone. Right now, it was looking like that was my future. My knees were going weak with fear.

The *dame blanche* muffled my mouth with her hand, suffocating the air out of my lungs.

Her damp touch felt strangely tempting—an escape from the fear. It was like she was luring me toward death, until I wanted to give in to her embrace. *La belle dame sans merci.* I wanted her to drag me under the water, deep below an icy surface where silence reigned. Where Aereus could never find me. A dark, angel-less place, a primordial home.

I clamped my eyes shut, desperate to stay in control of myself. *We're running out of time. Running out of time to get Adonis, to save ourselves from a horrendous fate.*

The *dame blanche*'s arms slid around me more tightly, the embrace of a desperate lover. If I gave in to her....

Distantly, I heard the shouts of angels echoing from the stairwell above us. They were coming for us. My heart slammed hard against my ribs.

Move. Now.

What had Kratos told me about mastering my impulses? He dwelled in his darkest memories. I needed to do that now, to get us out of here before it was too late.

In my mind's eye, I summoned the vision of dragons ripping Hazel from the earth, of the dragon who slaughtered Marcus, his body turning to ash on the pavement—

Grief pierced my chest, ripping me from the watery allure of the *dame blanche.* I slammed my elbows into her, knocking her away from me, and she fell backward.

Around me, the *dames blanches* writhed around the bodies of my companions, feeding from them.

The pain of iron still seared my skin. Hadn't Kratos said the *dames* were fae, also? That's why she had hissed when she touched me; the iron burned her skin, too.

I growled, my canines lengthening as I whirled on my attacker. A phantom breeze toyed with her white hair, and she let out a low, eerie wail as she glared at me.

Battle fury arced through my veins. As quick as a storm wind, I scooped iron dust off the floor and rushed for the *dame blanche.*

When she opened her lips to howl again, I shoved the iron into her mouth. She gagged, choking on it until her body began to hiss, steam rising from her flesh. She crumpled to the floor.

I whirled to survey the others. Kratos had just managed to free himself, and he swung his sword through one of the *dames.* She leapt away from him, and his blade *whooshed* harmlessly through the air.

"The dust!" I screamed. "The iron dust."

He caught my eye, and understanding sparked in his gaze. In the next moment, his Angelic words were clattering around us, reverberating in my skull like curses. Iron dust whirled into the air, swooping around the *dames blanches* and coating their ethereal skin. Agonized howls rose from their throats. As the dust covered them, a sound like a gale through a window crack whistled around us, and the *dames blanches* evaporated before our eyes. At last, nothing remained of them but a few wisps of steam and the dank scent of a riverbed.

I nodded at Kratos. "Nicely done. Now let's get the fuck out of here, because the Host is coming for us."

I broke into a sprint again, looking over my shoulder as I ran. Already, I could hear the sounds of Aereus's army reverberating off the ancient stone walls, just behind us. I pumped my arms faster, desperate to find my way to Adonis before we were captured.

I felt a slight sense of relief when Kratos began chanting in Angelic —I had no idea what the words meant, but hopefully he could stave off the oncoming horde for a bit.

The tug in my shoulder intensified. As we moved deeper into the dungeons, I felt an overwhelming need to wrap my arms around Adonis, to breathe in the intoxicating scent of myrrh.

But quickly, that desire was replaced a fiery rage. And that meant Aereus was near, getting closer. He was stoking my bloodlust to a fever pitch. In my mind's eye, an image arose—Aereus capturing us, strapping Hazel and me to one of his iron contraptions, spikes tearing at our flesh. White-hot fury ripped my mind apart, so intense my body shook uncontrollably.

Shouts rang out behind us, and an arrow whistled past my ear. Then, another.

"I can't hold them off any longer," said Kratos.

"Ruby!" Yasmin shouted. "Your magic."

I want to destroy him. I pivoted, facing the oncoming horde—my heart about to explode. Aereus was leading the charge.

The stones in my forehead blazed, a wild power ripping me apart. My canines lengthened, and a growl tore from my throat. As magic exploded from my body, images flooded my mind—a garden paradise. And me, running wild and naked alongside a river—hunting an angel. The enemy. I captured him, claws digging into his perfect skin, teeth tearing at his flesh in an orgy of blood. Ecstasy coursed through me. I'd been born to kill him. The beast taking down the angel, the way it was always meant to be.

Except, the symphony of the Old Gods crested around me. Cracks formed in my body, light beaming from them. The power of the Old Gods was going to rip me apart, tear through me like teeth through flesh.

Smack. I landed hard on the stone floor, my entire body shaking wildly. I rolled over to see Kratos staring down at me.

"You were frothing at the mouth. But you managed to make a shield."

My canines had pierced my lower lip, and I tasted salty blood. Apparently, I could always count on Kratos to smack me upside the head when I needed it.

Just to my left blazed a shield of pearly white light—with the angelic horde trapped on the other side. Somehow, without even realizing what I was doing, I'd managed to create a blockade. On the other side, fire burned in Aereus's eyes.

Slowly, I pushed myself to my feet.

Aereus pulled his sword from his scabbard. He was screaming—probably in Angelic—but the shield had silenced him.

Kratos was shouting back at him in Angelic, the words clamoring in my mind.

The Horseman of War slammed his sword against the shield. *Thunk.* It sounded like metal slamming against metal. *Thunk.*

The faintest of fractures appeared in the shield. We were still running on borrowed time.

CHAPTER 9

$\mathcal{H}$azel tugged my arm. "We need to keep going before he breaks through that thing."

Aereus's sword *thunked* behind us, and we took off running again.

My body was still shaking from the magical burst. I didn't want to think too long about that image in my mind—the one of me ripping apart an angel's flesh. The gray eyes—had they been Adonis's? I couldn't escape the sense that I was fated to kill him—the beast taking down the angel, destroying his otherworldly perfection. Was that my destiny?

Thunk.

I had no time to figure that out now, not when Aereus was hot on our heels.

When we rounded the next corner in the stone hall, we found a row of angelic guards standing before a dark hall. I nocked two arrows, letting them fly straight into two angels' hearts. Kratos flicked his wrist, and the other three fell to their knees before him. One by one, they pulled knives from their belts and plunged them into their own guts.

Kratos was starting to impress me more and more by the minute.

A dark, barren hall loomed in front of us, and a silence fell over us, heavy as damp earth.

Tension rippled over my skin as we moved through the dim hall. Empty cells, barred with iron, lined either side of us.

Thunk. Thunk. Distantly, the sound of sword hitting shield echoed around us, spurring me on.

A sense of panic was starting to climb up my throat. Was Adonis here at all? I'd been following a tug in my shoulder, and it was entirely possible I'd been imagining it.

"Adonis!" I shouted, fear tightening my chest.

A flash of white in the corner of my eye halted me in my tracks.

Thunk. Thunk.

I whirled to find a pale form in the corner of a cell—Muriel, on her own, her dress torn, blond hair bloodied. Devil's Bane curled around her body, streaming into her mouth. Thorns had scratched her skin, and red streaks marred her porcelain skin. Golden magic blazed around her body. Already, Kratos was using his magic to rip through the iron bars of the cell.

"Where is Adonis?" I demanded.

Hazel smacked my arm. "She can't talk, Ruby. Help her first, at least. You have plant powers, don't you?"

Right.

I rushed over to her, letting my fingers trace the Devil's Bane that trapped her. I didn't have much time to figure this out—I just had to get her out of here.

I closed my eyes, and energy buzzed from my stones. *Kill the angel,* the Old Gods sang....

I clenched my jaw. *Not now, fuckers.*

A feral snarl escaped my throat, and I flicked my fingers. The vines began to retreat from her, snaking out of her mouth and away from her body. She fell to the floor, and Kratos swooped in to catch her.

A stream of drool trickled from the corner of her mouth.

Thunk. Thunk.

"Where is Adonis?" I shouted again.

"Underground," she rasped.

My stomach dropped. Underground? Gods below. What kind of torture had they subjected him to?

I bent lower, gripping her arm—maybe a little too tightly. "Underground where?"

She lifted a limp arm, pointing farther down the corridor. "There's a door in the ground." Her eyes fluttered closed again.

Kratos scooped her up, but I was already moving on, ahead of the others. Our bond pulled me toward him.

Thunk. Thunk.

After a few more yards, a metal hatch interrupted the stone ground. I yanked it up, revealing darkness and the dank smell of a grave.

Thunk — The sound of shattering glass stopped my heart. They'd broken through the shield.

With a racing pulse, I dropped into the hole—not entirely sure where I was going. As I dropped down, a terrible thought struck me. What if Muriel had been in on this? What if this was all part of their trap? After all—I was supposed to be their target.

When my feet hit the ground, a wave of fear slammed into me, silencing my thoughts.

Terrifying, spiked iron instruments lined the walls—a gallery of torture.

And there—in a shadowy corner—I found Adonis.

At the sight of him, the world tilted below my feet.

Nails pinned him to a wooden wall—nails driven through every inch of him, each one wrapped in Devil's Bane. The agony must have been unbearable.

My blood roared in my ears.

Blood streaked his golden skin, staining the floor. Only his perfect face was unmarred. His eyes were closed, dark lashes sweeping against his cheeks.

I heard nothing now except the beating of my own heart. A shock of guilt slammed into me, as if I'd been the one to do this to him. That vision I'd had of him—the one where I'd been tearing his flesh off his bones—I'd enjoyed it. I closed my eyes, trying to shut it all out.

"Ruby!" Yasmin's voice this time. "We have to get out of here."

"I know." Hot tears poured down my cheeks, but I forced myself to think logically. How would I get the nails out of him? I had control over plants, but definitely not iron.

I'd need some angelic intervention.

"Kratos!" I screamed.

He was by my side in the next moment, feet thudding on the stone floor. He still gripped Muriel in his arms.

"They're almost here—" He stopped short at the sight of Adonis.

"Can you get the nails out of him?" I asked, panic rising. "Fast?"

The angelic horde thundered over us, and Yasmin was yelling something about blocking the entrance.

Without another word, Kratos nodded, then launched into an Angelic spell. The words tumbled from his lips. They rattled chaotically in my mind, but I could see the spell working—drawing the nails from his body. They clattered to the floor, and Adonis's ruined body started to slump. I rushed forward, catching him in my arms.

Without the Devil's Bane, he could heal on his own. But with that poison coursing through his veins, he'd be out of commission for weeks, his body decaying....

Instinct took over, and I slid my arm under his neck. His blood soaked my clothes, and I pressed my mouth to his in a kiss. Gently, my lips moved over his, and my ancient magic ignited between us. As I kissed him, I could feel myself pulling the toxins from his body into my own. Devil's Bane wasn't poisonous to a fae—in fact, it filled me with a strange sort of energy.

I heard Adonis moan—a low sound, either pain or pleasure, and his tongue brushed against mine. His eyelids slowly opened, and his fingers moved over my arm, tightening. He pulled away from the kiss.

"Ruby," he whispered.

Hazel and Kratos were shouting, urging us to get going, but I had to make sure Adonis could move.

"Can you heal yourself now?" I asked.

Pain etched his features, and his dark magic began to writhe around his body. It skimmed over my skin—cold and soothing at the same time, like a blanket of night. Magic curled around us.

My gaze flicked to the ceiling, where Kratos had sealed the opening, buying us a little time.

"Are you okay?" I asked Adonis.

He pulled himself from my embrace, then rose to his full height. "Of course I am. I was doing fine."

"You've got to be kidding me."

"It's Muriel we need to worry about."

Kratos still held Muriel in his arms. "We can worry later. We need to leave now."

"Speaking of which," Hazel interjected. "How the fuck do we get out of here?"

Adonis pointed to the far side of the room, where an iron maiden stood before a bare stone wall. "I think there's a tunnel behind that wall that leads to the upper levels. I haven't had much chance to explore, but I spent three days listening to water drip behind the walls. I think I may have gone temporarily insane."

"Can someone smash through the walls?" asked Yasmin.

Adonis pulled Muriel from Kratos's arms to start healing her.

Kratos pressed his ear against the wall. Then, he backed away, chanting in Angelic.

As he did, the metal door above us groaned open, and panic tightened my throat.

They're here.

I closed my eyes, and warm light burst from my body. I vibrated with the magic of the Old Gods—with blood and moss and the forgotten secrets of buried bones. The beast, taking down the angels, light exploding from within me until I thought I might die from the power of it all.

This time, Hazel snapped me out of it with fingernails digging into my skin.

When I opened my eyes again, I stared at the shimmering shield above us, my body trembling. It had worked—at least, until Aereus broke through it again.

Thunk. Thunk.

"Let's move." Kratos stood before a crumbled wall—where rock and dust had crashed to the floor to reveal a hollow cavern.

As I ran for it, someone blocked my path. Adonis had healed Muriel completely. But unfortunately for me, she kind of looked like she wanted to murder me.

Her cheeks reddened, and she pointed at me. "You betrayed us."

"Not now, Muriel." I pivoted to move past her, but she grabbed me by the hair.

In the next moment, I found myself entangled in an avalanche of dress ripping, face-scratching, and hair-pulling.

Really? An angel who had witnessed Adam and Eve's fall in the Garden of Eden—and this was how she fought? Like a pissed off fifth-grader? Disappointing.

I shoved her hard, then punched her once in the jaw. She staggered back, her hand on her face. "You gave up our location to Aereus, didn't you, animal?"

"If she had," Adonis barked, "she wouldn't be here rescuing us, would she?"

Thunk. Thunk. Thunk.

Muriel went silent—pouting at me, pretty much—but she wasn't stopping me, at least.

I pushed past her, running with the others into a dark stone passage. Not just one passage—a network of dank tunnels that branched off around us like spokes on a wheel.

Around us, the palace's alarm bells rang loudly, reverberating in my skull. And once more, the sound of a shattering shield rang out.

The sound of Aereus's Angelic spells traveled to us, and as they echoed through the passage, a wall of flames rose up around us. Smoke billowed through the air, and I screamed for my sister.

Aereus wanted to burn us alive, and chaos reigned.

A powerful wave of Adonis's icy magic rippled through the passages, snuffing out some of the flames. Still, black smoke bloomed all around, and I doubled over, coughing uncontrollably.

"Hazel!" I choked out, tears streaming from my eyes.

Aereus's powerful voice boomed through the passage, and a fresh wave of flames roared around us, black smoke choking the oxygen out of the air.

A battle of Angelic words clattered and roared around me—fire battling ice, the smoke only thickening.

"Hazel!"

A burst of coughing wracked my body, and smoke filled my lungs, until dizziness clouded my mind completely.

CHAPTER 10

I woke with a sharp intake of breath, filling my lungs with mercifully clear air. Iron dust covered my body, sapping my strength.

"Hazel," I gasped, but she wasn't near me. I was lying in Adonis's lap, looking up at his perfect face. He was still shirtless, and I could see the scars and gashes all over his chest. He'd hidden his midnight wings, making himself a little less conspicuous.

"Are you okay?" His gray eyes searched mine.

"Where's Hazel?" I rasped.

"Kratos got her out of the building. She's fine. You sucked in a lot of smoke."

The alarm bells still rang around us, and I pushed myself up to look around. We were in the marble hall with all the medieval art and confessional booths, and it seemed eerily still in here.

Adonis went still, frowning. "Someone's coming."

In the next moment, he was on his feet, pulling my hand toward one of the confessional booths. We hurried into it. It smelled of ancient wood in there, and light poured through the latticework onto ornate carvings in the dark oak.

A half-empty bottle of wine stood on a crooked chair. Seemed an angel had been indulging a bit in here.

In the cramped space, Adonis's powerful body pressed against mine. He leaned down, his dark power caressing me until I wanted to pull off my soot-covered dress and wrap my legs around him.

Focus, Ruby. You're about ten seconds away from death by angelic horde.

"I had a feeling you'd come for me here."

"I thought you were doing fine and didn't need me?"

He went quiet for a moment. "That's not entirely true."

"Once we get outside, I'll need you to fly out to the Jardin des Tuileries just long enough that we can make sure everyone is there. Then, we get out of France as fast as we can. But we need to wait until the coast is completely clear."

Outside, footfalls and the sounds of Angelic commands echoed off the ceiling. They were hunting for us, sending my heart into a wild race.

"I can hear your heart pounding," he whispered, warming my ear.

"Because my brain keeps trying to remind me of what Aereus will do to us if he finds us." I swallowed hard, and I traced my fingertips over one of the scars in his chest. Anger ignited when I thought of the agony Adonis must have endured. I wanted to drive nails right through Aereus until his enormous body ripped into pieces. Adrenaline surged through my veins. "Not to mention what he's already done to you."

Adonis stroked his hand down my chest, until it rested over my heart. "Calm yourself. You won't be able to think clearly if your emotions are overwhelming you."

Right. Panic was the enemy of strategy.

That said, the feel of Adonis's hand on my chest wasn't exactly calming—in fact, it sent my heart racing for a different reason. My breath sped up. "You're not helping me control my emotions, you know."

"I'm not?" he purred.

He traced his hand lower over my body, and warmth surged

through my core. Heat and raw power radiated off his body. He was like a dark star, luring me in with his gravitational pull.

I shook my head. "Not exactly."

He stroked his fingertips down my spine, and my back arched.

"Well, Ruby. As much as I want to touch you in all the right places and listen to your heart race faster, maybe we should formulate a plan."

I was practically panting now. "Oh, yeah?"

"You're the one with the power of the Old Gods. And I know from personal experience that powerful emotions will cloud judgment and lead to ruin—"

"Wait, what? Just generally feeling emotions leads to ruination?"

"Just trust me."

"If there's a horseman equivalent of a psychologist, you might want to meet with one at some point."

He pulled away from me, and I regretted the loss of his warmth.

"Whatever you do," he said, "try to stay calm until we can get out of Paris. Don't think about Aereus's torture machines, or the nails he drove through my bones. Think about—whatever it is you think about when you get that faraway look in your eyes. I've watched you closely, and I've seen the smile on your lips while you think about *something*." His dark brows drew together. "What exactly is it that you think about?"

Nothing weird. You. Naked, with soup. "Plants."

"Plants."

I nodded.

"Funny," he said. "I think about the same thing."

"You do?" *Interesting, because mine was a lie.*

"When I need to master my emotions, I think about my garden. The anemones, the myrtle trees, the river. It's my home, the place that has belonged to me and always will."

"That's … adorable. You daydream about your garden?"

"It requires my careful touch and my protection. It rewards me with beauty and comfort, and watching it thrive makes my heart joyful."

"You feel very strongly about your flowers. Careful, or gardening could lead to your ruination." I peered through one of the cracks, watching as the angels continued to stream through, searching for us.

"You'll need to glamour us to get us out of here." He looked through a crack. "Once the soldiers clear out of here."

"My magic won't work with all the iron dust covering my skin."

Adonis snatched the bottle of wine from the chair. "We'll just have to wash it off, then." He pulled down the top of my dress, exposing my bare skin beneath it. His exotic magic raised goosebumps on my skin, and even as the angelic soldiers hammered over the floor outside, I found myself completely transfixed by his eyes on my naked skin.

Adonis began pouring the wine over my chest and shoulders. Then he stroked his hand down my body, washing off the dust with the wine. Adonis tipped the bottle, and the red wine dripped over my body, washing off the dust with it.

As he did, I let my gaze roam over his body. I winced at the sight of his bare torso. His wounds were healing quickly, but I could still see every place where Aereus had gouged his skin with iron, all the divots and indentations. Aereus had scarred every inch of his golden skin.

"This must have been agony."

I expected him to brush it off like he usually did.

"It was," he said instead. He pulled my dress off the rest of the way, until I was standing in nothing but my underwear. Another slow pour of wine, and his hands roamed over my skin, washing off all the iron.

I reached up, brushing my thumb over his cheek. "When I kill Aereus, I'll make sure it's painful." In fact, I wanted to tear Aereus's head off his body and batter him to death with his own skull.

"At least my time here wasn't wasted."

"What do you mean?"

"Aereus has no idea how keen my hearing is," he said. "I listened in to his conversations with Johnny," he continued, letting the wine run over me. "And I know what they have planned. Aereus wants to call down an angel known as Metatron—ruler of the Heavenly Host."

With the iron washed off my bare skin, Adonis sat down on the bench. He pulled me onto his lap.

Slowly, he ran his fingertips inside the top of my panties.

"We need to get outside," I breathed.

"We will." He kissed my neck, and a hand ran up my thigh.

With his hands moving over my wet skin, I could hardly focus.

"Metatron," I repeated, trying to remember how to use words.

"The voice of the gods. Leader of the Heavenly Host. Ruthless."

His fingers moved higher, and my back arched. "Bad news, I take it?"

"He hates humanity," he added. "Hates demons, hates everything that can speak except angels."

Adonis's intoxicating scent curled around me, making my skin hot, my knees weak. As I gazed at his perfect face, I found my tongue running over my lips, and Adonis seemed transfixed by the movement.

I felt his magic intensifying around me, thrumming up my spine and over my breasts.

Adonis leaned in closer, licking some of the wine off my neck. I wrapped my arms around his back.

"There," he said, his breath warming my skin. "All clean."

"Apart from the wine."

Another stroke of his tongue on my neck, and molten heat warmed me from the inside out.

"Adonis," I managed. "We need to go. They're waiting for us."

"We'll finish this later."

I rose and snatched my dress from the floor. I pulled it on. My underwear stuck to my wine-damp skin. It'd be a cold trip over the English Channel.

"Before we go out, I'm going to create another decoy. We can at least confuse the angels as much as possible."

I closed my eyes, letting my mind fill with images of the Garden of Eden and the scent of crushed grapes. The air felt heavy with rain. Then, I imagined Adonis—his golden skin, his tattoos, his pale gray eyes and graceful sweep of midnight wings.

I called to mind an army of him, each one physically perfect—

except for the scarred skin. And by the side of each Adonis, I created a red-haired Ruby in her tattered dress.

I opened my eyes, then stood on my tiptoes to peer out the lattice-work window. There, outside, an army of us had stormed the Louvre. Aereus and Johnny would be completely confused. At least, I hoped.

"Want to have a look?" I asked.

Adonis peered outside and quirked a smile. "You can do this?"

"Not to brag, but I'm pretty amazing."

He frowned. "Is that how you see me?"

"Pretty good, right?"

"Not quite as devastating as the original, but you can work on it."

"This is why people get you confused with that dude who fell into the river looking at his own face."

"Narcissus. *Completely* different. Not nearly as good-looking."

"Stop talking. I need to glamour us now." I closed my eyes, and my body tingled as magic rippled over us.

I opened my eyes, and it was almost with a sense of regret that I watched him transform from a beautiful horseman into an ordinary angelic soldier. My own hair lightened from bright red to blond, my red-stained dress shimmering into a clean white gown.

When the glamour had completely taken hold, Adonis cracked open the confessional door, peering out. "Even with the illusions, we'll still have to move quickly. Johnny and Aereus will be able to smell you."

I stiffened. "Me in particular? Not you?"

"Fae have a particular smell. It wasn't so strong before, but with those gemstones, it's intensified."

This was news to me. "What do fae smell of, exactly?"

"Moss and dirt."

I blinked. "Is there not a better way you could have phrased that?"

"I happen to love the smell." He held up his hand, signaling for me to wait, until he whispered, "Now."

He pushed through the door into the hall, and we fell in line at a safe distance from the army of us. It was too bad I couldn't glamour them to smell like a forest floor, I supposed.

We broke into a run in the hall, moving among the illusions, until we reached an intersection of halls.

An angelic soldier burst from around the corner, slamming into me. I fell backward, and my head knocked against the hard marble floor.

The angel leapt on top of me, bloodlust glinting in his pale eyes. He sniffed the air, eyes shining.

CHAPTER 11

I reached for the knife at my belt, but there was no need.

Above us, Adonis flicked his wrist. The motion severed the angel at the waist, and the remains of the angel's body slumped onto mine.

The angel's blood drenched my glamoured white dress, and my nostrils flared, stones heating in my forehead. My feral side *liked* the smell of angel blood a little too much, and I had to fight the disturbing urge to taste it. My canines lengthened, and I flicked my tongue over them.

Adonis pulled the angel's torso off of me, and I snarled, fighting to keep control of myself. "Do you have any tidier ways of slaughtering?"

"You're one to talk. I've seen how you kill." Blood had spattered him, too. "Anyway, he was trying to kill you, and I didn't have time to make it pretty."

I stood up and narrowed my eyes at him. His body was shaking, tense. Shadows darkened the air around him, and darkness clouded his eyes. I'd never seen him so rattled before. He'd always managed to convey a cool exterior.

Even through the glamour, I recognized something in him that I knew well—but it was an emotion I'd never seen on Adonis before.

Bloodlust. I'd been in that state enough times to know what he was thinking now. Something along the lines of *more death.*

"Adonis." I gripped him by the shoulders. "Focus."

The shadows cleared from his eyes, and his eyebrows drew together. He stared at the blood staining my body. For just a moment, he looked strangely vulnerable. Then his jaw clenched, as if he were gaining mastery of himself. "Right."

We started moving again, heading for the main entrance. Adonis slammed through the doors into the piazza. Around the pyramid, anarchy had erupted. Angelic soldiers were moving among the illusions of Adonis and me, trying to fight phantoms. Swarms of angels and cherubs darkened the skies above us, searching for the real Ruby and Adonis among all the fakes.

We moved among them unnoticed, racing now for our meeting spot in the Jardin des Tuileries, where Uthyr awaited us. My feet pounded hard against the stones, and my breath grew ragged.

Almost there. Almost free. Adrenaline sparked through my veins as I spotted the shimmering contours of the dragon, shielded by my glamour.

I'd done it. I'd gotten Adonis out of his prison, and we were escaping Aereus's clutches.

"There!" I shouted to Adonis.

Before we took off, I just needed to make sure we were all here, all accounted for.

I pulled the glamour off the dragon, my gaze roaming over Yasmin, Muriel, Kratos…. My heart hammered hard in my chest.

Where the fuck was Hazel?

"Hazel!" Kratos shouted.

I spun, following his gaze, and fear hit me like a freight train.

There—before the pyramid—the Horseman of Famine had captured my sister. Johnny's Angelic words boomed in the air around us, echoing off the stone. I stared in horror as his incantation created an iron mask for her mouth, a collar for her neck.

Johnny held an iron knife aloft, ready to plunge it into her heart. "A fae for a fae!" he boomed. He pressed the knife into her collar bone, drawing blood. Crimson streaked down the front of her body. "Give yourself up, Ruby," he screeched, "and your sister lives."

My mind flashed with the horror of what awaited me if I gave myself up to these two horsemen. But if not me, then it was Hazel. *Shit.* I was out of options here. But there was no way in hell I was letting Johnny take my little sister.

My body shook with a mixture of fear and rage, and I let my glamour drop. All at once, the army of Adonises and Rubys vanished. The wind toyed with my red hair, and I stood across from Johnny in my wine-stained, tattered dress.

Aereus and his angelic horde swarmed above, but as soon as my glamour dropped, angels began swooping lower, circling around me.

I thought I could hear Adonis saying something to me—shouting—but I tuned him out. I took a step forward, ready to announce myself.

Suddenly, the air around us erupted with angelic magic. I fell to my knees at the sound, clamping my hands over my ears. Adonis's voice rang out with Angelic spells, clashing with Johnny's. From behind me, Kratos joined in, and I felt as if my own mind were at war with itself.

The Angelic language in its true form, spoken by native speakers, was something humans and fae were never meant to hear. In the magical battle, angels' bodies began to drop from the skies, blood streaming from their ears.

Even with my hands clamped over my ears, the spells boomed through my fingers, driving me mad.

Angels were never meant to walk the earth.

The song of the Old Gods was swelling within me, reacting to the curse of the Angelic language. I needed to kill the angels, to slaughter all of them. The gemstones in my forehead began to heat, urging me on to massacre the angels around me.

I felt like a battle was raging between the Angelic language and the Old Gods, and I could hardly hear my own thoughts between them. All I knew right now was that I wanted blood—angel blood.

Stay in control, Ruby. Kratos used emotional pain to master his impulses. Maybe physical would work just as well.

I gritted my teeth, pulling the knife from my belt. I sliced through my palm, drawing blood. The sharp sting cleared the cacophony from my mind, and my senses sharpened. I stared at Johnny, seeing him clearly again. He'd dropped his grip on Hazel, but she still lay at his feet, bound in iron.

Now, blood poured from Johnny's eyes, his nose, his ears, as Kratos and Adonis attacked him with magic. He was screaming in Angelic, and by the look of it, trying to fight back with defensive spells.

With the iron clamped around her skinny body, she'd be in agony. Not to mention the knife wound at her collarbone.

The sight of her streaked with blood sent fiery wrath burning through my veins. I didn't just want to hurt Johnny now. I didn't just want to put him in the ground. I wanted him dead. The Old Gods wanted him dead, and they were going to help me.

My body ached to use the full force of their magic, to let the light explode from my body. But I had to hold back. If I gave in to their desires completely, I'd die.

My gaze flicked to the skies, where Aereus circled among the other angels like a bird of prey. His Angelic words echoed off the stone walls.

Johnny was still on the ground, screaming out spells. I pulled the bow off my back and nocked an arrow, narrowing my eyes at him. I loosed two arrows in close succession, hitting him in his eye socket, then his throat. He fell to the ground, already succumbing to the effects of the Devil's Bane.

There's more where that came from, you skinny fuck.

I crossed to him, dropping the bow. I didn't need weapons now. In fact, I *was* a weapon—honed perfectly to destroy angels.

I licked my lips, already tasting blood. When I reached Johnny, he was grunting, struggling to stand. "I'm going to peel off your skin, fae whore!" he screeched.

I stepped over Hazel's prone body when I reached him, and I

yanked him up by the throat. Strength infused my body, and I lifted him into the air, squeezing his neck until his remaining eye bulged.

"The Old Gods have a message," I said in a voice that wasn't quite my own. "You don't belong here. You never did. Humans, demons, fae … we might be brutal and savage, but you created hell on earth."

He was screaming now, his shrieks music to my savage ears. I lifted my free hand to his face, and a dark smile curled my lips. Devil's Bane began to spool out of my fingernails, climbing into his mouth, his ears, his eye sockets. I sent the plants surging into his brain, suffocating it.

"You should have never come here with your Angelic language," I hissed. "None of you should have come."

I flicked my wrist, and Johnny's head exploded in a mist of flesh and bone.

One down, three to go.

I arched my back, feeling my canines lengthen. The Old Gods had awoken Feral Ruby, and she wanted more angel blood. I could end this all right here, get rid of them all.

I whirled, my gaze landing on the beautiful one with eyes the color of stormy skies. Already, Devil's Bane was spooling from my fingertips.

You're next.

I crossed to him, my body warming with light. I felt as if cracks were opening, ready to break me apart, ready to tear me to pieces.

You never should have come here.

But something in his eyes stopped me. I flicked my tongue over my teeth, transfixed by that flash of vulnerability in his eyes.

"Ruby."

As soon as he said my name, my mind began to clear again, the song of the Old Gods dimming to a hum.

Hazel. I needed to get her.

Just as I turned back to grab my sister, Aereus swooped down, his sword drawn.

My heart skipped a beat as he swung for Adonis.

Adonis raised his arm defensively, but it was too late. Blood arced through the air.

The Old Gods' gemstones sparked, urging me to use their power. Devil's Bane curled from my fingertips, reaching for Aereus. Even so, I knew it was too late.

Aereus had completely severed one of Adonis's arms, and he was lifting his sword again. Just as the tendrils of vines reached the Horseman of War, he brought his sword down again with a roar.

My mind went blank for a moment as horror slammed into me.

The horsemen couldn't kill each other, right? And yet—the sight of Adonis, felled by Aereus's sword, robbed me of breath. His blood spilled over the stones.

I had a vague sense that Kratos was shouting something at me, but panic had begun to climb up my throat, and it was hard to think clearly.

Aereus turned to me, his angelic voice booming cursed spells. As he did, pain ripped my body apart, searing me from the inside out. Something was hitting me, again and again.

Clutching my ribs, I fell hard to my knees. I was dimly aware of blood spilling from my mouth, then of someone tugging me by the hair, lifting me from the ground like a trophy.

As my vision began to darken, only one thought rang in my mind, carving through the chaos of the angelic warfare. In fact, it rang out with a stark, crystal clarity. *Hazel and I are going to die here.*

CHAPTER 12

I opened my eyes a crack, and the light burned them. Stone arched above me. Pain splintered my body, so sharp I couldn't think through the haze of agony. Something felt very wrong inside of me, as if my insides had been punctured over and over. It took me a moment to realize they probably had been.

Was I alive or dead? Which was the better option?

The paradise of the Old Gods called to me—the untamed garden where no questions would plague my mind.

The air smelled of cedar.

Before I could focus on anything clearly, the world around me began to dim, replaced with a vision—my phantom life. The one with the cottage, and Adonis sitting naked before the fireplace. It seemed so vivid I could almost reach out and touch him….

* * *

THE NEXT TIME I opened my eyes, the pain had left me completely, replaced by a dull calm. Rosy sunlight streamed in through the windows—and with it, the wisteria from outside the castle climbed in through the opening. Once again, the plants had snaked over the floor, reaching for me.

I nearly missed the beautiful, dark-haired angel slumped in a chair in the shadows, his eyes closed. *Adonis.*

No wonder I felt better.

Drakon, his dragonile, sat on the floor next to him, thumping his reptilian tail against the floor. He blinked his yellow eyes at me, looking awfully proud at having contributed to his master's rescue.

Adonis's eyes opened, looking more haunted than ever. Something was very wrong.

My chest clenched. "Where's Hazel?"

"She's fine. She's here, at Hotemet." His voice sounded toneless.

I licked my dry lips. "What happened?"

"Aereus's sword carved me in half."

"I saw that."

"I got better, and I smelled your blood all around me. Aereus nearly killed you. He used his magic to destroy your body."

"So that's what that pain was." I swallowed hard. "How did I get out of there?"

"Kratos." He opened his mouth and closed it again, and his gaze shuttered. "It's over now."

There was something he wasn't telling me.

He leaned forward, resting his hands on his knees. "The important thing is that Metatron is on his way."

Is that what was bothering him? "Okay. I'll kill him, just like I killed Johnny. Vines. Exploding head."

Adonis shook his head. "He's not like Johnny. He's much more powerful, and he will toy with your mind."

I tried to sit up, but pain speared my ribs. Even with Adonis's healing magic suffusing my body, I still felt like I'd been sliced open through my middle. Like my organs had been taken out, beaten up a bit, and stuffed back in.

A cough wracked my chest, and for a split second, I had the disturbing feeling that my intestines were about to fall out of place. I grimaced, clutching my gut. *Gods save me.*

Adonis rushed for the edge of my bed, his magic thickening in the air. "Lay down." A sharp command.

"I don't understand," I managed. "Last time I got hurt, I healed fast. And your magic has always healed me in instantly in the past. Why is it not working now?"

"Aereus used powerful spells on you. It's a miracle you're alive at all." He frowned, tracing his fingertips over the stones in my forehead. "If it weren't for these, I think you'd be vaporized right now."

I winced at the image. "Let's not dwell on that image too long, shall we?"

Adonis whispered under his breath in Angelic. His healing magic skimmed over my skin, taking the pain away and making my eyelids droop. As the agony left my body, a hint of euphoria washed over me. I could already smell the garden of Paradise. I reached for Adonis, but he pulled away from me.

"There's something you're not telling me," I managed.

That cold, haunted look in his eyes shut me up. "Get some sleep."

A command I couldn't refuse. When I closed my eyes, I was in the garden again.

* * *

As I slept, I was dully aware of Hazel's voice telling me long, rambling stories of her time in the dragon's lair.

I woke fully again at night, with moonlight streaming into the room onto Adonis. It silvered his skin and sparked in his pale eyes. "Ruby," he said quietly.

"How long has it been since we returned from Sadeckrav?" I asked.

"Three days. How are you feeling?"

Slowly, I pushed myself up onto my elbows. Now, only a dull pain throbbed in my ribs. "Fine. But let's cut to the chase. What's going on with Metatron? I need more details."

"I spotted him at the Tower of London with one or two members of the Heavenly Host. When I haven't been here, watching over you,

Kratos and I have been spying on him. We've seen him moving around the city, trying to meet secretly with other angels."

My throat tightened. "The Tower of London? That's where the Institute are located."

"Not anymore."

My breath sped up. "What about Yasmin's daughter?"

He nodded. "As soon as we returned here, she was reunited with the surviving members of the Institute. I helped her find her daughter, who was hiding out in the rookeries with her uncle."

"She's okay? Thank the gods."

"Yasmin was out of her mind when she heard what had happened. Metatron wanted to make a point about revolutions and submission to authority. The Tower walls are now decorated with the severed heads of members of the Institute. Only because of luck did Yasmin's daughter make it out of there alive."

I rubbed my eyes. "Okay, so you know where the Heavenly Host are hidden now? If we find them, you can just kill them all. Then we're done."

"I'm afraid it's not that simple."

Something in his tone sent a lick of dread up my spine. "What do you mean?"

"Metatron isn't an ordinary angel. He's the one who cursed Azazeyl when he fell. He's the one who split the fallen angel into seven earthly gods, damned to their own hells. He's the one who tasks the horsemen with destroying humanity. Frankly, he's a bit unpleasant."

"So what's he doing?"

"He's making his soldiers immortal. One by one. I can't kill them."

Panic began climbing up my throat. With an army of immortals, we didn't stand a chance. I needed to try my light magic again. "Let's go to the Tower."

"Can you even sit up?"

A sharp pain hit my side. Okay, so I couldn't just sit upright like that, using my abdominal muscles. Grunting, I rolled to the left. From there, I could push myself up with my arm until I was nearly sitting, as long as I didn't shift too much to the side—

"Balls!"

"You're not ready for this."

Almost up. "We need to end this now. If Metatron wins, I'll be dead. So I think a bit of abdominal discomfort is manageable."

Adonis quirked an eyebrow. "Have you mastered your light magic?"

Not even close. Still pretty sure the Old Gods wanted to kill me. "No, but I have to try before this immortal army gets any bigger." Wincing at the pain in my gut, I pushed myself off the bed to a standing position using my arms. And I nearly toppled over. "By the time we reach London, I'll be feeling much better. Just hit me with some of your opiate magic on the way." I gripped my stomach. "Any chance you can just defeat his immortality spell with a mortality spell?"

Adonis shook his head. "Metatron's Angelic spells are too powerful. He's the voice of the gods." Then, he fixed his gaze on me. "The magic of the Old Gods is the only thing that can combat him." A muscle tightened in his jaw. "If we let him continue, we won't stand a chance. There will be no way to defeat his army."

"There's a small chance I might start to lose my mind when I use the Old Gods' magic." And also … I might die. "If I start to look like I'm losing control, I need you to hurt me."

He scowled. "I'll handle you without hurting you. But you'll need to be fast. Blast him with that magic before he gets the chance to smell you. Just like you did when you blasted the Heavenly Host off the earth last time. If it starts to go wrong, and if the Old Gods start taking over, I'll stop you."

"Of course. Yes. I smell like the underside of a rock, so I need to be fast."

"Remember, magic doesn't have its own will. Someone always commands it. When I died, it was because the Old Gods wanted me dead. They were in control. You need to control their power instead. You need to command it, to direct it."

"How?"

"Make it a part of you."

Right. I had no idea how to do that, but considering the fate of the entire world was at stake, I had to at least try.

CHAPTER 13

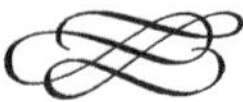

Glamoured as ravens, we swooped over the ruined city of London, the wind whipping at our skin. Steel-gray clouds covered the sky.

At the sight of the ravaged husks of buildings below us, a chill rippled over my skin. Things had gotten worse since I'd last been here. Yasmin had said that people were starting to organize, to get ready to fight back against the angels. Behind these crumbling walls, were people really willing to fight?

I tightened my arms around Adonis's back, my gaze sweeping over his features. He'd hardly spoken at all on our way here. Something had happened in Paris that he wasn't telling me, and it was starting to drive me crazy.

"Have you ever met him?" I asked.

"Who?"

"Metatron."

"Once. It was enough."

As we soared closer to the Tower, I caught a glimpse of a legion of angelic soldiers marching along Bethnal Green Road. Their weapons and armor gleamed in the dull light. It was a neighborhood I knew well—one of squat buildings, old pubs mixed with trendy new bars—all deserted since the Great Nightmare had begun. But as the angelic horde marched, I watched the structures crumble around them. Buildings shook, windows shattered, and pieces of plaster rained into the road.

Immortals.

The pavement cracked beneath the marching army.

My breath sped up. "What's happening to the buildings?"

Adonis's grip tightened on me, and he pulled me so close I could feel his heart beating through his clothes. "The Angelic language is used to create reality. It seems that Metatron is using it to break reality apart. He's practicing creating chaos."

I swallowed hard. "He wants to destroy it all, is that it? Everything on earth."

"Not exactly." A muscle clenched in his jaw. "First, he plans to make us suffer."

I shook my head. "Why?"

"Because we haven't sufficiently worshipped him, and it irritates him."

"So he's just an ordinary insecure asshole. Except he's also a godlike being with the power to destroy the fabric of the universe."

"That sums it up."

We flew further south, toward the Tower, and the swarm of angels kept marching through the street as steel bent and cement cracked around them.

At last we reached the Tower, and nervousness crawled up my spine. What kind of monster were we dealing with here?

"I can feel his power." A dark whisper from Adonis.

Was it just me, or was the Horseman of Death himself freaking out right now? That did nothing to assuage my nerves. Considering we didn't have a ton of hope, I wasn't going to tell him my own disturbing secret—the one about how the Old Gods wanted me dead.

"If we get close to him," said Adonis, "you'll need to act quickly. Even when you're glamoured, he'll be able to smell you."

"Right. Moss and dirt. Thanks for reminding me of that."

We swooped over the Tower walls, Adonis's wings beating like a heart.

"There," he said. "He's in the Tower church."

We dove lower over the Tower green—over the spot where traitors, heretics, and unwanted wives had fed the stones with their blood.

Angels milled around us, their bodies glowing with golden light.

We touched down on the cobblestones just in front of the church entrance. The iron gate and doors stood open, and pale light streamed out of the archway.

Already, I could feel Metatron's power thrumming over my skin. It felt alien—an invasive magic that belonged in the celestial realm. Not here.

As we stood at the precipice, my heart rate began to speed up, pulse racing. I had to remind myself that Metatron would see only a simple raven if he looked our way. One of many in the Tower. Not a big deal.

We took a step inside, and my breath caught at the sight before me. There, at the altar, stood Metatron. Golden wings cascaded from his back, which was turned toward us, and an angel knelt before him. The angel spoke in Angelic, so I had no idea what he was saying, but he seemed to be supplicating himself. He clasped his hands together, his head lowered before Metatron, like he was worshipping him.

Seemed like Metatron had found someone willing to pander to his overwhelming insecurity.

As we stood in the church's doorway, Metatron held out his hands to either side, and pearly, celestial light glowed from his body. He arched his back, and his powerful voice began to boom around us, echoing off the church's stone walls. He spoke in Angelic, and the raw power of the words pounded through my bones. As he chanted his spells, thin rays of light beamed from his skull. And everything the light touched began to disintegrate and dissolve, bits of the walls and ceiling crumbling to the floor.

My breath caught in my throat. I needed to see his face.

The angel at his feet seemed enraptured, his lips curled in an ecstatic smile. From the church walls, pieces of stone began to break, and cracks opened in the flagstones. As I listened to the spell, chaos rampaged through my skull—words and fragments of words, all disconnected, all jumbled and meaningless. *Pyramid puddle can open half luck mugger stem alter mag ord lish lake minst....*

I clamped my hands over my ears, trying to block out the chaos.

When Metatron had finished his spell, Adonis tugged on my arm, signaling that I had to hurry up. But I felt rooted in place, desperate to see his face.

I got my wish then. Metatron turned around, and the breath left my lungs.

Apart from the color of his wings, he looked nearly *exactly* like Adonis. Same gray eyes, same breathtaking beauty. But there was something colder about Metatron, something more alien. It was a divine beauty that simple, bestial creatures like me were never meant to see. *Never meant to be here.*

I took a steadying breath and stepped farther into the church. To Metatron, I still appeared as a raven, but I knew I only had a matter of seconds before he smelled me.

Now, the stones in my forehead began to tingle. The scent of a lush garden curled around me. Metatron's Angelic words clattered in my mind, but as the light began to warm up my body, it drowned out some of the chaos of his spells.

I stared at him—at this creature who didn't belong here—and rage begin to roil in my chest. The Old Gods didn't want him here, and a chorus of their voices rang in my mind. The Old Gods wanted to teach him a lesson, wanted to teach all the angels a lesson. It was something we should have done long ago, when they came to the Garden of Eden, when they brought their invasive magic to our world. Should have hunted them, fertilized the Garden with angel blood.

My canines began to lengthen. *Kill all of them.* My back arched, and light began to burst from my body, cracking through my skin. Here, I'd explode like a dying star.

I snarled, light beaming from my body, prepared to slaughter—

All at once, a soothing magic slipped into my mind, calming my rage. It was a blanket of night, of sleep, of the quietness of soil....

The chorus of the Old Gods dulled in my skull, and it took me a moment to realize that a beautiful man had wrapped his arms around me, and that he smelled like myrrh.

I blinked, realizing I was in the air. Adonis's arms were tight around me, and the fresh air outside kissed my skin.

I swallowed hard. "So, I guess that didn't go well. What happened, exactly? Did you see—did I look different?" Had he noticed that light was ripping me apart from the inside out, and that the Old Gods were trying to kill me?

"You were starting to attack me. I had to intervene."

Shit. "But my body looked normal."

He frowned. "I tell you that you were trying to kill me, and you're concerned about how your body looked?"

"I was just curious if the magic made me look different."

"Apart from the terrifying rage in your expression, no. Why?"

"I don't suppose I killed Metatron while I was at it?"

"No, but he shot a moderately annoyed look at you, like he didn't want a raven in his church."

"That's it? The Old Gods were screaming in my mind about angel blood fertilizing the Garden of Eden, and all I achieved was moderate annoyance?"

Adonis cocked his head. "He is very powerful. You'll need more time. Or more mastery. Or more … something. We'll work on it."

Adonis's skin looked paler than it should. No longer golden, it had taken on a porcelain hue, as if some of the blood had been drained from his body.

I touched his cheek. "Are you okay?"

"I'm fine. It's just that I think your magic affected me a little more than it did Metatron. I'll recover."

In the chilly air over the Tower of London, I scanned Adonis's perfect features, cold gray eyes, and dark eyelashes. "He's connected to you, isn't he? He looks just like you."

For a moment, a heavy silence fell over us. Then, without meeting my gaze, Adonis said, "He created me."

"But you had a mother." I blinked. "Do you mean he's your father?"

"I suppose you could call it that."

CHAPTER 14

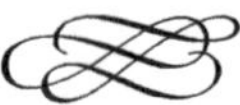

$\mathcal{E}$ver since our battle at the Louvre, I'd had the sense that Adonis had been keeping something from me. He was no longer flirtatious or seductive, no longer making eye contact. For some reason, he'd become colder and a little more distant, like something was haunting him.

When we returned from the Tower, he walked me to my room with shadows darkening the air around him, giving one-word answers to my questions.

Was it some kind of angelic daddy issues that had him acting strangely? I had no idea. But after a few hours of stewing in my room, I decided I should just ask him. We were supposed to be working together, weren't we? I needed to know the truth from him.

I crossed through the drafty stone hall toward his room, where I found the door slightly ajar. It creaked as I pushed it open further. I didn't see any signs of Adonis in here—just Drakon, sitting in the corner, lazily thumping his scaly tail up and down on the stone. He lifted his head, blinked his yellow eyes at me a few times, then fell back asleep.

Still, I could feel Adonis's power crackling over my body. It was only when I heard the running of water that I understood he was filling the tub.

"Adonis?" I called out.

"I'm in here." His voice came from an archway.

I felt torn between an overwhelming urge to see what he looked like in the bath, and my better judgment that told me maybe this was weird. I'd never actually slept with him. Maybe we weren't in "chatting in the bath" territory yet. "I'll come back later."

"It's fine."

Or maybe we were.

I crossed through the doorway, and found Adonis shoulder-deep in an enormous, circular stone tub. Light spilled in from latticed windows onto him, giving him a sort of halo.

He gripped a bar of soap, and given the redness of his skin, it looked like he'd been scrubbing at it. His dark tattoos snaked over his raw skin.

"What's wrong?" I asked.

"We just have a lot ahead of us if we're going to combat the chaos Metatron is creating." Steam curled the air around him.

My eyes swept over his muscled torso. "I'm not a psychologist, but I'm getting the sense that your father's presence here is bothering you."

"I have a mother. I don't have a father. Metatron impregnated my mother, just like he impregnated the mothers of Kratos, Johnny, and Aereus, but...."

"They're your half-brothers?"

A slow shrug. "If you want to call it that."

I crossed to him, sitting at the edge of his bathtub. I let my fingertip trail in the steaming water. It was practically scalding.

Droplets of water dotted his skin, and I had the strongest urge to lick them off.

Slowly, he raised his gaze to meet mine, and the raw vulnerability in his gray eyes pierced me to the core.

I cocked my head. "That's the first time you've looked at me since we returned from the Louvre. I mean really looked at me."

"Angels are cruel, cold creatures from the vast, unchanging landscape of the heavens. I've seen civilizations rise and fall, cities born only to crumble. I've seen the birth and death of gods. I speak a language humans were never meant to learn, and I kill people just by feeling too much." There was no feeling in his words now, no emotion. Just a cold, stark reality. "It's in my nature to kill and to destroy. It's what I was born to do."

"Bullshit. We're not born to do anything. We make ourselves. I'm a fae, a succubus, a spy, a demon. I'm a god and a beast, a dancer and a soldier. I wasn't born to be any one thing, and neither were you. We are what we create. We are our actions and our stories."

A slow tilt of his head, his eyes now pure ice. "And killing is what I do."

"Why is this coming up now? What happened?"

"When you flew over Paris, did you see the humans camped out in the fields? They lived in makeshift tents and huddled around bonfires. Mothers, fathers, children, babies...."

"Yeah. I remember. I saw some little kids toddling among the gardens."

"They're all dead now. You need to understand. Nature is cruel, and so am I."

My chest clenched. "How? Why?"

"I told you that powerful emotions can lead to ruination. If I feel too much, people die. When I found my mother's dead body, waves of death rippled off me. I slaughtered the entire city of Afeka nearby. I walked through the streets and found the dead littering the cobblestones. Young and old. And when I recovered at the Louvre, I smelled your blood all around me. I could no longer hear you through our bond. I was certain they'd killed you. You're still mortal. I couldn't control it, and a wave of death washed over the city. Our souls are immutable, Ruby. You might appear to be a succubus, a dancer, a soldier, but I've seen the real you."

I wanted to tear my gaze away from the pain in his eyes. "Enlighten me."

"The real you is wild and beautiful. And while you take on all these disguises, you're running from yourself. I can see it in your eyes sometimes. Fantasies draw you in. You're imagining a paradise that never existed, a Ruby that never existed."

I clenched my jaw, thinking of the fae I'd seen in the cottage. The happy couple, making soup. "Paradise does exist, it's just not handed to us on a plate. It's something we create. Did you see those two fae living in the cottage, when we were on our way to meet Kratos? It might not be a palace or a tropical island or whatever, but their simple life right now seems like paradise to me. That could be us."

"Us? When it's my destiny to slaughter thousands just by feeling emotions?"

I crossed my arms. "This 'my destiny is to slaughter' thing is horse-shit. If it was your inescapable destiny, you'd be doing it constantly. When was the last time you lost control and killed people?"

"A thousand years, maybe." He seemed lost in his own mind. "But it's just that rage poured off me when I thought you were dead. I think a part of me wanted everyone to die. The bloodlust was uncontrol-lable." He straightened, the water dripping off his skin in rivulets. "Has it occurred to you that maybe you're lying to yourself about what you really are? Do you really think you can just reinvent your-self, that you can just wipe the slate clean and start again? I've seen you covered in the blood of angels. I've seen you rip into flesh. That's the real you, and it terrifies you."

Irritation simmered. "You don't get to define me."

He traced his fingertip through the water, creating little ripples. "You're right. Just make sure you're not running from the darkest parts of you. You have a tendency to romanticize things."

He was annoying me now. "What makes you say that?"

"The fae you saw in the woods, the ones you think live in Paradise. I could smell the blood on them. Human and fae blood. They'd been eating their own species. How do you think they survived in this world? By being brutal and savage, the way nature designed them."

My stomach dropped. *No way.* "Blood could have been there for any reason."

"I should just let you believe in your fantasies, shouldn't I? It's almost heartbreaking to disabuse you of them. You have such a vibrant phantom life."

I swallowed hard. His words weren't *entirely* off the mark—in fact, he knew what I called my other life. And it did sometimes seem that my phantom life—the one with the garden and the cottage—was more real than the grim world around me.

"There's nothing wrong with having an active fantasy life."

He cocked his head, studying me intently. "What is that you see in your fantasies, anyway?"

The whole "soup fantasy" was a little embarrassing, and yet I felt an overwhelming urge to confess it. Like I just needed to get it off my chest. "You, eating soup by a fireplace." My cheeks heated. "Naked."

Not weird at all.

A wicked smile. "And that's the first problem with an active fantasy life. It pulls you away from the truth. I don't even like soup."

Of course the Horseman of Death did not sit by fireplaces with hot soup.

I hadn't convinced him of anything, but it seemed like maybe he'd lost the will to argue with me. I didn't want to argue with him anymore, either. Right now, I felt sick of talking, sick of words. I just wanted the peacefulness of an empty mind.

He leaned back, his stormy gaze boring into me. "Tell me more about this naked fantasy you have of me."

At those words, all I knew was that I really wanted was to feel his body beneath mine.

"It's more about the soup, honestly," I lied. "Minestrone." I licked my lips.

"I don't even know what that is. Do we have to focus on the soup aspects of this fantasy?"

Slowly, I tugged up the hem of my dress, showing off my thighs. "But it has parmesan and pancetta."

"I don't care about the pancetta. Keep pulling up your dress."

I lifted it another inch. "And zucchini. *Diced.*"

He gripped the edge of the tub. "Dress. Off."

"Some recipes call for butter." I pulled off my dress entirely, and the cool air whispered over my skin.

Adonis's body seemed to stiffen, his gray eyes brightening. "That's more like it."

"Your bath looks nice." The feel of his eyes on my body was electrifying.

I unhooked my bra, letting it fall to the floor. My body warmed, and I felt as if my breasts were swelling under his gaze.

Adonis's jaw dropped open, and he drank me in. My thighs clenched with anticipation. Then, I slid off my panties.

I stepped into the bath, the water scalding my porcelain skin until it turned pink. My legs slid against his as I lowered myself into the tub.

I nestled in across from him. His magic thrummed hot over my skin, and despite the warmth around me, goosebumps rose on my skin. "I said we can create Paradise, right? I'll show you."

I summoned glamour, transforming the air around us to create an illusion of blood red flowers—the same ones that lined the riverbed in Afeka. Then, I flicked my fingers, and the sparkling river appeared, curving out of the cavern of the afterworld. Adonis's home—and the home of the Old Gods. With a twitch of my fingers, myrtle tees sprang up around the river's edge.

For just a moment, I thought I glimpsed drops of blood on their leaves, but I blinked, shoving the image out of my mind. Something dark nagged at the recesses of my mind, but I ignored it, letting my leg slide against Adonis's.

A little more life glinted in his eyes now—a little hunger—and his mouth twitched in a dangerous smile. Sensuous magic pulsed off him, swirling around my body along with the steam. Deep within the eyes of an immortal being like him, you could find a union of opposites: hot and cold, dark and light, the beginning and the end.

My core throbbed at the sight of him. I'd never wanted someone so badly in my life.

"What other sort of paradise can you create for me?" His voice had become husky. His heavy-lidded eyes promised sex and danger all at once.

I flicked my wrist, and the vision of the garden disappeared, replaced by a steaming bowl of soup.

A short growl. "Not food."

The soup's surface glimmered red, and I frowned. I snapped my fingers, and the disturbingly crimson soup disappeared.

Adonis gripped the soap in his hands and leaned forward. With a gentle touch, he started soaping my skin, sliding his hands up my calves.

His fingertips lightly stroked my legs as he washed me, and I felt my knees falling open, inviting him in.

My breath came in short, sharp bursts, and I couldn't really focus on the illusions anymore. Not with the hungry look he was giving me. My body began to tremble with anticipation, legs opening wider. His hands moved farther up my thighs. I ached for him to keep going.

I wanted more contact with him, wanted to feel him inside me. But he was holding back. His powerful body skimmed against mine, his touch light. Already, I was arching into him, aching for more. His soapy thumbs brushed over my hardened nipples, a light touch that made my back curve into him. *More, more, more....* I moaned lightly.

Painfully slowly, he lowered his mouth to my throat, his lips hot against my skin. He was tasting me, exploring.

A louder moan this time. He lifted his face for a moment, gazing at me from under his dark lashes, a smile curling his lips. He was enjoying teasing me.

I wrapped my arms around his neck, my legs around his. He growled softly, skimming his hands farther up my body to cup my breasts. Liquid heat pulsed in my core, and I pulled him in closer to me. I rocked against him, feeling the hardness of his body.

His powerful back tensed, and then he whispered in my ear, "Not so fast. I'm going to take my time with you."

I didn't want him to take his time. I wanted him now, hard and fast. I stroked my hands down his back, feeling his body go rigid under my fingers. Then, I found his mouth with mine, pulling him in for a deep kiss. My tongue brushed against his, my hips moving against him, more urgently.

I smelled the scent of an exotic garden curling around me. *Paradise is here.*

My kiss deepened, desperate now. I *needed* him. "Adonis," I whispered.

I raked my fingernails down his back, then gripped his ass. I pulled him closer, guiding him into me. When he'd buried himself inside me, filling me completely, I moaned loudly, spurred on by pure need. My body tightened around him.

He stroked slowly between my legs, and I had the vague sense that I was moaning his name over and over. As ecstasy claimed my body, I could no longer quite remember how language worked.

As I shuddered against him, only one word rang in my mind. *Paradise.*

CHAPTER 15

e sat at the round dining table in the Celestial Room, with moonlight washing over us. There were four of us, joined together to discuss our plan of attack: Kratos, Yasmin, Adonis, and I.

I swirled the wine in my glass, thinking about the terrifying chaos Metatron could create using only his words. Now that we knew Metatron could create immortal angels, we had to come up with something. Fast.

Kratos glowed with golden light, gripping his wineglass so tightly it looked like it might break. "I am Conquest. I was born to lead an army. I can command legions of soldiers to victory at my behest and force my enemies into submission. I can orchestrate a large-scale attack using my mind, and subjugate our enemies. Only problem is that I'm several legions short of an army." He met my gaze. "What about your powers? Those gemstones? You managed to get the Heavenly Host off the earth once. Why can't you do it again?"

Because I'd die.

I shook my head. "I don't have control over that magic yet. It's too powerful for me. I'm working on it, but I need more time. If we can just do something to buy us time, then I'll be able to fight them." I paused, tapping my fingertips on the table. "This situation is admittedly not awesome. And neither of you happen to know any Angelic spells that could combat Metatron's magic? Can you make his army mortal, at least? Then Adonis could kill them."

"No," said Adonis. "Metatron is the voice of the gods. His Angelic is pure and perfect, and our magic won't combat him. Only you could do that, I think, with your light magic."

"The magic I can't control whatsoever?" I frowned. "Okay. How about we create an army? What about all the humans just barely clinging onto life in the rookeries and hovels around the country? They'll fight to survive." Granted, they might not want to follow the angel who'd been hunting them, but maybe we could persuade them somehow.

Yasmin shook her head. "Humans won't save us. We break a little too easily. We need to make our army out of demons."

"We don't exactly have a great relationship with the demon world," said Adonis. "And moreover, we can't kill the Heavenly Host anyway. They're immortal, remember?"

My throat tightened. "No, but we could buy ourselves some time. We can slam them all with Devil's Bane arrows and bullets and knock them out for weeks. Maybe during that time, I can learn to control my powers better."

"Frankly, that's the best we can hope for right now." Yasmin leaned on the table. "And what if I told you we could make our human allies a little more durable? That we could find someone to transform them into demons and fae?"

I cocked my head. "How is that possible?"

Yasmin paced over the flagstones, her brow furrowed. After Metatron's attack on the Tower, she seemed more determined than ever to help put an end to the Great Nightmare. "Azazeyl's power can do it."

I'd seen the statue of Azazeyl at Adonis's castle—the beautiful, pensive man with a snake coiled around his thigh. Maybe I'd seen him once or twice in my fantasies, too. He'd been the one to tempt Eve in the Garden of Eden. He was the one who brought the Angelic language to earth in the first place.

And yet … had she lost her mind? He didn't exist anymore. "He fractured into seven gods when he fell to earth. There is no Azazeyl."

She cocked her head. "Before he fell to earth, he visited the Garden of Eden, and he fathered a child with a human. His descendant lives, and she has the power to transform humans into demons."

"Who is this person?" Kratos asked.

"Our sources tell us that her name is Rosalind, and she lives in the Vampire Kingdom of Lilinor with a demigod named Caine. Grandson of Nyxobas. At least, they used to be vampires."

"Caine," said Adonis. "He's awful."

"What are you talking about?" I asked. "I've heard of him. My boyfriend, Marcus, was once a soldier in Caine's army. Caine is apparently mind-blowingly hot, and—" I stopped short, reading Adonis's irritated expression. "That's not important. He's a general and whatnot."

Adonis glared at me. "He's the demon who seduced Muriel five centuries ago. He intended to ruin her. He hates angels. And of course he does, because he's an incubus."

Yasmin let out a long sigh. "Well, his wife has the power of seven gods. So whoever Caine shagged four centuries ago will just have to deal with it."

Kratos rubbed his forehead. "Will the humans even agree to this? To become demons? And would the humans even agree to work with us after…."

He let the words die on his tongue—the likely words being something like *I hunted them like rats through the streets.*

Adonis looked at me. "You spent time in the rookeries. You know humans just like Yasmin does. What do you think?"

I drummed my fingertips on the table. "Kratos has a bit of a problematic reputation among the human populations, since his dogs had a habit of eating them."

Kratos's features darkened. "I hope they appreciate the sacrifice I've been making. My hounds have been starving on a diet of pigs."

I nodded. "I'm sure the humans will be very impressed."

"So you don't think it will work?" asked Adonis. "Our transformed army?"

I bit my lip. "I think they'll come around, eventually. We'll need to keep Kratos out of it until the humans are already committed. But when it comes down to it, I think they'll fight for their own survival."

"I think you're right," said Yasmin. "The will to live is a powerful thing."

"So where is this vampire kingdom?" asked Adonis.

Yasmin leaned on the table. "It can only be accessed through a portal. It's one of the magical realms, completely sealed off from this world ever since they battled the magic-hunters years ago. Someone will need to find a way in."

"I'll do that," said Kratos. "It will give you all some time to convince the humans to let me lead them while I'm not here, terrifying them with my presence. But are you sure Rosalind has this ability?"

Yasmin nodded. "One of our informants was a member of Caine's army when Rosalind transformed them all. He was once a vampire. Now, he's a hellhound." She chewed on her thumbnail. "Now, I just need to meet with some of the human leaders and convince them we're on their side." She shot me a piercing look. "I looked for your old friends, just like you asked, to see if we could better make inroads into the resistance. Your friend Alex ranks highly among them. He returned from his safe haven outside of London. Do you think he trusts you?"

I loosed a relieved breath. *He's safe.* "I'm not sure." Guilt pierced my chest. "He did at one point. We were close, even. But I disappeared when I started working for the Institute. He had no idea what I was doing. The last time I saw him, I was on a parapet with Johnny, aiming an arrow at him. Adonis helped to spare his life, so maybe he'd be willing to talk to us."

"We'll explain to him that you were working for us." She tapped her fingertip against her lip. "I'll try to arrange a meeting with the resistance leaders and Alex. You go on your own. No horsemen. It will be easier to persuade them without any apocalyptic agents milling around. And without me, for that matter."

CHAPTER 16

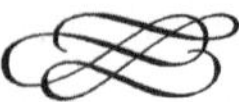

*H*igh above the streets, I clutched tightly to Adonis's neck. Under a starlit sky, we soared over London's perimeter, over the crumbling, shattered buildings, the abandoned streets. Empty cars littered the roads, gleaming in the moonlight. At night, I didn't even need to glamour us. Adonis's magic had us blending into the night sky like dark smoke.

Already, we were soaring over London's western edge. As we flew above an enormous Victorian cemetery, my pulse raced. Even from here I could see many of the graves had been disturbed, and piles of dirt lay next to dark holes.

My lip curled with disgust. Humans sometimes resorted to cannibalism in times of desperation, but they couldn't be surviving off old corpses. Right? I suppressed a shudder, burying the thought deep under the surface.

Then, I hugged Adonis a little closer. "It's nice of you to give me a ride, but I could have gone with Yasmin."

Adonis's powerful arms tightened around me, and he lowered his face to mine. "I want to stay as close to you as possible."

"I do have the power of the Old Gods protecting me."

"It didn't help you in Paris, did it?"

An image flashed in my mind—Adonis, falling beneath Aereus's sword, his body carved in two. "I was a little distracted. I saw the Horseman of War cut your head in half."

"Is that what threw you off? You were worried about me?"

"Yes."

"That's absolutely ridiculous. I can't die. Unless you kill me."

The very thought of it made my stomach flutter. "I know. But it looked like you died, and it was very visceral. It was an emotional reaction."

His midnight wings beat the air. "Has it occurred to you that we might be bad for each other?"

Cold wind rippled over me. "What do you mean?"

"You worry about me so much that you no longer can protect yourself, and I worry about you so much that I slaughter everyone around me. Not to mention the fact that you are the one living being who can kill me. We make each other vulnerable."

"That's what love is, my friend." As soon as the words were out of my mouth, my cheeks heated.

He pulled me in closer. "Is that right?" He honestly looked almost perplexed, as if this were some kind of foreign concept. "Yes, I think you're right."

"You're old as hell. You've never been in love before?"

"I thought it was a human concept. I didn't think it was something a horseman could feel." Warmth radiated from his powerful body. "But now you feel like my home, and like you've always belonged to me." His voice was a velvet caress that tingled over my skin.

My lips curled in a smile. "So how do I rank against your garden?"

"I'd say you have the advantage."

I nestled my head into his neck. I probably didn't need him flying with me to London. I could disguise myself completely. But the truth was that I liked his protectiveness. I liked that he wanted to keep me safe—just like I wanted to keep him safe. It had been a long time since anyone had tried to look after me.

As if hearing my thoughts, Adonis said, "Use our bond to stay in touch with me. I'll stay out of the way while you're meeting with the humans, but I won't go far."

"I will."

Westminster was our designated meeting point. While Metatron had taken over the Tower in the East, some of the humans had retreated to the old Anglo-Saxon part of the city. They'd taken over the Houses of Parliament and Westminster Cathedral, planning their resistance from there.

And as soon as we touched down in Westminster, Adonis was supposed to take off. When trying to persuade humans that we were on their side, we didn't need Death hanging around, glooming up the place.

As we swooped lower over Westminster, I found the old medieval buildings almost untouched. The Great Nightmare had destroyed most of the city, but at least it had left this place intact.

Under the darkness of night, Adonis soared down to the abandoned streets. An eerie silence had fallen over the city.

Flying through the shadows, we touched down behind the abandoned Jewel Tower—across the street from the cathedral.

Adonis lowered me to the ground, then leaned in to whisper in my ear. "Don't let me lose track of you again."

He traced his fingertips over my shoulder, right in the place where he'd marked me with the *theta*, and warmth spread through my body.

I cupped his face in my hands. "They're just human. It will be fine."

"I'll come back for you when I hear your call." Adonis turned, and the shadows around him seemed to absorb him as he walked away.

An oppressive silence hung over the city, and a shiver danced up my neck. For a thousand years, these streets were teeming with life. Now, it felt like an empty carapace.

I climbed up an old set of stairs until I reached the street. There, across from me, stood the ancient cathedral, where kings and queens had been crowned for a thousand years. Iridescent magic glimmered around it, sparkling like a canopy of stars. I felt reassured knowing that the humans here were smart enough to have protected the place—but concerned that they'd done it in such an ostentatious way. I doubted they understood what Metatron was capable of. Magic wouldn't protect them from his power, and a grand display like this would only attract his attention. Given the showiness of the magic, Metatron already knew they were here. He probably just didn't consider them much of a threat.

I surveyed the outside of the cathedral before crossing the road. Two human guards stood in front of the shimmering shield of magic. They clutched semiautomatic rifles.

I smoothed out my hair. I'd taken care with my outfit, hoping to convey "I'm a normal human here."

Before his untimely demise, Elan had left behind a multitude of cat sweatshirts. I'd chosen to wear one that depicted a cat eating pizza and tacos in front of a starry sky. I'd even painted my nails with chipped nail polish, just like a human would.

When you had to meet with people who might kill you, it helped to let them underestimate you. Plus, I knew enough about the human race to understand that they loved weird cat stuff. Just like anything else, this was a performance, and I had to dress the part. Except unlike with my burlesque shows, this performance had life-or-death consequences.

As soon as the guards saw me moving through the darkness, their bodies stiffened, rifles pointed at me.

"Don't you fucking move!" one of them shouted, spittle flying form his mouth.

Gods below. I guess I still conveyed some sense of threat even in the stupid cat sweatshirt.

I held up my hands, showing them I had no weapons. "Easy does it, gentlemen. The Council is expecting me." That's what the humans had started calling themselves. *The Council.*

One of the humans—a stocky fellow who looked like a squashed Chuck Norris—stepped forward. "What's the secret password?"

I sighed. I'd forgotten about the password. Or perhaps I'd temporarily repressed it. "Cock-arsing bollocks," I mumbled.

"What?"

"Cock-arsing bollocks," I said a little louder. Real mature, these guys.

Stocky Chuck Norris nodded, then shouted into the air, "Fuck-stick patrol!"

The magic shimmered away, and a large wooden door behind him groaned open.

CHAPTER 17

"Now," he barked. "Before we put the shield back up."

I hurried past them, moving quickly into the transept.

The city hadn't had electricity in months, but candles had been lit in sconces and chandeliers around the cathedral. Light danced over the ivory flagstones in Poets' Corner, where Chaucer, Spenser, and Tennyson had been buried centuries ago.

So here we were. The poets and thinkers who represented humanity's greatest gifts to the world, guarded by men who shouted *Fuckstick patrol* at each other.

My footsteps echoed off the high ceiling as I walked farther into the ancient space. There, on the ornate mosaic floor and among the gilt candleholders of Westminster's altar, stood three women. I searched in the shadows, but I didn't see Alex.

I raised a hand in greeting. "I'm Ruby."

The first person to step forward was a curvy young woman with shoulder-length hair, dressed in a Mickey Mouse T-shirt. Already, I was feeling confident about my taco-cat clothing choice.

"Lila here," she said. "Girl, they made you use bullshit passwords, didn't they?"

I nodded. "Cock-arsing bollocks."

"Charming." A second leader stepped forward—one with dewy skin and smooth, auburn hair. "You're Ruby, I take it. I'm Amber."

"I'm Brianna," said the last one—a young woman with a chin-length blond bob.

"We put those men in charge of security so they feel important," said Brianna. "Stops them from trying to make crucial decisions, but they get to choose the passwords."

I frowned. "Speaking of men, I thought Alex was supposed to be here."

Lila stepped closer to me, looking me up and down carefully. "Alex! Is this her?" she shouted into the shadows.

Alex stepped into the candlelight, a smile lighting up his face. "That's most definitely Ruby."

He looked even leaner than the last time I saw him, a ragged sweater hanging off his thin frame. I ran over to him, throwing my arms around his neck in a hug. "Alex! I missed you. Sorry about disappearing. And about pointing an arrow at you."

I pulled away from Alex, meeting the blonde's gaze. "So how did you three get to be leaders?"

"Each of us represents a faction of the resistance from different territories," said Brianna.

Lila shoved her hands in her pockets, eying me warily. "Probably best if we don't give too much information."

Pretty suspicious for a girl in a Mickey Mouse T-shirt.

I nodded at the exit. "I take it by the ostentatious display of magic that you're not too worried about the angels discovering your location."

Amber flicked her auburn hair over her shoulder. "We've got some of the world's best mages working with us. We want the angels to see what kind of power we have. The essence of Devil's Bane imbues that force field. If any angels touch it, their bodies will dissolve like ice in a lava flow."

This might be my chance to provide them with some valuable

information so they'd know I was on their side. "Yeah, that's not going to stop Metatron."

"Who?" asked Lila.

"Leader of the Heavenly Host, father of the horsemen, all around terrifying fuck-stick of an angel. To use your guard's term. He's been keeping the Heavenly Host in hiding and slowly transforming them into immortal beings. From what I understand, he is the most adept speaker of the Angelic language in the universe. I think he can break your shield. I think he can break everything."

Brianna's face paled. Then, she straightened. "In the worst-case scenario, the mages can transport us to one of the magical realms. The angels won't find us."

Lila folded her arms in front of her cartoon shirt. I wouldn't say the look on her face was exactly welcoming. "We're not transporting anywhere. This—London—is our home. They've invaded, and we're fighting back to protect us. You've been living with the angels. You really want us to trust you?" She moved closer to me, her shoes clacking off the floor.

"She's been working with the Institute," said Alex. "She's been undercover among the horsemen, gathering information, even before the resistance was formed."

Lila's jaw tightened. "I know that. But now she's working with the Hunter. Isn't that right? You want us to join an alliance with two of the horsemen who've been slaughtering us." Tears shone in her eyes, and her cheeks turned pink. "I watched one of my friends torn to pieces in the streets by his hounds." She pulled up the sleeve of her sweatshirt, displaying a brutal scar where some of the flesh had been torn off her arm. "His hounds did this to me."

Oh, balls.

I had known this was going to be a hard sell, and the taco cat on my sweatshirt might not be enough to smooth it over. But I didn't think it would be "watched my friend eaten by dogs" bad. Or "he ripped the flesh off my arms" bad.

I took a deep breath. I wanted to say that Kratos couldn't control it —that he'd been cursed by Metatron and forced to hunt. But this would just sound like a bunch of bullshit excuses to them. They'd never feel sympathy for him or care why he'd done it.

I had to appeal to something more powerful. A desperate will to live. "Yes, Kratos—the Hunter—is part of the alliance I want you to join. As I'm sure you know, he is no longer hunting humans. The simple fact is, a war has erupted between the horsemen. Two of the horsemen are trying to end life on earth as we know it. They want to kill all of us and start fresh. They want to create a race of humans born only to worship them and Metatron. The two horsemen who oppose them are willing to wage war against them, and we need to work with them. Because guess who's not going to win a war against immortal angels? Humans."

Alex frowned. "You think humans are weak against the angels, and maybe we are. So why are you so eager to form an alliance with us?"

And here's where my pitch got *really* difficult. "To give us the greatest chance of winning, we might need you to change a bit."

Amber furrowed her brow. "Change us? What are you talking about?"

"Look, I'm just going to lay it out for you," I said. "Right now, your chances of survival are not good. Metatron can get through your shields and slaughter you all within seconds."

"Even if that's true," said Brianna doubtfully, "How exactly are you proposing that we change?"

"We can make you more durable."

"Bollocks," said Lila. "How?"

"You'd have to stop being human."

"What are you on about?" snapped Lila.

"There's a way to convert you to demons and fae," I said. "Whatever species you choose. You'd have magic, maybe the ability to fly. As a demon, you could be immortal. As a fae, your life would extend for centuries."

"You've got to be bloody joking," said Lila.

"I definitely didn't come here to tell jokes."

"First," said Brianna, "you want us to accept the Hunter as an ally.

Now you want us to transform into the demons who have been attacking us since the Great Nightmare began."

This wasn't going well. "You'd still be you. Just more powerful. And more importantly, you'll be alive." I sighed. "Look, I'm not human, but I lived among you. Just like you, I watched my loved ones taken from me. The day angels came to earth, I watched a dragon shifter kill my boyfriend in front of my eyes. I watched my sister taken from me while Kratos flew through the skies above us."

I nodded at Alex.

"Alex and I lived in a rookery in Whitechapel, fighting gangs over rat meat, just like you've been doing. I remember the Hunter coming through the city at night. I remember trembling in fear when I heard his hounds howling. The Great Nightmare changed me. After everything I'd seen, I started getting scared of the dark. I slept in a windowless room, hiding my candle from the others because I couldn't face the shadows. This is our chance to come out into the light again. This is our chance to rebuild. You have two options. You can stay human and die, or you can adapt and survive. You're leaders. Lead. Your job is to make sure your people survive at all costs."

Amber shot me a fierce look. "Demons have done nothing on earth except feed from us. Humans have created everything you see here." She gestured at Poets' Corner. "Shakespeare, Darwin, Byron—all human. Galileo, Newton, Einstein—all human. We are earth's actors, its creators. We built civilization, and we're here to defend it. And now you want us to give all that up and become monsters? Leeches? What exactly are we defending if we become like them? We were born human, and we're meant to stay human."

"You can protect the other humans by adapting." I shook my head. "Clinging too hard to what you believe is your nature is dangerous. It's a shackle around your throat. Sometimes I'm a fae, sometimes a human. Sometimes I'm a succubus. None of these things are my destiny. We all have to adapt to survive, and the fact is, if you don't form an allegiance with us, human culture won't survive at all. No more poems, sculptures, or cathedrals. All this turns to ash. No more nursery rhymes or tacos or cat sweatshirts. Just a wasteland populated by human slaves created to worship the horsemen. Do you understand what I'm saying? You can either join us, or die. *Everything* dies."

Join or die. I think I'd seen that slogan on some old human propaganda, and it seemed like it might be effective. In fact, it seemed perhaps like the perfect note to end on.

I turned, crossing to the cathedral's doors. I'd done my job for now —planting a seed of an idea in their minds. They didn't seem like they were jumping at the chance to become a mob of vampires and ogres, and I didn't blame them. But surely they'd spent enough time scrambling for rat meat and dying from dysentery to know that death lingered for them around every corner.

I pushed open the enormous transept door into the cold night air, and the two guards nodded at me. I crossed into the shadowy street in front of Westminster, heading for my meeting spot with Adonis.

But as I moved closer to the old stairwell, Angelic words began to boom around me, clattering inside my skull until I couldn't hear my own thoughts. Words and fragments appeared and popped in my mind like bubbles.... *Pavem—blood—Marc—fera—drago—beast—*

I fell to the ground, my hands over my ears, trying to block it out. Through the chaos, one idea rang clearly.

Metatron is near.

And in the next moment, my world went black and silent as a grave.

CHAPTER 18

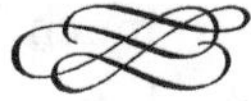

I woke in a tiny stone room, hanging from the ceiling in iron manacles, agony burning through my arms. Only the tips of my toes touched the slimy floor.

I knew my manacles were iron by the fact that they sent a deep, throbbing pain racing through my bones, from the wrists down through my shoulders. Also from the fact that my body felt completely drained of all energy, as if someone had sucked all the blood out of me.

I strained, trying to see around me. In the gloom, I couldn't see much beyond the slick stones. The air around me smelled damp and fusty, like old moss. Or like an old fae. As my eyes adjusted, I peered through an arched doorway. Through it, I could vaguely see a spiral staircase leading up to another floor. All I really knew was that I was hanging by my wrists in a vaulted room. Heavy shadows cloaked much of the space.

Something fluttered in the darkness, then burst into the air, cawing. My body tensed until I realized it was just a raven.

A wild guess told me I was in one of the old dungeons at the Tower. And also that I was pretty much screwed. With iron sapping my power and no one to hear me scream in a torture dungeon, it was looking a little bleak. Fear began to crawl up my spine.

If I needed to, I'd call to Adonis through our bond. But I wasn't going to panic just yet. I wanted to know exactly what my enemies had planned here before I called Adonis into the fray. For all I knew, this could be a trap.

Then—from the shadows—*he* appeared. Metatron glowed with pale light. His features looked so much like Adonis's, but he had that otherworldliness about him that disturbed me. He wore his dark hair longer, and it hung over his shoulders, melding with the shadows. His body seemed fuzzy, like I was looking at it through a Vaseline-smeared lens. I didn't quite have a sense of what he was wearing—just an ethereal, white glow around his body.

"Ruby." His voice knelled like a funeral bell. "The great savior. Are those little rocks in your head supposed to ward us all away?"

An uneven stream of water droplets dripped onto me from the ceiling, plunging onto my shoulder, cold and slimy. *Drip, drip ... drip.*

Faintly, the stones tingled. But with the iron digging into my skin, I couldn't summon any of their magic.

An icy wind rippled over me, and I shivered. It was only at this point that I realized I'd been strung up completely naked. "I was actually growing fond of that cat sweatshirt, you know. You fucking pervert."

"Oh, you misunderstand, little beast. I find you physically repulsive."

I narrowed my eyes at him. From what I could tell, he was telling the truth. He looked at my body with all the excitement of a high school student staring at a math problem about train velocity.

"Of course I find you repulsive," he continued. "It's just that beasts weren't meant to wear clothes. Humans certainly weren't. Don't you know the story of the Garden of Eden?"

The manacles were biting into my flesh, but I tried to keep myself from grunting, or from giving him the pleasure of hearing me struggle. "Yeah, I've heard of it once or twice."

"Humans—beasts like yourself—became self-conscious. They

learned they would die someday, that the consciousness they came to think of as eternal would cease to exist. It pained their simple minds. That was their punishment for hubris. They thought of themselves as angels. They weren't."

"Okay. So you're not into human or fae bodies. Good to know." I grimaced at the pain in my arms. "You do realize that I'm not a human, though, right?"

He sniffed the air. "You have a particularly strong fae smell. You smell of moss and dirt. Eons ago, your kind were angels. You chose to live as beasts here on earth. Fighting and fucking like animals. You are worse than humans. Have you ever seen a dog dressed in a suit? That's what you look like to me in your clothing."

"Yes, I get it. Shall we move on? I assume you have a point to all this."

Whatever it took, I needed to get out of these manacles. I just had no idea how. I craned my head, glancing behind me to find a sort of ladder. That was the rack, I thought. If I had to guess, they probably planned to tie me to that at some point for a bit of enhanced interrogations.

His lip twitched in a smile. "I understand you know Aereus."

Footfalls echoed out, and the Horseman of War stepped into the dim light. In his eyes, I didn't find the bland dispassion that Metatron displayed. Nope, Aereus was looking at me like I was a stripper at his prison release party.

This all just got more fun. "Did you know that your lovely son here has a prurient interest in animals?"

Metatron ignored me, taking another step closer. "It was the worst mistake an angel ever made—giving divine knowledge to the animals. I listened in on your little meeting in the cathedral. Very interesting. The humans are quite proud of their scientists and their poets. They don't commemorate the truth. Shall I show you what they leave out of Poets' Corner? The real work of humans. Their singular ability to devise creative ways to torture, maim, and kill. Everything we're going to do to you here in this prison was designed by humans. Remember that."

Oh, this didn't sound good. In fact, my mouth was starting to go dry, and I really wanted to puke.

The pain in my wrists was starting to take my breath away. "You have a very selective interpretation of history."

"Humans were given the gift of language, of magic," said Metatron. "And what did they do with it? They squandered it. Do you know that war and violence are the primary drivers of human technology and advancement? You all could have used their gifts for working with each other, but you didn't. That's why we need to burn it all and start again."

Metatron spoke a few words in Angelic, and a vision rose before my eyes.

A thin, blond woman lay strapped to a rack, dressed in only a tiny white dress. Two men flanked the rack, one of them with his meaty fists on a wooden wheel at her feet. When he began turning the wheel, her face contorted with pain. She appeared to shriek, then she lost consciousness.

"Anne Askew," said Metatron. "Tortured nearly to death, right here in the Tower. And for what? Some differences in theology that none of them were right about in the first place. They turned the handles so hard, that they ripped dear old Anne apart. They dislocated her elbows and knees, pulled all her joints out of their sockets. She screamed so loud they heard her outside the Tower walls. And when they finished, they carried her broken body to Smithfield—the meat market—where they burned her alive."

Bile rose in my throat, and I closed my eyes. I didn't want to see it, didn't want to hear it. I wanted to run back to the humans to listen to them talk about Darwin again. Still, I needed to keep him stalling, at least long enough until I could think of a plan.

The vision disappeared with a flick of Metatron's hand. "I know what's in your soul, little animal. I can see it smudged on your fore-head like a bloodstain. You dream of a simple life in a cottage. Like that fae couple you saw."

I swallowed hard. His ability to see into my mind bothered the hell out of me. I didn't mind him looking at my naked body, but reading my thoughts felt like a complete violation. "Is there a point to all this?" I snapped.

Aereus grinned. "We just want to break your mind before we break your body."

My gut churned. *Think of a plan, Ruby, think of a plan.*

"Pathetic, really," said Metatron. "Your dream of a fae utopia in the woods. You and my son. Do you really think he belongs with a creature like you? Eating soup?"

I didn't answer. His intrusion enraged me.

"He doesn't even like soup," Metatron continued.

"It's not about the soup!" I shouted. *Who doesn't like soup? It's so weird.*

"Would you like to see more from your little fae friends?" Metatron asked.

"No," I replied. "Not at all, actually."

"Too bad."

From the darkness, a second vision arose. It was that cottage I'd seen in the woods. An emaciated fae boy was walking toward it, his features gaunt. He knocked on the door, and the woman opened it.

The woman smiled, her cheeks dimpling. Then, she lunged for the boy. Her teeth were in his neck before he knew what hit him, blood pouring from his throat.

My heart clenched. Adonis had said he'd smelled blood when we passed that place.

My lip curled. "I get it. You don't like anyone who's not an angel."

After everything Metatron had showed me in here, part of me was starting to wonder if he was right. The smartest species on earth were also the most brutally sadistic. Beasts with the minds of angels—a dangerous combination. What if I'd been viewing everything through rose-tinted glasses, romanticizing a life that just didn't exist? Humans who used science to kill, fae who ate their own.

Maybe Adonis was right, and we were all slaves to our own natures.

He is Death; I am a beast, and all of us were born to hurt each other.

CHAPTER 19

"You must understand now." Metatron steepled his fingertips. "This is why it's time for a reckoning. If humans had worshipped me like they were supposed to in the first place, if they'd remained humble, none of us would be here. But they desired supremacy over each other, the way gods like me are supposed to reign supreme over the beasts." Metatron cocked his head. "Strange to me that all those people like dear old Anne allowed themselves to be tortured because of moderately different interpretations of religious texts. You were meant to worship me. You all got it wrong. What would you die for, Ruby? Shall we find out?"

One thing, and one thing alone: the people I love.

"Ahh. You'd die for my son. How sweet."

He was listening in on my thoughts again, and I wanted to rip his smug, glowing face off.

He moved closer to me, his eyes curious now. "Maybe torturing you isn't the worst thing, then. Maybe watching your loved ones die painful deaths would be worse."

I swallowed hard. "Would you kill your own son?"

"I can't kill him. Only you can do that. But if I hurt you enough, you'll give in. Beasts like you will always save themselves in the end, even if you make yourselves weak with your attachments. Love weakens you, just like the iron does. Because when you turn on Adonis, it will break you completely."

I shuddered. Metatron was a complete monster.

Faint light glinted off Aereus's armor, and he took a step forward. "Adonis will come for you, of course. We'll make you kill him. Then you die. Then the rest of the world. In just three days, my army of immortals will begin rampaging through one city after another. They will cleanse the world of the rest of the humans and demons who hid like rats in the sewers. Busy week, honestly."

Panic slammed me in the gut. In three days? We only had three days before everyone and everything died. Still, I tried to think clearly. If I managed to get out of here alive, this was my opportunity to gather some intelligence from them. I needed to know what their exact plan was.

What was the best way to get people to tell you things when they had all the power? Naked and chained to the ceiling, I couldn't exactly scare him into giving me information. I had to appeal to his weaknesses. Unfortunately, he didn't seem to have any, except for the fact that he was really hung up on the "worship me" thing.

"When you attack, people all over the world will tremble before you," I said, looking straight at Metatron. "Everyone will know your name."

He stared at me. Maybe that was a little too much. I needed him talking, not gaping at me.

Let me try that again. "I beg you to rethink this. As you march from one city to another, the people who remain will know the true meaning of fear and terror. Their last remaining moments on earth will be filled with thoughts of you instead of thoughts of their loved ones. I beseech you to change your mind."

The white light intensified around him. "They should think about me. I don't see what the problem is there."

I let my eyes go wider. "Can you picture it, Metatron? Can you picture the destruction, the fear?"

"We will make humans bleed from their ears," Aereus cut in, his face reddening. "From their chests and throats."

Metatron shot Aereus an irritated look, like a father who wanted his son to stop showing off at the dinner table. "The important thing isn't that as we kill, humans will know the true meaning of divine perfection through my presence. If they don't know it through worship, they will know it through my wrath."

What. An. Asshole.

"Of course!" I simpered. "Your divine power is overwhelming. I can feel it changing me already. Inspiring me with divine grace."

I closed my eyes, thinking of some kind of ecstatic state. "So amazing to be in the presence of a real god. I can imagine you moving first through the City of London, inspiring sacred terror. In fact, I'm having a vision. A divinely inspired vision. First, you'll move through Westminster, then you spread through the rest of London, then Kent...."

"I'm bored of hearing you speak," said Metatron. "And I have someone else I'd like you to meet."

With that, he turned and slipped into the darkness of the hallway.

Shit. That line of interrogation had gotten me nowhere, and I had a feeling he was about to introduce someone even more unpleasant to my afternoon.

Aereus stared at me, licking his lips. He took a few steps closer. "You think you're so smart. Bollocks. We're not even going the way you said. We start in East London, then we move up to Northampton-shire. Spread through the North, then Denmark, and on to the rest of Europe."

Okay, so forget about appealing to someone's ego. Maybe the best strategy was always "get the dumbest person in the room to tell you stuff."

"When?" I asked.

"We leave at dawn, three days from now. That's all the time you have left until all your human friends die."

In all likelihood, Aereus didn't see me as a threat, anyway. He probably didn't expect me to make it out of here alive at all.

My mouth went dry as I waited to see who Metatron was about to bring back. My torturer, I assumed. At this point, I was glad I hadn't told Adonis where I was. This was all part of a trap to lure him here, so they could try to torture me into killing him.

Would I break?

My throat tightened, and raw fear snaked over my skin. I must have let some of that fear slip through the bond, because for the first time, I felt something coming through the bond toward me. Not words, but a feeling. Adonis's fear, mirroring my own.

Footsteps echoed in the corridor outside, and then Metatron returned through the arched doorway. By his side was a squat man wielding a dull-looking axe.

Yep, this was about to get a whole lot worse.

Metatron stepped closer, his face still wearing a bored expression. "If Adonis doesn't come on his own, we'll have to entice him a bit. He can feel your emotions, can't he? Let's give him something to really feel."

Dried blood coated the blade. The man wore a shabby tunic that looked like it belonged to another century.

Metatron gestured to him. "May I introduce Jack Ketch, the most sadistic executioner in England's history. I revived him, just for this. I hope you appreciate the effort I went through. I'll leave you alone to his ministrations. As he cuts into your flesh, think about whether or not humans like him have made good use of their divine knowledge, or if Azazeyl should have left them as wordless beasts rutting in the shrubs."

Jack flashed me another crooked grin, giving me the distinct impression that he was a snaggle-toothed simpleton with no idea what the hell Metatron was talking about.

Aereus rubbed his hands together. "Perhaps I can help."

Metatron glared at him. "You enjoy it too much. You're at risk of falling. Enjoying sadistic acts is what beasts do. Come."

Aereus scowled, then followed his father through the doorway.

Jack gripped his axe, grinning to reveal rotten teeth. "Collar day for you, pretty thing. Oooh, but I'd love to flog you at the cart's arse."

No idea what he meant, but the creepiness came through just fine. If this was who Metatron spent time around, no wonder he hated humans.

My heart began to race. I tried to slow it, worried I'd draw Adonis here with the fear blazing through our bond. Once Adonis arrived, my torments would probably only get worse.

I surveyed the room again, now that my eyes had adjusted, and caught a glimpse of the dark leaves crawling around the stone walls. *Devil's Bane.* That's how they planned to subdue Adonis while they tortured me. Adrenaline sparked through my nerves, electrifying me.

Gods below. If I could only get out of the handcuffs, I could control the plants completely. Maybe I could even kill these fuckers. My gaze flicked upward, where the iron bit into my wrists. How the hell could I get this off me?

Jack grinned, staring at my thighs. "I'll start with your pretty shanks...."

Stupid of Metatron to leave me here alone, but maybe he had a hard time believing a tiny chick wearing a taco-cat sweatshirt could fuck anyone up. *Always let your enemy underestimate you.*

I widened my eyes and bit my lip. "Jack, you have such a fearsome reputation. I don't think I can ... I don't think I can take it...." I let my head loll to the side, as if I'd just fainted.

Whatever time period he was from, women probably fainted all the time. Maybe this unrealistic performance wasn't much of a stretch.

"Ooooh, you dimber wench," he burbled. "I'd like to get my nimble fingers on your crinkum crankum before I cut you open."

What. The. Fuck.

Through a slit in my eyes, I watched him lay down his axe. When he reached for me, I swung my legs, tightening them around his neck. I squeezed hard, trying to block out the unfortunate proximity of his face to my *crinkum crankum.*

I snapped his neck. Humans were such fragile things.

Jack fell to the ground—dead once more, like he was supposed to be.

Now, I needed to get out of the damn manacles. I had very thin wrists, and if had something to lubricate them a bit, I could probably slide them out....

Drip, drip ... drip.

Right. The ceiling slime.

I swung my body back just a little until I caught a rung with my toes. I scrambled back onto the ladder until my heels were resting on a rung. From there, I stepped my way up the ladder until the chains were slack, and I could reach the ceiling with my manacles. I began rubbing them against the dungeon slime—a sort of mixture of water, moss, and gods-knew-what—until it covered the iron completely. Then, I yanked the chains down to my foot, and used it to put pressure on the links between the manacles. Grimacing, I pressed hard on the chain, and the iron scraped against my wrists. With the help of the slime, I was able to scrape them down to my hands, though it took some skin off with it. Already, I could feel the iron poisoning my blood, and I wanted to puke.

From somewhere above, Metatron's voice was booming off the stones. *He's coming back.*

My heart slammed against my ribs as I caught a glimpse of his pearly glow on the stairwell. *He's going to kill me.*

Then—at last—I slid the manacles off, and magic surged through my bones. The gemstones in my forehead began to heat up, and I let my mind merge with the plants around me. Their spirits called to me, and I felt as if they were my children. I beckoned them closer, and the ropes of Devil's Bane began peeling off the wall, sliding across the floor toward me, until the vines had wrapped themselves around my body like a makeshift dress.

In the next moment, Metatron was standing before me, with Aereus close behind. Light beamed from my body, creating a sort of shield, exploding from the inside out. The magic of the Old Gods surged in my skull, but his words were confusing me, creating chaos until I could no longer remember what I was supposed to be doing....

As he spoke, rock and stone rained from the ceiling, slamming against the shield I'd created, threatening to smash through it.

Fight the angel ... magical myster ... longitu ... apple clipper sternum malc drip....

I clamped my hands over my ears, trying to drown out the noise so I could fight him. *He's going to kill ... he's ... kill ... shrill mockingbir ... oyster....*

Ravens burst out of the shadows, fluttering around me, and their caws echoed off the stone walls, drowning out the sounds of Angelic. Then, darkness crept in like a miasma. The shadows had a heaviness to them, vast and overwhelming, a disorienting void that sucked up everything around it—even my own light—until I could see only blackness. And with it—sweet, merciful silence.

Once, darkness terrified me beyond measure. Once, I'd slept with a candle burning by my bed all night. Now, by the soothing tinge of the darkness, I knew Adonis had come.

With the Angelic language dulled, I could focus on my plant magic again. In the darkness, I sent my vines out, searching for my enemies. Through my connection to the vines, I felt them wrap around Metatron and Aereus, squeezing them tighter. Then, Metatron launched into another of his spells, and I could feel the vines crumbling. My body ached as they fell to pieces—but along with their demise, the walls were crumbling around us too, debris raining down on us. Chaos, of course, was hard to control.

Before Metatron had a chance to utter another spell, I felt Adonis's arms around me. He curled his body around mine protectively. Then, we were zooming through the air at the speed of a tornado wind.

Stone shattered around us, and I shielded my head with my arms.

Adonis had burst through the rock walls to free us, and blood streaked his face as we soared into the London sky.

CHAPTER 20

In the forest outside Hotemet Castle, I walked between the oaks, my bow slung over my back. With each step, a dull pain shot up my legs. The iron from the manacles still poisoned my system.

I'd spent the past hour out here, practicing my magic. But each time I used a more powerful spell, I felt the Old Gods overwhelming me until I was certain I'd lose my mind.

Now, a cold wind whispered through the trees, skimming my bare legs and making me shiver. Clouds roiled in the sky, the color of iron, and the sun had begun to set.

Today, I wasn't quite as in love with nature. Since my escape from the Tower earlier, the forest didn't seem to hold the beauty that it once had. Particularly since I'd already happened upon a large blackbird eating a baby blackbird that writhed in the dirt, its body malformed. I was never one for superstitions, but that had to be a bad omen, right? It was the kind of image Aereus would have framed and stuck on his wall.

And yet the destructiveness of nature seemed like it was all around me now. Crushed acorns littered the ground—little seedlings that had never made it into trees, each one of them a failed life. What if Eden had only been a paradise because humans were too dumb to see the decay around them, just like I'd been?

Every living thing in this forest would die at some point. In the end, chaos ruled everything, and sometimes the old ate the young.

So that was the kind of mood I was in.

As I walked through an alder grove, a familiar soothing magic whispered over my body, tinged with myrrh. All it took was the scent of Adonis to heat my blood, and I'd moved on from *death whispers all around us* to *let's get naked in a bath again.* Even though, technically, he *was* Death.

I turned to find him walking toward me, a faint smile curling his sensual lips. Dark, finely cut clothes accentuated his perfect body, and he wore a sword slung over his back. "What are you doing brooding out here? Don't you know that's my job?"

"Just wondering if I've been wrong about nature and paradise and all that crap. And maybe the forest is a cemetery, where a seed of death lies within every berry and fern and apple tree. That kind of fun stuff."

"You definitely sound like me. Have I gotten into your head?" He looked mesmerized as he gazed at me, and he closed the distance between us. Then, he stroked the back of his knuckles down my cheek. "No. Metatron got in your head, didn't he?"

"Your dad is an asshole."

"I could have told you that." His pale eyes shone like beacons in the forest's gloom. "But death gives rise to new life, doesn't it? Plants grow from the soil fertilized by the dead. It's not an endpoint. It's just part of a cycle."

One last ray of sunlight broke free from the clouds, gilding the perfect planes of his face. Already, his presence was soothing me, his otherworldly beauty an antidote to the ugliness of nature. "I think I have an idea of how to convince the humans to join us."

He arched a perfect eyebrow. "How, exactly?"

"Metatron showed me images of people being tortured. I always knew it was something that happened in the world, something that humans did. But seeing it right before my eyes disturbed me on another level. What if I gave the humans a clear visual image of what they were facing?"

"Facing death, you mean?"

"The deaths of people they love. Metatron said that love makes us weak, but only if you define strength as an unyielding stubbornness. I saw a vision of a woman who died for an idea. Something theological. I'd die only to protect those I love, and so would most people. Love can give us strength, can push us to make the right choices: the will to survive, to protect those we care about. The strength to adapt when we need to. Life is too precious to waste on ideals like staying human just for the sake of it."

"You want to remind them that they're fighting for those they love."

"Exactly. What if I used my powers of illusion to convince humans? They need to see firsthand what can happen to their loved ones if they don't join us."

"Terrify them into compliance. I like your tactics."

"They need to understand that people's children will die if they don't join us."

"There's a little problem with your plan."

"Oh?"

"The entire resistance has disappeared."

I blinked. "Disappeared?"

"Yasmin has just told us. It seems there were mages among them."

"Yeah. They were very proud of their mages. The best mages in the world, apparently. But they didn't know what we know. We only have three days before everything ends."

Adonis cocked his head. "And, unfortunately, I think they might have overestimated their mages' abilities."

A chill snaked up my neck. "What happened, exactly?

"After you told them Metatron could get through their shields, they panicked. When a king from another realm offered them asylum in his kingdom, they jumped at the chance. He's supposedly offering them space in his castle."

"Why did they leave so fast?"

"They thought they could plan the resistance from there, unperturbed by the angels. They transported the entire army to a magical realm. Only one old woman stayed behind, unwilling to jump into an unknown kingdom. She didn't want to risk the journey. It seems they didn't leave time to research the realm, and they might have jumped somewhere completely inhospitable."

My stomach clenched. Alex was among them. Was he in trouble? "Do you have any idea how to find them?"

"I've found them through scrying, and I can get us there. I don't know much beyond the location, but I can open a portal in and out."

"You're sure you can get them out?"

He looked affronted. "Of course I can, Ruby. I'm more powerful than their idiot human mages."

"Let's go, then. Now. I've got my bow and arrow, and I'm ready to shoot things if I need to."

Adonis grabbed me by the hand, pulling me toward the river. The sun had now dipped lower behind the trees, and I shivered in the cooling air. Once we reached the river, Adonis pulled me toward the edge. The water flowed fast, shimmering like quicksilver in the darkening forest.

"Are you ready for a swim?"

Goosebumps covered my skin beneath my dress. It felt a little cold to jump in the river, but with Metatron on the verge of unleashing his army of immortals, time was running short.

As we stood at the edge of the river, Adonis spoke in Angelic, and his powerful magic rippled over my body, electrifying me. I stared at the river as its churning waters grew darker. Then, a few sparks of electricity ignited on its surface.

"Could this realm be dangerous?" I asked.

"Yes, but we can leave through a portal any time we need to."

Holding each other's hands, we jumped into the river. Icy water enveloped our bodies.

Underwater, Adonis pulled me close to his powerful chest, and warmth radiated from his body as we sank deeper below the surface. My lungs began to burn the deeper we went down.

In the water's darkness, eels swam around us, their bodies blazing with electric pulses. That was eerie. I was starting to have a very bad feeling about this location.

At last, Adonis tugged my hand, and we began swimming for the surface. We reached the top, and I gasped for air, resting my elbows on the lip of a stone basin. I caught my breath for a moment, heaving air into my lungs. Then, I hoisted myself out, flopping to the cobble-stones below like a dying fish.

My dress was completely soaked, and my teeth began to chatter as I looked around me. We were standing on a stone lane of a ramshackle old city. Rickety timber-frame buildings crowded the roads, their surfaces covered in thorny branches and—disconcertingly—Devil's Bane.

We'd just arrived through a drinking fountain that featured a gorgon spewing water. At the top of a stone obelisk in the fountain, an enormous copper spike speared the sky. Dark clouds roiled above us, and I shivered.

Here, night was falling quickly. I wasn't as scared of the dark as I'd once been—not since I'd stolen the power of the Old Gods. Still, this place gave me the heebie-jeebies. I shivered, relieved that I'd brought my bow and arrow with me.

From our spot in the town square, the street snaked up a hill. And on top of the hill itself stood a dark, tottering castle. Between its spindly copper spires, electricity sparked rhythmically, like a heartbeat.

I glanced at Adonis. On the journey here, he'd hidden his wings. He didn't look particularly concerned about our current situation, but then, he rarely did.

He narrowed his gray eyes. "Whoever rules this place has covered it in Devil's Bane. Maybe the king has heard about the Great Night-mare even from within his sealed-off realm. He certainly doesn't want angels or horsemen here."

A tavern sign creaked in the wind, its chipped surface reading *Adam & Lucifer,* with an image of a painted snake.

A man and a woman burst from the pub, slamming the wooden

door open and tumbling into the street. The woman's lips were painted red, and she wore vibrant skirts with a tight black bustier. Another woman followed behind her, breasts spilling out of her gown. Let no one say that this realm lacked for cleavage.

Still, something looked *off* about them—their movements a little jerky, eyes a little haunted.

Thunder boomed, and a spear of lightning cracked the sky, touching down on the copper post to our right. I jumped, practically leaping on Adonis before recovering myself.

His lip curled in a wry smile. "A little scared of lighting, are we?"

I scowled at him. "Don't be ridiculous."

I surveyed the buildings around us once more, the thin chimneys jutting from rooftops like crooked teeth. Copper spikes protruded from some of them, and electricity sparked from their points.

I reached out for the vines covering one of the buildings. "Can this Devil's Bane affect you even if it's not touching you?"

"With this much around me, it's already sapping my powers."

I swallowed hard. Guess we'd be counting on my powers here, although the iron had wrecked me a bit. "Think we're supposed to head up to that castle?"

"That would be my guess. But considering this world is hostile to angels, I think it's best if we walk instead of fly."

Even though the dark buildings around us looked like they were falling apart, a sensual and alluring scent floated on a warm breeze, skimming over my skin.

As we walked, my arm brushed against Adonis, and a shiver of pleasure rippled over my body. Here, my mind felt different, my body strangely heated. I glanced at Adonis, whose spine had stiffened.

He slid his gaze to me. "There's an aphrodisiac in the air. Designed to distract us."

Oh, shit. I had a feeling we were in trouble.

CHAPTER 21

"*R*ight," I breathed. "So, we have electric eels, lightning rods, aphrodisiacs. That all adds up to…."

"Yes?"

"I have no idea, actually. It's all just fucking weird, and I can't think straight."

Thunder rumbled over the horizon again and lightning ignited the sky, touching down on a lightning rod over the palace spires. The skies opened up and rain began hammering down from above.

I felt my nipples harden under my soaking wet dress. As we walked along the winding streets, the hairs stood up on the back of my neck, and I started to have the sense that someone was watching us.

My chest flushed, and I glanced at Adonis again, running my tongue over my lower lip. I couldn't stop thinking about how his body had felt pressed against mine underwater. My heart beat faster, chest and cheeks flushing. *It's only the aphrodisiac, confusing me.*

As we walked, some electric lights cast a flickering glow, sparking bright white over the tumbledown buildings. We passed another bar —this one called *The Sparking Frog.*

Another woman slammed through the door, this one with platinum curls piled high on her head. She smiled at me, her lips cherry red. Even if she had those same strange, jerky movements, her eyes looked heavy-lidded, a lustful expression on her features. She looked like she'd just been satiated, and I suddenly had a burning desire to feel like that, too. She tottered across the dark road.

I breathed in the exotic scent in the air, feeling as if my breasts were growing heavy and full, and I had the strongest desire to pull Adonis into an alleyway….

I gritted my teeth, trying to stay focused. We were here to find the resistance. My eyes slid to Adonis, roaming over his muscled form. Plenty of time for fucking later.

As if hearing my thoughts, he shot me a wicked smile, and I realized that I'd stopped walking just to stare at him. In fact, I was leaning against a ramshackle wall—a pub, maybe. My bow was pushing into my back, annoying me. It didn't matter. What mattered was that heat pulsed between my legs, and my body ached for Adonis's touch. I tugged up the hem of my dress, and Adonis's gaze devoured every inch of my exposed thighs.

"Adonis," I said. My legs trembled, and I yearned for him—for his dark power.

I clenched my fists, trying to remember what we were doing here. *The resistance. Resist. Resist.*

"Plenty of time for fucking later," I managed, even as his possessive hands were grabbing my hips. My arms found their way around his neck, and I pulled him closer. "Plenty of time for your mouth on my breasts, for me to rub against you, touching you everywhere…."

What was I talking about?

His hot mouth found its way to my neck, and he murmured against it. "I could hike up your dress and take you right here if you wanted."

Oh, gods, I wanted that more than I'd ever wanted anything in my life. The raw ache built in me so strongly, liquid heat surging through my body. Adonis's magic spiraled off of him, caressing my skin up my thighs, under my skirt, in all the places I wanted his fingers to reach.

Adonis reached down, grabbing my wrists and pinning them to

the wall. My back arched into him. He leaned down, brushing his lips over my throat. I felt my legs widening, and my hips pressed against him. I wanted his mouth to move lower. Instead, he brushed slow kisses up my neck until he locked his gaze on me once more—his gray eyes fierce and hungry. He was a man used to restraining himself. I wanted him to let go, for once to completely give in to pleasure. I wanted his hand to reach the apex of my legs.

His pale eyes pierced me, and I gazed into them helplessly, mesmerized by him.

I tugged at my wrists to free them, ready to move things faster, but he held me in place, staying in control. This slowness felt like pure agony, and I moaned.

"You belong with me," he said. "Do you know that? Life and death belong together."

Whatever. Just put those hands under my skirt and we're good.

Instead, he leaned in, claiming my mouth in a sensual kiss. He pressed his hard body against mine, and I groaned, opening my mouth to him. His tongue swept against mine, and molten heat arced through my blood. I wanted more of him.

Still kissing me, his hands traced down my arms, skimming over my breasts, my hips. I shivered, overcome by desire.

My body ached for him. He pulled away from the kiss, his fingers now on my thighs. He was torturing me with the lightness of his touch, and I gasped, rocking my hips into him.

I felt my breasts straining against the fabric of my sodden dress, and I tugged down the front of it, exposing my lacy pink bra. Adonis growled, kissing my neck again, teeth grazing my throat until the only words I could hear were *ache, need, want....*

"I want you now, Adonis," I whispered.

Maybe if I pulled off my dress and discarded my panties, I could get him to move faster. I could turn my back to him and get him to take me against the wall. I'd always wanted to fuck someone up against a rickety building covered in thorns and Devil's Bane, in the center of a strange town....

Oh, no, wait. Had I? That didn't quite sound right.

"Adonis," I whispered, gripping his hair. "Something's not right."

He hooked his fingers into the top of my panties, tugging them down. *Oh, gods, I need him to touch me.*

"Yeah," he muttered into my neck. "You're wearing too many clothes."

Air caressed my skin as my panties fell to the ground, and my legs opened wider. I started to tug on his belt.

And yet, somewhere in the back of my mind, I knew this wasn't what we were supposed to be doing. The hairs rose on the back of my neck, that feeling of being observed.

"Adonis," I said. "He's watching us."

Resist. Resist.

Adonis's body tensed, and he froze. All at once, his gaze cleared, jaw clenching, and he pulled away from me. He reached over my head, grabbing a thorny branch, and he yanked it from the wall. He clutched it tightly, until blood poured from his fist into the dirt.

Of course. That was how Adonis controlled himself—for centuries, when pleasure overtook him, he used pain to control it.

The sight of his blood was enough to clear some of the heat from my body, and I took a deep, shuddering breath. Then I leaned down, pulling up my panties again. I looked furtively around me, catching the eye of a woman in a red dress. She winked at me.

Gods below.

Blood dripped from Adonis's palms. "We're going to have to stay focused."

I took a deep, steadying breath. "So this is what it must be like to be a horseman, always trying to resist temptation? How did you manage for all that time?"

As we moved deeper into the city, the buildings started to look more stable, some now made of smooth stone. "Yes. I could have lovers, but I had to keep myself at an emotional distance. You know what can happen if I become emotionally overwhelmed. In the fourteenth century, I had a close friend, once. A siren named Esmerelda who I met on the shores of Sicily. We used to stay up late, studying the stars. She made me laugh with her impersonations of a drunk priest we knew. One night, a sea monster attacked her, and she nearly died. Death washed off me, killing scores of people with a plague."

Even though he was talking about something super morbid, another wave of that aphrodisiac washed over me. "What about Tanit and Kur? You're close to them."

"True, but nothing can kill those two. I don't have to worry."

"So what changed? Why aren't you running from me?"

"I can't. Your allure is a command I have to obey. I don't have a choice in this, any more than the earth can choose to stop orbiting the sun. No more than the ocean can stop crashing against the shore. Your body draws me in with an inexorable gravitational pull. My own will has nothing to do with it."

I frowned, not sure if I should be flattered—although I felt the exact same thing for him. "That sounds ... strangely like a prison sentence."

"It's a prison I'll happily inhabit," he said in a voice that was strangely dreamy for Adonis. Clearly, the aphrodisiac was affecting him again, too.

We reached a small park, where willow trees grew among tall grasses. Lightning cracked the sky, illuminating a few women milling around the park. In this part of the city, the women's dresses had become even shorter—just little lacy scraps, with black stockings that stopped mid-thigh, their breasts on display and nipples painted red....

No one would judge us here. We all wanted the same thing.

I breathed in the heavy scent of spring, and my body started to feel full again. We seemed to have drifted off course, and the tall grasses tickled my feet. I'd taken off my shoes at some point. That ache began pooling between my thighs again, and I grabbed Adonis by the shirt, giving in to that gravitational pull. I needed him near me, and the heat in my body was driving me insane. If I could just get rid of this overwhelming desire, we could move on to ... whatever it was we were doing here.

My fingers found their way into Adonis's shirt, exploring his muscled body, and he let out a low growl.

I couldn't remember why he didn't want to give in to me here, why he wouldn't just take me in the grass right now … there was some reason, but it was stupid, and I could entice him if I just pulled off my dress.

"Ruby," his lips were at my ear, his breath hot against my skin.

"You. Me. Now." My ability to phrase things elegantly seemed to have disappeared along with my shoes somewhere. Might as well discard the dress with it. I pulled up the hem of my dress, then tossed it into the grass. Lust lit me on fire.

A cool breeze kissed my skin, and Adonis's gaze raked over me, studying every curve. My pulse roared.

At the look he was giving me, raw need surged. I had a vague sense that we were outside somewhere, that people might be watching, and I really should have my dress on. But I couldn't quite stop myself. I kissed him deeply, rubbing against him as I tried to make the aching stop.

Adonis pulled down my bra, covering one of my nipples with his mouth. I hooked my leg around him, trying to draw him in closer to me. He pressed his hard body into me, teeth skimming my nipple. Then, his tongue swirled over it. He wanted me as badly as I wanted him.

My breath hitched in my throat. "Touch my crinkum crankum…."

He pulled away from my breast. "What?"

Shit. Had I said that out loud? I'd just killed the mood. Godsdamn executioner, getting in my head.

I swallowed hard. "I didn't say anything."

In the next moment, he was spinning me around so I faced the tree. His hands found their way into my panties, and he stroked me with such a light touch between my legs that I thought I might lose my mind.

"Adonis," I moaned, rolling my hips, my ass pressing against him.

His breath was hot against my ear. "Tell me you love me."

I'd say anything he wanted right now just to get him to touch me harder. And in any case, it was the truth. I shuddered as he stroked me again, too lightly. I pressed myself against his hand.

"I love you," I whispered.

Lightning cracked again. An adder slithered though the grass toward me, and I had a vague sense that I needed to get away from it … something about venom, but….

"Say it louder," Adonis whispered.

As it slithered up my leg, another wave of pleasure rippled through me. This was how Eve had felt in the Garden of Eden, when Azazeyl had tempted her. This was—

That's when the adder sank its fangs into my thigh.

"Ouch!" I shrieked.

Adonis's body stiffened, and he pulled away from me.

I gripped the adder by its neck—if you could say that a snake had a neck—and pulled it off me. Two red droplets bloomed on my thigh.

"That thing is venomous." He ripped it from my hand. In an instant, the snake went limp. Adonis didn't have to expend much effort to kill—it just kind of happened naturally for him.

The place where the adder had bitten me throbbed, and the pain was enough to bring me back down to earth.

"I need to get the venom out," said Adonis. In the next moment, he was on his knees, his head between my legs, his hot mouth on my thigh. His tongue moved expertly over my skin, sucking out the venom. Involuntarily, I felt my thighs clenching around his head, and I threaded my fingers into his hair.

When I'd imagined Adonis's head between my thighs, snake venom hadn't been in the picture, and yet I wasn't going to complain about the feel of his mouth on my skin.

If I could just get these panties off—

But just as I was thinking it, he pulled his head away. A droplet of blood glistened on his lower lip. "That's the venom out."

"Venom?" I blinked.

He stood. "From the adder bite."

"Right. Yes."

Adonis looked dazed, his eyes half-lidded with lust like mine. Then, he straightened, smoothing out his clothes. "We were on our way to the castle." He reached down to the ground, picked up my dress, and handed it to me.

"I know that. I've been thinking about it the whole time."

When lightning speared the sky again, I found that the women weren't quite as I'd imagined them. Their breasts weren't on display. They wore ordinary frocks, hems at their knees. A few men in suits were standing around, pretending to ignore us, even though I knew they'd seen everything.

With my cheeks reddening, I pulled my wet dress over my body, then snatched my weapons off the ground.

Keep it together, Ruby.

CHAPTER 22

We just barely managed to keep our clothes on the rest of the way up to the castle.

A long, crooked stone bridge spanned a moat between where we stood and the castle itself. Electric lights flickered inside the narrow castle windows. There were no guards here, no soldiers to protect the place.

"Any idea where we are?"

Adonis shook his head, staring at his palm. Blood still ran from the thorn wounds, pooling on the pavement. "No, but all the Devil's Bane is weakening me. My body isn't even healing like it should."

I swallowed hard. "Maybe this is a bad idea. Maybe I should come back with Hazel, or someone else impervious to the Devil's Bane."

He narrowed his eyes at me. "No way. You are not sending me away for my safety to come back with a teenaged fae."

I could already tell there was no arguing with him. And in any case, we really didn't have much time to lose.

"Let's see if we can get in there, then."

We stood before the castle's entrance, and a pulse of electricity surged between the spires above us. It had a clear rhythm to it, and I guessed there must have been some kinds of thin wires connecting them. Beneath our feet, a sheen of copper glinted from the cobblestones.

This whole city looked like it had been built to conduct electricity.

An eerie feeling rippled over me, and I suddenly felt very grateful for the bow and arrows I'd brought with me. Despite all the aphrodisia, this whole place creeped me out. I stared at the entrance—an ordinary-looking wooden door with what looked like an electric buzzer—wondering if we were just supposed to ring the doorbell. But before I crossed the stones toward it, a shudder whispered up my spine.

Loud, thumping footfalls turned my head, and I whirled to find a monstrous man looming over us. At the sight of his face, my mouth went dry.

He held a torch aloft, and it cast wavering light over his misshapen face. His skin looked piecemeal, like it had been poorly sewn together. It had a yellowish hue, stretched tightly over his bones. It was practically translucent, and I could see the sinews and muscles through it. He must have been at least eight feet tall, dressed in rags, with the dark lips of a corpse....

Suddenly the pieces were starting to come together in my mind. The emptied graves I'd seen in London, the missing corpses, the jerky movements of this city's inhabitants, the electricity everywhere.

"Somewhere in this city is a necromancer," I whispered. "We should be very careful."

Adonis stared at the corpse, his expression unimpressed. "Please don't tell me the festering bag of flesh before us is the king of this place."

Adonis had spent so much time being immortal, and completely immune to any kind of harm, that he really had no idea when to shut up. Even when Devil's Bane had made him vulnerable.

"Not a king," said the corpse.

Honestly, the fact that he could talk—and talk clearly—surprised me.

"Not a king," the creature repeated as he straightened. He pressed a hand to his fleshy chest. "A monster who roams this earth alone, scorned intensely by all who behold me for my wretchedness. Why do I live? I've been cursed with a countenance that inspires dread, and yet deep within my bosom—"

Adonis rolled his eyes. "Here we go."

The monster scowled, then cleared his throat. "Deep within my bosom, I hold feelings of affection. Yet other passions stir me like any other man—not least among them a venomous rage. Despair imbues my every thought, and I yearn for revenge. I shall draw sweet pleasure by indulging myself in your shrieks and torment as you die. For within my bosom—"

The rest of his monologue was cut off by a swing from Adonis's sword. The blade cut his meaty arm, slicing into it. The monster roared, even though no blood poured from his body.

"Stop it with the bosoms," Adonis snarled. "You sound like a twat."

The monster staggered back, but the blow hardly seemed to affect him. In the next moment, he was lunging for Adonis, wielding his torch like a weapon. "I shall incinerate you and relish the cries of your torment!"

I pulled an arrow from my quiver, nocking it. "I take it your death powers aren't working on him."

"No. He is unnatural, and so is his soul."

I loosed my arrow, and it found its mark in his chest. He kept stumbling onward, moving toward me with his torch, and I stepped backward.

"The gods should never have given the fire of knowledge to mankind," he bellowed. "For look what they've done with it. The world reviles me, and anguish pierces me to the marrow! I am malicious only because—"

Adonis swung for him again, his blade carving into the monster's side. "Please stop talking."

The monster howled, but he seemed undeterred. I nocked another arrow, and it sailed into his chest, protruding next to the other one. "I am alone!" he cried, thrusting his torch at us. "And palely loitering!"

The weapons weren't stopping him. Still, there was only one of him, and two of us.

At least, there *had* been only one of him. I gaped as more monsters stumbled from the shadows, their feet slamming against the stones.

"I thought you said you were tormented by solitude?" snapped Adonis. "There are dozens of you. What in the gods' names are you complaining about?"

"Each of us equally tormented by cruel solitude, for within our bosoms—"

One of my arrows slammed into his jaw, cutting off his rambling. But as soon as it did, I felt a searing heat scorching the back of my arm.

I whirled to find a new monster thrusting his torch at me. "The fires of knowledge burn you!"

"That is actual, literal fire," I shouted, gripping my arm. "You fucking knob-end."

Lucky for me, the rain had dampened my clothing, so nothing ignited.

But now, more monsters surrounded us, each one of them waving a torch and banging on about their bosoms and cruel visages. Most importantly, they all looked eager to light us on fire. My heart raced, and I loosed arrow after arrow.

My arrows were flying uselessly into them, striking their hearts, their lungs. And it didn't make a godsdamned bit of difference, because they just kept lumbering on, waving their torches.

They'd encircled us, closing us in, determined to burn us to death.

I backed up to Adonis, my arrow still raised. "Now might be a good time to use those wings."

"Already? I thought we were doing well here."

"Do you really want to stand here listening to their monologues?"

"You have a point."

In the next moment, his arms were encircling me, and he lifted me into the air, wings beating the rainy air. As he lifted me above the castle, I stared down at the undead mob below us. We'd escaped them, but they blocked the only entrance I could see to the castle.

I had no idea what could kill these fuckers, until another bold of lightning cracked the sky.

I had a feeling that electrical pulses had given life to these corpses. Was it possible that a powerful electrical current could also overwhelm them—overloading their synapses?

That electricity between the palace spires pulsed again, igniting the wires between the towers. As it did, an idea began to spark in my mind.

Rainwater covered the ground below us. Water conducted electricity, right?

The storm hammered against us, and I shifted in Adonis's arms. "Can you bring us over to those wires? The ones with the electricity running between them?"

"Why?" he murmured in my ear. "Are you planning on ending it all after listening to them speak for too long?"

"No, I think I have an idea." I reached behind my back, pulling an arrow from my quiver.

I'd just have to be *very* quick, or I really would end it all.

Adonis soared toward the wires that stretched between the spires. I watched them carefully, getting a feel for the rhythm of the electrical pulses. I had about five seconds between each one. "When I say 'now,' bring me right down to the wire."

"Are you going to tell me what in the gods' names this is about?"

"You'll just have to trust me."

When the next burst of electricity sparked and snapped along the wire, I said, "Now!"

One.

Adonis swooped lower until we were just over the copper wire.

Two.

I ripped it out of its mooring, the copper biting into my fingers.

Three. I quickly tied the wire to the end of my arrow.

Four. I raised my bow, then loosed the arrow. It soared into the crowd of monsters, touching down on the wet ground.

Five.

The next electrical pulse burst along the line, racing down the copper until it ignited within the crowd. Electricity singed the air as it surged through the monsters' bodies, and the scent of burning flesh curled all around us.

One by one, they fell to the ground.

"There." I nuzzled my face against Adonis's. "They're not tormented by solitude anymore."

"You could say that."

"Because they're dead," I added.

"I understood, yes."

During the next gap between electrical pulses, I yanked on the wire, pulling the arrow up from the ground. With one shot from my bow, it soared over the castle's spires in the other direction.

And just like that, I'd cleared the ground for our landing.

CHAPTER 23

$\mathcal{H}$e lowered us to the ground, and we stood before the fallen pile of monsters.

Honestly, there was no better antidote to an aphrodisiac than a pile of scorched, undead and re-dead monsters. The stench and the charred remains managed to dampen any remaining lust that might have heated my body. At least, for now.

I glanced at Adonis's hand, grimacing when I saw the blood still flowing from his palm. If we spent too long here, would he actually become mortal? And what other disturbing creatures would we run into?

I stared at the castle entrance. Unlike a traditional castle with an iron gate or portcullis, this one had a wooden door inset into a stone opening. The stone doorframe had been carved to look like some sort of clown with sharp teeth. I shuddered. I was no psychological expert, but clown-fascination never seemed like the hallmark of mental stability or social adjustment.

An electric light flickered above us, and I eyed the buzzer.

While I was mentally calculating another complex plan with my bow and arrow—in case something came running for us—Adonis reached over me, pushing the buzzer.

"Just like that. You're ringing the doorbell."

He shrugged.

After a few beats of silence, the castle door creaked open on its own, revealing an empty stone hallway. There were no defenses here to deter us. Had the king been expecting us? It only reinforced my sense that he'd been watching us.

We crossed into the hall, where the tall ceiling arched high above us. A crimson velvet carpet stretched out over the floor like the tongue of an enormous beast. I breathed in deeply, that floral aphrodisiac heating my blood again.

Lightbulbs crackled and sparked from the arched ceiling, and a rhythmic beat from distant music pulsed in the air. I glanced at the carpet, thinking of Adonis's tongue on my thighs. A smile curled my lips.

It was at this moment that I looked down at myself, realizing that at some point—probably in the last few seconds—I'd pulled down the top of my dress, exposing my sheer bra. The strap of my bow carved between my breasts. My nipples were standing at attention, and for a moment, the sight of them distracted me until I yanked my top up once more. *Keep it together, Agent Hudole.*

Adonis's hand around my waist didn't help the situation, and he leaned into me, breathing in deeply. I indulged myself in a quick kiss on his neck, licking his skin, tasting a hint of salt. Then, I forced myself to pull away again, thinking of the stench of scorched corpses.

Stay focused, Ruby. Stay focused. Corpse bosoms and scorched flesh.

At the top of the stairs, the doors opened into a red-velvet-draped hall. It had the shabby, faded grandeur of an old music hall—in fact, maybe it *was* an old music hall, crammed with people in vibrant clothing. Voices echoed off the high ceiling. A stage stood at one end of the hall, and balconies and box seats hung above us. Faded green and red paint chipped off the wood. I *liked* it here. In fact, I didn't really want to leave.

"This place is amazing," I breathed.

I could almost envision myself on the stage, giving the burlesque performance of my life. Some black tassels, a fan dance. In fact, I had the strongest urge to get up there right now.

Adonis's eyes were on me, blazing with intensity, and I could feel his magic strengthen, licking over my body. "It's going to be hard to focus in here," he said.

I licked my lips. "You have a knack for understatements."

Chandeliers with sparking lightbulbs illuminated the crowd. All around us, women wore thigh-high stockings and short, bright frocks. They sipped from bright green drinks, their cheeks and lips painted red. The men wore suits, many of them with thin mustaches and slick hair.

In corners and under tables all around the room, men and women were groping and straddling each other.

Waitresses tottered around the room—their movements jerky, just like the women I'd seen outside. The waitresses' skin looked stretched over their bones, nearly translucent. They were the undead ones—corpses raised from the dead by the necromancer.

Unlike the waitresses, all the guests were alive. I stared at a woman climbing onto a tabletop and beckoning a man closer, her eyes half-lidded with lust.

I licked my lips, my body growing warm, swelling against my sodden dress. In here, the perfumed scent overwhelmed me, and my breath quickened.

A haze of sweet-smelling smoke filled the air. Why were we here, again? That's right, we were here to enjoy ourselves.

A waitress lurched past us, and I plucked a glowing green drink from the tray. I took a sip, savoring the hint of anise, before Adonis snatched it from my hand. "Bad idea, Ruby."

His sharp gray eyes brought me down to earth again.

"Right." I blinked a few times, surveying the crowd. Although the guests were alive, everyone's eyes held a glazed expression.

Adonis leaned down, whispering in my ear. "The longer we stay here, the harder it will be to leave."

"I was starting to get that impression." Whoever ruled this place seemed like he was into both necromancy and mind control. And ... orgies. "Any idea where we are yet?"

Adonis furrowed his brow. "I'm beginning to get a sense. I think we may have wandered into the realm of a phantom king named Spring-Heeled Jack."

"Who?"

"In the nineteenth century, women all over London reported being attacked by a winged creature who'd fly at them and grope their breasts." Adonis linked his arm through mine, and we started walking. He leaned in, whispering in my ear as we moved deeper into the hall. "Sometimes he breathed out fire, blue and white flames. After a bit of groping, he'd bound away again. The rumors were that he was a hedonist who lived in almost total isolation. So, he built himself a small kingdom of revived corpses to keep him company and to indulge with him, only occasionally venturing out into London to claw at women's breasts."

Gods. "Oh, he sounds lovely. I hope we get to meet him."

"Now," added Adonis, "it seems he's found himself some living playthings from among the desperate resistance. And they're completely under his thrall."

In all likelihood, the drinks played a role in the mind control.... In fact, I was having a harder time than ever thinking clearly. Warmth flooded my veins.

Adonis was talking to me, but I couldn't focus on the content of what he was saying, just the rich timbre of his voice. It rumbled over my skin, caressing me. My back arched as I walked, hips swaying to the pulsing music.

Cool air whispered over my skin, and I realized I'd pulled up the hem of my dress. If I hadn't been wearing the bow slung over my back, I'd have pulled it off completely.

Now, Adonis's eyes looked as glazed as mine, and he stared at my body, fingers skimming my waist. Forget acting like angels. We were animals, and we might as well give into it.

I started to tug up the hem of his shirt, but he grabbed my wrists, leaning in to me, whispering in my ear.

Something about *resist ... resist....*

Right. The resistance. That's why we were here.

How could I clear this fucking fog from my mind? Adonis used physical pain, Kratos used mental pain. Right?

I closed my eyes, summoning my worst memories. The day Marcus had died. The fear in my mother's eyes when I'd bitten her arm. Adonis lying dead after I'd killed him.

Pain tightened my chest, and my mind began to clear again. I breathed deeply, tears stinging my eyes.

I smoothed out my dress. "Okay. I'm with you now. What were you saying to me?"

"You met some of the members of the resistance. Do you see them here?"

"Give me a sec." I grabbed Adonis by the hand, moving around in the crowd, until a spark of recognition ignited in my mind.

There, sipping from a glass of bright green cocktail, I found one of the leaders of the resistance. She now wore a lacy black dress, and her dark brown eyes held a glazed expression.

Bingo. At least I knew now we were in the right place, which meant all the reanimated corpses had been worth it.

"Lila!" I grabbed her arm, trying to catch her attention, but she just licked her lips.

The keen intelligence I'd seen in her expression before had disappeared. She sipped her cocktail, blinking at Adonis. "Yeah, so, like ... I think I spilled something on my tits, but I don't really care. Has that ever happened to you?"

Adonis's magic thickened in the air. "No, as a matter of fact. But we need to get you out of here. You and the rest of the resistance."

I reached for her cocktail glass. "You need to stop drinking this."

Lila scrunched her nose. "I don't know, because, like ... it makes me feel good. I don't really want to have to think, and this makes me not have to think. I kind of feel like I want a jam sandwich, but it might make my hands sticky." She began swaying rhythmically to the music again.

I caught a glimpse of Brianna, who spun in a circle, sloshing her green cocktail over the dance floor. "I think I'm flying!"

And this was what was left of our army.

CHAPTER 24

I frowned at Adonis. "So, I think the entire resistance is here, shitfaced and boning each other under tables. Any ideas? Because my instinct is just to start slapping them all until they snap out of it."

"It's not the worst idea you've ever had."

"It's not, is it?" I bit my lip. "Pain can throw people out of ecstatic states. You know all about that."

"Do you want me to stab them all in the heart? Because I think we might find our army at a disadvantage once they've all expired."

I shook my head. "We can use mental pain. Just like Kratos does. What if I showed them visions that would shock them out of it? I can use my illusion powers, now, and show them exactly what will happen to them if they don't get back to England and start fighting back."

Adonis looked down at his bleeding palm. "Try it. We don't have many other options, and we're running out of time."

I summoned my glamour—the one where I could project illusions—and conjured up images of what the future would hold if Metatron were allowed to carry out his plan.

On the stage, in front of the red curtain, I created an image of

London, and one of Westminster Cathedral's walls now stood before us on the stage. I littered the streets with bodies—piles of them, rotting before the Cathedral. I scanned the crowd around me, finding that they seemed completely unimpressed by the image. They pretty much kept swaying on the dance floor, tonguing each other.

"Wrong tactic," I said to Adonis. "The dead are too faceless, and no one cares about faceless dead people. I need to show them the deaths of people they care about."

I'd start with Lila first. She was both their leader, and absolutely adorable. I had no doubt that many of the people she led cared about her—particularly some of the men, given the way they were following her around right now.

I flicked my fingers, bringing up a new image—this one of Lila standing in a road. Aereus appeared on his red horse, galloping over the pavement. He drew his sword, and it burst into flames. Lila drew a gun, shooting at him, but the bullets didn't stop him.

Aereus carved his blade through her neck, and her body fell to the earth.

A few screams echoed off the tall ceiling. Good, good. I was starting to get to them.

Adonis stroked his chin. "His sword doesn't burn like that."

"I was taking artistic license."

"You made him cooler than he is."

"Shhh … I'm concentrating."

Now, I summoned an image of Brianna and Amber, running from Metatron. He raised his hands in the air, eyes blazing with flames, and he lit the two women on fire. They fell to the ground, their bodies writhing with fiery torment.

More screams erupted over the hall.

Adonis cocked his head. "The fiery eyes were a nice touch. Also inaccurate."

For my *pièce de resistance*, I plucked random members from the crowd, and envisioned them in the worst possible scenarios. Aereus breaking them on his torture wheel, pulling their bodies apart on the rack. Bodies being trampled, hanged, death in the streets. I conjured up the most disturbing images I could and displayed them over the hall. I nearly made myself sick with creative ways to maim and mutilate.

Screams erupted all over the hall, cutting through the miasma of euphoria.

When I'd finished, Adonis was staring at me with a mixture of horror and admiration. "I'm not sure if I want to kiss you or run away from you right now."

One by one, each person in the crowd began snapping out of their trances. Their eyes became alert, and suddenly they were pulling up their pants and smoothing out their dresses, making mortified eye contact with the people around them. Nervous chatter broke out, and a sense of pure panic tinged the air. I let the images continue to play on the stage so they wouldn't slip back into euphoria, keeping them focused on the real danger that lay ahead of them.

"Now, someone needs to tell them what's going on," said Adonis. "But I don't think it should come from me."

I reached out, grabbing Lila's arm. If they were going to listen to anyone right now, it would be one of their leaders.

She stared at me, her eyes wide, body trembling. "How did I end up here?"

"You've been mind-controlled by a phantom king and everyone has been fucking in a music hall. Easy mistake; it could happen to anyone."

Her jaw dropped. *"What?"*

"Look, you jumped into a sketchy realm, here. And the truth is, we don't have a lot of time left. Metatron is going to destroy the rest of the earth in just a few days, and we need to fight back. Now." I pointed at the stage. "Or everything you saw up there will come true."

"Not the flaming sword," added Adonis. "But the rest of it."

Lila bit her lip. "How do I know I can trust you?"

"Look at this situation." I waved at the crowd. "It's not a good one. And I'm the one getting you out of here."

Around us, the members of the resistance were panicking.

Lila grabbed my arm. "I'll have to find our mages to get us out of here. If we can find the portal—"

"I'll get us out of here faster," Adonis interrupted. "We just need you to tell your people what's going on so they'll follow."

"Right." Lila glanced at the balconies above us. "Some of my memories are starting to come back, now. There's a man with claw-like fingers, flames shooting out of his mouth. He swoops in and … I can't quite remember." Her body had gone rigid with tension. "We need to get out of here before *he* comes. I can't quite remember who he is, or what he does, but—"

"Spring-Heeled Jack," Adonis cut in. "Necromancer phantom-king pervert with claws. Now we're up to speed. I'm going outside to create a portal just on the other side of the undead, re-dead corpse pile. Lead everyone out there as soon as you can." And with that, Adonis took off, slipping through the crowd.

Lila began clambering to the top of a table, then cupped her hands around her mouth. "Members of the resistance!" Her voice echoed off the hall.

The panicked murmurs in the hall began to simmer down.

"We've made a terrible mistake," Lila shouted. "We never should have come here. We need to get back to London, now. We may only have a few days left before—" She pointed at the stage. "Before all that shite happens for real. One of our allies is creating a portal for us right now, just outside—"

A shriek cut through the air, and all heads turned to the ceiling. A blur of black and white swooped above us, zooming between the chandeliers.

Spring-Heeled Jack, I presumed.

That's when all hell broke loose.

An undead waitress next to me dropped her tray, and glass smashed on the floor. Her expression grew furious, and she pulled a knife from her garter belt.

Oh, balls. The phantom king was turning his undead servants on us.

From the darkest corners of the music hall, towering monsters—like the ones we'd seen outside—tottered into the crowd. I stared as one of them picked up a bespectacled member of the resistance, bashing him against the wall.

Some of the monsters brandished torches at the crowd members, bellowing about their tormented souls.

The monsters were turning on us.

"Out! Now!" I shrieked at the resistance. But no one could hear me above the din.

"My life is an accumulation of anguish!" One of the monsters boomed. "Since I cannot be loved, I will be feared!"

Oh, for fuck's sake.

"Start leading them outside," I shouted to Lila. She followed my command, already elbowing her way to the hall exit.

My pulse raced. Pandemonium had erupted, and I considered readying an arrow. But in close quarters like this, it wasn't the best weapon.

Unless…. If all the monsters and undead waitresses were following the phantom king's command, maybe I could just take him out. Would they all simply collapse?

I pulled an arrow from my quiver, then whirled to find the nearest torch-wielding monster. I lit the tip of the arrow in his flames, then nocked it. I scanned the ceiling, watching the phantom zoom between the chandeliers. He moved so quickly I could hardly track him, but I locked my gaze on him as he leapt down into the crowd. He wore a black cape and pointed velvet cap, and his eyes flashed with flames.

He plunged to the ground, grabbing for a woman's breasts with his clawed hands. She tried to land a punch, but he leapt toward the ceiling again before she could make contact.

Weird prick.

With my gaze trained on him, I loosed the flaming arrow. It grazed his cape, igniting. He shrieked, his eyes blazing, then set his sights on me.

I nocked another arrow, but he was already zooming toward me. With his cape flaming, he flew faster—too fast for me to track. He slammed into me and knocked me into the ground. The speed of his flight had already extinguished the flames.

I tried to shove him off me, but he slammed a fist into my skull. My thoughts went a bit woozy.

Quick as a flash, his clawed fingers were around my throat. He started to spit fire, but I kneed him hard in the balls.

He howled, and tears sprang from his eyes. As I looked into his face, my mind began to fog once more, clouded with a vision of a euphoric cabaret, women dancing in short skirts.

"Why did you have to ruin this for me?" Spittle flew from his mouth. "I lived here alone for far too long. The corpses were my friends." His lip curled, a faraway look in his eyes. "When the Great Nightmare began, I had so many corpses to choose from. All these beautiful dead women, here to serve my needs. Their flesh ready for the groping, no arguments from them." He clawed at my breasts. "But then I thought, why limit myself to the dead, when I could use my scientific knowledge to control the living? A whole army here to keep me company...."

I gritted my teeth, trying to focus. I needed to shove the cabaret visions out of my mind. *Blood on the pavement. Adonis's dead body....*

With images of death in my mind clearing my thoughts, I brought my knee up into his balls once more. The phantom's eyes widened, and I slammed my fist hard into his face. Then, I tugged on his cape, pulling him off me. Lightning-fast, I leapt up. I snatched an arrow from my quiver, then fired it into his chest.

As I stood over him, his body simply disappeared, leaving behind only a wisp of smoke. The floral scent intensified in the air.

When I looked around me, I found the crowd streaming out of the hall, fighting back against the monsters. I ran with them, struggling to keep my thoughts focused.

At last, we burst free into the open air. Rain hammered down and lighting cracked the sky. Adonis had created a portal—an enormous, black whirlpool. One by one, the humans plunged into it, not knowing exactly where they were going, or if we could be trusted, but only that they had to get the fuck away from the torch-wielding monsters.

Just after the last of the humans plunged into the portal, I grabbed Adonis's hand and jumped in with him.

We climbed out of the freezing river, dripping with sludgy water. By the time Adonis and I got out, Lila was already mid-speech, the entire resistance milling around the river's edge. Lila stood on a tree stump, shouting through her cupped hands.

It didn't seem like she was getting through to anyone, considering the entire crowd was jabbering over her. She needed help.

I crossed to her. "Lila."

She turned to me, fear shining in her eyes. "They don't understand what's happening. And I'm not sure I do, either. Can you explain it to them?"

I stepped onto the tree stump. "Members of the resistance!" I shouted, waiting for the crowd to fall into a reverent hush.

That did not happen.

"Shut the fuck up, everyone!" I shouted.

And that also did not work. I stared out at the crowd of resistance members, their colorful frocks soaked with river water, makeup streaking the women's faces. Just like Lila, I had no control over the panicked crowd. Maybe another visual would get their attention.

I took a deep breath, channeling my glamour magic. It tingled over my body as I summoned an image of a field of corpses—some of them with recognizable faces from the crowd before me. Aereus appeared from nowhere, his golden wings swooping behind him, flaming sword raised.

After he trampled the corpses, I envisioned them blackening and decomposing into the earth.

I could feel the mood dampen around me, turning from panic into complete despair. I swallowed hard. Perhaps I was hitting the mortality note a bit too hard. I had to lighten the mood with a bit of hope.

From the rotting corpse pile, I summoned the image of a golden flower—then another, and another. A field of golden flowers grew— then buildings, houses, a thriving city.

Life grows from death.

Now, a reverent hush *had* actually fallen over the crowd.

I cleared my throat. "I've been showing you images of what might happen in the next few days if we don't band together. I think you get the point now, right? We'll all die, probably in painful ways. But if we fight back—using whatever means necessary—we can survive this. And we can rebuild again. You may have to change and adapt—you might have to become something you're not. But we'll only win if we use every tool in our arsenal. Including adaptation. I'll let your leaders explain the rest to you, because—frankly, you don't even know who I am."

I nodded, stepping down from the tree stump, and gripped Lila by the shoulders. "Convince them. Convince them to become demons."

Okay, the speech had ended on kind of a lame note, but I think I had gotten the point across. For now, I was leaving out the part about how Kratos—the Hunter—would be leading them. The fact was, the Horseman of Conquest was a natural combat leader. He could survey the fighting from above, issue commands in their minds, coordinate it all with precision.

Just a bit inconvenient that he'd spent over a year trying to slaughter all of them with his dogs.

I moved deeper into the forest, searching for Adonis. It took me a moment to find him standing in the shadows of a towering oak, separated from the rest of the group. He was staring at something, but I couldn't quite see what.

Shivering, I crossed to him and stood by his side. He seemed to be staring into the dark forest.

"Umm … is there something I'm missing here?" I asked.

"Don't you see it?" He reached out, stroking his fingertip against the air. As he did, a faint silvery ripple spread outward from his fingertips.

"What the hell is that?" I asked.

"A shield. I just have no idea who created it."

Well, this was interesting.

From the other side, an arrow slammed against the shield, and a crack began to form, splintering the air before us.

I stared down at the arrow on the other side of the shield. When I crouched down to inspect further, I could see that the shaft was carved with tiny Angelic markings.

Somewhere out there in the forest, the Heavenly Host wanted to shoot their way through this shield.

I turned, rushing back to Lila. She was milling around with people in the crowd, and I grabbed her by the arm. "What did they say?" I asked.

Her eyes were wide. "I think your disturbing displays of death might have actually worked. You scared the shit out of them."

* * *

WE CROSSED the hall toward the Celestial Room, and I could feel the tension rippling off Adonis.

As soon as we'd stepped inside the castle, Hazel had been there to excitedly give us the answer to our shield mystery. Apparently, Kratos had returned with our new potential allies. Rosalind and Caine had arrived while we'd been off fighting undead monsters. Rosalind had thrown up a shield to protect us from the Heavenly Host, and now Caine was waiting to meet with us for some sort of discussion.

In the stone hallway, Adonis had gone completely silent.

"You don't seem particularly thrilled about seeing Caine," I said.

"He hates angels. He used to seduce them just to make them fall. Muriel was among them."

I frowned. "Has it occurred to you that maybe Muriel would be better as a demon? Because she kind of sucks as an angel."

"Really?" His eyebrows shot up. "She's not that bad."

"She's awful. But anyway, we need Caine to help us, so maybe you should let go of whatever happened five hundred years ago. Time to move on."

"I've moved on. I'm just not a hundred percent sure we can trust these people. You don't know what he's like."

I frowned. "Marcus trusted him. He must have changed after a few centuries. It's a long time to most people, you know."

The doors to the Celestial Room swung open. From the glass dome, moonlight streamed into the center of the room, piercing the incubus's dark aura that wafted around him like smoke.

Caine sat with his feet on the table, a glass of whiskey in his hand. Dark curls framed his chiseled features. He had similar coloring to Adonis—but his eyes were an eerie silver and his body was narrower, lips a little fuller. Shadowy magic bloomed around him, darkening the air. In his presence, the air felt a little cooler, and I shivered, hugging myself. For a moment, the ghost of dark wings appeared behind him. His magic smelled like a lightning storm.

Instantly—at the sight of Adonis—he narrowed his strange, pale eyes, and rose from his chair. They walked toward each other.

The two men squared off toward each other, in some kind of gorgeous alpha male stare-off.

"Incubus," said Adonis. "I believe we've met before."

"Horseman," said Caine, managing to lace the word with a considerable amount of disgust. "What do I know you from? Oh, that's right. You tried to kill me. Didn't work. I guess killing a demigod was a little harder than you thought, wasn't it?"

Well. This was going well.

Adonis slid his hands into his pockets, looking perfectly at ease, even though I could feel the tension rippling off his body. "Right. How could I forget? Little Caine, born in a whorehouse, descended from the god of the void. What a charming combination."

"You could write my biography. Is it just me, or are you fascinated by me?" Caine lifted his glass. "I'm drinking your whiskey. Am I right in thinking your kind isn't supposed to indulge? You wouldn't want to risk turning into a scary demon like me, would you? You might find yourself the star of stories meant to scare children, or perhaps enjoying yourself. How horrifying."

Adonis sauntered forward another step, his gait easy. "Remind me. How long has it been since you served as the Queen of Maremount's whore?"

"Just a few centuries. It was right before I tossed her body out the tower window." He sipped his whiskey. "Ah, now I remember why I love angels so much. Being judged by you is so much fun. Let's not indulge or enjoy life. The angels might frown at us." Caine stepped closer, his silver eyes trained on Adonis. "You'd never truly give in to pleasure or passion, now, would you? Always holding back. Does your girlfriend mind your restraint?"

Adonis's smile faltered a little. "Angels have a sense of responsibility that a waste of life like you would never understand."

Caine quirked a smile. "Is that the same sense of responsibility you feel when killing scores of people with plagues?"

I clapped my hands together. "Okay, so, we're all a little cranky today. A few naps and some cookies would be in order. But we're all supposed to be on the same side, aren't we?"

Shadows whirled around Caine. "You're not cursed anymore, horseman, are you? I can't see the curse on you."

"I pulled the curses off Adonis and Kratos," I said. "They're both free now."

Caine cocked his head. "You've found a way to fuck with impunity. Maybe I like your priorities."

"You haven't changed much, have you?" said Adonis. "Your mother must be so proud."

Caine shrugged. "She was a literal whore, so who knows. And yes,

I have changed. I command the Lilinor army now, and I'm married to a woman whose powers exceed my own. Which is why we're here."

I crossed my arms. "So, if you don't want to work with angels, why are you here?"

"My wife, Rosalind, is fond of humans. I have no idea why. She wanted to find out what you have to say in case she can help protect them." Caine looked at me for the first time, and his pale eyes bored into me. "An angel who loves a fae. Now that is interesting. Life and death, pleasure and restraint. Maybe death-horse here is more interesting than I'd given him credit for."

I took a deep breath. "Okay. Well, that's all the pleasantries out of the way; now let's get down to the real issue. Rosalind's shield is protecting us, but the angels' arrows are already cracking its surface."

"I don't see how that's possible." A female voice turned my head. I looked around to see a beautiful brunette woman. The faintest hints of colored magic whirled off her athletic body in fine tendrils—just wisps and glimmers. Somehow, she exuded power and vulnerability at the same time. "The shield shouldn't be able to crack. Caine and I built it together. We've been protecting Lilinor with a shield for years, and we're pretty good at it by now." She crossed to her husband, putting her arm around his waist.

"But you've never encountered an enemy like Metatron," said Adonis. "His angelic magic can destroy anything. He creates chaos, breaks things down. He will make you feel insane and destroy the fabric of the world around him."

"And we've got about two days until he wrecks the entire world." I shivered in my freezing gown. "Metatron is going to try to kill us all, and then slaughter everyone else on earth. In a couple of days, he'll be going on a killing spree all over the earth. Starting with London. We need your help to stop that from happening."

Caine sipped his whiskey. "Why not just escape to one of the magical realms? We were safe in Lilinor."

Adonis shook his head. "We'd never get every living creature on earth into a magical realm. And in any case, Metatron will probably come after those, too. He can move in and out of realms at will, and he's hell-bent on destroying demons. Lilinor is not safe, even with your shield up."

I could see Caine visibly stiffen. He wanted to protect his home. Good. He'd fight harder that way.

I crossed my arms. "Look, outside this castle, we have an entire army of humans who are reluctantly willing to transform into demons because they're terrified of dying. They're willing to fight with us."

Rosalind stared at me. "And you think they can defeat the Heavenly Host?"

"Not quite," I said. "But I think we can stop their death march for now."

"They're immortal." Adonis met my gaze. "Only Ruby can defeat the Heavenly Host. She just needs a little more time to work on it."

At least, I hoped to the seven hells that time was all I needed.

CHAPTER 26

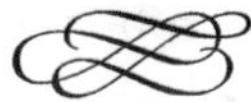

Kratos stood above me, his copper wings swooping behind him.

I sat in the grass, looking up at him. When speaking to Conquest, staring up from the ground only seemed like the natural order of things.

His body glowed with ethereal copper. "Have you convinced the members of the resistance to let themselves become transformed into immortal beings?"

"I showed them some images of their deaths."

"I saw. You do realize Aereus's sword can't really shoot flames?"

"What is it with you horsemen and realism? I took some liberties. It gets the point across. Anyway, it worked to set the stage. Lila, one of their leaders, did the rest of the convincing."

He cocked his head. "You know, I never before would have imagined that mortal beasts would take such convincing. Who *wouldn't* want to become a superior creature?"

"Right. Particularly when you all have such charming personalities," I said. "But, yes, they're on board now. Rosalind is already transforming them, one by one." I glanced at the fracturing shield once more. "It's, unfortunately, kind of a long process, and that thing won't last long."

"And they know that I'm to be their leader, right?"

I shook my head. "Not yet. I'm thinking that the news that the Hunter is their new leader will be a last-minute revelation. When they're too committed to back out."

"Devious. I like it." He frowned. "It hasn't escaped my attention that you tend to leave out crucial bits of information quite a lot. You tend to just tell one part of the story."

"The stories we tell shape reality. We have to be careful with them. So let's make sure this ends up being a story about victory, shall we?" I glanced at my legs. A silver chain attached cuffs on my ankle to a silver loop in the ground. In case I tried to rip the chains right out of the earth, I'd asked him to add a few spikes inside the loose cuff. The pain could rip me out of any kind of feral trance—one that might lead to my death.

Of course, I'd left out the "I might die" part of the story.

"You're sure these things will hold?" I asked.

"I've protected them with angelic magic. Only an angel would be able to get you out of them."

"You'd better fly away from me, now. And make sure Adonis is nowhere near me. If I explode with light, the Old Gods might kill you."

"Good luck." Kratos beat his wings, then took off into the sky. I watched him fly away, his copper glow growing smaller as he swooped over the castle's turrets.

I took a deep breath, staring up at the fracturing shield. I didn't want to practice this magic, but I had to. Once Metatron broke through, he and Aereus would come for us. First, they'd capture me. They'd torture me until I broke mentally, then they'd try to force me to kill Adonis and Kratos with my powers. Would I do it, if pushed hard enough? I really didn't want to find out, but I suspected everyone had a breaking point.

Then, they'd kill me and Hazel. In other words, a quick death was better than this outcome. When I thought of what could go wrong, panic rose in my chest.

My heart raced out of control. I tried to shut out my frantic thoughts, to center myself by tuning into the world around me. If I couldn't calm myself, I wouldn't be of any use to anyone. Right now, I had a task to achieve, and I needed to be able to focus on something other than my own probable death.

Focus on the moment. I lay in the grass, staring up at the night sky. Buttercups dotted the grasses nearby.

The stars looked a little different tonight, with the faint silver sheen of the shield. It also seemed like my vision was becoming increasingly keen ever since I'd gotten the gemstones. Another deep, centering breath. Now, I could see it all—particularly vivid was the bright swath of the Milky Way.

I exhaled, trying to force out my feelings of panic.

At least, until another angel soared above the shield, shooting an arrow at the dome of magic, just above my head. Particles of the shield fragmented, raining down on me.

Caine and Rosalind might be gods or demigods or whatever, but their shitty shield needed a little help from the Old Gods. And now, it was time to try to summon it.

I closed my eyes, channeling the magic of the Old Gods. Faintly, the gemstones in my forehead began heating. The song of the Old Gods whispered in the back of my mind.

Then, it fizzled out again. I blew a strand of hair out of my eyes. Seemed like I was bouncing between not being able to summon the magic at all and letting it overwhelm me until it was going to rip my mind and body apart.

Maybe I'd gone a little too far with calming myself down. The other times I'd summoned the Old Gods' power, I'd been blazing with adrenaline, scared for either myself or Adonis.

Just like with the resistance, fear could be a powerful motivator.

I sat up in the grass. Instead of channeling the Old Gods' light, I summoned an illusion—something that would make me wild with fury and fear. Adonis, on his knees, as Aereus slammed his sword through his head—just like I'd seen in Paris.

Already, my canines were growing longer, my feral side taking over.

At the sight of blood and gore before me, a mixture of rage and panic began to roil in my veins, and the gemstones grew hotter. My blood roared in my ears, and wild power ripped through me.

Images of a garden paradise bloomed in my mind like wildflowers, and I ran along the river's edge, hunting an angel....

I snarled, light beaming from my body. The symphony of the Old Gods built and crested in my mind. And as it did, cracks formed in my body, and I could feel that the light was going to destroy me from the inside out.

Creatures like me were never meant to toy with divine magic like this. The Old Gods wanted to punish me for stealing their magic.

As I felt the magic tearing me apart, it brought out the beast in me, desperate to live. I wanted to tear through flesh, I wanted—

A sharp pain in my ankle snapped me out of it. Jolted out of my trance, I stared down at the blood pouring from my ankle, staining the yellow buttercup petals.

So. That had gone well.

Frustration tightened my chest. *Well, this is fucking pointless.* I was a Bringer of Light, unable to use my powers without sacrificing my life.

The delicious smell of myrrh began to soothe me, and without turning my head, I knew Adonis was there.

"Still working on it, are you?" The moonlight sparked in his gray eyes.

"I told you to stay away from me while I was practicing. I'm not quite there yet. But I think I'm making progress." I heaved a heavy breath. "I'm lying. I'm making no progress whatsoever. Do you really think we can defeat Metatron? The resistance isn't even trained soldiers. They're just ordinary people who've been starving in hovels for years, eating rats."

Adonis stared up at the sky. "The truth is, I don't know what will happen, Ruby. But if you'd asked me months ago if I thought it would ever be possible to remove my curse and fall in love with a fae, I would've said no."

"The Old Gods are powerful," I said, "but I wasn't born to wield that power. Maybe humans and fae like me were never meant to have the tools of the divine beings. Maybe our minds can't handle it."

"I thought you didn't believe in destinies like that? Anyway, maybe there's power in opposite forces joining together. Look at us. You and I are the beginning and the end, we are life and death. We are strangely perfect together." He leaned down, ripping the silver chains from the earth. Then, he swept me into his arms, and I breathed in his delicious scent. His warmth and powerful magic enveloped me.

I slid down his body, then lay back on the grass. I held out my hand to Adonis. He lay next to me, his body warming mine. I curled into him, resting my head on his shoulder, and put my hand over his heart to feel its beat. Then, I turned my head to stare up at the stars blazing above us. I focused on the Milky Way, picturing it as it would appear from outer space, elegant swoops curving around a gaping black hole at the center.

Once again, I saw the seeds of death in the world around me. "Someday, everything in the universe will fall into a black hole, ripped apart by gravity. All the fires in the stars will die out, and the universe will lie a cold, abandoned wasteland. In the end, chaos consumes us all."

"You're in a cheerful mood, aren't you?"

A bright star above us flickered like a Christmas tree light. I pointed to it. "Do you see that? It's about to die. We're witnessing the death of a star."

"You're witnessing the death of a star two thousand years ago," he pointed out. "It died when I was still young. You're seeing its echo. And there are stars born out there that we can't yet see. Their creation is like us—a balance of forces, fusion and gravity."

He turned on his side, and his hand found its way to my waist.

"First you romanticize nature, now it's all death. If you can find a balance, maybe you can control your powers better. Nature isn't life or death. It's both. Accept your feral side. Accept your monstrous side. Neither of us are perfect. We are distinctly imperfect. You and I are both destructive, but that's not all we are. That's not the limit."

He traced his fingertips over my waist, and my blood heated.

"When I first saw you in the streets of London," said Adonis, "I saw your savage side. You were covered in blood, disguised as a demon. But there was life there, too—a spark of the divine in your eyes. You enthralled me. You woke something in my mind that I'd tried to keep dormant. You were dangerous to me. And even so, I took such a pleasure in killing the redcaps who wanted to hurt you. I will always take pleasure in killing anyone who wants to hurt you."

I quirked a smile. "Same. I'd quite happily eat Aereus's face off."

Adonis's eyebrows shot up. "I'd do it a bit more elegantly than you would, of course. And yet, even with your feral nature, you have an elegant side, too. When you danced for me, I couldn't take my eyes off the beauty of your body and the way it moved, the divine inspiration beneath every twirl. The way the fabric moved over your delicate skin, the light shining from behind the darkness in your eyes." He brushed his fingertips over my body, over my chest. "The flush of your chest. I knew there was a mystery there, one I needed to explore. You made me feel alive again, and vulnerable again. And then you pulled me back from the underworld. You had the power and the courage to raise Death from the dead. If anyone can take on Metatron, it's you."

"So you don't think we're bad for each other anymore? That we make each other too vulnerable?"

"When I smelled your blood all over the stones in Paris, I hadn't felt that sort of terror since my mother died. It swallowed me whole. I felt my heart breaking. The beauty that had awoken me again, that had revived me—it was just gone. So, yes, love is a vulnerability, but it's also my reason for living. And, yes, everything will end someday. In the end, even the immortals will be ripped apart by chaos. But we're here now—sparks of light in the darkness." He pointed at the stars. "And while we're here, still alive, there is divine order all around us."

I stared up at the Milky Way, thinking of its perfect whorls. It was a sort of divine order out there, wasn't it? And maybe it was an answer to the chaos. Like Adonis had said, maybe perfection could be found in the balance of opposites: life and death, chaos and order.

I remembered reading something in a magazine long ago about Fibonacci numbers—a series in which each number was the sum of the two numbers that came before it. One, one, two, three, five, eight, and so on. And when you divided them together, you got the golden ratio. Nature had a habit of using the golden ratio to create beautiful, elegant patterns of a predictable order. The swoops of seashells, the curves of floral patterns—natural beauty mimicked by painters.

I turned to my side, plucking a buttercup from the ground. There it was again, the spiraling, winding perfection of the petals.

Metatron created chaos wherever he went. But there was order within the swirling patterns of the stars. This math was the voice of the gods—celestial and earthly gods alike. If you knew where to look, you could find divinity in nature.

I twirled the buttercup in front of my eyes. I had power over plants, didn't I? Maybe nature could combat the chaos after all.

An idea began germinating my mind. "I want to try something."

"Oh?"

"I want to see exactly what I can do with plants. Buttercups, wild grasses, vines."

"I love you, Ruby, but I'm not sure we're going to defeat Metatron's immortal army with plants."

I frowned. "A minute ago, you were expressing complete confidence in me. What happened to that?"

"Well, you started talking about buttercups."

I sat up straight. "Maybe they're the answer to the chaos. There is order here. Have you heard of the Fibonacci sequence? Every number is the sum of the two numbers that came before it, and that gives us the golden ratio. It's in the distance between the whorls of stars in the Milky Way, or the spirals in a seashell. You can see it in the patterns of plants. Think about the number of petals that show up on a flower— it's usually one of those numbers. Whoever created the material world that we see around us used this pattern, over and over again. I think this is our answer."

He ran his fingertips up my arm, from my elbow up to my wrist, leaving trails of hot tingles in his wake. "And how do you plan to use these patterns?"

I shook my head. "I don't know yet. But I know I can control plants. I did it in your garden in Scotland, and when I killed Johnny." I took the buttercup and slowly stroked it down his perfect cheekbone.

It seemed to ignite something in him, and the next thing I knew, lust shone in his eyes. He hissed a breath, giving me a look that said "I'm about to jump your bones."

Maybe practicing magic could be fun instead of just painful. In fact, I had the strongest urge now to watch my plants climbing all over his perfect body.

I waved my fingertips over the buttercups, and my skin tingled and sizzled with ancient magic. One of the buttercup stems began lengthening and snaking over Adonis's torso. Heat blazed in his eyes, and he ran a hand over his mouth, as if he was still restraining himself, still keeping himself leashed.

Part of me wanted to see if I could get him to fully let go. Maybe in order to coax him to unleash himself, I had to confine him myself. I'd be his restraints, until he fought against them with all his power.

I hooked my leg over his waist and climbed on top of him, my dress riding up nearly to my hips. From where he lay, he had a view of my lacy panties. Then, I unbuttoned his shirt and pulled it off, feeling the sensuous thrill of his magic caressing my body.

I tried to focus on my magic, even with the heat sizzling over my skin and his body between my thighs. "Watch this." I flicked my fingertips again, and buttercup stems surged from the ground, wrapping themselves around his wrists. I clenched my thighs around his abs, his skin warm against mine.

He let out a low snarl. "Are we done talking about buttercups?"

"No, we're just getting started. I'm going to teach you to listen to me when I talk about plants. I need to practice."

A wry smile curled his lips. "You do realize I have enough physical strength to break through buttercup stems. "

I clenched my thighs tighter, then ran my hands up his chest to his throat. "Don't disobey me. I killed a man with these thighs. Don't think I won't squeeze you to death."

"If I may put in a request for my method of execution," he said, his velvety voice stroking my body, "I'd like to die in the same way."

I cocked my head. "Noted. If I ever have to put you down, you can die between my thighs. And if you don't drop the cocky attitude, that might be sooner than you'd like."

"What attitude?"

"You're magic-shaming me. You have no faith in my plants. You're a plantist, in fact."

"When it comes to killing angels, I just don't think flowers are likely to be as effective as the magic that can literally hurl angels off the earth. Maybe that's a personal quirk of mine."

Sure. As long as you're fine with your girlfriend dying.

I narrowed my eyes. "You think you can break free from the buttercup stems? Try it."

Adonis's cocky smile still curled his lips—until he tried tugging on the stems. Then, the amusement left his features pretty fast.

Still straddling him, I straightened. "Like I said, you need to listen to me when I talk about plants."

"You can talk all you want. But I need your dress off. Now." His commanding voice dripped with the promise of sex.

"Pretty assertive there for a guy trapped to the ground by buttercups."

"But you know as soon as I get out of this botanical prison, you'll be at my mercy, and I will touch you until you beg me to fuck you."

Already at his words, heat pulsed between my legs. I wanted to feel his masterful fingers at the apex of my thighs, but I also wanted to draw this out.

I flicked my fingertips again, and more strands of buttercups slid over his skin, trapping him to the earth.

I leaned down, stroking his face. "An angel, trapped in dirt like a beast." I nipped at his lower lip, my nipples hardening. "How delightful."

His body tensed beneath me. "As long as you keep your legs wrapped around me, I'm happy to be here."

My body reacted powerfully to him, core throbbing. I kissed him more deeply, and his tongue stroked against mine. I rocked my hips on top of him, and I felt as if my body was swelling with heat. The fabric of my dress felt too hot now, and my brain was screaming at me to pull it off. I complied, and the cold night air whispered over my skin. I leaned down again, my nipples grazing his chest, and I kissed him deeply. I rocked my hips against him, moaning.

"Ruby," he breathed, his voice husky. "I need you now." He yanked his wrists against the plant manacles.

I whispered in his ear, "First, I want to hear you say my plant powers are worth exploring."

His hips moved underneath me. "Is this really necessary?"

I brushed my fingertips over his waistband "Say it."

"They're worth exploring."

I leaned in, my body pressed against his, and I started kissing his neck. My tongue flicked over his skin, and I moved my body into his.

He groaned.

"Not good enough," I said. "Tell me you were wrong when you said my buttercups wouldn't do it. My magic is powerful. I should be worshipped…. You know. The kind of stuff Metatron would want to hear."

"Can we not talk about my father right now?"

"Say it."

"I was wrong. You are a goddess of plants and all other things, and I bow before you and worship you in all your magical glory. And, in particular, right now I'd like to worship your perfect curves and your mouth and your breasts and every other part of your body."

Sounded good to me. "Fine." I raised my hands, beckoning the plants toward me. They whipped off his body, freeing him.

Just as I'd anticipated, it had taken my restraining him to entice him to truly unleash himself. He snarled, and in one swift movement, he had me on my back in the grass. Already, he was tugging down my panties, desperate for me. I tore his pants off him, and he lunged for me—more beast than I was at that moment.

He kissed me deeply, and with every thrust of his tongue, my legs fell open a little wider, my back arching. We kissed with abandon, his tongue stroking mine. We were frantic for each other, desperate. From underneath, I rocked my hips against him. He slid into me, and I moved in tune with him until my mind fractured with pleasure.

CHAPTER 28

Alex and I stood at the edge of a crowd of humans, watching as Rosalind transformed them. Tendrils of her brightly colored magic snaked into the crowd, curling over the humans. Over the course of the past few hours, Rosalind had honed her ability to transform people. Now, she could reach several of them at a time. I stared as her magic curled around a human male, transforming his emaciated and stooped form into a powerful, silver-horned demon.

I glanced up at the shield, hearing the faint thuds of arrows raining against it. Pieces of the shield chipped and flaked off, and my body tensed.

With each direct hit, the cracks in the shield deepened further. At every faint thud, my heart lurched. Each point of contact meant we were one heartbeat closer to death.

My chest felt tight. "Whatever happens, things are about to change," I said to Alex.

"Good." Alex looked up at the shield arching above us. "How much time do you think we have till the Host come through that?"

"I honestly don't know. We're going to try to strengthen it, and I think I might have an idea of how to do that. But all of this magic is new to me."

"I don't know if we'll survive this," said Alex, "but I know I can't live like a hunted, starving animal anymore. I think death is better than the life I've had in the past year. Whatever happens next, I'm not going back to the rookeries."

I studied Alex for a moment. "What happened to you since I last saw you? Where are Lucy and Katie?"

"What happened to us? More of the same. More starvation, more watching people die. More disease around me. We live, we die. The horsemen toy with us, just like Famine did when he put me on that scaffold. And scaffold or not, all of us humans are just inches away from death in this world. Lucy and Katie are fine, though. They're living in an abandoned mansion right now."

"The last time I saw you—I mean before the resistance started—I was pointing an arrow at you. What was that like? Being abducted, nearly dying, then set free again?"

Alex folded his arms, moonlight washing over him. "I had no idea what the hell was going on when Johnny kidnapped us. We were just cooking our rats over a fire on our rooftop. I didn't even see him coming, just felt this insane hunger ripping me apart." He dropped my gaze, looking over my shoulder. "The hunger nearly drove me mad. I just kept thinking about how I could eat Katie, that she had some meat...." He blinked. "You know what? Never mind. Let's not finish that thought. Anyway, we all blacked out from extreme hunger, and next thing I know, I'm on a scaffold and you're pointing an arrow at me."

"You must have been terrified."

He scrunched his forehead. "Not really. I had no idea what was going on or why you were standing next to Famine, but I knew you'd never even consider shooting me."

Right. Probably best that I leave out the part about how I had, in fact, considered shooting him. "Of course, it never even crossed my mind. And the good news is, Johnny's dead now. I made his head explode. Then what happened to you once Adonis took you away from here?"

"The death angel led us out of the city to an abandoned mansion in

Northamptonshire. But I couldn't stay there with just the three of us. We were safe, but in total isolation. They were driving me mad, until I felt like I had nothing to live for anymore anyway. I came back to London, found the resistance, and joined up."

Something tingled over my skin, and it took me a moment to realize it was Rosalind's overwhelming magic, vibrating through the air.

I stared as her colored magic whirled off her body. Within the crowd, she was transforming a middle-aged woman. Before my eyes, the woman's graying, frizzled hair transformed into sleek brown curls, her body growing taller. Shimmering, silver wings grew from her shoulder blades. This frail human woman was turning into a valkyrie, a being that could ride the storm winds and rain death from above.

"Have you chosen what you're going to transform into?" I asked Alex.

"Incubus."

My eyebrows shot up. "Incubus. Really."

"They're gods of sex. Why would I choose anything else? I haven't gotten any action since the Great Nightmare began, but...." He peered into the crowd. "With some of those cute valkyrie ladies wandering around, I'm liking my chances as an incubus."

I nudged him with my elbow. "I have no doubt that you'll be knee-deep in a bit of the ol' how's-your-father soon," I said, trying out the British expression.

Alex grimaced.

"Yeah, that's creepy. Forget I said that."

"I'll pretend it never happened." Another arrow slammed into the shield, showering us with glimmering shield particles, and he frowned. "Do you honestly think we're going to get our army together in time?"

I closed my eyes, thinking of the buttercups and the Milky Way. "I might have a plan. And I think we need to institute it *now*."

* * *

AT THE NORTHERN edge of the domed shield, I stood by Adonis's side. To our right, Rosalind and Caine were frowning at their work, running fingertips over the cracks.

Apparently, it was news to both of them that they were fallible.

"This doesn't look good," Rosalind grumbled.

"Whatever happens," said Adonis, "we can't fight them here. An open battle against the Host would be suicide. They outnumber us, and their skill level outmatches our forces. They're all trained soldiers. But the Heavenly Host is used to a particular way of fighting. They march in formation. They've always done so. It's their vulnerability."

I nodded. "Our best chance at fighting them is guerrilla-style. We'll need to hide around the City of London, taking cover in some of the ruined buildings and towers. From our hidden vantage points, we can take shots at them with poison-tipped bullets and arrows. Metatron's chaos will be able to eat our weapons, destroy the buildings, everything around us. Even our soldiers, if we let them get close enough. I'm going to try to combat that as best I can. But we'll all have to do our best to stay hidden, so he doesn't know where to strike."

Caine's eyes gleamed like stars in the darkness. "And how are we supposed to fight this chaos power of his?"

"I'm working on it." I tapped my fingertip against the shield. "And this is our first test. When we go into battle with them, we need it to be on our terms, or we have no chance."

Rosalind let out a long breath. "They're going to smash through this any minute now."

Caine crossed his arms. "And you think that our combined magic can be strong enough to make the shield last."

"I have no idea," I said. "But it's worth a shot. I want to try to strengthen the shield with the Divine Order of the Old Gods—all four of us working together. Let's see what happens, okay?"

By my side, I could already feel Adonis's power intensifying, that forceful, dark magic that licked up and down my skin. He began chanting in Angelic, and I tuned out the words. His native language only distracted me.

I glanced at Caine and Rosalind, and the thin strands of magic that curled off their bodies. They closed their eyes, and Caine moved closer to his wife, slipping his arm around her waist. They seemed completely in tune with each other, their magic blending harmoniously, as if they'd done this a million times.

Already, I could see tendrils of their magic sliding over the shield, strengthening it. It spread over my body, raising goosebumps on my skin. Caine's magic was cold and electrifying at the same time, and it tingled up my spine. Rosalind's was almost overpowering—a heady mixture of the seven gods twining together, vibrating through my chest, my bones.

But we needed more to combat the chaos. We needed order. And with any luck, my ancient magic would be exactly what we needed.

I closed my eyes, tuning into the nature around me. Clematis and wild grapes grew on the oaks around me. Grapes ... the forbidden fruit from the Garden of Eden. It seemed fitting enough.

My mind filled with visions of the bright green Garden of Paradise, the burbling river.

In my phantom world, I found my way to a tree wrapped in grapevines—the forbidden tree of knowledge. I stroked my fingertips over the leaves. Patterns and perfect, ordered spirals whirled around me, until I started to realize that I wasn't alone here in my phantom world.

Now, within the garden, the four of us stood around the Tree of Knowledge—completely naked. My eyes roamed over Adonis, Caine, Rosalind—their perfect bodies pulsing with sensual magic. Adonis's powerful hand slid around my waist, his muscled body pressing against mine, pinning me to the tree. His mouth found its way to my neck. My back arched, warmth pooling in my body. My heart raced. Vines twined around our ribs, bringing the four of us together—

When I opened my eyes again, I found grapevines threading into the magic that slid over the shield. The vines had found their way into the cracks and fissures, sealing them shut. In fact, we now stood below an enormous dome of grape leaves.

"Holy shit." Rosalind smiled. "It worked! Are those grape leaves? What in the world…?"

Adonis traced his fingertips over the shield. "Ruby, you have channeled the magic of the Old Gods to perfection. It's the perfect antidote to Metatron's chaos."

"You had a vision. An ecstatic state." Caine's head was cocked, and he was studying me with those keen, pale eyes. "What did you see in your vision?"

I shifted uncomfortably. "Me? Nothing. Just leaves."

He arched an eyebrow. He didn't believe me. As an incubus, he was immediately tuned into sexual energy, which was mortifying. The gorgeous bastard was probably feeding off it right now.

"It's not important," I added. "The important thing is that we've bought ourselves time so we can finish building our army, and attack them on our own terms."

Another arrow thunked against the shield. This time, it bounced off harmlessly.

Apart from his piercing eyes, Caine practically blended into the darkness around him. As a grandson of Nyxobas, he wore night like a cloak. "If you want to truly catch them by surprise, we can attack at night. I'll make sure shadows hide us, so they'll never see us sneaking into the city."

"When do you want us to sneak into London?" asked Rosalind.

"Metatron has pledged to begin his attack in two days," said Adonis. "Before dawn breaks, we'll sneak into the city and wait for their march."

"When I interrogated Metatron in the Tower," I said, skimming over the details, "I learned the Host will be marching up Tower Hill first, then Minories and Aldgate High Street. We can hide ourselves all over East London, just northeast of the Tower. Alex and I spent enough time in that neighborhood to know which buildings are stable. I know we can't kill the Host, but the poison-tipped weapons will lay them out for a while. When I've mastered the power of the Old Gods, I'll send them all back home again."

Adonis was studying me closely. "The magic of the Old Gods is supposed to be able to counteract angelic magic. If you can find a way to break down Metatron's immortality spell using your light magic, I can destroy his entire army at once. An army of mortals before me doesn't stand a chance. Angelic bodies would litter the streets of London." His eyes looked a little too delighted. "Metatron's army would be reduced to ashy piles of corpses—"

I held up a hand. "I get it, Death, my love, but I'm not sure. I don't think I can use that kind of magic yet." Without dying. "I just don't have enough control."

Rosalind crossed her arms, staring at us. "You guys are kind of a weird couple. I like you, but you're weird."

But Adonis's stormy eyes were still on me. "If it comes down to it, Ruby, you have to use whatever powers are at your disposal. We won't get a second chance at this. And it it we lose, we all die."

His words sent a shiver up my spine. He had a point.

CHAPTER 29

We stood outside Hotemet Castle. With the shield's new vines blocking out most of the moonlight, our world had fallen into darkness, so Adonis had created glowing orbs to give us a bit of light. They now hovered above the army of demons, casting a golden glow over them.

I hugged myself tightly. Adonis and Rosalind had already taken off. Right now, they were on a reconnaissance mission, looking for traps and patrols around the City of London before our arrival.

Before she'd left, Rosalind had transformed our forces from a horde of emaciated humans into something quite terrifying. Along with their demonic bodies came demonic magic. They could now shoot arrows with precision and fly above the angelic forces. Each of them had a weapon laced with Devil's Bane.

Granted, Metatron could break all those weapons apart. But it would be my job to keep it all together.

I scanned the army, my gaze trailing over Alex, whose dark incubus wings swooped behind him. His pupils twinkled like a night sky. For a moment, I felt a chill looking at him—until he broke into his charming smile.

Hazel sidled up to me, then jabbed me with her elbow. "If you can make the angels mortal again, I can burn them all to death with Uthyr."

I shook my head. "If I had time to practice, I could make them all mortal, but I don't think it's going to happen today. The Old Gods only care about one thing: ridding the earth of the horsemen. When I use the light magic, Adonis might end up dead, or anything could happen. The best we can do for now is lay them out with Devil's Bane until I can get some mastery over the situation."

She glared at me. "You realize what happens if you take on Metatron and fail, right? Everything dies."

"Great pep talk—thanks, Hazel." I bit my lip, and a quiet fear clenched my chest. "Anyway, I won't let that happen. I'm not going to let you die." She didn't need to know the consequences right now. I just felt the need to reassure my little sister. "It will be fine, Hazel. I won't let anything bad happen to you. I just want you to stay here, behind the shield."

"That's stupid. I should be circling the city with a fire-breathing dragon, but instead we're supposed to rely on your plants."

"My plants fixed the damn shield. Anyway, you're sixteen, Hazel. You're staying behind the shield." I took a deep breath. "You're breaking my concentration right now."

"What are you trying to concentrate on? Making grass grow in preparation for the big battle? Must be exhausting."

I shot her a dirty look. "I have to convince this entire army of angel-hating former humans that they need to follow Kratos's orders. They agreed to transform into demons, but they don't yet know they're supposed to follow the Hunter."

"Why does it have to be him? I could lead them just as easily. On my dragon."

"He's Conquest, Hazel. He was made for this. He can mentally command thousands of soldiers. He can coordinate it all to perfection."

"So just tell them if they don't follow his commands, they'll probably die."

"I can't just tell them that. It has to be sophisticated. Like a whole inspiring battle speech performance."

She narrowed her eyes at me. "Fine. I'm going inside now. Have fun with your grass magic."

I loosed a long sigh, looking up at our shield. With the plants threaded through it, the shield now blocked us completely from the angels' view. No cherubs or sentinels or any other celestial creatures could see us.

Still, we had to march from here into London, and that meant leaving our dome of protection.

I turned back to the army of demons, and my gaze landed on Lila. The resistance leader was crossing toward me. She looked much the same as before, except now she had delicate wings that swooped from her back. Valkyrie seemed a fitting species for her.

"So, Ruby," she said. "Are you ready to give your little speech to tell them how well you know Kratos, and that he's actually loving and sweet and all that?"

I shook my head. "Not even remotely ready. Dancing is more my thing than speechmaking, and I honestly have no idea what to say. But I'll put on a good show if I can."

I crossed to the tree stump and climbed onto it, staring out at the sea of demonic faces before me. The thing was, burlesque was generally a silent affair. Dancing, fans, sequins, tassels. We weren't known for our oratory skills. But maybe I could borrow from some of the most inspiring speeches I vaguely remembered from history and English class.

I raised my hands. "Friends. Demons. Countrymen! Lend me your ears, for I have come to...." I couldn't remember how the rest of that went. "I have come to tell you that, they may kill us, but they'll never take our freedom!" That made no sense. If we were dead, we wouldn't be particularly free. "We shall fight on the beaches."

I cleared my throat. Not my best performance.

"Okay, look. You all want to live, right?" My voice boomed over the crowd. "We are facing an army of immortal angels with superior skills to ours. Kratos is a living embodiment of the concepts of conquest and victory. If he doesn't lead us, we'll probably die." I scratched my cheek. "Oh, yeah, and he will issue those commands in your mind, so if that happens, it's not a hallucination. Just do what he says."

The crowd of demonic soldiers began murmuring. I could feel the tension rippling off them in waves, the air buzzing with nervous energy.

I glanced at Lila, raising my eyebrows, and she shrugged.

"So, are we good? Please don't tell me I have to show you more images of your deaths at Aereus's hands, because I'm getting a little tired of that."

I raised my arrow. A sword really would have been better, but I didn't have one.

"Give me liberty, or give me death!"

I nodded, and a few sad claps broke the silence. I was dying up here.

At the front of the line of troops, Alex raised his sword, his dark wings swooping from his shoulder blades. "We can't stay within this shield, or we'll starve. We can't leave the shield without fighting back, or the angels will kill us by tomorrow morning. Just get us through this night alive. We'll worry about the rest later."

I turned, smiling at Kratos. I gave him the "thumbs up" symbol.

Okay, one more try. Maybe what they needed was a little more hope. If their lives were only despair and gloom, there wasn't much to fight for. *Put on a good show, Ruby. Give them something to love.*

I raised my arrow. "We're at the precipice between life and death right now. We have been since the Great Nightmare began—fighting for life among the ashes. We are going to war today for the people we love, and that love will give us strength. Our enemies love no one but themselves, and that gives us the advantage. So, when we're done, when we finally rid the earth of the angels who don't belong here, we will rebuild. We will plant fruit trees and vegetables. We will construct our homes again. We will find love and life in the ashes of death."

Silence greeted me, but I think I'd gotten through to them that time, and no one was arguing.

The golden light of the orbs glinted off Kratos's body, gilding him. Wordlessly, he took to the skies above the troops. Now, bestowed with an army, his body seemed to glow even more powerfully, his head burning with a halo.

Move to the portal. Already, I could hear him issuing commands in my mind, his voice deep and booming. Being able to fragment attention, to think about a thousand different things simultaneously, must be some kind of angelic ability.

Meet Caine there. Prepare to open it on my command.

CHAPTER 30

aine and Kratos flanked me as I stood before the shield, running my fingertips over it. As I touched it, the shield whirled in a spiral like the Milky Way.

I glanced at Caine. "You can help me open up a portal in the shield, right?"

"Everything except that wall of leaves you created."

"I'll handle that part."

For the first time, I saw Caine with his wings—beautiful, black-feathered wings that blended in the shadows behind him. "Adonis is ready for us. The streets of London are clear of angelic patrols. Metatron isn't expecting us. As the army slips out of this portal, they'll be cloaked with my shadows. The angelic patrols won't be able to see us at all."

My heart beat a rapid tattoo in my chest. "Good."

I ran my fingertips over the shield again, then met Caine's gaze. "Okay. Let's do this, incubus."

He closed his eyes, and his electric magic tingled over my skin, raising the hair on the back of my neck. I felt my back arching at its power.

Then, I pressed my palm against the shield, envisioning a hole opening within the leaves. I could feel their spirits melding with mine, their vibrations tuning into mine. The leaves whirled away from my fingertips, opening a portal in the shield.

Lead them through the portal. Kratos again.

My footsteps crunched over the leaves, and I listened to the rhythmic marching of the demon army behind us. Kratos somehow had us all marching in time with one another. As we moved deeper into the woods, Caine's shadows clung to me, whispering over my skin.

In silence, we moved through the forest, slipping through the trees. This was how the High Fae had once fought—firing arrows from behind the cover of trees. Silent, unseen by the enemy. Humans had a term for the sudden blood clots or paralytic seizures that plagued some of the elderly among them: strokes. That came from us —the fae. In the old days, we hid behind trees, shooting arrows into humans who'd wandered into our territory. A fairy-stroke.

And that's how we'd be taking on the angels today, using the ancient way of the fae. If it went well, they'd be struck down by unseen forces, unable to fight back.

Metatron would try to rip the world apart, and I just had to keep it together.

Caine and I led the troops deeper into the forest. I turned to him as we walked. "Are you worried about what could happen to Rosalind?"

His gaze was icy. "No. She has the power of seven gods. Why? You're worried about your horseman, aren't you? He's the embodiment of death. I don't think you need to worry."

No point lying when we were facing the possible end of the world. "Yeah, but I'm worried about him anyway."

"I thought you were the only person who could kill him."

"That's one of the things I'm worried about. If I have to use the full extent of my powers, Adonis could die. The Old Gods want to rid the earth of the horsemen."

"You're glamoured. You look like a human. A creature who wants to be human can't wield the power of gods."

"What?"

"I'm a demon. Half-incubus. I know what I am. I seduce, and I kill, and my powers are mine. Do you know who you are?"

At his words, I felt unsteady, like the world was tilting beneath my feet, and my heart began to beat a little faster. "Succubus, fae, human, dancer, spy." My answer didn't seem quite as satisfying as it had before.

His glacial eyes shone in the darkness. "And what do you feel when you try to use the gods' power?"

"My feral side comes out. Canines. Blood. Wrath. The whole nine yards."

"You're scared of your feral side. You're repressing it. That's why it takes over when you use the gods' power."

My pulse began to race, and I started to find myself annoyed. "What are you, some kind of demonic therapist?"

"Don't think I don't notice you trying to deflect what I'm saying."

For just a moment, my mind flashed with a memory I wished I'd kept hidden. My teeth, tearing into my mother's flesh. I'd left her permanently scarred. Scared of me, even. "My feral side is scary. Of course I'm scared of it. You should be, too, quite frankly."

"There are angels, and there are beasts. Creatures like us are in between, and you won't control your powers until you accept both sides of yourself. If you fight your feral impulses, they'll take over. The Old Gods can sense your weakness, and they will gain control. Believe me—I've fought the same battle with the God of Night. My powers came from him, but they're mine, now, and I wield them how I want."

* * *

AFTER MARCHING for hours through the darkness, we'd finally arrived in the City of London. Kratos's commands guided each of us into the city.

Separate from the rest. Move north. As we moved further south, toward the Tower, Conquest's voice boomed in my mind.

With a nod to Caine, I slipped away from the rest of the demonic horde.

You'll join Adonis, said Kratos.

The Horseman of Conquest still hoped I'd be able to destroy the immortality spell. If I could, Adonis would be at my side to slaughter them all within moments. I only wished I had more time to prepare until I was sure I could take them down.

I moved quietly through London's abandoned streets, following Kratos's directions. As I got closer to Adonis, I broke into a run, desperate to see him.

There's a tall, glass building to your right, said Kratos. *The door is open. Push through it.*

Once again, I had to marvel at Kratos's ability to multitask, each of us getting our own unique commands.

You'll join Adonis on the top floor.

I pushed through the door, finding myself in a dark stairwell. A few streams of moonlight shone through the doorway, glinting off shattered glass on the floor. It smelled faintly of rotting food in here. In the humid stairwell, I blew a strand of red hair out of my eyes.

While I climbed the dark stairs, I thought back to what Caine had said. Maybe he had a point. If I was going to take on the power of a god, I couldn't run from myself.

On the one hand, transforming, performing, putting on a show— that was all part of who I really was. But Caine was right, too. I was hiding a part of myself, one that I hardly ever showed to anyone. I hid my ears, my hair. I hated my feral side, and maybe I didn't want to be fae. I wanted the grace and elegance of angels.

I heaved a deep breath. If I was going to use the magic of the natural world, I couldn't reject it.

As I climbed another flight of stairs, I let the glamour shimmer away from my body. My true color.

I let the gemstones glow in my forehead. When I caught a glimpse of myself in the reflection of a door window, I saw my pointed ears sticking through pale, blond hair.

I could adapt, I could change, but I couldn't run from myself. Not if I wanted to wield true power.

Push through the door to your right, said Kratos in my mind.

How did he even know where I was? I was hidden in a darkened, abandoned building, and he seemed to know my every move.

I pressed through a heavy fire door, and a cold wind whispered through a shattered window. A few rays cast pale, silver light over the room. In the dim light, it took me a moment to find Adonis, until he said my name. I caught the gleam of his eyes. He sat by a broken window in the darkened room, the floor littered with bits of debris.

In the darkness, I could just barely see him smiling at me. "Ruby. The real Ruby."

I returned his smile. "We're fighting fae style today. So fae Ruby is here to kick some angel ass."

"I wouldn't want to spend the possible end of the world with anyone else."

I crouched next to him. "Let's try to be a little optimistic and imagine that it's not ending."

I knelt next to the window, taking care to avoid the shattered glass, and I peered out the broken window. Nothing seemed to move in the streets except a few drifting pieces of crumpled paper. The resistance's forces were well hidden, cloaked by tendrils of Caine's night magic. In the quiet darkness, a chill rippled over my skin.

CHAPTER 31

*D*espite the stillness, around the eastern edge of the old City of London, our soldiers were taking shelter in the rookeries and derelict tower buildings. Just like the old fae, the resistance was waiting to strike unseen—deadly, stealthy arrows and bullets would fly from the shadows.

I took a shuddering breath, meeting Adonis's gaze. The truth was, we didn't fully understand Metatron's powers, and I wasn't sure how long we'd have to attack his forces. I had to face the fact that chaos could take over before we had a chance to fight back. If it did, we could find ourselves ripped apart in the black hole of Metatron's magic.

Adonis reached for me. "You want me to be optimistic, but I can hear your heart racing with fear." He pulled me to his chest, and I could hear his heart beat, too. "Don't let death scare you, Ruby."

I wanted to stay like this forever, wrapped up in Adonis's arms. Or in our forest paradise. "I'm not ready for it to end yet," I said.

"Then let's try to make sure it doesn't."

His body tensed, and he released me. Then he crouched before the window, and I knelt by his side.

"I feel him now," he said. "I feel his magic."

The hair began to stand up on my nape. I felt it now, too, my body reacting to Metatron's otherworldly magic.

I readied my arrow, pointing it out the shattered window. Right now, thousands of us had our weapons trained through glass shards, ready to fire. Guns, arrows, grenades stuffed with shrapnel and Devil's Bane—we'd come well prepared.

Nausea turned my gut—a mixture of nerves and a reaction to Metatron's magic. My hands had begun shaking, and I tightened my fingers on my bow and arrow.

Overhead, the sky began transforming from midnight velvet into a bruise purple until streaks of red spread across the canopy.

My pulse began to race, and the Old Gods' magic simmered in my blood. Fear whispered through me. Distantly, the sound of marching trembled over the streets.

"They're coming," said Adonis from my side.

A few rays of light heralded the oncoming Heavenly Host. As their feet hammered against the pavement, I watched the stream of angels march up Minories. Then, just above his soldiers, soared Metatron himself. His ivory wings beat the air. Golden light radiated from his powerful body, and I found myself unable to tear my eyes away from him.

At any moment, the resistance would begin to attack.

Deep within my skull, Kratos's voice rumbled. *Resistance, prepare to fire. Ruby, ready your magic.*

I forced myself to rip my gaze from Metatron. My breath was coming in short, sharp bursts. As the legion moved closer within range, I set my sights set on a broad-shouldered angel at the front of the legion, whose ginger hair flowed down his back. His enormous white wings spread out behind him.

A cold sweat broke out over my body. As soon as we unleashed our arrows, Metatron would know we were here. He'd start ripping all of this apart with his magic. I had no way of knowing just how rapidly he could destroy a city.

Fire! Kratos's voice rang out like a bell in my mind.

Adonis and I loosed our arrows, and mine found its mark, right in the ginger angel's chest. At the same time, a hail of gunfire rang out, and explosions rocked the streets below. Smoke billowed into the air.

In our minds, Kratos kept commanding us to fire.

As poisoned-tipped bullets rained down on the Heavenly Host, I unleashed another arrow. Chaos ripped apart the army beneath us as the resistance hammered them with Devil's Bane. Through the haze of smoke, I couldn't even see Metatron.

So far, this was working beautifully.

Just as I was reaching into my quiver for another arrow, Metatron's voice rumbled over the horizon.

The Angelic words clanged in my mind, and I squeezed my eyes shut, trying to block out the anarchy. Words and pieces of words whirled around my mind, confusing me. *Buttercup, the brick, zebrek, manifold, lurking, crepusc, melaton, urge....*

Angelic was Adonis's native language, and it didn't seem to affect him. He just kept firing his arrows.

"Ruby," he said. "We need your power. He's starting to pull down the buildings."

I forced my eyes open and looked out the windows. What I saw sharpened my thoughts.

Metatron had simply begun tearing down the buildings where resistance members were hiding. Plaster, cement, and glass crumbled and fractured off the towering buildings around us. If this went on much longer, Metatron would bury the entire resistance in rubble.

I lowered my bow, tuning into the spirits of the plants that I could connect to around me. It wasn't much: grass, weeds, some clover—but I could use these plants as my own legion.

I let my body meld with their vibrations, their patterns, the divine order of their leaves and blades. Once I felt them responding to me, I commanded them to grow into the buildings, through the brick, through the glass. I sent them rushing through the steel, surging into stone. They sealed the materials together with perfect strength.

Ruby. Kratos's voice in my mind. *The streets just to your north are falling to pieces.*

I tuned into them, to the plants growing there, and I willed them to grow and to bind.

Still, the Heavenly Host were rallying. Those who'd survived the initial onslaught were taking to the air, trying to hunt down the snipers.

"The resistance are panicking," said Adonis from my side. "I can feel the raw fear of all the demons around us. And if they're panicking, they won't be thinking clearly."

Metatron's Angelic language rattled through my skull, and confusion danced in my skull.

Multitude, nurser, milget, rubbe....

Forget the demons. *I* was panicking.

He glanced at me. "I can hear your heartbeat. Everyone needs to stay calm if we're going to win this."

Like air breathing in and out of a bellows, dark magic pulsed from his body. Already, it soothed my mind and washed over my body in calming waves until I could think clearly again.

With my senses sharpened, I summoned another wave of plants, and grasses surged through the buildings' structures.

Gunfire and explosions rocked the streets, and dust clouded the air. Angelic soldiers took to the skies, wings furiously beating, searching for their attackers. But they weren't used to fighting unseen forces like this. We weren't playing by the rules of celestial warfare, and they had no idea how to handle it.

Through the smoke, I couldn't see Metatron, but I could see the angelic bodies littering the streets—burnt and tattered wings, blood staining the pavement. In the air, Metatron's soldiers frantically tried to ferret out the snipers' locations, but they made easy targets. It seemed our plan was actually working.

We were actually ripping apart the Heavenly Host.

While my plants sprouted from the earth, Metatron's magic began echoing around me, reverberating in my skull until nothing meant anything anymore.

Igloo, butters, legitro, melkan, resist, resist, resist—

I couldn't see where he was, couldn't fight back against him, but his magic kept intensifying. I clamped my hands over my ears. Metatron was the black hole at the center of the galaxy, and he was dragging us into his chaos. "Adonis! He's going to rip this world—!"

Before I could finish the sentence, a wave of his powerful celestial magic slammed into us. Glass shattered around me, and the steel began to warp. Panic climbed up my throat, and I screamed for Adonis, reached for him.

My fingers grasped at air, at smoke, and I felt myself falling through debris, an avalanche of shattered glass and plaster raining around us. For just a moment, Adonis's powerful arms grasped me in the air, the scent of myrrh blanketing us. He'd broken my fall, his wings slowly beating the air. Then, his body tensed as something slammed into us. With horror, I stared at the arrow protruding from his neck, the blood pouring from his wound.

He dropped his grip on me, and I felt myself falling.

CHAPTER 32

I slammed against rocky debris, and the fall knocked the wind out of me. Dust darkened the air above me, and I drew a ragged breath, filling my lungs with particles of plaster. Adonis's rescue attempt actually *had* saved me—I hadn't fallen too far to the ground, and I'd ended up on top of the rubble instead of buried beneath it.

Still, I was exposed here, and panic began climbing up my throat. I pushed myself up as fast as I could, frantically scanning for Adonis. Clouds of dust from fallen buildings filled the air around me, and I could hardly see a thing. Worse, my bow had been smashed to pieces in the fall.

I can't let Metatron get him. I can't let them take Adonis....

A sharp pain slammed into me from the back, and I fell forward on my hands. Jagged debris bit into my palms. Pain screamed through my shoulder. I glanced down at an arrow tip protruding near my collarbone.

With a trembling hand, I reached behind my back, my fingers grazing the shaft of an arrow lodged in my shoulder blade. Even if I had the strength, I wouldn't be able to yank it out where it had struck. Was I going to die here on my hands and knees?

Shaking, I turned my head to look at my attacker. An angel towered over me, pointing an arrow at me through the clouds of dust.

The wind toyed with his long, dark hair, and blood streaked his skin. "Are you the one they call the Light Bringer?"

Without waiting for an answer, he unleashed the arrow—this one hitting me in the other shoulder. Pain slammed into me.

As I STARED AT HIM, battle fury surged in my blood like molten lava. Time seemed to slow down, and I locked my gaze on him. Now, I could hear my own heartbeat roaring in my ears.

These fuckers wanted to destroy the world. But the truth was, that was too abstract for me to even worry about. What rang the most clearly in my mind was this: if the angels won, they'd be coming for Hazel and Adonis. And I couldn't let that happen. I'd fight for the ones I loved.

My pale hair whipped around my head, and my canines began lengthening.

Blood. The Old Gods wanted angel blood, and I was going to give it to them. I was going to end this now. Wrath flooded my mind as Feral Ruby took over. I couldn't feel the pain anymore.

As the dark-haired angel nocked another arrow, I lunged for him, slamming him to the ground. Instinct took over, and my teeth found their way to his throat. Blood poured from his neck, and his screams brought a smile to my lips. My fist slammed into his cheek, shattering bone, and then I was biting him again. He shrieked as I tore at his flesh.

The ancient fury of the Old Gods screamed in my mind. *Kill them all.*

Angel blood gave me strength. I rose to my knees, then snapped the arrow shafts in my shoulders. Grunting, I pulled out the arrows. I threw them down on the rubble.

From behind, another angel came at me with a sword. I ducked, then slashed at his gut with my claws. Blood sprayed from the wound. He dropped his sword, and I picked it up.

Shiny. Good for angel-killing. I wanted to sink it into angel hearts.

The stones in my forehead were heating up, desperate to rid the earth of this scourge. But there was some reason I couldn't do it, couldn't just give in to the blast of light....

I pivoted as another angel came for me through the rubble. My borrowed sword sliced through his angelic body. His blood smelled sweet to me. A frantic stab of pain—injured shoulders—tried to fight its way into my consciousness, but I pushed the thought out again. *Kill.*

Wild energy ran through my body. I felt at one with the wind and the jagged rubble beneath my feet. I cut my sword through another angelic soldier, glorying in the spray of blood as I severed his head from his neck. This was what I had been made for: a red-toothed beast born to slay angels.

I am blood, moss, bones, and earth, a creature of the damp caves. I am the feet pounding the leaves as you run from me. I am the rhythmic terror of your blood roaring in your ears.

My heart hammered like a war drum, life thrumming through my veins. My canines craved more blood. I couldn't quite remember to how to speak, couldn't make the words clear in my mind, but....

Had to find someone here, among the rubble. The man who smelled like myrrh. Gray eyes, dark wings.

From the skies above, an ivory-winged angel swooped down to me, slashing his sword.

He thought I was his prey. He was wrong.

I leapt into the air with the force of a wave crashing on the shore, and I slashed my sword through his neck. A beautiful crimson arc of blood.

Thrust. Kill. Draw blood. Come at me, fuckers. I will eat your hearts.

Their terrified hearts beat rhythmically, melding with their screams in a perfect battle song. They feared the Bringer of Light.

I whirled, my sword finding its way into the next enemy.

Vaguely, through the haze of bloodlust in my mind, I wondered where my lover was. Who he was. Who I was. Beast, or....

There was someone I needed to get to, needed to save.

The man with the red flower around his neck, the man who felt like home....

Around me, demons began climbing out of the rubble. Horns, teeth, wings—monsters, all of them. It took me a moment to remember they were on my side. We were all fighting angels.

My gaze flicked over a beautiful one with night magic—an incubus. He was fighting viciously, slicing his sword in graceful arcs through the angels around him.

Where's Adonis?

As some of my panic subsided, Feral Ruby began to grow quiet. Pain throbbed through my body once again, spearing my shoulder, my chest. The agony I'd been ignoring crashed into me, and I dropped my sword.

Find Adonis. Kratos's voice in my mind.

"Easier said than done!" I shouted. I couldn't see him through the dust, the smoke, the magic whirling around me. Now, tendrils of multicolored magic spooled around me—Rosalind's lethal magic curling around angelic soldiers. Demons from the resistance were climbing over the rubble, attacking the angels along with the magical assault. We still had a chance here.

I stumbled over the rubble, trying to feel for my bond with Adonis, that tug in my shoulder. But one of the arrows had ripped right through his mark.

As I touched my ravaged shoulder, Metatron's voice began blaring in my mind again. Anarchy roiled in my skull. Around me, I watched as our troops' weapons and armor began to flake and disintegrate— swords, arrows, guns, splintering into pieces. He was pulling us apart.

The breath left my lungs. Blood poured from my shoulder wound. I tried tuning into the spirits of the plants around me, to make them germinate in the weapons. But Metatron was speaking again, blocking out my own thoughts with his voice, until only one word pounded in my mind.

Beast. Beast. Beast.

He was mocking me, confusing me. And as he did, the world seemed to be fragmenting, falling to pieces. Parts of buildings, pavement, steel, and glass danced and ruptured in the air around me. And then, another angelic phrase ... *worship me.* It was an answer to the chaos, a beacon in the darkness. He had the answers I needed.

It felt like a command I couldn't ignore. I fell to my knees in the rubble, my hands in the dust, the jagged cement scraping at my skin.

I looked up from the ground, awed to find Metatron. Radiant light beamed from his head.

He spoke to me in my mind.

Ruby. I'm going to tear your mind apart, and your sister will be next. And I want you to die knowing that the man you love will be eternally punished for his transgressions.

His words cleared my mind again. I needed to stop this. I needed to stop it all....

I needed the Old Gods, even if it killed me. Even if they ripped my body apart with the power of their light.

My world tilted. Time seemed to slow down again, and Metatron's dark hair twisted and writhed in the wind. His mouth moved slowly, forming words he used as weapons.

A familiar scent hit me—myrrh. My gaze flicked to Adonis. He was crawling from the rubble, his dark wings coated in dust. His stormy gray eyes locked on me. His armor, his sword began to disintegrate before my eyes. And then, to my horror—even his wings began to fragment. Aereus swooped over him, moving in slow motion, his sword raised.

Unable to get up from my knees, I stared at Adonis, screaming his name. Aereus—the Horseman of War—raised his sword over Death's head.

If I used the magic of the Old Gods, I'd die.

But I didn't have a choice anymore.

As I met Adonis's gaze, light blazed from my body. I gave in to it, relinquishing control. The power of the Old Gods ripped me open, streaming from my ribs, my bones. I felt my lungs and organs expand, and agony fractured my mind.

Even as I fragmented, I could see the world slowly come together again—divine order and light slowly piecing together feathers, metal, stone—one particle at a time. But the magic was overpowering—a stolen force I couldn't control. My back arched, and ancient forces pulled me further apart.

When I looked up at Metatron, in his golden eyes, I saw something new. Something strangely human: fear.

With the last bit of strength in me, I pushed myself to my feet.

I was going to die, but Metatron was coming with me. I grasped his body in an embrace.

And I let the magic of the Old Gods erupt.

CHAPTER 33

As the pain left my body, everything around me seemed to crumble into atoms. I watched the world dissolve around me, until darkness replaced it.

I couldn't feel anything, couldn't place myself in space. I had no idea if I'd been here for a few seconds or for an eternity. Time didn't quite make sense anymore.

Until—a burst of light in the darkness.

I could hear my own breathing, my own heartbeat. I was here at the beginning and the end of it all. In the time before words and after them.

Nothing would last forever, and in the end, chaos would eat us all. But Adonis and I—we'd been sparks of light in the darkness.

I felt him here, in fact. I felt his soothing presence, his calming effect on my mind. Death, my lover, was with me, here, and he wanted to bring me back. I reached for him, trying to stroke him, embrace him, but I couldn't find him in the darkness. That light was too far from me. I wanted to feel his smooth skin under my fingertips, and they stroked helplessly through the air. *Nothing.*

Loneliness ate through me, and a rising sense of panic. I couldn't stay here forever on my own, separated from the people I loved.

Then, the distant chink of light expanded, swirling with green in the darkness, until light and matter began to bloom and piece together around me. A solid ground of soil formed beneath my feet.

From the void, a garden formed, until leaves from plants brushed my calves. I took a step, my feet sinking into the soil.

I blinked, my eyes dazzled by the azure sky. Okay, so this was death, and I was in Paradise. Not the worst outcome, I supposed.

Had the Old Gods just taken me here? Maybe they didn't hate me after all, because it seemed fairly heavenly here. In fact, the scent of the garden intoxicated me. Was this Eden?

Yes.

I caught a glimpse of Azazeyl slipping through the trees. This was where it had all begun, where minds had gone to war with bodies, creation with instinct, where the Old Gods had begun to fight the new.

I spotted a tree in the corner of my eye, its trunk wrapped in grapevines. I *needed* to know how the fruit tasted.

I hurried to it, then plucked one of the grapes from the tree. I popped it in my mouth. I bit down on it, and the sweet juice washed over my tongue. I swallowed, and golden, powerful magic spilled through my veins and filled my skull. As it did, I felt my body start to move again. As if by its own volition, my body twirled through the garden, my bare feet skimming across leaves and moss.

Long ago, when I'd danced, my mind had been silent. Peaceful.

Now, as I moved through the garden, perfect silence washed over me. I twirled, extending my arms as I moved. I pointed my toes, lifting my leg into the air. With every graceful arc of my arms, light beamed from my body. It was just like Caine had said. I was an angel and a beast, in a garden of life and death.

As I moved, words began to form in my mind. Angelic words. But now, they seemed like they belonged in my thoughts—like a skill I'd once had and lost, a sense that had once been native to me.

I couldn't run from the past, from the memories I wanted to forget. I couldn't ignore the blood staining my memories, my teeth piercing flesh. My feral side. It was a part of me.

But I could change the way the story was told. I could give it new meaning. Love and rage were primal, animal forces, but we could shape them with our stories.

I caught a glimpse of a perfect form moving through the trees. Azazeyl?

I moved toward him, his powerful magic drawing me closer. Gray eyes, midnight wings—it wasn't Azazeyl. It was Adonis, his night-kissed magic spooling from his body. I ran to him, and he wrapped his arms around me. I pressed my head to his chest, listening to his heartbeat.

Perfect spirals of magic whirled from him like the Milky Way.

Death, my lover, ruled this domain. But he wanted me back among the living. The smell of myrrh swept over me, raising goosebumps on my skin. I pulled his face to mine, kissing him.

With the kiss, life streamed back into my body, lighting me up.

When I opened my eyes again, I found myself in Adonis's arms.

Back in London, in a cloud of dust. Life suffused my body. He'd healed me completely, and I felt amazing. I stared at the gorgeous planes of his face, wanting to pull him in for another kiss. The sweet music of Paradise still played in my ears.

"You brought me back. Is it over? The battle?" I asked, warmth lighting up my body.

"No."

Well, fuck. That killed the mood. I'd just died, and my death hadn't even finished the job.

All at once, the roaring of battle noises returned to me. The clashing of swords, the agonized screams of people losing limbs. The brutal pounding of my own heart.

"Metatron is gone," said Adonis. "Banished to the Celestial realm by the Old Gods' power. That was your doing, when you grabbed him. But the rest of their army remains. Along with Aereus."

My heart hammered, and I pulled myself free from Adonis's embrace and rose to my feet.

Above us, winged demons were fighting the angels. I caught a brief glimpse of Caine, a blur of silver and black, rushing for an angel, his sword raised in the air.

Ruby. Kratos's voice boomed in my mind once more. *Can you kill Aereus?*

"Working on it!" I shouted.

My gemstones began simmering and tingling. I glanced overhead, where Aereus was locked in a battle with Kratos. They weren't far above us. In fact, I could probably drag War down from here. That fucker had nailed my boyfriend to a wooden plank, and I was still pissed about it.

Already, I could feel the Devil's Bane building in me, curling from my fingertips.

I flung out my wrists, and ropes of the plant spooled out of my body, wrapping around the Horseman of War.

I tugged on the vines, yanking him down to earth. He slammed hard on the rubble, and dust puffed in an enormous cloud around him.

He started to stand, roaring with rage. His very presence ignited wrath in my body. I wanted him to suffer. Strength rippled through me, and I grabbed him by the throat. I squeezed his neck, reveling in the pain etched across his features.

"I have a message. You don't belong here. You never did. Not because you're a horseman. Because you're an evil, stupid fuck who created hell on earth, and you don't even know why."

He screamed, and I lifted my free hand to his face. Devil's Bane spiraled out of my fingernails, surging into his mouth and his eye sockets, his nostrils. My plants ripped through his bones and veins, crawling through his wretched heart and arteries. He gurgled, his skin bulging and ripping apart.

"Your time on earth is over." I flicked my wrist, and his body exploded into particles of flesh and bone.

I glanced at Adonis, whose gray eyes had gone wide. He gripped a sword, ready to cut into more angels, but the sight of me exploding another horseman seemed to have distracted him, and he was giving me that look again, somewhere between horror and admiration.

But he didn't have long to stare, because already an angel was rushing up behind him, sword raised.

Adonis whirled, gracefully slashing his sword through the angel's neck. Headless, the angel fell into the rubble.

When I looked closer at the soldier from the Heavenly Host, I could now see the magical spells writhing in the air around him. The words snaked and curved around every one of them. It was the immortality spell.

I stared as the magic vibrated around the decapitated angel's neck, shimmering until his head appeared again.

Immortal.

Kratos's voice rang in my mind again. *Can you pull the immortality spell off the soldiers?*

It was just that a silver-haired angel was swinging for me. I ducked, and his blade whooshed over my head.

"Working on it!" I shouted again.

I unleashed a stream of Devil's Bane from my fingertips, and it surged into his body, ripping him apart from the inside out.

I glanced at Adonis, who was fighting through the angels around him.

I whirled, trying to keep the oncoming horde off of me. I was dimly aware of Kratos's commands in my mind. He was trying to direct our demonic allies to keep me safe, but there were just so many angels. I shot out another blast of Devil's Bane, and the magic curled around some of the soldiers around me.

Time to make them mortal again.

I arched my back, flinging out my arms. I was a black hole, pulling the golden magic toward me with an overpowering gravitational force.

The golden words spun through the air in perfect spirals that mirrored the Milky Way, ripping away from all of the angelic soldiers.

I pulled the immortality spells off one soldier after another—from the streets and the sky—and they spiraled into me.

. . .

As I MADE the enemy mortal once more, a blaze of fire seared the air above me.

Hazel, on her godsdamned dragon. She was picking off members of the Heavenly Host who flew in the sky. Their mortal bodies burned, and ash rained down from the heavens.

The angelic magic of immortality streamed into my body—words upon words—until I'd ripped every last spell from them.

"Your turn, Death." I glanced at Adonis, who was already rising into the air.

His back curved, as if in ecstasy. A chink of light broke through the clouds, and golden rays washed over him while his wings carried him into the air. He cast an enormous, dark shadow over the city.

Dark magic spiraled off of him in perfect arcs, like the curves of a seashell, and there was something beautiful and terrifying about it at the same time. The magical tendrils slipped over the Heavenly Host, curling around each victim. As soon as it touched them, each of them seized up, their eyes bulging.

Here he was—the bringer of death. His black wings beat the air. I couldn't help it—even if he was the man I loved, right now, he scared the crap out of me. I felt my knees going weak looking up at him. He looked like a god of death, and it was hard to reconcile this image with the Adonis who thought fondly of his garden. Still, it was like he said—we were both destructive monsters, but that wasn't all we were. It wasn't the limit.

I stared at one of the angels who'd been coming for me—a black-haired woman with silver eyes. As Adonis's dark magic spun around her, her skin began to turn purple. She was putrefying before my eyes. Holes formed in her flesh, and the scent of rot rolled off her.

My lip curled. My lover had a very, very disturbing skillset.

I closed my eyes to the horrifying sight before me. When I opened them again, piles of the angelic dead littered the streets.

Among the dead, the demonic forces began moving. I scanned the survivors, relieved every time my gaze landed on someone I cared about.

For just a moment, perfect silence reigned.

CHAPTER 34

$\mathcal{I}$ sank deeper into Kratos's bath—regrettably, without Adonis to keep me company this time.

I'd washed off the ash and blood of battle, although it couldn't, unfortunately, wash the image of the putrefying angels out of my mind. Their bodies now littered the streets. Perfect fertilization for the gardens and fields we needed to plant. We'd be rebuilding this world, one vegetable patch at a time. Already, the members of the former resistance were clearing London's streets of angel bodies. They had begun hauling them out to open fields and razing abandoned buildings to create more farmland.

The resistance had begun and ended in London, and now the entire world could rebuild. It would be a while before we got things back to normal again. Transportation between countries was limited, and we had to rely on growing our own food. Luckily, I could help in that regard.

I toweled off my body, marveling at the pale, golden glow emanating from my legs. The glow of immortality. Truthfully, I felt amazing.

When I straightened again, I nearly jumped out of my skin. Kratos was standing there in the doorway, his copper eyes locked on me.

"Gods below, Kratos. You need to stop watching me while I bathe."

"Why? I appreciate your beauty."

"It's creepy."

"Is it?"

It had taken me this long to understand that some of Kratos's creepiness was just an inability to understand normal social conventions. "What are you doing here?"

He straightened. "I wanted to thank you for ridding me of my curse."

I pulled the towel tightly around me. "Thank you for leading our army to victory."

"It's what I was born to do."

I smiled. "It's part of what you were born to do. But it's not the limit. You're free now, and you can do what you want." I studied him, his rigid posture of a commander. "What *are* you going to do next?"

I couldn't stop wondering if Kratos had finally gotten laid, but I wasn't going to come out and ask it.

"I'm going to get busy," he said.

"Interesting turn of phrase."

"...with rebuilding the world that I helped to destroy. I've learned that I don't like living in isolation. Humans and demons in London may not accept me, since they remember me as the Hunter. I was tempted to terrify them into submission so that they would accept and love me."

I narrowed my eyes. "That's not really how love works."

"But your human friend Alex suggested I can earn people's trust again by helping to recreate what was lost. After all, conquest isn't just about war. It's about taking over a new place and making it your own. It's about construction as much as it is about destruction."

I nodded. "The ruins of the world could definitely use your help."

His gaze slid over my bare shoulders. "I'd also like to fuck someone." His jaw tightened. "Obviously not you. I mean, I would like to have sex with you, but—"

"Maybe just stop talking."

"Right." He nodded curtly. "Good talk."

"I'll get dressed on my own."

Before leaving, he turned to me one last time. "Do you think you could pull the curse off Muriel? If she were into that kind of thing?"

I loosed a sigh. There was no way around it. I was involved in Kratos's love life.

"I will ask her what she thinks." *Even though she sucks.*

Without another word, Kratos turned and left me alone.

Now, I had some rebuilding of my own I wanted to do. I had spent so long thinking about my phantom life—the perfect vision of a cottage, a garden, a sylvan paradise. Now, I had the chance to try to make it real.

CHAPTER 35

I hammered another nail into the side of the oak plank. I'd wanted this cottage, dammit, and I was making it myself.

I'd promised the resistance we'd rebuild, and that was exactly what we were doing now. I was making my phantom life real.

It was a little different from my fantasy—not quite the forest. In fact, fields and gardens stretched out around me.

I stepped back from my creation, a smile curling my lips. Adonis had offered to make a cottage with magic—a perfect one, carved with the words of the gods. But I'd wanted to make something with my hands. I'd wanted to feel the wood beneath my fingertips. I didn't want it to be perfect. I wanted the crooked lines and unevenness of the nails. And I wanted it to be a surprise for him, compelled by some primal instinct to make a home for my family.

I took another step back. It was perfect in its imperfections.

Hazel sidled up to me, holding a sausage in her hand. She stared at the cottage. "Yeah, that thing looks like a piece of crap."

"Thanks, sis."

"You should just stay at Kratos's castle with me."

"This is my paradise," I said. "And you know what? I'm going to eat godsdamn soup in here. You can visit us from his castle."

She bit into her sausage. "Whatever."

Hazel turned to the garden behind us. "Did you make all this?"

I turned to survey my work. A blue river carved through the forest, and red anemones dappled its banks. "It's modeled after the garden where Adonis was born. He hasn't seen it yet."

There were seeds of death, here in Paradise, but that was okay. I rubbed my rounded belly. Death grew in me, too.

Hazel pointed at my stomach. "How's your little deathling?"

I swallowed hard. My mouth had been weirdly watery since I'd gotten pregnant. "It's making me puke three times a day, and I have an uncontrollable urge to eat a vat of soup. But Yasmin keeps telling me that's normal. It's not a horseman-spawn thing."

"Remind me never to get pregnant. I'm going back to the castle. Kratos is making me a gin and tonic. He's never had alcohol before a week ago, and between you and me, I think he likes the sauce too much, if you know what I mean."

I scowled. "I told him you're not allowed to drink."

"Oh, yeah. He said I'm not supposed to tell you." She paused, turning to frown at the cottage. "It's still missing something. I'm not sure what."

I narrowed my eyes at it. She was right. It *was* missing something.

It was missing Adonis's touch.

I crossed to the other side of the cottage. This is where I'd planted the vegetables—potatoes, carrots, cabbage. I was even growing garlic.

The crunching of footsteps through the leaves turned my head, and I smiled at the sight of Alex coming closer.

"I think this garden is a step up from our Bethnal Green garden."

"Want to help me catch some rabbits?" I asked. "I have rabbit stew plans. Adonis doesn't know that stew and soup are basically the same thing, and he's agreed to eat it."

"I don't mind setting some traps. As long as I never have to eat rat meat again."

"You know you're welcome to stay here at the castle. Kratos said it was fine, and he's got a billion rooms."

Alex wrinkled his nose. "I came here to say goodbye. I was fine letting him lead us into battle, because it meant we got to live. I was fine with recovering here. But I don't want to spend any more time around the Hunter than I have to. And anyway, I want to go back and rebuild the city. We have a lot of angel bodies to clear."

"Do you really think London can recover?" I asked.

"My lovely American friend—London is one thing I'm not worried about. Do you have any idea how many times that city has been burnt to the ground completely? Queen Boudicca slaughtered everyone, burnt it to the ground. A seventeenth-century baker lit the whole place up. Nothing remained when the fire was done except ashes and melted bones. The Luftwaffe bombed the ever-loving shit out of it.

"And you know what happened? Every time, Londoners just went back and recreated the same winding, meandering, nonsensical bull-shit streets we've been using for two thousand years. We are putting it back exactly like it's always been. We're rebuilding the crooked streets with ridiculous names like Poultry and Crutched Friars. In a few years' time, I could be passing out under pub tables again."

"Passing out under pub tables. Your aspirations are awe-inspiring."

"Hey, we survived all this because we knew how to fantasize, didn't we? You fantasized about cupcakes—"

"And cottages with soup." And Adonis naked.

"And I fantasized about having fun again. Being irresponsible again. Doing shit just for the hell of it instead of for survival. We survived this because we told stories of the good old days, and for just a few minutes, they felt real to us. Golden-flaked cupcakes, expensive burgers. Burlesque routines. That's why we're alive."

Our lives and souls were defined by the stories we told. "I call that the phantom life."

"What?"

"The life you create in your mind that seems almost as real as this one." I nodded at my vegetable garden. "You haven't had time to plant stuff yet. Take some of this with you. When I go back to London, I'm going to clear that entire field in Bethnal Green."

"The one with our shitty garden?"

"Yeah, except I'm going to make a not-shitty garden."

"Your words inspire me. And I'm taking some potatoes with me because my stomach is about to eat itself."

On the way out of the garden, Alex leaned down, pulling up a few potatoes and stashing them in the crook of his arm. I smiled as I watched him walk between the oaks. I had an overwhelming urge to make sure that man always stayed fed from now on.

I crossed to the potato patch, plucking a few out for myself, and I brushed the soil off them. I had my rabbit, potatoes, and carrots. Adonis and I would eat by the fire tonight.

Metatron had tried to get into my head, to convince me that paradise on earth wasn't possible. That a fae like me would always give in to her feral, bloodthirsty instincts. He'd tried to destroy my phantom life.

But I was here, now, and I might be a feral fae with stones in my head who sometimes tried to eat people, but that's not all I was.

* * *

I STIRRED THE STEW, breathing in its rich scent.

When the sunlight slanted lower through the trees, casting long shadows over the forest floor, I felt Adonis's presence—his rich, soothing magic that whispered over my skin. It felt like home now. Adonis had been spending his days healing the injured members of the resistance. We'd set up a triage system, and the most severely injured had been healed first.

During the nights, I'd come here to work on my little project.

I'd kept my work here hidden from him, because I wanted to surprise him. Admittedly, the cottage had been for myself.

But the garden outside, the one modeled after his home in Afeka—that was for him. Here, our two worlds could meld together.

I crossed out of the cottage into the vibrant garden outside. I'd built this cottage next to the river on purpose, at the mouth of a cave. The bright blue of the river mirrored the color of the gemstones still embedded in my forehead. Using my plant magic, I'd grown myrrh trees lining the river's edge. And among them, I'd created the blood-red anemones in the tall grasses, just like the one he wore around his neck.

I watched him as he walked along the river's edge, his blue-gray eyes glinting. I felt ridiculously proud of my work.

His dark, sensual magic slipped around me, raising goosebumps on my skin.

"This is perfect," he said.

I squinted in the dying sunlight. "Not quite perfect, but good enough." I grabbed his hand, leading him into the cottage. "I made us dinner."

"I don't actually need to eat."

"It doesn't matter. You can enjoy life, now, so enjoy it."

We crossed into the cottage, and Adonis swept his gaze over it. "It's beautiful. You made all this?"

"With my bare hands. Except I don't understand things like plumbing and electricity, so someone's going to have to magic that into existence before we stay here overnight."

The stew simmered in a cauldron over the stone fireplace, and Adonis crossed to it.

"Taste it," I said.

He plucked a ladle from the stone mantle and scooped out a small spoonful. When he tasted it, his eyes lit up. "This is delicious."

I beamed. "See? I knew you'd like soup. I mean—stew."

His forehead crinkled. "This is what soup is?"

"Yeah." Once again, I was staggered at how little time he'd spent eating in his two thousand years. I'd be spending the rest of our immortal lives working on changing that. "What did you think it was?"

"I think I had it confused with that dish of mashed fruit and lard."

I gagged. "I don't even want to know what that is."

He took another spoonful. "People eat it all the time. You light it on fire."

I blinked. *"What?"*

"At Christmas."

"Oh, that's Christmas pudding. Only the British eat that. Let's never speak of it again."

I crossed to the stew, stirring it again while the steam curled around me.

Adonis sidled up behind me and rubbed the gentle curve of my belly. "Do you know that I've never seen you look more perfect?" His voice caressed my body. "How's little Thanatos?"

"We're not calling him the Greek word for *death.*" I scowled. "Or her."

"It's a noble name. What were you thinking of?"

"Jackson for a boy."

His body went stiff. "Jackson's not even a real name. It's the surname of America's second-worst president."

"Thanatos is not a real name. It's the personification of a rather grim concept."

"It's been my name for several thousand years."

"It's also your horse's name. We're not naming our baby after your horse. You can't just keep calling everyone *Thanatos.*"

"Fine." He took another spoonful of the soup. "We'll think of a new name."

"Speaking of names." I turned to face him. "This cottage is missing something. It needs your mark."

"What do you mean?"

"I used my hands to build it. And I used the magic of the Old Gods to cover it in anemones. But it needs something from the angelic world. This is supposed to be our home together."

He pushed a strand of my pale, blond hair out of my eyes. "I think I have an idea."

He crossed outside and stood facing the cottage. He closed his eyes, and he began speaking in Angelic. I still couldn't understand what it meant, but the words no longer bothered me. They sounded beautiful on his tongue. As he spoke, golden Angelic letters etched into the sides of the cottage, beaming out from the wood. When he finished, he opened his eyes to stare at his work.

"What does it say?" I asked.

"It's just our story. You know, beautiful, angelic perfection meets argumentative beast-woman."

I gave him a shove. "Don't make me bring out my feral side."

"You scare me, woman. And I like it."

I stared at the cottage, at the golden words glowing among the ropes of flowers. Here, in our new home, the Old Gods melded with the new.

My phantom world—the stories I'd told myself—had come to life in front of my eyes.

CHAPTER 36

I held Liora up just under her shoulders, trying to coax a smile from her. Mornings were when she smiled the most, before the sounds and noises of the day started to annoy her and she yelped angrily.

"Come on, Liora. You woke me up four times last night. I deserve a smile." The corners of her lips turned up, and I beamed. "That's a smile! That's a good girl! Smile for Mommy!"

A few years ago, if I'd overheard this sickly-sweet tone, I'd have rolled my eyes, and now it was just flowing out of me like spit-up from a baby.

Liora stuffed a pudgy fist in her mouth, gnawing on it. She had her father's stormy gray eyes—almond-shaped, with dark eyelashes—and some of the fattest cheeks I'd ever seen on a baby. Faint, blond wisps grew on her head.

Liora was lucky—born into a world we were rebuilding. With the angelic invasion driven from the earth, we were starting to put the world back together just the way it had been.

I drew Liora in closer to me, sniffing her head. She had that perfect baby smell.

Adonis's footsteps creaked the floor behind me. "See?" He said. "Dirt and moss smells lovely."

From the floor of our cottage, I scowled at him. "That's not what she smells like."

He reached down, picking her up and cradling her in his arms. Light from the morning sun washed over him.

Adonis had lived for two thousand years thinking he was unable to father a child. And he had been, all that time. But when I'd pulled the curse off him, something had changed, I supposed. Death could create life.

I wasn't going to second-guess it, anyway. I had my imperfect paradise here, and I wasn't going to ruin it.

* * *

THANK you so much for reading the Spy Among the Fallen series.

Please read on for more from this world, including Liora's story. In the next series, you will also be reunited with Caine and Bael.

www.ingramcontent.com/pod-product-compliance
Lightning Source LLC
Chambersburg PA
CBHW060637310726

48982CB00003B/802